GA

'Lively, vigo
FANTASY AND SCIE

'A glittering array of imperial futures . . .
well-organized and good fun' LIBRARY
JOURNAL

# GALACTIC EMPIRES

## Brian Aldiss

A Legend Book
Published by Arrow Books Limited
62-65 Chandos Place, London WC2N 4NW

An imprint of Century Hutchinson Limited

London Melbourne Sydney Auckland
Johannesburg and agencies throughout
the world

*Galactic Empires Volume 1* and *Galactic Empires Volume 2* first published separately 1976 by St Martin's Press Inc., USA
Introductions and original material © 1976 Brian Aldiss
This Legend edition published 1988

This book is sold subject to the condition that it shall not, by way of trade or otherwise, be lent, resold, hired out, or otherwise circulated without the publisher's prior consent in any form of binding or cover other than that in which it is published and without a similar condition including this condition being imposed on the subsequent purchaser.

Printed and bound in Great Britain by
Anchor Brendon Limited, Tiptree, Essex

ISBN 0 09 952150 4

# ACKNOWLEDGEMENTS

"Been a Long, Long Time" by R. A. Lafferty
  Copyright © 1969 by Ultimate Publishing Co. Inc.
  permission of the author and his agent, Virginia Kidd
"The Possessed" by Arthur C. Clarke
  Copyright © Arthur C. Clarke 1953
"Protected Species" by H. B. Fyfe
  Copyright © 1951 by Street & Smith Publications
"All the Way Back" by Michael Shaara
  Copyright © Michael Shaara 1952
"The Star Plunderer" by Poul Anderson
  Copyright © 1952 by Love Romances Publishing Co.
  Inc.
"Foundation" by Isaac Asimov
  Copyright © 1951 by Isaac Asimov
  Reprinted by permission of Doubleday & Co. Inc.
"We're Civilized" by Mark Clifton and Alex
  Apostolides
  Copyright © 1953 by Mark Clifton & Alex Apostolides
"The Crime and Glory of Commander Suzdal" by Cord-
  wainer Smith
  Copyright © 1964 by Ziff-Davis Publishing Co. for
  Amazing Science Fiction Stories copyright 1971
  by Mrs. Geneviève Linebarger
"The Rebel of Valkyr" by Alfred Coppel
  Copyright © Alfred Coppel 1950
"Brightness Falls from the Air" by Idris Seabright
  Copyright © I. Seabright 1954
"Immigrant" by Clifford Simak
  Copyright © 1954 by Clifford Simak
"Resident Physician" by James White

Copyright © 1961 by Nova Publications Limited for
"New Worlds" September 1961
Reprinted by permission of the author and
E. J. Carnell Literary Agency
"Age of Retirement" by Mal Lynch
Copyright © 1954 by Street & Smith Publications Inc.
"Planting Time" by Pete Adams & Charles Nightingale
Copyright © 1975 by Pete Adams first published in
Antigrav (ed. Philip Strick) by Arrow Books Ltd.
Non-exclusive publication rights granted on behalf of
Mr. P. Adams & Mr. C. Nightingale

# GALACTIC EMPIRES
## Volume One

# CONTENTS

# INTRODUCTION

Galactic empires represent the ultimate absurdity in science fiction.

Galactic empires represent a promiscuous liaison between Science and Glamour, with Glamour generally in the ascendant.

Galactic empires represent the spectaculars of the sf field.

As such, galactic empires have often been condemned by the serious-minded. That may be less because of faults intrinsic in the genre than because the serious-minded are practised in condemnation. One can be fairly sensible and still get pleasure from reading about armoured chaps with flambeaux, drinking out of bellarmines and leading war-horses into starships before they dash across the parsecs at many times the speed of light.

You can, in other words, take these stories seriously. What you must not do is take them literally. Their authors didn't. There's a way of reading everything.

Most of these stories were written for fun. But there are levels of fun. It is the responsibility of an anthologist to get serious-minded on that score; but first—a quote from one of the stories in this volume (you will come on it in good time):

> Metal-clad heels struck the paving in harsh cadence as the twelve guards escorted Deralan down the centre of the Avenue of Kings. The once proud street had become a place of bazaars. Rael was a wise and sour old planet. To it had come the dregs

of a thousand planets, the sycophants, the cheats, with their smell of depravity, their swaggering insolence. One did not walk alone at night on Rael.

Tumbledown squalor is often an attraction in the galactic story. The streets of Rael are depraved with good inventions, but they take second place to the picturesque. In a thousand Raels, the authors instinctively escort us to the nearest low drinking booth rather than showing us how the sewage system functions (unless our hero escapes down it) or how the rates are gathered to the mutual benefit of all. They know our tastes.

What the authors do in the main is tell us a story adorned with alien creatures, swordplay, fascinating gadgets, and—for preference—beautiful princesses. The story itself is generally fairly traditional, the crux being resolved by quick wits, courage, and brute strength. If this sounds like the recipe for a fairy-tale, the point about fairy-tales is that they enchant us and enlarge our perceptions. As Michael Shaara puts it in his story:

The history of Earth and of all Mankind just faded and dropped away. They heard of great races and worlds beyond number, the illimitable government which was the Galactic Federation. The fiction, the legends, the dreams of a thousand years had come true in a moment, in the figure of a square little old man who was not from Earth. There was a great deal for them to learn and accept in the time of a single afternoon, on an alien planet.

Science is thin stuff beside this legendary material. I say that this is what the authors give us in the main. Yet there is a moral which blows ever and anon like a chill wind down Rael's High Street, through the galactic tale: that it is better to govern than be governed. In more than one tale included here, the governed become the governors in the course of the story. In case the message does not quite get home, we have a special department in Volume Two entitled "The Other End of the Stick", in which Mack Reynolds and colleagues take us properly to task. Mark Clifton and Alex Apostolides also have something cogent to say on the matter.

Morality is all very well, but give me luxury every time. There is an undeniable luxuriousness in the most characteristic of these stories, which shows itself in the asides. You have to love the throw-away explanation, which contains in a few lines the gaudiness of technology and the tudorishness of the past:

> He followed her swaying body along the drape-hung corridors, into small rooms and past oak-beamed doors. She came to a blank wall, reached up and pressed pink fingertips against a rose-red stone.
>
> "The whorls at the tips of my fingers set off a light-switch mechanism within the stone," she explained. "It's better than any key."
>
> Somewhere an engine hummed and the rock wall began to turn.

You have to love the way villains or heroes flee across the remote star galaxies in pursuit of each other. You have to love the way Elder Races, Hideous Secrets, Ancient Forces or plain sneaky old teleportators crop up at every turn. And you have to love the imperial women.

It must be said that most of these stories were written in an innocent age, before Women's Lib and often when the authors themselves were of an innocent age. So a distinctly romantic view is taken of girls like Daylya "whose beauty had been like a warm cry in the night." Cordwainer Smith's Commander is practically alone in having a wife whom he prosaically loves. The beauties you meet here are apt to materialise in sinister circumstances, and to dress—or undress—to kill, like Alys in the showiest of the tales in this volume.

> He watched the graceful line of her unadorned throat, the bare shoulders and breasts, the small waist, the flat, firm stomach—all revealed by the studied nakedness of the fashions of the Inner Marches. This was no child.

So we all fervently hope. Often a note of longing and despair sounds, when the heroine is lost. "He remembered the sound of her voice and the sweetness of her lips, and he loved her. A million years, and she was dust blowing on the night wind . . ."

Some commentators have claimed to find something sinister in the idea of a galactic civilization, linking it to American Imperialist designs. This seems to me absurd; the stories do not bear that sort of weight of interpretation. Nevertheless, it is noticeable that all the best exponents of galactic empires are American, with one exception (the greatest, Olaf Stapledon). Presumably the British, who had an empire, regarded the matter more matter-of-factly.

Another objection is that we are morally unfit to rule our own world as yet, so that to think of us spreading to other worlds is to offend mightily. This objection might have more strength if the authors were actually attempting prophecy or endeavouring to show us how we could in fact take over the galaxy. But of course nothing is further from the truth. They are interested in the perennial business of writers, of catching an audience by its collective ear and telling it a good tale and a few home truths at the same time. Prediction does not enter into it. (All I'm prepared to admit is that if Earth establishes or becomes incorporated in a galactic empire in, say, three hundred years, then clearly the idea was festering in our racial collective unconscious during the twentieth century—particularly that bit of the collective unconscious called Poul Anderson.)

C. S. Lewis—in general an astute critic of sf—brought another objection against the galactic story, when he complained that the author "then proceeds to develop an ordinary love-story, spy-story, wreck-story, or crime-story. This seems to me tasteless. Whatever in a work of art is not used, is doing harm." Lewis misses the point, amazingly for a keen follower of science fiction. We read the love-story, the spy-story, or whatever, *because* it takes place on a fifty-kilometre-long spaceship, *because* it is set on a planet where the sun goes into eclipse every hour on the hour, *because* it happens in the capital city of the greatest empire the universe has ever known. Our sensibilities are affected by these settings, and by the knowledge that we are reading about legendary characters living hundreds of years in our future. We would toss the story aside unread if it all took place in Leicester in 1976.

Am I then saying that this anthology contains mere escapism? If I am, then let me summon the spirit of C. S. Lewis again, this time on the side of justice (my side). He thought the charge of escapism a puzzling one. "I never fully understood it until my friend Professor Tolkein asked me the very simple question 'What class of men would you expect to be most preoccupied with, and most hostile to, the idea of escape?' and gave the obvious answer: jailers."

In this connection, I noticed when I had assembled the stories that the majority of them were first published in the fifties. This may be partly because a great many sf magazines—more than before or since—were then being printed. But a more significant part of the explanation is surely that that was the era of the Cold War, those frigid years when West and East confronted each other across a pile of H-bombs. The Earth was not particularly habitable to the imagination; it was a relief to go a-voyaging. (And you will notice that *radiation* appears as a sinister and often curiously unrealistic threat in a number of these stories.)

As in the previous anthologies in this series, I have confined myself virtually to selecting from sf magazines. There are many sf anthologies on the market; few of their editors appear to have studied anything but other anthologies. I am interested in rescuing from oblivion stories, not necessarily by famous authors, which—for one reason or another—can be read and enjoyed today.

The two volumes of this anthology contain twenty-six stories culled from fourteen different sources spanning thirty-four years. Some of those magazines were obscure, some well-loved. Most have gone the way of the dodo. They were great while they lasted; they formed another empire which has vanished.

We print the original blurbs which appeared with the

stories on first publication. Blurbs were a minor art-form in their own right. Where blurbs have not been available, they have been forged.

BRIAN ALDISS

Heath House
Southmoor
July 1975

# SECTION ONE

•

# RISE AND SHINE

*Germinating in regions far apart, these empires easily mastered any sub-utopian worlds that lay within reach. Thus they spread from one planetary system to another, till at last empire made contact with empire.*

*Then followed wars such as had never occurred before in our galaxy. Fleets of worlds, natural and artificial, manoeuvred among the stars to outwit one another, and destroyed one another with long-range jets of sub-atomic energy. As the tides of battle spread hither and thither through space, whole planetary systems were annihilated. Many a world spirit found a sudden end. Many a lowly race that had no part in the strife was slaughtered in the celestial warfare that raged around it.*

Olaf Stapledon: Star Maker

Some ideas are so powerful, lie so close to the foundations of human thinking, that they impose themselves in realms where they appear to have no rightful place. The idea of cycles or seasons is one such. Christian thought is familiar with the idea of an Eternal Kingdom but, "on Earth", in Reality, no kingdom lasts for ever. The ghostly galactic empires of sf also prove seasonal. So, for that matter, do galaxies themselves.

For those who live on the equator, or for those who live on planets without seasons, the cyclic nature of the universe may be less obtrusive. *May be.* But the basic conditions of life, being born, giving birth, dying, acquaint us forcefully with the meaning of seasonal change. In this section, we begin in Mother Nature's way, with the spring of empires.

Yet most of the stories in the section would belong almost as well at the end. Take the case of Jeff Otis, investigating some ruins on the planet of a binary star. Terrestrial civilization is reaching out into interplanetary space at last, and already five planetary systems have

5

been opened up. This one is now being made ready for colonization. And then Otis gets a little closer to one of the alien creatures. As H. B. Fyfe relates in his beautifully constructed story, the creature has a scrap of information which will change perspectives all round.

Curious the attraction that ruins have for science fiction writers. It is part of the gothic heritage of the literature and at the same time, I believe, a symbol of the way we see ourselves as living in the ruins of religious belief or of a deeper culture. Only in the last ten years has science fiction been paid any sort of critical attention; most critics have observed the startling way in which sf, by abandoning literalism and moving towards surrealism, provides a special kind of mirror for its own times. One might say that galactic empires have been invented because we have a longing for that sort of cosmic cohesion; their tendency is as much religious as materialist.

So don't be too surprised if all sorts of implications leap unexpectedly from these stories. The implication in Michael Shaara's story concerns evil and its relationship with the human race. It is a typical sf story in the way in which it takes large chunks of time and space for granted —a freedom for which many of us read sf. Inevitably, perspectives become changed in the process.

This was Shaara's first or second story to be published, incidentally. He was one of many new authors to appear in the early fifties. He has recently won a Pulitzer Prize for his Civil War novel, *The Killer Angels*.

The two opening stories, by Arthur C. Clarke and R. A. Lafferty, are brief. They serve as overtures to the grand theme of colonial expansion. They set the scene within a frame of reference. Clarke reminds us, in a vein characteristic of him, that the large and the small are connected; both are part of the processes at work in the universe. A process on the whole indifferent to man. It may be that man's incursions into the universe, if he gets that far, will be lemming-like, rather than a rational progression.

As for R. A. Lafferty, he reminds us—well, Lafferty is a very funny man, and he reminds us of that. We shall need a sense of humour as much as a blaster on the *Long Voyage Out*.

6

*You've heard the one about the monkeys, the type-writer, and the complete works of Shakespeare? So did Michael . . . but he set out to prove it—!*

●

# BEEN A LONG, LONG TIME
## by R. A. Lafferty

It doesn't end with one—it *Begins* with a whimper.

It was a sundering Dawn—Incandescence to which all later lights are less than candles—Heat to which the heat of all later suns is but a burnt-out match—the Polarities that set up the tension forever.

And in the middle was a whimper, just as was felt the first jerk that indicated that time had begun.

The two Challenges stood taller than the radius of the space that was being born; and one weak creature, Boshel, stood in the middle, too craven to accept either challenge.

"Uh, how long you fellows going to be gone?" Boshel snuffled.

The Creative Event was the Revolt rending the Void in two. The two sides formed, opposing Nations of Lightning split above the steep chasm. Two Champions had it out with a bitterness that has never passed—Michael wrapped in white fire—and Helel swollen with black and purple blaze. And their followers with them. It has been put into allegory as Acceptance and Rejection, and as Good

7

and Evil; but in the Beginning there was the Polarity by which the universes are sustained.

Between them, like a pigmy, stood Boshel alone in whimpering hesitation.

"Get the primordial metal out of it if you're coming with us," Helel growled like cracked thunder as he led his followers off in a fury to form a new settlement.

"Uh, you guys going to be back before night?" Boshel whimpered.

"Oh, get to Hell out of here," Michael roared.

"Keep the little oaf!" Helel snorted. "He hasn't enough brimstone in him to set fire to an outhouse."

The two great hosts separated, and Boshel was left alone in the void. He was still standing there when there was a second little jerk and time began in earnest, bursting the pod into a shower of sparks that traveled and grew. He was still standing there when the sparks acquired form and spin; and he stood there yet when life began to appear on the soot specks thrown off from the sparks. He stood there quite a long, long time.

"What are we going to do with the little bugger?" an underling asked Michael. "We can't have him fouling up the landscape forever."

"I'll go ask," said Mike, and he did.

But Michael was told that the responsibility was his; that Boshel would have to be punished for his hesitancy; and that it was up to Michael to select the suitable punishment and see that it was carried out.

"You know, he made time itself stutter at the start," Mike told the underling. "He set up a random that affected everything. It's got to be a punishment with something to do with time."

"You got any ideas?" the underling asked.

"I'll think of something," Michael said.

Quite a while after this, Michael was thumbing through a book one afternoon at a news-stand in Los Angeles.

"It says here," Michael intoned, "that if six monkeys were set down to six typewriters and typed for a long enough time, they would type all the words of Shakespeare exactly. Time is something we've got plenty of. Let's try it, Kitabel, and see how long it takes."

"What's a monkey, Michael?"

8

"I don't know."

"What's a typewriter?"

"I don't know."

"What's Shakespeare, Mike?"

"Anybody can ask questions, Kitabel. Get the things together and let's get the project started."

"It sounds like a lengthy project. Who will oversee it?"

"Boshel. It's a natural for him. It will teach him patience and a sense of order, and impress on him the majesty of time. It's exactly the punishment I've been looking for."

They got the things together and turned them over to Boshel.

"As soon as the project is finished, Bosh, your period of waiting will be over. Then you can join the group and enjoy yourself with the rest of us."

"Well, it's better than standing here doing nothing," Boshel said. "It'd go faster if I could educate the monkeys and let them copy it."

"No, the typing has to be random, Bosh. It was you who introduced the random factor into the universe. So, suffer for it."

"Any particular edition the copy has to correspond to?"

"The 'Blackstone Readers' Edition Thirty-Seven and a half Volumes in One that I have here in my hand will do fine," Michael said. "I've had a talk with the monkeys, and they're willing to stick with it. It took me eighty thousand years just to get them where they could talk, but that's nothing when we're talking about time."

"Man, are we ever talking about Time!" Boshel moaned.

"I made a deal with the monkeys. They will be immune to fatigue and boredom. I cannot promise the same for you."

"Uh, Michael, since it may be quite a while, I wonder if I could have some sort of clock to keep track of how fast things are going."

So Michael made him a clock. It was a cube of dressed stone measuring a parsec on each edge.

"You don't have to wind it, you don't have to do a thing to it, Bosh," Michael explained. "A small bird will come every millennium and sharpen its beak on this stone. You can tell the passing of time by the diminishing of the stone. It's a good clock, and it has only one moving part, the bird. I will not guarantee that your project will be finished by the time the entire stone is worn away, but you will be able to tell that time has passed."

"It's better than nothing," Boshel said, "but it's going to be a drag. I think this concept of time is a little Mediaeval, though."

"So am I," Michael said. "I tell you what I can do, though, Bosh. I can chain you to that stone and have another large bird dive-bomb you and gouge out hunks of your liver. That was in a story in another book on that news-stand."

"You slay me, Mike. That won't be necessary. I'll pass the time somehow."

Boshel set the monkeys to work. They were conditioned to punch the typewriters at random. Within a short period of time (as the Larger Creatures count time) the monkeys had produced whole Shakesperian words: "Let" which is found in scene two of act one of Richard III; "Go" which is in scene two of act two of Julius Caesar; and "Be" which occurs in the very first scene and act of The Tempest. Boshel was greatly encouraged.

Some time after this, one of the monkeys produced two Shakespearian words in succession. By this time, the home world of Shakespeare (which was also the home of the news-stand in Los Angeles where was born a great idea) was long out of business.

After another while, the monkeys had done whole phrases. By then, quite a bit of time had run out.

The trouble with that little bird is that its beak did not seem to need much sharpening when it did come once every thousand years. Boshel discovered that Michael had played a `dirty seraphic trick on him and had been feeding the bird entirely on bland custard. The bird would take two or three light swipes at the stone, and then be off for another thousand years. Yet after no more than a thousand visitations, there was an unmistakable scratch on the stone. It was a hopeful sign.

Boshel began to see that the thing could be done. A monkey—and not the most brilliant of them—finally produced a whole sentence: "What say'st thou, bully-rook?" And at that very moment another thing happened. It was surprising to Boshel, for it was the first time he had ever seen it. But he would see it milliards of times before it was finished.

A speck of cosmic dust, on the far outreaches of space, met another speck. This should not have been unusual; specks were always meeting specks. But this case was different. Each speck—in the opposite direction—had been the outmost in the whole cosmos. You can't get farther apart than that. The speck (a teeming conglomerate of peopled worlds) looked at the other speck with eyes and instruments, and saw its own eyes and instruments looking back at it. What the speck saw was itself. The cosmic tetradimensionate sphere had been completed. The first speck had met itself coming from the other direction, and space had been transversed.

Then it all collapsed.

The stars went out, one by one, and billion by billion. Nightmares of falling! All the darkened orbs and oblates fell down into the void that was all bottom. There was nothing left but one tight pod in the void, and a few out of context things like Michael and his associates, and Boshel and his monkeys.

Boshel had a moment of unease: he had become used to the appearance of the expanding universe. But he need not have been uneasy. It began all over again.

A few billion centuries ticked by silently. Once more, the pod burst into a shower of sparks that traveled and grew. They acquired form and spin, and life appeared again on the soot specks thrown off from those sparks.

This happened again and again. Each cycle seemed damnably long while it was happening; but in retrospect, the cycles were only like a light blinking on and off. And in the Longer Retrospect, they were like a high-frequency alternator, producing a dizzy number of such cycles every over-second, and continuing for tumbling ages. Yet Boshel was becoming bored. There was just no other word for it.

When only a few billion cosmic cycles had been completed, there was a gash in the clock-rock that you could hide a horse in. The little bird made very many journeys

11

back to sharpen its beak. And Pithekos Pete, the most rapid of the monkeys, had now random-written The Tempest, complete and perfect. They shook hands all around, monkeys and angel. It was something of a moment.

The moment did not last. Pete, instead of pecking at furious random to produce the rest of the plays, wrote his own improved version of The Tempest. Boshel was furious.

"But it's better, Bosh," Peter protested. "And I have some ideas about stage-craft that will really set this thing up."

"Of course it's better! We don't want them better. We want them just the same. Can't you monkeys realize that we are working out a problem of random probabilities? Oh, you clunker-heads!"

"Let me have that damned book for a month, Bosh, and I'll copy the plagued things off and we'll be finished," Pithekos Pete suggested.

"Rules, you lunk-heads, rules!" Boshel grated out. "We have to abide by the rules. You know that isn't allowed, and besides it would be found out. I have reason to suspect, and it cuts me to say this, that one of my own monkeys and associates here present is an informer. We'd never get by with it."

After the brief misunderstanding, things went better. The monkeys stayed with their task. And after a number of cycles expressed by nine followed by zeros in pica type sufficient to stretch around the universe at a period just prior to its collapse (the radius and the circumference of the ultimate sphere are, of course, the same), the first complete version was ready.

It was faulty, of course, and it had to be rejected. But there were less than thirty thousand errors in it; it presaged great things to come, and ultimate triumph.

Later (People, was it ever later!) they had it quite close. By the time that the gash in the clock-rock would hold a medium-sized solar system, they had a version with only five errors.

"It will come," Boshel said. "It will come in time. And time is the one thing we have plenty of."

Later—much, much later—they seemed to have it

12

perfect; and by this time, the bird had worn away nearly a fifth of the bulk of the great stone with its millennial visits.

Michael himself read the version and could find no error. This was not conclusive, of course, for Michael was an impatient and hurried reader. Three readings were required for verification, but never was hope so high.

It passed the second reading, by a much more careful angel, and was pronounced letter-perfect. But it was later at night when that reader had finished it, and he may have gotten a little careless at the end.

And it passed the third reading, through all the thirty-seven plays of it, and into the poems at the end. This was Kitabel, the scribing angel himself, who was appointed to that third reading. He was just about to sign the certification when he paused.

"There is something sticking in my mind," he said, and he shook his head to clear it. "There is something like an echo that is not quite right. I wouldn't want to make a mistake."

He had written "Kitab—", but he had not finished his signature.

"I won't be able to sleep tonight if I don't think of it," he complained. "It wasn't in the plays; I know that they were perfect. It was something in the poems—quite near the end—some dissonance. Either the bard wrote a remarkably malapropos line, or there was an error in the transcription that my eye overlooked but my ear remembered. I acknowledge that I was sleepy near the end."

"Oh, by all the worlds that were ever made, sign!" pleaded Boshel.

"You have waited this long, a moment more won't kill you, Bosh."

"Don't bet on it, Kit. I'm about to blow, I tell you."

But Kitabel went back and he found it—a verse in the Phoenix and the Turtle:

> From this session interdict
> Every fowl of tyrant wing,
> Save the eagle, feather'd king:
> Keep the obsequy so strict.

That is what the book itself said. And what Pithekos Pete had written was nearly, but not quite, the same thing:

> From this session interdict
> Every fowl of tyrant wingg,
>     ave the eaggle, feather'd kingg:
> Dam machine the g is sticked.

And if you ever saw an angel cry, words cannot describe to you the show that Boshel put on then.

They are still at it tonight, typing away at random, for that last sad near-victory was less than a million billion cycles ago. And only a moment ago—half way back in the present cycle—one of the monkeys put together no less than nine Shakespearian words in a row.

There is still hope. And the bird has now worn the rock down to about half its bulk.

*They moved towards the future—in quest for something hidden in the distant past.*

•

# THE POSSESSED
## by Arthur C. Clarke

And now the sun ahead was so close that the hurricane of radiation was forcing the Swarm back into the dark night of space. Soon it would be able to come no closer; the gales of light on which it rode from star to star could not be faced so near their source. Unless it encountered a planet very soon, and could fall down into the peace and safety of its shadow, this sun must be abandoned as had so many before.

Six cold outer worlds had already been searched and discarded. Either they were frozen beyond all hope of organic life, or else they harbored entities of types that were useless to the Swarm. If it was to survive, it must find hosts not too unlike those it had left on its doomed and distant home. Millions of years ago the Swarm had begun its journey, swept starward by the fires of its own exploding sun. Yet even now the memory of its lost birth-place was still sharp and clear, an ache that would never die.

There was a planet ahead, swinging its cone of shadow through the flame-swept night. The senses that the Swarm

15

had developed upon its long journey reached out toward the approaching world, reached out and found it good.

The merciless buffeting of radiation ceased as the black disc of the planet eclipsed the sun. Falling freely under gravity, the Swarm dropped swiftly until it hit the outer fringe of the atmosphere. The first time it had made planet-fall it had almost met its doom, but now it contracted its tenuous substance with the unthinking skill of long practice, until it formed a tiny, close-knit sphere. Slowly its velocity slackened, until at last it was floating motionless between earth and sky.

For many years it rode the winds of the stratosphere from Pole to Pole, or let the soundless fusillades of dawn blast it westward from the rising sun. Everywhere it found life, but nowhere intelligence. There were things that crawled and flew and leaped, but there were no things that talked or built. Ten million years hence there might be creatures here with minds that the Swarm could possess and guide for its own purposes; there was no sign of them now. It could not guess which of the countless life-forms on this planet would be the heir to the future, and without such a host it was helpless—a mere pattern of electric charges, a matrix of order and self-awareness in a universe of chaos. By its own resources the Swarm had no control over matter, yet once it had lodged in the mind of a sentient race there was nothing that lay beyond its powers.

It was not the first time, and it would not be the last, that the planet had been surveyed by a visitant from space —though never by one in such peculiar and urgent need. The Swarm was faced with a tormenting dilemma. It could begin its weary travels once more, hoping that ultimately it might find the conditions it sought, or it could wait here on this world, biding its time until a race had arisen which would fit its purpose.

It moved like mist through the shadows, letting the vagrant winds take it where they willed. The clumsy, ill-formed reptiles of this young world never saw its passing, but it observed them, recording, analyzing, trying to extrapolate into the future. There was so little to choose between all these creatures; not one showed even the first faint glimmerings of conscious mind. Yet if it left this

16

world in search of another, it might roam the universe in vain until the end of time.

At last it made its decision. By its very nature, it could choose both alternatives. The greater part of the Swarm would continue its travels among the stars, but a portion of it would remain on this world, like a seed planted in the hope of future harvest.

It began to spin upon its axis, its tenuous body flattening into a disc. Now it was wavering at the frontiers of visibility—it was a pale ghost, a faint will-of-the-wisp that suddenly fissured into two unequal fragments. The spinning slowly died away: the Swarm had become two, each an entity with all the memories of the original, and all its desires and needs.

There was a last exchange of thoughts between parent and child who were also identical twins. If all went well with them both, they would meet again in the far future here at this valley in the mountains. The one who was staying would return to this point at regular intervals down the ages; the one who continued the search would send back an emissary if ever a better world was found. And then they would be united again, no longer homeless exiles vainly wandering among the indifferent stars.

The light of dawn was spilling over the raw, new mountains when the parent swarm rose up to meet the sun. At the edge of the atmosphere the gales of radiation caught it and swept it unresisting out beyond the planets, to start again upon the endless search.

The one that was left began its almost equally hopeless task. It needed an animal that was not so rare that disease or accident could make it extinct, nor so tiny that it could never acquire any power over the physical world. And it must breed rapidly, so that its evolution could be directed and controlled as swiftly as possible.

The search was long and the choice difficult, but at last the Swarm selected its host. Like rain sinking into thirsty soil, it entered the bodies of certain small lizards and began to direct their destiny.

It was an immense task, even for a being which could never know death. Generation after generation of the lizards was swept into the past before there came the slightest improvement in the race. And always, at the

17

appointed time, the Swarm returned to its rendezvous among the mountains. Always it returned in vain: there was no messenger from the stars, bringing news of better fortune elsewhere.

The centuries lengthened into millennia, the millennia into eons. By the standards of geological time, the lizards were now changing rapidly. Presently they were lizards no more, but warm-blooded, fur-covered creatures that brought forth their young alive. They were still small and feeble, and their minds were rudimentary, but they contained the seeds of future greatness.

Yet not only the living creatures were altering as the ages slowly passed. Continents were being rent asunder, mountains being worn down by the weight of the unwearying rain. Through all these changes, the Swarm kept to its purpose; and always, at the appointed times, it went to the meeting place that had been chosen so long ago, waited patiently for a while, and came away. Perhaps the parent swarm was still searching or perhaps—it was a hard and terrible thought to grasp—some unknown fate had overtaken it and it had gone the way of the race it had once ruled. There was nothing to do but to wait and see if the stubborn life-stuff of this planet could be forced along the path to intelligence.

And so the eons passed . . .

Somewhere in the labyrinth of evolution the Swarm made its fatal mistake and took the wrong turning. A hundred million years had gone since it came to Earth, and it was very weary. It could not die, but it could degenerate. The memories of its ancient home and of its destiny were fading: its intelligence was waning even while its hosts climbed the long slope that would lead to self-awareness.

By a cosmic irony, in giving the impetus which would one day bring intelligence to this world, the Swarm had exhausted itself. It had reached the last stage of parasitism; no longer could it exist apart from its hosts. Never again could it ride free above the world, driven by wind and sun. To make the pilgrimage to the ancient rendezvous, it must travel slowly and painfully in a thousand little bodies. Yet it continued the immemorial custom, driven on by the desire for reunion which burned all the

18

more fiercely now that it knew the bitterness of failure. Only if the parent swarm returned and reabsorbed it could it ever know new life and vigor.

The glaciers came and went; by a miracle the little beasts that now housed the waning alien intelligence escaped the clutching fingers of the ice. The oceans overwhelmed the land, and still the race survived. It even multiplied, but it could do no more. This world would never be its heritage, for far away in the heart of another continent a certain monkey had come down from the trees and was looking at the stars with the first glimmerings of curiosity.

The mind of the Swarm was dispersing, scattering among a million tiny bodies, no longer able to unite and assert its will. It had lost all cohesion; its memories were fading. In a million years, at most, they would all be gone.

Only one thing remained—the blind urge which still, at intervals which by some strange aberration were becoming ever shorter, drove it to seek its consummation in a valley that long ago had ceased to exist.

Quietly riding the lane of moonlight, the pleasure steamer passed the island with its winking beacon and entered the fjord. It was a calm and lovely night, with Venus sinking in the west out beyond the Faroes, and the lights of the harbor reflected with scarcely a tremor in the still waters far ahead.

Nils and Christina were utterly content. Standing side by side against the boat rail, their fingers locked together, they watched the wooded slopes drift silently by. The tall trees were motionless in the moonlight, their leaves unruffled by even the merest breath of wind, their slender trunks rising whitely from pools of shadow. The whole world was asleep; only the moving ship dared to break the spell that had bewitched the night.

Then suddenly, Christina gave a little gasp and Nils felt her fingers tighten convulsively on his. He followed her gaze: she was staring out across the water, looking toward the silent sentinels of the forest.

"What is it, darling?" he asked anxiously.

"Look!" she replied, in a whisper Nils could scarcely hear. "There—under the pines!"

Nils stared, and as he did so the beauty of the night ebbed slowly away and ancestral terrors came crawling back from exile. For beneath the trees the land was alive: a dappled brown tide was moving down the slopes of the hill and merging into the dark waters. Here was an open patch on which the moonlight fell unbroken by shadow. It was changing even as he watched: the surface of the land seemed to be rippling downward like a slow waterfall seeking union with the sea.

And then Nils laughed and the world was sane once more. Christina looked at him, puzzled but reassured.

"Don't you remember?" he chuckled. "We read all about it in the paper this morning. They do this every few years, and always at night. It's been going on for days."

He was teasing her, sweeping away the tension of the last few minutes. Christina looked back at him, and a slow smile lit up her face.

"Of course!" she said. "How stupid of me!" Then she turned once more toward the land and her expression became sad, for she was very tender-hearted.

"Poor little things!" she sighed. "I wonder why they do it?"

Nils shrugged his shoulders indifferently.

"No one knows," he answered. "It's just one of those mysteries. I shouldn't think about it if it worries you. Look—we'll soon be in harbor!"

They turned toward the beckoning lights where their future lay, and Christina glanced back only once toward the tragic, mindless tide that was still flowing beneath the moon.

Obeying an urge whose meaning they had never known, the doomed legions of the lemmings were finding oblivion beneath the waves.

*When men arrived on the planet, they found ruins, and a few hard-to-see aliens. And they decided to protect the species—which was a mistaken idea based on inadequate understanding of the facts.*

●

# PROTECTED SPECIES
## by H. B. Fyfe

The yellow star, of which Torang was the second planet, shone hotly down on the group of men viewing the half-built dam from the heights above. At a range of eighty million miles, the effect was quite Terran, the star being somewhat smaller than Sol.

For Jeff Otis, fresh from a hop through space from the extra-bright star that was the other component of the binary system, the heat was enervating. The shorts and light shirt supplied him by the planet co-ordinator were soaked with perspiration. He mopped his forehead and turned to his host.

"Very nice job, Finchley," he complimented. "It's easy to see you have things well in hand here."

Finchley grinned sparingly. He had a broad, hard, flat face with tight lips and mere slits of blue eyes. Otis had been trying ever since the previous morning to catch a revealing expression on it.

He was uneasily aware that his own features were too frank and open for an inspector of colonial installations. For one thing, he had too many lines and hollows in his face, a result of being chronically underweight from space-hopping among the sixteen planets of the binary system.

Otis noticed that Finchley's aides were eying him furtively.

"Yes, Finchley," he repeated to break the little silence, "you're doing very well on the hydroelectric end. When are you going to show me the capital city you're laying out?"

"We can fly over there now," answered Finchley. "We have tentative boundaries laid out below those precolony ruins we saw from the 'copter."

"Oh, yes. You know, I meant to remark as we flew over that they looked a good deal like similar remnants on some of the other planets."

He caught himself as Finchley's thin lips tightened a trifle more. The co-ordinator was obviously trying to be patient and polite to an official from whom he hoped to get a good report, but Otis could see he would much rather be going about his business of building up the colony.

He could hardly blame Finchley, he decided. It was the fifth planetary system Terrans had found in their expansion into space, and there would be bigger jobs ahead for a man with a record of successful accomplishments. Civilization was reaching out to the stars at last. Otis supposed that he, too, was some sort of pioneer, although he usually was too busy to feel like one.

"Well, I'll show you some photos later," he said. "Right now, we— Say, why all that jet-burning down there?"

In the gorge below, men had dropped their tools and seemed to be charging toward a common focal point. Excited yells carried thinly up the cliffs.

"Ape hunt, probably," guessed one of Finchley's engineers.

"Ape?" asked Otis, surprised.

"Not exactly," corrected Finchley patiently. "That's common slang for what we mention in reports as Torangs. They look a little like big, skinny, gray apes;

but they're the only life large enough to name after the planet."

Otis stared down into the gorge. Most of the running men had given up and were straggling back to their work. Two or three, brandishing pistols, continued running and disappeared around a bend.

"Never catch him now," commented Finchley's pilot.

"Do you just let them go running off whenever they feel like it?" Otis inquired.

Finchley met his curious gaze stolidly.

"I'm in favor of anything that will break the monotony, Mr. Otis. We have a problem of morale, you know. This planet is a key colony, and I like to keep the work going smoothly."

"Yes, I suppose there isn't much for recreation yet."

"Exactly. I don't see the sport in it myself but I let them. We're up to schedule."

"Ahead, if anything," Otis placated him. "Well, now, about the city?"

Finchley led the way to the helicopter. The pilot and Otis waited while he had a final word with his engineers, then they all climbed in and were off.

Later, hovering over the network of crude roads being leveled by Finchley's bulldozers, Otis admitted aloud that the location was well-chosen. It lay along a long, narrow bay that thrust in from the distant ocean to gather the waters of the same river that was being dammed some miles upstream.

"Those cliffs over there," Finchley pointed out, "were raised up since the end of whatever civilization used to be here—so my geologist tells me. We can fly back that way, and you can see how the ancient city was once at the head of the bay."

The pilot climbed and headed over the cliffs. Otis saw that these formed the edge of a plateau. At one point, their continuity was marred by a deep gouge.

"Where the river ran thousands of years ago," Finchley explained.

They reached a point from which the outlines of the ruined city were easily discerned. From the air, Otis knew,

23

they were undoubtedly plainer than if he had been among them.

"Must have been a pretty large place," he remarked. "Any idea what sort of beings built it or what happened to them?"

"Haven't had time for that yet," Finchley said. "Some boys from the exploration staff poke around in there every so often. Best current theory seems to be that it belonged to the Torangs."

"The *animals* they were hunting before?" asked Otis.

"Might be. Can't say for sure, but the diggers found signs the city took more of a punch than just an earthquake. Claim they found too much evidence of fires, exploded missiles, and warfare in general—other places as well as here. So . . . we've been guessing the Torangs are degenerated descendents of the survivors of some interplanetary brawl."

Otis considered that.

"Sounds plausible," he admitted, "but you ought to do something to make sure you are right."

"Why?"

"If it *is* the case, you'll have to stop your men from hunting them; degenerated or not, the Colonial Commission has regulations about contact with any local inhabitants."

Finchley turned his head to scowl at Otis, and controlled himself with an obvious effort.

"Those *apes?*" he demanded.

"Well, how can you tell? Ever try to contact them?"

"Yes! At first, that is; before we figured them for animals."

"And?"

"Couldn't get near one!" Finchley declared heatedly. "If they had any sort of half-intelligent culture, wouldn't they let us make *some* sort of contact?"

"Offhand," admitted Otis, "I should think so. How about setting down a few minutes? I'd like a look at the ruins."

Finchley glared at his wrist watch, but directed the pilot to land at a cleared spot. The young man brought them down neatly and the two officials alighted.

24

Otis, glancing around, saw where the archaeologists had been digging. They had left their implements stacked casually at the site—the air was dry up here and who was there to steal a shovel?

He left Finchley and strolled around a mound of dirt that had been cleared away from an entrance to one of the buildings. The latter had been built of stone, or at least faced with it. A peep into the dim excavation led him to believe there had been a steel framework, but the whole affair had been collapsed as if by an explosion.

He walked a little way further and reached a section of presumably taller buildings where the stone ruins thrust above the sandy surface. After he had wandered through one or two arched openings that seemed to have been windows, he understood why the explorers had chosen to dig for their information. If any covering or decoration had ever graced the walls, it had long since been weathered off. As for ceiling or roof, nothing remained.

"Must have been a highly developed civilization just the same," he muttered.

A movement at one of the shadowed openings to his right caught his eye. He did not remember noticing Finchley leave the helicopter to follow him, but he was glad of a guide.

"Don't you think so?" he added.

He turned his head, but Finchley was not there. In fact, now that Otis was aware of his surroundings, he could hear the voices of the other two mumbling distantly back by the aircraft.

"Seeing things!" he grumbled, and started through the ancient window.

Some instinct stopped him half a foot outside.

*Come on, Jeff,* he told himself, *don't be silly! What could be there? Ghosts?*

On the other hand, he realized, there were times when it was just as well to rely upon instinct—at least until you figured out the origin of the strange feeling. Any spaceman would agree to that. The man who developed an animal sixth sense was the man who lived longest on alien planets.

He thought he must have paused a full minute or more, during which he had heard not the slightest sound except the mutter of voices to the rear. He peered into the the chamber, which was about twenty feet square and well if not brightly lit by reflected light.

Nothing was to be seen, but when he found himself turning his head stealthily to peer over his shoulder, he decided that the queer sensation along the back of his neck meant something.

*Wait, now,* he thought swiftly. *I didn't see quite the whole room.*

The flooring was heaped with wind-bared rubble that would not show footprints. He felt much more comfortable to notice himself thinking in that vein.

*At least, I'm not imagining ghosts,* he thought.

Bending forward the necessary foot, he thrust his head through the opening and darted a quick look to left, then to the right along the wall. As he turned right, his glance was met directly by a pair of very wide-set black eyes which shifted inward slightly as they got his range.

The Torang about matched his own six-feet-two, mainly because of elongated, gibbonlike limbs and a similarly crouching stance. Arms and legs, covered with short, curly, gray fur, had the same general proportions as human limbs, but looked half again too long for a trunk that seemed to be ribbed all the way down. Shoulder and hip joints were completely lean, rather as if the Torang had developed on a world of lesser gravity than that of the human.

It was the face that made Otis stare. The mouth was toothless and probably constructed more for sucking than for chewing. But the eyes! They projected like ends of a dumb-bell from each side of the narrow skull where the ears should have been, and focused with obvious mobility. Peering closer, Otis saw tiny ears below the eyes, almost hidden in the curling fur of the neck.

He realized abruptly that his own eyes felt as if they were bulging out, although he could not remember having changed his expression of casual curiosity. His back was getting stiff also. He straightened up carefully.

"Uh . . . hello," he murmured, feeling unutterably silly but conscious of some impulse to compromise between a tone of greeting for another human being and one of pacification to an animal.

26

The Torang moved then, swiftly but unhurriedly. In fact, Otis later decided, deliberately. One of the long arms swept downward to the rubble-strewn ground.

The next instant, Otis jerked his head back out of the opening as a stone whizzed past in front of his nose.

"Hey!" he protested involuntarily.

There was a scrabbling sound from within, as of animal claws churning to a fast start among the pebbles. Recovering his balance, Otis charged recklessly through the entrance.

"I don't know why," he admitted to Finchley a few minutes later. "If I stopped to think how I might have had my skull bashed in coming through, I guess I'd have just backed off and yelled for you."

Finchley nodded, but his narrow gaze seemed faintly approving for the first time since they had met.

"He was gone, of course," Otis continued. "I barely caught a glimpse of his rump vanishing through another window."

"Yeah, they're pretty fast," put in Finchley's pilot. "In the time we've been here, the boys haven't taken more than half a dozen. Got a stuffed one over at headquarters though."

"Hm-m-m," murmured Otis thoughtfully.

From their other remarks, he learned that he had not noticed everything, even though face to face with the creature. Finchley's mentioning the three digits of the hands or feet, for instance, came as a surprise.

Otis was silent most of the flight back to headquarters. Once there, he disappeared with a perfunctory excuse toward the rooms assigned him.

That evening, at a dinner which Finchley had made as attractive as was possible in a comparatively raw and new colony, Otis was noticeably sociable. The co-ordinator was gratified.

"Looks as if they finally sent us a regular guy," he remarked behind his hand to one of his assistants. "Round up a couple of the prettier secretaries to keep him happy."

"I understand he nearly laid hands on a Torang up at the diggings," said the other.

"Yep, ran right at it bare-handed. Came as close bagging it as anybody could, I suppose."

"Maybe it's just as well he didn't," commented the assistant. "They're big enough to mess up an unarmed man some."

Otis, meanwhile and for the rest of the evening, was assiduously busy making acquaintances. So engrossed was he in turning every new conversation to the Torangs and asking seemingly casual questions about the little known of their habits and possible past, that he hardly noticed receiving any special attentions. As a visiting inspector, he was used to attempts to entertain and distract him.

The next morning, he caught Finchley at his office in the sprawling one-story structure of concrete and glass that was colonial headquarters.

After accepting a chair across the desk from the coordinator, Otis told him his conclusions. Finchley's narrow eyes opened a trifle when he heard the details. His wide, hard-muscled face became slightly pink.

"Oh, for—! I mean, Otis, why must you make something big out of it? The men very seldom bag one anyway!"

"Perhaps because they're so rare," answered Otis calmly. "How do we know they're not intelligent life? Maybe if you were hanging on in the ruins of your ancestors' civilization, reduced to a primitive state, *you'd* be just as wary of a bunch of loud Terrans moving in!"

Finchley shrugged. He looked vaguely uncomfortable, as if debating whether Otis or some disgruntled sportsman from his husky construction crews would be easier to handle.

"Think of the overall picture a minute," Otis urged. "We're pushing out into space at last, after centuries of dreams and struggles. With all the misery we've seen in various colonial systems at home, we've tried to plan these ventures so as to avoid old mistakes."

Finchley nodded grudgingly. Otis could see that his mind was on the progress charts of his many projects.

"It stands to reason," the inspector went on, "that some day we'll find a planet with intelligent life. We're still new in space, but as we probe farther out, it's bound to happen. That's why the Commission drew up rules about native life forms. Or have you read that part of the code lately?"

Finchley shifted from side to side in his chair.

"Now, look!" he protested. "Don't go making *me* out a hardboiled vandal with nothing in mind but exterminating everything that moves on all Torang. *I* don't go out hunting the apes!"

"I know, I know," Otis soothed him. "But before the Colonial Commission will sanction any destruction of indigenous life, we'll have to show—*besides* that it's not intelligent—that it exists in sufficient numbers to avoid extinction."

"What do you expect me to do about it?"

Otis regarded him with some sympathy. Finchley was the hard-bitten type the Commission needed to oversee the first breaking-in of a colony on a strange planet, but he was not unreasonable. He merely wanted to be left alone to handle the tough job facing him.

"Announce a ban on hunting Torangs," Otis said. "There must be something else they can go after."

"Oh, yes," admitted Finchley. "There are swarms of little rabbit-things and other vermin running through the brush. But, I don't know—"

"It's standard practice," Otis reminded him. "We have many a protected species even back on Terra that would be extinct by now, but for the game laws."

In the end, they agreed that Finchley would do his honest best to enforce a ban provided Otis obtained a formal order from the headquarters of the system. The inspector went from the office straight to the communications center, where he filed a long report for the chief co-ordinator's office in the other part of the binary system.

It took some hours for the reply to reach Torang. When it came that afternoon, he went looking for Finchley.

He found the co-ordinator inspecting a newly finished canning factory on the coast, elated at the completion of one more link in making the colony self-sustaining.

"Here it is," said Otis, waving the message copy.

"Signed by the chief himself. 'As of this date, the apelike beings known as Torangs, indigenous to planet number and so forth, are to be considered a rare and protected species under regulations and so forth et cetera.'"

"Good enough," answered Finchley with an amiable shrug. "Give it here, and I'll have it put on the public address system and the bulletin boards."

Otis returned satisfied to the helicopter that had brought him out from headquarters.

"Back, sir?" asked the pilot.

"Yes . . . *no!* Just for fun, take me out to the old city. I never did get a good look the other day, and I'd like to before I leave."

They flew over the plains between the sea and the upjutting cliffs. In the distance, Otis caught a glimpse of the rising dam he had been shown the day before. This colony would go well, he reflected, as long as he checked up on details like preserving native life forms.

Eventually, the pilot landed at the same spot he had been taken on his previous visit to the ancient ruins. Someone else was on the scene today. Otis saw a pair of men he took to be archaeologists.

"I'll just wander around a bit," he told the pilot.

He noticed the two men looking at him from where they stood by the shovels and other equipment, so he paused to say hello. As he thought, they had been digging in the ruins.

"Taking some measurements in fact," said the sunburned blond introduced as Hoffman. "Trying to get a line on what sort of things built the place."

"Oh?" said Otis, interested. "What's the latest theory?"

"Not so much different from us," Hoffman told the inspector while his partner left them to pick up another load of artifacts.

"Judging from the size of the rooms, height of doorways, and such stuff as stairways," he went on, "they were pretty much our size. So far, of course, it's only a rough estimate."

"Could be ancestors of the Torangs, eh?" asked Otis.

"Very possible, sir," answered Hoffman, with a promptness that suggested it was his own view. "But we haven't dug up enough to guess at the type of culture they had,

30

or draw any conclusions as to their psychology or social customs."

Otis nodded, thinking that he ought to mention the young fellow's name to Finchley before he left Torang. He excused himself as the other man returned with a box of some sort of scraps the pair had unearthed, and strolled between the outlines of the untouched buildings.

In a few minutes, he came to the section of higher structures where he had encountered the Torang the previous day.

"Wonder if I should look in the same spot?" he muttered aloud. "No . . . that would be the *last* place the thing would return to . . . unless it had a lair thereabouts—"

He stopped to get his bearings, then shrugged and walked around a mound of rubble toward what he believed to be the proper building.

*Pretty sure this was it,* he mused. *Yes, shadows around that window arch look the same . . . same time of day—*

He halted, almost guiltily, and looked back to make sure no one was observing his return to the scene of his little adventure. After all, an inspector of colonial installations was not supposed to run around ghost-hunting like a small boy.

Finding himself alone, he stepped briskly through the crumbling arch—*and froze in his tracks.*

"I am honored to know you," said the Torang in a mild, rather buzzing voice. "We thought you possibly would return here."

Otis gaped. The black eyes projecting from the sides of the narrow head tracked him up and down, giving him the unpleasant sensation of being measured for an artillery salvo.

"I am known as Jal-Ganyr," said the Torang. "Unless I am given incorrect data, you are known as Jeff-Otis. That is so."

The last statement was made with almost no inflection, but some still-functioning corner of Otis' mind interpreted it as a question. He sucked in a deep breath, suddenly conscious of having forgotten to breathe for a moment.

"I didn't know . . . yes, that is so . . . I didn't know you Torangs could speak Terran. Or anything else. How—?"

31

He hesitated as a million questions boiled up in his mind to be asked. Jal-Ganyr absently stroked the gray fur of his chest with his three-fingered left hand, squatting patiently on a flat rock. Otis felt somehow that he had been allowed to waste time mumbling only by grace of disciplined politeness.

"I am not of the Torangs," said Jal-Ganyr in his wheezing voice. "I am of the Myrbs. You would possibly say Myrbii. I have not been informed."

"You mean that is your name for yourselves?" asked Otis.

Jal-Ganyr seemed to consider, his mobile eyes swiveling inward to scan the Terran's face.

"More than that," he said at last, when he had thought it over. "I mean I am of the race originating at Myrb, not of this planet."

"Before we go any further," insisted Otis, "tell me, at least, how you learned our language!"

Jal-Ganyr made a fleeting gesture. His "face" was unreadable to the Terran, but Otis had the impression he had received the equivalent of a smile and a shrug.

"As to that," said the Myrb, "I possibly learned it before you did. We have observed you a very long time. You would unbelieve how long."

"But then—" Otis paused. That must mean before the colonists had landed on this planet. He was half-afraid it might mean before they had reached this sun system. He put aside the thought and asked, "But then, why do you live like this among the ruins? Why wait till now? If you had communicated, you could have had our help rebuilding—"

He let his voice trail off, wondering what sounded wrong. Jal-Ganyr rolled his eyes about leisurely, as if disdaining the surrounding ruins. Again, he seemed to consider all the implications of Otis' questions.

"We picked up your message to your chief," he answered at last. "We decided time is to communicate with one of you.

"We have no interest in rebuilding," he added. "We have concealed quarters for ourselves."

Otis found that his lips were dry from his unconsciously having let his mouth hang open. He moistened them with the tip of his tongue, and relaxed enough to lean against the wall.

"You mean my getting the ruling to proclaim you a protected species?" he asked. "You have instruments to intercept such signals?"

"I do. We have," said Jal-Ganyr simply. "It has been decided that you have expanded far enough into space to make necessary we contact a few of the thoughtful among you. It will possibly make easier in the future for our observers."

Otis wondered how much of that was irony. He felt himself flushing at the memory of the "stuffed specimen" at headquarters, and was pecularily relieved that he had not gone to see it.

*I've had the luck,* he told himself. *I'm the one to discover the first known intelligent beings beyond Sol!*

Aloud, he said, "We expected to meet someone like you eventually. But why have you chosen me?"

The question sounded vain, he realized, but it brought unexpected results.

"Your message. You made in a little way the same decision we made in a big way. We deduce that you are one to understand our regret and shame at what happened between our races . . . long ago."

"Between—?"

"Yes. For a long time, we thought you were all gone. We are pleased to see you returning to some of your old planets."

Otis stared blankly. Some instinct must have enabled the Myrb to interpret his bewildered expression. He apologized briefly.

"I possibly forgot to explain the ruins." Again, Jal-Ganyr's eyes swiveled slowly about.

"They are not ours," he said mildly. "They are yours."

*There is one circumstance under which it is exceedingly difficult to establish communications with another individual—or race. A new author considers a point that could make technically adequate communications quite futile . . .*

●

# ALL THE WAY BACK
## by Michael Shaara

Great were the Antha, so reads the One Book of history, greater perhaps than any of the Galactic Peoples, and they were brilliant and fair, and their reign was long, and in all things they were great and proud, even in the manner of their dying—
*Preface to Loab: History of The Master Race.*

The huge red ball of a sun hung glowing upon the screen.

Jansen adjusted the traversing knob, his face tensed and weary. The sun swung off the screen to the right, was replaced by the live black of space and the million speckled lights of the farther stars. A moment later the sun glided silently back across the screen and went off at the left. Again there was nothing but space and the stars.

"Try it again?" Cohn asked.

Jansen mumbled: "No. No use," and he swore heavily. "Nothing. Always nothing. Never a blessed thing."

34

Cohn repressed a sigh, began to adjust the controls.

In both of their minds was the single, bitter thought that there would be only one more time, and then they would go home. And it was a long way to come to go home with nothing.

When the controls were set there was nothing left to do. The two men walked slowly aft to the freeze room. Climbing up painfully on to the flat steel of the beds, they lay back and waited for the mechanism to function, for the freeze to begin.

Turned in her course, the spaceship bore off into the open emptiness. Her ports were thrown open, she was gathering speed as she moved away from the huge red star.

The object was sighted upon the last leg of the patrol, as the huge ship of the Galactic Scouts came across the edge of the Great Desert of the Rim, swinging wide in a long slow curve. It was there on the massometer as a faint *blip,* and, of course, the word went directly to Roymer.

"Report," he said briefly, and Lieutenant Goladan—a young and somewhat pompous Higiandrian—gave the Higiandrian equivalent of a cough and then reported.

"Observe," said Lieutenant Goladan, "that it is not a meteor, for the speed of it is much too great."

Roymer nodded patiently.

"And again, the speed is decreasing"—Goladan consulted his figures—"at the rate of twenty-four dines per segment. Since the orbit appears to bear directly upon the star Mina, and the decrease in speed is of a certain arbitrary origin, we must conclude that the object is a spaceship."

Roymer smiled.

"Very good, lieutenant." Like a tiny nova, Goladan began to glow and expand.

A good man, thought Roymer tolerantly, his is a race of good men. They have been two million years in achieving space flight; a certain adolescence is to be expected.

"Would you call Mind-Search, please?" Roymer asked.

Goladan sped away, to return almost immediately with the heavy-headed non-human Trian, chief of the Mind-Search Section.

35

Trian cocked an eyelike thing at Roymer, with grave inquiry.

".Yes, commander?"

Those of Trian's race had no vocal apparatus. In the aeon-long history of their race it had never been needed.

"Would you stand by please?" said Roymer, and he pressed a button and spoke to the engaging crew. "Prepare for alien contact."

The abrupt change in course was noticeable only on the viewplate, as the stars slid silently by. The patrol vessel veered off, swinging around and into the desert, settled into a parallel course with the strange new craft, keeping a discreet distance of —approximately—a light-year.

The scanners brought the object into immediate focus, and Goladan grinned with pleasure. A spaceship, yes, Alien, too. Undoubtedly a primitive race. He voiced these thoughts to Roymer.

"Yes," the commander said, staring at the strange, small, projectilelike craft. "Primitive type. It is to be wondered what they are doing in the desert."

Goladan assumed an expression of intense curiosity.

"Trian," said Roymer pleasantly, "would you contact?"

The huge head bobbed up and down once and then stared into the screen. There was a moment of profound silence. Then Trian turned back to stare at Roymer, and there was a distinctly human expression of surprise in his eyelike things.

"Nothing," came the thought. "I can detect no presence at all."

Roymer raised an eyebrow.

"Is there a barrier?"

"No"—Trian had turned to gaze back into the screen— "a barrier I could detect. But there is nothing at all. There is no sentient activity on board that vessel."

Trian's word had to be taken, of course, and Roymer was disappointed. A spaceship empty of life—Roymer shrugged. A derelict, then. But why the decreasing speed? Pre-set controls would account for that, of course, but why? Certainly, if one abandoned a ship, one would not arrange for it to—

He was interrupted by Trian's thought:

36

"Excuse me, but there is nothing. May I return to my quarters?"

Roymer nodded and thanked him, and Trian went ponderously away. Goladan said:

"Shall we prepare to board it, sir?"

"Yes."

And then Goladan was gone to give his proud orders.

Roymer continued to stare at the primitive vessel which hung on the plate. Curious. It was very interesting, always, to come upon derelict ships. The stories that were old, the silent tombs that had been drifting perhaps, for millions of years in the deep sea of space. In the beginning Roymer had hoped that the ship would be manned, and alien, but—nowadays, contact with an isolated race was rare, extremely rare. It was not to be hoped for, and he would be content with this, this undoubtedly empty, ancient ship.

And then, to Roymer's complete surprise, the ship at which he was staring shifted abruptly, turned on its axis, and flashed off like a live thing upon a new course.

When the defrosters activated and woke him up, Jansen lay for a while upon the steel table, blinking. As always with the freeze, it was difficult to tell at first whether anything had actually happened. It was like a quick blink and no more, and then you were lying, feeling exactly the same, thinking the same thoughts even, and if there was anything at all different it was maybe that you were a little numb. And yet in the blink time took a great leap, and the months went by like—Jansen smiled—like fenceposts.

He raised a languid eye to the red bulb in the ceiling. Out. He sighed. The freeze had come and gone. He felt vaguely cheated, reflected that this time, before the freeze, he would take a little nap.

He climbed down from the table, noted that Cohn had already gone to the control room. He adjusted himself to the thought that they were approaching a new sun, and it came back to him suddenly that this would be the last one, now they would go home.

Well then, let this one have planets. To have come all

this way, to have been gone from home for eleven years, and yet to find nothing—

He was jerked out of the old feeling of despair by a lurch of the ship. That would be Cohn taking her off the auto. And now, he thought, we will go in and run out the telescope and have a look, and there won't be a thing.

Wearily, he clumped off over the iron deck, going up to the control room. He had no hope left now, and he had been so hopeful at the beginning. As they are all hopeful, he thought, as they have been hoping now for three hundred years. And they will go on hoping, for a little while, and then men will become hard to get, even with the freeze, and then the starships won't go out any more. And Man will be doomed to the System for the rest of his days.

Therefore, he asked humbly, silently, let this one have planets.

Up in the dome of the control cabin, Cohn was bent over the panel, pouring power into the board. He looked up, nodded briefly as Jansen came in. It seemed to both of them that they had been apart for five minutes.

"Are they all hot yet?" asked Jansen.

"No, not yet."

The ship had been in deep space with her ports thrown open. Absolute cold had come in and gone to the core of her, and it was always a while before the ship was reclaimed and her instruments warmed. Even now there was a sharp chill in the air of the cabin.

Jansen sat down idly, rubbing his arms.

"Last time around, I guess."

"Yes," said Cohn, and added laconically, "I wish Weizsäcker was here."

Jansen grinned. Weizsäcker, poor old Weizsäcker. He was long dead and it was a good thing, for he was the most maligned human being in the System.

For a hundred years his theory on the birth of planets, that every sun necessarily gave birth to a satellite family, had been an accepted part of the knowledge of Man. And then, of course, there had come space flight.

Jansen chuckled wryly. Lucky man, Weizsäcker. Now, two hundred years and a thousand stars later, there had been discovered just four planets. Alpha Centauri had one: a barren, ice-crusted mote no larger than the Moon;

38

and Pollux had three, all dead lumps of cold rock and iron. None of the other stars had any at all. Yes, it would have been a great blow to Weizsäcker.

A hum of current broke into Jansen's thought as the telescope was run out. There was a sudden beginning of light upon the screen.

In spite of himself and the wry, hopeless feeling that had been in him, Jansen arose quickly, with a thin trickle of nervousness in his arms. There is always a chance, he thought, after all, there is always a chance. We have only been to a thousand suns, and in the Galaxy a thousand suns are not anything at all. So there is always a chance.

Cohn, calm and methodical, was manning the radar.

Gradually, condensing upon the center of the screen, the image of the star took shape. It hung at last, huge and yellow and flaming with an awful brilliance, and the prominences of the rim made the vast circle uneven. Because the ship was close and the filter was in, the stars of the background were invisible, and there was nothing but the one great sun.

Jansen began to adjust for observation.

The observation was brief.

They paused for a moment before beginning the tests, gazing upon the face of the alien sun. The first of their race to be here and to see, they were caught up for a time in the ancient, deep thrill of space and the unknown Universe.

They watched, and into the field of their vision, breaking in slowly upon the glaring edge of the sun's disk, there came a small black ball. It moved steadily away from the edge, in toward the center of the sun. It was unquestionably a planet in transit.

When the alien ship moved, Roymer was considerably rattled.

One does not question Mind-Search, he knew, and so there could not be any living thing aboard that ship. Therefore, the ship's movement could be regarded only as a peculiar aberration in the still-functioning drive. Certainly, he thought, and peace returned to his mind.

But it did pose an uncomfortable problem. Boarding that ship would be no easy matter, not if the thing was inclined to go hopping away like that, with no warning. There were two hundred years of conditioning in Roymer, it would be impossible for him to put either his ship or his crew into an unnecessarily dangerous position. And wavery, erratic spaceships could undoubtedly be classified as dangerous.

Therefore, the ship would have to be disabled.

Regretfully, he connected with Fire Control, put the operation into the hands of the Firecon officer, and settled back to observe the results of the actions against the strange craft.

And the alien moved again.

Not suddenly, as before, but deliberately now, the thing turned once more from its course, and its speed decreased even more rapidly. It was still moving in upon Mina, but now its orbit was tangential and no longer direct. As Roymer watched the ship come about, he turned up the magnification for a larger view, checked the automatic readings on the board below the screen. And his eyes were suddenly directed to a small, conical projection which had begun to rise up out of the ship, which rose for a short distance and stopped, pointed in on the orbit towards Mina at the center.

Roymer was bewildered, but he acted immediately. Firecon was halted, all protective screens were reestablished, and the patrol ship back-tracked quickly into the protection of deep space.

There was no question in Roymer's mind that the movements of the alien had been directed by a living intelligence, and not by any mechanical means. There was also no doubt in Roymer's mind that there was no living being on board that ship. The problem was acute.

Roymer felt the scalp of his hairless head beginning to crawl. In the history of the galaxy, there had been discovered but five nonhuman races, yet never a race which did not betray its existence by the telepathic nature of its thinking. Roymer could not conceive of a people so alien that even the fundamental structure of their thought process was entirely different from the Galactics.

Extra-Galactics? He observed the ship closely and shook his head. No. Not an extra-Galactic ship certainly, much too primitive a type.

40

Extraspatial? His scalp crawled again.

Completely at a loss as to what to do, Roymer again contacted Mind-Search and requested that Trian be sent to him immediately.

Trian was preceded by a puzzled Goladan. The orders to alien contact, then to Firecon, and finally for a quick retreat, had affected the lieutenant deeply. He was a man accustomed to a strictly logical and somewhat ponderous course of events. He waited expectantly for some explanation to come from his usually serene commander.

Roymer, however, was busily occupied in tracking the alien's new course. An orbit about Mina, Roymer observed, with that conical projection laid on the star; a device of war; or some measuring instrument?

The stolid Trian appeared—walking would not quite describe how—and was requested to make another attempt at contact with the alien. He replied with his usual eerie silence and in a moment, when he turned back to Roymer, there was surprise in the transmitted thought.

"I cannot understand. There is life there now."

Roymer was relieved, but Goladan was blinking.

Trian went on, turning again to gaze at the screen.

"It is very remarkable. There are two life-beings. Human-type race. Their presence is very clear, they are"—he paused briefly—"explorers, it appears. But they were not there before. It is extremely unnerving."

So it is, Roymer agreed. He asked quickly: "Are they aware of us?"

"No. They are directing their attention on the star. Shall I contact?"

"No. Not yet. We will observe them first."

The alien ship floated upon the screen before them, moving in slow orbit about the star Mina.

Seven. There were seven of them. Seven planets, and three at least had atmospheres, and two might even be inhabitable. Jansen was so excited he was hopping around the control room. Cohn did nothing, but grin widely with a wondrous joy, and the two of them repeatedly shook hands and gloated.

"Seven!" roared Jansen. "Old lucky seven!"

Quickly then, and with extreme nervousness, they ran

spectrograph analyses of each of those seven fascinating worlds. They began with the central planets, in the favorable temperature belt where life conditions would be most likely to exist, and they worked outwards.

For reasons which were as much sentimental as they were practical, they started with the third planet of this fruitful sun. There was a thin atmosphere, fainter even than that of Mars, and no oxygen. Silently they went on to the fourth. It was cold and heavy, perhaps twice as large as Earth, had a thick envelope of noxious gases. They saw with growing fear that there was no hope there, and they turned quickly inwards toward the warmer area nearer the sun.

On the second planet—as Jansen put it—they hit the jackpot.

A warm, green world it was, of an Earthlike size and atmosphere; oxygen and water vapor lines showed strong and clear in the analysis.

"This looks like it," said Jansen, grinning again.

Cohn nodded, left the screen and went over to man the navigating instruments.

"Let's go down and take a look."

"Radio check first." It was the proper procedure. Jansen had gone over it in his mind a thousand times. He clicked on the receiver, waited for the tubes to function, and then scanned for contact. As they moved in toward the new planet he listened intently, trying all lengths, waiting for any sound at all. There was nothing but the rasping static of open space.

"Well," he said finally, as the green planet grew large upon the screen, "if there's any race there, it doesn't have radio."

Cohn showed his relief.

"Could be a young civilization."

"Or one so ancient and advanced that it doesn't *need* radio."

Jansen refused to let his deep joy be dampened. It was impossible to know what would be there. Now it was just as it had been three hundred years ago, when the first Earth ship was approaching Mars. And it will be like this —Jansen thought—in every other system to which we go. How can you picture what there will be? There is

42

nothing at all in your past to give you a clue. You can only hope.

The planet was a beautiful green ball on the screen.

The thought which came out of Trian's mind was tinged with relief.

"I see how it was done. They have achieved a complete stasis, a perfect state of suspended animation which they produce by an ingenious usage of the absolute zero of outer space. Thus, when they are—frozen, is the way they regard it—their minds do not function, and their lives are not detectable. They have just recently revived and are directing their ship."

Roymer digested the new information slowly. What kind of a race was this? A race which flew in primitive star ships, yet it had already conquered one of the greatest problems in Galactic history, a problem which had baffled the Galactics for millions of years. Roymer was uneasy.

"A very ingenious device," Trian was thinking, "they use it to alter the amount of subjective time consumed in their explorations. Their star ship has a very low maximum speed. Hence, without this—freeze—their voyage would take up a good portion of their lives."

"Can you classify the mind-type?" Roymer asked with growing concern.

Trian reflected silently for a moment.

"Yes," he said, "although the type is extremely unusual. I have never observed it before. General classification would be Human-Four. More specifically, I would place them at the Ninth level."

Roymer started. "The Ninth level?"

"Yes. As I say, they are extremely unusual."

Roymer was now clearly worried. He turned away and paced the deck for several moments. Abruptly, he left the room and went to the files of alien classification. He was gone for a long time, while Goladan fidgeted and Trian continued to gather information plucked across space from the alien minds. Roymer came back at last.

"What are they doing?"

"They are moving in on the second planet. They are

43

about to determine whether the conditions are suitable there for an establishment of a colony of their kind."

Gravely, Roymer gave his orders to navigation. The patrol ship swung into motion, sped off swiftly in the direction of the second planet.

There was a single, huge blue ocean which covered an entire hemisphere of the new world. And the rest of the surface was a young jungle, wet and green and empty of any kind of people, choked with queer growths of green and orange. They circled the globe at a height of several thousand feet, and to their amazement and joy, they never saw a living thing; not a bird or a rabbit or the alien equivalent, in fact nothing alive at all. And so they stared in happy fascination.

"This is it," Jansen said again, his voice uneven.

"What do you think we ought to call it?" Cohn was speaking absently. "New Earth? Utopia?"

Together they watched the broken terrain slide by beneath them.

"No people at all. It's ours." And after a while Jansen said: "New Earth. That's a good name."

Cohn was observing the features of the ground intently.

"Do you notice the kind of . . . circular appearance of most of those mountain ranges? Like on the Moon, but grown over and eroded. They're all almost perfect circles."

Pulling his mind away from the tremendous visions he had of the colony which would be here, Jansen tried to look at the mountains with an objective eye. Yes, he realized with faint surprise, they were round, like Moon craters.

"Peculiar," Cohn muttered. "Not natural, I don't think. Couldn't be. Meteors not likely in this atmosphere. What in—?"

Jansen jumped. "Look there," he cried suddenly, "a round lake!"

Off toward the northern pole of the planet, a lake which was a perfect circle came slowly into view. There was no break in the rim other than that of a small stream which flowed in from the north.

"That's not natural," Cohn said briefly, "someone built that."

They were moving on to the dark side now, and Cohn turned the ship around. The sense of exhilaration was too new for them to be let down, but the strange sight of a huge number of perfect circles, existing haphazardly like the remains of great splashes on the surface of the planet, was unnerving.

It was the sight of one particular crater, a great barren hole in the midst of a wide red desert, which rang a bell in Jansen's memory, and he blurted:

"A war! There was a war here. That one there looks just like a fusion bomb crater."

Cohn stared, then raised his eyebrows.

"I'll bet you're right."

"A bomb crater, do you see? Pushes up hills on all sides in a circle, and kills—" A sudden, terrible thought hit Jansen. Radioactivity. Would there be radioactivity here?

While Cohn brought the ship in low over the desert, he tried to calm Jansen's fears.

"There couldn't be much. Too much plant life. Jungles all over the place. Take it easy, man."

"But there's not a living thing on the planet. I'll bet that's why there was a war. It got out of hand, the radioactivity got everything. We might have done this to Earth!"

They glided in over the flat emptiness of the desert, and the counters began to click madly.

"That's it," Jansen said conclusively, "still radioactive. It might not have been too long ago."

"Could have been a million years, for all we know."

"Well, most places are safe, apparently. We'll check before we go down."

As he pulled the ship up and away, Cohn whistled.

"Do you suppose there's really not a living thing? I mean, not a bug or a germ or even a virus? Why, it's like a clean new world, a nursery!" He could not take his eyes from the screen.

They were going down now. In a very little while they would be out and walking in the sun. The lust of the feeling was indescribable. They were Earthmen freed forever from the choked home of the System, Earthmen gone out

45

to the stars, landing now upon the next world of their empire.

Cohn could not control himself.

"Do we need a flag?" he said grinning. "How do we claim this place?"

"Just set her down, man," Jansen roared.

Cohn began to chuckle.

"Oh, brave new world," he laughed, "that has *no* people in it."

"But why do we have to contact them?" Goladan asked impatiently. "Could we not just—"

Roymer interrupted without looking at him.

"The law requires that contact be made and the situation explained before action is taken. Otherwise it would be a barbarous act."

Goladan brooded.

The patrol ship hung in the shadow of the dark side, tracing the alien by its radioactive trail. The alien was going down for a landing on the daylight side.

Trian came forward with the other members of the Alien Contact Crew, reported to Roymer. "The aliens have landed."

"Yes," said Roymer, "we will let them have a little time. Trian, do you think you will have any difficulty in the transmission?"

"No. Conversation will not be difficult. Although the confused and complex nature of their thought-patterns does make their inner reactions somewhat obscure. But I do not think there will be any problem."

"Very well. You will remain here and relay the messages."

"Yes."

The patrol ship flashed quickly up over the north pole, then swung inward toward the equator, circling the spot where the alien had gone down. Roymer brought his ship in low and with the silence characteristic of a Galactic, landed her in a wooded spot a mile east of the alien. The Galactics remained in their ship for a short while as Trian continued his probe for information. When at last the Alien Contact Crew stepped out, Roymer and Goladan were in the lead. The rest of the crew faded quietly into the jungle.

As he walked through the young orange brush, Roymer regarded the world around him. Almost ready for repopulation, he thought, in another hundred years the radiation will all be gone, and we will come back. One by one the worlds of that war will be reclaimed.

He felt Trian's directions pop into his mind.

"You are approaching them. Proceed with caution. They are just beyond the next small rise. I think you had better wait, since they are remaining close to their ship."

Roymer sent back a silent yes. Motioning Goladan to be quiet, Roymer led the way up the last rise. In the jungle around him the Galactic crew moved silently.

The air was perfect; there was no radiation. Except for the wild orange color of the vegetation, the spot was a Garden of Eden. Jansen felt instinctively that there was no danger here, no terrible blight or virus or any harmful thing. He felt a violent urge to get out of his spacesuit and run and breathe, but it was forbidden. Not on the first trip. That would come later, after all the tests and experiments had been made and the world pronounced safe.

One of the first things Jansen did was get out the recorder and solemnly claim this world for the Solar Federation, recording the historic words for the archives of Earth. And he and Cohn remained for a while by the air lock of their ship, gazing around at the strange yet familiar world into which they had come.

"Later on we'll search for ruins," Cohn said. "Keep an eye out for anything that moves. It's possible that there are some of them left and who knows what they'll look like. Mutants, probably, with five heads. So keep an eye open."

"Right."

Jansen began collecting samples of the ground, of the air, of the nearer foliage. The dirt was Earth-dirt, there was no difference. He reached down and crumbled the soft moist sod with his fingers. The flowers may be a little peculiar—probably mutated, he thought—but the dirt is honest to goodness dirt, and I'll bet the air is Earth-air.

He rose and stared into the clear open blue of the sky,

feeling again an almost overpowering urge to throw open his helmet and breathe, and as he stared at the sky and at the green and orange hills, suddenly, a short distance from where he stood, a little old man came walking over the hill.

They stood facing each other across the silent space of a foreign glade. Roymer's face was old and smiling; Jansen looked back at him with absolute astonishment.

After a short pause, Roymer began to walk out onto the open soil, with Goladan following, and Jansen went for his heat gun.

"Cohn!" he yelled, in a raw brittle voice, "Cohn!"

And as Cohn turned and saw and froze, Jansen heard words being spoken in his brain. They were words coming from the little old man.

"Please do not shoot," the old man said, his lips unmoving.

"No, don't shoot," Cohn said quickly. "Wait. Let him alone." The hand of Cohn, too, was at his heat gun.

Roymer smiled. To the two Earth-men his face was incredibly old and wise and gentle. He was thinking: Had I been a nonhuman they would have killed me.

He sent a thought back to Trian. The Mind-Searcher picked it up and relayed it into the brains of the Earthmen, sending it through their cortical centers and then up into their conscious minds, so that the words were heard in the language of Earth. "Thank you," Roymer said gently. Jansen's hand held the heat gun leveled on Roymer's chest. He stared, not knowing what to say.

"Please remain where you are," Cohn's voice was hard and steady.

Roymer halted obligingly. Goladan stopped at his elbow, peering at the Earthmen with mingled fear and curiosity. The sight of fear helped Jansen very much.

"Who are you?" Cohn said clearly, separating the words.

Roymer folded his hands comfortably across his chest, he was still smiling.

"With your leave, I will explain our presence."

Cohn just stared.

"There will be a great deal to explain. May we sit down and talk?"

Trian helped with the suggestion. They sat down.

The sun of the new world was setting, and the conference went on. Roymer was doing most of the talking. The Earthmen sat transfixed.

It was like growing up suddenly, in the space of a second.

The history of Earth and of all Mankind just faded and dropped away. They heard of great races and worlds beyond number, the illimitable government which was the Galactic Federation. The fiction, the legends, the dreams of a thousand years had come true in a moment, in the figure of a square little old man who was not from Earth. There was a great deal for them to learn and accept in the time of a single afternoon, on an alien planet.

But it was just as new and real to them that they had discovered an uninhabited, fertile planet, the first to be found by Man. And they could not help but revolt from the sudden realization that the planet might well be someone else's property—that the Galactics owned everything worth owning.

It was an intolerable thought.

"How far," asked Cohn, as his heart pushed up in his throat, "does the Galactic League extend?"

Roymer's voice was calm and direct in their minds.

"Only throughout the central regions of the galaxy. There are millions of stars along the rim which have not yet been explored."

Cohn relaxed, bowed down with relief. There was room then, for Earthmen.

"This planet. Is it part of the Federation?"

"Yes," said Roymer, and Cohn tried to mask his thought. Cohn was angry, and he hoped that the alien could not read his mind as well as he could talk to it. To have come this far—

"There was a race here once," Roymer was saying, "a humanoid race which was almost totally destroyed by war. This planet has been uninhabitable for a very long time. A few of its people who were in space at the time of the last attack were spared. The Federation established them elsewhere. When the planet is ready, the descendants of those survivors will be brought back. It is their home."

Neither of the Earthmen spoke.

"It is surprising," Roymer went on, "that your home world is in the desert. We had thought that there were no habitable worlds—"

"The desert?"

"Yes. The region of the galaxy from which you have come is that which we call the desert. It is an area almost entirely devoid of planets. Would you mind telling me which star is your home?"

Cohn stiffened.

"I'm afraid our government would not permit us to disclose any information concerning our race."

"As you wish. I am sorry you are disturbed. I was curious to know—" He waved a negligent hand to show that the information was unimportant. We will get it later, he thought, when we decipher their charts. He was coming to the end of the conference, he was about to say what he had come to say.

"No doubt you have been exploring the stars about your world?"

The Earthmen both nodded. But for the question concerning Sol, they long ago would have lost all fear of this placid old man and his wide-eyed, silent companion.

"Perhaps you would like to know," said Roymer, "why your area is a desert."

Instantly, both Jansen and Cohn were completely absorbed. This was it, the end of three hundred years of searching. They would go home with the answer.

Roymer never relaxed.

"Not too long ago," he said, "approximately thirty thousand years by your reckoning, a great race ruled the desert, a race which was known as the Antha, and it was not a desert then. The Antha ruled hundreds of worlds. They were perhaps the greatest of all the Galactic peoples; certainly they were as brilliant a race as the galaxy has ever known.

"But they were not a good race. For hundreds of years, while they were still young, we tried to bring them into the Federation. They refused, and of course we did not force them. But as the years went by the scope of their knowledge increased amazingly; shortly they were the technological equals of any other race in the galaxy. And then

50

the Antha embarked upon an era of imperialistic expansion.

"They were superior, they knew it and were proud. And so they pushed out and enveloped the races and worlds of the area now known as the desert. Their rule was a tyranny unequaled in Galactic history."

The Earthmen never moved, and Roymer went on.

"But the Antha were not members of the Federation, and, therefore, they were not answerable for their acts. We could only stand by and watch as they spread their vicious rule from world to world. They were absolutely ruthless.

"As an example of their kind of rule, I will tell you of their crime against the Apectans.

"The planet of Apectus not only resisted the Antha, but somehow managed to hold out against their approach for several years. The Antha finally conquered and then, in retaliation for the Apectans' valor, they conducted the most brutal of their mass experiments.

'They were a brilliant people. They had been experimenting with the genes of heredity. Somehow they found a way to alter the genes of the Apectans, who were humanoids like themselves, and they did it on a mass scale. They did not choose to exterminate the race, their revenge was much greater. Every Apectan born since the Antha invasion, has been born without one arm."

Jansen sucked in his breath. It was a very horrible thing to hear, and a sudden memory came into his brain. Caesar did that, he thought. He cut off the right hands of the Gauls. Peculiar coincidence. Jansen felt uneasy.

Roymer paused for a moment.

"The news of what happened to the Apectans set the Galactic peoples up in arms, but it was not until the Antha attacked a Federation world that we finally moved against them. It was the greatest war in the history of Life.

"You will perhaps understand how great a people the Antha were when I tell you that they alone, unaided, dependent entirely upon their own resources, fought the rest of the Galactics, and fought them to a standstill. As the terrible years went by we lost whole races and planets— like this one, which was one the Antha destroyed—and yet we could not defeat them.

51

"It was only after many years, when a Galactic invented the most dangerous weapon of all, that we won. The invention—of which only the Galactic Council has knowledge—enabled us to turn the suns of the Antha into novae, at long range. One by one we destroyed the Antha worlds. We hunted them through all the planets of the desert; for the first time in history the edict of the Federation was death, death for an entire race. At last there were no longer any habitable worlds where the Antha had been. We burned their worlds, and ran them down in space. Thirty thousand years ago, the civilization of the Antha perished."

Roymer had finished. He looked at the Earthmen out of grave, tired old eyes.

Cohn was staring in open-mouth fascination, but Jansen—unaccountably felt a chill. The story of Caesar remained uncomfortably in his mind. And he had a quick, awful suspicion.

"Are you sure you got all of them?"

"No. Some surely must have escaped. There were too many in space, and space is without limits."

Jansen wanted to know: "Have any of them been heard of since?"

Roymer's smile left him as the truth came out. "No. Not until now."

There were only a few more seconds. He gave them time to understand. He could not help telling them that he was sorry, he even apologized. And then he sent the order with his mind.

The Antha died quickly and silently, without pain.

Only thirty thousand years, Roymer was thinking, but thirty thousand years, and they came back out to the stars. They have no memory now of what they were or what they have done. They started all over again, the old history of the race has been lost, and in thirty thousand years they came all the way back.

Roymer shook his head with sad wonder and awe. The most brilliant people of all.

Goladan came in quietly with the final reports.

"There are no charts," he grumbled, "no maps at all. We will not be able to trace them to their home star."

52

Roymer did not know, really, what was right, to be disappointed or relieved. We cannot destroy them now, he thought, not right away. He could not help being relieved. Maybe this time there will be a way, and they will not have to be destroyed. They could be——

He remembered the edict—the edict of death. The Antha had forged it for themselves and it was just. He realized that there wasn't much hope.

The reports were on his desk and he regarded them with a wry smile. There was indeed no way to trace them back. They had no charts, only a regular series of course-check coordinates which were present on their home planet and which were not decipherable. Even at this stage of their civilization they had already anticipated the consequences of having their ship fall into alien hands. And this although they lived in the desert.

Goladan startled him with an anxious question:

"What can we do?"

Roymer was silent.

We can wait, he thought. Gradually, one by one, they will come out of the desert, and when they come we will be waiting. Perhaps one day we will follow one back and destroy their world, and perhaps before then we will find a way to save them.

Suddenly, as his eyes wandered over the report before him and he recalled the ingenious mechanism of the freeze, a chilling, unbidden thought came into his brain.

And perhaps, he thought calmly, for he was a philosophical man, they will come out already equipped to rule the galaxy.

The paper spaceships are on their way. The galaxy, like the Wild West, is wide open.

What surprises humankind met with in the galaxy was a matter for speculation, and the authors answered the question according to their own temperaments. Almost every science fiction writer took a look at interplanetary empires at one time or another and, whether they talked of federalism or colonialism, produced their own interpretation. Robert Heinlein, E. E. Smith, Van Vogt, Beam Piper, Henry Kuttner, James Blish—each offered his own version. E. E. Smith's multi-specific galactic culture, spreading over the six volumes of the Lensman saga, has become particularly famous.

All authors agreed on one item: power was needed to establish or to maintain any sort of empire. This section contains three interesting interpretations of how that power might be wielded.

Mark Clifton and Alex Apostolides, in *We're Civilized!*, demonstrate the immorality of power—and we feel that immorality most forcibly when it is wielded against us. Carl Sagan was recently talking on the question of communicating with other intelligences in the galaxy. At one point, "Let's consider what we should do," he said, "if they chose to get in touch with us——" And an urgent voice from the audience said, "Don't answer the phone!" No doubt that gentleman had read Clifton and Apostolides' story.

The Asimov story represents the first section of his "Foundation", trilogy, which has been voted the most popular sf book ever written. This story appeared in *Astounding Science Fiction* in 1942, and immediately captured the imagination of readers. It is not hard to see why.

There is one comic moment when the Mayor of Terminus jumps up and cries "The Galaxy is going to pot!" In the hands of sf writers, this is what it constantly does. But Asimov's human-ruled galaxy has special qualities, in particular the quality which distinguished him from many of his fellow-writers: he is for order. Like H. G. Wells, whom Asimov has emulated in turning from fiction to extensive scientific popularization, he is against the untidiness of war and killing. Just as his robots are governed by rules which prevent them harming men (whereas before Asimov's day robots were constantly running amok), so his Foundation-ruled galaxy is designed to work in orderly fashion according to the programming of Hari Seldon's psycho-history.

The currency on Terminus is made—as currencies generally are—of a rare metal: steel. It is characteristic of Asimov's method that the Foundation, destined to play such a powerful role in the history of the galaxy over the next ten thousand years, is set on a world virtually without metals.

The power in this story is the power of an intellectual idea: that the seeds of the Renaissance are sewn on Terminus. To the ordinary people, this idea becomes almost a religious belief—a development the scientists of Terminus constantly have to fight against.

There are signs, I believe, that Asimov intended Terminus to be something of a utopia, with no metals, no warlike intent, and no psychologists. Armed with all these interesting intentions, he can be forgiven for making the one politician, Lord Dorwin, a parody of an eighteenth-century English statesman, down to his lisp and snuff-box ("over-adorned and poor workmanship at that," Hardin notes).

So Foundation is that rare thing, an attempt at an intellectual galactic empire. Poul Anderson's empire starts from very different directions. It is an out-and-out adventure story with a starry background and a galaxy swarming with semi-human savages. Within three paragraphs, we are watching a big grey barbarian "spin on his heels, stagger and scream with all four hands clutching his belly, and sink slowly to his knees" to die.

This appetite for mad or multi-shaped aliens is, of

course, deplorably un-solemn, and the reverse of Asimov's rather austere stage-setting. It was the fashion at one time in science fiction circles to deprecate such imaginative swash-buckle. The feeling was that it acted as a barrier against a general acceptance of sf.

One sees the force of this line of argument; I have been at least partly convinced by it myself. But the other side of the argument has greater force. Stories like *The Star Plunderer* epitomize what sf once was, before it became acceptable. When sf writers began taking themselves seriously, they tended to abandon their imaginations and rely instead on the predictions of think-tanks or on extrapolations from scientific journals and population statistics; the result was a descent into greyness, a loss of the original driving force, an espousal of literalism.

Literalism is something we shall encounter rarely in this anthology, or in its companions in the series. Poul Anderson gives us a savage empire and a go-getting Earthman, "a blend of all humanity". It's the sort of tale at which the youthful Anderson excelled, told with considerable emotional clout. Just for a treat, we have another Poul Anderson in the second volume.

We will continue later the argument about motley galactic empires and what they may or may not represent. Meanwhile, let's get into that stinking Gorzuni slave-ship . . .

*Empires start oddly . . . one grew from a mutiny in
the hold of a Gorzuni slave-ship.*

●

# THE STAR PLUNDERER
## by Poul Anderson

The following is a part, modernized but otherwise au-
thentic, of that curious book found by excavators of
the ruins of Sol City, Terra—the Memoirs of Rear
Admiral John Henry Reeves, Imperial Solar Navy.
Whether or not the script, obviously never published
or intended for publication, is a genuine record left by
a man with a taste for dramatized reporting, or
whether it is pure fiction, remains an open question;
but it was undoubtedly written in the early period of
the First Empire and as such gives a remarkable picture of the times and especially of the Founder. Actual events may or may not have been exactly as
Reeves described, but we cannot doubt that in any
case they were closely similar. Read this fifth chapter
of the Memoirs as historical fiction if you will, but remember that the author must himself have lived
through that great and tragic and triumphant age
and that he must have been trying throughout the

book to give a true picture of the man who even in
his own time had become a legend.

Donvar Ayeghen,
President of the Galactic Archeological Society

They were closing in now. The leader was a gray bulk
filling my sight scope, and every time I glanced over the
wall a spanging sleet of bullets brought my head jerking
down again. I had some shelter from behind which to
shoot in a fragment of wall looming higher than the rest,
like a single tooth left in a dead man's jaw, but I had to
squeeze the trigger and then duck fast. Once in a while
one of their slugs would burst on my helmet and the gas
would be sickly-sweet in my nostrils. I felt ill and dizzy
with it.

Kathryn was reloading her own rifle, I heard her swearing as the cartridge clip jammed in the rusty old weapon.
I'd have given her my own, except that it wasn't much
better. It's no fun fighting with arms that are likely to
blow up in your face but it was all we had—all that poor
devastated Terra had after the Baldics had sacked her
twice in fifteen years.

I fired a burst and saw the big gray barbarian spin on
his heels, stagger and scream with all four hands clutching
his belly, and sink slowly to his knees. The creatures
behind him howled, but he only let out a deep-throated
curse. He'd be a long time dying. I'd blown a hole clear
through him, but those Gorzuni were tough.

The slugs wailed around us as I got myself down under
the wall, hugging the long grass which had grown up
around the shattered fragments of the house. There was
a fresh wind blowing, rustling the grass and the big war-
scarred trees, sailing clouds across a sunny summer sky,
so the gas concentration was never enough to put us out.
But Jonsson and Hokusai were sprawled like corpses
there against the broken wall. They'd taken direct hits
and they'd sleep for hours.

Kathryn knelt beside me, the ragged, dirty coverall like
a queen's robe on her tall young form, a few dark curls
falling from under her helmet for the wind to play with.
"If we get them mad enough," she said, "they'll call for

61

the artillery or send a boat overhead to blow us to the Black Planet."

"Maybe," I grunted. "Though they're usually pretty eager for slaves."

"John—" She crouched there a moment, the tiny frown I knew too well darkening her blue eyes. I watched the way leaf-shadows played across her thin brown face. There was a grease smudge on the snub nose, hiding the freckles. But she still looked good, really good, she and green Terra and life and freedom and all that I'd never have again!

"John," she said at last, "maybe we should save them the trouble. Maybe we should make our own exit."

"It's a thought," I muttered, risking a glance above the wall.

The Gorzuni were more cautious now, creeping through the gardens toward the shattered outbuilding we defended. Behind them, the main estate, last knot of our unit's resistance, lay smashed and burning. Gorzuni were swarming around it, dragging out such humans as survived and looting whatever treasure was left. I was tempted to shoot at those big furry bodies but I had to save ammunition for the detail closing in on us.

"I don't fancy life as the slave of a barbarian outworlder," I said. "Though humans with technical training are much in demand and usually fairly well treated. But for a woman—" The words trailed off. I couldn't say them.

"I might trade on my own mechanical knowledge," she said. "And then again I might not. Is it worth the risk, John, my dearest?"

We were both conditioned against suicide, of course. Everyone in the broken Commonwealth navy was, except bearers of secret information. The idea was to sell our lives or liberty as exorbitantly as possible, fighting to the last moment. It was a stupid policy, typical of the blundering leadership that had helped lose us our wars. A human slave with knowledge of science and machinery was worth more to the barbarians than the few extra soldiers he could kill out of their hordes by staying alive till captured.

But the implanted inhibition could be broken by a person of strong will. I looked at Kathryn for a moment, there in the tumbled ruins of the house, and her eyes met mine and rested, deep-blue and grave with a tremble of tears behind the long smoky lashes.

"Well—" I said helplessly, and then I kissed her.

It was our big mistake. The Gorzuni had worked closer than I realized and in Terra's gravity—about half of their home planet's—they could move like a sunbound comet. One of them came soaring over the wall behind me, landing on his clawed splay feet with a crash that shivered in the ground. His wild "Whoo-oo-oo-oo!" was hardly out of his mouth before I'd blown the horned, flat-faced head off his shoulders. But there was a gray mass swarming behind him, and Kathryn yelled and fired into the thick of another attack from our rear.

Something stung me, a bright sharp pain and then a bomb exploding in my head and a long sick spiral down into blackness. The last thing I saw was Kathryn, caught in the four arms of a soldier. He was half again as tall as she, he'd twisted the barrel off her gun as he wrenched it from her hands, but she was giving him a good fight. A hell of a good fight. Then I didn't see anything else for some time.

They herded us aboard a tender after dark. It was like a scene from some ancient hell—night overhead and around, lit by a score of burning houses like uneasy furnaces out there in the dark, and the long, long line of humans stumbling toward the boat with kicks and blows from the guards to hurry them along.

A house was aflame not far off, soaring red and yellow fire glancing off the metal of the ship, picking a haggard face from shadow, glimmering in human tears and . in steely unhuman eyes. The shadows wove in and out, hiding us from each other save when a gust of wind blew up the fire. Then we felt a puff of heat and looked away from each other's misery.

Kathryn was not to be seen in that weaving line. I groped along with my wrists tied behind me, now and then jarred by a gun-butt as one of the looming figures grew impatient. I could hear the sobbing of women and

63

the groaning of men in the dark, before me, behind me, around me as they forced us into the boat.

"Jimmy. Where are you, Jimmy?"

"They killed him. He's lying there dead in the ruins."

"O God, what have we done?"

"My baby. Has anyone seen my baby? I had a baby and they took him away from me."

"Help, help, help, help help—"

A mumbled and bitter curse, a scream, a whine, a rattling gasp of breath, and always the slow shuffle of feet and the sobbing of the women and the children.

We were the conquered. They had scattered our armies. They had ravaged our cities. They had hunted us through the streets and the hills and the great deeps of space, and we could only snarl and snap at them and hope that the remnants of our navy might pull a miracle. But miracles are hard to come by.

So far the Baldic League had actually occupied only the outer planets. The inner worlds were nominally under Commonwealth rule but the government was hiding or nonexistent. Only fragments of the navy fought on without authority or plan or hope, and Terra was the happy hunting ground of looters and slave raiders. Before long, I supposed bitterly, the outworlders would come in force, break the last resistance, and incorporate all the Solar System into their savage empire. Then the only free humans would be the extrasolar colonists, and a lot of them were barbaric themselves and had joined the Baldic League against the mother world.

The captives were herded into cells aboard the tender, crammed together till there was barely room to stand. Kathryn wasn't in my cell either. I lapsed into dull apathy.

When everyone was aboard, the deckplates quivered under our feet and acceleration jammed us cruelly against each other. Several humans died in that press. I had all I could do to keep the surging mass from crushing in my chest but of course the Gorzuni didn't care. There were plenty more where we came from.

The boat was an antiquated and rust-eaten wreck, with half its archaic gadgetry broken and useless. They weren't technicians, those Baldics. They were barbarians who had learned too soon how to build and handle spaceships and firearms, and a score of their planets united by a military genius had gone forth to overrun the civilized Commonwealth.

But their knowledge was usually by rote; I have known many a Baldic "engineer" who made sacrifices to his converter, many a general who depended on astrologers or haruspices for major decision. So trained humans were in demand as slaves. Having a degree in nuclear engineering myself, I could look for a halfway decent berth, though of course there was always the possibility of my being sold to someone who would flay me or blind me or let me break my heart in his mines.

Untrained humans hadn't much chance. They were just flesh-and-blood machines doing work that the barbarians didn't have automatics for, rarely surviving ten years of slavery. Women were the luxury trade, sold at high prices to the human renegades and rebels. I groaned at that thought and tried desperately to assure myself that Kathryn's technical knowledge would keep her in the possession of a non-human.

We were taken up to a ship orbiting just above the atmosphere. Airlocks were joined, so I didn't get a look at her from outside, but as soon as we entered I saw that she was a big interstellar transport of the Thurnogan class used primarily for carrying troops to Sol and slaves back, but armed for war. A formidable fighting ship when properly handled.

There were guards leaning on their rifles, all of Gorzuni race, their harness worn any way they pleased and no formality between officers and men. The barbarian armies' sloppy discipline had blinded our spit-and-polish command to their reckless courage and their savage gunnery. Now the fine-feathered Commonwealth navy was a ragged handful of hunted, desperate men and the despised outworlders were harrying them through the Galaxy.

This ship was worse than usual, though. I saw rust and mold on the unpainted plates. The fluoros were dim and in some places burned out. There was a sickening pulse in the gravity generators. The cabins had long ago been stripped of equipment and refurnished with skins, stolen household goods, cooking pots, and weapons. The Gorzuni were all as dirty and unkempt as their ship. They lounged about gnawing on chunks of meat, drinking, dicing, and glancing up now and then to grin at us.

A barbarian who spoke some Anglic bellowed at us to strip. Those who hesitated were cuffed so the teeth rattled in their heads. We threw the clothes in a heap and moved forward slowly past a table where a drunken Gorzuni and a very sober human sat. Medical inspection.

The barbarian "doctor" gave each of us the most cursory glance. Most were waved on. Now and then he would look closer, blearily, at someone.

"Sickly," he grunted. "Never make the trip alive. Kill."

The man or woman or child would scream as he picked up a sword and chopped off the head with one expert sweep.

The human sat halfway on the desk, swinging one leg and whistling softly. Now and again the Gorzuni medic would glance at him in doubt over some slave. The human would look closer. Usually he shoved them on. One or two he tapped for killing.

I got a close look at him as I went by. He was below medium height, strongly built, dark and heavy-faced and beak-nosed, but his eyes were large and blue-gray, the coldest eyes I have ever seen on a human. He wore a loose colorful shirt and trousers, rich material probably stolen from some Terran villa.

"You filthy bastard," I muttered.

He shrugged, indicating the iron slave-collar welded about his neck. "I only work here, Lieutenant," he said mildly. He must have noticed my uniform before I shucked it.

Beyond the desk, a Gorzuni played a hose on us, washing off blood and grime, and then we were herded down the long corridors and by way of wooden ladders (the drop-shafts and elevators weren't working it seemed) to the cells. Here they separated men and women. We went into adjoining compartments, huge echoing caverns of metal with bunks tiered along the walls, food troughs, and sanitary facilities the only furnishing.

Dust was thick on the corroded floor, and the air was cold and had a metallic reek. There must have been about five hundred men swarming hopelessly around after the barred door clanged shut on us.

There were windows between the two great cells. We made a rush for them, crying out, pushing and crowding and snarling at each other for first chance to see if our women still lived.

I was large and strong. I shouldered my way through the mob up to the nearest window. A man was there already, flattened against the wall by the sweating bodies behind, reaching through the bars to the three hundred women who swarmed on the other side.

"Agnes!" he shrieked. "Agnes, are you there? Are you alive?"

I grabbed his shoulder and pulled him away. He turned with a curse, and I fed him a mouthful of knuckles and sent him lurching back into the uneasy press of men. "Kathryn!" I howled.

The echoes rolled and boomed in the hollow metal caves, crying voices, prayers and curses and sobs of despair thrown back by the sardonic echoes till our heads shivered with it. "Kathryn! Kathryn!"

Somehow she found me. She came to me and the kiss through those bars dissolved ship and slavery and all the world for that moment. "Oh, John, John, John, you're alive, you're here. Oh, my darling——"

And then she looked around the metal-gleaming dimness and said quickly, urgently: "We'll have a riot on our hands, John, if these people don't calm down. See what you can do with the men. I'll tackle the women."

It was like her. She was the most gallant soul that ever walked under Terran skies, and she had a mind which flashed in an instant to that which must be done. I wondered myself what point there was in stopping a murderous panic. Those who were killed would be better off, wouldn't they? But Kathryn never surrendered so I couldn't either.

We turned back into our crowds, and shouted and pummeled and bullied, and slowly others came to our aid until there was a sobbing quiet in the belly of the slave ship. Then we organized turns at the windows. Kathryn and I both looked away from those reunions, or from the people who found no one. It isn't decent to look at a naked soul.

67

The engines began to thrum. Under way, outward bound to the ice mountains of Gorzun, no more to see blue skies and green grass, no clean salt smell of ocean and roar of wind in tall trees. Now we were slaves and there was nothing to do but wait.

# II

There was no time aboard the ship. The few dim fluoros kept our hold forever in its uneasy twilight. The Gorzuni swilled us at such irregular intervals as they thought of it, and we heard only the throb of the engines and the asthmatic sigh of the ventilators. The twice-normal gravity kept most of us too weary even to talk much. But I think it was about forty-eight hours after leaving Terra, when the ship had gone into secondary drive and was leaving the Solar System altogether, that the man with the iron collar came down to us.

He entered with an escort of armed and wary Gorzuni who kept their rifles lifted. We looked up with dull eyes at the short stocky figure. His voice was almost lost in the booming vastness of the hold.

"I'm here to classify you. Come up one at a time and tell me your name and training, if any. I warn you that the penalty for claiming training you haven't got is torture, and you'll be tested if you do make such claims."

We shuffled past. A Gorzuni, the drunken doctor, had a tattoo needle set up and scribbled a number on the palm of each man. This went into the human's notebook, together with name, age, and profession. Those without technical skills, by far the majority, were shoved roughly back. The fifty or so who claimed valuable education went over into a corner.

The needle burned my palm and I sucked the breath between my teeth. The impersonal voice was dim in my ears: "Name?"

"John Henry Reeves, age twenty-five, lieutenant in the Commonwealth navy and nuclear engineer before the wars." I snapped the answers out, my throat harsh and a bitter taste in my mouth. The taste of defeat.

"Hmmm." I grew aware that the pale chill eyes were

68

resting on me with an odd regard. Suddenly the man's thick lips twisted in a smile. It was a strangely charming smile, it lit his whole dark face with a brief radiance of merriment. "Oh, yes, I remember you, Lieutenant Reeves. You called me, I believe, a filthy bastard."

"I did," I almost snarled. My hand throbbed and stung, I was unwashed and naked and sick with my own helplessness.

"You may be right at that," he nodded. "But I'm in bad need of a couple of assistants. This ship is a wreck. She may never make Gorzun without someone to nurse the engines. Care to help me?"

"No," I said.

"Be reasonable. By refusing you only get yourself locked in the special cell we're keeping for trained slaves. It'll be a long voyage, the monotony will do more to break your spirit than any number of lashings. As my assistant you'll have proper quarters and a chance to move around and use your hands."

I stood thinking. "Did you say you needed two assistants?" I asked.

"Yes. Two who can do something with this ruin of a ship."

"I'll be one," I said, "if I can name the other."

He scowled. "Getting pretty big for the britches you don't have, aren't you?"

"Take it or leave it," I shrugged. "But this person is a hell of a good technician."

"Well, nominate him, then, and I'll see."

"It's a her. My fiancée, Kathryn O'Donnell."

"No." He shook his dark curly head. "No woman."

"No man, then." I grinned at him without mirth.

Anger flamed coldly in his eyes. "I can't have a woman around my neck like another millstone."

"She'll carry her own weight and more. She was a j.g. in my own ship, and she fought right there beside me till the end."

The temper was gone without leaving a ripple. Not a stir of expression in the strong, ugly, olive-skinned face that looked up at me. His voice was as flat. "Why didn't you say so before? All right, then, Lieutenant. But the gods help you if you aren't both as advertised!"

69

It was hard to believe it about clothes—the difference they made after being just another penned and naked animal. And a meal of stew and coffee, however ill prepared, scrounged at the galley after the warriors had messed, surged in veins and bellies which had grown used to swilling from a pig trough.

I realized bleakly that the man in the iron collar was right. Not many humans could have remained free of soul on the long, heart-cracking voyage to Gorzun. Add the eternal weariness of double weight, the chill dark grimness of our destination planet, utter remoteness from home, blank hopelessness, perhaps a touch of the whip and branding iron, and men became tamed animals trudging meekly at the heels of their masters.

"How long have you been a slave?" I asked our new boss.

He strode beside us as arrogantly as if the ship were his. He was not a tall man for even Kathryn topped him by perhaps five centimeters and his round-skulled head barely reached my shoulder. But he had thick muscular arms, a gorilla breadth of chest and the gravity didn't seem to bother him at all.

"Going on four years," he replied shortly. "My name, by the way, is Manuel Argos, and we might as well be on first-name terms from the start."

A couple of Gorzuni came stalking down the corridor, clanking with metal. We stood aside for the giants, of course, but there was no cringing in Manuel's attitude. His strange eyes followed them speculatively.

We had a cabin near the stern, a tiny cubbyhole with four bunks, bleak and bare, but its scrubbed cleanliness was like a breath of home after the filth of the cell. Wordlessly, Manuel took one of the sleazy blankets and hung it across a bed as a sort of curtain. "It's the best privacy I can offer you, Kathryn," he said.

"Thank you," she whispered.

He sat down on his own bunk and looked up at us. I loomed over him, a blond giant against his squatness. My family had been old and cultured and wealthy before the wars, and he was the nameless sweepings of a hundred slums and spaceports, but from the first there was never any doubt of who was the leader.

70

"Here's the story," he said in his curt way. "I knew enough practical engineering in spite of having no formal education to get myself a fairly decent master in whose factories I learned more. Two years ago he sold me to the captain of this ship. I got rid of the so-called chief engineer they had then. It wasn't hard to stir up a murderous quarrel between him and a jealous subordinate. But his successor is a drunken bum one generation removed from the forests.

"In effect, I'm the engineer of this ship. I've also managed to introduce my master, Captain Venjain, to marijuana. It hits a Gorzuni harder than it does a human, and he's a hopeless addict by now. It's partly responsible for the condition of this ship and the laxness among the crew. Poor leadership, poor organization. That's a truism."

I stared at him with a sudden chill along my spine. But it was Kathryn who whispered the question: "Why?"

"Waiting my chance," he snapped. "I'm the one who made junk out of the engines and equipment. I tell them it's old and poorly designed. They think that only my constant work holds the ship together at all but I could have her humming in a week if I cared to. I can't wait too much longer. Sooner or later someone else is going to look at that machinery and tell them it's been deliberately haywired. So I've been waiting for a couple of assistants with technical training and a will to fight. I hope you two fit the bill. If not—" he shrugged. "Go ahead and tell on me. It won't free you. But if you want to risk lives that won't be very long or pleasant on Gorzun, you can help me to take over the ship!"

I stood for some time looking at him. It was uncanny, the way he had sized us up from a glance and a word. Certainly the prospect was frightening. I could feel sweat on my face. My hands were cold. But I'd follow him. Before God, I'd follow him!

Still—"Three of us?" I jeered. "Three of us against a couple of hundred warriors?"

"There'll be more on our side," he said impassively. After a moment's silence he went on: "Naturally, we'll have to watch ourselves. Only two or three of them know

71

Anglic. I'll point them out to you. And of course our work is under surveillance. But the watchers are ignorant. I think you have the brains to fool them."

"I—" Kathryn stood reaching for words. "I can't believe it," she said at last. "A naval vessel in this condition—"

"Things were better under the old Baldic conquerors," admitted Manuel. "The kings who forged the League out of a hundred planets still in barbaric night, savages who'd learned to build spaceships and man atom-blasts and little else. But even they succeeded only because there was no real opposition. The Commonwealth society was rotten, corrupt, torn apart by civil wars, its leadership a petrified bureaucracy, its military forces scattered over a thousand restless planets, its people ready to buy peace rather than fight. No wonder the League drove everything before it!

"But after the first sack of Terra fifteen years ago, the barbarians split up. The forceful early rulers were dead, and their sons were warring over an inheritance they didn't know how to rule. The League is divided into two hostile regions now and I don't know how many splinter groups. Their old organization is shot to hell.

"Sol didn't rally in time. It was still under the decadent Commonwealth government. So one branch of the Baldics has now managed to conquer our big planets. But the fact that they've been content to raid and loot the inner worlds instead of occupying them and administering them decently shows the decay of their own society. Given the leadership, we could still throw them out of the Solar System and go on to over-run their home territories. Only the leadership hasn't been forthcoming."

It was a harsh, angry lecture, and I winced and felt resentment within myself. "Damn it, we've fought," I said.

"And been driven back and scattered." His heavy mouth lifted in a sneer. "Because there hasn't been a chief who understood strategy and organization, and who could put heart into his men."

"I suppose," I said sarcastically, "that you're that chief."

His answer was flat and calm and utterly assured. "Yes."

72

In the days that followed I got to know more about Manuel Argos. He was never loath to talk about himself.

His race, I suppose, was primarily Mediterranean-Anatolian, with more than a hint of negro and oriental, but I think there must have been some forgotten nordic ancestor who looked out of those ice-blue eyes. A blend of all humanity, such as was not uncommon these days.

His mother had been a day laborer on Venus. His father, though he was never sure, had been a space prospector who died young and never saw his child. When he was thirteen he shipped out for Sirius and had not been in the Solar System since. Now, at forty, he had been spaceman, miner, dock walloper, soldier in the civil wars and against the Baldics, small-time politician on the colony planets, hunter, machinist, and a number of darker things.

Somewhere along the line, he had found time to do an astonishing amount of varied reading, but his reliance was always more on his own senses and reason and intuition than on books. He had been captured four years ago in a Gorzuni raid on Alpha Centauri, and had set himself to study his captors as cold-bloodedly as he had studied his own race.

Yes, I learned a good deal about him but nothing of him. I don't think any living creature ever did. He was not one to open his heart. He went wrapped in loneliness and dreams all his days. Whether the chill of his manner went into his soul, and the rare warmth was only a mask, or whether he was indeed a yearning tenderness sheathed in armor of indifference, no one will ever be sure. And he made a weapon out of that uncertainty, a man never knew what to await from him and was thus forever strained in his presence, open to his will.

"He's a strange sort," said Kathryn once, when we were alone. "I haven't decided whether he's crazy or a genius."

"Maybe both, darling," I suggested, a little irritably. I didn't like to be dominated.

"Maybe. But what is sanity, then?" She shivered and crept close to me. "I don't want to talk about it."

The ship wallowed on her way, through a bleak glory of stars, alone in light-years of emptiness with her cargo of

73

hate and fear and misery and dreams. We worked, and waited, and the slow days passed.

The laboring old engines had to be fixed. Some show had to be made for the gray-furred giants who watched us in the flickering gloom of the power chambers. We wired and welded and bolted, tested and tore down and rebuilt, sweltering in the heat of bursting atoms that rolled from the anti-radiation shields, deafened by the whine of generators and thud of misadjusted turbines and deep uneven drone of the great converters. We fixed Manuel's sabotage until the ship ran almost smoothly. Later we would on some pretext throw the whole thing out of kilter again. "Penelope's tapestry," said Manuel, and I wondered that a space tramp could make the classical allusion.

"What are we waiting for?" I asked him once. The din of the generator we were overhauling smothered our words. "When do we start our mutiny?"

He glanced up at me. The light of his trouble lamp gleamed off the sweat on his ugly pockmarked face. "At the proper time," he said coldly. "For one thing, it'll be when the captain goes on his next dope jag."

Meanwhile two of the slaves had tried a revolt of their own. When an incautious guard came too near the door of the men's cell one of them reached out and snatched his gun from the holster and shot him down. Then he tried to blast the lock of the bars. When the Gorzuni came down to gas him, his fellow battled them with fists and teeth till the rebels were knocked out. Both were flayed living in the presence of the other captives.

Kathryn couldn't help crying when we were back in our cabin. She buried her face against my breast and wept till I thought she would never stop weeping. I held her close and mumbled whatever foolish words came to me.

"They had it coming," said Manuel. There was contempt in his voice. "The fools. The blind stupid fools! They could at least have held the guard as a hostage and tried to bargain. No, they had to be heroes. They had to shoot him down. Now the example has frightened all the others. Those men deserved being skinned."

After a moment, he added thoughtfully: "Still, if the fear-emotion aroused in the slaves can be turned to hate

74

it may prove useful. The shock has at least jarred them from their apathy."

"You're a heartless bastard," I said tonelessly.

"I have to be, seeing that everyone else chooses to be brainless. These aren't times for the tender-minded, you. This is an age of dissolution and chaos, such as has often happened in history, and only a person who first accepts the realities of the situation can hope to do much about them. We don't live in a cosmos where perfection is possible or even desirable. We have to make our compromises and settle for the goals we have some chance of attaining." To Kathryn, sharply: "Now stop that snuffling. I have to think."

She gave him a wide-eyed tear-blurred look.

"It gives you a hell of an appearance." He grinned nastily. "Nose red, face swollen, a bad case of hiccoughs. Nothing pretty about crying, you."

She drew a shuddering breath and there was anger flushing her cheeks. Gulping back the sobs, she drew away from me and turned her back on him.

"But I stopped her," whispered Manuel to me with a brief impishness.

# III

The endless, meaningless days had worn into a timelessness where I wondered if this ship were not the Flying Dutchman, outward bound forever with a crew of devils and the damned. It was no use trying to hurry Manuel, I gave that up and slipped into the round of work and waiting. Now I think that part of his delay was on purpose, that he wanted to grind the last hope out of the slaves and leave only a hollow yearning for vengeance. They'd fight better that way.

There wasn't much chance to be alone with Kathryn. A brief stolen kiss, a whispered word in the dimness of the engine room, eyes and hands touching lightly across a rusty, greasy machine. That was all. When we returned to our cabin we were too tired, generally, to do much except sleep.

I did once notice Manuel exchange a few words in the

75

slave pen with Ensign Hokusai, who had been captured with Kathryn and myself. Someone had to lead the humans, and Hokusai was the best man for that job. But how had Manuel known? It was part of his genius for understanding.

The end came suddenly. Manuel shook me awake. I blinked wearily at the hated walls around me, feeling the irregular throb of the gravity field that was misbehaving again. More work for us. "All right, all right," I grumbled. "I'm coming."

When he flicked the curtain from Kathryn's bunk and aroused her, I protested. "We can handle it. Let her rest."

"Not now!" he answered. Teeth gleamed white in the darkness of his face. "The captain's off in never-never land. I heard two of the Gorzuni talking about it."

That brought me bolt awake, sitting up with a chill along my spine. "Now—?"

"Take it easy," said Manuel. "Lots of time."

We threw on our clothes and went down the long corridors. The ship was still. Under the heavy shuddering drone of the engines, there was only the whisper of our shoes and the harsh rasp of the breath in my lungs. Kathryn was white-faced, her eyes enormous in the gloom. But she didn't huddle against me. She walked between the two of us and there was a remoteness over her that I couldn't quite understand. Now and then we passed a Gorzuni warrior on some errand of his own, and shrank aside as became slaves. But I saw the bitter triumph in Manuel's gaze as he looked after the titans.

Into the power chambers where the machines loomed in a flickering red twilight like heathen gods there were three Gorzuni standing there, armed engineers who snarled at us. One of them tried to cuff Manuel. He dodged without seeming to notice and bent over the gravity generator and signaled me to help him lift the cover.

I could see that there was a short circuit in one of the field coils, inducing a harmonic that imposed a flutter on the spacewarping current. It wouldn't have taken long to fix. But Manuel scratched his head, and glanced back at the ignorant giants who loomed over our shoulders. He began tracing wires with elaborate puzzlement.

He said to me: "We'll work up to the auxiliary atom-converter. I've fixed that to do what I want."

I knew the Gorzuni couldn't understand us, and that human expressions were meaningless to them, but an uncontrollable shiver ran along my nerves.

Slowly we fumbled to the squat engine which was the power source for the ship's internal machinery. Manuel hooked in an oscilloscope and studied the trace as if it meant something. "Ah-hah!" he said.

We unbolted the antiradiation shield, exposing the outlet valve. I knew that the angry, blood-red light streaming from it was harmless, that baffles cut off most of the radioactivity, but I couldn't help shrinking from it. When a converter is flushed through the valve, you wear armor.

Manuel went over to a workbench and took a gadget from it which he'd made. I knew it was of no use for repair but he'd pretended to make a tool of it in previous jobs. It was a lead-plated flexible hose springing from a magnetronic pump, with a lot of meters and switches haywired on for pure effect. "Give me a hand, John," he said quietly.

We fixed the pump over the outlet valve and hooked up the two or three controls that really meant something. I heard Kathryn gasp behind me, and the dreadful realization burst into my own brain and numbed my hands. There wasn't even a gasket—

The Gorzuni engineer strode up to us, rumbling a question in his harsh language, his fellows behind him. Manuel answered readily, not taking his gaze off the wildly swinging fake meters.

He turned to me, and I saw the dark laughter in his eyes. "I told them the converter is overdue for a flushing out of waste products," he said in Anglic. "As a matter of fact, the whole ship is."

He took the hose in one hand and the other rested on a switch of the engine. "Don't look, Kathryn," he said tonelessly. Then he threw the switch.

I heard the baffle plates clank down. Manuel had shorted out the automatic safety controls which kept them up when the atoms were burning. I threw a hand over my own eyes and crouched.

The flame that sprang forth was like a bit of the sun. It

77

sheeted from the hose and across the room. I felt my skin shriveling from incandescence and heard the roar of cloven air. In less than a second, Manuel had thrown the baffles back into place but his improvised blaster had torn away the heads of the three Gorzuni and melted the farther wall. Metal glowed white as I looked again, and the angry thunders boomed and echoed and shivered deep in my bones till my skull rang with it.

Dropping the hose, Manuel stepped over to the dead giants and yanked the guns from their holsters. "One for each of us," he said.

Turning to Kathryn: "Get on a suit of armor and wait down here. The radioactivity is bad, but I don't think it'll prove harmful in the time we need. Shoot anyone who comes in."

"I—" Her voice was faint and thin under the rolling echoes, "I don't want to hide—"

"Damn it, you'll be our guard. We can't let those monsters recapture the engine room. Now, null gravity!" And Manuel switched off the generator.

Free fall yanked me with a hideous nausea. I fought down my outraged stomach and grabbed a post to get myself back down to the deck. Down—no. There was no up and down now. We are floating free. Manuel had nullified the gravity advantage of the Gorzuni.

"All right, John, let's go!" he snapped.

I had time only to clasp Kathryn's hand. Then we were pushing off and soaring out the door and into the corridor beyond. Praise all gods, the Commonwealth navy had at least given its personnel free-fall training. But I wondered how many of the slaves would know how to handle themselves.

The ship roared around us. Two Gorzuni burst from a side cabin, guns in hands. Manuel burned them as they appeared, snatched their weapons, and swung on toward the slave pens.

The lights went out. I swam in a thick darkness alive with the rage of the enemy. "What the hell—" I gasped.

Manuel's answer came dryly out of blackness: "Kathryn knows what to do. I told her a few days ago."

At the moment I had no time to realize the emptiness

within me from knowing that those two had been talking without me. There was too much else to do. The Gorzuni were firing blind. Blaster bolts crashed lividly down the halls. Riot was breaking loose. Twice a lightning flash sizzled within centimeters of me. Manuel fired back at isolated giants, killing them and collecting their guns. Shielded by the dark, we groped our way to the slave pens.

No guards were there. When Manuel began to melt down the locks with lower-power blasting I could dimly see the tangle of free-floating naked bodies churning and screaming in the vast gloom. A scene from an ancient hell. The fall of the rebel angels. Man, child of God, had stormed the Stars and been condemned to Hell for it.

And now he was going to burst out!

Hokusai's flat eager face pressed against the bars. "Get us out," he muttered fiercely.

"How many can you trust?" asked Manuel.

"About a hundred. They're keeping their heads, see them waiting over there? And maybe fifty of the women."

"All right. Bring out your followers. Let the rest riot for a while. We can't do anything to help them."

The men came out, grimly and silently, hung there while I opened the females' cage. Manuel passed out such few guns as we had. His voice lifted in the pulsing dark.

"All right. We hold the engine room. I want six with guns to go there now and help Kathryn O'Donnell keep it for us. Otherwise the Gorzuni will recapture it. The rest of us will make for the arsenal."

"How about the bridge?" I asked.

"It'll keep. Right now the Gorzuni are panicked. It's part of their nature. They're worse than humans when it comes to mass stampedes. But it won't last and we have to take advantage of it. Come on!"

Hokusai led the engine room party—his naval training told him where the chamber would be—and I followed Manuel, leading the others out. There were only three or four guns between us but at least we knew where we were going. And by now few of the humans expected to live or cared about much of anything except killing Gorzuni. Manuel had timed it right.

We fumbled through a livid darkness, exchanging shots with warriors who prowled the ship firing at everything

79

that moved. We lost men but we gained weapons. Now and again we found dead aliens, killed in the rioting, and stripped them too. We stopped briefly to release the technicians from their special cage and then shoved violently for the arsenal.

The Gorzuni all had private arms, but the ship's collection was not small. A group of sentries remained at the door, defending it against all comers. They had a portable shield against blaster bolts. I saw our flames splatter off it and saw men die as their fire raked back at us.

"We need a direct charge to draw their attention, while a few of us use the zero gravity to soar 'overhead' and come down on them from 'above,' " said Manuel's cold voice. It was clear, even in that wild lightning-cloven gloom. "John, lead the main attack."

"Like hell!" I gasped. It would be murder. We'd be hewed down as a woodman hews saplings. And there was Kathryn waiting— Then I swallowed rage and fear and lifted a shout to the men. I'm no braver than anyone else but there is an exaltation in battle, and Manuel used it as calculatingly as he used everything else.

We poured against them in a wall of flash, a wall that they ripped apart and sent lurching back in tattered fragments. It was only an instant of flame and thunder, then Manuel's flying attack was on the defenders, burning them down, and it was over. I realized vaguely that I had a seared patch on my leg. It didn't hurt just then, and I wondered at the minor miracle which had kept me alive.

Manuel fused the door and the remnants of us swarmed in and fell on the racked weapons with a terrible fierceness. Before we had them all loaded a Gorzuni party charged us but we beat them off.

There were flashlights too. We had illumination in the seething dark. Manuel's face leaped out of that night as he gave his crisp, swift orders. A gargoyle face, heavy and powerful and ugly, but men jumped at his bidding. A party was assigned to go back to the slave pens and pass out weapons to the other humans and bring them back here.

Reinforcements were sent to the engine room. Mortars and small antigrav cannon were assembled and loaded.

The Gorzuni were calming too. Someone had taken charge and was rallying them. We'd have a fight on our hands.

We did!

I don't remember much of those fire-shot hours. We lost heavily in spite of having superior armament. Some three hundred humans survived the battle. But many of them were badly wounded. But we took the ship. We hunted down the last Gorzuni and flamed those who tried to surrender. There was no mercy in us. The Gorzuni had beaten it out, and now they faced the monster they had created. When the lights went on again three hundred weary humans lived and held the ship.

# IV

There was a conference in the largest room we could find. Everyone was there, packed together in sweaty silence and staring at the man who had freed them. Theoretically it was a democratic assembly called to decide our next move. In practice Manuel Argos gave his orders.

"First, of course," he said, his soft voice somehow carrying through the whole great chamber, "we have to make repairs, both of battle damage and of the deliberately mishandled machinery. It'll take a week, I imagine, but then we'll have us a sweet ship. By that time, too, you'll have shaken down into a crew. Lieutenant Reeves and Ensign Hokusai will give combat instruction. We're not through fighting yet."

"You mean—" A man stood up in the crowd. "You mean, sir, that we'll have opposition on our return to Sol? I should think we could just sneak in. A planet's too big for blockade, you know, even if the Baldics cared to try."

"I mean," said Manuel calmly, "that we're going on to Gorzun."

It would have meant a riot if everyone hadn't been so tired. As it was, the murmur that ran through the assembly was ominous.

"Look, you," said Manuel patiently, "we'll have us a first-class fighting ship by the time we get there, which none of the enemy has. We'll be an expected vessel, one of their own, and in no case do they expect a raid on their home planet. It's a chance to give them a body blow. The Gorzuni don't name their ships, so I propose we christen ours now—the Revenge."

It was sheer oratory. His voice was like an organ. His words were those of a wrathful angel. He argued and pleaded and bullied and threatened and then blew the trumpets for us. At the end they stood up and cheered for him. Even my own heart lifted, and Kathryn's eyes were wide and shining. Oh, he was cold and harsh and over-bearing, but he made us proud to be human.

In the end, it was agreed, and the Solar ship *Revenge*, Captain Manuel Argos, First Mate John Henry Reeves, resumed her way to Gorzun.

In the days and weeks that followed, Manuel talked much of his plans. A devastating raid on Gorzun would shake the barbarian confidence and bring many of their outworld ships swarming back to defend the mother world. Probably the rival half of the Baldic League would seize its chance and fall on a suddenly weakened enemy. The *Revenge* would return to Sol, by that time possessed of the best crew in the known universe, and rally mankind's scattered forces. The war would go on until the System was cleared——

"—and then, of course, continue till all the barbarians have been conquered," said Manuel.

"Why?" I demanded. "Interstellar imperialism can't be made to pay. It does for the barbarians because they haven't the technical facilities to produce at home what they can steal elsewhere. But Sol would only be taking on a burden."

"For defense," said Manuel. "You don't think I'd let a defeated enemy go off to lick his wounds and prepare a new attack, do you? No, everyone but Sol must be dis-armed, and the only way to enforce such a peace is for Sol to be the unquestioned ruler." He added thoughtfully: "Oh, the empire won't have to expand forever. Just till it's big enough to defend itself against all comers. And a bit of economic readjustment could make it a paying proposition, too. We could collect tribute, you know."

"An empire—?" asked Kathryn. "But the Common-wealth is democratic—"

"Was democratic!" he snapped. "Now it's rotted away.

Too bad, but you can't revive the dead. This is an age in history such as has often occurred before when the enforced peace of Caesarism is the only solution. Maybe not a good solution but better than the devastation we're suffering now. When there's been a long enough period of peace and unity it may be time to think of reinstating the old republicanism. But that time is many centuries in the future, if it ever comes. Just now the socio-economic conditions aren't right for it."

He took a restless turn about the bridge. A million stars of space in the viewport blazed like a chill crown over his head. "It'll be an empire in fact," he said, "and therefore it should be an empire in name. People will fight and sacrifice and die for a gaudy symbol when the demands of reality don't touch them. We need a hereditary aristocracy to put on a good show. It's always effective, and the archaism is especially valuable to Sol just now. It'll recall the good old glamorous days before space travel. It'll be even more of a symbol now than it was in its own age. Yes, an empire, Kathryn, the Empire of Sol. Peace, ye underlings!"

"Aristocracies decay," I argued. "Despotism is all right as long as you have an able despot but sooner or later a meathead will be born——"

"Not if the dynasty starts with strong men and women, and continues to choose good breeding stock, and raises the sons in the same hard school as the fathers. Then it can last for centuries. Especially in these days of gerontology and hundred-year active lifespans."

I laughed at him. "One ship, and you're planning an empire in the Galaxy!" I jeered. "And you yourself, I suppose, will be the first emperor?"

His eyes were expressionless. "Yes," he said. "Unless I find a better man, which I doubt."

Kathryn bit her lip. "I don't like it," she said. "It's—cruel."

"This is a cruel age, my dear," he said gently.

Gorzun rolled black and huge against a wilderness of stars. The redly illuminated hemisphere was like a sickle of blood as we swept out of secondary drive and rode our gravbeams down toward the night side.

Once only were we challenged. A harsh gabble of words came over the transonic communicator. Manuel answered smoothly in the native language, explaining that our vision set was out of order, and gave the recognition signals contained in the code-book. The warship let us pass.

Down and down and down, the darkened surface swelling beneath us, mountains reaching hungry peaks to rip the vessel's belly out, snow and glaciers and a churning sea lit by three hurtling moons. Blackness and cold and desolation.

Manuel's voice rolled over the intercom: "Look below, men of Sol. Look out the viewports. This is where they were taking us!"

A snarl of pure hatred answered him. That crew would have died to the last human if they could drag Gorzun to oblivion with them. God help me, I felt that way myself.

It had been a long, hard voyage even after our liberation, and the weariness in me was only lifted by the prospect of battle. I'd been working around the clock, training men, organizing the hundred units a modern warcraft needs. Manuel, with Kathryn for secretary and general assistant, had been driving himself even more fiercely, but I hadn't seen much of either of them. We'd all been too busy.

Now the three of us sat on the bridge watching Gorzun shrieking up to meet us. Kathryn was white and still, the hand that rested on mine was cold. I felt a tension within myself that thrummed near the breaking point. My orders to my gun crews were strained. Manuel alone seemed as chill and unruffled as always. There was steel in him. I sometimes wondered if he really was human.

Atmosphere screamed and thundered behind us. We roared over the sea, racing the dawn, and under its cold colorless streaks of light we saw Gorzun's capital city rise from the edge of the world.

I had a dizzying glimpse of squat stone towers, narrow canyons of streets, and the gigantic loom of spaceships on the rim of the city. Then Manuel nodded and I gave my firing orders.

Flame and ruin exploded beneath us. Spaceships burst open and toppled to crush buildings under their huge mass. Stone and metal fused, ran in lava between crumbling walls. The ground opened and swallowed half the town. A blue-white hell of atomic fire winked through the sudden roil of smoke. And the city died.

We slewed skyward, every girder protesting, and raced for the next great spaceport. There was a ship riding above it. Perhaps they had been alarmed already. We never knew. We opened up ,and she fired back, and while we maneuvered in the heavens the *Revenge* dropped her bombs. We took a pounding, but our force-screens held and theirs didn't. The burning ship smashed half the city when it fell.

On to the next site shown by our captured maps. This time we met a cloud of space interceptors. Ground missiles went arcing up against us. The *Revenge* shuddered under the blows. I could almost see our gravity generator smoking as it tried to compensate for our crazy spins and twists and lurchings. We fought them, like a bear fighting a dog pack, and scattered them and laid the base waste.

"All right," said Manuel. "Let's get out of here."

Space became a blazing night around us as we climbed above the atmosphere. Warships would be thundering on their way now to smash us. But how could we locate a single ship in the enormousness between the worlds? We went into secondary drive, a tricky thing to do so near a sun, but we'd tightened the engines and trained the crew well. In minutes we were at the next planet, also habitable. There were only three colonies there. We smashed them all.

The men were cheering. It was more like the yelp of a wolf pack. The snarl died from my own face and I felt a little sick with all the ruin. Our enemies, yes. But there were many dead. Kathryn wept, slow silent tears running down her face, shoulders shaking.

Manuel reached over and took her hand. "It's done, Kathyrn," he said quietly. "We can go home now."

He added after a moment, as if to himself: "Hate is a useful means to an end but damned dangerous. We'll have to get the racist complex out of mankind. We can't conquer anyone, even the Gorzuni, and keep them as inferiors and hope to have a stable empire. All races must be equal." He rubbed his strong square chin. "I think I'll borrow a leaf from the old Romans. All worthy individuals, of any race, can become terrestrial citizens. It'll be a stabilizing factor."

"You," I said, with a harshness in my throat, "are a megalomaniac." But I wasn't sure any longer.

It was winter in Earth's northern hemisphere when the *Revenge* came home. I walked out into snow that crunched under my feet and watched my breath smoking white against the clear pale blue of the sky. A few others had come out with me. They fell on their knees in the snow and kissed it. They were a wild-looking gang, clad in whatever tatters of garment they could find, the men bearded and long-haired, but they were the finest, deadliest fighting crew in the Galaxy now. They stood there looking at the gentle sweep of hills, at blue sky and ice-flashing trees and a single crow hovering far overhead, and tears froze in their beards.

Home.

We had signalled other units of the Navy. There would be some along to pick us up soon and guide us to the secret base on Mercury, and there the fight would go on. But now, just now in this eternal instant, we were home.

I felt weariness like an ache in my bones. I wanted to crawl bear-like into some cave by a murmuring river, under the dear tall trees of Earth, and sleep till spring woke up the world again. But as I stood there with the thin winter wind like a cleansing bath around me, the tiredness dropped off. My body responded to the world which two billion years of evolution had shaped it for and I laughed aloud with the joy of it.

We couldn't fail. We were the freemen of Terra fighting for our own hearthfires and the deep ancient strength of the planet was in us. Victory and the stars lay in our hands, even now, even now.

I turned and saw Kathryn coming down the airlock gangway. My heart stumbled and then began to race. It had been so long, so terribly long. We'd had so little time but now we were home, and she was here and I was here and all the world was singing.

Her face was grave as she approached me. There was something remote about her and a strange blending of pain with the joy that must be in her too. The frost crackled in her dark unbound hair, and when she took my hands her own were cold.

"Kathryn, we're home," I whispered. "We're home, and free, and alive. O Kathryn, I love you!"

She said nothing, but stood looking at me forever and forever until Manuel Argos came to join us. The little stocky man seemed embarrassed—the first and only time I ever saw him quail, even faintly.

"John," he said, "I've got to tell you something."

"It'll keep," I answered. "You're the captain of the ship. You have authority to perform marriages. I want you to marry Kathryn and me, here, now, on Earth."

She looked at me unwaveringly, but her eyes were blind with tears. "That's it, John," she said, so low I could barely hear her. "It won't be. I'm going to marry Manuel."

I stood there, not saying anything, not even feeling it yet.

"It happened on the voyage," she said, tonelessly. "I tried to fight myself, I couldn't. I love him, John. I love him even more than I love you, and I didn't think that was possible."

"She will be the mother of kings," said Manuel, but his arrogant words were almost defensive. "I couldn't have made a better choice."

"Do you love her too," I asked slowly, "or do you consider her good breeding stock?" Then: "Never mind. Your answer would only be the most expedient. We'll never know the truth."

It was instinct, I thought with a great resurgence of weariness. A strong and vital woman would pick the most suitable mate. She couldn't help herself. It was the race within her and there was nothing I could do about it.

"Bless you, my children," I said.

They walked away after awhile, hand in hand under the high trees that glittered with ice and sun. I stood watching them until they were out of sight. Even then, with a long and desperate struggle yet to come, I think I knew that those were the parents of the Empire and the glorious Argolid dynasty, that they carried the future within them.

And I didn't give a damn.

*It's a characteristic of a decadent civilization that their "scientists" consider all knowledge already known—that they spend their time making cyclopedic gathering of that knowledge. But that Foundation was something rather tricky——*

•

# FOUNDATION
## by Isaac Asimov

Hari Seldon was old and tired. His voice, roared out though it was, by the amplifying system, was old and tired as well.

There were few in that small assemblage that did not realize that Hari Seldon would be dead before the next spring. And they listened in respectful silence to the last official words of the Galaxy's greatest mind.

"This is the final meeting," that tired voice said, "of the group I had called together over twenty years ago." Seldon's eyes swept the seated scientists. He was alone on the platform, alone in the wheel chair to which a stroke had confined him two years before, and on his lap was the last volume—the fifty-second—of the minutes of previous meetings. It was opened to the last page.

He continued: "The group I called together represented the best the Galactic Empire could offer of its philosophers, its psychologists, its historians, and its physical scientists. And in the twenty years since, we have considered the greatest problem ever to confront any group of fifty men—perhaps the greatest ever to confront any number of men.

"We have not always agreed on methods or on procedure. We have spent months and, doubtless, years on futile debates over relatively minor issues. On more than one occasion, sizable sections of our group threatened to break away altogether.

"And yet"—his old face lit in a gentle smile—"we solved the problem. Many of the original members died and were replaced by others. Schemes were abandoned; plans voted down; procedures proven faulty.

"Yet we solved the problem; and not one member, while yet alive, left our group. I am glad of that."

He paused, and allowed the subdued applause to die.

"We have done; and our work is over. The Galactic Empire is falling, but its culture shall not die, and provision has been made for a new and greater culture to develop therefrom. The two Scientific Refuges we planned have been established: one at each end of the Galaxy, at Terminus and at Star's End. They are in operation and already moving along the inevitable lines we have drawn for them.

"For us is left only one last item, and that fifty years in the future. That item, already worked out in detail, will be the instigation of revolts in the key sectors of Anacreon and Loris. It will set that final machinery in motion to work itself out in the millennium that follows."

Hari Seldon's tired head dropped. "Gentlemen, the last meeting of our group is hereby adjourned. We began in secret; we have worked throughout in secret; and now end in secret—to wait for our reward a thousand years hence with the establishment of the Second Galactic Empire."

The last volume of minutes closed, and Hari Seldon's thin hand fell away from it.

"I am finished!" he whispered.

Lewis Pirenne was busily engaged at his desk in the one well-lit corner of the room. Work had to be co-ordinated.

Effort had to be organized. Threads had to be woven into a pattern.

Fifty years now; fifty years to establish themselves and set up Encyclopedia Foundation Number One into a smoothly working unit. Fifty years to gather the raw material. Fifty years to prepare.

It had been done. Five more years would see the publication of the first volume of the most monumental work the Galaxy had ever conceived. And then at ten-year intervals—regularly—like clockwork—volume after volume after volume. And with them there would be supplements; special articles on events of current interest, until——

Pirenne stirred uneasily, as the muted buzzer upon his desk muttered peevishly. He had almost forgotten the appointment. He shoved the door release and out of an abstracted corner of one eye saw the door open and the broad figure of Salvor Hardin enter. Pirenne did not look up.

Hardin smiled to himself. He was in a hurry, but he knew better than to take offense at Pirenne's cavalier treatment of anything or anyone that disturbed him at his work. He buried himself in the chair on the other side of the desk and waited.

Pirenne's stylus made the faintest scraping sound as it raced across paper. Otherwise, neither motion nor sound. And then Hardin withdrew a two-credit coin from his vest pocket. He flipped it and its stainless-steel surface caught glitters of light as it tumbled through the air. He caught it and flipped it again, watching the flashing reflections lazily. Stainless steel made good medium of exchange on a planet where all metal had to be imported.

Pirenne looked up and blinked. "Stop that!" he said querulously.

"Eh?"

"That infernal coin tossing. Stop it."

"Oh." Hardin pocketed the metal disk. "Tell me when you're ready, will you? I promised to be back at the City Council meeting before the new aqueduct project is put to a vote."

Pirenne sighed and shoved himself away from the desk. "I'm ready. But I hope you aren't going to bother me with city affairs. Take care of that yourself, please. The Encyclopedia takes up all my time."

"Have you heard the news?" questioned Hardin, phlegmatically.

"What news?"

"The news that the Terminus City ultra-wave set received two hours ago. The Royal Governor of the Prefect of Anacreon has assumed the title of king."

"Well? What *of* it?"

"It means," responded Hardin, "that we're cut off from the inner regions of the Empire. Do you realize that Anacreon stands square across what was our last remaining trade route to Santanni and to Trantor and to Vega itself? Where is our metal to come from? We haven't managed to get a steel or aluminum shipment through in six months and now we won't be able to get any at all, except by grace of the King of Anacreon."

Pirenne *tch-tched* impatiently. "Get them through him, then."

"But can we? Listen, Pirenne, according to the charter which established this Foundation, the Board of Trustees of the Encyclopedia Committee has been given full administrative powers. I, as Mayor of Terminus City, have just enough power to blow my own nose and perhaps to sneeze if you countersign an order giving me permission. It's up to you and your Board then. I'm asking you in the name of the City, whose prosperity depends upon uninterrupted commerce with the Galaxy, to call an emergency meeting——"

"Stop! A campaign speech is out of order. Now, Hardin, the Board of Trustees has not barred the establishment of a municipal government on Terminus. We understand one to be necessary because of the increase in population since the Foundation was established fifty years ago, and because of the increasing number of people involved in non-Encyclopedia affairs. *But* that does not mean that the first and *only* aim of the Foundation is no longer to publish the definitive Encyclopedia of all human knowledge. We are a State-supported, scientific institution, Hardin. We cannot—must not—*will* not interfere in local politics."

"Local politics! By the Emperor's left big toe, Pirenne,

this is a matter of life and death. The planet, Terminus, by itself cannot support a mechanized civilization. It lacks metals. You know that. It hasn't a trace of iron, copper, or aluminum in the surface rocks, and precious little of anything else. What do you think will happen to the Encyclopedia if this watchamacallum King of Anacreon clamps down on us?"

"On *us*? Are you forgetting that we are under the direct control of the Emperor himself? We are not part of the Prefect of Anacreon or of any other prefect. Memorize that! We are part of the Emperor's personal domain and no one touches us. The Empire can protect its own."

"Then why didn't it prevent the Royal Governor of Anacreon from kicking over the traces? And only Anacreon? At least twenty of the outermost prefects of the Galaxy, the entire Periphery as a matter of fact, have begun steering things their own way. I tell you I feel darned uncertain of the Empire and its ability to protect us."

"Hokum! Royal Governors, Kings—what's the difference? The Empire is always shot through with a certain amount of politics and with different men pulling this way and that. Governors have rebelled, and, for that matter, Emperors have been deposed or assassinated before this. But what has that to do with the Empire itself? Forget it, Hardin. It's none of our business. We are first of all and last of all—scientists. And our concern is the Encyclopedia. Oh, yes, I'd almost forgotten. Hardin!"

"Well?"

"Do something about that paper of yours!" Pirenne's voice was angry.

"The Herminus City *Journal*? It isn't mine; it's privately owned. What's it been doing?"

"For weeks now it has been recommending that the fiftieth anniversary of the establishment of the Foundation be made the occasion for public holidays and quite inappropriate celebrations."

"And why not? The radium clock will open the First Vault in three months. I would call that a big occasion, wouldn't you?"

"Not for silly pageantry, Hardin. The First Vault and its opening concern the Board of Trustees alone. Anything of importance will be communicated to the peo-

92

ple. That is final and please make it plain to the *Journal*."

"I'm sorry, Pirenne, but the City Charter guarantees a certain minor matter known as freedom of the press."

"It may. But the Board of Trustees does not. I am the Emperor's representative on Terminus, Hardin, and have full powers in this respect."

Hardin's expression became that of a man counting to ten, mentally. He said grimly: "In connection with your status as Emperor's representative, then, I have a final piece of news to give you."

"About Anacreon?" Pirenne's lips tightened. He felt annoyed.

"Yes. A special envoy will be sent to us from Anacreon. In two weeks."

"An envoy? Here? From Anacreon?" Pirenne chewed that. "What for?"

Hardin stood up, and shoved his chair back up against the desk. "I give you one guess."

And he left—quite unceremoniously.

Anselm haut Rodric—"haut" itself signifying noble blood —Sub-prefect of Pluema and Envoy Extraordinary of his Highness of Anacreon—plus half a dozen other titles— was met by Salvor Hardin at the spaceport with all the imposing ritual of a state occasion.

With a tight smile and a low bow, the sub-prefect had flipped his blaster from its holster and presented it to Hardin butt first. Hardin returned the compliment with a blaster specifically borrowed for the occasion. Friendship and good will were thus established, and if Hardin noted the barest bulge at Haut Rodric's shoulder, he prudently said nothing.

The ground car that received them then—preceded, flanked, and followed by the suitable cloud of minor functionaires—proceeded in a slow, ceremonious manner to Cyclopedia Square, cheered on its way by a properly enthusiastic crowd.

Sub-prefect Anselm received the cheers with the complaisant indifference of a soldier and a nobleman.

He said to Hardin, "And this city is all your world?"

Hardin raised his voice to be heard above the clamor. "We are a young world, your eminence. In our short his-

93

tory we have had but few members of the higher nobility visiting our poor planet. Hence, our enthusiasm."

It is certain that "higher nobility" did not recognize irony when he heard it.

He said thoughtfully: "Founded fifty years ago. Hm-m-m! You have a great deal of unexploited land here, mayor. You have never considered dividing it into estates?"

"There is no necessity as yet. We're extremely centralized; we have to be, because of the Encyclopedia. Some day, perhaps, when our population has grown——"

"A strange world! You have no peasantry?"

Hardin reflected that it didn't require a great deal of acumen to tell that his eminence was indulging in a bit of fairly clumsy pumping. He replied casually, "No—nor nobility."

Haut Rodric's eyebrows lifted. "And your leader—the man I am to meet?"

"You mean Dr. Pirenne? Yes! He is the Chairman of the Board of Trustees—and a personal representative of the Emperor."

"*Doctor?* No other title? A *scholar?* And he rates above the civil authority?"

"Why, certainly," replied Hardin, amiably. "We're all scholars more or less. After all, we're not so much a world as a scientific foundation—under the direct control of the Emperor."

There was a faint emphasis upon the last phrase that seemed to disconcert the sub-prefect. He remained thoughtfully silent during the rest of the slow way to Cyclopedia Square.

If Hardin found himself bored by the afternoon and evening that followed, he had at least the satisfaction of realizing that Pirenne and Haut Rodric—having met with loud and mutual protestations of esteem and regard—were detesting each other's company a good deal more.

Haut Rodric had attended with glazed eye to Pirenne's lecture during the "inspection tour" of the Encyclopedia Building. With polite and vacant smile, he had listened to the latter's rapid patter as they passed through the vast storehouses of reference films and the numerous projection rooms.

It was only after he had gone down level by level into and through the composing departments, editing departments, publishing departments, and filming departments that he made his first comprehensive statement.

"This is all very interesting," he said, "but it seems a strange occupation for grown men. What good is it?"

It was a remark, Hardin noted, for which Pirenne found no answer, though the expression of his face was most eloquent.

The dinner that evening was much the mirror image of the events of that afternoon, for Haut Rodric monopolized the conversation by describing—in minute technical detail and with incredible zest—his own exploits as battalion head during the recent war between Anacreon and the neighboring newly proclaimed Kingdom of Smyrno.

The details of the sub-prefect's account were not completed until dinner was over and one by one the minor officials had drifted away. The last bit of triumphant description of mangled spaceships came when he had accompanied Pirenne and Hardin onto the balcony and relaxed in the warm air of the summer evening.

"And now," he said, with a heavy joviality, "to serious matters."

"By all means," murmured Hardin, lighting a long cigar of Vegan tobacco—not many left, he reflected—and teetering his chair back on two legs.

The Galaxy was high in the sky and its misty lens shape stretched lazily from horizon to horizon. The few stars here at the very edge of the universe were insignificant twinkles in comparison.

"Of course," said the sub-prefect, "all the formal discussions—the paper signing and such dull technicalities, that is—will take place before the—— What is it you call your Council?"

"The Board of Trustees," replied Pirenne, coldly.

"Queer name! Anyway, that's for tomorrow. We might as well clear away some of the underbrush, man to man, right now, though. Hey?"

"And this means——" prodded Hardin.

"Just this. There's been a certain change in the situation

95

out here in the Periphery and the status of your planet has become a trifle uncertain. It would be very convenient if we succeeded in coming to an understanding as to how the matter stands. By the way, mayor, have you another one of those cigars?"

Hardin started and produced one reluctantly.

Anselm haut Rodric sniffed at it and emitted a clucking sound of pleasure. "Vegan tobacco! Where did you get it?"

"We received some last shipment. There's hardly any left. Space knows when we'll get more—if ever."

Pirenne scowled. He didn't smoke—and, for that matter, detested the odor. "Let me understand this, your eminence. Your mission is merely one of clarification?"

Haut Rodric nodded through the smoke of his first lusty puffs.

"In that case, it is soon over. The situation with respect to Encyclopedia Foundation Number One is what it always has been."

"Ah! And what is it that it always has been?"

"Just this: A State-supported scientific institution and part of the personal domain of his august majesty, the Emperor."

The sub-prefect seemed unimpressed. He blew smoke rings. "That's a nice theory, Dr. Pirenne. I imagine you've got charters with the Imperial Seal upon it—but what's the actual situation? How do you stand with respect to Smyrno? You're not fifty parsecs from Smyrno's capital, you know. And what about Konom and Daribow?"

Pirenne said: "We have nothing to do with any prefect. As part of the Emperor's——"

"They're not prefects," reminded Haut Rodric; "they're kingdoms now."

"Kingdoms then. We have nothing to do with them. As a scientific institution——"

"Science be dashed!" swore the other, via a bouncing soldiery oath that ionized the atmosphere. "What the devil has that got to do with the fact that we're liable to see Terminus taken over by Smyrno at any time?"

"And the Emperor? He would just sit by?"

Haut Rodric calmed down and said: "Well, now, Dr. Pirenne, you respect the Emperor's property and so does

Anacreon, but Smyrno might not. Remember, we've just signed a treaty with the Emperor—I'll present a copy to that Board of yours tomorrow—which places upon us the responsibility of maintaining order within the borders of the old Prefect of Anacreon on behalf of the Emperor. Our duty is clear, then, isn't it?"

"Certainly. But Terminus is not part of the Prefect of Anacreon."

"And Smyrno——"

"Nor is it part of the Prefect of Smyrno. It's not part of any prefect."

"Does Smyrno know that?"

"I don't care what it knows."

*"We* do. We've just finished a war with her and she still holds two stellar systems that are ours. Terminus occupies an extremely strategic spot, between the two nations."

Hardin felt weary. He broke in: "What is your proposition, your eminence?"

The sub-prefect seemed quite ready to stop fencing in favor of more direct statements. He said briskly: "It seems perfectly obvious that, since Terminus cannot defend itself, Anacreon must take over the job for its own sake. You understand we have no desire to interfere with internal administration——"

"Uh-huh," grunted Hardin, dryly.

"—but we believe that it would be best for all concerned to have Anacreon establish a military base upon the planet."

"And that is all you would want—a military base in some of the vast unoccupied territory—and let it go at that."

"Well, of course, there would be the matter of supporting the protecting forces."

Hardin's chair came down on all four, and his elbows went forward on his knees. "Now we're getting to the nub. Let's put it into language. Terminus is to be a protectorate and to pay tribute."

"Not tribute. Taxes. We're protecting you. You pay for it."

Pirenne banged his hand on the chair with sudden violence. "Let me speak, Hardin. Your eminence, I don't care a rusty half-credit coin for Anacreon, Smyrno, or all your local politics and petty wars. I tell you this is a State-supported tax-free institution."

"State-supported? But *we* are the State, Dr. Pirenne, and we're not supporting."

Pirenne rose angrily. "Your eminence, I am the direct representative of——"

"——his august majesty, the Emperor," chorused Anslem haut Rodric sourly, "and I am the direct representative of the King of Anacreon. Anacreon is a lot nearer, Dr. Pirenne."

"Let's get back to business," urged Hardin. "How would you take these so-called taxes, your eminence? Would you take them in kind: wheat, potatoes, vegetables, cattle?"

The sub-prefect stared. "What the devil? What do we need with those? We've got hefty surpluses. Gold, of course. Chromium or vanadium would be even better, incidentally, if you have it in quantity."

Hardin laughed. "Quantity! We haven't even got iron in quantity. Gold! Here, take a look at our currency." He tossed a coin to the envoy.

Haut Rodric bounced it and stared. "What is it? Steel?"

"That's right."

"I don't understand."

"Terminus is a planet practically without metals. We import it all. Consequently, we have no gold, and nothing to pay unless you want a few thousand bushels of potatoes."

"Well—manufactured goods."

"Without metal? What do we make our machines out of?"

There was a pause and Pirenne tried again. "This whole discussion is wide of the point. Terminus is not a planet, but a scientific foundation preparing a great encyclopedia. Space, man, have you no respect for science?"

"Encyclopedias don't win wars." Haut Rodric's brows furrowed. "A completely unproductive world, then—and practically unoccupied at that. Well, you might pay with land."

"What do you mean?" asked Pirenne.

"This world is just about empty and the unoccupied land is probably fertile. There are many of the nobility on Anacreon that would like an addition to their estates."

"You can't propose any such—"

"There's no necessity of looking so alarmed, Dr. Pirenne. There's plenty for all of us. If it comes to what it comes, and you co-operate, we could probably arrange it so that you lose nothing. Titles can be conferred and estates granted. You understand me, I think."

Pirenne sneered, "Thanks!"

And then Hardin said ingenuously: "Could Anacreon supply us with adequate quantities of praseodymium for our atomic-power plant? We've only a few years' supply left."

There was a gasp from Pirenne and then a dead silence for minutes. When Haut Rodric spoke it was in a voice quite different from what it had been till then:

"You have atomic power?"

"Certainly. What's unusual in that? I imagine atomic power is fifty thousand years old now. Why shouldn't we have it? Except that it's a little difficult to get praseodymium."

"Yes . . . yes." The envoy paused and added uncomfortably: "Well, gentlemen, we'll pursue the subject tomorrow. You'll excuse me—"

Pirenne looked after him and gritted through his teeth: "That insufferable, dull-witted donkey! That—"

Hardin broke in: "Not at all. He's merely the product of his environment. He doesn't understand much except that 'I got a gun and you ain't'."

Pirenne whirled on him in exasperation. "What in space did you mean by the talk about military bases and tribute? Are you crazy?"

"No. I merely gave him rope and let him talk. You'll notice that he managed to stumble out with Anacreon's real intentions—that is, the parceling up of Terminus into landed estates. Of course, I don't intend to let that happen."

"*You* don't intend. *You* don't. And who are you? And may I ask what you meant by blowing off your mouth about our atomic-power plant? Why, it's just the thing that would make us a military target."

"Yes," grinned Hardin. "A military target to stay away from. Isn't it obvious why I brought the subject up? It happened to confirm a very strong suspicion I had had."

"And that was what?"

"'That Anacreon no longer has an atomic-power economy—and that, therefore, the rest of the Periphery no longer has one as well. Interesting, wouldn't you say?'"

"Bah!" Pirenne left in fiendish humor, and Hardin smiled gently.

He threw his cigar away and looked up at the outstretched Galaxy. "Back to oil and coal, are they?" he murmured—and what the rest of his thoughts were he kept to himself.

When Hardin denied owning the *Journal*, he was perhaps technically correct, but no more. Hardin had been the leading spirit in the drive to incorporate Terminus into an autonomous municipality—he had been elected its first mayor—so it was not surprising that, though not a single share of *Journal* stock was in his name, some sixty percent was controlled by him in more devious fashions.

There were ways.

Consequently, when Hardin began suggesting to Pirenne that he be allowed to attend meetings of the Board of Trustees, it was not quite coincidence that the *Journal* began a similar campaign. And the first mass meeting in the history of the Foundation was held, demanding representation of the City in the 'national' government.

And, eventually, Pirenne capitulated with ill grace.

Hardin, as he sat at the foot of the table, speculated idly as to just what it was that made physical scientists such poor administrators. It might be merely that they were too used to inflexible fact and far too unused to pliable people.

In any case, there was Tomaz Sutt and Jord Fara on his left; Lundin Crast and Yate Fulham on his right; with Pirenne, himself, presiding. He knew them all, of course, but they seemed to have put on an extra-special bit of pomposity for the occasion.

Hardin half dozed through the initial formalities and

then perked up when Pirenne sipped at the glass of water before him by way of preparation and said:

"I find it very gratifying to be able to inform the Board that, since our last meeting, I have received word that Lord Dorwin, Chancellor of the Empire, will arrive at Terminus in two weeks. It may be taken for granted that our relations with Anacreon will be smoothed out to our complete satisfaction as soon as the Emperor is informed of the situation."

He smiled and addressed Hardin across the length of the table. "Information to this effect has been given the *Journal*."

Hardin snickered below his breath. It seemed evident that Pirenne's desire to strut this information before him had been one reason for his admission into the sacrosanctum.

He said evenly: "Leaving vague expressions out of account, what do you expect Lord Dorwin to do?"

Tomaz Sutt replied. He had a bad habit of addressing one in the third person when in his more stately moods.

"It is quite evident," he observed, "that Mayor Hardin is a professional cynic. He can scarcely fail to realize that the Emperor would be most unlikely to allow his personal rights to be infringed."

"Why? What would he do in case they were?"

There was an annoyed stir. Pirenne said, "You are out of order," and, as an after-thought, "and are making what are near-treasonable statements, besides."

"Am I to consider myself answered?"

"Yes! If you have nothing further to say—"

"Don't jump to conclusions. I'd like to ask a question. Besides this stroke of diplomacy—which may or may not prove to mean anything—has anything concrete been done to meet the Anacreonic menace?"

Yate Fulham drew one hand along his ferocious red mustache. "You see a menace there, do you?"

"Don't you?"

"Scarcely"—this with indulgence. "The Emperor—"

"Great space!" Hardin felt annoyed. "What is this? Every once in a while someone mentions 'Emperor' or 'Empire' as if it were a magic word. The Emperor is fifty thousand parsecs away, and I doubt whether he gives a damn about us. And if he does, what can he do? What there was of the imperial navy in these regions is in the hands of the four kingdoms now and Anacreon has its share. Listen, we have to fight with guns, not with words.

"Now, get this. We've had two months of grace so far, mainly because we've given Anacreon the idea that we've got atomic weapons. Well, we all know that that's a little white lie. We've got atomic power, but only for commercial uses, and darn little at that. They're going to find that out soon, and if you think they're going to enjoy being jollied along, you're mistaken."

"My dear sir—"

"Hold on; I'm not finished." Hardin was warming up. He liked this. "It's all very well to drag chancellors into this, but it would be much nicer to drag a few great big siege guns fitted for beautiful atomic bombs into it. We've lost two months, gentlemen, and we may not have another two months to lose. What do you propose to do?"

Said Lundin Crast, his long nose wrinkling angrily: "If you're proposing the militarization of the Foundation, I won't hear a word of it. It would mark our open entrance into the field of politics. We, Mr. Mayor, are a scientific foundation and nothing else."

Added Sutt: "He does not realize, moreover, that building armaments would mean withdrawing men—valuable men—from the Encyclopedia. That cannot be done, come what may."

"Very true," agreed Pirenne. "The Encyclopedia first—always."

Hardin groaned in spirit. The Board seemed to suffer violently from Encyclopedia on the brain.

He said icily: "Has it ever occurred to the Board that it is barely possible that Terminus may have interests other than the Encyclopedia?"

Pirenne replied: "I do not conceive, Hardin, that the Foundation can have any interest other than the Encyclopedia."

"I didn't say the Foundation; I said *Terminus*. I'm afraid you don't understand the situation. There's a good million of us here on Terminus, and not more than a hundred and fifty thousand are working directly on the Encyclopedia. To the rest of us, this is *home*. We were born here. We're living here. Compared with our farms and our homes and our factories, the Encyclopedia means little to us. We want them protected—"

He was shouted down.

"The Encyclopedia first," ground out Crast. "We have a mission to fulfill."

"Mission, hell," shouted Hardin. "That might have been true fifty years ago. But this is a new generation."

"That has nothing to do with it," replied Pirenne. "We are scientists."

And Hardin leaped through the opening. "Are you, though? That's a nice hallucination, isn't it? Your bunch here is a perfect hallucination, isn't it? Your bunch here is a perfect example of what's been wrong with the entire Galaxy for thousands of years. What kind of science is it to be stuck out here for centuries classifying the work of scientists of the last millennium? Have you ever thought of working onward, *extending* their knowledge and improving upon it? No! You're quite happy to stagnate. The whole Galaxy is, and has been for space knows how long. That's why the Periphery is revolting; that's why communications are breaking down; that's why petty wars are becoming eternal; that's why whole systems are losing atomic power and going back to barbarous techniques of chemical power.

"If you ask me," he cried, *"the Galaxy is going to pot!"*

He paused and dropped into his chair to catch his breath, paying no attention to the two or three that were attempting simultaneously to answer him.

Crast got the floor. "I don't know what you're trying to gain by your hysterical statements, Mr. Mayor. Certainly, you are adding nothing constructive to the discussion. I move, Mr. Chairman, that the last speaker's remarks be placed out of order and the discussion be resumed from the point where it was interrupted."

Jord Fara bestirred himself for the first time. Up to this point Fara had taken no part in the argument even at its hottest. But now his ponderous voice, every bit as ponderous as his three-hundred-pound body, burst its bass way out.

"Haven't we forgotten something, gentlemen?"

"What?" asked Pirenne, peevishly.

"That in a month we celebrate our fiftieth anniversary."
Fara had a trick of uttering the most obvious platitudes
with great profundity.

"What of it?"

"And on that anniversary," continued Fara, placidly,
"Hari Seldon's First Vault will open. Have you ever considered what might be in the First Vault?"

"I don't know. Routine matters. A stock speech of congratulations, perhaps. I don't think any significance need
be placed on the First Vault—though the *Journal*"—and
he glared at Hardin, who grinned back—"did try to make
an issue of it. I put a stop to that."

"Ah," said Fara, "but perhaps you are wrong. Doesn't
it strike you"—he paused and put a finger to his round
little nose—"that the Vault is opening at a very convenient time?"

"Very *in*convenient time, you mean," muttered Fulham.
"We've got some other things to worry about."

"Other things more important than a message from
Hari Seldon? I think not." Fara was growing more pon-
tifical than ever, and Hardin eyed him thoughtfully. What
was he getting at?

"In fact," said Fara, happily, "you all seem to forget
that Seldon was the greatest psychologist of our time and
that he was the founder of our Foundation. It seems reasonable to assume that he used his science to determine
the probable course of the history of the immediate future.
If he did, as seems likely, I repeat, he would certainly
have managed to find a way to warn us of danger and,
perhaps, to point out a solution. The Encyclopedia was
very dear to his heart, you know."

An aura of puzzled doubt prevailed. Pirenne hemmed.
"Well, now, I don't know. Psychology is a great science,
but—there are no psychologists among us at the moment,
I believe. It seems to me we're on uncertain ground."

Fara turned to Hardin. "Didn't you study psychology
under Alurin?"

Hardin answered, half in reverie: "Yes. I never completed my studies, though. I got tired of theory. I wanted
to be a psychological engineer, but we lacked the facilities,

104

so I did the next best thing—I went into politics. It's practically the same thing."

"Well, what do you think of the First Vault?"

And Hardin replied cautiously, "I don't know."

He did not say a word for the remainder of the meeting —even though it got back to the subject of the Chancellor of the Empire.

In fact, he didn't even listen. He'd been put on a new track and things were falling into place—just a little. Little angles were fitting together—one or two.

And psychology was the key. He was sure of that.

He was trying desperately to remember the psychological theory he had once learned—and from it he got one thing right at the start.

A great psychologist such as Seldon could unravel human emotions and human reactions sufficiently to be able to predict broadly the historical sweep of the future.

And that meant—hm-m-m!

Lord Dorwin took snuff. He also had long hair, curled intricately and, quite obviously, artificially; to which were added a pair of fluffy, blond sideburns, which he fondled affectionately. Then, too, he spoke in over-precise statements and left out all the r's.

At the moment, Hardin had no time to think of more of the reasons for the instant detestation in which he had held the noble chancellor. Oh, yes, the elegant gestures of one hand with which he accompanied his remarks and the studied condescension with which he accompanied even a simple affirmative.

But, at any rate, the problem now was to locate him. He had disappeared with Pirenne half an hour before— passed clean out of sight, blast him.

Hardin was quite sure that his own absence during the preliminary discussions would quite suit Pirenne.

But Pirenne had been seen in this wing and on this floor. It was simply a matter of trying every door. Halfway down, he said, "Ah!" and stepped into the darkened room. The profile of Lord Dorwin's intricate hairdo was unmistakable against the lighted screen.

Lord Dorwin looked up and said: "Ah, Hahdin. You ah looking foah us, no doubt?" He held out his snuffbox

—overadorned and poor workmanship at that, noted Hardin—and was politely refused, whereat he helped himself to a pinch and smiled graciously.

Pirenne scowled and Hardin met that with an expression of blank indifference.

The only sound to break the short silence that followed was the clicking of the lid of Lord Dorwin's snuffbox. And then he put it away and said:

"A gweat achievement, this Encyclopedia of yoahs, Hahdin. A feat, indeed, to rank with the most majestic accomplishments of all time."

"Most of us think so, milord. It's an accomplishment not quite accomplished as yet, however."

"Fwom the little I have seen of the efficiency of yoah Foundation, I have no feahs on that scoah." And he nodded to Pirenne, who responded with a delighted bow.

Quite a love feast, thought Hardin. "I wasn't complaining about the lack of efficiency, milord, as much as of the definite excess of efficiency on the part of the Anacreonians—though in another and more destructive direction."

"Ah, yes, Anacweon." A negligent wave of the hand. "I have just come from theah. Most bahbawous planet. It is thowoughly inconceivable that human beings could live heah in the Pewiphewy. The lack of the most elementawy wequiahments of a cultuahed gentleman; the absence of the most fundamental necessities foah comfoht and convenience—the uttah disuetude into which they—"

Hardin interrupted dryly: "The Anacreonians, unfortunately, have all the elementary requirements for warfare and all the fundamental necessities for destruction."

"Quite, quite." Lord Dorwin seemed annoyed, perhaps at being stopped midway in his sentence. "But we ahn't to discuss business now, y'know. Weally, I'm othah-wise concuhned. Doctah Piwenne, ahn't you going to show me the second volume? Do, please."

The lights clicked out and for the next half-hour Hardin might as well have been on Anacreon for all the attention they paid him. The book upon the screen made little sense to him, nor did he trouble to make the attempt to follow, but Lord Dorwin became quite humanly excited at times. Hardin noticed that during these moments of excitement the chancellor pronounced his *r*'s.

When the lights went on again. Lord Dorwin said: "Mah-velous. Twuly mahvelous. You ah not, by chance, intewested in ahchaeology, ah you, Hahdin?"

"Eh?" Hardin shook himself out of an abstracted reverie. "No, milord, can't say I am. I'm a psychologist by original intention and a politician by final decision."

"Ah! No doubt intewesting studies. I, myself, y'know" —he helped himself to a giant pinch of snuff—"dabble in ahchaeology."

"Indeed?"

"His lordship," interrupted Pirenne, "is most thoroughly acquainted with the field."

"Well, p'haps I am, p'haps I am," said his lordship complacently. "I *have* done an awful amount of wuhk in the science. Extwemely well-read, in fact. I've gone thwough all of Jawdun, Obijasi, Kwomwill . . . oh, all of them, y'know."

"I've heard of them, of course," said Hardin, "but I've never read them."

"You should some day, my deah fellow. It would amply repay you. Why, I cutainly considah it well wuhth the twip heah to the Pewiphewy to see this copy of Lameth. Would you believe it, my libwawy totally lacks a copy. By the way, Doctah Piwenne, you have not fohgotten yoah pwomise to twansdevelop a copy foah me befoah I leave?"

"Only too pleased."

"Lameth, you must know," continued the chancellor, pontifically, "pwesents a new and most intewesting addition to my pwevious knowledge of the 'Owigin Question'."

"Which question?" asked Hardin.

"The 'Owigin Question.' The place of the owigin of the human species, y'know. Suahly you must know that it is thought that owiginally the human wace occupied only one planetawy system."

"Well, yes, I know that."

"'Of cohse, no one knows exactly which system it is— lost in the mists of antiquity. Theah ah theawies, howevah. Siwius, some say. Othahs insist on Alpha Centauwi, oah on Sol, oah on 61 Cygni—all in the Siwius sectah, you see."

"And what does Lameth say?"

"Well, he goes off along a new twail completely. He

twies to show that ahchaeological wemains on the thuhd
planet of the Ahctuwian System show that humanity existed theah befoah theah wah any indications of space-
twavel."

"And that means it was humanity's birth planet?"

"P'haps. I must wead it closely and weigh the evidence
befoah I can say foah cuhtain. One must see just how
weliable his obsuhvations ah."

Hardin remained silent for a short while. Then he said,
"When did Lameth write his book?"

"Oh—I should say about eight hundwed yeahs ago. Of
cohse, he has based it lahgely on the pwevious wuhk of
Gleen."

"Then why rely on him? Why not go to Arcturus and
study the remains for yourself?"

Lord Dorwin raised his eyebrows and took a pinch of
snuff hurriedly. "Why, whatevah foah, my deah fellow."

"To get the information firsthand, of course."

"But wheah's the necessity? It seems an uncommonly
woundabout and hopelessly wigmawolish method of getting anywheahs. Look heah, now, I've got the wuhks of
all the old mastahs—the gweat ahchaeologists of the past.
I weigh them against each othah—balance the disagwee-
ments—analyze the conflicting statements—decide which
is pwobably cowwect—and come to a conclusion. That is
the scientific method. At least"—patronizingly—"as *I* see
it. How insuffewably cwude it would be to go to Ahctuwus,
oah to Sol, foah instance, and blundah about, when the
old mastahs have covahed the gwound so much moah ef-
fectually than we could possibly hope to do."

Hardin murmured politely, "I see."

Scientific method, hell! No wonder the Galaxy was going to pot.

"Come, milord," said Pirenne, "I think we had better
be returning."

"Ah, yes. P'haps we had."

As they left the room, Hardin said suddenly, "Milord,
may I ask a question?"

Lord Dorwin smiled blandly and emphasized his answer with a gracious flutter of the hand. "Cuhtainly, my
deah fellow. Only too happy to be of service. If I can help

you in any way fwom my pooah stoah of knowledge—"

"It isn't exactly about archaeology, milord."

"No?"

"No. It's this: Last year we received news here in Terminus about the explosion of a power plant on Planet V of Gamma Andromeda. We got the barest outline of the accident—no details at all. I wonder if you could tell me exactly what happened."

Pirenne's mouth twisted. "I wonder you annoy his lordship with questions on totally irrelevant subjects."

"Not at all, Doctah Piwenne," interceded the chancellor. "It is quite all wight. Theah isn't much to say concuhning it in any case. The powah plant did explode and it was quite a catastwophe, y'know. I believe sevewal million people wah killed and at least half the planet was simply laid in wuins. Weally, the govuhnment is sewiously considewing placing seveah westwictions upon the indiscwiminate use of atomic powah—though that is not a thing for genewal publication, y'know."

"I understand," said Hardin. "But what was wrong with the plant?"

"Well, weally," replied Lord Dorwin indifferently, "who knows? It had bwoken down some yeahs pweviously and it is thought that the weplacements and wepaiah wuhk was most infewiah. It is *so* difficult these days to find men who *weally* undahstand the moah technical details of ouah powah systems." And he took a sorrowful pinch of snuff.

"You realize," said Hardin, "that the independent kingdoms of the Periphery have lost atomic power altogether?"

"Have they? I'm not at all suhpwised. Barbawous planets—Oh, but my deah fellow, don't call them independent. They ahn't, y'know. The tweaties we've made with them ah pwoof of that. They acknowledge the soveweignty of the Empewah. They'd have to, of cohse, oah we wouldn't tweat with them."

"That may be so, but they have considerable freedom of action."

"Yes, I suppose so. Considewable. But that scahcely mattahs. The Empiah is fah bettah off, with the Pewiphewy thwown upon its own wesoahces—as it is, moah oah less. They ahn't any good to us, y'know. *Most* bahbawous planets. Scahcely civilized."

109

"They were civilized in the past. Anacreon was one of the richest of the outlying provinces. I understand it compared favorably with Vega itself."

"Oh, but, Hahdin, that was centuwies ago. You can scahcely dwaw conclusion fwom that. Things wah diffewent in the old gweat days. We ahn't the men we used to be, y'know. But, Hahdin, come, you ah a most puhsistent chap, I've told you I simply won't discuss business today. Doctah Piwenne did pwepayah me foah you. He told me you would twy to badgah me, but I'm fah too old a hand foah that. Leave it foah next day."

And that was that.

This was the second meeting of the Board that Hardin had attended, if one were to exclude the informal talks the Board members had had with the now-departed Lord Dorwin. Yet the mayor had a perfectly definite idea that at least one other, and possibly two or three, had been held, to which he had somehow never received an invitation.

Nor, it seemed to him, would he have received notification of this one had it not been for the ultimatum.

At least, it amounted to an ultimatum, though a superficial reading of the visigraphed document would lead one to suppose that it was a friendly interchange of greetings between two potentates.

Hardin fingered it gingerly. It started off floridly with a salutation from "His Puissant Majesty, the King of Anacreon, to his friend and brother, Dr. Lewis Pirenne, Chairman of the Board of Trustees, of the Encyclopedia Foundation Number One," and it ended even more lavishly with a gigantic, multicolored seal of the most involved symbolism.

But it was an ultimatum just the same.

Hardin said: "It turned out that we didn't have much time after all—only three months. But little as it was, we threw it away unused. This thing here gives us a week. What do we do now?"

Pirenne frowned worriedly. "There must be a loophole. It is absolutely unbelievable that they would push matters to extremities in the face of what Lord Dorwin has assured us regarding the attitude of the Emperor and the Empire."

Hardin perked up. "I see. You have informed the King of Anacreon of this alleged attitude?"

"I did—after having placed the proposal to the Board for a vote and having received unanimous consent."

"And when did this vote take place?"

Pirenne climbed onto his dignity. "I do not believe I am answerable to you in any way, Mayor Hardin."

"All right. I'm not that vitally interested. It's just my opinion that it was your diplomatic transmission of Lord Dorwin's valuable contribution to the situation"—he lifted the corner of his mouth in a sour half-smile—"that was the direct cause of this friendly little note. They might have delayed longer otherwise—though I don't think the additional time would have helped Terminus any, considering the attitude of the Board."

Said Yate Fulham: "And just how do you arrive at that remarkable conclusion, Mr. Mayor?"

"In a rather simple way. It merely required the use of that much-neglected commodity—common sense. You see, there is a branch of human knowledge known as symbolic logic, which can be used to prune away all sorts of clogging deadwood that clutters up human language."

"What about it?" said Fulham.

"I applied it. Among other things, I applied it to this document here. I didn't really need to for myself because I knew what it was all about, but I think I can explain it more easily to five physical scientists by symbols rather than by words."

Hardin removed a few sheets of paper from the pad under his arm and spread them out. "I didn't do this myself, by the way," he said. "Muller Holk of the Division of Logic has his name signed to the analyses, as you can see."

Pirenne leaned over the table to get a better view and Hardin continued: "The message from Anacreon was a simple problem, naturally, for the men who wrote it were men of action rather than men of words. It boils down easily and straightforwardly to the unqualified statement, which in symbols is what you see, and which in words,

111

roughly translated, is, 'You give us what we want in a week, or we beat the hell out of you and take it anyway'."

There was silence as the five members of the Board ran down the line of symbols, and then Pirenne sat down and coughed uneasily.

Hardin said, "No loophole, is there, Dr. Pirenne?"

"Doesn't seem to be."

"All right." Hardin replaced the sheets. "Before you now you see a copy of the treaty between the Empire and Anacreon—a treaty, incidentally, which is signed on the Emperor's behalf by the same Lord Dorwin who was here last week—and with it a symbolic analysis."

The treaty ran through five pages of fine print and the analysis was scrawled out in just under half a page.

"As you see, gentlemen, something like ninety percent of the treaty boiled right out of the analysis as being meaningless, and what we end up with can be described in the following interesting manner:

"Obligations of Anacreon to the Empire: *None!*

"Powers of the Empire over Anacreon: *None!*"

Again the five followed the reasoning anxiously, checking carefully back to the treaty, and when they were finished, Pirenne said in a worried fashion, "That seems to be correct."

"You admit, then, that the treaty is nothing but a declaration of total independence on the part of Anacreon and a recognition of that status by the Empire?"

"It seems so."

"And do you suppose that Anacreon doesn't realize that, and is not anxious to emphasize the position of independence—so that it would naturally tend to resent any appearance of threats from the Empire? Particularly when it is evident that the Empire is powerless to fulfill any such threats, or it would never have allowed independence."

"But then," interposed Sutt, "how would Mayor Hardin account for Lord Dorwin's assurances of Empire support? They seemed—" He shrugged. "Well, they seemed satisfactory."

Hardin threw himself back in the chair. "You know, that's the most interesting part of the whole business. I'll admit I had thought his lordship a most consummate donkey when I first met him—but it turned out that he was actually an accomplished diplomat and a most clever man. I took the liberty of recording all his statements."

There was a flurry, and Pirenne opened his mouth in horror.

"What of it?" demanded Hardin. "I realize it was a gross breach of hospitality and a thing no so-called gentleman would do. Also, that if his lordship had caught on, things might have been unpleasant; but he didn't, and I have the record, and that's that. I took that record, had it copied out and sent that to Holk for analysis, also."

Lundin Crast said, "And where is the analysis?"

"That," replied Hardin, "is the interesting thing. The analysis was the most difficult of the three by all odds. When Holk, after two days of steady work, succeeded in eliminating meaningless statements, vague gibberish, useless qualifications—in short, all the goo and dribble—he found he had nothing left. Everything cancelled out.

"Lord Dorwin, gentlemen, in five days of discussion *didn't say one damned thing*, and said it so you never noticed. *There* are the assurances you had from your precious Empire."

Hardin might have placed an actively working stench bomb upon the table and created no more confusion than existed after his last statement. He waited, with weary patience, for it to die down.

"So," he concluded, "when you sent threats—and that's what they were—concerning Empire action to Anacreon, you merely irritated a monarch who knew better. Naturally, his ego would demand immediate action, and the ultimatum is the result—which brings me to my original statement. We have one week left and what do we do now?"

"It seems," said Sutt, "that we have no choice but to allow Anacreon to establish military bases on Terminus."

"I agree with you there," replied Hardin, "but what do we do toward kicking them off again at the first opportunity?"

Yate Fulham's mustache twitched. "That sounds as if you have made up your mind that violence must be used against them."

"Violence," came the retort, "is the last refuge of the incompetent. But I certainly don't intend to lay down the welcome mat and brush off the best furniture for their use."

"I still don't like the way you put that," insisted Fulham. "It is a dangerous attitude; the more dangerous because we have noticed lately that a sizable section of the populace seems to respond to all your suggestions just so. I might as well tell you, Mayor Hardin, that the Board is not quite blind to your recent activities."

He paused and there was general agreement. Hardin shrugged.

Fulham went on: "If you were to inflame the City into an act of violence, you would achieve elaborate suicide—and we don't intend to allow that. Our policy has but one cardinal principle, and that is the Encyclopedia. Whatever we decide to do or not to do will be so decided because it will be the measure required to keep that Encyclopedia safe."

"Then," said Hardin, "you come to the conclusion that we must continue our intensive campaign of doing nothing."

Pirenne said bitterly: "You have yourself demonstrated that the Empire cannot help us; though how and why it can be so, I don't understand. If compromise is necessary—"

Hardin had the nightmarelike sensation of running at top speed and getting nowhere. "There *is* no compromise? Don't you realize that this bosh about military bases is a particularly inferior grade of drivel? Haut Rodric told us what Anacreon was after—outright annexation and imposition of its own feudal system of landed estates and peasant-aristocracy economy upon us. What is left of our bluff of atomic power may force them to move slowly, but they will move nonetheless."

He had risen indignantly, and the rest rose with him—except for Jord Fara.

And then Jord Fara spoke. "Everyone will please sit down. We've gone quite far enough, I think. Come, there's no use looking so furious, Mayor Hardin; none of us have been committing treason."

"You'll have to convince me of that!"

Fara smiled gently. "You know you don't mean that. Let me speak!"

His little shrewd eyes were half closed, and the perspiration gleamed on the smooth expanse of his chin. "There seems no point in concealing that the Board has come to the decision that the real solution to the Anacreonian problem lies in what is to be revealed to us when the First Vault opens six days from now."

"Is that your contribution to the matter?"

"Yes."

"We are to do nothing, is that right, except to wait in quiet serenity and utter faith for the *deus ex machina* to pop out of the First Vault?"

"Stripped of your emotional phraseology, that's the idea."

"Such unsubtle escapism! Really, Dr. Fara, such folly smacks of genius. A lesser mind would be incapable of it."

Fara smiled indulgently. "Your taste in epigrams is amusing, Hardin, but out of place. As a matter of fact, I think you remember my line of argument concerning the First Vault about three weeks ago."

"Yes, I remember it. I don't deny that it was anything but a stupid idea from the standpoint of deductive logic alone. You said—stop me when I make a mistake—that Hari Seldon was the greatest psychologist in the System; that, hence, he could foresee the tight and uncomfortable spot we're in now; that, hence, he established the First Vault as a method of telling us the way out."

"You've got the essence of the idea."

"Would it surprise you to hear that I've given considerable thought to the matter these last weeks?"

"Very flattering. With what result?"

"With the result that pure deduction is found wanting. Again what is needed is a little sprinkling of common sense."

"For instance?"

"For instance, if he foresaw the Anacreonian mess, why not have placed us on some other planet nearer the Galactic centers? Why put us out here at all if he could see in advance the break in communication lines, our isolation from the Galaxy, the threat of our neighbors—and our helplessness because of the lack of metals on Terminus? That above all! Or if he foresaw all this, why not have warned the original settlers in advance that they might have had time to prepare, rather than wait, as he is doing, until one foot is over the cliff, before doing so?

"And don't forget this. Even though he could foresee the problem *then*, we can see it equally well *now*. Therefore, if he could foresee the solution then, we should be able to see the solution now. After all, Seldon was not a magician. There are no trick methods of escaping from a dilemma that he can see and we can't."

"But, Hardin," reminded Fara, "we can't!"

"But you haven't *tried*. You haven't tried once. First, you refused to admit that there was a menace at all! Then you reposed an absolutely blind faith in the Emperor! Now you've shifted it to Hari Seldon. Throughout you have invariably relied on authority or on the past—never on yourselves."

His fists balled spasmodically. "It amounts to a diseased attitude—a conditioned reflex that shunts aside the independence of your minds whenever it is a question of opposing authority. There seems no doubt ever in your minds that the Emperor is more powerful than you are, or Hari Seldon wiser. And that's wrong, don't you see?"

For some reason, no one cared to answer him.

Hardin continued: "It isn't just you. It's the whole Galaxy. Pirenne heard Lord Dorwin's idea of scientific research. Lord Dorwin thought the way to be a good archaeologist was to read all the books on the subject—written by men who were dead for centuries. He thought that the way to solve archaeological puzzles was to weigh opposing authorities. And Pirenne listened and made no objections. Don't you see that there's something wrong with that?"

Again the note of near-pleading in his voice. Again no answer.

He went on: "And you men and half of Terminus as well are just as bad. We sit here, considering the Encyclopedia the all-in-all. We consider the greatest end of science to be the classification of past data. It *is* important, but is there no further work to be done? We're receding and forgetting, don't you see? Here in the Periphery

116

they've lost atomic power. In Gamma Andromeda, a power plant has blown up because of poor repairs, and the Chancellor of the Empire complains that atomic technicians are scarce. And the solution? To train new ones? Never! Instead, they're to restrict atomic power."

And for the third time: "Don't you *see?* It's Galaxy-wide. It's a worship of the past. It's a deterioration—*a stagnation!*"

He stared from one to the other and they gazed fixedly at him.

Fara was the first to recover. "Well, mystical philosophy isn't going to help us here. Let us be concrete. Do you deny that Hari Seldon could easily have worked out historical trends of the future by simple psychological technique?"

"No, of course not," cried Hardin. "But we can't rely on him for a solution. At best, he might indicate the problem, but if ever there is to be a solution, we must work it out ourselves. He can't do it for us."

Fulham spoke suddenly. "What do you mean—'indicate the problem'? We *know* the problem."

Hardin whirled on him. "You think you do? You think Anacreon is all Hari Seldon is likely to be worried about. I disagree! I tell you, gentlemen, that as yet none of you has the faintest conception of what is really going on."

"And you do?" questioned Pirenne, hostilely.

"I think so!" Hardin jumped up and pushed his chair away. His eyes were cold and hard. "If there's one thing that's definite, it is that there's something smelly about the whole situation; something that is bigger than anything we've talked about yet. Just ask yourself this question: Why was it that among the original population of the Foundation not one first-class psychologist was included, except Bor Alurin? And *he* carefully refrained from training his pupils in more than the fundamentals."

A short silence and Fara said: "All right. Why?"

"Perhaps because a psychologist might have caught on to what this was all about—and too soon to suit Hari Seldon. As it is, we've been stumbling about, getting misty glimpses of the truth and no more. And that is what Hari Seldon wanted."

He laughed harshly. "Good day, gentlemen!"

He stalked out of the room.

Mayor Hardin chewed at the end of his cigar. It had gone out but he was past noticing that. He hadn't slept the night before and he had a good idea that he wouldn't sleep this coming night. His eyes showed it.

He said wearily, "And that covers it?"

"I think so." Yohan Lee put a hand to his chin. "How does it sound?"

"Not too bad. It's got to be done, you understand, with impudence. That is, there is to be no hesitation; no time to allow them to grasp the situation. Once we are in position to give orders, why, give them as though you were born to do so, and they'll obey out of habit. That's the essence of a coup."

"If the Board remains irresolute for even—"

"The Board? Count them out. After tomorrow, their importance as a factor in Terminus affairs won't matter a rusty half-credit."

Lee nodded slowly. "Yet it is strange that they've done nothing to stop us so far. You say they weren't entirely in the dark."

"Fara indicated as much. And Pirenne's been suspicious of me since I was elected. But, you see, they never had the capacity of really understanding what was up. Their whole training has been authoritarian. They are sure that the Emperor, just because he is the Emperor, is all-powerful. And they are sure that the Board of Trustees, simply because it is the Board of Trustees acting in the name of the Emperor, cannot be in a position where it does not give the orders. That incapacity to recognize the possibility of revolt is our best ally."

He heaved out of his chair and went to the water cooler. "They're not bad fellows, Lee, when they stick to their Encyclopedia—and we'll see that that's where they stick in the future. They're hopelessly incompetent when it comes to ruling Terminus. Go away, now, and start things rolling. I want to be alone."

He sat down on the corner of his desk and stared at the cup of water.

Space! If only he were as confident as he pretended! The Anacreonians were landing in two days and what had

118

he to go on but a set of notions and half-guesses as to what Hari Seldon had been driving at these past fifty years? He wasn't even a real, honest-to-goodness psychologist—just a fumbler with a little training trying to outguess the greatest mind of the age.

If Fara were right; if Anacreon were all the problem Hari Seldon had foreseen; if the Encyclopedia were all he was interested in preserving—then what price *coup d'état?*

He shrugged and drank his water.

The First Vault was furnished with considerably more than six chairs, as though a larger company had been expected. Hardin noted that thoughtfully and seated himself wearily in a corner just as far from the other five as possible.

The Board members did not seem to object to that arrangement. They spoke among themselves in whispers, which fell off into sibilant monosyllables, and then into nothing at all. Of them all, only Jord Fara seemed even reasonably calm. He had produced a watch and was staring at it somberly.

Hardin glanced at his own watch and then at the glass cubicle—absolutely empty—that dominated half the room. It was the only unusual feature of the room, for aside from that there was no indication that somewhere a speck of radium was wasting away toward that precise moment when a tumbler would fall, a connection be made and—

The lights went dim!

They didn't go out, but merely yellowed and sank with a suddenness that made Hardin jump. He had lifted his eyes to the ceiling lights in startled fashion, and when he brought them down the glass cubicle was no longer empty.

A figure occupied it—a figure in a wheel chair!

It said nothing for a few moments, but it closed the book upon its lap and fingered it idly. And then it smiled, and the face seemed all alive.

It said, "I am Hari Seldon." The voice was old and soft.

Hardin almost rose to acknowledge the introduction and stopped himself in the act.

The voice continued conversationally: "I can't see you, you know, so I can't greet you properly. I don't even

119

know how many of you there are, so all this must be conducted informally. If any of you are standing, please sit down; and if you care to smoke, I wouldn't mind." There was a light chuckle. "Why should I? I'm not really here."

Hardin fumbled for a cigar almost automatically, but thought better of it.

Hari Seldon put away his book—as if laying it upon a desk at his side—and when his fingers let go, it disappeared.

He said: "It is fifty years now since this Foundation was established—fifty years in which the members of the Foundation have been ignorant of what it was they were working toward. It was necessary that they be ignorant, but now the necessity is gone.

"The Encyclopedia Foundation, to begin with, is a fraud, and always has been!"

There was the sound of a scramble behind Hardin and one or two muffled exclamations, but he did not turn around.

Hari Seldon was, of course, undisturbed. He went on: "It is a fraud in the sense that neither I nor my colleagues care at all whether a single volume of the Encyclopedia is ever published. It has served its purpose, since by it we extracted an imperial charter from the Emperor, by it we attracted the hundred thousand scientists necessary for our scheme, and by it we managed to keep them preoccupied while events shaped themselves, until it was too late for any of them to draw back.

"In the fifty years that you have worked on this fraudulent project—there is no use in softening phrases—your retreat has been cut off, and you have now no choice but to proceed on the infinitely more important project that was, and is, our real plan.

"To that end we have placed you on such a planet and at such a time that in fifty years you were maneuvered to the point where you no longer have freedom of action. From now on, and into the centuries, the path you must take is inevitable. You will be faced with a series of crises, as you are now faced with the first, and in each case your freedom of action will become similarly circum-

120

scribed so that you will be forced along one, and only one, path.

"It is that path which our psychology has worked out—and for a reason.

"For centuries Galactic civilization has stagnated and declined, though only a few ever realized that. But now, at least, the Periphery is breaking away and the political unity of the Empire is shattered. Somewhere in the fifty years just past is where the historians of the future will place an arbitrary line and say: 'This marks the Fall of the Galactic Empire.'

"And they will be right, though scarcely any will recognize that Fall for additional centuries.

"And after the Fall will come inevitable barbarism, a period which, our psychohistory tells us, should, under ordinary circumstances, last from thirty to fifty thousand years. We cannot stop the Fall. We do not wish to; for Empire culture has lost whatever virility and worth it once had. But we can shorten the period of barbarism that must follow—down to a single thousand of years.

"The ins and outs of that shortening, we cannot tell you; just as we could not tell you the truth about the Foundation fifty years ago. Were you to discover those ins and outs, our plan might fail; as it would have, had you penetrated the fraud of the Encyclopedia earlier; for then, by knowledge, your freedom of action would be expanded and the number of additional variables introduced would become greater than our psychology could handle.

"But you won't, for there are no psychologists on Terminus, and never were, but for Alurin—and he was one of us.

"But this I can tell you: Terminus and its companion Foundation at the other end of the Galaxy are the seeds of the Renascence and the future founders of the Second Galactic Empire. And it is the present crisis that is starting Terminus off to that climax.

"This, by the way, is a rather straight-forward crisis, much simpler than many of those that are ahead. To reduce it to its fundamentals, it is this: You are a planet suddenly cut off from the still-civilized centers of the Galaxy, and threatened by your stronger neighbors. You are a small world of scientists surrounded by vast and rapidly expanding reaches of barbarism. You are an island of atomic power in a growing ocean of more primitive energy; but are helpless despite that, because of your lack of metals.

"You see, then, that you are faced by hard necessity, and that action is forced on you. The nature of that action —that is, the solution to your dilemma—is, of course, obvious!"

The image of Hari Seldon reached into open air and the book once more appeared in his hand. He opened it and said:

"But whatever devious course your future history may take, impress it always upon your descendants that the path has been marked out, and that at its end is a new and greater Empire!"

And as his eyes bent to his book, he flicked into nothingness, and the lights brightened once more.

Hardin looked up to see Pirenne facing him, eyes tragic and lips trembling.

The chairman's voice was firm but toneless. "You were right, it seems. If you will see us tonight at six, the Board will consult with you as to the next move."

They shook his hand, each one, and left; and Hardin smiled to himself. They were fundamentally sound at that; for they were scientists enough to admit that they were wrong—but for them, it was too late.

He looked at his watch. By this time, it was all over. Lee's men were in control and the Board was giving orders no longer.

The Anacreonians were landing their first spaceships tomorrow, but that was all right, too. In six months, *they* would be giving orders no longer.

In fact, as Hari Seldon had said, and as Salvor Hardin had guessed since the day that Anselm haut Rodric had first revealed to him Anacreon's lack of atomic power— the solution to this first crisis was obvious.

Obvious as all hell!

*Naturally, the superior race should win . . . but superior by which standards . . . and whose?*

●

# WE'RE CIVILIZED!
## by Mark Clifton and
## Alex Apostolides

The females and children worked among the lichen growth, picking off the fattest, ripest leaves for their food and moisture, completing their arc of the circle of symbiosis.

The males worked at the surface of the canals, or in open excavations. Their wide, mutated hands chipped into the rock-hard clay, opening a channel which was to be filled with sand and then sealed off with clay on all sides and surface. That water might seep through the sand without evaporation, without loss, from the poles to the equator of Mars—seep unimpeded, so that moisture might reach the lichen plants of everyone, so that none might thirst or hunger.

The seepage must flow. Not even buried in the dim racial memory had there ever been one who took more than his share, for this would be like the fingers of one hand stealing blood from the fingers of the other.

Among the Mars race there were many words for con-

123

tentment, kinship of each to all. There were words to express the ecstasy of watching the eternal stars, by night and by day, through the thin blackish atmosphere. There were words to express the joy of opening slitted nostrils to breathe deeply in those protected places where the blowing sands did not swirl, of opening folds of rubbery skin to catch the weak rays of the distant Sun.

But there were no words for "mine" as separate from "yours." And there was no urge to cry out, "Why am I here? What is the purpose of it all?"

Each had his purpose, serene, unquestioning. Each repaired or extended the seepage canals so that others, unborn, might know the same joys, and ecstasies as they. The work was in itself a part of the total joy, and they resisted it no more than healthy lungs resist clear, cool air.

So far back that even the concept of beginnings had been forgotten, the interwoven fabric of their symbolic interdependence seeped through their lives as naturally at the precious water seeped through the canal sands. As far back as that, they had achieved civilization.

Their kind of civilization.

Captain Griswold maintained an impassive face. (Let that, too, be a part of the legend.) Without expression, he looked through the screen at the red land flashing below the ship. But unconsciously he squared his shoulders, breathed deeply, enjoying the virile pull of his uniform over his expanding chest. Resolutely he pushed aside the vision of countless generations of school children, yet to come, repeating the lesson dutifully to their teachers.

"Captain Thomas H. Griswold took possession of Mars, June 14, 2018."

No, he must not allow any mood of vanity to spoil his own memories of this moment. It was beside the point that his name would rank with the great names of all times. Still, the history of the moment could not be denied.

Lieutenant Atkinson's voice broke through his preoccupation, and saved him the immodest thought of wondering if perhaps his cap visor might not be worn a little more rakishly to one side. He must father a custom, something distinctive of those who had been to Mars—

"Another canal, sir."

Below them, a straight line of gray-green stretched to the horizon, contrasting sharply with the red ferrous oxide of the landscape. An entire planet of ferrous oxide—iron—steel for the already starving technology of the Western Alliance. The captain felt a momentary irritation that even this narrow swath displaced the precious iron ore.

Obviously these canals served no purpose. His ship had circled the planet at its equator, and again from pole to pole. Canals everywhere, but nothing else. Enough time and fuel had been wasted. They must land. Obviously there was no intelligent life. But the history of the moment must not be marred by any haste. There must be no question within the books yet to be written. There must be no accredited voice of criticism raised.

"My compliments to Mr. Berkeley," he said harshly to Lt. Atkinson, "and would he kindly step to the control room?" He paused and added dryly, "at his convenience."

Mister Berkeley, indeed. What was it they called the civilian—an ethnologist? A fellow who was supposed to be an authority on races, civilizations, mores and customs of groups. Well, the man was excess baggage. There would be no races to contact here. A good thing, too. These civilian experts with their theories—show them a tooth and they'll dream up a monster. Show them a fingernail paring and they'll deduce a civilization from it. Nonsense!

"You wanted to see me, Captain?" The voice was young, quiet, controlled.

Without haste, Captain Griswold turned and faced Berkeley. Not only a theorist, but a young theorist. These super-bright young men with their sharp blue eyes. A lot of learning and no knowledge. A lot of wisdom and no common sense. He carefully controlled his voice, concealing his lack of respect for the civilian.

"Well, Mr. Berkeley, we have quartered the globe. We have seen no evidence of civilization."

"You discount the canals, Captain?" Berkeley asked, as if more from curiosity than refutation.

"I must discount them," the captain answered decisively. "Over all the planet we have seen no buildings, not even ruins, no evidence at all that intelligence exists here."

125

"I consider straight lines, running half the length of a world, to be evidence of something, sir." It was a flat statement, given without emphasis.

Arguments! Arguments! Little men who have to inflate themselves into a stature of importance—destroy the sacred history of the moment. But quietly now. There must be no memory of petty conflict.

"Where are their buildings, Mr. Berkeley?" he asked with patient tolerance. "Where are their factories? The smoke from their factories? The highways? The transportation facilities? Where are the airplanes? Even this thin air would support a fast jet. I do not require they have spaceships, Mr. Berkeley, to concede them intelligence. I do not require they be the equal of Man. I also have some scientific training. And my training tells me I cannot recognize the existence of something where there is no evidence at all."

"The canals," Berkeley answered. His voice also was controlled, for he, too, knew the history of this moment. But his concern was not for his own name in the history books. He knew only too well what its writers did to individuals for the sake of expediency. His concern was that this moment never be one of deep shame for Man. "Perhaps they have no buildings, no factory smoke, because they don't need them. Perhaps they don't have highways because they don't want to go anywhere. Perhaps their concept of living is completely unlike ours."

Griswold shrugged his shoulders. "We speak an entirely different language, Mr. Berkeley."

"I'm afraid you're right, Captain," Berkeley sighed. "And it might be a tragic thing that we do. Remember, European man spoke a different language from that of the American Indian, the Mayan, Polynesian, African, Indonesian—" He broke off as if the list were endless. "I ask only that we don't hasten into the same errors all over again."

"We can't hover here above the surface forever," Griswold said irritably. "We have quartered the globe. The other experts are anxious to land, so they can get to their work. We have made a search for your civilization and we have not found it."

126

"I withdraw all objections to landing, Captain. You are entirely correct. We must land."

The intercom on the wall squawked into life.

"Observation to Control. Observation to Control. Network of canals forming a junction ahead."

"Prepare for landing, Lieutenant Atkinson," Griswold commanded sharply. "At the junction." He turned and watched the screen. "There, Mr. Berkeley, dead ahead. A dozen—at least *a* dozen of your canals joining at one spot. Surely, if there were a civilization at all, you would find it at such a spot." Slowly and carefully, he constructed the pages of history. "I do not wish the implication ever to arise that this ship's commander, or any of its personnel, failed to cooperate in every way with the scientific authorities aboard."

"I know that, Captain," Berkeley answered. "And I agree. The junction, then."

The sigh of servo-mechanism, the flare of intolerably hot blue flame, and the ship stood motionless above the junction of canals. Ponderously, slowly, she settled; held aloft by the pillars of flame beneath her, directly above the junction, fusing the sand in the canals to glass, exploding their walls with steam. Within their warm and protected burrows beside the canals, slitted nostrils closed, iris of eyes contracted, fluted layers of skin opened and pulled tight, and opened again convulsively in the reflexes of death.

There was a slight jar only as the ship settled to the ground, bathed in the mushrooming flame.

"A good landing, Lieutenant," Captain Griswold complimented. "A good landing, indeed."

His head came up and he watched the screen to see the landscape reappear through the dust and steam.

"Prepare to disembark in approximately six hours, Lieutenant. The heat should have subsided sufficiently by then. The ship's officers, the civ—er—scientific party, a complement of men. I will lead the way. You, lieutenant, will carry the flag and the necessary appurtenances to the ceremony. We will hold it without delay."

Berkeley was watching the screen also. He wondered what the effect of the landing heat would be on the canals.

He wondered why it had been considered necessary to land squarely on the junction; why Man always, as if instinctively, does the most destructive thing he can.

He shrugged it away. Wherever they landed might have been the wrong place.

Farther along the canals, where the heat had not reached, the Mars race began to emerge from their protecting burrows. They had seen the meteor hurtling downward, and it was part of their conditioning to seek their burrows when any threatening phenomenon occurred.

Flaming meteors had fallen before, but never in the interlocked racial mind was there memory of one which had fallen directly on a canal junction. Within the fabric of their instinct, they sensed the fused sand, the broken clay walls, the water boiling through the broken walls, wasted. They sensed the waters on the other side of the barrier seeping onward, leaving sand unfilled. Within the nerves of their own bodies they felt the anticipated pangs of tendril roots searching down into the sand for water, and not finding it.

The urgency came upon them, all within the region, to remove this meteor; restore the canals as soon as the heat would permit. They began to gather, circling the meteor, circling the scorched ground around it. The urgency of getting at it before there was too much water lost drove them in upon the hot ground.

The unaccustomed heat held them back. They milled uncertainly, in increasing numbers, around the meteor.

Since Captain Griswold had not asked him to leave the control room during landing operations, Berkeley still stood and watched the screen. At the first appearance of the Mars race emerging from the soil, he exclaimed in great excitement:

"There they are! There they are, Captain!"

Griswold came over and stood beside him, watching the screen. His eyes widened.

"Horrible," he muttered in revulsion. The gorge arose in his throat and stopped his speech for a moment. But history took possession of him again. "I suppose we will get accustomed to their appearance in time," he conceded.

"They're the builders, Captain. Wonderful!" Berkeley exulted. "Those shovel-shaped forelimbs—they're the builders!"

"Perhaps," Griswold agreed. "But in the way a mole or gopher—still, if they were intelligent enough to be trained for mining operations—but then you certainly cannot call these things intelligent, Mr. Berkeley."

"How do we know, Captain?"

But the Captain was looking about vainly for buildings, for factory smoke, for highways.

"Lieutenant Atkinson!" he called.

"Yes, sir."

"Send an immediate order throughout the ship. The Mars things are not to be molested." He glanced at Berkeley as he gave the order, and then glanced away. "Double the complement of men on the landing party and see that they are fully armed." Then back to Berkeley, "A good leader guards against every contingency. But there will be no indiscriminate slaughter. You may be assured of that. I am as anxious as you that Man—"

"Thank you, Captain," Berkeley answered. "And the planting of the flag? The taking possession?"

"Well, now, Mr. Berkeley, what shall we do, now that we have seen some—things? Go away? Leave an entire planet of iron ore to be claimed later by Eastern Alliance? The enemy is not far behind us in their technology, Mr. Berkeley."

He warmed to his theme, his head came up, his shoulders back.

"Suppose these things are intelligent. Suppose they do have feelings of one kind or another. What would happen to them if the Eastern Alliance laid claim to this planet? Under us, at least, they will have protection. We will set aside reservations where they may live in peace. Obviously they live in burrows in the ground; I see no buildings. Their total food supply must be these miserable plants. What a miserable existence they have now!

"We will change that. We will provide them with adequate food, the food to fill their empty stomachs—if they have stomachs. We will clothe their repulsive nakedness. If they have enough sense to learn, we will give them the pride of self-employment in our mines and factories.

We would be less than human, Mr. Berkeley, if we did not acknowledge our duty."

The light of noble intention shone in his face. He was swept away with his own eloquence.

"If," he finished, "we take care of the duty, the destiny will take care of itself!"

That was very good. He hoped they would have the grace to quote him on that. It was a fine summing up of his entire character.

Berkeley smiled a rueful smile. There was no stopping it. It was not a matter of not planting the flag, not taking possession. The captain was right. If not the Western Alliance, then certainly the Eastern Alliance. His quarrel was not with the captain nor with the duty, but with the destiny. The issue was not to be decided now. It had already been decided—decided when the first apeman had crept into the tree nest of another and stolen his mate.

Man takes. Whether it be by barbaric rapine, or reluctant acceptance of duty through carefully contrived diplomacy, Man takes.

Berkeley turned and made his way out of the control room.


Outside, the soil shifted in its contortions of cooling. The wind whispered dryly over the red landscape, sending up little swirls of dust, eternally shifting it from one place to another. The soil was less hot, and as it cooled, the Mars race pressed inward. Theirs was the urgency to get at this meteor as quickly as possible, remove it, start the water flowing once more.

"Observation reports ground cool enough for landing!" The magic words seemed to sing into the control cabin.

"Summon all landing party," Captain Griswold commanded immediately.

The signal bells rang throughout the ship. The bell in the supercargo cabin rang also. With the other scientists, Berkeley dressed in his protecting suit, fitted the clear glassite oxygen helmet over his head, fastened it. Together with the rest, he stood at the designated airlock to await the captain's coming.

And the captain did not keep them waiting. At precisely the right moment, with only a flicker of a side glance at the photographic equipment, the captain strode ahead of his officers to the airlock. The sealing doors of the corridor behind them closed, shutting off the entire party, making the corridor itself into a great airlock.

There was a long sigh, and the great beams of the locks moved ponderously against their weight. There was the rush of air from the corridor as the heavier pressure rushed out through the opening locks, to equalize with the thin air of Mars. With the air rushed outward fungus spores, virus, microbes; most of them to perish under the alien conditions, but some to survive—and thrive.

The red light above the lock was blinking on-off-on-off.

The officers, the scientists, the armed men, watched the light intently. It blinked off for the last time. The locks were open. The great ramp settled to the ground.

In ordered, military file, the captain at their head, the landing party passed down the corridor, through the locks, out upon the ramp beneath the blue-black sky; and down to the red soil. Captain Griswold was the first man to set foot on Mars, June 14, 2018. The photographers were second.

Now the Mars race was moving closer to the ship, but the ground was still too hot for their unprotected feet. The pressing need for removing the meteor possessed them. The movement of the men disembarking from the ship was to them no more than another unintelligible aspect of this incredible meteor.

The sound of a bugle pierced the thin air, picked up by the loudspeaker from the ship, reverberating through their helmets. The landing party formed a semi-circle at the foot of the ramp.

Captain Griswold, his face as rigidly set as the marble statuary of him to follow, reached out and took the flag from Lieutenant Atkinson. He planted it firmly, without false motion, in the framework one of the men had set upon the baked ground to receive it.

He pointed to the north, the south, the east, the west. He brought his hands together, palms downward, arms fully outstretched in front of him. He spread his arms wide open and down, then back together and up, completing a circle which encompassed all the planet. He held out his right hand and received the scroll from Lieutenant Atkinson.

With a decisive gesture, not quite theatrical, he unfurled the scroll. He read in a voice firm enough to impress all posterity:

"By virtue of authority invested in me from the Supreme Council of the Western Alliance, the only true representatives of Earth and Man, I take possession of all this planet in the name of our President, the Supreme Council, the Western Alliance, Earth, and in the name of God."

The ground was cool enough now that their feet might bear it. The pain was great, but it was lost in the greater pain of feeling the killing obstruction the great meteor had brought to their canals. The Mars race began to press inward, inexorably.

It was in the anticlimactic moment, following the possession ceremony, when men milled around in uncertainty, that Lt. Atkinson saw the Mars race had come closer and were still moving.

"The monsters!" he exclaimed in horror. "They're attacking!"

Berkeley looked, and from the little gestures of movement out of his long training he deduced their true motive.

"Not against us!" he cried. "The ship."

Perhaps his words were more unfortunate than his silence might have been; for the ship was of greater concern to Captain Griswold than his own person.

"Halt!" Griswold shouted toward the approaching Mars race. "Halt or I'll fire!"

The Mars race paid no heed. Slowly they came forward, each step on the hot ground a torture, but a pain which could be borne. The greater torture, the one they could not bear, was the ache to press against this meteor, push it away, that they might dig the juncture clean again. As a man whose breath is stopped fights frantically for air, concerned with nothing else, so they felt the desperation of drying sands.

They came on.

"For the last time," Griswold shouted, "halt!" He made

132

a motion with his hands, as if to push them back, as if to convey his meaning by signs. Involuntarily, then, his eyes sought those of Berkeley. A look of pleading, helplessness. Berkeley met the glance and read the anxiety there, the tragic unwillingness of the man to arouse posterity's rage or contempt.

It was a brief glance only from both men and it was over. Captain Griswold's head came up; his shoulders straightened in the face of the oncoming monsters. They were close now, and coming closer. As always, the experts were free with their advice when it was not needed. When the chips were down, they could do no more than smirk and shrug a helpless shoulder.

He gave the command, and now there was no uncertainty.

"Fire!"

The celebration was being held in the Great Stadium, the largest, most costly structure that Man had ever built. It was a fitting structure for the more important football games; and used on occasion, if they could be fitted in without upsetting the schedule, for State affairs. Now the stadium was filled to capacity, its floor churned by the careless feet of the thousands upon thousands who had managed to obtain an entrance.

From the quarter-mile-high tiers of seats, from the floor of the stadium, the shouts welled up, washing over the platform at the North end.

"Griswold! Griswold!"

It was not yet time for history to assess the justice of the massacre.

The President raised his hand. The battery of video cameras picked up each move.

"Our hopes, our fears, our hearts, our prayers rode through every space-dark, star-flecked mile with these glorious pioneers." He turned then to the captain. "For the people of Earth, *Admiral* Griswold, this medal. A new medal for a Guider of Destiny, Maker of Empire, Son of Man!"

The voice faltered, stopped.

The crowd on the floor of the stadium was pressing outward from the center, screaming in pain and terror. At

133

the moment when the people should be quiet, rapt in reverence, they were emptying the floor of the stadium. But not willingly. They were being pressed back and out, as a great weight pushes its way through water. Those who could move outward no farther were crushed where they stood.

And then the ship appeared.

Hazy of outline, shimmering with impossible angles, seen by its glinting fire of light rather than by its solid form, as if its reality were in some other dimension and this only a projection, the ship appeared.

The President's hand reached out and gripped Griswold's shoulder as he leaned back and back, trying to determine its vast height. A silence then clutched the crowd—a terrified silence.

A full minute passed. Even on the platform, where all the pioneers of Mars were assembled with Earth's dignitaries, even there the people cowered back away from this unseeable, unknowable horror.

But one man leaned forward instead, frantically studying the shimmering outline of the ship. One man— Berkeley.

With the training of the ethnologist, a man who really can deduce an entire civilization from mystifying data, he recognized the tremendous import.

At the end of that minute, without warning, a group of figures hovered in the air near the floor of the stadium.

Quickly, Berkeley's eyes assessed their form, their color, the increasing solidity of the humanoids. There are some movements, some gestures, common to all things of intelligence—the pause, the resolution, the lift of pride.

"No!" he screamed and started forward. "Oh, no! We're civilized. We're intelligent!" He was pulled back, as in his terror he tried to leap from the platform to get at the humanoids.

Held there, unable to move, he read the meaning of the actions of the group hovering near the ship. One flashed a shining tentacle around, as if to point to the stadium, the pitifully small spaceship on display, the crowds of people.

The leader manifestly ignored him. He flowed forward a pace, his ovoid head held high in pride and arrogance.

He pointed a tentacle toward the south end of the stadium, and a pillar of leaping flame arose; fed with no fuel, never to cease its fire, the symbol of possession.

He pointed his tentacles to the north, the south, the east, the west. He motioned with his tentacles, as if to encircle all of Earth.

He unfurled a scroll and began to read.

# SECTION TWO

•

# MATURITY OR BUST

*In cycle after cycle, civilization would emerge from barbarism, mechanization would bring the people into uneasy contact, national wars and class wars would breed the longing for a better world order, but breed it in vain. Disaster after disaster would undermine the fabric of civilization. Gradually barbarism would return. Aeon after aeon, the process would repeat itself . . .*

Olaf Stapledon: *Star Maker*

Olaf Stapledon's synoptic view of the universe is far removed from the fun and games of magazine science fiction. Nevertheless, his cyclic approach was generally adopted. Its intellectual respectability was vouched for by Oswald Spengler in *The Decline of the West*.

Magazine sf, which began as a continuity when Hugo Gernsback founded his *Amazing Stories* in 1926, was in general a sort of cheer-leader for technology. However often the robots ran amok, they were seen as good things in themselves, needing only to be controlled to increase the sum of human happiness. It appears that the later generation of writers who produce the sort of science-fantasy incorporated in this anthology were in general of a different view. Their opinion might be roughly summarised in the words of Arnold Toynbee: "With the increase in our power, our sense of responsibility and our sense of distress increases." Toynbee has said that the growth of science and technology makes more acute the disparity between the real and the ideal.

If this is so, then the galactic empire does make a contribution to one of the central problems of our time, sharing as it does both the real and the ideal; that it manages this via swordplay, suppurating aliens, and gadgets is an indication that philosophers are not being addressed.

The warning has already been given: take your galactic empire with a pinch of salt. It is a gaudy balloon launched for the hell of it. See how high it goes before it pops.

Clifford Simak, however, keeps a straight face as he tells his story of Selden Bishop, the bright kid from Earth who passes all his exams, qualifying for a place on Kimon, that planet at the galactic rainbow's end. There was a time when Simak was everyone's favourite author. A Simak story was unmistakeable. When everyone else appeared to be describing big tough heroes going out and giving alien races what-for, Simak would tell you about this little old Earthman sitting on his verandah, whittling a stick, when up comes this green guy. The green guy has a funny big machine come down out of the skies. The two of them get talking, and the little old Earthman takes a can of oil and fixes the green man's funny big machine, and in exchange this green guy makes the little old Earthman's crops grow a durn sight better'n his neighbour's ever do. Or words to that effect. Simak was the poet of rural space. People were always clearing off to Jupiter or wherever, and leaving Earth as green and pleasant as it used to be. Remember *City*?

*Immigrant* is a little different. But it does have that leisurely Simak quality. Surely somewhere on Kimon they have sense enough to hand out degrees in Stick-whittling.

It is a pity to say anything about Idris Seabright's story. Let her tell you about the bird people, who were really too delicate for empire.

Empires were generally in trouble. The empire Alfred Coppel portrays is only just holding together. Fans of galactic empires like ray-guns and swordplay. The trick is to marry the two convincingly. Coppel, with a mad, bold stroke, has FTL ships loaded to the hull with warriors and their horses, lit by smokey oil lamps. The picturesque can hardly be carried further.

When I wrote to Mr. Coppel asking permission to publish his story here, I mentioned his recent successful novel, *Thirty-Four East*, and wondered whether he still recalled his early fantasy with affection. It appears that he does.

Moreover, he expanded *Rebel of Valkyr* into a trilogy of novels, writing under the pen-name of Robert Cham Gilman. If you enjoy this long story, you might try hunting down the trilogy, the volumes of which are entitled *The Rebel of Rhada, The Navigators of Rhada,* and *The Starkahn of Rhada.*

Like Robert Gilman, Cordwainer Smith is an alias. So, for that matter, is Idris Seabright. Smith wrote several stories centering round his empire before he died. He called its government The Instrumentality—an appropriate name, for there is something scalpel-like about Smith's extraordinary imagination. Inventing a whole race of cats? Flinging them back in time? Preposterous. Amazing. Admirable.

Most writers write about life as it is or as they think it ought to be. Cordwainer Smith wrote about a heaven-and-hell which seemed more real to him than life.

Off his gallant Commander goes, with his imaginary companions . . .

*Do not read this story; turn the page quickly. The story may upset you. Anyhow, you probably know it already. It is a very disturbing story. Everyone knows it. The glory and the crime of Commander Suzdal have been told in a thousand different ways. Don't let yourself realize that the story really is the truth.*

*It isn't. Not at all. There's not a bit of truth to it. There is no such planet as Arachosia, no such people as klopts, no such world as Catland. These are all just imaginary, they didn't happen, forget about it, go away and read something else.*

●

# THE CRIME AND THE GLORY OF COMMANDER SUZDAL

## by Cordwainer Smith

### *The Beginning*

Commander Suzdal was sent forth in a shell-ship to explore the outermost reaches of our galaxy. His ship was called a cruiser, but he was the only man in it. He was equipped with hypnotics and cubes to provide him the semblance of company, a large crowd of friendly people who could be convoked out of his own hallucinations.

The Instrumentality even offered him some choice in his imaginary companions, each of whom was embodied in a small ceramic cube containing the brain of a small animal but imprinted with the personality of an actual human being.

Suzdal, a short, stocky man with a jolly smile, was blunt about his needs:

"Give me two good security officers. I can manage the ship, but if I'm going into the unknown, I'll need help in meeting the strange problems which might show up."

The loading official smiled at him, "I never heard of a cruiser commander who *asked* for security officers. Most people regard them as an utter nuisance."

"That's all right," said Suzdal. "I don't."

"Don't you want some chess players?"

"I can play chess," said Suzdal, "all I want to, using the spare computers. All I have to do is set the power down and they start losing. On full power, they always beat me."

The official then gave Suzdal an odd look. He did not exactly leer, but his expression became both intimate and unpleasant. "What about other companions?" he asked, with a funny little edge to his voice.

"I've got books," said Suzdal, "a couple of thousand. I'm going to be gone only a couple of years Earth time."

"Local-subjective, it might be several thousand years," said the official, "though the time will wind back up again as you reapproach Earth. And I wasn't talking about books," he repeated, with the same funny, prying lilt to his voice.

Suzdal shook his head with momentary worry, ran his hand through his sandy hair. His blue eyes were forthright and he looked straightforwardly into the official's eyes. "What do you mean, then, if not books? Navigators? I've got them, not to mention the turtlemen. They're good company, if you just talk to them slowly enough and then give them plenty of time to answer. Don't forget, I've been out before. . . ."

The official spat out his offer: "Dancing girls. WOMEN. Concubines. Don't you want any of those? We could even cube your own wife for you and print her mind on a cube for you. That way she could be with you every week that you were awake."

Suzdal looked as though he would spit on the floor in

sheer disgust. "Alice? You mean, you want me to travel around with a ghost of her? How would the real Alice feel when I came back? Don't tell me that you're going to put my wife on a mousebrain. You're just offering me delirium. I've got to keep my wits out there with space and time rolling in big waves around me. I'm going to be crazy enough, just as it is. Don't forget, I've been out there before. Getting back to a real Alice is going to be one of my biggest reality factors. It will help me to get home." At this point, Suzdal's own voice took on the note of intimate inquiry, as he added, "Don't tell me that a lot of cruiser commanders ask to go flying around with imaginary wives. That would be pretty nasty, in my opinion. Do many of them do it?"

"We're here to get you loaded on board ship, not to discuss what other officers do or do not do. Sometimes we think it good to have a female companion on the ship with the commander, even if she is imaginary. If you ever found anything among the stars which took on female form, you'd be mighty vulnerable to it."

"Females, among the stars? Bosh!" said Suzdal.

"Strange things have happened," said the official.

"Not that," said Suzdal. "Pain, craziness, distortion, panic without end, a craze for food—yes, those I can look for and face. They will be there. But females, no. There aren't any. I love my wife. I won't make females up out of my own mind. After all, I'll have the turtle-people aboard, and they will be bringing up their young. I'll have plenty of family life to watch and to take part in. I can even give Christmas parties for the young ones."

"What kind of parties are those?" asked the official.

"Just a funny little ancient ritual that I heard about from an Outer Pilot. You give all the young things presents, once every local-subjective year."

"It sounds nice," said the official, his voice growing tired and final. "You still refuse to have a cube-woman on board. You wouldn't have to activate her unless you really needed her."

"You haven't flown, yourself, have you?" asked Suzdal.

It was the official's turn to flush. "No," he said, flatly.

"Anything that's in that ship, I'm going to think about. I'm a cheerful sort of man, and very friendly. Let me just

146

get along with my turtle-people. They're not lively, but they are considerate and restful. Two thousand or more years, local-subjective, is a lot of time. Don't give me additional decisions to make. It's work enough, running the ship. Just leave me alone with my turtle-people. I've gotten along with them before."

"You, Suzdal, are the commander," said the loading official. "We'll do as you say."

"Fine," smiled Suzdal. "You may get a lot of queer types on this run, but I'm not one of them."

The two men smiled agreement at one another and the loading of the ship was completed.

The ship itself was managed by turtle-men, who aged very slowly, so that while Suzdal coursed the outer rim of the galaxy and let the thousands of years—local count—go past while he slept in his frozen bed, the turtle-men rose generation by generation, trained their young to work the ship, taught the stories of the earth that they would never see again, and read the computers correctly, to awaken Suzdal only when there was a need for human intervention and for human intelligence. Suzdal awakened from time to time, did his work and then went back. He felt that he had been gone from earth only a few months.

Months indeed! He had been gone more than a subjective ten-thousand years, when he met the siren capsule.

It looked like an ordinary distress capsule. The kind of thing that was often shot through space to indicate some complication of the destiny of man among the stars. This capsule had apparently been flung across an immense distance, and from the capsule Suzdal got the story of Arachosia.

The story was false. The brains of a whole planet—the wild genius of a malevolent, unhappy race—had been dedicated to the problem of ensnaring and attracting a normal pilot from Old Earth. The story which the capsule sang conveyed the rich personality of a wonderful woman with a contralto voice. The story was true, in part. The appeals were real, in part. Suzdal listened to the story and it sank, like a wonderfully orchestrated piece of grand opera, right into the fibers of his brain. It would have been different if he had known the real story.

147

Everybody now knows the real story of Arachosia, the bitter terrible story of the planet which was a paradise, which turned into a hell. The story of how people got to be something different from people. The story of what happened way out there in the most dreadful place among the stars.

He would have fled if he knew the real story. He couldn't understand what we now know:

Mankind could not meet the terrible people of Arachosia without the people of Arachosia following them home and bringing to mankind a grief greater than grief, a craziness worse than mere insanity, a plague surpassing all imaginable plagues. The Arachosians had become *un*-people, and yet, in their innermost imprinting of their personalities, they remained people. They sang songs which exalted their own deformity and which praised themselves for what they had so horribly become, and yet, in their own songs, in their own ballads, the organ tones of the refrain rang out,

*And I mourn Man!*

They knew what they were and they hated themselves. Hating themselves they pursued mankind.

Perhaps they are still pursuing mankind.

The Instrumentality has by now taken good pains that the Arachosians will never find us again, has flung networks of deception out along the edge of the galaxy to make sure that those lost ruined people cannot find us. The Instrumentality knows and guards our world and all the other worlds of mankind against the deformity which has become Arachosia. We want nothing to do with Arachosia. Let them hunt for us. They won't find us.

How could Suzdal know that?

This was the first time someone had met the Arachosians, and he met them only with a message in which an elfin voice sang the elfin song of ruin, using perfectly clear words in the old common tongue to tell a story so sad, so abominable, that mankind has not forgotten it yet. In its essence the story was very simple. This is what

Suzdal heard, and what people have learned ever since then.

The Arachosians were settlers. Settlers could go out by sailship, trailing behind them the pods. That was the first way.

Or they could go out by planoform ship, ships piloted by skilful men, who went into space-two and came out again and found man.

Or for very long distances indeed, they could go out in the new combination. Individual pods packed into an enormous shell-ship, a gigantic version of Suzdal's own ship. The sleepers frozen, the machines waking, the ship fired to and beyond the speed of light, flung below space, coming out at random and homing on a suitable target. It was a gamble, but brave men took it. If no target was found, their machines might course space forever, while the bodies, protected by freezing as they were, spoiled bit by bit, and while the dim light of life went out in the individual frozen brains.

The shell-ships were the answers of mankind to an over-population, which neither the old planet Earth nor its daughter planets could quite respond to. The shell-ships took the bold, the reckless, the romantic, the wilful, sometimes the criminals out among the stars. Mankind lost track of these ships, over and over again. The advance explorers, the organized Instrumentality, would stumble upon human beings, cities and cultures, high or low, tribes or families, where the shell-ships had gone on, far, far beyond the outermost limits of mankind, where the instruments of search had found an earth-like planet, and the shell-ship, like some great dying insect, had dropped to the planet, awakened its people, broken open, and destroyed itself with its delivery of newly re-born men and women, to settle a world.

Arachosia looked like a good world to the men and women who came to it. Beautiful beaches, with cliffs like endless rivieras rising above. Two bright big moons in the sky, a sun not too far away. The machines had pretested the atmosphere and sampled the water, had already scattered the forms of old earth life into the atmosphere and in the seas so that as the people awakened they heard the singing of earth birds and they knew that earth fish had already been adapted to the oceans and flung in, there to multiply. It seemed a good life, a rich life. Things went well.

Things went very, very well for the Arachosians.

This is the truth.

This was, thus far, the story told by the capsule.

But here they diverged.

The capsule did not tell the dreadful, pitiable truth about Arachosia. It invented a set of plausible lies. The voice which came telepathically out of the capsule was that of a mature, warm happy female—some woman of early middle age with a superb speaking contralto.

Suzdal almost fancied that he talked to it, so real was the personality. How could he know that he was being beguiled, trapped?

It sounded right, *really* right.

"And then," said the voice, "the Arachosian sickness has been hitting us. Do not land. Stand off. Talk to us. Tell us about medicine. Our young die, without reason. Our farms are rich, and the wheat here is more golden than it was on earth, the plums more purple, the flowers whiter. Everything does well—except people.

"Our young die . . ." said the womanly voice, ending in a sob.

"Are there any symptoms?" thought Suzdal, and almost as though it had heard his question, the capsule went on.

"They die of nothing. Nothing which our medicine can test, nothing which our science can show. They die. Our population is dropping. People, do not forget us! Man, whoever you are, come quickly, come now, bring help! But for your own sake, do not land. Stand off-planet and view us through screens so that you can take word back to the Home of Man about the lost children of mankind among the strange and outermost stars!"

Strange, indeed!

The truth was far stranger, and very ugly indeed.

Suzdal was convinced of the truth of the message. He had been selected for the trip because he was good-natured, intelligent, and brave; this appeal touched all three of his qualities.

Later, much later, when he was arrested, Suzdal was

asked, "Suzdal, you fool, why didn't you test the message? You've risked the safety of all the mankinds for a foolish appeal!"

"It wasn't foolish!" snapped Suzdal. "That distress capsule had a sad, wonderful womanly voice and the story checked out true."

"With whom?" said the investigator, flatly and dully.

Suzdal sounded weary and sad when he replied to the point. "It checked out with my books. With my knowledge." Reluctantly he added, "And with my own judgment . . ."

"Was your judgment good?" said the investigator.

"No," said Suzdal, and let the single word hang on the air as though it might be the last word he would ever speak.

But it was Suzdal himself who broke the silence when he added, "Before I set course and went to sleep, I activated my security officers in cubes and had them check the story. They got the real story of Arachosia, all right. They cross-ciphered it out of patterns in the distress capsule and they told me the whole real story very quickly, just as I was waking up."

"And what did you do?"

"I did what I did. I did that for which I expect to be punished. The Arachosians were already walking around the outside of my hull by then. They had caught my ship. They had caught me. How was I to know that the wonderful, sad story was true only for the first twenty full years that the woman told about. And she wasn't even a woman. Just a klopt. Only the first twenty years . . ."

Things had gone well for the Arachosians for the first twenty years. Then came disaster, but it was not the tale told in the distress capsule.

They couldn't understand it. They didn't know why it had to happen to them. They didn't know why it waited twenty years, three months and four days. But their time came.

We think it must have been something in the radiation of their sun. Or perhaps a combination of that particular sun's radiation and the chemistry, which even the wise machines in the shell-ship had not fully analyzed, which

151

reached out and was spread from within. The disaster hit. It was a simple one and utterly unstoppable.

They had doctors. They had hospitals. They even had a limited capacity for research.

But they could not research fast enough. Not enough to meet this disaster. It was simple, monstrous, enormous. *Femininity became carcinogenetic.*

Every woman on the planet began developing cancer at the same time, on her lips, in her breasts, in her groin, sometimes along the edge of her jaw, the edge of her lip, the tender portions of her body. The cancer had many forms, and yet it was always the same. There was something about the radiation which reached through, which reached into the human body, and which made a particular form of desoxycorticosterone turn into a subform— unknown on earth—of pregnandiol, which infallibily caused cancer. The advance was rapid.

The little baby girls began to die first. The women clung weeping to their fathers, their husbands. The mothers tried to say goodbye to their sons.

One of the doctors, herself, was a woman, a strong woman.

Remorselessly, she cut live tissue from her living body, put it under the microscope, took samples of her own urine, her blood, her spit, and she came up with the answer: *There is no answer.* And yet there was something better and worse than an answer.

If the sun of Arachosia killed everything which was female, if the female fish floated upside down on the surface of the sea, if the female birds sang a shriller, wilder song as they died above the eggs which would never hatch, if the female animals grunted and growled in the lairs where they hid away with pain, female human beings did not have to accept death so tamely. The docor's name was Astarte Kraus.

## The Magic of the Klopts

The human female could do what the animal female could not. She could turn male. With the help of equipment from the ship, tremendous quantities of testosterone

152

were manufactured, and every single girl and woman still surviving was turned into a man. Massive injections were administered to all of them. Their faces grew heavy, they all returned to growing a little bit, their chests flattened out, their muscles grew stronger, and in less than three months they were indeed men.

Some lower forms of life had survived because they were not polarized clearly enough to the forms of male and female, which depended on that particular organic chemistry for survival. With the fish gone, plants clotted the oceans, the birds were gone but the insects survived; dragonflies, butterflies, mutated versions of grasshoppers, beetles, and other insects swarmed over the planet. The men who had lost women worked side by side with the men who had been made out of the bodies of women.

When they knew each other, it was unutterably sad for them to meet. Husband and wife, both bearded, strong, quarrelsome, desperate and busy. The little boys somehow realizing that they would never grow up to have sweethearts, to have wives, to get married, to have daughters.

But what was a mere world to stop the driving brain and the burning intellect of Dr. Astarte Kraus? She became the leader of her people, the men and the men-women. She drove them forward, she made them survive, she used cold brains on all of them.

(Perhaps, if she had been a sympathetic person, she would have let them die. But it was the nature of Dr. Kraus not to be sympathetic—just brilliant, remorseless, implacable against the universe which had tried to destroy her.)

Before she died, Dr. Kraus had worked out a carefully programed genetic system. Little bits of the men's tissues could be implanted by a surgical routine in the abdomens, just inside the peritoneal wall, crowding a little bit against the intestines, an artificial womb and artificial chemistry and artificial insemination by radiation, by heat, made it possible for men to bear boy children.

What was the use of having girl children if they all died? The people of Arachosia went on. The first generation lived through the tragedy, half insane with the grief and disappointment. They sent out message capsules

153

and they knew that their message would reach Earth in 6 million years.

As new explorers, they had gambled on going further than other ships went. They had found a good world, but they were not quite sure where they were. Were they still within the familiar galaxy, or had they jumped beyond. to one of the nearby galaxies? They couldn't quite tell. It was a part of the policy of old earth not to overequip the exploring parties for fear that some of them, taking violent cultural change or becoming aggressive empires, might turn back on earth and destroy it. Earth always made sure that it had the advantages.

The third and fourth and fifth generations of Arachosians were still people. All of them were male. They had the human memory, they had human books, they knew the words "mama," "sister," "sweetheart," but they no longer really understood what these terms referred to.

The human body, which had taken five million years on earth to grow, has immense resources within it, resources greater than the brain, or the personality, or the hopes of the individual. And the bodies of the Arachosians decided things for them. Since the chemistry of femininity meant instant death, and since an occasional girl baby was born dead and buried casually, the bodies made the adjustment. The men of Arachosia became both men and women. They gave themselves the ugly nickname, "klopt." Since they did not have the rewards of family life, they became strutting cockerels, who mixed their love with murder, who blended their songs with duels, who sharpened their weapons and who earned the right to reproduce within a strange family system which no decent earthman would find comprehensible.

But they did survive.

And the method of their survival was so sharp, so fierce, that it was indeed a difficult thing to understand.

In less than four hundred years the Arachosians had civilized into groups of fighting clans. They still had just one planet, around just one sun. They lived in just one place. They had a few spacecraft they had built themselves. Their science, their art and their music moved forward with strange lurches of inspired neurotic genius, because they lacked the fundamentals in the human personality itself, the balance of male and female, the family, the operations of love, of hope, of reproduction. They survived, but they themselves had become monsters and did not know it.

Out of their memory of old mankind they created a legend of old earth. Women in that memory were deformities, who should be killed. Misshapen beings, who should be erased. The family, as they recalled it, was filth and abomination which they were resolved to wipe out if they should ever meet it.

They, themselves, were bearded homosexuals, with rouged lips, ornate earrings, fine heads of hair, and very few old men among them. They killed off their men before they became old; the things they could not get from love or relaxation or comfort, they purchased with battle and death. They made up songs proclaiming themselves to be the last of the old men and the first of the new, and they sang their hate to mankind when they should meet, and they sang "Woe is earth that we should find it," and yet something inside them made them add to almost every song a refrain which troubled even them,

*And I mourn Man!*

They mourned mankind and yet they plotted to attack all of humanity.

# The Trap

Suzdal had been deceived by the message capsule. He put himself back in the sleeping compartment and he directed the turtle-men to take the cruiser to Arachosia, wherever it might be. He did not do this crazily or wantonly. He did it as a matter of deliberate judgment. A judgment for which he was later heard, tried, judged fairly and then put to something worse than death.

He deserved it.

He sought for Arachosia without stopping to think of the most fundamental rule: How could he keep the Arachosians, singing monsters that they were, from following him home to the eventual ruin of earth? Might not their condition be a disease which could be contagious, or might not their fierce society destroy the other societies of men and leave earth and all of other men's worlds in ruin? He did not think of this, so he was heard, and tried and punished much later. We will come to that.

# The Arrival

Suzdal awakened in orbit off Arachosia. And he awakened knowing he had made a mistake. Strange ships clung to his shell-ship like evil barnacles from an unknown ocean, attached to a familiar water craft. He called to his turtle-men to press the controls and the controls did not work.

The outsiders, whoever they were, man or woman or beast or god, had enough technology to immobilize his ship. Suzdal immediately realized his mistake. Naturally, he thought of destroying himself and the ship, but he was afraid that if he destroyed himself and missed destroying the ship completely there was a chance that his cruiser, a late model with recent weapons would fall into the hands of whoever it was walking on the outer dome of his own cruiser. He could not afford the risk of mere individual suicide. He had to take a more drastic step. This was not time for obeying earth rules.

His security officer—a cube ghost wakened to human form—whispered the whole story to him in quick intelligent gasps:

"They are people, sir.

"More people than I am.

"I'm a ghost, an echo working out of a dead brain.

"These are real people, Commander Suzdal, but they are the worst people ever to get loose among the stars. You must destroy them, sir!"

"I can't," said Suzdal, still trying to come fully awake. "They're *people*."

"Then you've got to beat them off. By any means, sir. By any means whatever. Save Earth. Stop them. Warn Earth."

"And I?" asked Suzdal, and was immediately sorry that he had asked the selfish, personal question.

"You will die or you will be punished," said the security officer sympathetically, "and I do not know which one will be worse."

"Now?"

"Right now. There is no time left for you. No time at all."

"But the rules . . . ?"

"You have already strayed far outside of rules."

There were rules, but Suzdal left them all behind.

Rules, rules for ordinary times, for ordinary places, for understandable dangers.

This was a nightmare cooked up by the flesh of man, motivated by the brains of man. Already his monitors were bringing him news of who these people were, these seeming maniacs, these men who had never known women, these boys who had grown to lust and battle, who had a family structure which the normal human brain could not accept, could not believe, could not tolerate. The things on the outside were people, and they weren't. The things on the outside had the human brain, the human imagination, and the human capacity for revenge, and yet Suzdal, a brave officer, was so frightened by the mere nature of them that he did not respond to their efforts to communicate.

He could feel the turtle-women among his crew aching with fright itself, as they realized who was pounding on their ship and who it was that sang through loud announcing machines that they wanted *in, in, in.*

Suzdal committed a crime. It is the pride of the Instrumentality that the Instrumentality allows its officers to commit crimes or mistakes or suicide. The Instrumentality does the things for mankind that a computer can not do. The Instrumentality leaves the human brain, the human choice in action.

The Instrumentality passes dark knowledge to its staff, things not usually understood in the inhabited world, things prohibited to ordinary men and women because the officers of the Instrumentality, the captains and the sub-chiefs and the chiefs must know their jobs. If they do not, all mankind might perish.

Suzdal reached into his arsenal. He knew what he was doing. The larger moon of Arachosia was habitable. He could see that there were earth plants already on it, and earth insects. His monitors showed him that the Arachosian men-women had not bothered to settle on the planet. He threw an agonized inquiry at his computers and cried out:

"Read me the age it's in!"

The machine sang back, "More than thirty million years."

Suzdal had strange resources. He had twins or quadruplets of almost every earth animal. The earth animals were carried in tiny capsules no larger than a medicine capsule and they consisted of the sperm and the ovum of the higher animals, ready to be matched for sowing, ready to be imprinted; he also had small life-bombs which could surround any form of life with at least a chance of survival.

He went to the bank and he got cats, eight pairs, sixteen earth cats, *felis domesticus*, the kind of cat that you and I know, the kind of cat which is bred, sometimes for telepathic uses, sometimes to go along on the ships and serve as auxiliary weapons when the minds of the pinlighters direct the cats to fight off dangers.

He coded these cats. He coded them with messages just as monstrous as the messages which had made the men-women of Arachosia into monsters. This is what he coded:

> Do not breed true.
> Invent new chemistry.
> You will serve man.
> Become civilized.
> Learn speech.
> You will serve man.
> When man calls you will serve man.
> Go back, and come forth.
> Serve man.

These instructions were no mere verbal instructions. They were imprints on the actual molecular structure of the animals. They were charges in the genetic and biological coding which went with these cats. And then

Suzdal committed his offense against the laws of mankind. He had a chronopathic device on board the ship. A time distorter, usually to be used for a moment or a second or two to bring the ship away from utter destruction.

The men-women of Arachosia were already cutting through the hull.

He could hear their high, hooting voices screaming delirious pleasure at one another as they regarded him as the first of their promised enemies that they had ever met, the first of the monsters from old earth who had finally overtaken them. The true, evil people on whom they, the men-women of Arachosia would be revenged.

Suzdal remained calm. He coded the genetic cats. He loaded them into life-bombs. He adjusted the controls of his chronopathic machine illegally, so that instead of reaching one second for a ship of 80,000 tons, they reached two million years for a load of less than four kilos. He flung the cats into the nameless moon of Arachosia.

And he flung them back in time.

And he knew he did not have to wait.

He didn't.

## The Catland Suzdal Made

The cats came. Their ships glittered in the naked sky above Arachosia. Their little combat craft attacked. The cats who had not existed a moment before, but who had then had two million years in which to follow a destiny printed right into their brains, printed down their spinal cords, etched into the chemistry of their bodies and personalities. The cats had turned into people of a kind, with speech, intelligence, hope, and a mission. Their mission was to attach themselves to Suzdal, to rescue him, to obey him, and to damage Arachosia.

The cat ships screamed their battle warnings.

"This is the day of the year of the promised age. And *now come cats!*"

The Arachosians had waited for battle for 4,000 years and now they got it. The cats attacked them. Two of the cat craft recognized Suzdal, and the cats reported,

"Oh Lord, oh God, oh Maker of all things, oh Commander of Time, oh Beginner of Life, we have waited since Everything began to serve You, to serve Your Name, to obey Your Glory! May we live for You, may we die for You. We are Your people."

Suzdal cried and threw his message to all the cats.

"Harry the klopts but don't kill them all!"

He repeated "Harry them and stop them until I escape." He flung his cruiser into non-space and escaped.

Neither cat nor Arachosian followed him.

And that's the story, but the tragedy is that Suzdal got back. And the Arachosians are still there and the cats are still there. Perhaps the Instrumentality knows where they are, perhaps the Instrumentality does not. Mankind does not really want to find out. It is against all law to bring up a form of life superior to man. Perhaps the cats are. Perhaps somebody knows whether the Arachosians won and killed the cats and added the cat science to their own and are now looking for us somewhere, probing like blind men through the stars for us true human beings to meet, to hate, to kill. Or perhaps the cats won.

Perhaps the cats are imprinted by a strange mission, by weird hopes of serving men they don't recognize. Perhaps they think we are all Arachosians and should be saved only for some particular cruiser commander, whom they will never see again. They won't see Suzdal, because we know what happened to him.

## The Trial of Suzdal

Suzdal was brought to trial on a great stage in the open world. His trial was recorded. He had gone in when he should not have gone in. He had searched for the Arachosians without waiting and asking for advice and reinforcements. What business was it of his to relieve a distress ages old? What business indeed?

And then the cats. We had the records of the ship to show that something came out of that moon. Spacecraft, things with voices, things that could communicate with the human brain. We're not even sure, since they transmitted directly into the receiver computers, that they spoke an earth language. Perhaps they did it with some sort of direct telepathy. But the crime was, *Suzdal had succeeded.*

By throwing the cats back two million years, by coding them to survive, coding them to develop civilization, coding them to come to his rescue, he had created a whole new world in less than one second of objective time.

His chronopathic device had flung the little life-bombs back to the earth of the big moon over Arachosia and in less time than it takes to record this, the bombs came back in the form of a fleet built by a race, an earth race, though of cat origin, two million years old.

The court stripped Suzdal of his name and said, "You will not be named Suzdal any longer."

The court stripped Suzdal of his rank.

"You will not be a commander of this or of any other navy, neither imperial nor of the Instrumentality."

The court stripped Suzdal of his life. "You will not live longer, former Commander, and former Suzdal."

And then the court stripped Suzdal of death.

"You will go to the planet Shayol, the place of uttermost shame from which no one ever returns. You will go there with the contempt and hatred of mankind. We will not punish you. We do not wish to know about you any more. You will live on, but for us you will have ceased to exist."

That's the story. It's a sad, wonderful story. The Instrumentality tries to cheer up all the different kinds of mankind by telling them it isn't true, it's just a ballad.

Perhaps the records do exist. Perhaps somewhere the crazy klopts of Arachosia breed their boyish young, deliver their babies, always by Caeserean, feed them always by bottle, generations of men who have no fathers and who have no idea of what the word *mother* might be. And perhaps the Arachosians spend their crazy lives in endless battle with intelligent cats who are serving mankind that may never come back.

That's the story.

Furthermore, it isn't true.

*. . . From the Dark Ages of Space emerged the Second Empire . . . ruled by a child, a usurper and a fool! The Great Throne of Imperial Earth commanded a thousand vassal worlds—bleak, starved worlds that sullenly whispered of galactic revolt . . . At last, like eagles at a distant eyrie, the Star-kings gathered . . . not to whisper, but to strike!*

●

# THE REBEL OF VALKYR
## by Alfred Coppel

Out of the dark ages of the Interregnum emerged the Second Empire. Once again in the space of a millennium, the banner of Imperial Earth waved above the decimated lands of the inhabited worlds. Four generations of conquerors, heirs to the greatness of the Thousand Emperors, had recreated the Galactic Empire, by force of arms. But technology, the Great Destroyer, was feared and forbidden. Only witches, warlocks and sorcerers remembered the old knowledge, and the mobs, tortured by the racial memories of the awful destruction of the Civil Wars, stoned these seekers and burned them in the squares of towns built amid the rubble of the old wars. The ancient, mighty spaceships—indestructible, eternal —carried men and horses, fire and sword across the Galaxy at the bidding of the warlords. The Second

Empire—four generations out of isolated savagery
—feudal, grim; a culture held together by bonds
forged of blood and iron and the loyalty of the warrior star-kings . . .
——Quintus Bland,
ESSAYS ON GALACTIC HISTORY

# I

Kieron, Warlord of Valkyr, paced the polished floor
angrily. The flickering lights of the vast mirrored chamber
glinted from the jewels in his ceremonial harness and
shimmered down the length of his silver cape. For a moment, the star-king paused before the tall double doors
of beaten bronze, his strong hands toying with the hilt of
his sword. The towering Janizaries of the Palace Guard
stood immobile on either side of the arching doorway,
their great axes resting on the flagstones. It was as though
the dark thoughts that coursed through Kieron's mind
were—to them—unthinkable. The huge warriors from
the heavy planets of the Pleiades were stolid, loyal, unimaginative. And even a star-king did not dream of as-
saulting the closed portals of the Emperor's chambers.

Kieron's fingers opened and closed spasmodically over
the gem-crusted pommel of his weapon; his dark eyes
glittered with unspent fury. Muttering an oath, he turned
away from the silent door and resumed his pacing. His
companion, a brawny man in the plain battle harness of
Valkyr, watched him quietly from under bushy yellow
brows. He stood with his great arms folded over the plaits
of grizzled yellow hair that hung to his waist, his deeply-
lined face framed by the loosened lacings of a winged
helmet. A huge sword hugged his naked thigh; a massive
blade with worn and sweat-stained hilt.

The lord of Valkyr paused in his angry pacing to glare
at his aide. "By the Great Destroyer, Nevitta! How long
are we to stand this?"

"Patience, Kieron, patience." The old warrior spoke
with the assurance of life-long familiarity. "They try us
sorely, but we have waited three weeks. A little longer can
do no harm."

"Three weeks!" Kieron scowled at Nevitta. "Will they *drive* us into rebellion? Is that their intention? I swear I would not have taken this from Gilmer himself!"

"The great Emperor would never have dealt with us so. The fighting men of Valkyr were ever closest to his heart, Kieron. This is a way of doing that smacks of a woman's hand." He spat on the polished floor. "May the Seven Hells claim her!"

Kieron grunted shortly and turned again toward the silent door. Ivane! Ivane the Fair . . . Ivane the schemer. What devil's brew was she mixing now? Intrigue had always been her weapon—and now that Gilmer was gone and she stood by the Great Throne . . .

Kieron cursed her roundly under his breath. Nevitta spoke the truth. There was Ivane's hand in this, as surely as the stars made Galaxies!

Three weeks wasted. Long weeks. Twenty-one full days since their ships had touched the Imperial City. Days of fighting through the swarms of dilettantes and favor-seekers that thronged the Imperial Palace. There had been times when Kieron had wanted to cut a path through the fawning dandies with his sword!

Gilmer of Kaidor lay dead a full year and still the new Court was a madhouse of simpering sycophants. Petitions were being granted by the score as the favorites collected their long-delayed largess from the boy-Emperor Toran. And Kieron knew well enough that whatever favors were granted came through the ambitious hands of the Consort Ivane. She might not be allowed to wear the crown of an Empress without the blood of the Thousand Emperors in her veins, but by now no one at Court denied that she was the fountain-head of Imperial favor. Yet that wasn't really enough for her, Kieron knew. Ivane dreamed of better things. And because of all this hidden by-play, the old favorites of the warrior Gilmer were snubbed and refused audience. A new inner circle was building, and Kieron of Valkyr was not—it was plain to see—to be included. He was prevented even from presenting his just complaints to the Emperor Toran.

Other matters, he was told again and again, occupied His Imperial Majesty's attention. Other matters! Kieron could

164

feel the anger hot and throbbing in his veins. What other matters could there be of more importance to a sovereign than the loyalty of his finest fighting men? Or if Toran was a fool as the courtiers privately claimed, then surely Ivane had more intelligence than to keep a Warlord of the Outer Marches cooling his heels in antechambers for three weeks! The Lady Ivane, herself so proud, should know how near to rebellion were the warrior peoples of the Periphery.

Under such deliberate provocations it was difficult to loyally ignore the invitation of Freka of Kalgan to meet with the other star-kings in grievance council. Rebellion was not alluring to one like Kieron who had spent his boyhood fighting beside Gilmer, but there was a limit to human endurance, and he was fast reaching it.

"Nevitta," Kieron spoke abruptly. "Were you able to find out anything concerning the Lady Alys?"

The grizzled warrior shook his head. "Nothing but the common talk. It is said that she has secluded herself, still mourning for Gilmer. You know, Kieron, how the little princess loved her father."

The lord of Valkyr frowned thoughtfully. Yes, it was true enough that Alys had loved Gilmer. He could remember her at the great Emperor's side after the battle of Kaidor. Even the conquered interregnal lords of that world had claimed that Gilmer would have surrendered the planet if they had been able to capture his daughter. The bond between father and daughter had been a close one. Possibly Alys *had* secluded herself to carry on with her mourning—but Kieron doubted it. That would not have been Gilmer's way, nor his daughter's.

"Things would be different here," said Nevitta with feeling, "if the little princess ruled instead of Toran."

Very different, thought Kieron. The foolish Toran bid fair to lose what four generations of loyal fighters had built up out of the rubble of the dark ages. Alys, the warrior princess, would add to the glory of the Imperium, not detract from it. But perhaps he was prejudiced in her favor, reflected Kieron. It was hard not to be.

He recalled her laughing eyes and her courage. A slim child, direct in manner and bearing. Embarrassing him before his roaring Valkyrs with her forthright protesta-

165

tions of love. The armies had worshipped her. A lovely child—with pride of race written into her patrician face. But compassionate, too. Gravely comforting the dying and the wounded with a touch or a word.

Eight years had passed since bloody Kaidor. The child of twelve would be a woman now. And, thought Kieron anxiously, a threat to the ascendant power of the Consort Ivane . . .

The tall bronze doors swung open suddenly, and Kieron turned. But it was not the Emperor who stood there framed in the archway, nor even the Consort. It was the gem-bedecked figure of Landor, the First Lord of Space.

Kieron snorted derisively. First Lord! The shades of the mighty fighters who had carried that title through a thousand of Imperial Earth's battles must have been sickened by young Toran's . . . or Ivane's . . . choice of the mincing courtier who now stood before him.

The more cynical courtiers said that Landor had won his honors in Ivane's bed, and Kieron could well believe it. Out in the vast emptinesses of the Edge men lived by different standards. Out there a woman was a woman—a thing to be loved or beaten, cherished or enjoyed and cast off—but not a touchstone to wealth and power. Kieron had loathed Landor on sight, and there was no reason enough to believe that the First Lord reciprocated most completely. It was not wise for anyone, even a Warlord, to openly scorn the Consort's favorites—but restraint was not one of the lord of Valkyr's virtues, though even Nevitta warned him to take care, Assassination was a fine art in the Imperial City, and one amply subsidized by the First Lord of Space.

"Well, Landor?" Kieron demanded, disdaining to use Landor's title.

Landor's smoothly handsome features showed no expression. The pale eyes veiled like a serpent's.

"I regret," the First Lord of Space said easily, "that His Imperial Majesty had retired for the night, Valkyr. Under the circumstances . . ." He spread his slender hands in a gesture of helplessness.

The lie was obvious. Through the open doorway of the royal chambers came the murmuring sound of laughter

166

and the reedy melody of a minstrel's pipes in the age-old ballad of *Lady Greensleeves*. Kieron could hear Toran's uncertain voice singing:

> Greensleeves was all my joy,
> Greensleeves was all my joy,
> And who but Lady Greensleeves?

Kieron could imagine the boy—lolling foolishly before the glittering Ivane, trying to win with verses what any man could have for a pledge of loyalty to the Consort.

The Valkyr glared at Landor. "I'm not to be received, is that it? By the Seven Hells, why don't you say what you mean?"

Landor's smile was scornful. "You out-worlders! You should learn how to behave, really. Perhaps later . . ."

"Later be damned!" snapped Kieron. "My people are starving *now!* Your grubbing tax-gatherers are wringing us dry! How long do you think they'll stand for it? How long do you imagine *I* will stand for it?"

"Threats, Valkyr?" asked the First Lord, his eyes suddenly venomous. "Threats against your Emperor? Men have been whipped to death for much less."

"Not men of Valkyr," retorted Kieron.

"The men of Valkyr no longer hold the favored position they once did, Kieron. I counsel you to remember that."

"True enough," Kieron replied scornfully. "Under Gilmer, fighting men were the power of the Empire. Now Toran rules with the hands of women . . . and dancing masters."

The First Lord's face darkened at the insult. He laid a hand on the hilt of his ornate sword, but the Valkyr's eyes remained insolent. The huge Nevitta stirred, measuring the Pleiadene Janizaries at the door, ready for trouble.

But Landor had no stomach for sword-play—particularly with as young and supple a fighter as the Warlord of Valkyr. His own ready tongue was a better weapon than steel. With an effort, he forced himself to smile. It was a cold smile, pregnant with subtle danger.

"Harsh words, Valkyr. And unwise. I shall not forget them. I doubt that you will be able to see His Majesty, since I do not believe the tribulations of a planet of savages would concern him. You waste your time here. If you have other business, you had better be about it."

It was Kieron's turn to feel the hot goad of anger. "Are those Toran's words or Ivane's dancing master?"

"The Consort Ivane, of course, agrees. If your people cannot pay their taxes, let them sell a few of their brats into service," Landor said smoothly.

The die was cast, then, thought Kieron furiously. All hope for an adjustment from Toran was gone and only one course lay open to him now.

"Nevitta! See that our men and horses are loaded tonight and the ships made ready for space!"

Nevitta saluted and turned to go. He paused, looked insolently at the First Lord, and deliberately spat on the floor. Then he was gone, his spurs ringing metallically as he disappeared through the high curving archway.

"Savage," muttered Landor.

"Savage enough to be loyal and worthy of any trust," said Kieron; "but you would know nothing of that."

Landor ignored the thrust. "Where do you go now, Valkyr?"

"Off-world."

"Of course," Landor smiled thinly, his eyebrows arching over pale, shrewd eyes. "Off-world."

Kieron felt a stab of suspicion. How much did Landor know? Had his spies pierced Freka the Unknown's counter-espionage cordon and brought work of the star-kings gathering on Kalgan?

"It cannot concern you where I go now, Landor," said Kieron grimly. "You've won here. But . . ." Kieron stepped a pace nearer the resplendent favorite. "Warn your tax-gatherers to go armed when they land on Valkyr. Well armed, Landor."

Kieron turned on his heel and strode out of the antechamber, his booted heels staccato on the flagstones, silver cape flaunting like a proud banner.

# II

Past the tall arch of the Emperor's antechamber lay the Hall of the Thousand Emperors. Kieron strode through it, the flickering flames of the wall-sconces casting long shadows out behind him—shadows that danced and whirled on the tapestried walls and touched the composed faces of the great men of Earth.

These were brooding men; men who stared down at him out of their thousand pasts. Men who had stood with a planet for a throne and watched their Empire passing in ordered glory from horizon to horizon across the night sky of Earth—men worshipped as gods on out-world planets, who watched and guided the tide of Empire until it crashed thundering on the shores of ten thousand worlds beyond Vega and Altair. Men who sat cloaked in sable robes with diamond stars encrusted and saw their civilization built out from the Great Throne, tier on shining tier until at last it reached the Edge and strained across the awful gulf for the terrible seetee suns of mighty Andromeda itself . . .

The last few of the men like gods had watched the First Empire crumble. They had seen the wave of annihilation sweeping in from the Outer Marches of the Periphery; had seen their gem-bright civilization shattered with destructive forces so hideous that the spectre of the Great Destroyer hung like a mantle of death over the Galaxy, a thing to be shunned and feared forever. And thus had come the Interregnum.

Kieron had no eyes for these brooding giants; his world was not the world they had known. It was in the next chamber that the out-world warrior paused. It was a vast and empty place. Here there were but five figures and space for a thousand more. This was the Empire that Kieron knew. This Empire he had fought for and helped secure; a savage, darkling thing spawned in the dark ages of the Interregnum, a Galaxy-spanning fief of star-kings and serfs—of warlocks and spaceships—of light and shadow. This Empire had been born in the agony of a

Galaxy and tempered in the bitter internecine wars of re-conquest.

Before the image of Gilmer of Kaidor, Kieron stopped. He stood in silence, looking into the face of his dead liege. The hour was late and the Hall deserted. Kieron knelt, suddenly filled with sadness. He was on his way to rebellion against the Empire that he had helped this stern-faced man to expand and hold—rebellion against the power of Imperial Earth, personified by the weak-faced boy standing draped in the sable mantle of sovereignty in the next niche. Kieron looked from father to son. By its composure and its nearness to the magnetic features of the great Gilmer, the face of young Toran seemed to draw character and strength. It was an illusion, Kieron knew.

The young Valkyr felt driven hard. His people hungered. Military service was no longer enough for the Imperial Government as it had been for decades. Money was demanded, and there was no-money on Valkyr. So the people hungered—and Kieron was their lord. He could not stand by and see the agony on the faces of his warrior maids as their children weakened, nor could he see his proud warriors selling themselves into slavery for a handful of coins. The Emperor would not listen. Kieron had recourse only to the one thing he knew . . . the sword.

He bowed his head and asked the shade of Gilmer for forgiveness.

A slight movement caught his battle-sharpened eye as someone stirred behind a fluted column. Kieron's sword whispered as it slid from the scabbard, the gemmed hilt casting shards of light into the dimness of the colonnade.

Treading softly, Kieron eased his tall frame into the shadows, weapon alert. The thought of assassination flashed across his mind and he smiled grimly. Could it be that Landor had his hirelings after him already?

Kieron saw the shadowy shape slip from the colonnade out onto the great curving terrace that bordered the entire west wing of the Palace. Eyes narrowed under his black brows, the lord of Valkyr followed.

The stars gleamed in the moonless night, and far below, Kieron could see the flickering torchlights of the Imperial

City fanning out to the horizon like the spokes of some fantastic, glittering wheel. The dark figure ahead had vanished.

Kieron sheathed his sword and drew his poniard. It was far too dark for swordplay, and he did not wish to risk letting the assassin escape. Melting into the shadows of the colonnade again, he made his way parallel to the terrace, alert for any sign of movement. Presently, the figure appeared again beside the balustrade, and the Valkyr moved swiftly and quietly up behind. With a cat-like movement, he slipped his free arm about the slight shape, pulling it tight against himself. The poniard flashed in his upraised hand, the slender blade reflecting the starlight.

The weapon did not descend . . .

Against his forearm, Kieron felt a yielding softness, and the hair that brushed his cheek was warm and perfumed.

He stood transfixed. The girl twisted in his grasp and broke free with a gasping cry. Instantly, a blade gleamed in her hand and she had launched herself at the Valkyr furiously. Her voice was tight with rage.

"Murdering butcher! *You dare . . . !*"

Kieron caught her upraised arm and wrenched the dagger from her grasp. She clawed at him, kicking, biting, but never once calling aloud for aid. At last Kieron was able to pin her to a column with his weight, and he held her there, arms pinioned to her sides.

"You hellcat!" he muttered against her hair. "Who are you?"

"You know well enough, you murdering lackey! Why don't you kill me and go collect your pay, damn you!" gritted the girl furiously. "Must you manhandle me too?"

Kieron gasped. *"I* kill *you!"* He caught the girl's hair and pulled her head back so that her features would catch the faint glow of light from the city below. "Who are you, hell-cat?"

The light outlined his own features and the Arms of Valkyr on the clasp of his cloak at his throat. The girl's eyes widened. Slowly the tenseness went out of her and she relaxed against him.

"Kieron! Kieron of Valkyr!"

* * *

Kieron was still alert for some trick. Landor could have hired a female assassin just as well as a man.

"You know me?" he asked cautiously.

*"Know* you!" She laughed suddenly, and it was a silvery sound in the night. "I *loved* you . . . beast!"

"By the Seven Hells, you speak in riddles! Who are you?" the Valkyr demanded irritably.

"And I thought you had come to kill me," mused the girl in self-reproach. "My own Kieron!"

"I'm not your Kieron or anyone else's, Lady," said Kieron rather stiffly, "and you'd better explain why you were watching me in the Hall of Emperors before I'll let you go."

"My father warned me that you would forget me. I did not think you would be so cruel," she taunted.

"I knew your father?"

"Well enough, I think."

"I've had a hundred wenches—and known some of their fathers, too. You can't expect me to . . ."

"Not *this* wench, Valkyr!" the girl exploded furiously.

The tone carried such command that Kieron involuntarily stepped back, but still keeping the girl's hands pinned to her sides.

"If you had spoken so on Kaidor, I'd have had the skin stripped from your back, outworld savage!" she cried.

Kaidor! Kieron felt the blood drain away from his face. This, then, was . . . Alys.

"Ha! So you remember now! Kaidor you can recall, but you have forgotten me! Kieron, you always were a beast!"

Kieron felt a smile spreading across his face. It was good to smile again. And it was good to know that Alys was . . . safe.

"Highness . . ."

"Don't 'Highness' me!"

"Alys, then. Forgive me. I could not have known you. After all it has been eight years . . ."

"And there have been a hundred wenches . . ." mimicked the girl angrily.

Kieron grinned. "There really haven't been that many. I boasted."

172

"Any would be too many!"

"You haven't changed, Alys, except that you . . ."

"Have grown so? Spare me that!" She glared at him, eyes flaming in the shadows. Then suddenly she was laughing again, a silvery laugh that hung like a bright thread in the soft tapestry of night sounds. "Oh, Kieron, it is good to see you again!"

"I thought to hear from you, Alys, when we reached Earth—but there was nothing. No word of any kind. I was told you were in seclusion still mourning Gilmer."

Alys bowed her head. "I will never stop mourning him." She looked up, her eyes suddenly bright with unshed tears. "Nor will you. I saw you kneeling inside. I thought then that it might be you. No one kneels to Gilmer now but the old comrades." She walked to the balustrade and stood looking out over the lights of the Imperial City. Kieron watched the play of emotions over her face, caught suddenly by her beauty.

"I tried to reach you, Kieron—tried hard. But my servants have been taken from me since I was caught spying on Ivane. And I'm kept under cover now, permitted out only after dark—and then only on the Palace grounds. Ivane has convinced Toran that I'm dangerous. The people like me because I was father's favorite. My poor stupid little brother! How that woman rules him. . . !"

Kieron was aghast. "You spied on Ivane? In heaven's name, why?"

"That woman is a born plotter, Kieron. She isn't satisfied with a Consort's coronet. She's brewing something. Emissaries have come to her from certain of the star-kings and *others* . . ."

"Others?"

Alys' voice was hushed. "A warlock, Kieron! He has been seeing Ivane privately for more than a year. An awful man!"

Superstition stirred like a quickening devil inside the Valkyr. The shuddering horror of the dark and bloody tales he had heard all his life about the warlocks who clung to the knowledge of the Great Destroyer rose like a wave of blackness within him.

Alys felt the same dark tide rising in her. She moved

173

closer to Kieron, her slim body trembling slightly against his. "The people would tear Ivane to pieces if they knew," she whispered.

"You *saw* this warlock?" asked Kieron sick with dread. Alys nodded soundlessly.

Kieron fought down his fears and wondered uneasily what Ivane's connection could be with such a pariah. The warlocks and witches were despised and feared above all other creatures in the Galaxy.

"His name?" Kieron asked.

"Geller. Geller of the Marshes. It is said that he is a conjurer of devils . . . *and that he can create homunculi!* Out of the very filth of the marches! Oh, Kieron!" Alys shuddered.

An awful plan was forming in Kieron's mind. He was thinking that Ivane must be stripped of the spells and powers of this devil-man. With such powers at her command there might be nothing impossible of attainment. Even the crown of the Imperium itself . . .

"Where," Kieron asked slowly, "can this warlock be found?"

"On the street of the Black Flame, in the city of Neg . . . on Kalgan."

*"Kalgan!"* Kieron's heart contracted. Was there a connection? Kalgan! What had Ivane to do with that lonely planet beyond the dark veil of the Coalsack? Was it coincidence? Out of all the thousands of worlds in space . . . Kalgan.

"Is there something wrong, Kieron? You know this man?"

Kieron shook his head. It had suddenly become more than imperative that he go to Kalgan. The mystery of the Imperial Consort's connection with a warlock of Kalgan must be unraveled. And the star-kings were gathering . . .

The Valkyr was suddenly taken with a new and different fear. If Alys had spied on Ivane, then she must be in danger here. Ivane would never tolerate interference with her plans from Gilmer's daughter.

"Alys, are you a prisoner here?"

"More, I'm afraid," the girl said sadly. "I'm a reminder to Toran of the days of our father. One that he would like to eliminate, I think."

Kieron studied her in the starlight. His eyes sought the thick golden hair that brushed her shoulders, the glittering metallic skirt that hung low on her hips, outlining the slim thighs. He watched the graceful line of her unadorned throat, the bare shoulders and breasts, the small waist, the flat, firm stomach—all revealed by the studied nakedness of the fashions of the Inner Marches. This was no child. The thought of her in danger shook him badly.

"Toran would not dare harm you, Alys," said Kieron uncertainly. There had been a time when he could have said such a thing with perfect assurance, but since the death of Gilmer, the Imperial City was like an over-civilized jungle—full of beasts of prey.

"No, Toran wouldn't . . . alone," said Alys; "but there are Ivane and Landor." She laughed, suddenly gay; her eyes, seeking Kieron's, were shining. "But not now! You are here, Kieron!"

The Valkyr felt his heart contract. "Alys," he said softly, "I leave Earth tonight. For Kalgan."

"For Kalgan, Kieron?" Alys' eyes widened. "To seek that warlock?"

"For another reason, Alys." Kieron paused uneasily. It was hard to speak to Gilmer of Kaidor's daughter about rebellion. Yet he could not lie to her. He temporized.

"I have business with the lord of Kalgan," he said.

Alys' face was shadowed and her voice when she spoke was sad. "Do the star-kings gather, Kieron? Have they had all they can stand of Toran's foolish rule?"

Kieron nodded wordlessly.

The girl flared up with a sudden imperious anger. "That fool! He is letting the favorites drive the Empire to ruin!" She looked up at Kieron pleadingly. "Promise me one thing, Kieron."

"If I can."

"That you will not commit yourself to any rebellion until we have spoken again."

"Alys, I . . ."

"Oh, Kieron! Promise me! If there is no other way, then fight the Imperial House. But give me one chance to save what my father and his father died for . . . !"

"And mine," added Kieron somberly.

"You know that if there is no other way, I won't try to

dissuade you. But while you are on Kalgan, I'll speak to Toran. Please, Kieron, promise me that Valkyr will not rebel until we have tried everything." Her eyes shone with passion. "Then if it comes to war, I'll ride by your side!"

"Done, Alys," said Kieron slowly. "But take care when you speak to Toran. Remember there is danger here for you." He wondered briefly what Freka the Unknown would think of his sudden reluctance to commit the hundred spaceships and five thousand warriors of Valkyr to the coming rebellion. A thought struck him and quickly he discarded it. For just an instant he had wondered if Geller of the Marshes and the mysterious Freka the Unknown might be the same . . . Stranger things had happened. But Alys had described Geller as old, and Freka was known to be a six-and-one-half foot warrior, the perfect "type" of the star-king caste.

"One thing more, Alys," Kieron said; "I will leave one of my vessels here for your use. Nevitta and a company will remain, too. Keep them by you. They will guard you with their lives." He slipped his arm about her, holding her to him.

"Nevitta?" Alys said with a slow smile. "Nevitta of the yellow braids and the great sword? I remember him."

"The braids are greying, but the sword is as long as ever. He can guard you for me, and keep you safe."

The girl's smile deepened at the words 'for me' but Kieron did not notice. He was deep in planning. "Be very careful, Alys. And watch out for Landor."

"Yes, Kieron," the girl breathed meekly. She looked up at the tall outworld warrior's face, lips parted.

But Kieron was looking up at the stars of the Empire, and there was uneasiness in his heart. He tightened his arm about Alys, holding her closer to him as though to protect her from the hot gaze of those fiery stars.

# III

The spaceship was ancient, yet the mysterious force of the Great Destroyer chained within the sealed coils between the hulls drove it with unthinkable speed across the star-shot darkness. The interior was close and smoky, for the only light came from oil lamps turned low to slow the fouling of the air. Once, there had been light without fire in the thousand-foot hulls, but the tiny orbs set into the ceilings had failed for they were not of a kind with the force in the sealed, eternal coils.

On the lower decks, the horses of the small party of Valkyr warriors aboard stomped the steel deck-plates, impatient in their close confinement; while in the tiny bubble of glass at the very prow of the ancient vessel, two shamen of the hereditary caste of Navigators drove the pulsing starship toward the spot beyond the veil of the Coalsack where their astrolabes and armillary spheres told them that the misty globe of Kalgan lay.

Many men—risking indictment as warlocks or sorcerers —had tried to probe the secrets of the Great Destroyer and compute the speed of these mighty spacecraft of antiquity. Some had even claimed a speed of 100,000 miles per hour for them. But since the starships made the voyage from Earth to the agricultural worlds of Proxima Centauri in slightly less than twenty-eight hours, such calculations would place the nearest star-system an astounding *two million eight hundred thousand* miles from Earth —a figure that was as absurd to all Navigators as it was inconceivable to laymen.

The great spaceship bearing the Warlord of Valkyr's blazon solidified into reality near Kalgan as its great velocity diminished. It circled the planet to kill speed and nosed down into the damp air of the grey world. The high cloud cover passed, it slanted down into slightly clearer air. Kalgan did not rotate: in its slow orbit around the red giant parent star, the planet turned first one face, and then another to the slight heat of its sun. Great oceans covered the poles, and the central land mass was like a craggy girdle of rock and soil around the bulging equator. Only in the twilight zone was life endurable, and the city of Neg, stronghold of Freka the Unknown, was the only urban grouping on the planet.

Neg lay sullen in the eternal twilight when at last Kieron's spaceship landed outside the gates and the debarkation of his retinue had begun; the spaceport, however, was ablaze with flares and torches, and the lord of Kalgan had sent a corps of drummers—signal honors—to

177

greet the visiting star-king. The hot, misty night air throbbed with the beat of the huge kettle-drums, and weapons and jewelled harness flashed in the yellow light of the flames.

At last the debarkation was complete, and Kieron and his warriors were led by a torch-bearing procession of soldiery into the fortified city of Neg—along ancient cobbled streets—through small crowded squares—and finally to the Citadel of Neg itself. The residence of Freka the Unknown, Lord of Kalgan.

The people they passed were a silent, sullen lot. Dull, brutish faces. The faces of slaves and serfs held in bondage by fear and force. These people, Kieron reflected, would go mad in a carnival of destruction if the heavy hand of their lord should falter.

He turned his attention from the people of Neg to the massive Citadel. It was a powerful keep with high walls and turreted outworks. It spoke of Kalgan's bloody history in every squat, functional line. A history of endless rebellion and uprising, of coups and upheavals. Warrior after warrior had set himself up as ruler of this sullen world only to fall before the assaults of his own vassals. It had ever been the policy of the Imperial Government never to interfere with these purely local affairs. It was felt that out of the crucibles of domestic strife would arise the best fighting men, and they, in turn, could serve the Imperium. As long as Kalgan produced its levy of fighting men and spaceships, no one on Earth cared about the local government. So Kalgan wallowed in blood.

Out of the last nightmare had come Freka. He had risen rapidly to power on Kalgan—and *stayed* in power. Hated by his people, he nevertheless ruled harshly, for that was his way. Kieron had been told that this warrior who had sprung out of nowhere was different from other men. The Imperial courtiers claimed that he cared nothing for wine or women, and that he loved only battle. It would take such a man, thought Kieron studying the Citadel, to take and hold a world like Kalgan. It would take such a man to want it!

If Freka of Kalgan loved bloodshed, he would be happy when this coming council of star-kings ended, the Valkyr reflected moodily. He knew himself how near to rebellion he was, and the other lords of the Outer Marches, the lords of Auriga, Doorn, Quintain, Helia—all were ready to strike the Imperial crown from Toran's foolish head.

Kieron was escorted with his warriors to a luxurious suite within the Citadel. Freka, he was informed, regretted his inability to greet him personally, but intended to meet all the gathered star-kings in the Great Hall within twelve hours. Meanwhile, there would be entertainment for the visiting warriors, and the hospitality of Kalgan. Which hospitality, claimed the hawk-faced steward pridefully, was without peer in the known Universe!

An imp of perversity stirred in Kieron. He found that he did not completely trust Freka of Kalgan. There was a premeditated cold-bloodedness about this whole business of the star-kings' grievance council that alerted him to danger. There should have been less smoothness and efficiency in the way the visitors were handled, Kieron thought illogically, remembering the troubles he, himself, had gone to whenever outworld rulers had visited Valkyr. He was suddenly glad that he had warned Nevitta to use extreme caution should it be necessary to bring Alys to Kalgan. It was possible he was being over-suspicious, but he could not forget that Alys herself had seen a warlock from Kalgan in familiar conversation with the woman really to blame for the danger that smouldered among the worlds of the Empire.

The drums told the Valkyr that the other star-kings were arriving. Torches flared in the courtyards of the Citadel, and the hissing roar of spaceships landing told of the eagles gathering.

Through the long, featureless twilight, the sounds continued. Freka made no appearances, but the promised entertainment was forthcoming and lavish. Food and wine in profusion were brought to the apartments of the Valkyrs. Musicians and minstrels came too, to sing and play the love songs and warchants of ancient Valkyr while the warriors roared approval.

Kieron sat on the high seat reserved for him and watched the dancing yellow light of the flambeaux light up the stone rooms and play across the ruddy faces of his warriors as they drank and gamed and quarreled.

Dancing girls were sent them, and the Valkyrs howled with savage pleasure as the naked bodies, glistening with scented oils, gyrated in the barbaric rhythms of the sword dances, steel whirring in bright arcs above the tawny heads. The long, gloomy twilight passed unregretted in the warm, flame-splashed closeness of the Citadel. Kieron watched thoughtfully as more women and fiery vintages were brought into the merrymaking. The finest wines and the best women were passed hand to hand over the heads of laughing warriors to Kieron's place, and he drank deeply of both. The wines were heady, the full lips of the sybaritic houris bittersweet, but Kieron smiled inwardly— if Freka the Unknown sought to bring him into the gathering of the star-kings drunk and satiated and amenable to suggestion, the lord of Kalgan knew little of the capacity of the men of the Edge.

The hours passed and revelry filled the Citadel of Neg. Life on the outer worlds was harsh, and the gathering warriors took full measure of the pleasures placed at their disposal by the lord of Kalgan. The misty, eternal dusk rang with the drinking songs and battle-cries, the quarreling and lovemaking of warriors from a dozen outworld planets. Each star-king, Kieron knew, was being entertained separately, plied with wine and woman-flesh until the hour for the meeting came.

The sands had run their course in the glass five times before the trumpets blared through the Citadel, calling the lords to the meeting. Kieron left his men to enjoy themselves, and with an attendant in the harness of Kalgan made his way toward the Great Hall.

Through dark passageways that reeked of ancient violence, by walls hung with tapestries and antique weapons, they went; over flagstones worn smooth by generations. This keep had been old when the reconquering heirs to the Thousand Emperors rode their chargers into the Great Hall and dictated their peace terms to the interregnal lords of Kalgan.

The hall was a vast, vaulted stone room filled with the smoky heat of torches and many bodies. It teemed with be-jewelled warriors, star-kings, warlords, aides and attendants. For just a moment the lord of Valkyr regretted having come into the impressive gathering alone. Yet it was unimportant. These men were—for the most part—his peers and friends; the warrior kings of the Edge.

Odo of Helia was there, filling the room with his great laughter; and Theron, the Lord of Auriga; Kleph of Quintain; and others. Many others. Kieron saw the white mane of his father's friend Eric, the Warlord of Doorn, the great Red Sun beyond the Horsehead Nebula. Here was an aggregation of might to give even a Galactic Emperor pause. The warlike worlds of the Edge, gathered on Kalgan to decide the issue of war against the uneasy crown of Imperial Earth.

Questions coursed through Kieron's mind as he stood among the star-kings. Alys—pleading with Toran—what success could she have against the insidious power of the Consort? Was Alys in danger? And there was Geller, the mysterious warlock of the Marshes. Kieron felt he must seek out the man. There were questions that only Geller could answer. Yet at the thought of a warlock—a familiar of the Great Destroyer—Kieron's blood ran cold.

The Valkyr looked about him. That there was power enough here to crush the forces of Earth, there was no doubt. But what then? When Toran was stripped of his power, who would wear the crown? The Empire was a necessity—without it the dark ages of the Interregnum would fall again. For four generations the mantle of shadows had hovered over the youngling Second Empire. Not even the most savage wanted a return of the lost years of isolation. The Empire must live. But the Empire would need a titular head. If not Toran, the foolish weak boy, then who? Kieron's suspicions stirred. . . .

A rumble of tympani announced the entrance of the host. The murmuring voices grew still. Freka the Unknown had entered the Great Hall.

Kieron stared. The man was—magnificent! The tall figure was muscled like a statue from the Dawn Age; sinews rippling under the golden hide like oiled machinery, grace and power in every movement. A mane of hair the color of fire framed a face of classic purity—ascetic, almost inhuman in its perfection. The pale eyes that swept the assemblage were like drops of molten silver. Hot, but with a cold heat that seared with an icy touch. Kieron shivered. This man was already half a god. . . .

Yet there was something in Freka that stirred resentment in the Valkyr. Some indefinable lack that was sensed rather than seen. Kieron knew he looked upon a magnificent star-king, but there was no warmth in the man.

Kieron fought down the unreasonable dislike. It was not his way to judge men so emotionally. *Perhaps,* thought the Valkyr, *I imagine the coldness.* But it was there!

Yet when Freka spoke, the feeling vanished, and Kieron felt himself transported by the timbre and resonant power of the voice.

"Star-kings of the Empire!" Freka cried, and the sound of his words rolled out over the gathering like a wave, gaining power even as he continued: "For more than a hundred years you and your fathers have fought for the glory and gain of the Great Throne! Under Gilmer of Kaidor you carried the gonfalon of Imperial Earth to the Edge and planted it there under the light of Andromeda itself! Your blood was shed and your treasure spent for the new Emperors! And what is your reward? *The heavy hand of a fool!* Your people writhe under the burden of excessive taxation—your women starve and your children are sold into slavery! You are in bondage to a foolish boy who squats like a toad on the Great Throne . . ."

Kieron listened breathlessly as Freka of Kalgan wove a web of half-truths around the assembled warriors. The compelling power of the man was astounding.

"The worlds writhe in the grip of an idiot! Helia, Doorn, Auriga, Valkyr, Quintain . . ." He called the roll of the warrior worlds. "Yes, and Kalgan, too! There is not enough wealth in the Universe to satiate Toran and the Great Throne! And the Court laughs at our complaints! At us! The star-kings who are the fists of the Empire! How long will we endure it? How long will we maintain Toran on a throne that he is too weak to hold?"

*Toran,* thought Kieron grimly, always Toran. Never a word of Ivane or Landor or the favorites who twisted Toran around their fingers.

Freka's voice dropped low and he leaned out over the first row of upturned faces. "I call upon you—as you love your people and your freedom—to join with Kalgan and rid the Empire of this weakling and his money-grubbing and neglect!"

In the crowd, someone stirred. All but this one seemed hypnotized. It was old Eric of Doorn who stepped forward.

"You speak treason! You brought us here to discuss grievances, and you preach rebellion and treason, I say!" he shouted angrily.

Freka turned cold eyes on the old warrior.

"If this is treason," he said ominously, "it is the Emperor's treason—not ours."

Eric of Doorn seemed to wilt under the icy gaze of those inhuman eyes. Kieron watched him step back into the circle of his followers, fear in his aging face. There was a power in Freka to quell almost any insurrection here, thought the Valkyr uneasily. He, himself, was bound by the promise he had made to Alys, but it was only that that kept him from casting in his lot with the compelling lord of Kalgan. Such a feeling was unreason itself, he knew, and he fought against it, drawing on his reserves of information to strengthen his resolve to obstruct Freka if he could. Yet it was easy to understand how this strange man had sprung out of obscurity and made himself master of Kalgan. Freka was a creature made for leadership.

Kieron stood away from the crowd and forced himself to speak. All his earlier suspicions were growing like a suffocating cloud within him. Someone was being fooled and used, and it was *not* the lord of Kalgan!

"You, Freka!" he cried, and the lords turned to listen. "You shout of getting rid of Toran—but what do you offer in his place?"

Freka's eyes were like steel now, glinting dully in the light of the wall-torches.

"Not myself. Is that what you feared?" The fine mouth curled scornfully. "I ask no man to lay down his life so that *I* may take for myself the Great Throne and the sable mantle of Emperor! I renounce here and now any claim to the Imperial Crown! When the time is right, I will make my wishes known."

The crowd of star-kings murmured approvingly. Freka had won them.

"A vote!" someone cried. "Those who are with Freka and against Toran! A vote!"

Swords leaped from scabbards and glittered in the torchlight while the chamber rang to a savage cheer. Here was war and loot to satisfy the savage heart! The sack of Imperial Earth herself! Even old Eric of Doorn's sword was reluctantly raised. Kieron alone remained silent, sword sheathed.

Freka looked down at him coldly.

"Well, Valkyr? Do you ride with us?"

"I need more time to consider," said Kieron carefully.

Freka's laughter was like a lash. "Time! Time to worry about risking his skin! Valkyr needs time!"

Kieron felt his quick anger surging. The blood pounded in his temples, throbbing, pulsing, goading him to fight. His hand closed on the hilt of his sword and it slipped half out of the sheath. But Kieron caught himself. There was something sinister in this deliberate attempt to ruin him —to brand him a coward before his peers. A man faced two choices here, apparently; follow Freka into rebellion, or be branded craven. Kieron glared into the cold eyes of the Kalgan lord. The temptation to challenge him was strong—as strong as Kieron's whole background and training in the harsh warrior-code of the Edge. But he could not. Not yet. There were too many irons in the fire to be watched. There was Alys and her plea to Toran. There was the plight of his people. He could not risk the danger to himself of driving a blade through Freka's throat, no matter how his blood boiled with rage.

He turned on his heel and strode from the Great Hall, the laughter of Freka and the star-kings ringing mockingly in his ears.

# IV

Kieron awoke in darkness. Of the fire on the hearth, only embers remained and the stone rooms were silent but for the sound of sleeping men. The single Valkyr sentry was at his elbow, whispering him into wakefulness. Kieron threw back the fur coverlets and swung his feet over the edge of the low couch.

"What is it?" he asked.

"Nevitta, sir."

"Nevitta! Here?" Kieron sprang to his feet, fully awake now. "Is there a woman with him?"

"A slave-girl, sir. They wait in the outer chamber."

Kieron reached for his harness and weapons, threading his way through his sleeping men. In the dimly lit antechamber, Nevitta stood near the muffled figure of Alys. Kieron went immediately to the girl, and she threw back her hood, baring her golden head to the torchlight. Her eyes were bright with the pleasure of seeing Kieron again, but there was anger in them, too. The lord of Valkyr knew at once that she had not succeeded with Toran.

"What happened, Nevitta?"

"An attempt was made on the little princess' life, sir."

"*What?*" Kieron felt the blood drain from his face.

"As I say, Kieron." The old Valkyr's face was grim. "We had to fight our way out of the Palace."

"I never had a chance to speak to Toran," the girl said sombrely. "It was all that could be done to reach the spaceship. Even the Janizaries tried to stop us. Two of your men died for me, Kieron."

"Who did this thing?" asked Kieron ominously.

"The men who attacked the princess' quarters," said Nevitta deliberately, "wore the harness of Kalgan."

That hit Kieron like a physical blow . . . hard. *"Kalgan!* And you brought her *here?* You fool, Nevitta!"

The old Valkyr nodded agreement. "Yes, Kieron. Fool is the proper word . . ."

"No!" Alys spoke up imperiously. "It was my command that brought us here. I insisted."

"By the Seven Hells! Why?" demanded Kieron. "Why here? You could have been safe on Valkyr! I know it was my order to bring you here, but after what happened . . ."

"The princess would not hear of seeking safety, Kieron," said Nevitta. "When Kalgan proved its treachery by trying to assassinate her, she could think only of your danger here . . . unwarned. She would risk her life to bring you this news, Kieron."

Kieron turned to face the girl. She looked up at him, eyes bright, lips parted.

"What could make a princess risk her life . . ." Kieron began numbly.

"Kieron . . ." The girl breathed his name softly. "I was so afraid for you."

The Valkyr reached slowly for the clasp of her cloak and unfastened it. The heavy mantle dropped unnoticed to the flagstones. Alys stood, swaying slightly, parted lips inviting. Kieron watched the throbbing pulse in her white throat and felt his own pounding. He took a step toward her, his arms closing about her yielding suppleness. His mouth sought her lips.

Unnoticed, Nevitta slipped from the antechamber and silently closed the door after him . . .

Kieron stood before the arched window, staring out into the eternal, misty dusk of Kalgan, his heart heavy. Behind him, Alys lay on the low couch. Her bright hair lay in tumbled profusion about her face as she watched her lover at the window. Kieron turned to look at her, feeling the impact of her warm beauty. He began to pace the floor, wracking his brains for a lead to his next move in the subtle war of treachery and intrigue that had taken shape around him.

He had ordered his men ready for attack, but for the moment there was little need for that kind of vigilance. What was needed was more information. Carefully, he marshalled what few facts he had at his disposal.

The connection between Freka and the plotters in the Imperial City which he had suspected was proved at last by the attempt on Alys' life by men of Kalgan. The star-kings were being used to fight a battle not their own. But whose? Freka's . . . or Ivane's? No matter which, they were being tricked into striking the Imperial Crown from Toran's head, and the gain to them and their people would be—more oppression.

The treatment he himself had received in the Imperial Court made sense now. Landor sought to drive him into the arms of Freka's revolt. Only Alys had spared him.

Now, the star-kings must be warned. But by the code of the Edge, Kieron must prove to them that he was not the craven coward that Freka's laughter had branded him. And he needed *proof*. Proof of the monstrous structure of treachery and intrigue that had sprung up out of a woman's cupidity and an unknown star-king's cold inhumanity.

Kieron stared moodily down into the damp courtyard beneath the open window. In the early dawn it was deserted. Then, quite suddenly, there was activity in the walled-in square. An officer of the Citadel guard escorted a heavily cloaked figure into the yard, and with every evidence of great respect, withdrew. The solitary figure paced the wet cobbles nervously.

Who, wondered Kieron, would be treated with such obvious obsequiousness and yet left in a back courtyard to await the summons of Freka of Kalgan? A sudden thought struck him. It could be only someone who should not be seen by the star-kings and their attendants that filled the Citadel of Neg to overflowing.

Kieron studied the cloaked nobleman with renewed interest. It seemed to him that he had seen that mincing walk before . . .

*Landor!*

Kieron flung open the door to the outer chamber. His startled men gathered about him. Alys was on her feet behind him. He signalled for Nevitta and four men to enter.

"Nevitta! Tear down that wall tapestry and cut it into shreds . . . Alys, tie the strips together and make a rope of it! Make certain the knots are secure enough to bear a man's weight . . . That's Landor down there!"

Kicking off his spurred boots, Kieron eased himself over the ledge of the window. The courtyard was thirty feet below, but the ancient walls of the Citadel were rough and full of the ornate projections of Interregnal architecture. Kieron let himself down, feeling the mist wet on his face. Twice he almost lost his footing and pitched to the courtyard floor. Alys stared down at him from the window, whitefaced.

He was ten feet from the bottom when Landor looked up. Recognition was instant. There was a moment of stunned silence, and Kieron dropped the remaining distance to land cat-like on his feet, blade in hand.

"Kieron!" Landor's face was grey.

The Valkyr advanced purposefully. "Yes, Landor! Kieron! I wasn't supposed to see you here, was I? And you don't dare raise an outcry or the others will see you, too! That would raise quite a smell in the Consort's pretty brew, wouldn't it?"

Landor shrank back, away from the gleaming blade in Kieron's hand.

"Draw, Landor," said Kieron softly. "Draw now, or I'll kill you where you stand."

In a panic, the First Lord of Space drew his sword. He knew himself to be no match for the Valkyr star-king, and at the first touch of blades, he turned and fled for the gate. He banged hard against the heavy panels. The gate was locked. Kieron followed him deliberately.

"Cry for help, Landor," Kieron suggested with a short, hard laugh. "The place is full of fighting-men."

Landor was wide-eyed. "Why do you want to kill me, Kieron," he cried hoarsely; "what have I done to you . . . ?"

"You've taxed my people and insulted me, and if that were not enough there would still be your treachery with Freka—tricking me and the others into rebellion so that Ivane can seize the crown! That's more than enough reason to kill you. Besides . . ." Kieron smiled grimly, "I just don't like you, Landor. I'd enjoy spilling some of your milky blood."

"Kieron! I swear, Kieron . . ."

"Save it, dancing master!" Kieron touched Landor's loosely held weapon with his own. "Guard yourself!"

Landor uttered an animal cry of desperation and lunged clumsily at the Valkyr. Kieron's sword made a glittering encirclement and the First Lord's weapon clattered on the cobblestones twenty feet away.

Kieron's eyes were cold as he advanced on the now thoroughly terrorized courtier. "Kneel down, Landor. A lackey should always die on his knees."

The First Lord threw himself to the cobbles, his arms around the outworlder's knees. He was grey with fright and babbling for mercy, his eyes tightly shut. Kieron reversed his sword and brought the heavy hilt down sharply on Landor's head. The courtier sighed and pitched forward. Kieron sheathed his weapon and picked the unconscious man up like a sack of meal. Time was short. The guards would be returning to escort Landor to Freka. Kieron picked up the courtier's fallen sword. There must be no sign of struggle in the courtyard.

The Valkyr carried Landor over to where Alys and Nevitta had lowered their improvised rope. He trussed Landor up like a butchered boar and called to them. "Haul him up!"

Landor disappeared into the window and the rope came down again. Kieron climbed hand over hand after the vanished courtier. Within seconds he stood among his warriors again, and the courtyard was empty.

"Landor!" Kieron splashed wine in the unconscious man's face. "Landor, wake up!"

The courtier stirred and opened his eyes. Immediately they filmed with fear. A hostile circle of faces looked down at him. Kieron, his dark eyes flaming. Alys . . . the great red face of Nevitta, framed by the winged helmet . . . other savage looking Valkyrs. It was to Landor a scene from the legendary Seventh Hell of the Great Destroyer.

"If you want to live, talk," said Kieron. "What are you doing here on Kalgan? It must be a message of importance you carry. Ivane would have sent someone else if it weren't."

"I . . . I carry no message, Kieron."

Kieron nodded to Nevitta who drew his dagger and placed it against Landor's throat.

"We have no time for lies, Landor," said Kieron.

To emphasize the point, Nevitta pressed the blade tighter against the pulse in the First Lord's neck. Landor screamed.

"Don't . . . !"

"Talk—or I'll cut the gizzard out of you!" Nevitta growled.

"All right! All right! But take the knife away . . . !"

"Ivane sent you here."

Landor nodded soundlessly.

"Why?"

"I . . . I . . . was to tell Freka that . . . that his men failed to . . . to . . ."

"To kill me!" finished Alys angrily. "What else?"

189

"I . . . was also to tell him that the rest of the plan was . . . was . . . carried out . . . successfully."

"Damn you, don't talk in riddles!" Kieron said. "What 'plan'?"

"The Emperor is dead," Landor blurted, eyes wild with terror. "But not by my hand! I swear it! Not by my hand!"

Alys choked back a cry of pain.

"Toran! Poor . . . Toran . . ."

Kieron took the terrified courtier by the throat and shook him.

"You filthy swine! Who did it? *Who killed the Emperor?*"

"*Ivane!*" gasped Landor. "The people do not know he is dead and she awaits the star-king's invasion to proclaim herself Empress! . . . In the god's name, Kieron, don't kill me! I speak the truth!"

"Freka helped plan this?" demanded Kieron.

"He is Ivane's man," stammered Landor, "but I know nothing of him! Nothing, Kieron! The warlock Geller brought him to Ivane five years ago . . . that is all I know!"

Geller of the Marshes . . . again. Kieron felt the awful dread seeping through his anger. Somehow the connection between Geller and Freka must be discovered. Somehow . . . !

Kieron turned away from the terrified Landor. The picture was shaping now. Freka and Ivane. The star-king's rebellion. Toran . . . murdered.

"Keep this hound under guard!" ordered Kieron.

Landor was led away, shaken and weak.

"Nevitta!"

"Sir?"

"You and the princess will go back to the ship as you came. She must be taken to safety at once. As soon as that pig is missed, we'll have visitors . . ."

"No, Kieron! I won't go!" cried Alys.

"You must. If you are captured on Kalgan now it will mean a *carte blanche* for Ivane."

"But then you must come!"

"I can't. If I tried to leave here now, Freka would detain me by force. I know his plans." He turned again to

190

ing like a black flame just beyond his range of vision. He saw Freka again and tried to reach him. Again he failed, blocked by a Kalgan soldier. A thrown sword whistled past him and imbedded itself in the last Valkyr's chest. The man sank to the floor in silence, and Kieron fought alone.

He saw the blade of an officer descending, but he could not ward it off. And as it fell, a great hissing roar sounded beyond the open window. Kieron almost smiled. Alys was safe . . .

He lifted his sword to parry the descending stroke. Weakened, the best he could do was deflect it slightly. The blade caught him a glancing blow on the side of the head and he staggered to his knees. He tried to raise his weapon again . . . tried to fight on . . . but he could not. Slowly, reluctantly, he sank to the floor as darkness welled up out of the bloody flagstones to engulf him . . .

# V

Kieron stirred, the pulsing ache in his side piercing the reddish veil of unconsciousness. Under him, he could feel wet stones that stank of death and filth. He moved painfully, and the throbbing agony grew worse, making him teeter precariously between consciousness and the dark.

He was stiff and cold. Hurt badly, too, he thought vaguely. His wounds had not been tended. Very carefully, he opened his eyes. They told him what he had already known. He was in a dark cell, filthy and damp. A sick chill shook him. Teeth chattering, huddled on the stone floor, Kieron sank again into unconsciousness.

When he awoke again, he was burning with fever and a cold bowl of solidified, greasy gruel lay beside him. His tongue felt thick and swollen, but the sharp agony of his wounded side had subsided to a dull hurt. With a great effort, he dragged himself into a corner of the dungeon and propped himself up facing the iron-bound door.

His searching hands found that he had been stripped of his harness and weapons. He was naked, smeared with filth and dried blood. As he moved he felt a renewed flow of warmth flooding down from his torn flank. The wound

Nevitta. "She goes with you, Nevitta. By force if necessary.

"Return to Valkyr and gather the tribes. We can do nothing without men at our backs. One of the ships will remain here with me and the men. We will try to get clear after we are certain that—" He looked over at the slim girl, his eyes sombre—"that Her Majesty is safe."

The Valkyr warriors in the room straightened, a subtle change in their expression as they watched Alys. A gulf had suddenly opened between this girl and their chieftain. They felt it too. One by one they dropped to their knees before her. Alys made a protesting gesture, her eyes bright with tears. She saw the chasm opening, and fought it futilely. But when Kieron, too, went to his knees, she knew it was so. In one fleeting moment, they had changed from lover and beloved to sovereign and vassal.

She forced back the tears and raised her head proudly; as Galactic Empress, Heiress to the Thousand Emperors, she accepted the homage of her fighting men.

"My lord of Valkyr," she said in a low, unsteady voice. "My love and affection for you—and these warriors will never be forgotten. If we live . . ."

Kieron rose to his full height, naked sword extended in his hands.

"Your Imperial Majesty," he spoke the words formally and slowly, regretting what was gone. "The men of Valkyr are yours. To the death."

Kieron watched Nevitta and Alys vanish down the long, gloomy hall outside the Valkyr chambers—to all appearances a warrior chieftain and his slave-girl ordered away by their master. Even then, thought Kieron bleakly, there was danger. He saw them pass one sentry, two . . . three . . . They turned the corner and were gone, Kieron's hopes and fears riding with them.

Already, there were sounds of confusion in the Citadel of Neg. Men were searching for the vanished Landor. Searching quietly, reflected Kieron with grim satisfaction, for the visiting star-kings must not know that Freka the Unknown held familiar audience with the Imperial First Lord of Space. Spur of the moment hunting parties and entertainments were keeping the visitors occupied while the Kalgan soldiery searched.

Kieron weighed his chances of escape and found them small indeed. They dared not stir from their quarters in the Citadel until the roar of Nevitta's spaceship told that the Empress was safely away. And meanwhile, the search for Landor drew nearer.

An hour passed, the sand in the glass running with agonizing slowness. Once Kieron thought he heard the beat of hooves on the drawbridge of the Citadel, but he could not be certain.

Two hours. Kieron paced the floor of the Valkyr chambers, his twelve remaining warriors armed, alert, watching him. Nervously he fingered the hilt of his sword.

Another hour in the grey, eternal twilight. Still no sound of a spaceship rising. Kieron's anxiety grew to gargantuan proportions. The search for Landor came closer steadily. Kieron could hear the soldiers tramping the stone corridors and causeways of the Citadel.

Suddenly there was a knock at the barred door to the Valkyrs' quarters.

"Open! In the name of the lord of Kalgan!"

A Valkyr near the door replied languidly. "Our master sleeps. Go away."

The knocking continued. "It is regretted that we must disturb him, but a slave of the household has escaped. We must search for him."

"Would you disturb the Warlord of Valkyr's repose for a slave, barbarians?" demanded the warrior at the door in a hurt tone of voice. "Go away."

The officer in the hallway was beginning to lose patience.

"Open, I say! Or we'll break in!"

"Do," offered the Valkyr pleasantly. "I have a sword that has been too long dry."

How Landor must be sweating in that back room, Kieron thought wryly, thinking that the Valkyrs would rather kill him than let his message reach Freka. But Landor's death would serve no useful purpose now. Time! Time was needed. Time enough to let Nevitta get Alys out of danger!

Kieron stepped to the door, hoping that some warriors of the Outer Marches might possibly be within earshot and catch the implication of his words. "Kieron of Valkyr speaks!" he cried. "We have Landor of Earth here! Landor, the First Lord—is *that* the slave you seek?"

But the only response was the sudden crash of a ram against the panels of the wooden door. Kieron prepared to fight. Still, no sound of a spaceship rising . . .

The door collapsed, and a flood of Kalgan warriors poured into the room, weapons flashing.

Savagely, the Valkyrs closed with them, and the air rang with the metallic clash of steel. No mercy was asked and none was given. Kieron cut a circle of death with his long, out-world weapon, the fighting blood of a hundred generations of warriors singing in his ears. The savage chant of the Edge rose above the confused sounds of battle. A man screamed in agony as his arm was severed by a blow from a Valkyr blade, and he waved the stump desperately, spattering the milling men with dark blood. A Valkyr warrior went down, locked in a death-embrace with a Kalgan warrior, driving his dagger into his enemy again and again even as he died. Kieron crossed swords with a guardsman, forcing him backward until the Kalgan slipped on the flagstones made slippery with blood and went down with a sword-cut from throat to groin.

The Valkyrs were cutting down their opponents, but numbers were beginning to tell. Two Valkyrs went down before fresh onslaughts. Another, and another, and still another. Kieron felt the burning touch of a dagger wound. He looked down and saw that a thrust from someone in the *melee* had slashed him to the bone. His side was slick with blood and the white ribs showed along the ten inch gash.

Now, Kieron stood back to back with his two remaining companions. The other Valkyrs were down, lying still on the bloody floor. Kieron caught a glimpse of Freka's tall figure behind his guardsman and he lunged for him, suddenly blind with fury. Two Kalgan guards engaged him, and he lost sight of Freka. A Valkyr went down with a thrust in the belly. Kieron took another wound in the arm. He could not tell how badly hurt he was, but faintness from the loss of blood was telling on him. It was getting hard to see clearly. Darkness seemed to be flicker-

had reopened. Sweat was streaking the caked blood on his cheek. His mind wandered in a feverish delirium—a nightmare dream in which the tall, coldly arrogant figure of Freka seemed to fill all space and all time. Kieron's over-bright eyes glittered with animal hate. . . .

Somehow, he felt that the hated Kalgan was nearby. He tried to keep his eyes open, but the lids seemed weighted. His head sagged and the fever took him again into the ebony darkness of some fantastic intergalactic night where wierd shapes danced and whirled in hideous joyousness . . .

The rattling of the door-lock woke him. It might have been minutes later or days. Kieron had no way of knowing. He felt light-headed and giddy. He watched the door open with fever-bright eyes. A jailer carrying a flambeau entered and the light blinded Kieron. He shielded his face with his hand. There was a voice speaking to him. A voice he knew . . . and hated. With a shuddering effort, he took a grip on his staggering mind, his hate sustaining him now. Moving his hands away from his face, he looked up— into the icy eyes of Freka the Unknown.

"So you're awake at last," the Kalgan said.

Kieron made no reply. He could feel the fury burning deep inside him.

Freka held a jewelled dagger in his hands, toying with it idly. Kieron watched the shards of light leaping from the faceted gems in the liquid torchlight. The slender blade shimmered, blue and silvery in the Kalgan's hands.

"I have been told that the Lady Alys was with you— here on Kalgan. Is this true?"

Alys . . . Kieron thought vaguely of her for a moment, but somehow the picture brought sadness. He put her out of his mind and squinted up at Freka's gemmed dagger, unable to take his eyes from the glittering weapon.

"Can you speak?" demanded Freka. "Was Toran's sister with you?"

Kieron watched the weapon, a feral brillance growing like a flame in his dark eyes.

Freka shrugged. "Very well, Kieron. It makes no difference. Does it interest you to know that the armies are gathering? Earth will be ours within four weeks." His voice was cold, unemotional. "You realize, of course, that you cannot be allowed to live."

Kieron said nothing. Very carefully he gathered his strength. The dagger . . . the dagger . . . !

"I will not risk war with Valkyr by killing you now. But you will be tried by a council of star-kings on Earth when we have done what we must do . . ."

Kieron stared hard at the slender weapon, his hate pounding in his fevered mind. He drew a deep, shuddering breath. Freka spun the blade idly, setting the jewels afire.

"We should have taken you the moment Landor was missed," mused the Kalgan. "But . . . it really doesn't matter now . . ."

Kieron's taut muscles uncoiled in a snakelike, lashing movement. He hit Freka below the knees with all his fevered strength and the Kalgan went down without a sound, the slim dagger clattering on the slimy floor of the cell. The guard leaped forward. Kieron's searching hand closed about the hilt of the dagger. With a sound of pure animal rage in his throat he drove it into Freka's unprotected chest. Twice again his hand rose and fell, and then the guard caught him full in the face with a booted foot and the light of the torch faded again into inky blackness . . .

In the darkness, time lost its meaning. Kieron woke a dozen times, feeling the dull throbbing ache of his wounds and then fading again into unconsciousness. He ate—or was fed—enough to keep him alive, but he had no memory of it. He floated in a red-tinged sea of black, unreal, frightening. He screamed or sobbed as the phantasms of his sick dreams dictated, but through it all ran a single thread of elation. Freka, the hated one, was dead. No horror of nightmare or delirium could strip him of that one grip on life. Freka was dead. He remembered vaguely the feel of the dagger plunging again and again into his tormentor's breast. Sometimes he even forgot why he had hated Freka, but he clung to the knowledge that he had killed him the way a drowning man clings to the last suffocating breath.

Sounds filtered into Kieron's dungeon. Sounds that were familiar. The hissing roar of spaceships. Then later the awful susurration of mob sounds. Kieron lay sprawled on the stones of his cell-floor, not hearing, lost in the fantasmagoric stupor of delirium. His wounds still untended, only the magnificent body of a warrior helped him cling to the thread of life.

Other sounds came. The crash of rams and the clatter of falling masonry. The shrieks of men and women dying. The ringing cacophony of weapons and the curses of fighting men. Hours passed and the din grew louder, closer, in the heart of the Citadel of Neg itself. The torches on the outer cellblocks guttered out and were left untended. The sounds of fighting rose to a wild pitch, interlaced with the inhuman, animal sounds of a mob gone mad.

At last Kieron stirred, some of the familiar sounds of battle striking buried chords in his fevered mind. He listened to the advancing clash of weapons until it rang just beyond his dungeon door.

He dragged himself into his corner again and crouched there, the feral light in his eyes brilliant now. His hands itched for killing. He flexed the fingers painfully and waited.

The silence was sudden and as complete as the hush of the tomb.

Kieron waited.

The door flung wide, and men bearing torches rushed into the cell. Kieron lunged savagely for the first one, hands seeking a throat.

*"Kieron!"* Nevitta threw himself backward violently. Kieron clung to him, his face a fevered mask of hate. "Kieron! It is I . . . Nevitta!"

Kieron's hands fell away from the old warrior and he stood swaying, squinting against the light of the torches. "Nevitta . . . Nevitta?"

A wild laugh came from the prisoner's cracked lips. He looked about him, into the strained faces of his own fighting men.

He took one step and pitched forward into the arms of Nevitta, who carried him like a child up into the light, tears streaking his grizzled cheeks . . .

For three weeks Alys and Nevitta nursed Kieron, sucking the poison of his untended wounds with their mouths and bathing him to break the fiery grip of the fever. At last

197

they won. Kieron opened his eyes—and they were sane and clear.

"How long?" Kieron asked faintly.

"We were gone from Kalgan twenty days . . . you have lain here twenty-one," Alys said thankfully.

"Why did you come back here?" Kieron demanded bitterly. "You have lost an Empire!"

"We came for you, Kieron," Nevitta said. "For our king."

"But . . . Alys . . ." Kieron protested.

"I would not have the Great Throne, Kieron," said Alys, "if it meant leaving you to rot in a cell!"

Kieron turned his face to the wall. Because of him, the star-kings fought Ivane's battle. And by now they would have won. The only thing that had been done was the killing of the treacherous Freka. He held Kalgan now, for the Valkyrs had returned seeking their Warlord after Freka's plan had stripped the planet of fighting men—and the mobs had done the Valkyr's work for them. But two worlds were not an Empire of stars. Alys had been cheated. Because of him.

No! thought Kieron, by the Seven Hells, no! They could not be defeated so easily. There were five thousand warriors with him now. If need be, he would fight the Imperium's massed forces to win Alys' rightful place on the throne of Gilmer of Kaidor!

"Let me up," Kieron demanded. "If we hit them on Earth before they have a chance to consolidate, there's still a chance!"

"There is no hurry, Kieron," said Nevitta holding him in the bed with a great hand. "Freka and the star-kings have already . . ."

"Freka!" Kieron sat bolt upright.

"Why, yes . . ." murmured Nevitta in perplexity. "Freka."

"That's impossible!"

"We have had information from the Imperial City, Kieron. Freka is there," said Alys.

Kieron sank back on the pillows. Had he dreamed killing the Kalgan? No! It wasn't possible! He had driven the blade into his chest three times . . . driven it deep.

With an effort he rose from the bed. "Order my charger, Nevitta!"

"But sir!"

"Quickly, Nevitta! There is no time!"

Nevitta saluted reluctantly and withdrew.

"Help me with my harness, Alys," ordered Kieron forgetful of majesty.

"Kieron, you can't ride!"

"I have to ride, Alys. Listen to me. I drove a dagger into Freka three times . . . and he has not died! One man can tell us why, and we must know. *That man is Geller of the Marshes!*"

Neg was a shambles. The advent of the Valkyrs had been a signal for the brutish population to go mad. Mobs had thronged the streets, smashing, killing and looting. The few Kalgan warriors left behind to guard the city had had to aid the Valkyrs in restoring order. It seemed to Kieron, as he rode along the now sullenly silent streets, that Kalgan and Neg had been deliberately abandoned as having served a purpose. If Freka still lived, as they said, then he was something unique among men, and not meant for so unimportant a world as Kalgan.

Shops and houses had been gutted by fire. Goods of all kinds were strewn about the streets, and here and there a body—twisted and dismembered—awaited the harassed burial detachments that roamed the shattered megalopolis.

Kieron and Alys rode slowly toward the marshy slums of the lower city, Nevitta following them at a short distance. The three war horses, creatures bred to war and destruction, paced along easily, flaring nostrils taking in the familiar smells of a ruined city.

Along the street of the Black Flames there was nothing left standing whole. Every hovel, every tenement had been gutted and looted by the mobs. Presently, Kieron drew rein before a shuttered shanty between two structures of fire-blackened stone.

Nevitta rode up with a protest. "Why do you seek this beloved of demons, Kieron?" he asked fearfully. "No good can come of this!"

Kieron stared at the shanty. It stared back at him with

veiled ghoulish eyes. The writhing mists shrouded the grey
street in the eternal twilight of Kalgan. Kieron felt his
hands trembling on the reins. This was the lair of the warlock.

The stench of the marshes was thick and now the mists
turned to soft rain. Kieron dismounted.

"Wait for me here," he ordered Nevitta and Alys.

With pounding heart, he drew his sword and started
for the door that gaped like the black mouth of a plague
victim. Alys touched his elbow, disregarding his instructions. Her eyes were bright with fear, but she followed
him closely. Secretly glad of her companionship, Kieron
breathed a prayer to his Valkyr gods and stepped inside. . . .

The place was a wreck. Old books lay everywhere,
ripped and tattered. In a corner, someone had tried to
make a bonfire of a pile of manuscripts and broken furniture and had half succeeded.

"The mob has been here," Alys said succinctly.

Kieron led the way through the rubble toward the door
of a back room. Carefully, he pushed it ajar with the
point of his blade. It creaked menacingly, revealing another chamber—one filled with strange machines and
twisted tubes of glass. Great black boxes stood along one
wall, coils of bright wire running into the jumbled mass of
shattered machines that dominated the center of the
room. The air of the cold, silent room had a strange and
unpleasant tang. The smell, thought the Valkyr, of the
Great Destroyer!

The tip of his sword touched one of the bright copper
coils springing from the row of black boxes along the wall,
and a tiny blue spark leaped up the blade. Kieron yanked
his weapon away, his heart racing wildly. A thin curl of
smoke hung in the air, and the steel of the blade was
pitted. Kieron fought down the urge to run in terror.

"I'm afraid, Kieron!" whispered Alys, clinging to him.

Kieron took her hand and moved cautiously around the
pile of broken machinery. He found Geller then, and tried
to stop Alys from seeing.

"The Great Destroyer he served failed him," Kieron
said slowly.

The warlock was dead. The mob, terrified—and hating

what they could not understand—had killed him cruelly. The staring eyes mocked Kieron, the blackened tongue lolled stupidly out of the dry lips. Geller's mystery, thought Kieron, was still safe with him. . . .

On the way out, Kieron stopped and picked up the remnants of a book of sigils. It was incredibly old, for the characters on the cover were those of the legendary First Empire. With some difficulty he made out the title.

" 'Perpetually Regenerating Warps and their Application in Interstellar Engines' . . . ."

The words meant nothing to him. He dropped the magic book and picked up two others. This time his eyes widened.

"What is it, Kieron?" Alys asked fearfully.

"Long ago," Kieron said thoughtfully, "on Valkyr, it was said that the ancients of the First Empire were familiar with the secrets of the Great Destroyer . . ."

"That's true. That is why the Interregnum came, and the dark ages," said Alys.

"I wonder," mused Kieron looking at the books. "What was this Geller known best for?"

Alys shuddered. "For his homunculi."

"The ancients, it is said, knew many things. Even how to make . . . artificial servants. Robots, they were called." He handed her the book. "Can you read this ancient script?"

Alys read aloud, her voice unsteady.

" 'First Principles of Robotics.' "

"And this one?"

" 'Incubation and Gestation of Androids' . . . !"

Kieron of Valkyr stood in the silent, wrecked laboratory of the dead warlock Geller, his medieval mind trying to break free of the bondage of a millennium of superstition and ignorance. He understood now . . . many things.

# VI

Like great silver fish leaping up into the bowl of night, the ships of the Valkyr fleet rose from Kalgan. Within the pulsing hulls five thousand warriors rode, ready for battle. Against the mighty forces of the assembled star-kings, the army of Valkyr counted for almost nothing; but the savage fighting men of the Edge carried with them their talisman—Alys Imperatrix, uncrowned sovereign of the Galaxy, Heiress to the Thousand Emperors—the daughter of their beloved warrior-prince, Gilmer, conqueror of Kaidor.

In the lead vessel, Nevitta dogged the harried Navigators, urging greater speed. Below decks, the war chargers snorted and stomped the steel decks, sensing the tension of the coming clash in the close, smoky air of the spaceships.

Kieron stood beside the forward port with Alys, looking out into the strangely distorted night of space. As speed increased, the stars vanished and the night that pressed against the flanks of the hurtling ship grew grey and unsteady. Still velocity climbed, and then beyond the great curving glass screen there was nothing. Not blackness, or emptiness. A soul-chilling nothingness that twisted the mind and refused to be accepted by human eyes. Hyperspace.

Kieron drew the draperies closed and the observation lounge of the huge ancient liner grew dim and warm.

"What's ahead, Kieron?" the girl asked with a sigh. "More fighting and killing?"

The Valkyr shook his head. "Your Imperium, Your Majesty," he said formally, "a crown of stars that a thousand generations have gathered for you. That lies ahead."

"Oh, Kieron! Can't you forget the Empire for the space of an hour?" Alys demanded angrily.

The Warlord of Valkyr looked at his Empress in perplexity. There were times when women were hard to fathom.

"Forget it, I say!" the girl cried, her eyes suddenly flaming.

"If Your Majesty wishes, I'll not speak of it again," said Kieron stiffly.

Alys took a step toward him. "There was a time when you looked at me as a woman. When you *thought* of me as a woman! Am I so different now?"

Kieron studied her slim body and sensuously patrician face. "There was a time when I thought of you as a child, too. Those times pass. You are now my Empress. I am

202

your vassal. Command me. I'll fight for you. Die for you, if need be. Anything. But by the Seven Hells, Alys, don't torture me with favors I can't claim!"

"So I must command then?" She stamped her foot angrily. "Very well, I command you, Valkyr!"

"Lady, I'll never be a Consort!"

The girl's face flushed. "Did I ask it? I know I can't make a lapdog out of you, Kieron."

"Stop it, Alys," Kieron muttered heavily.

"Kieron," she said softly, "I've loved you since I was a child. I love you now. Does that mean nothing to you?"

"Everything, Alys." Lust rose as he felt the tensions in her.

"Then for the space of this voyage, Kieron, forget the Empire. Forget everything except that I love you. Take what I offer you. There is no Empress here . . ."

The silver fleet speared down into the atmosphere of the mother planet. Earth lay beneath them like a globe of azure. The spaceships fanned out into a wedge as they split the thin cold air high above the sprawling megalopolis of the Imperial City.

The capital lay ringed about with the somnolent shapes of the star-kings' great armada. Somewhere down there, Kieron knew, Freka waited. Freka the Unknown. The unkillable? Kieron wondered. For weapons he had his sword and a little knowledge. He prayed it would be enough. It had to be. Five thousand warriors could not defeat the assembled might of the star-kings.

Shunning the spaceport, Kieron led his fleet to a landing on the grassy esplanade that surrounded the city. As the hurried debarkation of men and horses began, Kieron could see a cavalry force massing before the gates to oppose them. He cursed and urged his men to greater speed. Horses reared and neighed; weapons glinted in the late afternoon sunlight.

Within the hour the debarkation was complete, and Kieron sat armed and mounted before the serried ranks of his warriors. The afternoon was filled with the flash of steel and the blazing glory of gonfalons as he ordered his ranks for battle . . . a battle that he hoped with all his heart to avoid.

Across the plain, the Valkyr could make out the pennon of Doorn in the first rank of the advancing defenders. Kieron ordered Nevitta to stay by the Empress in the rear ranks and to escort her forward with all ceremony if he called for her.

Alys rode a white charger and had clad herself in the panoply of a Valkyr warrior maid. Her hips were girded in a harness of linked steel plates, her long legs free to ride astride. Over her chest and breasts was laced a hauberk of chain mail that shimmered in the slanting sunlight. On her head a Valkyr's winged helmet—and from under it her golden hair fell in cascades of light to her shoulders. A silver cloak stood out behind her as she galloped past the ranks of Valkyrs, and they cheered her as she went. Kieron, watching her, thought she resembled the ancient war-goddess of his own world—imperious, regal.

With a cry, Kieron ordered his riders forward and the glittering ranks swept forward across the esplanade like a turbulent wave, spear-heads agleam, gonfalons fluttering. He rode far ahead, seeking a meeting with old Eric of Doorn, his father's friend.

He signalled, and the two surging masses of warriors slowed as the two star-kings rode to a meeting between the armies. Kieron raised an open right hand in the sign of truce and old Eric did likewise. Their caparisoned chargers tossed their heads angrily at being restrained and eyed each other with white-rimmed eyes.

Kieron drew rein, facing the old star-king.

"I greet you," he said formally.

"Do you come in friendship, or in war?" asked Eric.

"That will depend on the Empress," Kieron replied.

The lord of Doorn smiled, and there was scorn on his face. He was remembering Kalgan and Kieron's reluctance. "You will be pleased to know, then, that the Imperial Ivane bids you enter her city in peace—so that you may do her homage and throw yourself on her mercy for your crimes against Kalgan."

Kieron gave a short, steely laugh. So Ivane had already learned of the Valkyr sack of Kalgan. "I do not know any 'Imperial Ivane,' Eric," he said coldly. "When I spoke of the Empress, I meant the true Empress, Alys, the daugh-

204

ter of your lord and mine, Gilmer of Kaidor." He signalled Alys and Nevitta forward.

The gonfalons of the Valkyr line dipped in salute as Alys trotted through the ranks. She drew rein, facing the amazed Eric.

"Noble lady!" he gasped. "We were told you were dead!"

"And so I might have been, had Ivane had her way!"

The old star-king stammered in confusion. There was more here than he could understand. Only a week before, he and the other star-kings had done homage to Ivane and hailed her as their savior from the oppressions of the Emperor Toran, and the nearest living kin to the late Gilmer. And now . . . !

Eric frowned. "If we have been made fools, Freka must answer for this!"

"And now," asked Kieron grimly, "do we enter the city in peace or do we cut our way in?"

Eric signalled his men to swing in beside the ranked Valkyrs and the whole mass of armed men moved through the fading afternoon toward the gates of the Imperial City.

It was dusk by the time the cavalcade reached the walls of the Imperial Palace. Kieron called a halt and ordered his men to rest on their arms. Taking only Nevitta and Alys with him, he joined Eric of Doorn in challenging the Janizaries of the Palace Guard.

They were passed by the stolid Pleiadenes without comment, for the lord of Doorn was known as a vassal of the Imperial Ivane. Faces set, the small party strode up the wide curving stairway that led into the Hall of the Great Throne. The courtiers had been warned by the shouts of the people in the streets that something was happening, and they had already begun to gather in the Throne Room.

He had come a long way, thought Kieron, from the day when he had stood before the Throne begging an audience with Toran. Now, everything hung on his one chance to prove his case—and Alys'—to the assembled nobles.

Kieron noted with some concern that the Palace Guards

205

were gathering too. They covered each exit to the chamber, cutting off retreat.

By now, the Hall of the Great Throne was jammed with courtiers and star-kings, all tensely silent—waiting. Nor did they wait long.

With a blast of trumpets and a rolling of tympani, Ivane entered the Throne Room. Some of the courtiers knelt, but others stood in confusion, looking from Alys to Ivane and back again.

Kieron studied Ivane coldly. She was, he had to admit, a regal figure. A tall woman with hair the color of jet. A face that seemed chiseled out of marble. Dark, predatory eyes and a figure like a Dawn Age goddess. She stood before the Great Throne of the Empire, mantled in the sable robe of the Imperium—a robe as black as space and spangled with diamonds to resemble the stars of the Imperial Galaxy. On her head rested the irridium tiara of Imperatrix.

Ivane swept the Hall with a haughty stare that stung like a lash. When her eyes found Alys standing beside Kieron, they brightened, became feral.

"Guards!" she commanded. "Seize that woman! She is the killer of the Emperor Toran!"

A murmuring filled the chamber. The Janizaries pressed forward. Kieron drew his sword and leaped to the dais beside Ivane. She did not shrink back from him.

"Touch her, and Ivane dies!" shouted Kieron, his point at Ivane's naked breast. The murmuring subsided and the Janizaries pulled up short.

"Now, you are all going to listen to me!" shouted Kieron from the dais. "This woman under my blade is a murderess and plotter, and I can prove it!"

Ivane's face was strained and white. Not from fear of his sword, Kieron knew.

"In the Palace dungeons you will likely find Landor . . ." Kieron continued. "He will be there because he knew of Ivane's plottings and talked too much when he had a dagger at his throat. He will confirm what I say!

"This woman plotted to usurp the Imperium *as long as five years ago!* It may have been longer . . ." He turned to Ivane. "How long does it take to incubate an *android,* Ivane? A year? Two? And then to train him, school him so that every move he makes is intended to further your aims? How long does all that take?"

Ivane uttered a scream of terror now. "Freka! Call Freka!"

Kieron dropped his sword point and stepped away from Ivane as though she were contaminated. There was little danger from *her* now—but there was still another.

Freka appeared at the edge of the dais, his tall form towering above the courtiers. "You called for me, Imperial Ivane?"

Ivane stared at Kieron with hate-filled eyes. "You have failed me! *Kill him now!*"

Kieron whirled and caught Freka's blade on his own. The courtiers drew back, giving them room to fight. No one made a move to interfere. It was known that Valkyrs had sacked the city of Neg, and according to the warrior code the two warlords must be allowed to fight to the death if they wished.

Kieron made no attack. Instead he retreated before the expressionless Freka.

"Did you know, Freka," asked Kieron softly, "that Geller of the Marshes is dead? He was your father in a way, wasn't he?"

Freka made no reply, and for a moment the only sound in the hushed chamber was the ring of blades.

Suddenly Kieron lunged. His sword pierced Freka from breast to back. The Valkyr stepped back and pulled his blade clear. The crowd gasped, for Freka the Unknown did not fall . . .

"Are you really unkillable?" breathed Kieron. "I wonder!"

Again he lunged under the mechanical guard of the Kalgan. Again his blade sank deep. Freka backed away for a moment, still alert and unwounded.

Kieron shouted derisively at the star-kings: "Great warriors! Do you see? You have followed the leadership of an android! A homunculus spawned by the warlock Geller!"

A gasping roar went up in the chamber. A sound of superstitious horror and growing anger.

Kieron parried a thrust and brought his blade down on

207

Freka's sword arm. Hard. A sword clattered to the flag-stones—still gripped by a slowly relaxing hand. There was no blood. The android still moved in, eyes expressionless, his one hand reaching for his enemy. Kieron struck again. A clean cut opened from shoulder to belly, slicing the artificial tendons and leaving the android helpless but still erect. Kieron raised and lowered his blade in glittering arcs. Freka . . . or the thing that had been Freka . . . collapsed in a grotesque heap. Still it moved. Kieron passed his point again and again through the quivering mass until at long last it was still. Somewhere a woman fainted.

A thick silence fell over the assemblage. All eyes turned to Ivane. She stood staring at the remnants of the thing that had been . . . almost . . . a man. Her hand fluttered at her throat.

Alys' voice cut through the heavy stillness. "Arrest that woman for the murder of my brother Toran!"

But the crowd of courtiers was thinking of other things. Jaded and cynical, they had seen with their own eyes that Ivane was a familiar of the dreaded Great Destroyer. Someone cried: "Witch! Burn her!"

The mass of courtiers and warriors swept forward, screaming for the kill. Kieron leaped for the dais, his sword still bared.

"I'll kill the first one who sets foot on the Great Throne!" he cried.

But Ivane had heard the crowd sounds. The black mantle slipped from her shoulders, and she stood stripped to the waist, like a marble goddess—her eyes recapturing some of their icy hauteur. Then, before she could be stopped, she had taken a jewelled dagger and driven it deep into her breast.

Kieron caught her as she fell, feeling the warm blood staining his hands. He eased her down on the foot of the Great Throne and laid his ear to her breast.

There was no pulse. Ivane was dead.

Before the assembled Court, the Warlord of Valkyr knelt before his Empress. The star-kings had gone, and the Valkyrs were the last outworld warriors remaining in the Imperial City. Now, they too, would take their leave.

The Empress sat on the Great Throne, mantled in sable. Somehow, the huge throne and the vast vaulted chamber seemed to make her look small and frail.

"Your Imperial Majesty," said Kieron, "have we your leave to go?"

Alys' eyes were bright with tears. She leaned forward so that none but Kieron might hear. "Stay a while yet, Kieron. At least let us say our goodbyes alone and not . . ." She looked about the crowded Throne Room, ". . . not here."

Kieron shook his head mutely. Aloud, he said again, "Have I Your Majesty's permission to return to Valkyr?"

"Kieron . . .!" whispered Alys. "Please . . ."

He looked up at her once, pain in his eyes, but he did not speak.

Alys knew then that the gulf had opened between them again; that this time, it was for the rest of their lives. The tears came and streaked her cheeks as she lifted her head and spoke for all the Court to hear.

"Permission is granted, My Lord of Valkyr. You . . . you may return to Valkyr." And then she whispered, "And my love goes with you, Kieron!"

Kieron raised her jewelled hands to his lips and kissed them. . . . Then he arose and turned on his heel to stride swiftly from the Great Hall.

*The problems of inter-galactic sociology are incisively
extrapolated by Idris Seabright in this brief, yet comprehensive study of a culture uneasily propped up by
"bread and circuses." For all the luminous beauty of
her story-telling, it is a poignant picture that Miss
Seabright sketches—that of a once creative citizenry
using its triumphs to gratify no more than a lust for
vicarious blood-letting. You will, of course, be struck
by the parallel between this empire of the future and
that one of our not too remote past, the Roman. One
hopes no actual future culture will fail to heed the
lesson the Romans imperially ignored: even slaves
and gladiators are human and can love.*

•

# BRIGHTNESS FALLS FROM
# THE AIR
## by Idris Seabright

Kerr used to go into the tepidarium of the identification
bureau to practise singing. The tepidarium was a big
room, filled almost from wall to wall by the pool of glittering preservative, and he liked its acoustics. The bodies
of the bird people would drift a little back and forth in
the pellucid fluid as he sang, and he liked to look at them.
If the tepidarium was a little morbid as a place to prac-

tise singing, it was (Kerr used to think) no more morbid than the rest of the world in which he was living. When he had sung for as long as he thought good for his voice—he had no teacher—he would go to one of the windows and watch the luminous trails that meant the bird people were fighting again. The trails would float down slowly against the night sky as if they were made of star dust. But after Kerr met Rhysha, he stopped all that.

Rhysha came to the bureau one evening just as he was going on duty. She had come to claim a body. The bodies of the bird people often stayed in the bureau for a considerable time. Ordinary means of transportation were forbidden to the bird people because of their extra-terrestrial origin, and it was hard for them to get to the bureau to identify their dead. Rhysha made the identification—it was her brother—paid the bureau's fee from a worn purse, and indicated on the proper form the disposal she wanted made of the body. She was quiet and controlled in her grief. Kerr had watched the televised battles of the bird people once or twice, but this was the first time he had ever seen one of them alive and face to face. He looked at her with interest and curiosity, and then with wonder and delight.

The most striking thing about Rhysha was her glowing, deep turquoise plumage. It covered her from head to heels in what appeared to be a clinging velvet cloak. The colouring was so much more intense than that of the bodies in the tepidarium that Kerr would have thought she belonged to a different species than they.

Her face, under the golden top-knot, was quite human, and so were her slender, leaf-shaped hands; but there was a fantastic, light-boned grace in her movements such as no human being ever had. Her voice was low, with a 'cello's fullness of tone. Everything about her, Kerr thought, was rare and delightful and curious. But there was a shadow in her face, as if a natural gaiety had been repressed by the overwhelming harshness of circumstance.

"Where shall I have the ashes sent?" Kerr asked as he took the form.

She plucked indecisively at her pink lower lip. "I am not sure. The manager where we are staying has told us we must leave tonight, and I do not know where we will

211

go. Could I come back again to the bureau when the ashes are ready?"

It was against regulations, but Kerr nodded. He would keep the capsule of ashes in his locker until she came. It would be nice to see her again.

She came, weeks later, for the ashes. There had been several battles of the bird people in the interval, and the pool in the tepidarium was full. As Kerr looked at her, he wondered how long it would be before she too was dead.

He asked her new address. It was a fantastic distance away, in the worst part of the city, and after a little hesitation he told her that if she could wait until his shift was over he would be glad to walk back with her.

She looked at him doubtfully. "It is most kind of you, but—but an earthman was kind to us once. The children used to stone him."

Kerr had never thought much about the position of the non-human races in his world. If it was unjust, if they were badly treated he had thought it no more than a particular instance of the general cruelty and stupidity. Now anger flared up in him.

"That's all right," he said harshly. "If you don't mind waiting."

Rhysha smiled faintly. "No, I don't mind," she said.

Since there were still some hours to go on his shift, he took her into a small reception room where there was a chaise longue. "Try to sleep," he said.

A little before three he came to rouse her, and found her lying quiet but awake. They left the bureau by a side door.

The city was as quiet at this hour as it ever was. All the sign projectors, and most of the street lights, had been turned off to save power, and even the vast, disembodied voices that boomed out of the air all day long and half the night were almost silent. The darkness and quiescence of the city made it seem easy for them to talk as they went through the streets.

Kerr realised afterwards how confident he must have been of Rhysha's sympathy to have spoken to her as freely as he did. And she must have felt an equal confidence in him, for after a little while she was telling him fragments of her history and her people's past without reserve.

212

"After the earthmen took our planet," she said, "we had nothing left they wanted. But we had to have food. Then we discovered that they liked to watch us fight."

"You fought before the earthmen came?" Kerr asked.

"Yes. But not as we fight now. It was a ritual then, very formal, with much politeness and courtesy. We did not fight to get things from each other, but to find out who was brave and could give us leadership. The earth people were impatient with our ritual—they wanted to see us hurting and being hurt. So we learned to fight as we fight now, hoping to be killed.

"There was a time, when we first left our planet and went to the other worlds where people liked to watch us, when there were many of us. But there have been many battles since then. Now there are only a few left."

At the cross street a beggar slouched up to them. Kerr gave him a coin. The man was turning away with thanks when he caught sight of Rhysha's golden top-knot. "God-damned Extey!" he said in sudden rage. "Filth! And you, a man, going around with it! Here!" He threw the coin at Kerr.

"Even the beggars!" Rhysha said. "Why is it, Kerr, you hate us so?"

"Because we have wronged you," he answered, and knew it was the truth. "Are we always so unkind, though?"

"As the beggar was? Often . . . it is worse."

"Rhysha, you've got to get away from here."

"Where?" she answered simply. "Our people have discussed it so many times! There is no planet on which there are not already billions of people from earth. You increase so fast!

"And besides, it doesn't matter. You don't need us, there isn't any place for us. We cared about that once, but not any more. We're so tired—all of us, even the young ones like me—we're so tired of trying to live."

"You mustn't talk like that," Kerr said harshly. "I won't let you talk like that. You've got to go on. If we don't need you now, Rhysha, we will."

From the block ahead of them there came the wan glow of a municipal telescreen. Late as the hour was, it was surrounded by a dense knot of spectators. Their eyes were fixed greedily on the combat that whirled dizzily over the screen.

Rhysha tugged gently at Kerr's sleeve. "We had better go around," she said in a whisper. Kerr realised with a pang that there would be trouble if the viewers saw a "man" and an Extey together. Obediently he turned.

They had gone a block further when Kerr (for he had been thinking) said: "My people took the wrong road, Rhysha, about two hundred years ago. That was when the council refused to accept, even in principle, any form of population control. By now we're stifling under the pressure of our own numbers, we're crushed shapeless under it. Everything has had to give way to our one basic problem, how to feed an ever-increasing number of hungry mouths. Morality has dwindled into feeding ourselves. And we have the battle sports over the telecast to keep us occupied.

"But I think—I believe—that we'll get into the right road again sometime. I've read books of history, Rhysha. This isn't the first time we've chosen the wrong road. Some day there'll be room for your people, Rhysha, if only—" he hesitated—"if only because you're so beautiful."

He looked at her earnestly. Her face was remote and bleak. An idea came to him. "Have you ever heard anyone sing, Rhysha?"

"Sing? No, I don't know the word."

"Listen, then." He fumbled over his repertory and decided, though the music was not really suited to his voice, on Tamino's song to Pamina's portrait. He sang it for her as they walked along.

Little by little Rhysha's face relaxed. "I like that," she said when the song was over. "Sing more, Kerr."

"Do you see what I was trying to tell you?" he said at last, after many songs. "If we could make songs like that, Rhysha, isn't there hope for us?"

"For you, perhaps. Not us," Rhysha answered. There was anger in her voice. "Stop it, Kerr. I do not want to be waked."

But when they parted she clasped hands with him and told him where they could meet again. "You are really our friend," she said without coquetry.

When he next met Rhysha, Kerr said: "I brought you a present. Here." He handed her a parcel. "And I've some news, too."

Rhysha opened the little package. An exclamation of pleasure broke from her lips. "Oh, lovely! What a lovely thing! Where did you get it, Kerr?"

"In a shop that sells old things, in the back." He did not tell her he had given ten days' pay for the little turquoise locket. "But the stones are lighter than I realised. I wanted something that would be the colour of your plumage."

Rhysha shook her head. "No, this is the colour it should be. This is right." She clasped the locket around her neck and looked down at it with pleasure. "And now, what is the news you have for me?"

"A friend of mine is a clerk in the city of records. He tells me a new planet, near gamma Cassiopeiae, is being opened for colonisation.

"I've filed the papers, and everything is in order. The hearing will be held on Friday. I'm going to appear on behalf of the Ngayir, your people, and ask that they be allotted space on the new world."

Rhysha turned white. He started toward her, but she waved him away. One hand was still clasping her locket, that was nearly the colour of her plumage.

The hearing was held in a small auditorium in the basement of the Colonisation building. Representatives of a dozen groups spoke before Kerr's turn came.

"Appearing on behalf of the Ngayir," the arbitrator read from a form in his hand, "S 3687 Kerr. And who are the Ngayir, S-Kerr? Some Indian group?"

"No, sir," Kerr said. "They are commonly known as the bird people."

"Oh, a conservationist!" The arbitrator looked at Kerr not unkindly. "I'm sorry, but your petition is quite out of order. It should never have been filed. Immigration is restricted by executive order to terrestrials. . . .

Kerr dreaded telling Rhysha of his failure, but she took it with perfect calm.

"After you left I realised it was impossible," she said.

"Rhysha, I want you to promise me something. I can't

tell you how sure I am that humanity is going to need your people sometime. It's true, Rhysha. I'm going to keep trying. I'm not going to give up.

"Promise me this, Rhysha: promise me that neither you nor the members of your group will take part in the battles until you hear from me again."

Rhysha smiled. "All right, Kerr."

Preserving the bodies of people who have died from a variety of diseases is not without its dangers. Kerr did not go to work that night or the next or for many nights. His dormitory chief, after listening to him shout in delirium for some hours, called a doctor, who filled out a hospital requisition slip.

He was gravely ill, and his recovery was slow. It was nearly five weeks before he was released.

He wanted above all things to find Rhysha. He went to the place where she had been living and found that she had gone, no one knew where. In the end, he went to the identification bureau and begged for his old job there. Rhysha would, he was sure, think of coming to the bureau to get in touch with him.

He was still shaky and weak when he reported for work the next night. He went into the tepidarium about nine o'clock, during a routine inspection. And there Rhysha was.

He did not know her for an instant. The lovely turquoise of her plumage had faded to a dirty drab. But the little locket he had given her was still around her neck.

He got the big jointed tongs they used for moving bodies out of the pool, and put them in position. He lifted her out very gently and put her down on the edge of the pool. He opened the locket. There was a note inside.

"Dear Kerr," he read in Rhysha's clear, handsome script, "you must forgive me for breaking my promise to you. They would not let me see you when you were sick, and we were all so hungry. Besides, you were wrong to think your people would ever need us. There is no place for us in your world.

"I wish I could have heard you sing again. I liked to hear you sing. Rhysha."

Kerr looked from the note to Rhysha's face, and back

216

at the note. It hurt too much. He did not want to realise that she was dead.

Outside, one of the vast voices that boomed portentously down from the sky half the night long began to speak: "Don't miss the newest, fastest battle sport. View the Durga battles, the bloodiest combats ever televised. Funnier than the bird people's battles, more thrilling than an Anda war, you'll . . ."

Kerr gave a cry. He ran to the window and closed it. He could still hear the voice. But it was all that he could do.

*After many years of work, the child graduates from grammar school—and is a freshman in high school. After more years of work—he gets to be a freshman again. And if he is very, very wise, he might even get to be a kindergarten student again ...*

●

# IMMIGRANT
## by Clifford D. Simak

He was the only passenger for Kimon and those aboard the ship lionized him because he was going there.

To land him at his destination the ship went two light-years out of its way, an inconvenience for which his passage money, much as it had seemed to him when he'd paid it back on Earth, did not compensate by half.

But the captain did not grumble. It was, he told Seldon Bishop, an honor to carry a passenger for Kimon.

The businessmen aboard sought him out and bought him drinks and lunches and talked expansively of the markets opening up in the new-found solar systems.

But despite all their expansive talk, they looked at Bishop with half-veiled envy in their eyes and they said to him: "The man who cracks this Kimon situation is the one who'll have it big."

One by one, each of them contrived to corner him for

private conversations and the talk, after the first drink, always turned to billions if he ever needed backing.

Billions—while he sat there with less than twenty credits in his pocket, living in terror against the day when he might have to buy a round of drinks. For he wasn't certain that his twenty credits would stretch to a round of drinks.

The dowagers towed him off and tried to mother him; the young things lured him off and did not try to mother him. And everywhere he went, he heard the whisper behind the half-raised hand:

"To Kimon!" said the whispers. "My dear, you know what it takes to go to Kimon! An I.Q. rating that's positively fabulous and years and years of study and an examination that not one in a thousand passes."

It was like that all the way to Kimon.

# II

Kimon was a galactic El Dorado, a never-never land, the country at the rainbow's foot. There were few who did not dream of going there, and there were many who aspired, but those who were chosen were a very small percentage of those who tried to make the grade and failed.

Kimon had been reached—either discovered or contacted would be the wrong word to use—more than a hundred years before by a crippled spaceship out of Earth which landed on the planet, lost and unable to go farther.

To this day no one knew for sure exactly what had happened, but it is known that in the end the crew destroyed the ship and settled down on Kimon and had written letters home saying they were staying.

Perhaps the delivery of those letters, more than anything else, convinced the authorities of Earth that Kimon was the kind of place the letters said it was—although later on there was other evidence which weighed as heavily in the balance.

There was, quite naturally, no mail service between Kimon and Earth, but the letters were delivered, and in a most fantastic, although when you think about it, a most logical way. They were rolled into a bundle and placed in a sort of tube, like the pneumatic tubes that are used in industry for inter-departmental communication and the tube was delivered, quite neatly, on the desk of the World Postal Chief in London. Not on the desk of a subordinate, mind you, but on the desk of the chief himself. The tube had not been there when he went to lunch; it was there when he came back, and so far as could be determined, despite a quite elaborate investigation, no one had been seen to place it there.

In time, still convinced that there had been some sort of hoax played, the postal service delivered the letters to the addressees by special messengers who in their more regular employment were operatives of the World Investigative Bureau.

The addressees were unanimous in their belief the letters were genuine, for in most cases the handwriting was recognized and in every letter there were certain matters in the context which seemed to prove that they were *bona fide*.

So each of the addressees wrote a letter in reply and these were inserted in the tube in which the original letters had arrived and the tube was placed meticulously in the same spot where it had been found on the desk of the postal chief.

Then everyone watched and nothing happened for quite some time, but suddenly the tube was gone and no one had seen it go—it had been there one moment and not there the next.

There remained one question and that one soon was answered. In the matter of a week or two the tube reappeared again, just before the end of office hours. The postal chief had been working away, not paying much attention to what was going on, and suddenly he saw that the tube had come back again.

Once again it held letters and this time the letters were crammed with sheafs of hundred-credit notes, a gift from the marooned spacemen to their relatives, although it should be noted immediately that the spacemen themselves probably did not consider that they were marooned.

The letters acknowledged the receipt of the replies that

had been sent from Earth and told more about the planet Kimon and its inhabitants.

And each letter carefully explained how come they had hundred-credit notes on Kimon. The notes as they stood, the letters said, were simply counterfeits, made from bills the spacemen had in their pockets, although when Earth's fiscal experts and the Bureau of Investigation men had a look at them there was no way in which you could tell them from the real thing.

But, the letters said, the Kimonian government wished to make right the matter of the counterfeiting. To back the currency the Kimonians, within the next short while, would place on deposit with the World bank materials not only equivalent to their value, but enough additional to set up a balance against which more notes could be issued.

There was, the letters explained, no money as such on Kimon, but since Kimon was desirous of employing the men from Earth, there must be some way to pay them, so if it was all right with the World bank and everyone else concerned ...

The World bank did a lot of hemming and hawing and talked about profound fiscal matters and deep economic principles, but all this talk dissolved to nothing when in the matter of a day or two several tons of carefully shielded uranium and a couple of bushels of diamonds were deposited, during the afternoon coffee hour, beside the desk of the bank's president.

With evidence of this sort, there was not much the Earth could do except accept the fact that the planet Kimon was a going concern, that the Earthmen who had landed there were going to stay, and to take the entire situation at face value.

The Kimonians, the letters said, were humanoid and had parapsychic powers and had built a culture which was miles ahead of Earth or any other planet so far discovered in the galaxy.

Earth furbished up a ship, hand-picked a corps of its most persuasive diplomats, loaded down the hold with expensive gifts, and sent the whole business out to Kimon.

Within minutes after landing, the diplomats had been

221

quite undiplomatically booted off the planet. Kimon, it appeared, had no desire to ally itself with a second-rate, barbaric planet. When it wished to establish diplomatic relationships it would say so. Earth people might come to Kimon if they wished and settle there, but not just any Earth person. To come to Kimon, the individual would have to possess not only a certain minimum IQ, but must also have an impressive scholastic record.

And that was the way it was left.

You did not go to Kimon simply because you wished to go there; you worked to go to Kimon.

First of all, you had to have the specified IQ rating and that ruled out ninety-nine per cent or better of Earth's population. Once you had passed the IQ test, you settled down to grueling years of study, and at the end of the years of study you wrote an examination and, once again, most of the aspirants were ruled out. Not more than one in a thousand who took the examinations passed.

Year after year, Earth men and women dribbled out to Kimon, settled there, prospered, wrote their letters home.

Of those who went out, none came back. Once you had lived on Kimon, you could not bear the thought of going back to Earth.

And yet, in all those years, the sum of knowledge concerning Kimon, its inhabitants and its culture, was very slight indeed. What knowledge there was, the only knowledge that there was, was complied from the letters delivered meticulously once each week to the desk of the postal chief in London.

The letters spoke of wages and salaries a hundred times the wage and salary that was paid on Earth, of magnificent business opportunities, of the Kimonian culture and the Kimonians themselves, but in no detail, of culture or of business or any other factor, were the letters too specific.

And perhaps the recipients of the letters did not mind too much the lack of specific information, for almost every letter carried with it a sheaf of notes, all crisp and new, and very very legal, backed by tons of uranium, bushels of diamonds, stacked bars of gold and other similar knicknacks deposited from time to time beside the desk of the World bank's president.

222

It became, in time, the ambition of every family on the Earth to send at least one relative to Kimon, for a relative on Kimon virtually spelled an assured and sufficient income for the rest of the clan for life.

Naturally the legend of Kimon grew. Much that was said about it was untrue, of course. Kimon, the letters protested, did not have streets paved with solid gold, since there were no streets. Nor did Kimonian damsels wear gowns of diamond-dust—the damsels of Kimon wore not much of anything.

But to those whose understanding went beyond streets of gold and gowns of diamonds, it was well understood that in Kimon lay possibilities vastly greater than either gold or diamonds. For here was a planet with a culture far in advance of Earth, a people who had schooled themselves or had naturally developed parapsychic powers. On Kimon one could learn the techniques that would revolutionize galactic industry and communications; on Kimon one might discover philosophy that would set mankind overnight on a new and better—and more profitable?—path.

The legend grew, interpreted by each according to his intellect and his way of thought, and grew and grew and grew . . .

Earth's government was very helpful to those who wished to go to Kimon, for government as well as individuals, could appreciate the opportunities for the revolution of industry and the evolution of human thought. But since there had been no invitation to grant diplomatic recognition, Earth's government sat and waited, scheming, doing all it could to settle as many of its people on Kimon as was possible. But only the best, for even the densest bureaucrat recognized that on Kimon Earth must put its best foot forward.

Why the Kimonians allowed Earth to send its people was a mystery for which there was no answer. But apparently Earth was the only other planet in the galaxy which had been allowed to send its people. The Earthmen and the Kimonians, of course, both were humanoid, but this was not an adequate answer, either, for they were not the only humanoids in the galaxy. For its own comfort, Earth assumed that a certain common understanding, a similar outlook, a certain parallel evolutionary trend—with Earth a bit behind, of course—between Earth and Kimon might account for Kimon's qualified hospitality.

But be that as it may, Kimon was a galactic El Dorado, a never-never land, a planet to get ahead, the place to spend your life, the country at the rainbow's end.

# III

Selden Bishop stood in the parklike area where the gig had landed him, for Kimon had no spaceports, as it likewise failed in having many other things.

He stood, surrounded by his luggage, and watched the gig drive spaceward to rendezvous with the liner's orbit.

When he could see the gig no longer, he sat down on one of his bags and waited.

The park was faintly Earthlike, but the similarity was only in the abstract, for in each particular there was a subtle difference that said this was an alien planet. The trees were too slim and the flowers just a shade too loud and the grass was off a shade or two from the grass you saw on Earth. The birds, if they were birds, were more lizardlike than the birds of Earth and their feathers were put on wrong and weren't quite the color one associated with plumage. The breeze had a faint perfume upon it that was no perfume of Earth, but an alien odor that smelled like a color looked and Bishop tried to decide, but couldn't, which color it might be.

Sitting on his bag, in the middle of the park, he tried to drum up a little enthusiasm, tried to whistle up some triumph that he finally was on Kimon, but the best that he could achieve was a thankfulness that he'd made it with the twenty still intact.

He would need a little cash to get along on until he could find a job. But, he told himself, he shouldn't have to wait too long before he found a job. The thing, of course, was not to take the first one offered him, but to shop around a little and find the one for which he was best fitted. And that, he knew, might take a little time.

Thinking of it, he wished that he had more than a

twenty. He should have allowed himself a bigger margin, but that would have meant something less than the best luggage he could buy and perhaps not enough of it, off-the-rack suits instead of tailored, and all other things accordingly.

It was, he told himself, important that he make the best impression, and sitting there and thinking it over, he couldn't bring himself to regret the money he had spent to make a good impression.

Maybe he should have asked Morley for a loan. Morley would have given him anything he asked and he could have paid it back as soon as he got a job. But he had hated to ask, for to ask, he now admitted, would have detracted from his new-found importance as a man who had been selected to make the trip to Kimon. Everyone, even Morley, looked up to a man who was set to blast for Kimon, and you couldn't go around asking for a loan or for other favors.

He remembered the last visit he had with Morley, and looking back at it now, he saw that while Morley was his friend, that last visit had a flavor, more or less, of a diplomatic job that Morley had to carry out.

Morley had gone far and was going farther in the diplomatic service. He looked like a diplomat and he talked like one and he had a better grasp, old heads at the department said, of Sector Nineteen politics and economics than any of the other younger men. He wore a clipped mustache that had a frankly cultivated look and his hair was always quite in place and his body, when he walked, was like a panther walking.

They had sat in Morley's diggings and had been all comfortable and friendly and then Morley had gotten up and paced up and down the room with his panther walk.

"We've been friends for a long, long time," said Morley. "We've been in lots of scrapes together."

And the two of them had smiled, remembering some of the scrapes they had been in together.

"When I heard you were going out to Kimon," Morley said, "I was pleased about it naturally. I'd be pleased at anything that came your way. But I was pleased, as well, for another reason. I told myself here finally was a man who could do a job and find out what we want."

"What do you want?" Bishop had asked and, as he remembered it, he had asked it as if he might be asking whether Morley wanted Scotch or bourbon. Although, come to think of it, he never would have asked that particular question, for all the young men in the alien relations section religiously drank Scotch. But, anyhow, he asked it casually, although he sensed that there was nothing casual at all about the situation.

He could smell the scent of cloak and dagger and he caught a sudden glimpse of huge official worry and for an instant he was a little cold and scared.

"There must be some way to crack that planet," Morley had told him, "but we haven't found it yet. So far as the Kimonians are concerned, none of the rest of us, none of the other planets, officially exist. There's not a single planet accorded diplomatic status. On Kimon there is not a single official representative of any other people. They don't seem to trade with anyone, and yet they must trade with someone, for no planet, no culture can exist in complete self-sufficiency. They must have diplomatic relations somewhere, with someone. There must be some reason, beyond the obvious one that we are an inferior culture, why they do not recognize Earth. For even in the more barbaric days of Earth there was official recognition of many governments and peoples who were cultural inferiors to the recognizing nation."

"You want me to find out all this?"

"No," said Morley. "Not all that. All we want are clues. Somewhere there is the clue that we are looking for, the hint that will tell us what the actual situation is. All we need is the opening wedge—the foot in the door. Give us that and we will do the rest."

"There have been others," Bishop told him. "Thousands of others. I'm not the only one who ever went to Kimon."

"For the last fifty years or more," said Morley, "the section has talked to all the others, before they went out, exactly as I'm talking to you now."

"And you've gotten nothing?"

"Nothing," said Morley. "Or almost nothing. Or nothing, anyhow, that counted or made any sense."

"They failed—"

"They failed," Morley told him, "because once on Kimon they forgot about Earth . . . well, not forgot about it, that's not entirely it. But they lost all allegiance to it. They were Kimon-blinded."

"You believe that?"

"I don't know," said Morley. "It's the best explanation that we have. The trouble is that we talk to them only once. None of them come back. We can write letters to them, certainly. We can try to jog them—indirectly, of course. But we can't ask them outright."

"Censorship?"

"Not censorship," said Morley, "although they may have that, too; but mostly telepathy. The Kimonians would know if we tried to impress anything too forcibly upon their minds. And we can't take the chance of a single thought undoing all the work that we have done."

"But you're telling me."

"You'll forget it," Morley said. "You will have several weeks in which you can forget it—push it to the back of your mind. But not entirely—not entirely."

"I understand," Bishop had told him.

"Don't get me wrong," said Morley. "It's nothing sinister. You're not to look for that. It may be just a simple thing. The way we comb our hair. There's some reason —perhaps many little ones. And we must know those reasons."

Morley had switched it off as quickly as he had begun it, had poured another round of drinks, had sat down again and talked of their school days and of the girls they'd known and of week-ends in the country.

It had been, all in all, a very pleasant evening.

But that had been weeks ago, and since then he'd scarcely remembered it and now here he was on Kimon, sitting on one of his bags in the middle of a park, waiting for a welcoming Kimonian to show up.

All the time that he'd been waiting, he had been prepared for the Kimonian's arrival. He knew what a Kimonian looked like and he should not have been surprised.

But when the native came, he was.

For the native was six-foot ten, and almost a godlike being, a sculptured humanoid who was, astonishingly, much more human than he had thought to find.

One moment he had sat alone in the little parklike glade and the next the native was standing at his side.

Bishop came to his feet and the Kimonian said, "We are glad you are here. Welcome to Kimon, sir."

The native's inflection was as precise and beautiful as his sculptured body.

"Thank you," Bishop said, and knew immediately that the two words were inadequate and that his voice was slurred and halting compared with the native's voice. And, looking at the Kimonian, he had the feeling that by comparison, he cut a rumpled, seedy figure.

He reached into his pocket for his papers and his fingers were all thumbs, so that he fumbled for them and finally dug them out—dug is the word exactly—and handed them to the waiting being.

The Kimonian flicked them—that was it, flicked them—then he said "Mr. Selden Bishop. Very glad to know you. Your IQ rating, 160, is very satisfactory. Your examination showing, if I may say so, is extraordinary. Recommendations good. Clearance from Earth in order. And I see you made good time. Very glad to have you."

"But—" said Bishop. Then he clamped his mouth shut tight. He couldn't tell this being he'd merely flicked the pages and could not possibly have read them. For, obviously he had.

"You had a pleasant flight, Mr. Bishop?"

"A most pleasant one," said Bishop and was filled with sudden pride that he could answer so easily and urbanely.

"Your luggage," said the native, "is in splendid taste."

"Why, thank you—" then was filled with rage. What right had this person to patronize his luggage!

But the native did not appear to notice.

"You wish to go to the hotel?"

"If you please," said Bishop, speaking very tightly, holding himself in check.

"Please allow me," said the native.

Bishop blurred for just a second—a definite sense of blurring—as if the universe had gone swiftly out of focus,

228

then he was standing, not in the parklike glade, but in a one-man-sized alcove off a hotel lobby, with his bags stacked neatly beside him.

# IV

He had missed the triumph before, sitting in the glade, waiting for the native, after the gig had left him, but now it struck him, a heady, drunken triumph that surged through his body and rose in his throat to choke him.

This was Kimon! He finally was on Kimon! After all the years of study, he finally was here—the fabulous place he'd worked for many years to reach.

A high IQ, they'd said behind their half-raised hands— a high IQ and many years of study, and a stiff examination that not more than one in every thousand passed.

He stood in the alcove, with the sense of hiding there, to give himself a moment in which to regain his breath at the splendor of what had finally come to pass, to gain the moment it would take for the unreasoning triumph to have its way with him and go.

For the triumph was something that must not be allowed to pass. It was something that he must not show. It was a personal thing and as something personal it must be hidden deep.

He might be one of a thousand back on Earth, but here he stood on no more than equal footing with the ones who had come before him. Perhaps not quite on equal footing, for they would know the ropes and he had yet to learn them.

He watched them in the lobby—the lucky and the fabulous ones who had preceded him, the glittering company he had dreamed about during all the weary years—the company that he presently would join, the ones of Earth who were adjudged fit to go to Kimon.

For only the best must go—the best and smartest and the quickest. Earth must put her best foot forward for how otherwise would Earth ever persuade Kimon that she was a sister planet?

At first the people in the lobby had been no more than a crowd, a crowd that shone and twinkled, but with that curious lack of personality which goes with a crowd. But now, as he watched, the crowd dissolved into individuals and he saw them, not as a group, but as the men and women he presently would know.

He did not see the bell captain until the native stood in front of him, and the bell captain, if anything, was taller and more handsome than the man who'd met him in the glade.

"Good evening, sir," the captain said. "Welcome to the Ritz."

Bishop stared. "The Ritz? Oh, yes, I had forgotten. This place is the Ritz."

"We're glad to have you with us," said the captain. "We hope your stay will prove to be a long one."

"Certainly," said Bishop. "That is, I hope so, too."

"We had been notified," the captain said, "that you were arriving, Mr. Bishop. We took the liberty of reserving rooms for you. I trust they will be satisfactory."

"I am sure they will be," Bishop said.

As if anything on Kimon could be unsatisfactory!

"Perhaps you will want to dress," the captain said. "There still is time for dinner."

"Oh, certainly," said Bishop. "Most assuredly I will."

And wished he had not said it.

"We'll send up the bags," the captain said. "No need to register. That is taken care of. If you'll permit me sir."

# V

The rooms were satisfactory.

There were three of them.

Sitting in a chair, Bishop wondered how he'd ever pay for them.

Remembering the lonely twenty credits, he was seized with a momentary panic.

He'd have to get a job sooner than he planned, for the twenty credits wouldn't go too far with a layout like this one. Although he supposed if he asked for credit it would be given him.

But he recoiled from the idea of asking for credit, of being forced to admit that he was short of cash. So far he'd done everything correctly. He'd arrived aboard a liner and not a battered trader; his luggage—what had the native said?—it was in splendid taste; his wardrobe was all that could be expected; and he hoped that he'd not communicated to anyone the panic and dismay he'd felt at the luxury of the suite.

He got up from the chair and prowled about the room. There was no carpeting, for the floor itself was soft and yielding and you left momentary tracks as you walked, but they puffed back and smoothed out almost immediately.

He walked over to a window and stood looking out of it. Evening had fallen and the landscape was covered with a dusty blue—and there was nothing absolutey nothing, but rolling countryside. There were no roads that he could see and no lights that would have told of other habitations.

Perhaps, he thought, I'm on the wrong side of the building. On the other side there might be streets and roads and homes and shops.

He turned back to the room and looked at it—the Earth-like furniture so quietly elegant that it almost shouted, the beautiful, veined marble fireplace, the shelves of books, the shine of old wood, the matchless paintings hanging on the wall, and the great cabinet that filled almost one end of the room.

He wondered what the cabinet might be. It was a beautiful thing, with an antique look about it and it had a polish—not a wax, but of human hands and time.

He walked toward it.

The cabinet said: "Drink, sir?"

"I don't mind if I do," said Bishop, then stopped stock-still, realizing that the cabinet had spoken and he had answered it.

A panel opened in the cabinet and the drink was there.

"Music?" asked the cabinet.

"If you please," said Bishop.

"Type?"

"Type? Oh, I see. Something gay, but maybe just a little sadness too. Like the blue hour of twilight spreading over Paris. Who was it used that phrase? One of the old writers. Fitzgerald. I'm sure it was Fitzgerald."

The music told about the blue hour stealing over that city far away on Earth and there was soft April and dis-

231

tant girlish laughter and the shine of the pavement in slanting rain.

"Is there anything else you wish, sir?" asked the cabinet.

"Nothing at the moment."

"Very well, sir. You will have an hour to get dressed for dinner."

He left the room, sipping his drink as he went—and the drink had a certain touch to it.

He went into the bedroom and tested the bed and it was satisfactorily soft. He examined the dresser and the full-length glass and peeked into the bathroom and saw that it was equipped with an automatic shaver and massager, that it had a shower and tub, an exercising machine and a number of other gadgets that he couldn't place.

And the third room.

It was almost bare by the standards of the other two. In the center of it stood a chair with great flat arms and on each of the arms many rows of buttons.

He approached the chair cautiously, wondering what it was—what kind of trap it was. Although that was foolish, for there were no traps on Kimon. This was Kimon, the land of opportunity, where a man might make a fortune and live in luxury and rub shoulders with an intelligence and a culture that was the best yet found in the galaxy.

He bent down over the wide arms of the chair and found that each of the buttons was labeled. They were labeled "History," "Poetry," "Drama," "Sculpture," "Literature," "Painting," "Astronomy," "Philosophy," "Physics," "Religions" and many other things. And there were several that were labeled with words he'd never seen and had no meaning to him.

He stood in the room and looked around at its starkness and saw for the first time that it had no windows, but was just a sort of box—a theater, he decided, or a lecture room. You sat in the chair and pressed a certain button and—

But there was no time for that. An hour to dress for dinner, the cabinet had said, and some of that hour was already gone.

The luggage was in the bedroom and he opened the bag

that held his dinner clothes. The jacket was badly wrinkled.

He stood with it in his hands, staring at it. Maybe the wrinkles would hang out. Maybe—

But he knew they wouldn't.

The music stopped and the cabinet asked: "Is there something that you wish, sir?"

"Can you press a dinner jacket?"

"Surely, sir, I can."

"How soon?"

"Five minutes," said the cabinet. "Give me the trousers, too."

# VI

The bell rang and he went to the door.

A man stood just outside.

"Good evening," said the man. "My name is Montague, but they call me Monty."

"Won't you come in, Monty?"

Monty came in and surveyed the room.

"Nice place," he said.

Bishop nodded. "I didn't ask for anything at all. They just gave it to me."

"Clever, these Kimonians," said Monty. "Very clever, yes."

"My name is Selden Bishop."

"Just come in?" asked Monty.

"An hour or so ago."

"All dewed up with what a great place Kimon is."

"I know nothing about it," Bishop told him. "I studied it, of course."

"I know," said Monty, looking at him slantwise. "Just being neighborly. New victim and all that, you know."

Bishop smiled because he didn't quite know what else to do.

"What's your line?" asked Monty.

"Business," said Bishop. "Administration's what I'm aiming at."

"Well, then," Monty said, "I guess that lets you out. You wouldn't be interested."

"In what?"

"In football. Or baseball. Or cricket. Not the athletic type."

"Never had the time."

"Too bad," Monty said. "You have the build for it."

The cabinet asked: "Would the gentleman like a drink?"

"If you please," said Monty.

"And another one for you, sir?"

"If you please," said Bishop.

"Go in and get dressed," said Monty. "I'll sit down and wait."

"Your jacket and trousers, sir," said the cabinet.

A door swung open and there they were, cleaned and pressed.

"I didn't know," said Bishop, "that you went in for sports out here."

"Oh, we don't," said Monty. "This is a business venture."

"Business venture?"

"Certainly. Give the Kimonians something to bet on. They might go for it. For a while at least. You see, they can't bet—"

"I don't see why not—"

"Well, consider for a moment. They have no sports at all, you know. Wouldn't be possibe. Telepathy. They'd know three moves ahead what their opponents were about to do. Telekinesis. They could move a piece or a ball or what-have-you without touching a finger to it. They—"

"I think I see," said Bishop.

"So we plan to get up some teams and put on exhibition matches. Drum up as much enthusiasm as we can. They'll come out in droves to see it. Pay admission. Place bets. We, of course, will play the bookies and rake off our commissions. It will be a good thing while it lasts."

"It won't last, of course."

Monty gave Bishop a long look.

"You catch on fast," he said. "You'll get along."

"Drinks, gentlemen," the cabinet said.

Bishop got the drinks, gave one of them to his visitor.

"You better let me put you down," said Monty. "Might as well rake in what you can. You don't need to know too much about it."

234

"All right," Bishop told him, agreeably. "Go ahead and put me down."

"You haven't got much money," Monty said.

"How did you know that?"

"'You're scared about this room," said Monty.

"Telepathy?" asked Bishop.

"You pick it up," said Monty. "Just the fringes of it. You'll never be as good as they are. Never. But you pick things up from time to time—a sort of sense that seeps into you. After you've been here long enough."

"I had hoped that no one noticed."

"A lot of them will notice, Bishop. Can't help but notice, the way you're broadcasting. But don't let it worry you. We all are friends. Banded against the common enemy, you might say. If you need a loan—"

"Not yet," said Bishop. "I'll let you know."

"Me," said Monty, "Me or anyone. We all are friends. We got to be."

"Thanks."

"Not at all. Now you go ahead and dress. I'll sit and wait for you. I'll bear you down with me. Everyone's waiting to meet you."

"That's good to know," said Bishop. "I felt quite a stranger."

"Oh, my, no," said Monty. "No need to. Not many come, you know. They'll want to know of Earth."

He rolled the glass between his fingers.

"How about Earth?" he asked.

"How about—"

"Yes, it still is there, of course. How is it getting on? What's the news?"

# VII

He had not seen the hotel before. He had caught a confused glimpse of it from the alcove off the lobby with his luggage stacked beside him, before the bell captain had showed up and whisked him to his rooms.

But now he saw that it was a strangely substantial fairyland, with fountains and hidden fountain music, with the spidery tracery of rainbows serving as groins and arches,

235

with shimmery columns of glass that caught and reflected and duplicated many times the entire construction of the lobby so that one was at once caught up in the illusion that here was a place that went on and on forever and at the same time you could cordon off a section of it in one's mind as an intimate corner for a group of friends.

It was illusion and substantiality, beauty and a sense of home—it was, Bishop suspected, all things to all men and what you wished to make it. A place of utter magic that divorced one from the world and the crudities of the world, with a gaiety that was not brittle and a sentimentality that stopped short of being cheap, and that transmitted a sense of well being and of self-importance from the very fact of being a part of such a place.

There was no such place on Earth, there could be no such place on Earth, for Bishop suspected that something more than human planning, more than human architectural skill had gone into its building. You walked in an enchantment and you talked with magic and you felt the sparkle and the shine of the place live within your brain.

"It gets you," Monty said. "I always watch the faces of the newcomers when they first walk in it."

"It wears off after a time," said Bishop, not believing it.

Monty shook his head. "My friend, it does not wear off. It doesn't surprise you quite so much, but it stays with you all the time. A human does not live long enough for a place like this to wear thin and commonplace."

He had eaten dinner in the dining room which was old and solemn, with an ancient other-worldness and a hushed tiptoe atmosphere, with Kimonian waiters at your elbow, ready to recommend a certain dish or a vintage as one that you should try.

Monty had coffee while he ate and there had been others who had come drifting past to stop a moment and welcome him and ask him of Earth, always using a studied casualness, always with a hunger in their eyes that belied the casualness.

"They make you feel at home," said Monty, "and they mean it. They are glad when a new one comes."

He did feel at home—more at home than he had ever felt in his life before, as if already he was beginning to fit in. He had not expected to fit in so quickly and he was

236

slightly astonished at it—for here were all the people he had dreamed of being with, and he finally was with them. You could feel the magnetic force of them, the personal magnetism that had made them great, great enough to be Kimon-worthy, and looking at them, he wondered which of them he would get to know, which would be his friends.

He was relieved when he found that he was not expected to pay for his dinner or his drinks, but simply sign a chit, and once he'd caught onto that, everything seemed brighter, for the dinner of itself would have taken quite a hole out of the twenty nestling in his pocket.

With dinner over and with Monty gone somewhere into the crowd, he found himself in the bar, sitting on a stool and nursing a drink that the Kimonian bartender had recommended as being something special.

The girl came out of nowhere and floated up to the stool beside him and she said:

"What's that you're drinking, friend?"

"I don't know," said Bishop. He made a thumb toward the man behind the bar. "Ask him to make you one."

The bartender heard and got busy with the bottles and the shaker.

"You're fresh from Earth," said the girl.

"Fresh is the word," said Bishop.

"It's not so bad," she said. "That is, if you don't think about it."

"I won't think about it," Bishop promised. "I won't think of anything."

"Of course, you do get used to it," she said. "After a while you don't mind the faint amusement. You think, what the hell, let them laugh all they want to so long as I have it good. But the day will come—"

"What are you talking about?" asked Bishop. "Here's your drink. Dip your muzzle into that and—"

"The day will come when we are old to them, when we don't amuse them any longer. When we become passé. We can't keep thinking up new tricks. Take my painting, for example—"

"See here," said Bishop, "you're talking way above my head."

"See me a week from now," she said. "The name's

237

Maxine. Just ask to see Maxine. A week from now, we can talk together. So long, Buster."

She floated off the stool and suddenly was gone.

She hadn't touched her drink.

# VIII

He went up to his rooms and stood for a long time at a window, staring out into the featureless landscape lighted by a moon.

Wonder thundered in his brain, the wonder and the newness and the many questions, the breathlessness of finally being here, of slowly coming to a full realization of the fact that he was here, that he was one of that glittering, fabulous company he had dreamed about for years.

The long grim years peeled off him, the years of books and study, the years of determined driving, the hungry, anxious, grueling years when he had lived a monkish life, mortifying body and soul to drive his intellect.

The years fell off and he felt the newness of himself as well as the newness of the scene. A cleanness and a newness and the sudden glory.

The cabinet finally spoke to him.

"Why don't you try the live-it, sir?"

Bishop swung sharply around.

"You mean—"

"The third room," said the cabinet. "You'll find it most amusing."

"The live-it!"

"That's right," said the cabinet. "You pick it and you live it."

Which sounded like something out of the Alice books.

"It's safe," said the cabinet. "It's perfectly safe. You can come back any time you wish."

"Thank you," Bishop said.

He went into the room and sat down in the chair and studied the buttons on the arms.

History?

Might as well, he told himself. He knew a bit of history. He'd been interested in it and taken several courses and did a lot of supplemental reading.

He punched the "History" button.

A panel in the wall before the chair lit up and a face appeared—the face of a Kimonian, the bronzed and golden face, the classic beauty of the race.

Aren't any of them homely? Bishop wondered. None of them ugly or crippled, like the rest of humanity?

"What type of history, sir?" the face in the screen asked him.

"Type?"

"Galactic, Kimonian, Earth—almost any place you wish."

"Earth, please," said Bishop.

"Specifications?"

"England," said Bishop. "October 14, 1066. A place called Senlac."

And he was there.

He was no longer in the room with its single chair and its four bare walls, but he stood upon a hill in sunny autumn weather with the gold and red of trees and the blueness of the haze and the shouts of men.

He stood rooted in the grass that blew upon the hillside and saw that the grass had turned to hay with its age and sunshine—and out beyond the grass and hill, grouped down on the plain, was a ragged line of horsemen, with the sun upon their helmets and flashing on their shields, with the leopard banners curling in the wind.

It was October 14th and it was Saturday and on the hill stood Harold's hosts behind their locked shield wall and before the sun had set new forces would have been put in motion to shape the course of empire.

Taillefer, he thought. Taillefer will ride in the fore of William's charge, singing the *"Chanson de Roland"* and wheeling his sword into the air so that it became a wheel of fire to lead the others on.

The Normans charged and there was no Taillefer. There was no one who wheeled his sword into the air, there was no singing. There was merely shouting and the hoarse crying of men riding to their death.

The horsemen were charging directly at him and he wheeled and tried to run, but he could not outrun them and they were upon him. He saw the flash of polished hoofs and the cruel steel of the shoes upon the hoofs, the glinting lance point, the swaying, jouncing scabbard, the red and green and yellow of the cloaks, the dullness of the armor, the open roaring mouths of men—and they were upon him. And passing through him and over him as if he were not there.

He stopped stock-still, heart hammering in his chest, and, as if from somewhere far off, he felt the wind of the charging horses that were running all around him.

Up the hill there were hoarse cries of "Ut! Ut!" and the high, sharp ring of steel. Dust was rising all around him and somewhere off to the left a dying horse was screaming. Out of the dust a man came running down the hill. He staggered and fell and got up and ran again and Bishop could see the blood poured out of the ripped armor and washed down across the metal, spraying the dead, sere grass as he ran down the hill.

The horses came back again, some of them riderless, running with their necks outstretched, with the reins flying in the wind, with foam dashing from their mouths.

One man sagged in the saddle and fell off, but his foot caught in the stirrup and his horse, shying, dragged him sidewise.

Up on top the hill the Saxon square was cheering and through the settling dust he saw the heap of bodies that lay outside the shield wall.

*Let me out of here!* Bishop was screaming to himself. *How do I get out of here! Let me out—*

He was out, back in the room again, with its single chair and the four blank walls.

He sat there quietly and he thought:

*There was no Taillefer.*

*No one who rode and sang and tossed the sword in air.*

*The tale of Taillefer was no more than the imagination of some copyist who had improved upon the tale to while away his time.*

But men had died. They had run down the hill, staggering with their wounds, and died. They had fallen from their horses and been dragged to death by their frightened mounts. They had come crawling down the hill, with minutes left of life and with a whimper in their throats.

He stood up and his hands were shaking.

He walked unsteadily into the next room.

"You are going to bed, sir?" asked the cabinet.

"I think I will," said Bishop.

"Very good, then, sir. I'll lock up and put out."

"That's very good of you."

"Routine, sir," said the cabinet. "Is there anything you wish?"

"Not a thing," said Bishop. "Good night."

"Good night," said the cabinet.


# IX

In the morning he went to the employment agency which he found in one corner of the hotel lobby.

There was no one around but a Kimonian girl, a tall, statuesque blonde, but with a grace to put to shame the most petite of humans. A woman, Bishop thought, jerked out of some classic Grecian myth, a blond goddess come to life and beauty. She didn't wear the flowing Grecian robe, but she could have. She wore, truth to tell, but little, and was all the better for it.

"You are new," she said.

He nodded.

"Wait, I know," she said. She looked at him: "Selden Bishop, age twenty-nine Earth years, IQ, 160."

"Yes, ma'am," he said.

She made him feel as if he should bow and scrape.

"Business administration, I understand," she said.

He nodded, bleakly.

"Please sit down, Mr. Bishop, and we will talk this over."

He sat down and he was thinking: It isn't right for a beautiful girl to be so big and husky. Nor so competent.

"You'd like to get started doing something," said the girl.

"That's the thought I had."

"You specialized in business administration. I'm afraid there aren't many openings in that particular field."

"I wouldn't expect too much to start with," Bishop told her with what he felt was a becoming modesty and a realistic outlook. "Almost anything at all, until I can prove my value."

"You'd have to start at the very bottom. And it would take two years of training. Not in method only, but in attitude and philosophy."

"I wouldn't—"

He hesitated. He had meant to say that he wouldn't mind. But he would mind. He would mind a lot.

"But I spent years," he said. "I know—"

"Kimonian business?"

"Is it so much different?"

"You know all about contracts, I suppose."

"Certainly I do."

"There is not such a thing as a contract on all of Kimon."

"But—"

"There is no need of any."

"Integrity?"

"That, and other things as well."

"Other things?"

"You wouldn't understand."

"Try me."

"It would be useless, Mr. Bishop. New concepts entirely so far as you're concerned. Of behavior. Of motives. On Earth, profit is the motive—"

"Isn't it here?"

"In part. A very small part."

"The other motives—"

"Cultural development for one. Can you imagine an urge to cultural development as powerful as the profit motive?"

Bishop was honest about it. "No, I can't," he said.

"Here," she said, "it is the more powerful of the two. But that's not all. Money is another thing. We have no actual money. No coin that changes hands."

"But there is money. Credit notes."

"For the convenience of your race alone," she said. "We created your money values and your evidence of wealth so that we could hire your services and pay you—and I might add that we pay you well. We have gone through all the motions. The currency that we create is as valid as anywhere else in the galaxy. It's backed by deposits in

242

Earth's banks and it is legal tender so far as you're concerned. But Kimonians themselves do not employ money."

Bishop floundered. "I can't understand," he said.

"Of course you can't," she said. "It's an entirely new departure for you. Your culture is so constituted that there must be a certain physical assurance of each person's wealth and worth. Here we do not need that physical assurance. Here each person carries in his head the simple book-keeping of his worth and debts. It is there for him to know. It is there for his friends and business associates to see at any time they wish."

"It isn't business, then," said Bishop. "Not business as I think of it."

"Exactly," said the girl.

"But I am trained for business. I spent—"

"Year and years of study. But on Earth's methods of business, not on Kimon's."

"But there are business men here. Hundreds of them."

"Are there?" she asked.

And she was smiling at him. Not a superior smile, not a taunting one—just smiling at him.

"What you need," she said, "is contact with Kimonians. A chance to get to know your way around. An opportunity to appreciate our point of view and get the hang of how we do things."

"That sounds all right," said Bishop. "How do I go about it?"

"There have been instances," said the girl, "when Earth people sold their services as companions."

"I don't think I'd care much for that. It sounds . . . well, like baby sitting or reading to old ladies or . . ."

"Can you play an instrument or sing?"

Bishop shook his head.

"Paint? Draw? Dance?"

He couldn't do any of them.

"Box, perhaps," she said. "Physical combat. That is popular at times, if it's not overdone."

"You mean prize fighting?"

"I think that is one way you describe it."

"No, I can't," said Bishop.

"That doesn't leave much," she said as she picked up some papers.

"Transportation?" he asked.

"Transportation is a personal matter."

And of course it was, he told himself. With telekinesis, you could transport yourself or anything you might have a mind to move—without mechanical aid.

"Communications," he said weakly. "I suppose that is the same?"

She nodded.

With telepathy, it would be.

"You know about transportation and communications, Mr. Bishop?"

"Earth variety," said Bishop. "No good here, I gather."

"None at all," she said. "Although we might arrange a lecture tour. Some of us would help you put your material together."

Bishop shook his head. "I can't talk," he said.

She got up.

"I'll check around," she said. "Drop in again. We'll find something that you'll fit."

"Thanks," he said and went back to the lobby.

# X

He went for a walk.

There were no roads or paths.

There was nothing.

The hotel stood on the plain and there was nothing else.

No buildings around it. No village. No roads. Nothing.

It stood there, huge and ornate and lonely, like a misplaced wedding cake.

It stood stark against the skyline, for there were no other buildings to blend into it and soften it and it looked like something that someone in a hurry had dumped down and left.

He struck out across the plain toward some trees that he thought must mark a watercourse and he wondered why there were no paths or roads, but suddenly he knew why there were no paths or roads.

He thought about the years he had spent cramming

business administration into his brain and remembered the huge book of excerpts from the letters written home from Kimon hinting at big business deals, at responsible positions.

And the thought struck him that there was one thing in common in all of the excerpts in the book—that the deals and positions were always hinted at, that no one had ever told exactly what he did.

Why did they do it? he asked himself. Why did they fool us all?

Although, of course, there might be more to it than he knew. He had been on Kimon for somewhat less than a full day's time. I'll look around, the Grecian blonde had said—I'll look around, we'll find somewhere that you fit.

He went on across the plain and reached the line of trees and found the stream. It was a prairie stream, a broad, sluggish flow of crystal water between two grassy banks. Lying on his stomach to peer into the depths, he saw the flash of fishes far below him.

He took off his shoes and dangled his feet in the water and kicked a little to make the water splash, and he thought:

They know all about us. They know about our life and culture. They know about the leopard banners and how Senlac must have looked on Saturday, October 14, 1066, with the hosts of England massed upon the hilltop and the hosts of William on the plain below.

They know what makes us tick and they let us come; because they let us come, there must be some value in us.

What had the girl said, the girl who had floated to the stool and then had left with her drink still untouched? Faint amusement, she had said. You get used to it, she had said. If you don't think too much about it, you get used to it.

See me in a week, she had said. In a week you and I can talk. And she had called him Buster.

Well, maybe she had a right to call him that. He had been starry-eyed and a sort of eager beaver. And probably ignorant-smug.

They know about us and how do they know about us?

Senlac might have been staged, but he didn't think so— there was a strange, grim reality about it that got under your skin, a crawling sort of feeling that told you it was true, that that was how it had happened and had been. That there had been no Taillefer and that a man had died with his guts dragging in the grass and that the Englishmen had cried "Ut! Ut!" which might have meant almost anything at all or nothing just as well, but probably had meant "Out."

He sat there, cold and lonely, wondering how they did it. How they had made it possible for a man to punch a button and to live a scene long dead, to see the death of men who had long been dust mingled with the earth.

There was no way to know, of course.

There was no use to guess.

Technical information, Morley Reed had said, that would revolutionize our entire economic pattern.

He remembered Morley pacing up and down the room and saying: "We must find out about them. We must find out."

And there was a way to find out.

There was a splendid way.

He took his feet out of the water and dried them with handfuls of grass. He put his shoes back on and walked back to the hotel sitting by himself.

The blond goddess was still at her desk in the Employment Bureau.

"About that baby sitting job," he said.

She looked startled for a moment—terribly, almost childishly startled, but her face slid swiftly back to its goddess-mask.

"Yes, Mr. Bishop."

"I've thought it over," he said. "If you have that kind of job I'll take it."

# XI

He lay in bed, sleepless, for a long time that night and took stock of himself and of the situation and he came to a decision that it might not be as bad as he thought it was.

There were jobs to be had, apparently. The Kimonians even seemed anxious that you should get a job. And even if it weren't the kind of work a man might want, or the kind that he was fitted for, it at least would be a start. From that first foothold a man could go up—a clever man, that is. And all the men and women, all the Earthians on Kimon, certainly were clever. If they weren't clever, they wouldn't be there to start with.

All of them seemed to be getting along. He had not seen either Monty or Maxine that evening, but he had talked to others and all of them seemed to be satisfied— or at least keeping up the appearance of being satisfied. If there were general dissatisfaction, Bishop told himself, there wouldn't even be the appearance of being satisfied, for there is nothing that an Earthian likes better than some quiet and mutual griping. And he had heard none of it—none of it at all.

He had heard some more talk about the starting of the athletic teams and had talked to several men who had been enthusiastic about it as a source of revenue.

He had talked to another man named Thomas who was a gardening expert at one of the big Kimonian estates and the man had talked for an hour or more on the growing of exotic flowers. There had been a little man named Williams who had sat in the bar beside him and had told him enthusiastically of his commission to write a book of ballads based on Kimonian history and another man named Jackson who was executing a piece of statuary for one of the native families.

If a man could get a satisfactory job, Bishop thought, life could be pleasant here on Kimon.

Take the rooms he had. Beautiful appointments, much better than he could expect at home. A willing cabinet-robot who dished up drinks and sandwiches, who pressed clothes, turned out and locked up, and anticipated your no-more-than-half-formed wish. And the room—the room with the four blank walls and the single chair with the buttons on its arm. There, in that room, was instruction and entertainment and adventure. He had made a bad choice in picking the battle of Hastings for his first test of it, he knew now. But there were other places, other times, other more pleasant and less bloody incidents that one could experience.

It was experience, too—and not merely seeing. He had really been walking on the hilltop. He had tried to dodge the charging horses, although there'd been no reason to, for apparently, even in the midst of a happening, you stood by some special dispensation as a thing apart, as an interested but unreachable observer.

And there were, he told himself, many happenings that would be worth observing. One could live out the entire history of mankind, from the prehistoric dawnings to the day before yesterday—and not only the history of mankind, but the history of other things as well, for there had been other categories of experience offered—Kimonian and Galactic—in addition to Earth.

Some day, he thought, I will walk with Shakespeare. Someday I'll sail with Columbus. Or travel with Prester John and find the truth about him.

For it was truth. You could sense the truth.

And how the truth?

That he could not know.

But it all boiled down to the fact that while conditions might be strange, one could still make a life of it.

And conditions would be strange, for this was an alien land and one that was immeasurably in advance of Earth in culture and in its technology. Here there was no need of artificial communications nor of mechanical transportation. Here there was no need of contrasts since the mere fact of telepathy would reveal one man to another so there'd be no need of contracts.

You have to adapt, Bishop told himself.

You'd have to adapt and play the Kimon game, for they were the ones who would set the rules. Unbidden he had entered their planet and they had let him stay, and staying, it followed that he must conform.

"You are restless, sir," said the cabinet from the other room.

"Not restless," Bishop said. "Just thinking."

"I can supply you with a sedative. A very mild and pleasant sedative."

"Not a sedative," said Bishop.

"Then, perhaps," the cabinet said, "you would permit me to sing you a lullaby."

"By all means," said Bishop. "A lullaby is just the thing I need."

So the cabinet sang him a lullaby and after a time Bishop went to sleep.

# XII

The Kimonian goddess at the employment bureau told him next morning that there was a job for him.

"A new family," she said.

Bishop wondered if he should be glad that it was a new family or if it would have been better if it had been an old one.

"They've never had a human before," she said.

"It's fine of them," said Bishop, "to finally take one in."

"The salary," said the goddess, "is one hundred credits a day."

"One hundred—"

"You will only work during days," she said. "I'll teleport you there each morning and in the evening they'll teleport you back."

Bishop gulped. "One hundred— What am I to do?"

"A companion," said the goddess. "But you needn't worry. We'll keep an eye on them and if they mistreat you—"

"Mistreat me?"

"Work you too hard or—"

"Miss," said Bishop, "for a hundred bucks a day I'd—"

She cut him short. "You will take the job?"

"Most gladly," Bishop said.

"Permit me—"

The universe came unstuck, then slapped back together.

He was standing in an alcove and in front of him was a woodland glen with a waterfall and from where he stood he could smell the cool, mossy freshness of the tumbling water. There were ferns and trees, huge trees like the gnarled oaks the illustrators like to draw to illustrate King Arthur and Robin Hood and other tales of very early Britain—the kind of oaks from which the Druids had cut the mistletoe.

A path ran along the stream and up the incline down

249

which the waterfall came tumbling and there was a blowing wind that carried music and perfume.

A girl came down the path and she was Kimonian, but she didn't seem as tall as the others he had seen and there was something a little less goddesslike about her.

He caught his breath and watched her and for a moment he forgot that she was Kimonian and thought of her only as a pretty girl who walked a woodland path. She was beautiful, he told himself—she was lovely.

She saw him and clapped her hands.

"You must be he," she said.

He stepped out of the cubicle.

"We have been waiting for you," she told him. "We hoped there'd be no delay, that they'd send you right along."

"My name," said Bishop, "is Selden Bishop and I was told—"

"Of course you are the one," she said. "You needn't even tell me. It's lying in your mind."

She waved an arm about her.

"How do you like our house?" she asked.

"House?"

"Of course, silly. This. Naturally it's only the living room. Our bedrooms are up in the mountains. But we changed this just yesterday. Everyone worked so hard at it. I do hope you like it. Because, you see, it is from your planet. We thought it might make you feel at home."

"House," he said again.

She reached out a hand and laid it on his arm.

"You're all upset," she said. "You don't begin to understand."

Bishop shook his head. "I just arrived the other day."

"But do you like it?"

"Of course I do," said Bishop. "It's something out of the old Arthurian legend. You'd expect to see Lancelot or Guinevere or some of the others riding through the woods."

"You know the stories?"

"Of course I know the stories. I read my Tennyson."

"And you will tell them to us?"

He looked at her, a little startled.

"You mean you want to hear them."

"Why, yes, of course we do. What did we get you for?"

And that was it, of course.

What had they got him for?

"You want me to begin right now?"

"Not now," she said. "There are the others you must meet. My name is Elaine. That's not exactly it, of course. It is something else, but Elaine is as close as you'll ever come to saying it."

"I could try the other name. I'm proficient at languages."

"Elaine is good enough," she said carelessly. "Come along."

He fell in behind her on the path and followed up the incline.

And as he walked along, he saw that it was indeed a house—that the trees were pillars holding up an artificial sky that somehow failed to look very artificial and that the aisles between the trees ended in great windows which looked out on the barren plain.

But the grass and flowers, the moss and ferns, were real and he had a feeling that the trees must be real as well.

"It doesn't matter if they're real or not," said Elaine. "You couldn't tell the difference."


They came to the top of the incline into a parklike place, where the grass was cut so closely and looked so velvety that he wondered for a moment if it were really grass.

"It is," Elaine told him.

"You catch everything I think," he said. "Isn't—"

"Everything," said Elaine.

"Then I mustn't think."

"Oh, but we want you to," she told him. "That is part of it."

"Part of what you got me for?"

"Exactly," said the girl.

In the middle of the parklike area was a sort of pagoda, a flimsy thing that seemed to be made out of light and shadow rather than anything with substance, and all around it were a half a dozen people.

They were laughing and chatting and the sound of them

was like the sound of music—very happy, but at the same time, sophisticated music.

"There they are," cried Elaine.

"Come along," she said.

She ran and her running was like flying and his breath caught in his throat at the slimness and the grace of her.

He ran after her and there was no grace in his running. He could feel the heaviness of it. It was a gambol rather than a run, an awkward lope in comparison to the running of Elaine.

Like a dog, he thought. Like an overgrown puppy trying to keep up, falling over its own feet, with its tongue hanging out and panting.

He tried to run more gracefully and he tried to erase the thinking from his mind.

*Mustn't think. Mustn't think at all. They catch everything. They will laugh at you.*

They *were* laughing at him.

He could feel their laughter, the silent, gracious amusement that was racing in their minds.

She reached the group and waited.

"Hurry up," she called and while her words were kindly, he could feel the amusement in the words.

He hurried. He pounded down upon them. He arrived, somewhat out of breath. He felt winded and sweaty and extremely uncouth.

"This is the one they sent us," said Elaine. "His name is Bishop. Is that not a lovely name?"

They watched him, nodding gravely.

"He will tell us stories," said Elaine. "He knows the stories that go with a place like this."

They were looking kindly at him, but he could sense the covert amusement, growing by the moment.

She said to Bishop: "This is Paul. And that one over there is Jim. Betty. Jane. George. And the one on the end is Mary."

"You understand," said Jim, "those are not our names."

"They are approximations," said Elaine. "The best that I could do."

"They are as close," said Jane, "as he can pronounce them."

252

"If you'd only give me a chance," said Bishop, then stopped short.

That was what they wanted. They wanted him to protest and squirm. They wanted him to be uncomfortable.

"But of course we don't," said Elaine.

*Mustn't think. Must try to keep from thinking. They catch everything.*

"Let's all sit down," said Betty. "Bishop will tell us stories."

"Perhaps," Jim said to him, "you will describe your life on Earth. I would be quite interested."

"I understand you have a game called chess," said George. "We can't play games, of course. You know why we can't. But I'd be very interested in discussing with you the technique and philosophy of chess."

"One at a time," said Elaine. "First he will tell us stories."

They sat down on the grass, in a ragged circle.

All of them were looking at him, waiting for him to start.

"I don't quite know where to start," he said.

"Why, that's obvious," said Betty. "You start at the beginning."

"Quite right," said Bishop.

He took a deep breath.

"Once, long ago, in the island of Britain, there was a great king whose name was Arthur—"

"Ycelpt," said Jim.

"You've read the stories?"

"The word was in your mind."

"It's an old word, an archaic word. In some versions of the tales—"

"I would be most interested sometime to discuss the word with you," said Jim.

"Go on with your story," said Elaine.

He took another deep breath.

"Once, long ago, in the island of Britain, there was a great king whose name was Arthur. His queen was Guinevere and Lancelot was his staunchest knight—"

253

# XIII

He found the writer in the desk in the living room and pulled it out. He sat down to write a letter.

He typed the salutation:

Dear Morley:

He got up and began pacing up and down the room.

What would he tell him?

What could he tell him?

That he had safely arrived and that he had a job?

That the job paid a hundred credits a day—ten times more than a man in his position could earn at any Earth job?

He went back to the writer again.

He wrote:

Just a note to let you know that I arrived here safely and already have a job. Not too good a job perhaps, but it pays a hundred a day and that's better than I could have done on Earth.

He got up and walked again.

There had to be more than that. More than just a paragraph.

He sweated as he walked.

What could he tell him?

He went back to the writer again:

In order to learn the conditions and the customs more quickly I have taken a job which will keep me in touch with the Kimonians. I find them to be a fine people, but sometimes a little hard to understand. I have no doubt that before too long I shall get to understand them and have a genuine liking for them.

He pushed back his chair and stared at what he'd written.

254

It was, he told himself, like any one of a thousand other letters he had read.

He pictured in his mind those other thousand people, sitting down to write their first letter from Kimon, searching in their minds for the polite little fables, for the slightly colored lie, for the balm that would salve their pride. Hunting for the words that would not reveal the entire truth:

> I have a job of entertaining and amusing a certain family. I tell them stories and let them laugh at me. I do this because I will not admit that the fable of Kimon is a booby trap and that I've fallen into it—

No, it would never do to write like that.
Nor to write:

> I'm sticking on in spite of them. So long as I make a hundred a day, they can laugh as much as they want to laugh. I'm staying here and cleaning up no matter what—

Back home he was one of the thousand. Back home they talked of him in whispers because he made the grade.

And the businessmen on board the ship, saying to him: "The one who cracks this Kimon business is the one who'll have it big," and talking in terms of billions if he ever needed backing.

He remembered Morley pacing up and down the room. A foot in the door, he'd said: "Some way to crack them. Some way to understand them. Some little thing—no big thing, but some little thing. Anything at all except the deadpan face that Kimon turns toward us."

Somehow he had to finish the letter. He couldn't leave it hanging and he had to write it.

He turned back to the writer:

> I'll write you later at a greater length. At the moment I'm rushed.

He frowned at it.

But whatever he wrote, it would be wrong. This was no worse than any of another dozen things that he might write.

Must rush off to a conference.
Have an appointment with a client.
Some papers to go through.

All of them were wrong.
What was a man to do?
He wrote:

Think of you often. Write me when you can.

Morley would write him. An enthusiastic letter, a letter with a fine shade of envy tingeing it, the letter of a man who wanted to be, but couldn't be on Kimon.

For everyone wanted to go to Kimon. That was the hell of it.

You couldn't tell the truth, when everyone would give their good right arm to go.

You couldn't tell the truth, when you were a hero and the truth would turn you into a galactic heel.

And the letters from home, the prideful letters, the envious letters, the letters happy with the thought you were doing so well—all of these would be only further chains to bind you to Kimon and to the Kimon lie.

He said to the cabinet: "How about a drink?"

"Yes, sir," said the cabinet. "Coming right up, sir."

"A long one," Bishop said, "and a strong one."

"Long and strong it is, sir."

# XIV

He met her in the bar.

"Why, if it isn't Buster!" she said, as though they met there often.

He sat on the stool beside her.

"That week is almost up," he said.

She nodded. "We've been watching you. You're standing up real well."

"You tried to tell me."

"Forget it," said the girl. "Just a mistake of mine. It's a waste of time telling any of them. But you looked intelligent and not quite dry behind the ears. I took pity on you."

She looked at him over the rim of her glass.

"I shouldn't have," she said.

"I should have listened."

"They never do," said Maxine.

"There's another thing," he said. "Why hasn't it leaked out? Oh, sure, I have written letters, too. I didn't admit what it was like. Neither did you. Nor the man next to you. But someone, in all the years we've been here—"

"We are all alike," she said. "Alike as peas in the pod. We are the anointed, the hand-picked, stubborn, vanity-stricken, scared. All of us got here. In spite of hell and high water we got here. We let nothing stand in our way and we made it. We beat the others out. They're waiting back there on Earth—the ones that we beat out. They'll never be quite the same again. Don't you understand it? They had pride, too, and it was hurt. There's nothing they would like better than to know what it's really like. That's what all of us think of when we sit down to write a letter. We think of the belly laughs by those other thousands. The quiet smirks. We think of ourselves skulking, making ourselves small so no one will notice us—"

She balled a fist and rapped against his shirt front.

"That's the answer, Buster. That's why we never write the truth. That's why we don't go back."

"But it's been going on for years. For almost a hundred years. In all that time someone should have cracked—"

"And lost all this?" she asked. "Lost the easy living. The good drinking. The fellowship of lost souls. And the hope. Don't forget that. Always the hope that Kimon can be cracked."

"Can it?"

"I don't know. But if I were you, Buster, I wouldn't count on it."

"But it's no kind of a life for decent—"

"Don't say it. We aren't decent people. We are scared and weak, every one of us. And with good reason."

"But the life—"

257

"You don't lead a decent life, if that was what you were about to say. There's no stability in us. Children? A few of us have children and it's not so bad for the children as it is for us, because they know nothing else. A child who is born a slave is better off, mentally, than a man who once knew freedom."

"We aren't slaves," said Bishop.

"Of course not," Maxine said. "We can leave any time we want to. All we got to do is walk up to a native and say 'I want to go back to Earth.' That's all you need to do. Any single one of them could send you back—*swish* —just like they send the letters, just like they whisk you to your work or to your room."

"But no one has gone back."

"Of course no one has," she said.

They sat there, sipping at their drinks.

"Remember what I told you," she said. "Don't think. That's the way to beat it. Never think about it. You got it good. You never had it so good. Soft living. Easy living. Nothing to worry about. The best kind of life there is."

"Sure," said Bishop. "Sure that's the way to do it."

She slanted her eyes at him.

"You're catching on," she said.

They had another round.

Over in the corner a group had gotten together and was doing some impromptu singing. A couple were quarreling a stool or two away.

"It's too noisy in this place," Maxine said. "Want to see my paintings?"

"Your paintings?"

"The way I make my living. They are pretty bad, but no one knows the difference."

"I'd like to see them."

"Grab hold then."

"Grab—"

"My mind, you know. Nothing physical about it. No use riding elevators."

He gaped at her.

"You pick it up," said Maxine. "You never get too good. But you pick up a trick or two."

"But how do I go about it?"

"Just let loose," she said. "Dangle. Mentally, that is. Try to reach out to me. Don't try to help. You can't."

He dangled and reached out, wondering if he was doing it the way it should be done.

The universe collapsed and then came back together.

They were standing in another room.

"That was a silly thing for me to do," Maxine said. "Some day I'll slip a cog and get stuck in a wall or something."

Bishop drew a deep breath.

"Monty could read me just a little," he said. "Said you picked it up—just at the fringes."

"You never get too good," said Maxine. "Humans aren't . . . well, aren't ripe for it, I guess. It takes millennia to develop it."

He looked around him and whistled.

"Quite a place," he said.

It was all of that.

It didn't seem to be a room at all, although it had furniture. The walls were hazed in distance and to the west were mountains, peaked with snow, and to the east a very sylvan river and there were flowers and flowering bushes everywhere, growing from the floor. A deep blue dusk filled the room and somewhere off in the distance there was an orchestra.

A cabinet-voice said. "Anything, madam?"

"Drinks," said Maxine. "Not too strong. We've been hitting the bottle."

"Not too strong," said the cabinet. "Just a moment, madam."

"Illusion," Maxine said. "Every bit of it. But a nice illusion. Want a beach. It's waiting for you if you just think of it. Or a polar cap. Or a desert. Or an old chateau. It's waiting in the wings."

"Your painting must pay off," he said.

"Not my painting. My irritation. Better start getting irritated, Buster. Get down in the dumps. Start thinking about suicide. That's a sure-fire way to do it. Presto, you're kicked upstairs to a better suite of rooms. Anything to keep you happy."

259

"You mean the Kimonians automatically shift you?"

"Sure. You're a sucker to stay down there where you are."

"I like my layout," he told her. "But this—"

She laughed at him. "You'll catch on," she said.

The drinks arrived.

"Sit down," Maxine said. "Want a moon?"

There was a moon.

"Could have two or three," she said, "but that would be over-doing it. One moon seems more like Earth. Seems more comfortable."

"There must be a limit somewhere," Bishop said. "They can't keep on kicking you upstairs indefinitely. There must come a time when even the Kimonians can't come up with anything that is new and novel."

"You wouldn't live long enough," she told him, "for that to come about. That's the way with all you new ones. You underestimate the Kimonians. You think of them as people, as Earth people who know just a little more. They aren't that, at all. They're alien. They're as alien as a spider-man despite their human form. They conform to keep contact with us."

"But why do they want to keep contact with us? Why—"

"Buster," she said, "that's the question that we never ask. That's the one that can drive you crazy."

# XV

He had told them about the human custom of going out on picnics and the idea was one that they had never thought of, so they adopted it with childish delight.

They had picked a wild place, a tumbled mountain area, filled with deep ravines, clothed in flowers and trees and with a mountain brook with water that was as clear as glass and as cold as ice.

They had played games and romped. They had swam and sunbathed and they had listened to his stories, sitting in a circle, needling him and interrupting him, picking arguments.

But he had laughed at them, not openly, but deep inside himself, for he knew now that they meant no harm, but merely sought amusement.

Weeks before he had been insulted and outraged and humiliated, but as the days went on he had adapted to it —had forced himself to adapt. If they wished a clown, then he would be a clown. If he were court fool, with bells and parti-colored garments, then he must wear the colors well and keep the bells ringing merrily.

There was occasional maliciousness in them and some cruelty, but no lasting harm. And you could get along with them, he told himself, if you just knew how to do it.

When evening came they had built a fire and had sat around it and had talked and laughed and joked, for once leaving him alone. Elaine and Betty had been nervous. Jim had laughed at them for their nervousness.

"No animals will come near a fire," he said.

"There are animals?" Bishop had asked.

"A few," said Jim. "Not many of them left."

He had lain there, staring at the fire, listening to their voices, glad that for once they were leaving him alone. Like a dog must feel, he thought. Like a pup hiding in a corner from a gang of rowdy children who are always mauling it.

He watched the fire and remembered other days—outings in the country and walking trips when they had built a fire and lay around it, staring at the sky, seeing the old, familiar skies of Earth.

And here again was another fire.

And here, again, a picnic.

The fire was Earth and so was the picnic—for the people of Kimon did not know of picnics. They did not know of picnics and there might be many other things of which they likewise did not know. Many other things, perhaps. Barbaric, folkish things.

Don't look for the big things, Morley had said that night. Watch for the little things, for the little clues.

They liked Maxine's paintings because they were primitives. Primitives, perhaps, but likewise not very good. Could it be that paintings also had been something the Kimonians had not known until the Earthmen came?

Were there, after all, chinks in the Kimonian armor. Little chinks like picnics and paintings and many other little things for which they valued the visitors from Earth?

Somewhere in those chinks might be the answer that he sought for Morley.

He lay and thought, forgetting to shield his mind, forgetting that he should not think because his thoughts lay open to them.

Their voices had faded away and there was a solemn night-time quiet. Soon, he thought, we'll all be going back —they to their homes and I to the hotel. How far away, he wondered. Half a world or less? And yet they'd be there in the instant of a thought.

Someone, he thought, should put more wood on the fire.

He roused himself to do it, standing up.

And it was not until then that he saw he was alone.

He stood there, trying to quiet his terror.

They had gone away and left him.

They had forgotten him.

But that couldn't be. They'd simply slipped off in the dark. Up to some prank, perhaps. Trying to scare him. Talking about the animals and then slipping out of sight while he lay dreaming at the fire. Waiting now, just outside the circle of the firelight, watching him, drinking in his thoughts, reveling in his terror.

He found wood and put it on the fire. It caught and blazed.

He sat down nonchalantly, but he found that his shoulders were hunched instinctively, that the terror of aloneness in an alien world still sat by the fire beside him.

Now, for the first time, he realized the alienness of Kimon. It had not seemed alien before except for those few minutes he had waited in the park after the gig had landed him, and even then it had not been as alien as an alien planet should be because he knew that he was being met, that there would be someone along to take care of him.

That was it, he thought. Someone to take care of me. We're taken care of—well and lavishly. We're sheltered and guarded and pampered—that was it, *pampered*. And for what reason?

Any minute now they'd tire of their game and come back into the circle of the firelight.

Maybe, he told himself, I should give them their money's worth. Maybe I should act scared, maybe I should shout out for them to come and get me, maybe I should glance around, out into the darkness, as if I were afraid of those animals that they talked about. They hadn't talked too much, of course. They were too clever for that, far too clever. Just a passing remark about existent animals, then on to something else. Not stressing it, not laying it on too thick. Not over-doing it. Just planting a suggestion that there were animals one could be afraid of.

He sat and waited, not as scared as he had been before, having rationalized away the fear that he first had felt. Like an Earth campfire, he thought. Except it isn't Earth. Except it's an alien planet.

There was a rustle in the bushes.

They'll be coming now, he thought. They've figured out that it didn't work. They'll be coming back.

The bushes rustled again and there was the sound of a dislodged stone.

He did not stir.

They can't scare me, he thought.

They can't scare—

He felt the breath upon his neck and leaped into the air, spinning as he leaped, stumbling as he came down, almost falling in the fire, then on his feet and scurrying to put the fire between him and the thing that had breathed upon his neck.

He crouched across the fire from it and saw the teeth in the gaping jaws. It raised its head and slashed, as if in pantomime and he could hear the clicking of the teeth as they came together and the little moaning rumble that came from the massive throat.

A wild thought came to him: It's not an animal at all. This is just part of the gag. Something they dreamed up. If they can build a house like an English wood, use it for a day or two, then cause it to disappear as something for

263

which they have no further use, surely it would be a second's work to dream up an animal.

The animal padded forward and he thought: Animals should be afraid of fire. All animals are afraid of fire. It won't get me if I stay near the fire.

He stooped and grabbed a brand.

*Animals are afraid of fire.*

But this one wasn't.

It padded round the fire. It stretched out its neck and sniffed.

It wasn't in any hurry, for it was sure of him.

Sweat broke out on him and ran down his sides.

The animal came with a smooth rush, whipping around the fire.

He leaped, clearing the fire, to gain the other side of it.

The animal checked itself, spun around to face him.

It put its muzzle to the ground and arched its back. It lashed its tail. It rumbled.

He was frightened now, cold with a fright that could not be laughed off.

It might be an animal.

It must be an animal.

No gag at all, but an animal.

He paced back toward the fire. He danced on his toes, ready to run, to dodge, to fight if he had to fight. But against this thing that faced him across the fire, he knew, there was no fighting chance. And yet, if it came to fighting, he could do no less than fight.

The animal charged.

He ran.

He slipped and fell and rolled into the fire.

A hand reached down and jerked him from the fire, flung him to one side, and a voice cried out, a cry of rage and warning.

Then the universe collapsed and he felt himself flying apart and, as suddenly, he was together once again.

He lay upon a floor and he scrambled to his feet. His hand was burned and he felt the pain of it. His clothes were smoldering and he beat them out with his uninjured hand.

A voice said, "I'm sorry, sir. This should not have happened."

The man was tall, much taller than the Kimonians he had seen before. Nine feet, perhaps. And yet not nine feet, actually. Not anywhere near nine feet. He was no taller, probably, than the taller men of Earth. It was the way he stood that made him seem so tall, the way he stood and looked and the way his voice sounded.

And the first Kimonian, Bishop thought, who had ever shown age. For there was a silvering of the temple hairs and his face was lined, like the faces of hunters or of sailors may be lined from squinting into far distances.

They stood facing one another in a room which, when Bishop looked at it, took his breath away. There was no describing it, no way to describe it—you felt as well as saw it. It was a part of you and a part of the universe and a part of everything you'd ever known or dreamed. It seemed to thrust extensions out into unguessed time and space and it had a sense of life and the touch of comfort and the feel of home.

Yet, when he looked again, he sensed a simplicity that did not square with his first impressions. Basic simplicities that tied in with the simple business of living out one's life, as if the room and the folks who lived within its walls were somehow integrated, as if the room were trying its best not to be a room, but to be a part of life, so much a part of life that it could pass unnoticed.

"I was against it from the first," said the Kimonian. "Now I know that I was right. But the children wanted you—"

"The children?"

"Certainly. I am Elaine's father."

He didn't say Elaine, however. He said the other name —the name that Elaine had said no Earthman could pronounce.

"Your hand?" asked the man.

"It's all right," said Bishop. "Only burned a little."

And it was as if he had not spoken, as if he had not said the words—but another man, a man who stood off to one side and spoke the words for him.

He could not have moved if he'd been paid a million.

"This is something," said the Kimonian, "that must be recompensed. We'll talk about it later."

"Please, sir," said the man who talked for Bishop. "Please, sir, just one thing. Send me to my hotel."

He felt the swiftness of the other's understanding—the compassion and the pity.

"Of course," said the tall man. "With your permission, sir."

# XVI

Once there were some children (human children, playfully) who had wanted a dog—a little playful puppy. But their father said they could not have a dog because they would not know how to treat him. But they wanted him so badly and begged their father so that he finally brought them home a dog, a cunning little puppy, a little butterball, with a paunchy belly and four wobbly legs and melting eyes, filled with the innocence of puppyhood.

The children did not treat him as badly as you might have imagined that they would. They were cruel, as all children are. They roughed and tumbled him; they pulled his ears and tail; they teased him. But the pup was full of fun. He liked to play and no matter what they did he came back for more. Because, undoubtedly, he felt very smug in this business of associating with the clever human race, a race so far ahead of dogs in culture and intelligence that there was no comparison at all.

But one day the children went on a picnic and when the day was over they were very tired, and forgetful, as children are very apt to be. So they went off and left the puppy.

That wasn't a bad thing really. For children will be forgetful, no matter what you do, and the pup was nothing but a dog.

The cabinet said: "You are very late, sir."

"Yes," said Bishop, dully.

"You hurt somewhere, sir. I can sense the hurt."

"My hand," said Bishop. "I burned it in a fire."

A panel popped open in the cabinet.

"Put it in there," said the cabinet. "I'll fix it in a jiffy."

Bishop thrust his hand into the opening. He felt finger-like appendages going over it, very gently and soothing.

"It's not a bad burn, sir," said the cabinet, "but I imagine it is painful."

Playthings, Bishop thought.

This hotel is a dollhouse—or a doghouse.

It is a shack, a tacked-together shack like the boys of Earth build out of packing cases and bits of board and paint crude, mystic signs upon.

Compared to that room back there it is no more than a hovel, although, come to think of it, a very gaudy hovel.

Fit for humans, good enough for humans but a hovel just the same.

*And we?* he thought.

*And we?*

The pets of children. The puppy dogs of Kimon.

Imported puppy dogs.

"I beg your pardon, sir," said the cabinet. "You are not puppy dogs."

"What's that?"

"You will pardon me, sir. I should not have spoken out. But I wouldn't have wanted you to think—"

"If we aren't pets, what are we?"

"You will excuse me, sir. It was a slip. I quite assure you. I should not have—"

"You never do a thing," said Bishop bitterly, "without having it all figured out. You or any of them. For you are one of them. You spoke because they wanted you to speak."

"I can assure you that's not so."

"You would deny it, naturally," said Bishop. "Go ahead and do your job. You haven't told me all they wanted you to tell me. Go ahead and finish."

"It's immaterial to me what you think," the cabinet told him. "But if you thought of yourself as playmates . . ."

"That's a hot one," Bishop said.

"Infinitely better," said the cabinet, "than thinking of yourself as a puppy dog."

"So that's what they want me to think."

"They don't care," the cabinet said. "It all is up to you. It was a mere suggestion, sir."

So, all right, it was a mere suggestion.

So, all right, they were playmates and not pets at all.

The kids of Kimon inviting the dirty, ragged, runny-nosed urchins from across the tracks to play with them.

Better to be an invited kid, perhaps, than an imported dog.

But even so, it was the children of Kimon who had engineered it all—who had set up the rules for those who wished to come to Kimon, who had built the hotel, had operated it and furnished it with the progressively more luxurious and more enticing rooms, who had found the so-called jobs for humans, who had arranged the printing of the credits.

And, if that were so, then it meant that not merely the people of Earth, but the government of Earth, had negotiated, or had attempted to negotiate with the children of another race. And that would be the mark of the difference, he thought, the difference between us.

Although, he told himself, that might not be entirely right.

Maybe he *had* been wrong in thinking, in the first flush of his bitterness, that he was a pet.

Maybe he *was* a playmate, an adult Earthman downgraded to the status of a child—and a stupid child, at that.

Maybe, if he had been wrong on the pet angle, he was wrong in the belief as well, that it had been the children of Kimon who had arranged the immigration of the Earth folk.

And if it hadn't been simply a childish matter of asking if some kids from across the tracks, if the adults of Kimon had had a hand in it, what was the set-up then? A school project, a certain phase of progressive education? Or a sort of summer camp project, designed to give the deserving but under-privileged, Earthman a vacation away from the squalor of their native planet? Or simply a safe way in which the children of Kimon might amuse and occupy themselves, be kept from underfoot?

We should have guessed it long ago, Bishop told himself. But even if some of us might have entertained the thought, that we were either pet or playmate, we would have pushed it far away from us, would have refused to recognize it, for our pride is too tender and too raw for a thought like that.

"There you are, sir," said the cabinet. "Almost as good as new. Tomorrow you can take the dressing off."

He stood before the cabinet without answering. He withdrew his hand and let it fall to his side, like so much dead weight.

Without asking if he wanted it, the cabinet produced a drink.

"I made it long and strong," said the cabinet. "I thought you needed it."

"Thank you," Bishop said.

He took the drink and stood there with it, not touching it, not wanting to touch it until he'd finished out the thought.

And the thought would not finish out.

There was something wrong. Something that didn't track.

*Our pride is too raw and tender*—

There was something there, some extra words that badly needed saying.

"There is something wrong, sir?"

"Nothing wrong," said Bishop.

"But your drink."

"I'll get around to it."

The Normans had sat their horses on that Saturday afternoon, with the leopard banners curling in the breeze, with the pennons on their lances fluttering, with the sun upon their armor and the scabbards clinking as the horses pranced. They had charged, as history said they had, and they were beaten back. That was entirely right, for it had not been until late afternoon that the Saxon wall was broken and the final fight around the dragon standard had not taken place until it was nearly dark.

But there had been no Taillefer, riding in the fore to throw up his sword and sing.

On that history had been wrong.

A couple of centuries later, more than likely, some copyist had whiled away a monotonous afternoon by writing into the prosaic story of the battle the romance and the glitter of the charge of Taillefer. Writing it in protest against the four blank walls, against his Spartan food, against the daily dullness when spring was in the air and a man should be in the fields or woods instead of shut indoors, hunched with his quills and inkpots.

And that is the way it is with us, thought Bishop. We write the half-truth and the half-lie in our letters home. We conceal a truth or we obscure a fact, or we add a line or two that, if not a downright lie, is certainly misleading.

We do not face up to facts, he thought. We gloss over the man crawling in the grass, with his torn-out guts snagging on the brambles. We write in the Taillefer.

And if we only did it in our letters, it would not be so bad. But we do it to ourselves. We protect our pride by lying to ourselves. We shield our dignity by deliberate indignation.

"Here," he said to the cabinet, "have a drink on me."

He set the glass, still full, on the top of the cabinet.

The cabinet gurgled in surprise.

"I do not drink," it said.

"Then take it back and put it in the bottle."

"I can't do that," said the cabinet, horrified. "It's already mixed."

"Separate it, then."

"It can't be separated," wailed the cabinet. "You surely don't expect me—"

There was a little swish and Maxine stood in the center of the room.

She smiled at Bishop.

"What goes on?" she asked.

The cabinet wailed at her. "He wants me to unmix a drink. He wants me to separate it, the liquor from the mix. He knows I can't do that."

"My, my," she said, "I thought you could do anything."

"I can't unravel a drink," the cabinet said primly. "Why don't you take it off my hands?"

"That's a good idea," said the girl. She walked forward and picked up the drink.

"What's wrong with you?" she asked Bishop. "Turning chicken on us?"

"I just don't want a drink," said Bishop. "Hasn't a man got a right to—"

"Of course," she said. "Of course you have."

She sipped the drink, looking at him above the rim.

"What happened to your hand?"

"Burned it."

"You're old enough not to play with fire."

"You're old enough not to come barging into a room this way," Bishop told her. "One of these days you'll reassemble yourself in the precise spot where someone else is standing."

She giggled. "That would be fun," she said. "Think of you and me—"

"It would be a mess," said Bishop.

"Invite me to sit down," said Maxine. "Let's act civilized and social."

"Sure, sit down," said Bishop.

She picked out a couch.

"I'm interested in this business of teleporting yourself," said Bishop. "I've never asked you before but you told me—"

"It just came to me," she said.

"But you can't teleport. Humans aren't parapsychic—"

"Some day, Buster, you'll blow a fuse. You get so steamed up."

He went across the room and sat down beside her.

"Sure, I get steamed up," he said. "But—"

"What now?"

"Have you ever thought . . . well, have you ever tried to work at it? Like moving something else, some object— other than yourself?"

"No, I never have."

"Why not?"

"Look, Buster. I drop in to have a drink with you and to forget myself. I didn't come primed for a long technical discussion. I couldn't anyway. I just don't understand. There's so much we don't understand."

She looked at him and there was something very much like fright brimming in her eyes.

"You pretend that you don't mind," she said. "But you do mind. You wear yourself out pretending that you don't mind at all."

"Then let's quit pretending," Bishop said. "Let's admit—"

She had lifted the glass to drink and now, suddenly, it slipped out of her hand.

"Oh—"

The glass halted before it struck the floor. It hovered for a moment, then it slowly rose. She reached out and grasped it.

And then it slipped again from her suddenly shaking hand. This time it hit the floor and spilled.

"Try it again," said Bishop.

She said: "I never tried. I don't know how it happened. I just didn't want to drop it, that was all. I wished I hadn't dropped it and then—"

"But the second time—"

"You fool," she screamed, "I tell you I didn't try. I wasn't putting on an exhibition for you. I tell you that I don't know what happened."

"But you did it. It was a start."

"A start?"

"You caught the glass before it hit the floor. You teleported it back into your hand."

"Look, Buster," she said grimly, "quit kidding yourself. They're watching all the time. They play little tricks like that. Anything for a laugh."

She rose, laughing at him, but there was a strangeness in her laughing.

"You don't give yourself a chance," he told her. "You are so horribly afraid of being laughed at. You got to be a wise guy."

"Thanks for the drink," she said.

"But, Maxine—"

"Come up and see me sometime."

"Maxine! Wait!"

But she was gone.

# XVII

Watch for the clues, Morley had said, pacing up and down the room. Send us back the clues and we will do the rest.

A foot in the door is all we expect from you. Give us a foot inside the door and that is all we need.

Let us look for facts.

The Kimonians are a race more culturally advanced than we are, which means, in other words, that they are further along the road of evolution, farther from the ape. And what does it take to advance along the evolutionary road beyond the high tide of my own race of Earth?

Not mere intelligence alone, for that is not enough.

What then would it take to make the next major stride in evolution?

Perhaps philosophy rather than intelligence—a seeking for a way to put to better use the intelligence that one already had, a greater understanding and a more adequate appreciation time of human values in relation to the universe.

And if the Kimonians had that greater understanding, if they had won their way through better understanding to closer brotherhood with the galaxy, then it would be inconceivable that they'd take the members of another intelligent race to serve as puppy dogs for children. Or even as playmates for their children, unless in the fact of playing with their children there be some greater value, not to their child alone, but to the child of Earth, than the happiness and wonder of such association. They would be alive to the psychic damage that might be done because of such a practice, would not for a moment run the danger of that damage happening unless out of it might come some improvement or some change.

He sat and thought of it and it seemed right, for even on his native planet, history showed increasing concern with social values with the improvement of the culture.

And something else.

Parapsychic powers must not come too soon in human evolution, for they could be used disastrously by a culture that was not equipped emotionally and intellectually to handle them. No culture which had not reached an adult stage could have parapsychic powers, for they were nothing to be fooled around with by an adolescent culture.

In that respect at least, Bishop told himself, the Kimonians are the adults and we are the adolescents. In comparison with the Kimonians, we have no right to consider ourselves any more than children.

It was hard to take.

He gagged on it.

Swallow it, he told himself. Swallow it.

The cabinet said: "It is late, sir. You must be getting tired."

"You want me to go to bed?"

"It's a suggestion, sir."

"All right," he said.

He rose and started for the bedroom, smiling to himself.

Sent off to bed, he thought—just as a child is sent.

And going.

Not saying: "I'll go when I am ready."

Not standing on your adult dignity.

Not throwing a tantrum, not beating your heels upon the floor and howling.

Going off to bed—like a child when it is told to go.

Maybe that's the way, he thought. Maybe that's the answer. Maybe that's the *only* answer.

He swung around.

"Cabinet."

"What is it, sir?"

"Nothing," Bishop said. "Nothing at all . . . that is. Thanks for fixing up my hand."

"That's quite all right," said the cabinet. "Good night."

Maybe that's the answer.

To act like a child.

And what does a child do?

He goes to bed when he is told.

He minds his elders.

He goes to school.

He—

Wait a minute!

*He goes to school.*

He goes to school because there is a lot to learn. He goes to kindergarten so he can get into first grade and he goes to high school so he can go to college. He realizes there is a lot to learn, that before he takes his place in the adult world it must be learned and that he has to work to learn.

But I went to school, Bishop told himself. I went

274

for years and years. I studied hard and I passed an examination that a thousand others failed to pass. I qualified for Kimon.

But just suppose.

You went to kindergarten to qualify for first grade.

You went to high school to qualify for college.

You went to Earth to qualify for Kimon.

You might have a doctorate on Earth, but still be no more than a kindergarten youngster when you got to Kimon.

Monty knew a bit of telepathy and so did some of the others. Maxine could teleport herself and she had made the glass stop before it hit the floor. Perhaps the others could, too.

And they'd just picked it up.

Although just telepathy or stopping a glass from hitting the floor would not be all of it. There'd be much more of it. Much more to the culture of Kimon than the parapsychic arts.

Maybe we are ready, he thought. Maybe we've almost finished with our adolescence. Maybe we are on the verge of being ready for an adult culture. Could that be why the Kimonians let us in, the only ones in the galaxy they are willing to let in?

His brain reeled with the thought.

On Earth only one of every thousand passed the examination that sent them on to Kimon. Maybe here on Kimon only another one in every thousand would be qualified to absorb the culture that Kimon offered them.

But before you could even start to absorb the culture, before you could start to learn, before you ever went to school, you'd have to admit that you didn't know. You'd have to admit that you were a child. You couldn't go on having tantrums. You couldn't be a wise guy. You couldn't keep on polishing up false pride to use as a shield between you and the culture that waited for your understanding.

Morley, Bishop said, I may have the answer—the answer that you're awaiting back on Earth.

But I can't tell it to you. It's something that can't be told. It's a thing that each one must find out for himself.

And the pity of it is that Earth is not readily equipped

to find it out. It is not a lesson that is often taught on Earth.

Armies and guns could not storm the citadel of Kimonian culture, for you simply could not fight a war with a parapsychic people. Earth aggressiveness and business cunning likewise would fail to crack the dead-pan face of Kimon.

There is only one way, Morley, Bishop said, talking to his friend. There is only one thing that will crack this planet and that is humility.

And Earthmen are not humble creatures.

Long ago they forgot the meaning of humility.

But here it's different.

Here you have to be different.

You start out by saying I don't know.

Then you say I want to know.

Then you say I'll work hard to learn.

Maybe, Bishop thought, that's why they brought us here, so that the one of us in every thousand who has a chance of learning would get that chance to learn. Maybe they are watching, hoping that there may be more than one in every thousand. Maybe they are more anxious for us to learn than we are to learn. For they may be lonely in a galaxy where there are no others like them.

Could it be that the ones at this hotel were the failures, the ones who had never tried, or who might have tried and could not pass.

And the others—the one out of every thousand—where were they?

He could not even guess.

There were no answers.

It all was supposition.

It was a premise built upon a pipe-dream—built on wishful thinking.

He'd wake up in the morning and know that it was wrong.

He'd go down to the bar and have a drink with Maxine or with Monty and laugh at himself for the things that he'd dreamed up.

School, he'd told himself. But it wouldn't be a school— at least not the kind of school he'd ever known before.

I wish it could be so, he thought.

The cabinet said, "You'd better get off to bed, sir."

"I suppose I should," said Bishop. "It's been a long, hard day."

"You'll want to get up early," said the cabinet, "so you aren't late for school."

## ii *The Health Service in the Skies*

•

It must be confessed that many of the operations of a galactic empire have yet to be revealed. Authors prefer to concentrate on such problems as how you get from planet A to planet B when they are hundreds of light-years apart, or who sits on which council or throne. The emphasis is on power, whether in the Main Drive or in the driving seat. We have here three stories which investigate interesting side-issues.

Hal Lynch turns his attention on the good old Space Patrol and tells us who mans it, if that is the appropriate phrase. Pete Adams and Charles Nightingale—as yet not two of the most famous names in sf—deal with the sexual problems of galactic travellers, laughing all the way to the nearest mossy bank.

It seems to have occurred only to James White that, with aliens getting shot up all over the inhabited universe, pretty capacious galactic hospitals will be needed for the wounded. In fact, White's famous space-going Sector General deals mainly with civilian casualties. The case on hand would baffle Dr. Kildare, who never had to cope with a patient possessing five large mouths. That Big Health Service in the Skies is used to anything.

Mr. White lavishes much ingenuity on the aliens who pass through Sector General. The adventures of his medico, Conway, are detailed in two volumes, *Hospital Station* and *Star Surgeon*. For a change, the central character is a pacifist. Here is an external view of the gigantic station.

"Far out on the galactic rim, where star systems were sparse and the darkness was nearly absolute, Sector Twelve General Hospital hung in space. In its three hundred and eighty-four levels were repro-

281

duced the environments of all the intelligent life-forms known to the Galactic Federation, a biological spectrum ranging from the ultra-frigid methane life-forms through the more normal oxygen- and chlorine-breathing types up to the exotic beings who existed by the direct absorption of hard radiation. Its thousands of viewports were constantly ablaze with light—light in the dazzling variety of colour and intensity necessary for the visual equipment of its extra-terrestrial patients and staff—so that to approaching ships the great hospital looked like a tremendous cylindrical Christmas tree."

Enter one dying criminal weighing one thousand pounds and looking like a giant upright pear . . .

*In this new story of the gigantic Sector General Hospital in space, Dr. Conway is posed with a particularly sticky problem—to diagnose and cure a sick alien who is both immortal and apparently a murderer.*

●

# RESIDENT PHYSICIAN
## by James White

The patient being brought into the observation ward was a large specimen—about one thousand pounds mass, Conway estimated—and resembled a giant, upright pear. Five thick, tentacular appendages grew from the narrow head section and a heavy apron of muscle at its base gave evidence of a snail-like, although not necessarily slow, method of locomotion. The whole body surface looked raw and lacerated, as though someone had been trying to take its skin off with a wire brush.

To Conway there was nothing very unusual about the physical aspect of the patient or its condition, six years in space Sector General Hospital having accustomed him to much more startling sights, so he moved forward to make a preliminary examination. Immediately the Monitor Corps lieutenant who had accompanied the patient's trolley into the ward moved closer also. Conway tried to ignore the feeling of breath on the back of his neck and took a closer look at the patient.

Five large mouths were situated below the root of each tentacle, four being plentifully supplied with teeth and the other one housing the vocal apparatus. The tentacles themselves showed a high degree of specialisation at their extremities; three of them were plainly manipulatory, one bore the patient's visual equipment and the remaining member terminated in a horn-tipped, boney mace. The head was featureless, being simply an osseus dome housing the patient's brain.

There wasn't much else to be seen from a superficial examination. Conway turned to get his deep probe gear, and walked on the Monitor officer's feet.

"Have you ever considered taking up medicine seriously, Lieutenant?" he said irritably.

The lieutenant reddened, his face making a horrible clash of colour against the dark green of his uniform collar. He said stiffly, "This patient is a criminal. It was found in circumstances which indicate that it killed and ate the other member of its ship's crew. It has been unconscious during the trip here, but I've been ordered to stand guard on it just in case. I'll try to stay out of your way, Doctor."

Conway swallowed, his eyes going to the vicious-looking, horny bludgeon with which, he had no doubt, the patient's species had battered their way to the top of their evolutionary tree. He said drily. "Don't try too hard, Lieutenant."

Using his eyes and a portable x-ray scanner Conway examined his patient thoroughly inside and out. He took several specimens, including sections of the affected skin, and sent them off to Pathology with three closely-written pages of covering notes. Then he stood back and scratched his head.

The patient was warm-blooded, oxygen-breathing, and had fairly normal gravity and pressure requirements which, when considered with the general shape of the beastie, put its physiological classification as EPLH. It seemed to be suffering from a well-developed and widespread epithelioma, the symptoms being so plain that he really should have begun treatment without waiting for the Path report. But a cancerous skin condition did not, ordinarily, render a patient deeply unconscious.

That could point to psychological complications, he knew, and in that case he would have to call in some specialised help. One of his telepathic colleagues was the obvious choice, if it hadn't been for the fact that telepaths could only rarely work minds that were not already telepathic and of the same species as themselves. Except for the very odd instance, telepathy had been found to be a strictly closed circuit form of communication. Which left his GLNO friend, the empath Dr. Prilicla . . .

Behind him the Lieutenant coughed gently and said, "When you've finished the examination, Doctor, O'Mara would like to see you."

Conway nodded. "I'm going to send someone to keep an eye on the patient," he said, grinning, "guard them as well as you've guarded me."

Going through to the main ward Conway detailed an Earth-human nurse—a very good-looking Earth-human nurse—to duty in the observation ward. He could have sent in one of the Tralthan FLGIs, who belonged to a species with six legs and so built that beside one of them an Earthy elephant would have seemed a fragile, sylph-like creature, but he felt that he owed the Lieutenant something for his earlier bad manners.

Twenty minutes later after three changes of protective armour and a trip through the chlorine section, a corridor belonging to the AUGL water-breathers and the ultra-refrigerated wards of the methane life-forms, Conway presented himself at the office of Major O'Mara.

As Chief Psychologist of a multi-environmental hospital hanging in frigid blackness at the Galactic rim, he was responsible for the mental well-being of a Staff of ten thousand entities who were composed of eighty-seven different species. O'Mara was a very important man at Sector General. He was also, on his own admission, the most approachable man in the hospital. O'Mara was fond of saying that he didn't care who approached him or when, but if they hadn't a very good reason for pestering him with their silly little problems then they needn't expect to get away from him again unscathed. To O'Mara the medical staff were patients, and it was the generally held belief that the high level of stability among that variegated and often touchy bunch of e-ts was due to them being too scared of O'Mara to go mad. But today he was in an almost sociable mood.

"This will take more than five minutes so you'd better sit down, Doctor," he said sourly when Conway stopped before his desk. "I take it you've had a look at our cannibal?"

Conway nodded and sat down. Briefly he outlined his findings with regard to the EPLH patient, including his suspicion that there might be complications of a psychological nature. Ending, he asked, "Do you have any other information on its background, apart from the cannibalism?"

"Very little," said O'Mara. "It was found by a Monitor patrol vessel in a ship which, although undamaged, was broadcasting distress signals. Obviously it became too sick to operate the vessel. There was no other occupant, but because the EPLH was a new species to the rescue party they went over its ship with a fine-tooth comb, and found that there should have been another person aboard. They discovered this through a sort of ship's log cum personal diary kept on tape by the EPLH, and by study of the airlock tell-tales and similar protective gadgetry the details of which don't concern us at the moment. However, all the facts point to there being two entities aboard the ship, and the log tape suggests pretty strongly that the other one came to a sticky end at the hands, and teeth, of your patient."

O'Mara paused to toss a slim sheaf of papers on to his lap and Conway saw that it was a typescript of the relevant sections of the log. He had time only to discover that the EPLH's victim had been the ship's doctor, then O'Mara was talking again.

"We know nothing about its planet of origin," he said morosely, "except that it is somewhere in the other galaxy. However, with only one quarter of our own

286

Galaxy explored, our chances of finding its home world are negligible—"

"How about the Ians," said Conway, "maybe they could help?"

The Ians belonged to a culture originating in the other galaxy which had planted a colony in the same sector of the home galaxy which contained the Hospital. They were into a chrysalis stage at adolescence and metamorphosized from a ten-legged crawler into a beautiful, winged life-form. Conway had had one of them as a patient three months ago. The patient had been long since discharged, but the two GKNM doctors, who had originally come to help Conway with the patient, had remained at Sector General to study and teach.

"A Galaxy's a big place," said O'Mara with an obvious lack of enthusiasm, "but try them by all means. However, to get back to your patient, the biggest problem is going to come *after* you've cured it."

"You see, Doctor," he went on, "this particular beastie was found in circumstances which show pretty conclusively that it is guilty of an act which every intelligent species we know of considers a crime. As the Federation's police force, among other things the Monitor Corps is supposed to take certain measures against criminals like this one. They are supposed to be tried, rehabilitated or punished as seems fit. But how can we give this criminal a fair trial when we know nothing at all about its background, a background which just might contain the possibility of extenuating circumstances? At the same time we can't just let it go free . . ."

"Why not?" said Conway. "Why not point it in the general direction from whence it came and administer a judicial kick in the pants?"

"Or why not let the patient die," O'Mara replied, smiling, "and save trouble all round?"

Conway didn't speak. O'Mara was using an unfair argument and they both knew it, but they also knew that nobody would be able to convince the Monitor enforcement section that curing the sick and punishing the malefactor were not of equal importance in the Scheme of Things.

"What I want you to do," O'Mara resumed, "is to find

out all you can about the patient and its background after it comes to and during treatment. Knowing how soft-hearted, or soft-headed you are, I expect you will side with the patient during the cure and appoint yourself an unofficial counsel for the defence. Well, I won't mind that if in so doing you obtain the information which will enable us to summon a jury of its peers. Understood?"

Conway nodded.

O'Mara waited precisely three seconds, then said, "If you've nothing better to do than laze about in that chair . . ."

Immediately on leaving O'Mara's office Conway got in touch with Pathology and asked for the EPLA report to be sent to him before lunch. Then he invited the two Ian GKNMs to lunch and arranged for a consultation with Prilicla regarding the patient shortly afterwards. With these arrangements made he felt free to begin his rounds.

During the two hours which followed Conway had no time to think about his newest patient. He had fifty-three patients currently in his charge together with six doctors in various stages of training and a supporting staff of nurses, the patients and medical staff comprising eleven different physiological types. There were special instruments and procedures for examining these extra-terrestrial patients, and when he was accompanied by a trainee whose pressure and gravity requirements differed both from those of the patient to be examined and himself, then the "routine" of his rounds could become an extraordinarily complicated business.

But Conway looked at all his patients, even those whose convalescence was well advanced or whose treatment could have been handled by a subordinate. He was well aware that this was a stupid practice which only served to give him a lot of unnecessary work, but the truth was, promotion to a resident Senior Physician was still too recent for him to have become used to the large-scale delegation of responsibility. He foolishly kept on trying to do everything himself.

After rounds he was scheduled to give an initial mid-wifery lecture to a class of DBLF nurses. The DBLFs were furry, multipedal beings resembling outsize cater-pillars and were native to the planet Kelgia. They also breathed the same atmospheric mixture as himself, which meant that he was able to do without a pressure suit. To this purely physical comfort was added the fact that talking about such elementary stuff as the reason for Kelgian females conceiving only once in their lifetime and then producing quads who were invariably divided equally in sex, did not call for great concentration on his part. It left a large section of his mind free to worry about the alleged cannibal in his observation ward.

# 2

Half an hour later he was with the two Ian doctors in the Hospital's main dining hall—the one which catered for Tralthan, Kelgian, human and the various other warm-blooded, oxygen-breathers on the Staff—eating the inevitable salad. This in itself did not bother Conway unduly, in fact, lettuce was downright appetising compared with some of the things he had had to eat while playing host to other e-t colleagues, but he did not think that he would ever get used to the gale they created during lunch.

The GKNM denizens of Ia were a large, delicate, winged life-form who looked something like a dragonfly. To their rod-like but flexible bodies were attached four insectile legs, manipulators, the usual sensory organs and three tremendous sets of wings. Their table manners were not actually unpleasant—it was just that they did not sit down to dine, they hovered. Apparently eating while in flight aided their digestions as well as being pretty much a conditioned reflex with them.

Conway set the Path report on the table and placed the sugar bowl on top of it to keep it from blowing away. He said, ". . . You'll see from what I've just been reading to you that this appears to be a fairly simple case. Unusually so, I'd say, because the patient is remarkably clear of harmful bacteria of any type. Its symptoms indicate a form of epithelioma, that and nothing else, which makes its unconsciousness rather puzzling. But maybe some information on its planetary environment, sleeping periods and so on, would clarify things, and that is why I wanted to talk to you.

"We know that the patient comes from your galaxy. Can you tell me anything at all about its background?"

The GKNM on Conway's right drifted a few inches back from the table and said through its Translator, "I'm afraid I have not yet mastered the intricacies of your physiological classification system, Doctor. What does the patient look like?"

"Sorry, I forgot," said Conway. He was about to explain in detail what an EPLH was, then he began sketching on the back of the Path report instead. A few minutes later he held up the result and said, "It looks something like that."

Both Ians dropped to the floor.

Conway who had never known the GKNMs to stop either eating or flying during a meal was impressed by the reaction.

He said, "You know about them, then?"

The GKNM on the right made noises which Conway's Translator reproduced as a series of barks, the e-t equivalent of an attack of stuttering. Finally it said, "We know of them. We have never seen one of them, we do not know their planet of origin, and before this moment we were not sure that they had actual physical existence. They . . . they are gods, Doctor."

*Another VIP . . .* I thought Conway, with a sudden sinking feeling. His experience with VIP patients was that their cases were *never* simple. Even if the patient's condition was nothing serious there were invariably complications, none of which were medical.

"My Colleague is being a little too emotional," the other GKNM broke in. Conway had never been able to see any physical difference between the two Ians, but somehow this one had the air of being a more cynical, world-weary dragonfly. "Perhaps I can tell you what little is known, and deduced, about them rather than enumerate all the things which are not . . ."

The species to which the patient belonged was not a numerous one, the Ian doctor went on to explain, but their sphere of influence in the other galaxy was tremendous. In the social and psychological sciences they were very well advanced, and individually their intelligence and

290

mental capacity was enormous. For reasons known only to themselves they did not seek each other's company very often, and it was unheard of for more than one of them to be found on any planet at the same time for any lengthy period.

They were always the supreme ruler on the worlds they occupied. Sometimes it was a beneficent rule, sometimes harsh—but the harshness, when viewed with a century or so's hindsight, usually turned out to be beneficence in disguise. They used people, whole planetary populations, and even interplanetary cultures, purely as a means to solve the problems which they set themselves, and when the problem was solved they left. At least this was the impression received by not quite unbiased observers.

In a voice made flat and emotionless only because of the process of Translation the Ian went on. ". . . Legends seem to agree that one of them will land on a planet with nothing but its ship and a companion who is always of a different species. By using a combination of defensive science, psychology and sheer business acumen they overcome local prejudice and begin to amass wealth and power. The transition from local authority to absolute planetary rule is gradual, but then they have plenty of time. They are, of course, immortal."

Faintly, Conway heard his fork clattering on to the floor. It was a few minutes before he could steady either his hands or his mind.

There were a few extra-terrestrial species in the Federation who possessed very long life-spans, and most of the medically advanced cultures—Earth's included—had the means of extending life considerably with rejuvenation treatments. Immortality, however, was something they did *not* have, nor had they ever had the chance to study anyone who possessed it. Until now, that was. Now Conway had a patient to care for, and cure and, most of all, investigate. Unless . . . but the GKNM was a doctor, and a doctor would not say immortal if he merely meant long-lived.

"Are you sure?" croaked Conway.

The Ian's answer took a long time because it included the detailing of a great many facts, theories and legends concerning these beings who were satisfied to rule nothing

291

less than a planet apiece. At the end of it Conway was still not sure that his patient was immortal, but everything he had heard seemed to point that way.

Hesitantly, he said, "After what I've just heard perhaps I shouldn't ask, but in your opinion are these beings capable of committing an act of murder and cannibalism—"

"No!" said one Ian.

"Never!" said the other.

There was, of course, no hint of emotion in the Translated replies, but their sheer volume was enough to make everyone in the dining hall look up.

A few minutes later Conway was alone. The Ians had requested permission to see the legendary EPLH and then dashed off full of awe and eagerness. Ians were nice people. Conway thought, but at the same time it was his considered opinion that lettuce was fit only for rabbits. With great firmness he pushed his slightly mussed salad away from him and dialled for steak with double the usual accessories.

This promised to be a long, hard day.

When Conway returned to the observation ward the Ians had gone and the patient's condition was unchanged. The Lieutenant was still guarding the nurse on duty— closely—and was beginning to blush for some reason. Conway nodded gravely, dismissed the nurse and was giving the Path report a rereading when Dr. Prilicla arrived.

Prilicla was a spidery, fragile, low-gravity being of classification GLNO who had to wear G-nullifiers constantly to keep from being mashed flat by a gravity which most other species considered normal. Besides being a very competent doctor Prilicla was the most popular person in the hospital, because its empathic faculty made it nearly impossible for the little being to be disagreeable to anyone. And, although it also possessed a set of large, iridescent wings it sat down at mealtimes and ate spaghetti with a fork. Conway liked Prilicla a lot.

Conway briefly described the EPLH's condition and background as he saw it, then ended, ". . . I know you can't get much from an unconscious patient, but it would help me if you could—"

"There appears to be a misunderstanding here, Doctor," Prilicla broke in, using the form of words which was the nearest it ever came to telling someone they were wrong. "The patient is conscious . . ."

*"Get back!"*

Warned as much by Conway's emotional radiation at the thought of what the patient's boney club could do to Prilicla egg-shell body as his words, the little GLNO skittered backwards out of range. The Lieutenant edged closer, his eyes on the still motionless tentacle which ended in that monstrous bludgeon. For several seconds nobody moved or spoke, while outwardly the patient remained unconscious. Finally Conway looked at Prilicla. He did not have to speak.

Prilicla said, "I detect emotional radiation of a type which emanates only from a mind which is consciously aware of itself. The mental processes themselves seem slow and, considering the physical size of the patient, weak. In detail, it is radiating feelings of danger, helplessness and confusion. There is also an indication of some overall sense of purpose."

Conway sighed.

"So it's playing 'possum," said the Lieutenant grimly, talking mostly to himself.

The fact that the patient was feigning unconsciousness worried Conway less than it did the Corpsman. In spite of the mass of diagnostic equipment available to him he subscribed firmly to the belief that a doctor's best guide to any malfunction was a communicative and co-operative patient. But how did one open a conversation with a being who was a near deity . . . ?

"We . . . we are going to help you," he said awkwardly. "Do you understand what I'm saying?"

The patient remained motionless as before.

Prilicla said, "There is no indication that it heard you, Doctor."

"But if it's conscious . . ." Conway began, and ended the sentence with a helpless shrug.

He began assembling his instruments again and with Prilicla's help examined the EPLH again, paying special attention to the organs of sight and hearing. But there was no physical or emotional reaction while the examination was in progress, despite the flashing lights and a considerable amount of ungentle probing. Conway could see no evidence of physical malfunction in any of the sensory organs, yet the patient remained completely unaware of all outside stimulus. Physically it was unconscious, insensible to everything going on around it, except that Prilicla insisted that it wasn't.

*What a crazy, mixed-up demi-god,* thought Conway. Trust O'Mara to send him the weirdies. Aloud he said. "The only explanation I can see for this peculiar state of affairs is that the mind you are receiving has severed or blocked off contact with all its sensory equipment. The patient's condition is not the cause of this, therefore the trouble must have a psychological basis. I'd say the beastie is urgently in need of psychiatric assistance.

"However," he ended, "the head-shrinkers can operate more effectively on a patient who is physically well, so I think we should concentrate on clearing up this skin condition first . . ."

A specific had been developed at the hospital against epithelioma of the type affecting the patient, and Pathology had already stated that it was suited to the EPLH's metabolism and would produce no harmful side-effects. It took only a few minutes for Conway to measure out a test dosage and inject subcutaneously. Prilicla moved up beside him quickly to see the effect. This, they both knew, was one of the rare, rapid-action miracles of medicine—its effect would be apparent in a matter of seconds rather than hours or days.

Ten minutes later nothing at all had happened.

"A tough guy," said Conway, and injected the maximum safe dose.

Almost at once the skin in the area darkened and lost its dry, cracked look. The dark area widened perceptibly as they watched, and one of the tentacles twitched slightly.

"What's its mind doing?" said Conway.

"Much the same as before," Prilicla replied, "but with mounting anxiety apparent since the last injection. I detect feelings of a mind trying to make a decision . . . of making a decision . . ."

Prilicla began to tremble violently, a clear sign that the

294

emotional radiation of the patient had intensified. Conway had his mouth open to put a question when a sharp, tearing sound dragged his attention back to the patient. The EPLH was heaving and throwing itself against its restraining harness. Two of the anchoring straps had parted and it had worked a tentacle free. The one with the club . . .

Conway ducked frantically, and avoided having his head knocked off by a fraction of an inch—he felt that ultimate in blunt instruments actually touch his hair. But the Lieutenant was not so lucky. At almost the end of its swing the boney mace thudded into his shoulder, throwing him across the tiny ward so hard that he almost bounced off the wall. Prilicla, with whom cowardice was a prime survival characteristic, was already clinging with its suckertipped legs to the ceiling, which was the only safe spot in the room.

From his position flat on the floor Conway heard other straps go and saw two more tentacles flailing about. He knew that in a few minutes the patient would be completely free of the harness and able to move about the room at will. He scrambled quickly to his knees, crouched, then dived for the berserk EPLH. As he hung on tightly with his arms around its body just below the roots of the tentacles Conway was nearly deafened by a series of barking roars coming from the speaking orifice beside his ear. The noise translated as "Help me! Help me!" Simultaneously he saw the tentacle with the great, boney bludgeon at its tip swing downwards. There was a crash and a three-inch hollow appeared on the floor at the point where he had been lying a few seconds previously.

Tackling the patient the way he had done might have seemed foolhardy, but Conway had been trying to keep his head in more ways than one. Clinging tightly to the EPLH's body below the level of those madly swinging tentacles, Conway knew, was the next safest place in the room.

Then he saw the Lieutenant . . .

The Lieutenant had his back to the wall, half lying and half sitting up. One arm hung loosely at his side and in the other hand he held his gun, steadying it between his knees, and one eye was closed in a diabolical wink while the other sighted along the barrel. Conway shouted desperately for him to wait, but the noise from the patient drowned him out. At every instant Conway expected the flash and shock of exploding bullets. He felt paralysed with fear, he couldn't even let go.

Then suddenly it was all over. The patient slumped on to its side, twitched and became motionless. Holstering his unfired weapon the Lieutenant struggled to his feet. Conway extricated himself from the patient and Prilicla came down off the ceiling.

Awkwardly, Conway said, "Uh, I suppose you couldn't shoot with me hanging on there?"

The Lieutenant shook his head. "I'm a good shot, Doctor. I could have hit it and missed you all right. But it kept shouting, 'Help me' all the time. That sort of thing cramps a man's style . . ."

# 3

It was some twenty minutes later, after Prilicla had sent the Lieutenant away to have a cracked humerus set and Conway and the GLNO were fitting the patient with a much stronger harness, that they noticed the absence of the darker patch of skin. The patient's condition was now exactly the same as it had been before undergoing treatment. Apparently the hefty shot which Conway had administered had had only a temporary effect, and that was decidedly peculiar. It was in fact downright impossible.

From the moment Prilicla's empathic faculty had been brought to bear on the case Conway had been sure that the root of the trouble was psychological. He also knew that a severely warped mind could do tremendous damage to the body which housed it. But this damage was on a purely physical level and its method of repair— the treatment developed and proved time and time again by Pathology—was a hard, physical fact also. And no mind, regardless of its power or degree of malfunction, should be able to ignore, to completely negate, a physical fact. The Universe had, after all, certain fixed laws.

So far as Conway could see there were only two possible explanations. Either the rules were being ignored because the Being who had made them had also the right to ignore them or somehow, someone—or some combination of circumstances of mis-read data—was pulling a fast one. Conway infinitely preferred the second theory because the first one was altogether too shattering to consider seriously. He desperately wanted to go on thinking of his patient with a small P . . .

Nevertheless, when he left the ward Conway paid a visit to the office of Captain Bryson, the Monitor Corps Chaplain, and consulted that officer at some length in a semi-professional capacity—Conway believed in carrying plenty of insurance. His next call was on Colonel Skempton, the officer in charge of Supply, Maintenance and Communications at the Hospital. There he requested complete copies of the patient's log—not just the sections relevant to the murder—together with any other background data available to be sent to his room. Then he went to the AUGL theatre to demonstrate operative techniques on submarine life-forms, and before dinner he was able to work in two hours in the Pathology department during which he discovered quite a lot about his patient's immortality.

When he returned to his room there was a pile of typescript on his desk that was nearly two inches thick. Conway groaned, thinking of his six-hour recreation period and how he was going to spend it. The thought obtruded of how he would have *liked* to spend it, bringing with it a vivid picture of the very efficient and impossibly beautiful Nurse Murchison whom he had been dating regularly of late. But Murchison was currently with the FGLI Maternity Section and their free periods would not coincide for another two weeks.

In the present circumstances perhaps it was just as well, Conway thought, as he settled down for a good long read.

The Corpsmen who had examined the patient's ship had been unable to convert the EPLH's time units into the Earth-human scale with any accuracy, but they had been able to state quite definitely that many of the taped logs were several centuries old and a few of them dated back

297

to two thousand years or more. Conway began with the oldest and sifted carefully through them until he came to the most recent. He discovered almost at once that they were not so much a series of taped diaries—the references to personal items were relatively rare—as a catalogue of memoranda, most of which was highly technical and very heavy going. The data relevant to the murder, which he studied last, was much more dramatic.

*. . . My physician is making me sick,* the final entry read, *it is killing me. I must do something. It is a bad physician for allowing me to become ill. Somehow I must get rid of it . . .*

Conway replaced the last sheet on its pile, sighed, and prepared to adopt a position more conducive to creative thinking; i.e. with his chair tipped far back, feet on desk and practically sitting on the back of his neck.

*What a mess,* he thought.

The separate pieces of the puzzle—or most of them, anyway—were available to him now and required only to be fitted together. There was the patient's condition, not serious so far as the Hospital was concerned but definitely lethal if not treated. Then there was the data supplied by the two Ians regarding this God-like, power-hungry but essentially beneficent race and the companions—who were never of the same species—who always travelled or lived with them. These companions were subject to replacement because they grew old and died while the EPLHs did not. There were also the Path reports, both the first written one he had received before lunch and the later verbal one furnished during his two hours with Thornnastor, the FGLI Diagnostician-in-Charge of Pathology. It was Thornnastor's considered opinion that the EPLH patient was not a true immortal, and the Considered Opinion of a Diagnostician was as near to being a rock-hard certainty as made no difference. But while immortality had been ruled out for various physiological reasons, the tests had shown evidence of longevity or rejuvenation treatments of the unselective type.

Finally there had been the emotion readings furnished by Prilicla before and during their attempted treatment of the patient's skin condition. Prilicla had reported a steady radiation pattern of confusion, anxiety and help-lessness. But when the EPLH had received its second injection it had gone berserk, and the blast of emotion exploding from its mind had, in Prilicla's own words, nearly fried the little empath's brains in their own ichor. Prilicla had been unable to get a detailed reading on such a violent eruption of emotion, mainly because it had been tuned to the earlier and more gentle level on which the patient had been radiating, but it agreed that there was evidence of instability of the schizoid type.

Conway wriggled deeper into his chair, closed his eyes and let the pieces of the puzzle slide gently into place.

It had begun on the planet where the EPLHs had been the dominant life-form. In the course of time they had achieved civilisation which included interstellar flight and an advanced medical science. Their life-span, lengthy to begin with, was artificially extended so that a relatively short-lived species like the Ians could be forgiven for believing them to be immortal. But a high price had had to be paid for their longevity: reproduction of their kind, the normal urge towards immortality of race in a species of mortal individuals, would have been the first thing to go; then their civilisation would have dissolved—been forced apart, rather—into a mass of star-travelling, rugged individualists, and finally there would have been the psychological rot which set in when the risk of purely physical deterioration had gone.

Poor demi-gods, thought Conway.

They avoided each other's company for the simple reason that they'd already had too much of it—century after century of each other's mannerisms, habits of speech, opinions and the sheer, utter boredom of looking at each other. They had set themselves vast, sociological problems —taking charge of backward or errant planetary cultures and dragging them up by their bootstraps, and similar large-scale philanthropies—because they had tremendous minds, they had plenty of time, they had constantly to fight against boredom and because basically they must have been nice people. And because part of the price of such longevity was an ever-growing fear of death, they had to have their own personal physicians—no doubt the most efficient practitioners of medicine known to them—constantly in attendance.

Only one piece of the puzzle refused to fit and that was the odd way in which the EPLH had negated his attempts to treat it, but Conway had no doubt that that was a physiological detail which would soon become clear as well. The important thing was that he now knew how to proceed.

Not every condition responded to medication, despite Thornnastor's claims to the contrary, and he would have seen that surgery was indicated in the EPLH's case if the whole business had not been so be-fogged with considerations of who and what the patient was and what it was supposed to have done. The fact that the patient was a near-deity, a murderer and generally the type of being not to be trifled with were details which should not have concerned him.

Conway sighed and swung his feet to the floor. He was beginning to feel so comfortable that he decided he had better go to bed before he fell asleep.

Immediately after breakfast next day Conway began setting up things for the EPLH's operation. He ordered the necessary instruments and equipment sent to the observation ward, gave detailed instructions regarding its sterilisation—the patient was supposed to have killed one doctor already for allowing it to become sick, and a dim view would be taken if another one was the cause of it catching something else because of faulty aseptic procedures—and requested the assistance of a Tralthan surgeon to help with the fine work. Then half an hour before he was due to start Conway called on O'Mara.

The Chief Psychologist listened to his report and intended course of action without comment until he had finished, then he said, "Conway, do you realise what could happen to this hospital if that thing got loose? And not just physically loose, I mean. It is seriously disturbed mentally, you say, if not downright psychotic. At the moment it is unconscious, but from what you tell me its grasp of the psychological sciences is such that it could have us eating out of its manipulatory appendage just by talking at us.

"I'm concerned as to what may happen when it wakes up."

It was the first time Conway had heard O'Mara confess to being worried about anything. Several years back when a runaway spaceship had crashed into the hospital, spreading havoc and confusion through sixteen levels, it was said that Major O'Mara had expressed a feeling of concern on that occasion also . . .

"I'm trying not to think about that," said Conway apologetically. "It just confuses the issue."

O'Mara took a deep breath and let it out slowly through his nose, a mannerism of his which could convey more than twenty scathing sentences. He said coldly, "Somebody should think about these things, Doctor. I trust you will have no objection to *me* observing the coming operation . . . ?"

To what was nothing less than a politely worded order there could be no reply other than an equally polite, "Glad to have you, sir."

When they arrived in the observation ward the patient's "bed" had been raised to a comfortable operating height and the EPLH itself was strapped securely into position. The Tralthan had taken its place beside the recording and anaesthetizing gear and had one eye on the patient, one on its equipment and the other two directed towards Prilicla with whom it was discussing a particularly juicy piece of scandal which had come to light the previous day. As the two beings concerned were PVSJ chlorebreathers the affair could have only an academic interest for them, but apparently their academic interest was intense. At the sight of O'Mara, however, the scandalmongering ceased forthwith. Conway gave the signal to begin.

The anaesthetic was one of several which Pathology had pronounced safe for the EPLH life-form, and while it was being administered Conway found his mind going off at a tangent towards his Tralthan assistant.

Surgeons of that species were really two beings instead of one, a combination of FGLI and OTSB. Clinging to the leathery back of the lumbering, elephantine Tralthan was a diminutive and nearly mindless being who lived in symbiosis with it. At first glance the OTSB looked like a furry ball with a long ponytail sprouting from it, but a closer look showed that the ponytail was composed of scores of fine manipulators most of which incorporated sensitive visual organs. Because of the *rapport* which existed between the Tralthan and its symbiote the FGLI-OTSB combination were the finest surgeons in the Galaxy. Not all Tralthans chose to link up with a symbiote, but FGLI medics wore them like a badge of office.

Suddenly the OTSB scurried along its host's back and huddled atop the dome-like head between the eye-stalks, its tail hanging down towards the patient and fanning out stiffly. The Tralthan was ready to begin.

"You will observe that this is a surface condition only," Conway said, for the benefit of the recording equipment, "and that the whole skin area looks dead, dried-up and on the point of flaking off. During the removal of the first skin samples no difficulty was encountered, but later specimens resisted removal to a certain extent and the reason was discovered to be a tiny rootlet, approximately one quarter of an inch long and invisible to the naked eye. My naked eye, that is. So it seems clear that the condition is about to enter a new phase. The disease is beginning to dig in rather than remain on the surface, and the more promptly we act the better."

Conway gave the reference numbers of the Path reports and his own preliminary notes on the case, then went on, ". . . As the patient, for reasons which are at the moment unclear, does not respond to medication I propose surgical removal of the affected tissue, irrigation, cleansing and replacement with surrogate skin. A Tralthan-guided OTSB will be used to insure that the rootlets are also excised. Except for the considerable area to be covered, which will make this a long job, the procedure is straightforward—"

"Excuse me, Doctors," Prilicla broke in, "the patient is still conscious."

An argument, polite only on Prilicla's side, broke out between the Tralthan and the little empath. Prilicla held that the EPLH was thinking thoughts and radiating emotions and the other maintained that it had enough of the anaesthetic in its system to render it completely insensible to everything for at least six hours. Conway broke in just as the argument was becoming personal.

"We've had this trouble before," he said irritably. "The patient has been physically unconscious, except for a few minutes yesterday, since its arrival, yet Prilicla detected the presence of rational thought processes. Now the same effect is present while it is under anaesthetic. I don't know how to explain this, it will probably require a surgical investigation of its brain structure to do so, and that is something which will have to wait. The important thing at the moment is that it is physically incapable of movement or of feeling pain. Now shall we begin?"

To Prilicla he added, "Keep listening just in case . . ."

# 4

For about twenty minutes they worked in silence, although the procedure did not require a high degree of concentration. It was rather like weeding a garden, except everything which grew was a weed and had to be removed one plant at a time. He would peel back an affected area of skin, the OTSB's hair-thin appendages would investigate, probe and detach the rootlets, and he would peel back another tiny segment. Conway was looking forward to the most tedious operation of his career.

Prilicla said, "I detect increasing anxiety linked with a strengthening sense of purpose. The anxiety is becoming intense . . ."

Conway grunted. He could think of no other comment to make.

Five minutes later the Tralthan said, "We will have to slow down, Doctor. We are at a section where the roots are much deeper . . ."

Two minutes later Conway said, "But I can *see* them! How deep are they now?"

"Four inches," replied the Tralthan. "And Doctor, they are visibly lengthening as we work."

"But that's impossible!" Conway burst out; then, "We'll move to another area."

303

He felt the sweat begin to trickle down his forehead and just beside him Prilicla's gangling, fragile body began to quiver—but not at anything the patient was thinking. Conway's own emotional radiation just then was not a pleasant thing, because in the new area and in the two chosen at random after that the result was the same. Roots from the flaking pieces of skin were burrowing deeper as they watched.

"Withdraw," said Conway harshly.

For a long time nobody spoke. Prilicla was shaking as if a high wind was blowing in the ward. The Tralthan was fussing with its equipment, all four of its eyes focussed on one unimportant knob. O'Mara was looking intently at Conway, also calculatingly and with a large amount of sympathy in his steady grey eyes. The sympathy was because he could recognise when a man was genuinely in a spot and the calculation was due to his trying to work out whether the trouble was Conway's fault or not.

"What happened, Doctor?" he said gently.

Conway shook his head angrily. "I don't know. Yesterday the patient did not respond to medication, today it won't respond to surgery. Its reactions to anything we try to do for it are crazy, impossible! And now our attempt to relieve its condition surgically has triggered off—something—which will send those roots deep enough to penetrate vital organs in a matter of minutes if their present rate of growth is maintained, and you know what that means . . ."

"The patient's sense of anxiety is diminishing," Prilicla reported. "It is still engaged in purposeful thinking."

The Tralthan joined in then. It said, "I have noticed a peculiar fact about those root-like tendrils which join the diseased flakes of skin with the body. My symbiote has extremely sensitive vision, you will understand, and it reports that the tendrils seem to be rooted at each end, so that it is impossible to tell whether the growth is attacking the body or the body is deliberately holding on to the growth."

Conway shook his head distractedly. The case was full of mad contradictions and outright impossibilities. To begin with no patient, no matter how fouled up mentally, should be able to negate the effects of a drug powerful enough to bring about a complete cure within half an hour, and all within a few minutes. And the natural order of things was for a being with a diseased area of skin to slough it off and replace it with new tissue, not hang on to it grimly no matter what. It was a baffling, hopeless case.

Yet when the patient had arrived it had seemed a simple, straightforward case—Conway had felt more concern regarding the patient's background than its condition, whose cure he had considered a routine matter. But somewhere along the way he had missed something. Conway was sure, and because of this sin of omission the patient would probably die during the next few hours. Maybe he had made a snap diagnosis, been too sure of himself, been criminally careless.

It was pretty horrible to lose a patient at any time, and at Sector General losing a patient was an extremely rare occurrence. But to lose one whose condition no hospital anywhere in the civilised galaxy would have considered as being serious . . . Conway swore luridly, but stopped because he hadn't the words to describe how he felt about himself.

"Take it easy, son."

That was O'Mara, squeezing his arm and talking like a father. Normally O'Mara was a bad-tempered, bull-voiced and unapproachable tyrant who, when one went to him for help, sat making sarcastic remarks while the person concerned squirmed and shamefacedly solved his own problems. His present uncharacteristic behaviour proved something, Conway thought bitterly. It proved that Conway had a problem which Conway could not solve himself.

But in O'Mara's expression there was something more than just concern for Conway, and it was probably that deep down the psychologist was a little glad that things had turned out as they did. Conway meant no reflection on O'Mara's character, because he knew that if the Major had been in his position he would have tried as hard if not harder to cure the patient, and would have felt just as badly about the outcome. But at the same time the Chief

Psychologist must have been desperately worried about the possibility of a being of great and unknown powers, who was also mentally unbalanced, being turned loose on the Hospital. In addition O'Mara might also be wondering if, beside a conscious and alive EPLH, he would look like a small and untutored boy . . .

"Let's try taking it from the top again," O'Mara said, breaking in on his thoughts. "Is there anything you've found in the patient's background that might point to it wanting to destroy itself?"

"*No!*" said Conway vehemently. "To the contrary! It would want desperately to live. It was taking unselective rejuvenation treatments, which means that the complete cell-structure of its body was regenerated periodically. As the process of storing memory is a product of ageing in the brain cells, this would practically wipe its mind clean after every treatment . . ."

"That's why those taped logs resembled technical memoranda," O'Mara put in. "That's exactly what they were. Still, I prefer our own method of rejuvenation even though we won't live so long, regenerating damaged organs only and allowing the brain to remain untouched . . ."

"I know," Conway broke in, wondering why the usually taciturn O'Mara had become so talkative. Was he trying to simplify the problem by making him state it in non-professional terms? "But the effect of continued longevity treatments, as you know yourself, is to give the possessor an increasing fear of dying. Despite loneliness, boredom and an altogether unnatural existence, the fear grows steadily with the passage of time. That is why it always travelled with its own private physician, it was desperately afraid of sickness or an accident befalling it between treatments, and that is why I can sympathise to a certain extent with its feelings when the doctor who was supposed to keep it well allowed it to get sick, although the business of eating it afterwards—"

"So you are on its side," said O'Mara drily.

"It could make a good plea of self-defence," Conway retorted. "But I was saying that it was desperately afraid of dying, so that it would be constantly trying to get a better, more efficient doctor for itself . . . Oh!"

"Oh, what?" said O'Mara.

It was Prilicla, the emotion sensitive who replied. It said, "Doctor Conway has just had an idea."

"What is it, you young whelp? There's no need to be so damn secretive . . . !" O'Mara's voice had lost its gentle fatherly tone, and there was a gleam in his eye which said that he was glad that gentleness was no longer necessary. "What *is* wrong with the patient?"

Feeling happy and excited and at the same time very much unsure of himself, Conway stumbled across to the intercom and ordered some very unusual equipment, checked again that the patient was so thoroughly strapped down that it would be unable to move a muscle, then he said, "My guess is that the patient is perfectly sane and we've been blinding ourselves with psychological red herrings. Basically, the trouble is something it ate."

"I had a bet with myself you would say that sometime during this case," said O'Mara. He looked sick.

The equipment arrived—a slender, pointed wooden stake and a mechanism which would drive it downwards at any required angle and controlled speeds. With the Tralthan's help Conway set it up and moved it into position. He chose a part of the patient's body which contained several vital organs which were, however, protected by nearly six inches of musculature and adipose, then he set the stake in motion. It was just touching the skin and descending at the rate of approximately two inches per hour.

"What the blazes is going on?" stormed O'Mara. "Do you think the patient is a vampire or something!"

"Of course not," Conway replied. "I'm using a wooden stake to give the patient a better chance of defending itself. You wouldn't expect it to stop a steel one, would you." He motioned the Tralthan forward and together they watched the area where the stake was entering the EPLH's body. Every few minutes Prilicla reported on the emotional radiation. O'Mara paced up and down, occasionally muttering to himself.

The point had penetrated almost a quarter of an inch when Conway noticed the first coarsening and thickening of the skin. It was taking place in a roughly circular area, about four inches in diameter, whose centre was the wound created by the stake. Conway's scanner showed a spongy, fibrous growth forming under the skin to a depth of half an inch. Visibly the growth thickened and grew opaque to his scanner's current setting, and within ten minutes it had become a hard, boney plate. The stake had begun to bend alarmingly and was on the point of snapping.

"I'd say the defences are now concentrated at this one point," Conway said, trying to keep his voice steady, "so we'd better have it out."

Conway and the Tralthan rapidly incised around and undercut the newly-formed bony plate, which was immediately transferred into a sterile, covered receptacle. Quickly preparing a shot—a not quite maximum dose of the specific he had tried the previous day—Conway injected, then went back to helping the Tralthan with the repair work on the wound. This was routine work and took about fifteen minutes, and when it was finished there could be no doubt at all that the patient was responding favourably to treatment.

Over the congratulations of the Tralthan and the horrible threats of O'Mara—the Chief Psychologist wanted some questions answered, fast—Prilicla said, "You have effected a cure, Doctor, but the patient's anxiety level has markedly increased. It is almost frantic."

Conway shook his head, grinning. "The patient is heavily anaesthetised and cannot feel anything. However, I agree that at this present moment . . ." He nodded toward the sterile container. ". . . its personal physician must be feeling pretty bad."

In the container the excised bone had begun to soften and leak a faintly purplish liquid. The liquid was rippling and sloshing gently about at the bottom of the container as if it had a mind of its own. Which was, in fact, the case . . .

Conway was in O'Mara's office winding up his report on the EPLH and the Major was being highly complimentary in a language which at times made the compliments indistinguishable from insults. But this was O'Mara's way, Conway was beginning to realise, and the Chief Psychologist was polite and sympathetic only when he was professionally concerned about a person.

308

He was still asking questions.

". . . An intelligent, amoebic life-form, an organised collection of submicroscopic, virus-type cells, would make the most efficient doctor obtainable," said Conway in reply to one of them. "It would reside within its patient and, given the necessary data, control any disease or organic malfunction from the inside. To a being who is pathologically afraid of dying it must have seemed perfect. And it was, too, because the trouble which developed was not really the doctor's fault. It came about through the patient's ignorance of its own physiological background.

"The way I see it," Conway went on, "the patient had been taking its rejuvenation treatments at an early stage of its biological life-time. I mean that it did not wait until middle or old age before regenerating itself. But on this occasion, either because it forgot or was careless or had been working on a problem which took longer than usual, it aged more than it had previously and acquired this skin condition. Pathology says that this was probably a common complaint with this race, and the normal course would be for the EPLH to slough off the affected skin and carry on as usual. But our patient, because the type of its rejuvenation treatment caused memory damage, did not know this, so its personal physician did not know it either."

Conway continued, "This, er, resident physician knew very little about the medical background of its patient-host's body, but its motto must have been to maintain the *status quo* at all costs. When pieces of its patient's body threatened to break away it held on to them, not realising that this could have been a normal occurrence like losing hair or a reptile periodically shedding its skin, especially as its master would have insisted that the occurrence was not natural. A pretty fierce struggle must have developed between the patient's body processes and its Doctor, with the patient's mind also ranged against its doctor. Because of this the doctor had to render the patient unconscious the better to do what it considered to be the right thing.

"When we gave it the test shots the doctor neutralised them. They were a foreign substance being introduced into its patient's body, you see. And you know what happened when we tried surgical removal. It was only when we

309

threatened underlying vital organs with that stake, forcing the doctor to defend its patient at that one point . . ."

"When you began asking for wooden stakes," said O'Mara drily, "I thought of putting *you* in a tight harness."

Conway grinned. He said, "I'm recommending that the EPLH takes his doctor back. Now that Pathology has given it a fuller understanding of its employer's medical and physiological history it should be the ultimate in personal physicians, and the EPLH is smart enough to see that."

O'Mara smiled in return. "And I was worried about what it might do when it became conscious. But it turned out to be a very friendly, likeable type. Quite charming, in fact."

As Conway rose and turned to go he said slyly, "That's because it's such a good psychologist. It is pleasant to people *all* the time . . ."

He managed to get the door shut behind him before the paperweight hit it.

*The course of evolution shows that the highest*
*achievement of one species becomes an embryonic*
*development in succeeding higher forms. And so, too,*
*perhaps, with cultural evolution.*

●

# AGE OF RETIREMENT
## by Hal Lynch

Eighty miles below us was the south continent of the
planet Uriel. I gave the order, and we roared down,
down toward the city of Sathos that had never known night,
where the light of four moons filled the sky when the sun
was gone. The *Spacebolt* swooped lower over the city, and
we dropped our blackness bombs. An inky cloud rose out
of Sathos behind us as we arced to return.

I looked across at my troopers, waiting beside the belly-
hatch. "The word is that the city's cleaned out, except for
the flickos, and you know just where they'll be hiding.
When you hit the streets, blast anything that moves!"
Sergeant Kregg grinned, and signaled his boys to switch
on their null-gravs. We were over the city again.

"OK, sergeant, let's go get 'em!" I yelled. I led the drop
down through the open hatch and into the blackness of
Sathos, where the flicko gang waited. They hadn't expected a blackness bomb, they were scattered and con-

fused, but they still knew how to fight. The stun-guns crackled as my troopers dropped into the streets and started hunting the flickos down. Sergeant Kregg and I went after the leaders, who were holed up in their dive downtown. They had a nauseator spraying the streets in front of the place, but the sergeant and I managed to keep out of its line of fire while we moved up. We located them on the third floor; it was already getting lighter now.

From behind a set of steps, the sergeant shouted our we're-here-to-help-you summons. They answered with a nauseator blast, but they couldn't reach him. I fired a couple of stun-shots from my side of the street, but they were protected, too.

"Stubborn!" said Kregg. "You'n' me can pick 'em off, though, soon's it gets light enough."

"Let's use sleep-gas; I'm in a hurry," I said. His face filled with disappointment. "That's an order, sergeant!"

The gas did the job. Soon we had them all "cuffed and counted." Kregg called the ship down while I recorded the operation details.

"Any injuries, sergeant?"

"One o' them has a skinned elbow; that's all, sir." He and the troopers herded our prisoners aboard, then he came back.

"Fastest operation I've ever seen," he said confidentially. "I'll bet it's a Space Patrol record, sir!"

I knew it was, and felt good about it, but I couldn't let him know it, of course. I just grunted and snapped back his salute. "Turn 'em over to the local psychomedics and bring your troop back to Mars Headquarters. I'm going back with the ship; I'm returning by mattercaster, to make the commander's step-down. Take over, sergeant!"

There were a few old folks at the mattercaster station, but they stepped aside for my blue-and-gold uniform.

"Right in here, captain!" said the attendant, leading me to the nearest booth. I felt a twinge of regret as I settled myself on the cushions. I'd have preferred to have flown my ship back. The *Spacebolt* was certainly the trimmest, fastest ship in the whole sector, and it would have been fitting to have flown her in, but we'd run out of time. Even traveling by mattercaster I'd be lucky to be in time for the ceremony.

When I stepped out of the Patrol receiving booth on Mars I found Wenda waiting for me. She saluted me smartly; prettier than ever in her dress uniform. I realized inwardly that I'd have to watch myself. I'd have to stay away from her if I didn't want to wash myself out a couple of years too early.

"Tommy, I've never been to a Final Review before," she whispered as we hurried down the corridor. "Are they very exciting?"

"Almost as dull as traveling by mattercaster." I didn't mean it, of course. They were wonderful. But I wasn't going to enjoy this one at all.

We started down the steps. "I wonder how the chief's taking it? I mean, knowing this is the last one, and all."

"I suppose he's got used to the idea," she said indifferently. We could hear the crowd milling around out on the field now.

Suddenly I just had to tell somebody how I felt. "It's not fair, Wenda, *it's just not fair!*"

She stopped, and looked at me worriedly. "You mean making the chief step down? It's for the good of the Patrol, Tommy—you know that. It gives the younger officers a chance."

"They'll get plenty of chance! Wenda, the chief's as good as he ever was. He can handle anything they throw at him, he—"

"Compulsory retirement at his age is one of the most important Patrol regs! Now, hush—we'll be late!"

As we came out onto the parade ground Colonel Croslake stepped over to meet us. He saluted, and shook my hand.

"Congratulations, Tommy!" he smiled. "I just heard you stopped another afflicted gang!"

"Tommy! You never told me!" said Wenda.

"I picked 'em up on Uriel. It was short and sweet; we were lucky. A little shooting, but no real trouble."

The colonel clapped me on the shoulder. "Keep up that sort of work and you'll be staff rank in no time." *I'd better hurry,* I thought to myself. *The way things are, I'd better hurry!* "Uh-oh. Guess we'd better fall in. There go the bugles!"

We found our places while the call sounded. Across

the parade ground row upon row of pink-cheeked cadets "snapped to," and stood stiff and silent. In the quiet we could hear the distant noises of the rocket sheds, and the faint stir as the first of the troops marched onto the lower end of the field. Then the color guard appeared, followed by the band, playing the inevitable "Patrol Alert," and after them the top brass, trim and stern in their new dress blues.

Last of all came the chief, with Halligan, his successor, walking beside him. He already looked older, somehow, and different, though he still marched straight as a ramrod and every inch a soldier. He took his place in the reviewing stand: the band struck up "The Colors," and the chief watched his troops march past in review for the last time. Picked men, they were, from all his old campaigns, here to see the Supreme Commander of the Space Patrol step down. I'm not ashamed to say I felt like crying.

After the last of the troops had passed there was a moment of silence, then the chief made a little speech. I don't remember what he said but it was great. The way he said it made it great. Afterwards he unbuckled his ceremonial belt and fastened it around Commander Halligan's waist while the band struck up "Honor of the Patrol" and we sang it with tears streaming down our cheeks. Then we cheered until we were hoarse while he went to each one of his staff and shook his hand. While we were cheering I suddenly saw my older brother, Bill, standing in the little crowd of older people at the edge of the field.

Our new CO, Commander Halligan, made a speech, too, but it was sort of an anticlimax. Then we stood Retreat and the chief's Final Review was over. I'd have liked to have had the chance to say something to him personally, but I knew I could never get to him in the crowd. So, as soon as Halligan called "Dismiss!" I went to find Bill. I avoided Wenda and struggled through the crowd of swarming cadets and troopers to where my brother waited. He grinned down at me.

"Hi, cap'n!" He looked like a stranger in his civvies. We talked for a minute or two about the family—I hadn't seen as much of them recently as I should have—then I led him away from the crowd, down toward the rocket sheds. Things were quieting, and the sun was going down.

314

"How are things in that, uh . . . philosophy school?" I asked, to be polite.

"Interesting—even exciting, sometimes."

"I'll bet!"

"I mean it, Tommy. We came across a relationship between music and social thought the other day, that— Well, I'll explain it to you sometime. It's new, and it's wonderful, and it has all kinds of possibilities. By the way, I hear we're going to get your chief, now that he's retired."

"In your school? You're crazy, Bill!"

"He's got quite a brain, that one. We can use him."

I stopped walking. "Listen, Bill, I've got to talk to you," I said. "I don't understand this thing. I just don't get it."

"What's the trouble?"

"Why does the chief have to step down *now?* He's the best we've ever had! Why did they make him quit?"

"If by 'they' you mean outsiders, you're wrong, Tommy. Compulsory retirement is the Patrol's own regulation. It wasn't forced on them from outside. Members of the Patrol staff set the age limit themselves. And, of course, it's been set for everybody; the chief's rank doesn't make any difference. He had to step down just as I had to when I reached his age. We just aren't any good any more, kid."

I grabbed his arm. "Don't give me that! Before I took my last duty-tour I spent some time up in the library. I was looking through some old visobooks, and I found some stories of the Patrol . . . of the Patrol of a hundred years ago. They had troopers as old as thirty, then!"

"Sure, kid, I know. And you may not know it, but if you check on law-forces that go back before the Patrol you'll find they used to have even older men. They recruited at an older age, too. But by the time the Patrol came along it had been found that older men just didn't have the speed of reaction, or the coordination to keep up the pace. So they started retiring men younger, and recruiting men younger.

"Then there was another factor: much less killing. Murderers are rarer than Mars clouds these days, but I guess you noticed in those stories that most of the criminals used deadly weapons. In these days of stun-guns

315

and sleep-gas, bringing in the troublemakers is a lot less dangerous. That's helped to lower the recruiting age, and in turn, the retirement age."

"What criminals?"

"It's an old word for afflicteds. You never paid enough attention to history, Tommy. You'll have to specialize in it after you step down."

"I don't even want to think about stepping down," I growled. "I've still got two more years. Maybe . . . maybe if I ever get on the staff, I'll be able to change that retirement reg!"

Bill seemed to find that amusing. "Not a chance, Tommy. They've tried, and it just doesn't work out any other way. When you reach sixteen, Final Review and out you go—for the good of the service!"

"Are you trying to tell me my coordination will be shot at sixteen?"

"Look at me," he grinned. "At nineteen I'm finished." Then he got serious. "No, kid, it isn't that. Something else is missing—a certain spirit, or idealism, or maybe a kind of instinct. You see, our race has changed in the last couple of centuries, Tommy. For one thing, our educational system's been put into high gear, we take on responsibilities sooner than our great-grandfathers did, and by the same token we . . . uh, we settle down a little sooner. Our expansion into space has brought us into contact with dozens of other cultures, some of them centuries older and wiser than ours. So, somehow, we've settled down, as a people, to a different outlook on life than our ancestors had."

It seemed to me he was getting way off the subject, but I let him talk. We turned and started back toward the parade ground; the sun had set and it was getting pretty dark.

"Tommy, we've started on the big adventure," he went on. "We've started on the biggest exploration of all, the exploration of ourselves. That's become so important to us that we don't have time, or inclination, for other things.

"But there are still afflicteds, and I guess there always will be no matter how much the world changes. Somebody's got to take the time and the trouble and the thought to round 'em up and bring 'em in for treatment. Somebody who still has the patience to take authority and routine without sinking into corruption, who can think without brooding and act without anxiety over consequences. Somebody who can fight without hate and live without sorrow, somebody who can give his whole heart to a cause that gives him little or nothing in return.

"So we've turned the job over to you, the younger generation. We've given you the weapons and the know-how, and you've supplied the—heart."

"Bill, I don't understand a word of what you're talking about. I don't get it."

"You will, Tommy, you will," he said quietly in the darkness. "In a few years you'll see what I mean. The Patrol's found out that after your fifteenth year you somehow 'put away these things.' The glory dies away, as new yearnings come, until you find yourself a stranger to what you used to be. So the Patrol makes you step down before you reach that point, Tommy. Compulsory retirement, before you stop caring, any more."

*"Stop caring about the Patrol? That's crazy!"*

"Trouble is, Tommy, you don't care when you're grown up."

*"You are my honey, honeysuckle, I am the bee . . ."*
*The way these honies could suckle was enough to*
*give anyone a buzz.*

●

# PLANTING TIME

## by Pete Adams and
## Charles Nightingale

Randy Richmond was bored, excessively, intolerably, and
what felt like eternally, bored. He was so bored, in fact,
that he no longer wondered what kind of programme the
hypnoconditioner had pumped into him back at Sector
X113 before he got fired off into space again. Whatever it
was, it had as usual made no impression at all.

The hypnoconditioner was supposed to alter the time-
sense, to relax the intellect into a placid exploration of the
more charming byways of spatial mathematics or of any
other fashionable problem that currently had the planetbound research teams stumped. As a result, you were expected to end your trip across the stars not only as fresh
as if it had begun that same morning but also in an inspired state approaching the level of genius. Giant mental
leaps for mankind had been predicted from this treatment, but Randy had yet to hear of a single plus-light

traveller emerging from the experience wih anything but ideas of the most fundamental nature, inventive as some of these were reputed to have been.

He supposed that somebody somewhere must at last have noticed that plus-light travel seemed to act more as a physical than a mental stimulus, because the more recent Spacegoer's Companions had begun to develop remarkably sophisticated accessories. Computers had always been essential furniture in space, of course, but the new CMP DIRAC-deriv. Mk. IV Astg. multi-media computers could provide every imaginable form of entertainment and several unimaginable ones when the pilot ran out of steam. You didn't need to ginger them up with a surreptitious screwdriver like the old models. They were a lot of fun.

Yet even they had their limitations, and after nine months in plus-light with his current Companion, its voluptuous frame enfolding the tiny cabin like an insanely plastic eider-down, Randy found himself sighing for a reality the computer could never provide. Headed for a particularly obscure K-class star located at the end of the galaxy's spiral arm, he still had to face another nine months of confinement. Books, films, tapes and artworks had been exhausted of their potency, and Randy was reduced to watching the Companion's animated reversioning of Beardsley's "Under the Hill" illustrations, one of the *Classical Favourites* videotapes. It was evident from the increasingly bizarre departures from the original that the computer shared the pilot's suspicion that his passions might never rise again.

It was at this critical point, so perfectly timed as almost to invite certain conclusions about the computer's motives, that the Companion announced the desirability of a planet call in order to replenish the ship's chemical supplies. A star was located only a few hours distant, possessing an E-type planet stocked with the appropriate materials from which the ship could synthesise what it needed. According to the file, the planet was inhabited by a human-type race at a fairly primitive stage of development; well aware of the strict Federation directives on matters of inter-cultural contact, Randy aimed to land on one of the many uninhabited islands scattered across the oceanic Northern hemisphere.

319

Finally the computer selected a lush, cone-shaped island which according to the infra-detectors supported no animal life likely to present any major problems, and the ship settled itself down with something of a flourish. The Companions always enjoyed the chance to show off, and landings had been known at which the computers burst out with flags, fireworks, and the Home Planets Anthem, ruining all hopes of peaceful contact with the local life forms. But on this occasion the ship's door merely whispered open and with enormous relief Randy stepped outside.

He was on an open grassy plain close to the sparkling sapphire sea, a beach of fine white sand crusting its edges. Here and there the grassland featured intriguing pod-shaped plants with superbly velvet green leaves. Occasional trees bore fruits which the Companion stated to be acceptable to the human constitution, and Randy gave them enthusiastic attention; they collapsed succulently in his hands, revealing juices and flesh that were intoxicatingly flavoured. When at last he could eat no more, he ran into the clear, astonishing shallows of the ocean and washed nine months of plus-light from his mind. He rolled in the sun, laughed and shouted, jumped over his own shadow, and did most of the foolish things you'd expect, and in due time he was quiet again, stuck with the one problem that the scents and breezes of the island did nothing to solve.

Part of the trouble was that the ship didn't need him. Its glistening ground serpent, directed by the computer, probed the planet's surface for suitable mineral veins, while the Companion's laboratory section hummed with self-satisfied activity. Samples were tested, ores smelted, reagents mixed and centrifuges whirled; bursts of blue-grass music punctuated the murmuring litany of equations, a racket to which the pilot had become resigned as indication that the computer was deep in thought. He shrugged away the sense of impotence that threatened all too soon to return, and set out to explore the island. It would be good to walk himself into a natural sleep for a change, instead of having to accept one of the computer's nauseating dozee drugs which, whatever the shape and colour (and the range seemed infinite), always gave him nightmares of quite shattering decadence.

The coastline was a delight, composed of clear colours in sudden sweeps and curves. A sun of muted gold hung in the sky as though the afternoon would last forever, and the air tasted of perfume, a kind that seemed to bring back unexpected memories of fulfilment. Dreamily following his nose, Randy strolled through a clump of trees that took him out of sight of the ship, and halted abruptly in their shadow while all considerations of the penalities for cultural interference drained from his mind. On the green plain beyond, reality shimmered as if the light-waves themselves were melting in the heat. Then his vision cleared, and there appeared before him, seated on a couch of velvet leaves, a creature of such spectacular beauty that he found himself vowing feverishly never again to waste his time with the 3-D pull-out pin-downs from *Stagman* magazine.

She appeared not to have seen him as she gazed out to sea with mysterious hooded eyes, her body languid and relaxed on the couch. She wore nothing but a short blue shift of some intricately worked material, and the sunlight lapped across her skin to make a tapestry of glowing curves and enticing shadows. Softly Randy moved to her side and amazingly she turned to welcome him, making a tentative movement with her hand which he took as an invitation. He sat down, paused for a moment on the edge of conversation, then reached instead to stroke the dark brown hair that swept like a long veil down her back. Words were unnecessary for the messages pouring between them in the electric air, and the lady showed no sign of wanting a language lesson.

She sighed like the murmur of leaves in midsummer and stretched herself out before him, the hem of her garment rising gently to reveal dark and appetising areas of accessibility. Her scent was all cinnamon, musk, and pure violets, stifling rational thought. Randy toppled drunkenly into her and was enfolded by flesh that writhed delicately against his own, and by hair that seemed to caress him with gently powdered tendrils as he plunged and gasped and shook. The afternoon exploded in golden fragments.

Afterwards, Randy slid from the couch and lay on the white sand convinced, as the Companion had never been able to convince him, that he now stood a chance of understanding his place in the universe. It was as though beings from some outer galaxy were suddenly aware of his presence, but as they stirred to greet him he began to fear the hollow echo of their thoughts, the dissonant music of their knowledge, and he sank back into wakefulness. A mist of writhing green and purple shapes lay briefly over his eyes, and warning voices whispered instantly forgotten messages. But the girl still sat placidly on her couch and at the sight of her, Randy's confusion melted away. Purpose and anticipation pulled him briskly to his feet.

To his surprise, her welcome was not repeated. She smiled in an absent-minded fashion and returned her gaze to the ocean. When he tried to caress her as before, her flesh seemed actually to crawl with distaste, she made no move to lie back, and her shift stayed clamped demurely to her knees. Randy was half inclined to force the issue, but the Federation directives had once more begun to hover at the back of his mind and at last he gave up. Promising to return soon with priceless gifts, an offer to which she paid not the slightest attention, he resumed his exploration of the island.

The coastline dipped again, and the girl soon disappeared behind him. The rich grass rippled in the heat and the air quivered with a spice that made his blood surge; beside him, the ocean flashed a million reflections of the sky. Shading his eyes, he blinked with disbelief at a new girl who lay ahead on her couch of velvet, her body undulating in unmistakable delight at his approach. She could have been the sister of the gorgeous creature he had just left; the same dark hair cascaded over the same perfect slopes of the back, the same kaleidoscope of delicate lights and shadows was picked out by the sun across the smooth and supple limbs, the same sweet savour drifted teasingly across the grass. She even wore a similar shift, although this one was red. It was intricately textured with tiny patterns that changed and flowed as he tried to follow them, their writhing designs suggesting an elusive and haunting symbolism.

Disinclined to question the gifts that fate so seldom

322

placed in his path, Randy made reverent haste towards the startlingly beautiful phenomenon that awaited him. Again words could be discarded as unnecessary; her eyes, deep violet pools of promise, beckoned him with unequivocal invitations, fully reinforced by the receptive and compliant body. He became mindless, drawn into a frenzy of sensations that mingled and mounted, until a nova flared and he sank at last into a dream-like state where the girl's every movement and gesture seemed part of an obscure but vital communication between one end of the universe and the other. He stared fascinated into her eyes, while a haze of glorious colours spiralled around the couch, and then he must have slept, for there was a time when the grasses and creepers that carpeted the island appeared to explore him with their tendrils and the moss grew restless beneath his back. The sun was a deeper gold and had dipped lower in the sky when Randy splashed ocean over his head and returned refreshed to his delightful partner.

Close to her, he found desire reviving as strongly as if it had never been satisfied, but when he reached again for the girl she was as unyielding as a block of wood, and her gaze was coldly out to sea. Try as he might, he was unable to rekindle her interest in the healthy athletic pursuits he had in mind. She ignored him so completely that he couldn't even be sure she understood what he wanted. Eventually Randy decided he would have to leave her there and hope she'd be around next day in more amenable mood. He kissed the motionless mouth and wandered back in the direction of the ship.

He splashed in the shallows along the dappled coast, the sand crunching beneath his feet, the breeze stirring across the grass dunes and probing the clumps of trees. The girl in the blue shift was still sunbathing where he had left her, and he halted on the edge of the water, uncertain whether to wave and rush by or stop to talk about old times.

Her perfume settled the matter. As he approached, led by the nose, she stirred and stretched and her smile got inside his body and tuned it up like an orchestra. She reached for him with irresisitible urgency and once more he felt himself swept into her on an unthinking torrent of enjoyment. Ripping away the shift completely, he abandoned himself to an extraordinary symphony of exotic rhythms and caresses. It was as if the planet itself had opened up to swallow him, the grass and the giant green leaves closing above his head.

The climax seemed to scatter him around the landscape like fragments of a bursting pod. For a long time he lay unable to move, with fantastic visions of strange beings and unearthly music wandering through his mind. The colours of the waning afternoon ran slowly together into a magnificent sunset, and when he finally staggered to his feet it was growing dark. The girl lay on her couch in a tight ball and he could do nothing to rouse her. Reluctant to carry her back to the ship and risk arousing the Companion's suspicion about his illegal activities, he draped the torn shift and some of the big velvet leaves over her as some form of protection against the night, and made his way alone across the grass.

The computer was rather stuffy having been left on its own for so long but at last it consented, after some argument, to turn the lights out. Randy fell instantly asleep on his bunk as dozee capsules bounced unheeded across his chest to the floor.

When he awoke the next morning, the Companion was strangely silent, although lights pulsed here and there on its console. The datadials indicated that the task of chemical restocking was now complete, but there was no indication that any resumption of the journey had been calculated. Debating whether to give the thing a kick in the fusebox, Randy suddenly noticed that the ship's door was wide open, revealing sea and sand and sunlight. The spiced air of the island summoned him, and gladly he responded.

It was crowded out there. Green couches were spread around in the sun, thickly clustered near the ship but also dotted across the grass in all directions as far as Randy could see, covering the island. And on them reclined girls of every description, of all sizes, all colours. They all wore shifts of the familiar design, in hues of rainbow miscellany, although red and blue were obvious favourites. Otherwise the girls were only alike in that they were blindingly beautiful and their deep clear eyes were fixed on Randy as if their lives had been specially constructed

324

for this one ecstatic moment. As he appeared, a wave of delight surged across his audience, and he thought he heard the island itself sigh in the shimmering silence of the morning. His fans were waiting and there was much to be done. Their perfume tugged him forward.

For several hours, Randy was extremely busy. Arms, bodies and legs ensnared him in a thicket of willing flesh, and hunger and pleasure pursued each other with frantic urgency. He ploughed and dug his way across this incredible plantation of sunsoaked skin, discarded garments, and voluptuous welcome, until his responses became too painful to be worth the continuing effort, and the pauses between bouts were shadowed with uneasy dreams in which his whole being became fragmented and seemed to crumble into sand with untraceable finality. Dimly he congratulated himself on his performance, and at last he ventured to hope that he might spend the rest of his days without again setting eyes on another female form.

Breaking free from the eager ranks of his admirers, he splashed and floated in the warm ocean until a modest confidence returned to his legs that they could hold him upright once more. The girls fortunately made no attempt to follow him, but gazed in worship from the shoreline, undulating pensively on their couches. Randy chewed some fruit and wandered at the water's edge, keeping out of reach; maintaining a polite smile, he eyed the girls dispassionately and did some hard thinking.

Suddenly he noticed among the sunbathers the girl in blue he had left wrapped in leaves the night before. Evidently her night out had proved far from beneficial. She lay apart from the others, unmoving on the stained and fraying couch, her shift draped over her limbs like a rotten shroud. The tawny skin that had shone out to him yesterday was now pallid and dull, sagging in places to create hollows of emaciation, and her mane of dark hair had coagulated into a limp, repellent mess. Horrified at this apparent consequence of his attentions, Randy made his way towards her; the Companion had assured him that under normal circumstances there could be no possible compatibility between the local bacteria and Randy's own collection of extra-galactic viruses, but the circumstances

325

had strayed rather far from the normal. If the girl was in trouble, Randy was likely to be in trouble too.

In the first automatic move of diagnosis, he took her hand. It parted immediately from the sagging mass of her body and rested soggily in his grip, greenish matter dripping from the severed wrist. The fingers broke and oozed together in his palm, and the thumb dropped to the ground with a soft squelch. Shaking off the decaying tissue in revulsion, he turned the girl's face towards him. It slipped under his touch, and his fingers sank into the black jelly where her eyes had been.

Randy left in a hurry, clambering heedlessly across a landscape of enchanting smiles. The island heaved beneath his feet, and the sun beat like a hammer on his skull. When he got to the ship he was crawling and had the impression that he was making a lot of noise. He fell through the doorway and dragged the hatch shut.

The computer received Randy's confession in utter contempt. If he had only bothered, said the Companion, to study all the information available before charging out of the ship like some Jugoslavian nudist (the doubtless apocryphal ardour of this legendary race was the basis for one of the more memorable sagas of the spaceways), he might have avoided making so spectacular a fool of himself. He should be aware, added the Companion, that nothing was unknown to or unforeseen by the CMP DIRAC-deriv Mk IV Astg multi-media computers, and that exploits such as Randy's not only had no hope of being kept secret but were even so predictable as to be exactly calculable according to a now-proven constant in which $x$ was equal to fifteen plus-light square roots divided simultaneously by point seven recurring. During the hours in which Randy had been neglecting his duties, stated the Companion, it had taken the opportunity to prepare a thesis on this very subject, demonstrating a breadth of vision so extraordinary that the Companion made so bold as to be confident that the highest intergalactic honours would be accorded to it when the voyage was completed. With a modest cough, the Companion disgorged a six-hundred-page volume of computer print-outs, handsomely bound in leather with gold edgings. Randy might care, suggested the Companion, to browse through this epoch-making work while preparing his own report to the Federation, although they were unlikely to treat his case with much sympathy if he presented it in his usual inarticulate manner.

Wearily dropping the book into the recycler, Randy pressed the Bowman button (the emergency control known only to the pilot in plus-light ships), and let the Companion sing nursery rhymes for half an hour while he consumed a soothe-tube of nerve paste. Relaxing on the control couch, he then re-engaged the information banks of the computer and summoned up all available facts and references about the planet they were on. The Companion had neglected to mention, of course, that the place had actually been visited before, so that instead of the usual brief list of aerial survey data there were voluminous technical and ecological reports, mostly incomprehensible to the non-specialist. They rolled across the information screen and Randy scowled his way through them without finding anything helpful. Such biological deductions as had been made seemed in no way related to his own experiences, and only one group of the exploring team had been anywhere near the islands of the Northern hemisphere, their purpose and conclusions connected merely with the botanical.

After presenting all the main texts, the computer automatically began to turn up the footnotes and addenda. Letting these run at double speed, Randy was about to give up hope when a small picture flashed by that struck a faint chord. He turned back and stared for a long time. The brightly coloured illustration showed the cross-section of a flower, and the accompanying article, under a severe Latin headline, was a report by one of the botanists.

Of the three species of *Bacchantius* growing on the planet Rosy Lee, perhaps the most unusual is *Gigantiflora*. The plant is herbaceous, and perenniates by means of thick starchy tubers. It flowers annually in the correct conditions and is a member of the family *Phorusorchidacae*, the local orchid family. (See ref. Axaia p. 74,418 for description of the parallel evolution of flowering plants on E-type worlds. See ref. Modoinisk p. 731,111 for detailed parameters of E-type conditions.)

Normally the *Gigantiflora* flowers only after sensing the airborne waste products of the humanoid species *Gaggus gaggus* which inhabits the planet Rosy Lee. The buds take some five months to mature but require no external stimulus to begin formation. When fully developed, they lie dormant under a thick covering of velvety green leaves. Once the presence of a humanoid has aroused the flowering response the buds rise above the leaves over-night and open just before dawn. The flowers are huge and strikingly shaped. Specimens examined ranged from 1.3716 m to 1.8315 m in height.

Pollination is by pseudo-copulation, as in many species of plant, but is exceptional in this case in that the pollinat-ing agent is the male *Gaggus*. The flowers are exact replicas of native women, and their whole structure, com-posed of united sepals and petals, is complete in almost every external detail. One of the few visible differences is the threadlike though robust stem emerging from the small of the plant's back.

The petal, analogous to the lip in other *orchidacae,* is primarily bright red or blue, although other shades based on these colours can often be found. Giving the appear-ance of a short garment, it is united to the perianth only by a tiny join at the nape of the neck and may be re-moved completely without any noticeable damage, al-though it quickly shrivels.

The flowers have a very powerful scent, and while the chemical structure of this has yet to be determined it is known to have pronounced hallucinatory and aphrodisi-acal properties, which it is thought acted originally to pre-vent the *Gaggus* from discovering the true nature of the girl that apparently confronts him. Under the influence of the scent, for example, the male finds the eyes of the plant lifelike and mobile, whereas in reality they are the least successful part of the imitation.

Capable of a quite sophisticated series of mechanical movements and reactions, *Gigantiflora* will on being dis-turbed by a suitable stimulus go through motions resem-bling those of a primitive coquette. The native male *Gaggus* is often completely addicted to the pleasures afforded by these flowers, to the extent that he will neglect his own wife. The female *Gaggus,* on the other hand, destroys these plants whenever she finds them. The theory appears tenable that the population of Rosy Lee is maintained at a low level by the waste of male effort expended on cultivating *Gigantiflora*.

The pollen develops before the gynoceum and forms a thick powder on the plant's "pubic" area. During pseudocopulation this pollen adheres to the male, and when next he amuses himself with a *Gigantiflora* it is transferred to the area surrounding the new flower's "navel" —which is in fact the stigma, thus completing the pollination. Directly after this process the flower is able to discourage further attempts by the same male, becoming rigid and unapproachable so that self-pollination is avoided.

The seeds of the planet are dust-like and blow many miles, even across oceans. On some of the planet's many uninhabited islands, whole colonies of the plants may be found; as the *Gaggus* is disinclined to travel, lacking any great incentive or energy to do so, these colonies presumably never reach the flowering stage. When members of the present expedition landed in one such island, the flowers appeared by the second day in numbers approaching infestation proportions, the effect resembling that of an overcrowded brothel. Since the team was wholly female, it was not possible to judge the effect on a male, but the sight, smell, and hallucinatory vapours were such as to convince us that the effect would be overpowering even for a civilized man.

I must confess (the report added, taking a suddenly personal tone), that while as a botanist I found the flowers fascinating, as a woman I found them profoundly disturbing, almost disgusting. Even when I was cutting portions of the petal from the "face", an unsettling exercise, the plant's lower half made several attempts to seduce me, although as far as we were aware only males could inspire the pollination mechanism. The fact that in uninhabited regions the flowers might react to women as well leads to interesting speculation about alternative means of pollination. And although every member of our team professed disgust for the flowers, several plants unquestionably set seed during our stay on the island despite the impossibility of self-pollination.

Further research could doubtless be pursued in this area, but while this would be diverting enough for the specialists involved, no particular value can be anticipated from it. We are familiar in botany with the basic principles of pseudocopulation, studied in detail on Terra in the last century. (Ref: *Wild Flowers of the World* by Everard & Morley, reprinted under the *Treasures of Antiquity* label: "The insect-like form of the lip and the scent of the flower in the *Ophrys* attract the males of certain insects and stimulates them into abortive attempts at copulation. During this pseudo-copulation the insects pick up pollinia or transfer pollen to the stigmas. Some tropical orchids have likewise been shown to possess particular scents which excite insects sexually.") A Research Priority Rating is accordingly recommended at no more than Z-Grade.

Some technicalities followed about the morphology and cytology of the plant, but Randy had read far enough. His head hurt as a torrent of ideas and schemes poured through his mind, and he realized that the hypnoconditioning he'd gone through at Sector X113 was, thanks to his uniquely exhausted condition, at last getting the chance to work. In dizzy flashes of inspiration, he saw that he was destined to become the greatest gardener ever known. He grabbed a screwdriver and got started.

The rest of course is history. Randy waited on Rosy Lee long enough to collect the ten pods of seeds he was later to refer to in his autobiography as his offspring, and within a few months he appeared on the "dry" planet Bergia (where prostitution is illegal) as the proprietor of "The Pleasure Gardens of Rosy Lee." The uproar led to a court case, a magnificent specimen of *Bacchantius Gigantiflora* was produced before the enraptured judge, and all charges were dismissed. The galaxy rang with the news, and Randy's fortune was made. He was able to make the unprecedented purchase of a plus-light ship—his own—from the Federation, complete with Ship's Companion.

Plus-light travel being as complicated as it is, few were in a position to track down the planet where Randy got his supplies, but those who made it to the islands of Rosy Lee said they found there only desert scrubland and bleak crags. The place had an atmosphere of terror, they said, and they were glad to leave; the *Gaggus* population, however, seemed undisturbed despite the odd preference on the part of the males for a species of cauliflower with a stench like rotten pulp.

It seems that Randy and his screwdriver, whirled to the heights of creativity by the hypnoconditioning that ran through his brain, had converted the Ship's Companion to new levels of chemical accomplishment. When the computer had finished with Rosy Lee, the aphrodisiac breeze that drifted across the planet had acquired a tang that went unnoticed by the *Gaggus* nose but which filled the human senses with stark revulsion. Thus Randy and his brood preserve a comfortable monopoly. The Companion, too, proved to be an unrivalled teacher; the girls in the "Pleasure Gardens", now a universal attraction, are renowned as much for their seductive conversation as for their physical skills. Naturally they are all experts in bluegrass music. And the hybrid strains developed with the aid of the computer become more delectable year by year, especially those highly prized specimens reputed to resemble famous beauties of the past. The Cleopatra Convulser, the Bardot Brainstorm, and the Lovelace Paralyzer have passed into legend.

So that, girls, is the story of the famed horticulturalist Randy Richmond, known throughout the galaxy (although the plus-light pilots have, I believe, a slightly different version) as "Mr. Greenfingers". All strength to his compost, and may his flyspray never dwindle! Now, dig in. Another batch of conservationists just stopped by our greenhouse.

# GALACTIC EMPIRES
## Volume Two

# ACKNOWLEDGEMENTS

"Escape to Chaos" by John D. MacDonald
   Copyright © 1951 by Fictioneers, Inc.
"Concealment" by A. E. van Vogt
   Copyright © 1943 by Street & Smith Publications
   Copyright renewed 1970 by A. E. van Vogt
"To Civilize" by Algis Budrys
   Copyright © Columbia Publications Inc.
   Reprinted by permission of the author and the author's
   agent Candida Donadio and Associates Inc.
"Beep" by James Blish
   Copyright © 1954 by James Blish
"Down the River" by Mack Reynolds
   Copyright © Startling Stories 1950, Better Publications
   Inc.
"The Bounty Hunter" by Avram Davidson
   Copyright © 1958 by King-Size Publications Inc.
   Reprinted by permission of the author and E. J. Carnell
   Literary Agency
"Not Yet the End" by Fredric Brown
   Copyright © 1941 by Captain Future
"Tonight the Stars Revolt" by Gardner F. Fox
   Copyright © 1952 by Gardner F. Fox
"Final Encounter" by Harry Harrison
   Copyright © 1964 by Galaxy Publishing Corporation
   Reprinted by permission of the author and his agent
   A. P. Watt & Son
"Lord of a Thousand Suns" by Poul Anderson
   Copyright © 1951 by Love Romances Publishing Co.,
   Inc.
"Big Ancestor" by F. L. Wallace
   Copyright © 1955 by F. L. Wallace
"The Interlopers" by Roger Dee
Copyright © 1954 by Roger Dee Aycock

# CONTENTS

# INTRODUCTION

There is no point in pretending to distinguish the galactic empire story as a genre. Generally speaking, such stories form part of what is known as "space opera" — to which the first two anthologies in this series were devoted. The galactic empire is a sort of crystallisation of space opera; there are others, of which Sword-and-Sorcery is one.

Some stories use the imperial background to make a moral point; didacticism is perenially popular in science fiction and Mack Reynolds provides a good example in this volume. But it is the playful aspect of the galactic empire which mainly strikes a reader.

This aspect led many readers, including a lot of sf fans, to despise space opera and the galactic scene. Now, there are good literary reasons why a wide canvas, such as these stories demand, will defeat all but the Michelangelos of sf — and we have too few of them — thus more thoughtful writers (and perhaps the ones we might call the better artists) eschewed the galactic manner. But to dismiss it just because it is playful is not good enough.

The two editors who have wielded most power since sf magazines came into being are undoubtedly Hugo Gernsback, founder of *Amazing Stories* and thus of magazine sf, and John W. Campbell, who edited *Astounding Science Fiction* (later *Analog*) for more than thirty years. Both these influential men took a certain attitude to mankind and mankind's activities. Their philosophy was utilitarian. Campbell's was the more formidable intellect, but he believed, no less than Gernsback, that greater human units made for a greater humanity, rather than for less humanity.

Both editors tolerated, nay, fostered space opera in their pages, but it was space opera strongly oriented towards the machine. Campbell saw man as a tool-making animal; he loved to talk about the thumb as the opposed digit which distinguished man from the other primates and gave him a better grasp of weapons, thus setting him on the path to the stars. And his influence was strong on the writers who wrote for him, writers such as Arthur C. Clarke. That great imaginative moment in the Kubrick-Clarke film, *2001: A Space Odyssey*, when a bone used by the early man as a killing weapon is hurled triumphantly into the air, to be transformed into a space station, is a Campbell image, the image of *homo faber*.

This Campbellian view of man naturally predisposed him to advocate larger and larger doses of technology. Or perhaps it was the other way round, and his belief in the dosages made him see man as primarily a worker. Whichever way it was, *Astounding* rarely admitted stories which showed mankind growing away from technology. Technology, after all, may merely be a manifestation of racial puberty, rather like motor bikes — to be abandoned for all the rest of our species' life-span. Other races may ascend to a high and creative level of civilization without carrying technics much further than the potter's wheel. But such speculation would have been heresy in *Astounding*. The unorthodox are particularly hot on their own orthodoxies.

Campbell was brilliantly clever. Yet he preferred — and the preference brought his eventual decline as an editor — to ignore the fact that the contents of his beautiful magazine were *play*, mind games, and, in Campbell's heyday, the best mind games in the business. His writers, too, following his example, liked to justify sf in terms of how accurately its predictions were fulfilled, or how well it served as propaganda for the space race, or how strongly it influenced American kids to become physicists when they grew up. This was sf as function, sf as just another tool.

The writers who wrote for other magazines often felt otherwise. They believed that sf should be a game, if a serious one, that its merits were integral, not applied. They understood *homo ludens;* and so their products were denigratingly referred to as escapism by the *faber* brigade.

Some philosophers have argued that *homo ludens* has played a supreme role in history, a role that the upstart *homo faber* has tended to edit out. The most distinguished contribution to this theory is J. Huizinga's *Homo Ludens*, which has recently received massive support from

Lewis Mumford in *The Myth of the Machine.* In general, sf has been approached and evaluated from the utilitarian standpoint, and conscripted willy-nilly under the *faber* banner. The result has been undue encouragement of an sf grounded in a little grey philosophy of man churning away into futurity as a unit of an amorphous technocracy. At least, such has been more or less the official view — in New York as in Moscow — and one which probably played a part in hastening the notorious sf revolt, the New Wave, of the mid-sixties, with its emphasis on doing one's own thing, however obnoxiously. But it is noticeable that when a madman enters the sf field, just plainly enjoying himself, he generates an immediate and enthusiastic following. The early A. E. van Vogt, Alfred Bester, Michael Moorcock, and R. A. Lafferty, are examples of this, while public speaking up and down the country has convinced me that probably the most popular of all short story writers is not Ray Bradbury, as commonly supposed, but Robert Sheckley, an imaginative joker whose ramshackle worlds and leaky spaceships have immediate appeal.

A galactic empire, in short, is not intended as a blueprint for a future utopia. That might not be much fun, though no doubt a few trendy sociologists would recommend it to their class. A galactic empire is ramshackle and anachronistic, full of miscegenation worlds, leaky spaceships, and naked slaves working by torchlight in uranium mines. A galactic empire owes more to Cecil B. de Mille than to Einstein: it is the Spectacular of sf.

This unashamed escapism is not incompatible with profundity of thought. Here we may recall the question J. R. R. Tolkein asked C. S. Lewis, "What class of men would you expect to be most preoccupied with, and most hostile to, the idea of escape?" He answered his own question: "Jailers."

I quoted Tolkein's remark in the introduction to the first volume of this anthology. This introduction has been an attempt to restate what I said there in different terms.

There's more than one way of killing a cat, or of sneaking up on a galactic empire.

# SECTION 2 (continued)
## MATURITY OR BUST

### *i "You Can't Impose Civilization by Force"*

•

*The issue of this appalling struggle in the minds of these former imperialists depended on the extent to which specialization for empire had affected them. In a few young worlds, in which specialization had not gone deep, a period of chaos was followed by a period of reorientation and world-planning, and in due season by sane utopia. But in most of these worlds no escape was possible. Either chaos persisted till racial decline set in, and the world sank to the human, the sub-human, the merely animal states; or else, in a few cases only, the discrepancy between the ideal and the actual was so distressing that the whole race committed suicide.*

Olaf Stapledon: *Star Maker*

One thing is certain. Men unify only to achieve strength, whether the strength of religion, knowledge, or power. And unification leads to various ills; once you have joined, you are apt to stay joined, whether or not you want out.

Unification also leads to complexity, and in this section mature empires reflect that complexity. Our four distinguished authors, van Vogt, John D. MacDonald, Algis Budrys, and James Blish, were writing for the amusement of their readers in generally despised popular magazines, yet they touch on a weird sort of truth. A friendly reviewer of the first book in this series said, "*Space Opera* is all good, unpretentious, and proud fun, yet one can't help but suspect that these tales touch some of the mythopoeic archetypal well-springs deep in every id." Large words, but I agree — though it may all depend on the circuit diagrams

345

in one's id. These stories seem to me to have the quality described.

Talking of the circuit diagrams of the id, no science fiction writer could boast more elaborate circuits than the late James Blish. All learning was his province. He was a great man for making connections. His splendid Cities in Flight saga explores one of the seminal connections of the modern age, the sibling relationship between space and time; while his formidable life of Roger Bacon, *Doctor Mirabilis*, examines the multitudinous relationships between science and religion — a theme developed in fictional counterpoint in Blish's most famous novel, *A Case of Conscience*, and later in *Black Easter* and *The Day After Judgement*. These threads can also be traced through "Beep," the slice of galactic history we present here.

One of Blish's preoccupations was with the problem of sin, which he appeared to deal with sometimes as if it were merely an intellectual question. With hindsight, we can observe that sin in "Beep" is conspicuous by its absence, to deploy that phrase precisely. The story can be interpreted as being about a machine which abolishes sin, root and branch — sin in fact, sin as concept.

"Beep" is a think-piece, and it forms a central think-piece to this volume. It is a story I greatly admire. When I first read it in *Galaxy* I was less impressed by its intellectual qualities than by a haunting image, which embodies much of the glamour of sf, the image contained in these lines:

"I've heard the commander of a worldline cruiser, travelling from 8873 to 8704 along the world-line of the planet Hathshepa, which circles a star on the rim of NGC 4725, calling for help across eleven million light years — but what kind of help he was calling for, or will be calling for, is beyond my comprehension."

This passage was picked up by Emsh, who illustrated it on its first appearance. He contributed a design showing a whirlpool of space-time, with the cruiser trapped along its spiral.

One of the ingenuities of "Beep" lies within its title, and in the correspondence of that title to the effect of the story, which unpacks a world of implications from a meaningless seed of noise. "Beep" tackles headlong one of the central problems of galactic empires: the problem of how to deal with, and if possible overcome, immensely long lines of communication. The Dirac transmitter proves a remarkably effective answer; and Blish shows us what paradoxically good side-effects it generates, including having one of the main characters almost forcibly married to a transvestite lady of mixed ancestry — which marriage he enjoys.

When writing the story, Blish perhaps felt that with free will removed from human affairs there would be no more sin. His assumptions about predestination are interesting and uncomfortable (a lot of Jim's lines of thought were interesting and uncomfortable). He depicts human consciousness as "just along for the ride"; elsewhere, it is described as "Helpless." Events rule. I once wrote a story ("Not for an Age") in which I depicted a human consciousness as carried along helpless to interfere with events. It was, and remains, my idea of hell. Yet Blish manages to make it sound almost utopian. The world he portrays in "Beep" is an extremely happy one, happier than any other world-view in the anthology; as one of the characters says, "The news is always good."

To make the connection between instant communication and redemption (freedom from sin) is a remarkable jump. Blish embodies it symbolically by the tender care taken to see that lovers meet as planned. All this is even more remarkable when we consider that most sf writers use the posit of instant communication to further aims of conquest and aggression. In "Beep," it brings peace. Was Blish trying to equate instant with perfect communication. How else explain why his all-powerful Service is incorruptible?

Science fiction stories often leave strange vapour trails in the skies of our minds. I find myself wondering at the way in which Blish has planted two people in disguise, one in the inner, one in the outer, story; though they assume the disguises for devious purposes, neither meets disapproval or anything stronger when discovered. Perhaps that is how it should be in a utopia. If you remove reasons for aggression, would aggression disappear? But one cannot ask such questions in this construct of Blish's, since cause and effect are proven inoperative by the Dirac transmitter.

If you grant that "Beep" is utopian in disposition then you have to grant that it is a very rare sort of story indeed. Although utopias and dystopias are traditionally associated with science fiction, no galactic empire to my knowledge could be remotely regarded as utopian. "Beep" is the one exception. In his wisdom, James Blish did a lot of strange things.

Algis Budrys' early short stories showed wisdom. Then he stopped writing. He has recently reappeared on the science fiction scene disguised as a reviewer; perhaps that experience will tempt him back to fiction, to show us all how it should be done. Meanwhile, I advise readers to seek out his novel, *Who?* (recently filmed) and, especially, *Rogue Moon*. One line in "To Civilize" remains in my memory: "You can't impose civilization by force." It is something that people, and not only sf writers, tend to forget.

These stories are garnered from obscure magazines, some of which were never published in Britain: *Super Science Stories* did appear over there in an emaciated edition. Above cover scenes showing such delights as New York in flames ran their proud legend, "Read It Today — Live It Tomorrow."

It is unlikely that the world of *Escape to Chaos* will ever see actuality, but that is hardly to the point. John D. MacDonald — famous for his polished thrillers — posits an amazingly complex civilization, hemmed cheek-by-jowl by other galaxies of similar probability. Among them moves the splendid City of Transition. Van Vogt himself might envy such a grand design.

Not that the Old Master has anything to fear. His Imperial Battleship *Star Cluster* moves through a galaxy inhabited by many races with many different abilities. Will the future see such things? The question remains open. But it should be remembered that space travel itself was once a similar mad dream; science fiction readers were among the scattered few who believed in its possibility. Van Vogt, at this stage of his career, always carried belief, even when his subject matter seemed frankly incredible. Over thirty years later, the magic remains, even if we are less easy to impress.

In this story and ones linked with it, van Vogt captured a sensuous interpretation of space which connects not only with the future but with man's early experience of the cosmos. Van Vogt's great storms in space, his light-year wide streams of particles — so "modern" when they first appeared — draw us back to ages when our everyday lives were less sundered from the elements and the night skies more omni-present. Technology has weaned us from Mother Nature; electricity and the water closet blacken the mind's eye. Now we have space travel, and we no longer believe in it, except as a quasimilitary exercise.

But *once* it was believed in, before we built water-tight bulwarks against sky and moor and forest and sea. Long before science fiction was thought of, great voyages were cosmic in scope, and responsibe minds leapt up to embrace the wanderer and his tale. Homer, first voice of the Western psyche, takes us to the margins of the known, where gods and goddesses form part of the traffic of Man, extending the dimensions of his experience. The ancient Epic of Gilgamesh celebrates the belief that if you navigate your ship to the edge of the oceans you may be able to join the great stream of stars and sail upwards into the heavens, where the secret of Creation is. The familiar names of the constellations tell us of an ancient and intimate relationship between man on Earth and the far stars.

One of the impulses behind modern science fiction — particularly the adventure-impulse behind such stories as Poul Anderson's and Gardner Fox's — is extremely ancient. And, we hope, inextinguishable.

349

*At bay against his dissolving skies he fought — the last champion of a star-spanning dynasty which never existed save to die!*

•

# ESCAPE TO CHAOS
## By John D. MacDonald

The third son of Shain, the rebel son, the traitor to Empire, was pursued thrice across the Galaxy, was trapped five times and five times he escaped. Now he stood in the blue and eternal dusk of a cobalt city on Zeran, one of the old planets, a planet of many histories, of many peoples, of the sadness of things lost beyond regaining. Zeran kept its face always toward the vast pink-orange sun that bore it, a half billion miles away.

Three years before, Shain had listened to the reports of the activities of his third son, Andro. Shain lay on the couch and ate of the fruit the women had brought him. He listened. "Andro said to Telka of Vereen, 'How long will you permit my father to oppress you?' Andro said to Clangaron of Lell, 'When the uprising comes, you must be ready to join us.'"

"Enough!" Shain said in the voice of Empire. He dropped seeds to the soft amber floor, selected another fruit. There was a small wet sound as he bit into it. He chewed, swallowed, yawned. "Have him killed," he said languidly.

Three years later Andro stood alone in the dusk of the city of endless blue. He stood alone with heavy shoulders braced against the wall at the end of a forgotten alley. His burns suppurated and they weakened him, but his hand was firm on the grip of the weapon. Forty ships there were, and now there were none. Seven thousand had pledged their loyalty beyond death, and of the seven thousand the last one, the girl, Daylya, had died as he dragged her from the ruin of the last ship.

He was a big man and he waited with a big man's patience. He waited and it was hate that gave him the strength to stand against his hurt. Once he smiled as he thought of what it had cost them. Four times seven thousand. Five times forty ships. Rumor among all the planets of Empire would make those totals greater. The deeds of Andro would be whispered in quiet places. And one day another one would dare, and win. Andro had shown them, shown all of them that revolt, even unsuccessful revolt, was possible, and to many it would seem a good way to die.

The wars of nations on ancient earth had been the rationalization for the founding of what had become galactic empire. For centuries as man had exploded across the star wastes, Empire had been weak. And then when the galactic wars began, star against star, cluster against cluster, Empire had regained its old strength merely by seeming necessary.

And the House of Galvan had ruled Empire for several thousand years. Shain of Galvan was no better and no worse than the average, Andro knew. The House of Galvan had not permitted itself to become weak. The men went to the far wild planets to find the strong-thighed mothers of Empire. The men of the House of Galvan were big. But the House had ruled too long. They had ruled from a time of enlightenment through to a time of superstition and stagnation. Andro, the youngest son, had not been as cleverly and carefully indoctrinated into the mores of Empire as his eldest brother, Larrent, as the middle brother, Masec. He had read much, of the olden times. Then, steeped in the rich traditions of early days, he had looked around him.

He had seen the prancing perfumed artists, claiming

an ultimate reality in incomprehensible daubs. He had visited the slave markets of Simpar and Chaigan, and had been sickened. He had seen that the ships were old ships, the weapons old weapons, and the old songs forgotten. He had seen the dusty rotting machines that had been the hope of man, while ten thousand laborers built, by hand and whip, a temple to the glory of the House of Galvan.

And he had said, "This is the dark age of Empire. We have had enough."

Even as youngest son in the great palaces and fortifications of the heart of Empire, on the green and gold planet called Rael at the heart of the Galaxy, he had only to raise a languid hand to acquire forty slave women, the rarest of wines, or the tax-tribute of a dozen planets for a hundred years.

And he said, "We have had enough."

And Shain said, "Have him killed."

And Larrent and Masec said, "Have him killed."

Death was close. The last ship had crashed near the wall of the empty blue city. The burns on his left side were deep enough to hold his doubled fist, and each time the wave of weakness lasted a bit longer. He wanted to take one more, or two, or three or even a dozen with him. Another fragment to add to the legend, to be said in an awed whisper, "And when they finally trapped him alone, on Zeran, he . . ."

Andro coughed and it was a cat-weak sound in the eternal dusk. Deralan, Chief of Empire Police, had personally headed this final, successful chase. And Andro knew that wiry, dour Deralan was a cautious man. Andro had felt the streets shudder as the ships had landed in a circle around the blue city. The ring of Deralan's men would be advancing toward the heart of the city, searching each building with care, the ring growing closed, tighter as they neared the center.

When he breathed there was a bubbling in the deepest part of the highest wound on his left side. His legs started to bend. He braced them once more, lifted his heavy head in time to see a flicker of movement at the end of the alley. All weakness was forgotten as he raised the weapon a trifle.

There was hard amusement in him as he thought how the pursuers must feel. Each one of the previous five escapes had bordered on the miraculous. Now they would be expecting a further miracle.

"No miracles this time," he said, and knew that the border-line of delirium had caused him to speak aloud.

A shadow appeared at the end of the alley. He lifted the weapon, sighted carefully. The firmness on which his feet were braced opened with an oiled abruptness. It wrenched his wounds so that he screamed out in agony. As he fell he saw the vast rim of the orange star directly overhead before the opening clapped shut far above him and he fell through an emptiness that was blacker than deep space.

Sarrz, Deputy Director of the Bureau of Socionetics, was a round little man with squirrel-bright eyes and a face like a plaster death mask. It was situations exactly like this which made him realize that his EC — Emotional Conditioning — was getting a bit frayed around the edges. He could not prevent a thalamic reaction to such ... stupidity. There was really no other word for it.

He turned in his chair so that he would not have to look at the two of them, so that he could regain some of his control. Framed in the window, thirty yards across and fifteen yards high, was most of the City of Transition. It looked, Sarrz sometimes thought, like several thousand bridal cakes with raspberry frosting. Beyond the ten thousand foot towers which marked the four corners of the city was darkness.

In the name of energy conservation Transition was now resting on a .8 gravity planet in Era Middle 6 in a high index probability. Transition was imitating a mountain, hence the opacity beyond the slip towers.

Sarrz realized that his pride in the Field Teams was possibly a bit unreasonable. He spoke without turning toward the two members of the team.

"The quality of your indoctrination is questionable,"

he said softly. "I shall conduct this on a primer basis. What is Transition?"

He knew by the voice that the younger of the two, the female, had spoken. She was the atavistic type — a throwback to a higher index of sensuality and emotional sway. A mistake to have ever let her go out.

"Transition," Calna said, "is an operational station in probability space-time. There are three such stations. This one operates on the socionetic level through the medium of Field Teams." She used the exact words of the basic manual.

"Excellent," he said with a trace of irony. "Please continue, Agent."

Her voice faltered a bit. "There are twenty-six known galactic civilizations with a high probability index, and many thousand more . . . distant."

He turned and stared at her. With her sturdy figure and overlong hair she looked like one of the old prints. "Is that the right word?"

"Not distant. Less available," she corrected.

Sarrz leaned back in his chair. "Much better. Continue, please."

The male agent was obviously uncomfortable. He kept fingering the tunic insignia. Calna said, rapidly, "With the discovery and application of the Oxton Effect, it became apparent that there was no need to limit any galactic civilization to the space-time rigidity previously known. With easy slip between the twenty-six civilizations with high probability index, it was believed that a unification on twenty-six space-time levels could be accomplished. Research had shown that only three space-time levels could be unified immediately. This was done. The unified civilization of three space-time aspects set itself the task of bringing the social level of the remaining twenty-three up to the point where unification could be undertaken."

"And how could this be done?" Sarrz asked in silky tone.

The girl flushed. "Field Teams, trained in Socionetics, and based at Transition, were assigned to the twenty-three lagging cultures. It was discovered that if the Field

354

Teams acted openly, as agents from a parallel space-time, their efforts caused a deviation in probability of the culture development so that the civilization resulting became less probable, and hence could not be kept within slip range. It could still be reached, of course, as can the several thousand less probable ones, but only with exorbitant power expenditure."

"I see," said Sarrz, as though he were hearing it for the first time. He leaned forward a bit. "And have we ever lost one of these parallel space-time cultures through too obvious meddling?"

"One," the girl said. "Several years ago. It was number seventeen on the program chart."

Sarrz was ready for the kill. He leaned forward a fraction of an inch more. "How can you be certain that it isn't two that we have lost, Agent? How can you be certain that your violation of all standing instructions hasn't lost us number four as well?"

The girl flushed and then turned pale. "You sit here in Transition and lose touch with the Field Team problems," she said boldly. "Solin and I have been on the case for over five years. As soon as we were well enough educated in language and customs to walk among them as subjects of the Empire, we found out that our hope was Andro, youngest son of the ruler. You do not know, Deputy Director, how hard we tried to get close enough to Andro to control him, control his rashness, so as to improve his timing. He led the revolt against Empire when his followers were too few, his resources too slim. Five times we managed to save him. I could not stand by and see him killed in an alley. I could not face beginning again. And let me absolve Solin here, my teammate, from any responsibility. He made the strongest protest possible. I went ahead on my own authority. And I do not think we have forced number four out of range, into a low probability index."

Sarrz closed his eyes for long seconds, opened them suddenly and stared at the girl. "You were trained, Agent. You were told the danger of obvious middling. You were told how long these things can continue. You knew that it may be two thousand years before we can steer that culture to the point where acceptance and unification can be considered. Knowing all these things about you, Agent, you leave me with but one conclusion. That you became personally and emotionally so involved with this Andro savage that you lost your head and tried, very sentimentally, to save him. Is that not true?" She turned her eyes from him. "Answer me?" he said softly.

"I . . . I don't know. Possibly it is true."

"Agent, there are seven hundred teams operating in that parallel culture. Most of them are attempting to activate a technistic renaissance. Others are directing the subjects of that Empire in equally necessary paths. Other teams, such as the one you two form, have been operating on the socio-political level. Up until now there has not been one violation of security."

Sarrz stood up and walked to the window. He whirled. "Think of it once! Think of what you've done! One tiny little ship and a galaxy of two billions of habitable planets is pushed forever out of our reach! What did you do with him?"

Solin said in a low tone, "We cut the passage and as he fell, we resealed it. He was unconscious by the time we floated him down to the chamber. He was badly hurt. Calna stayed with him and I set up the field, returned to our ship and activated the field, removing both of them from the city. He was almost gone. We rebuilt the tissues, took him in deep sleep to the dark side of that planet, to one of the dead cities which they have lost the skill to visit, and placed him on the zero metabolic level. Then we . . . grew worried and came back."

"So you grew worried, did you?" Sarrz said with acid sweetness. "What am I to tell the Director?"

"If only they hadn't spotted him as he escaped from the ship," Solin said.

"I've been going over your detailed reports," Sarrz said, with a sudden note of hope in his voice. "This Deralän, he who headed the pursuit, isn't he a very ambitious one?"

"Very," Solin said.

"Then there's our chance! This sixth escape by Andro

will ruin Deralan. Shain will probably have him shot. Shain will want proof of Andro's death. Is there any distinctive mark on this Andro?"

"A tattoo of the royal House of Calvan on the upper portion of the right arm."

"Go into slip at once, Solin. Take a square of the skin with the tattoo on it. Use your finder to contact the Field Team on Rael. Give the little trophy to either Agent of the Team. It will be placed in Deralan's hand before he has his audience with Shain. I don't think Deralan will ask any questions."

"But then," said Calna, in a thin voice, "when Andro reappears . . ."

"He won't reappear. He'll sleep there for ten thousand years, if it seems necessary."

The girl stood up, one hand at her throat. "You can't do that!"

"You have no hand in any more discussion of either policy or procedure, girl. You are no longer an Agent. You will receive all the usual pensions. Report to field five at once. They'll have orders on you. You are being sent back to our own space-time. Any planet preference?"

"Earth," the girl said softly.

For a moment Sarrz forgot his irritation with her. "Indeed! I guess I never noticed origin on your card. Do you know, this is the first time I have ever actually met anyone from our planet of origin."

She lifted her chin, with a look of pride. "It is a good place," she said. "It is a good place to know, and a good place to go back to."

"I am sorry," Sarrz said with a gentleness. "Possibly you were never right for this sort of work. I am truly sorry."

"Why can not Andro be released to recruit new personnel for his revolt?" she asked. "Wouldn't it save time?"

The irritation came back into Sarrz' voice. "Release him and he knows that he did not escape through his own powers. He knows he was helped, and to him it would be help through the good offices of the supernatural. He would at once relate this last escape to the previous five, and become, through his new convictions, a son of the gods rather than a revolutionary. Rebellion would change from a social to a quasi-religious basis, and we know that in order to keep number four within the high probability index range, we must hasten development along the *same* lines as would normally occur. We have plotted their culture curve. We can accelerate it without affecting probability, but we cannot redraw the curve on a new basis without losing them forever, or at least until slip becomes possible for lesser probabilities, and our technicians in symbolics say that will never occur."

"So," Calna said in a dead tone, "you will leave him there. A living death."

"There is no room for sentimentality in our work," Sarrz said.

Calna turned and left the Deputy Director's headquarters. The door orifice folded softly shut behind her.

Earth was always the origin. Symbolics made that clear. Ten thousand times ten thousand, Earth was the planet of origin. In the beginnings of the science of Symbolic Probability, it was thought all deviations were of equal value. The result would be, if it could be vizualized at all, in the shape of a fan, with an infinity of lines diverging from a fixed point, lines equally spaced.

This concept did not take into account the limitations on culture deviation. Always it was humankind, and reactions — social reactions — are limited, so it became a problem of dividing infinity by the finite. The result is infinity also, but the lines were no longer equally spaced from the common point. They were bundled. Each spacetime frame was thus co-existent with its sister probabilities. And as long as they were bundled, grouped, you could slip from one sister probability into the next.

The space-time frame in which the conception originated had tried to jump extra-galactic space and had been hurled back. It was a rigid boundary to further expansion, until, of course, it was found that there were twenty-six superimposed home galaxies in the probability grouping.

The small golden pyramidal ships quivered, shimmered, became milky and disappeared in one frame to reappear in the next. So mated were three of the probability frames that the languages, the mores, even the fads and fashions were co-existent. Had it not been possible to slip to one of the other two, the slip would have been accomplished in the other direction within a matter of months rather than years. Three were ready for unification. Twenty-three needed acceleration in their own charted culture line. One was lost. One day it would be twenty-five times two billion planets. Symbolic Probability indicated that there were other bundles of space-time frames in which complete unity and cross travel had been achieved, but their probabilities were so divergent, and on so low an index that slip could not be accomplished.

Slip was the only word that would fit the mode of travel. Travel in a dimension for which there was no name. A dimension folded upon itself, so that the little golden ships were neither up nor down nor sideways. They neither shrank nor expanded. They "slipped" across a probability matrix into a sister reality without positional change. So close were the co-existences that it explained everything that had ever gone bump in the night, shadows half-seen out of the corner of the eye. You left your own frame and entered the sister frame which had been brushing at the sensory tendrils through generations of superstition. And the frame you left behind was the frame which, through its very closeness, had appeared to rap on tables and speak through trumpets.

Calna stepped from the express strip onto a local strip and then across the increasingly lower strips to the platform of field five. The planet on which Transition rested, was in Era 6, a frame not ready for unification. She had been assigned to Era 4. Eras one, two and three were the unified ones, and, with her loss of Agent standing, the only ones available to her. Possibly, in her lifetime, another would be unified. Era twenty, she had heard, was almost ready. Transition rested in Era 6, next to space stations constructed in Eras one, two and three.

She turned and looked back across the city she would

never see again. To the great mass of peoples in Eras one, two, and three, the three great cities constructed to slip across probability lines were more rumor than actuality. Only trained minds could comprehend the enormity of the task the three unified cultures had set themselves. Only highly specialized people could aid in the task.

To the average man and woman of the three basic eras, it was merely a new and wondrous and inexplicable advantage to be able to enjoy three contiguous environments. Those with ample means arranged title to the same piece of property co-existent on three probability levels. The slip field was installed in a central doorway with minimal controls. Each room was three rooms. For the very wealthy, proper positioning of the co-existent homes could result in three climates to be enjoyed. The ideal was a tropic warmth in one, eternal springtime in the next, and a crisp and endless October in the third.

She turned her back on Transition. There was a thickness in her throat. She knew that she should feel shame at the enormity of her mistake — and yet she could not. She knew that her identification with Andro had been too intense, and yet she did not wish it any other way.

"Ex-Agent to Era One," she said crisply to the routing clerk. He eyed her curiously. Ex-Agents were rare. Dead Agents were not so rare. Resignation was unheard of. And so the routing clerk knew that the change of status had been disciplinary.

The customary respect shown to Agents was markedly lacking. He stared at her until she flushed. "Why the delay?" she asked angrily.

He winked. "Are your pensions going to be big enough for two of us?" he asked, leering.

"I can still put you on report," she said.

"But you won't." He yawned. "Take the one at the end of the platform."

She walked out and down the platform. She saw it and felt lost. It was one of the rooted ships, built only for the slip between frames. Unlike the Agent ships, it could not leap like a golden arrow from planet to planet within any frame. It would contain no survival equipment. The minimal controls would be no more complex than the buttons in an elevator.

Once she was in that stodgy ship there would be no turning back. She slowed her pace as she neared it. The ship beyond was a true Agent's ship, with its double control panel, one for probability change, one for positional change. She could see the new seal beside the insignia and knew that this ship had just been completely checked and re-equipped.

She turned and glanced back. The routing clerk had his back to her. She moved quickly then. It had to be done in seconds. She darted into the Agent's ship. In her mind was the great stabbing pain that came with disobedience. It was the same pain she had felt when overruling Solin and rescuing Andro. Conditioning caused that pain, and should have made disobedience impossible. But, as in the rescue of Andro, there was something in her that fought the pain, made it endurable.

She knew that to slip to Era 4 would mean capture within seconds. She picked Era 18 at random. As she hit the lever with the base of her palm, she heard the suck-snap of the port behind her. As the ship began to fade around her she heard the clangor of the alarm. In thirty seconds they could track her. As the ship shimmered back into life in Era 18, she dropped her hands to the lower panel and shot it straight up at maximum takeoff. As the planet dwindled in the screen, she chopped the ship over onto SL drive, counted slowly to ten, swung it out of SL twenty light-years from the planet, slipped over into Era 22, picked a random course change, put it back into SL for a twenty count. After nine Era shifts in which she kept away from the basic eras and from Era 4, she knew that pursuit was out of the question.

The strain of escape had kept her from thinking of the consequences of her act. Now that she was safe for a time, she felt slack, exhausted. She wept for the first time since she was a child. When there were no more tears, she slept.

# II

## *Calna*

Sarrz stood at attention facing the Director. The words that had lashed out at him made him feel faint and dizzy. There was contempt on the Director's gaunt face.

Sarrz tried again. He said, "But no Agent has disobeyed a——"

"Be still! What order had you started to give when I put you under arrest?"

"I had ordered Agent Solin to go to Era 4 and destroy the body of Andro. I thought she would immediately try to . . . you see, there's an emotional attachment . . . seemed logical that . . ."

"Do you remember your history, Sarrz? What, in its simplest sense, was cancer?"

"Why . . . uncontrolled cell growth, starting with one rebel cell and——"

"Any Agent, Sarrz, equipped with an Agent's ship, is very, very close to being impregnable. We are dealing with an unbalanced Agent, for the first time in socionetic history. You would have fixed it so that she would have returned to that place and found this Andro destroyed. Revenge is a typical emotion in an unbalanced mind. What, then, would keep her from using the ship and her mobility to intrude in the most destructive possible way on all probability frames within our reach?"

Sarrz blanched. "But . . ."

"One rebel cell in our structure, Sarrz. Remember that. If we are not to lose twenty-two sister galaxies, we must eliminate her. Possibly you think this is an alarmist reaction. Agent Calna ceased to be predictable when she prejudiced the entire operation in Era four. Angered and hurt she can force twenty-two cultures off their extrapolated pattern. Saying that she retains enough loyalty to refrain from doing that is mere wishful thinking. I want every available Field Team briefed and assigned to the planet Era four calls Zeran. I want a trap that she won't see on the way in, and can't slip out of. Is that clear?"

"It is clear," Sarrz said with an effort.

"In the meantime proceed with your plan of presenting Shain, through Solin and the team of Rael, with proof of the death of his youngest son. But warn Solin not to kill Andro. Not under any circumstances. Once we have the girl, Andro can be safely killed."

When Deralan had been young, he had not feared space flight. He stood as a guest on the bridge of the flagship of the police fleet returning to Rael. He was returning to report to Shain the utter destruction of the remnants of Andro's rebel force. And the sixth escape of Andro himself.

Deralan was a realist. The execution would be swift, and relatively painless. For a time he had considered lying to Shain. But lying led straight to the rooms of evil repute under the main palace, and there Deralan would scream until Shain found the truth and permitted him to die.

In his youth he had accepted the great, roaring, shuddering, thundering ships as a part of life that would never change. Now he knew of the great fields where tens of thousands of the ships moldered away, as no one had the skill to repair them. If the drive failed in flight, the crew and passengers were dead. It was that simple.

And many had failed. Abilities had been lost, somehow. He could see the sign of those lost abilities in the puffy face of the captain of the flag ship now standing before the vast control board, watching his officers complete the intricate procedure for landing. Deralan felt a vast bitterness. They were like monkeys firing a gun. The monkey pulled the trigger and the gun went bang. Ask the monkey to explain the principle of expansion of gasses. The officers pulled switches in the order prescribed in the space flight manuals. The ship landed. It was that simple. If one switch was pulled and somewhere in the guts of the ship a coil failed, that was too bad, and very very fatal.

Routine repairs could be made. New tubes, oxygenation equipment — things on that level. But what made the ship take off, accelerate to ten lights, deaccelerate and land — what induced the normal gravity under any acceleration — what force adapted the view screens to the acceleration — all those things were mysteries, lost in the ancient past when men were wiser, stronger.

Deralan thought sourly that Andro had not been very far-sighted. All he had to do was wait. He could die knowing that within a thousand years there would be no more ships that would function. With no more ships, the House of Galvan would rule one planet rather than a galaxy. Each inhabited planet would be isolated, left to go its own way, to find its own answers, maybe win its way back to space. The ships would die and Empire would die with them.

Now the face of Rael was so close that it filled all of the view screen, the tiny drift of cloud appearing flat against the surface. Deralan's mind kept returning to the report the three men had given him. He could not suppress a thin eerie feeling of awe and concern. "I saw him. He seemed to be hurt. He had a weapon. As I aimed, he dropped out of sight. We went back there. There was no place for him to get out. There was no hole for him to drop through. He was just . . . gone."

Shain would not be amused by that story. Three of them had seen it. Deralan had isolated the three who had seen it happen. After considering all sides of the question he had killed them. His power over his men was that of life and death, with no questions asked. Their eye-witness account was an embarrassing factor, an unnecessary factor in the equation. Deralan felt no regret, and no satisfaction over it.

He knew that he did not dare lie to Shain, and yet he wished to continue to live. It was impasse.

The fleet landed, a far smaller fleet than had set out in pursuit of Andro. A guard of honor awaited Deralan as he disembarked. They formed a hollow square around him. Deralan smiled. Shain hadn't been thinking of honor when he sent the guard. Shain had been thinking of escape.

Metal-clad heels struck the paving in harsh cadence as the twelve guards escorted Deralan down the center of the Avenue of Kings. The once-proud street had become a place of bazaars. Rael was a wise and sour old planet. To it had come the dregs of a thousand planets, the sycophants, the cheats, with their smell of depravity, their swaggering insolence. One did not walk alone at night on Rael.

The aimless crowds opened to let the guard through. Some of them jeered at the guards and then fell suddenly silent as they recognized Deralan, feared almost as much as Shain himself and his elder sons.

A drunk reeled too close to the guard. The man at the front left corner of the hollow square reversed his ceremonial short-sword with a practised gesture and smashed the man's skull with the heavy grip.

They marched through the stink of the bazaars, past the crones that vended remedies for every ill, past the street girls in their rags, past men who turned with jerky quickness to hide a wanted face from the keen eye of Deralan. The main palace towered at the end of the Avenue of Kings. They marched through three gates so huge that the men did not have to change formation. Only the fourth gate was so narrow that they shifted to a column of twos. Deralan was midway along the column.

Just as they passed through the gate a screaming girl came racing from the side, her eyes wide with panic. A bearded man chased her. In her fright she ran directly into Deralan, staggering him. The guards cursed and shoved her roughly back into the grasp of the bearded man. Deralan fingered the object the girl had thrust into his hand. It had a soft texture. In the great main hall of the palace he risked a glance at it. For a moment he did not know what it was. When he at last understood what it was, his mind reeled with the shock, and his mouth went dry.

But Deralan was a realist and an opportunist. They took him back through the corridors to the private apartments of Shain. Shain was a ruin of what had been an enormous, powerful man. Years of debauch had left him looking like a pig carved of cold lard.

"Your report told me nothing," Shain said.

Deralan straightened up from the ceremonial bow. "Forgive me," he said. "I possibly took a childish pleasure in anticipating this moment."

"I have some childish pleasures waiting, if I don't like your report."

Deralan bowed again, advanced and handed the object to Shain. "My proof, your imperial majesty."

Shain unfolded the soft square. He stared at it. Then he threw back his great head and began to laugh. He laughed until tears squeezed out of the small eyes and rolled down the white heavy cheeks. Deralan took a deep breath. He knew that he was out of danger.

"How did you do it?" Shain demanded.

"We searched the city. I found him myself, and killed him. It was your wish."

"You did well. Tonight we shall celebrate your victory . . . and . . . and the death of the best of my three sons, and death of the only one fit to be Emperor."


Always, in a limited world, the machines grew more powerful. Machines were a form of inbreeding. Man turned his attentions onto his own pleasures and comforts and the machines grew, giving sage electronic attention to the complexities of equations with a thousand variables. And man grew softer within his limitations.

But now, with multiple realities waiting to be merged, the machines were of little help. Properly guided, the machines had indicated the possibility of multiple space-time frames, had assisted in finding a way to reach them. But once reached, it was once again up to man to work with hands and eyes and heart to achieve that unity which would weld twenty-five conditional realities into one world.

The Agents were recruited from those who, in less pressing times, would be termed malcontents, would be difficult to control, manage. All of them were, in one sense atavistic.

The Agent was man. His tools were provided by the machines. And no tools in history equaled the golden pyramidial agent ships. They were the extension of the Agent, the way the stone ax fitted the horny palm of the Neanderthal. On SL drive they could span the galaxy in a mouth. The webbed forces, interlocked and convoluted like the surface of a brain, shimmered constantly along the five planes of the ships. They were very close to being invulnerable. They could dive into a planet crust, protecting the Agent in much the way an insect would be protected while held in the palm of an iron fist as the fist was driven into loam. They could move in any direction except time, and at speeds beyond contractive effects. Yet it was the Man and not the Ship.

Calna entered Era 4 at the galactic rim. She was lost. It took long hours of feeding data into the computers to arrive at exact position. Since exact position was only exact in relation to any known object, she calculated her speed in relation to Zeran's sun in the invisible distance. She established course corrections. The ship flickered once and was gone. Twenty hours later the alarm brought her out of deep sleep a hundred million miles from Zeran. She had set the protective web so that light was bent around the tiny ship. She risked observation, in three-second intervals, returning to objective invisibility each time. She knew that she could be detected only by a chance intersection of her path from the galactic rim. It was a risk she had to take.

She stretched the weakness of sleep from her body and tried to think clearly. She was afraid. She suspected weakness in herself that implied an eventual failure. The rescue of Andro was, in Sarrz' terms, weakness. Emotionality. In all probability it would make her reactions predictable. And so she had to fight for a cold objectivity. What made it most difficult was that thoughts of Andro made her heart pound and her face flush. Agents were taught to consider the peoples of backward frames as pawns to be moved at will, sacrificed for the sake of socionetic gambits. But she thought of Andro in the way of a woman rather than an Agent. Yet, even if she were to rescue Andro and take him out of reach of the Field Teams who were undoubtedly waiting, what would he think of her? What would he see in this strong-bodied woman of a more mature culture? This woman with the grey-bright eyes and the hair like ripened grain in a September sun.

She remembered the harsh and shameful joy with which she had seen the death of the woman, Daylya whose beauty had been like a warm cry in the night.

Andro was, above all else, a strong proud man. He would not react kindly to being aided by a woman who, in all except brute muscle, equaled or surpassed his own strength.

The possibility that they had already killed him was like the first rasp of the knifeblade against her throat. She knew how she would plan it were she in charge of those attempting to intercept her. She would make the path to Andro's black and quiet tomb very simple. And escape impossible. By a focus of power five other Agent ships could hold her ship in stasis. She sensed that they were waiting.

She knew the exact location of Andro's body. It was in a crypt in the small room of the highest tower in a frozen city abandoned for half of time. The body would be hard and tough as granite. If there were some way to snatch it up on the run. . . .

Anything could be transferred from planet to ship provided the proper field were built around the item to be transferred. A field was created by a tiny generator no larger than a plum. It could be set to create a field a foot across, or five miles across. But it had to be placed in position.

The item could be received inside the ship, or received within any given range of the ship. She made her plan. It was dependent on deceiving them through apparently descending to land near the crypt. Their reaction times would be trigger-fast. It would be close, and with no possibility of fumbling.

She boldly dropped the ship's screens and streaked toward the dark side of Zeran. She came down through the blackness with her view screens adjusted so that the ruined city stood out as though bathed in a great light. The adjusted generator lay in the small disposal port. The port switch was hooked in with the computer which in turn was hooked up with the aiming screen. She waited without breathing, her hands on the lower panel, fingertips moist on the controls. The interval of drop was to be twenty seconds. The instant she heard the click, she chopped the ship into SL drive and winked away into space. She felt for a fractional part of a second the drag of the focused power of the other Agent ships. It was as though, for that moment, her ship flew through molten lead. For the moment there was nothing for her to do. She had set the ship to come out of SL at exactly twenty seconds from the moment of the drop. The port was ready and skin-gravity set to hold any pair that would escape, heat screen ready to combat the cold of space.

She put her hand on the main port control. The moment she felt the tiny, twisting dislocation that meant the end of SL, she tripped the control and the port yawned. The receiving area was set outside the open port. With the suddenness of an explosion the entire top of the tower appeared in the receiving area, swung over and thudded against the ship. Using the top panel she slipped ship and tower into Era 20 to give her a few more moments of grace.

The rough stone of the tower was flat against the open port. Using the hand blower she crumbled a hole through the stone, exposing one corner of the black crypt. She widened the hole, caught the crypt with the focused beam of the attractor, angled it through the port. Ignoring the crumbled stone that had drifted in, she shut the port and tried to flee.

The ship did not move. She cried out, and fought the controls. Her hands flashed across the panels as she tried combinations of controls. Higher and higher rose the thin whine of the ship's screens, fighting the holding force. She applied all power to a straight SL drive, feeling the heat rising within the ship. The ship grew hotter and she waited, her jaw set, until she could scent the acrid odor of the scorched tendrils of her hair. Then, with one fast motion, she cut off everything in the ship. The pursuers were in the position of a man who runs to break down a door when the door opens just before his shoulder touches it. Calna's ship gave a tiny lurch and she was ready to take advantage of it. She slipped to Era 1, and immediately to Era 25, and applied full SL drive the moment the new frame had been attained.

The ship whipped off into freedom, and she laughed aloud with a note of hysteria. She used a completely random pattern of slip and direction, taking no chances, working for long hours on the twin panels until she knew that pursuit was impossible. She knew the danger of awakening Andro in too unfamiliar an environment. The chance of madness was too great.

In Era 11, one of the most backward ones, she found the planet she wanted. In more sophisticated probability frames, it had been turned into a rest planet for Agents. It was uninhabited in all frames except the basic three. The best aspect of it was that it was not the last place they'd look for her. Anticipating her reaction, they would look at once in the last place. It was neither the best nor the worst, thus a median chance in several billion.

She drifted low across the springtime face of the planet and selected a place where a crystal stream came down across rocks to form a pool beside a slant of lush green grass. She tucked the ship between the mighty roots of a fairyland tree so tall that clouds brushed its crown. This was a planet on which one felt elfin. Small and wild and free. The vastness of the trees and the boulders and the utter stillness were the artifacts of magic.

She opened the purloined crypt and laid her fingers against the marble coldness of Andro's cheek. All body functions were suspended. She moved quickly and lightly as she prepared the twin injections that would bring him slowly up to the threshold of life once again. The tips of the needles had to be heated before she could put them into the vein on his inner arm.

She made the injections and then laid her head against his broad chest. It was like listening to a stone. It was the coldness of death and she felt small and afraid. With no circulation of the blood, with the blood itself as still and hard as the red veins in marble, it took a long time for the effect to spread from the point of innoculation.

The heart, at last, gave a slow thud. She counted to thirty before she heard the next thud. Each time the interval decreased by a full second. Body warmth began to return. When he took his first fluttering, shallow breath, she straightened up and smiled down at him. There was color in his face again.

With the help of the small attractor she unhooked from her belt, she lifted him effortlessly and carried him through the port and placed him on the fresh-scented grass at the edge of the deep blue pool.

Then, motivated by a force that was strange to her, she used the cleansing chamber of the ship, webbed fresh garments for herself in a brighter color than ever before.

# III

## *Revolt on Simpar*

The slip towers glowed, grew misty and indistinct. The City of Transition gave a delicate shrug of raspberry shoulders and slipped from Era 6 to Era 4. The risk of thus hastening the deviation from plotted culture line was great. But the Director felt that coordination could better be obtained within the target era than from outside. As yet no method of direct communication between eras had been devised. Field Team reports could be received at Transition and orders could go out only if the city were in the era which ex-Agent Calna had made so critical.

Sarrz felt lost. The Director had stepped in to handle direct coordination of Field Teams. Sarrz was left without a function. Though it irked him, it did give him a chance to review the entire picture. As with all directing heads in Socionetics, Sarrz had a good background in Symbolic Probability. With the idle and aimless feeling of mental doodling, he decided to equate the index of probability of the loss of further spacetime frames.

He took the small table which held the computor and swung it around within easy reach. He put it on alphabetic scale and ignored, as he fed in the data, the glow of the "insufficient data" light. He had the direct loss of one era, the pending loss of a second, plus areas of disturbance in three more.

He read off the index and it startled him. He cleared the computer and tried again. Same result. He sat and listened to the quickening thud of his heart. The index of probability of all sister space-time frames being lost was almost grotesquely high, so high that complete data would have to be within itself improbable in order to level off the result based on incomplete data.

The inference was that some outside factor was at work, some unequated factor. There was a parallel in astronomy. Find the deviation and then look for the cause.

Suddenly Sarrz realized that this matter was of highest importance. The Director must be informed, and at once.

He reached for the switch that would enable him to communicate with the Director.

And that was the way they found him. His heart had stopped as his fingertips had touched the switch.

Animal caution did not desert Andro as he recovered consciousness. He neither stirred nor opened his eyes. He remained quite still and concentrated on bringing all senses up to peak awareness. Hearing — the soft rush and babble of water, a crackling stir, as of wind in leaves. Scent — the spiced smell of brush and forest and wild places. Touch — brush of grass against his arm. Warm air against his body. He remembered the deepness of the burn wounds. He concentrated his sensory attention on the wounded areas and could find no message of pain from the scorched nerve ends. He increased the depth of his respiration and could not detect the quick knives that had stabbed him with each breath as he stood in the blue shadows of the alley.

He remembered those who had joined him, and who had lost. Grief was deep and slow and still. Daylya and all the others. His fault. And born of impatience. Had he waited, grown a bit stronger, planned more thoroughly. . . .

His ear picked up the whisk of grass against an approaching foot. Fingertips touched his chest over his heart. He opened his eyes just enough to see the figure outlined against the sky, bending over him. The equation was simple. Once all your allies are dead, all who remain are enemies.

Andro struck with clenched fist, with a roll that brought the heavy muscles of shoulder and back into the blow. He rolled onto hands and knees and jumped up onto his feet, weaving a little from weakness. He stood under a strange sky near the mightiest tree he had ever seen and looked down on the crumpled unconscious figure of a woman. She wore a toga-like garment of lime yellow, a wide belt from which small unknown devices dangled. Her hair had the clarity and purity of the white fall of water into the deep blue pool a few yards away. On the angle of her jaw was the spreading stain of the force of the blow. He stood and waited and listened for others. There was no sound but the water and the wind. He bent over and fingered her jaw clumsily. The bone did not feel loose and broken under his fingers.

It was then that he remembered his wounds. He looked at his side, and found a strange thing. The skin was clear, firm, healthy over the wounds, and he would have thought he had dreamed the wounds were it not for the untanned pallor of the new skin.

He looked at the woman again, and he frowned. The alley floor had given way under him and he had fallen into darkness. The woman was connected with that phenomenon in some way. At the moment she was helpless. Yet the devices on the belt she wore were a promise that she might not remain helpless. He rolled her over and

373

looked for a place to unhook the belt. It seemed to have no fastening and it fitted too tightly around her slim waist to be slipped down over her hips. He contented himself with unhooking the small devices. He could not guess their uses. Yet they had a gleam that spoke of efficiency, utility. There were six of them. He carried them carefully in his cupped hands and placed them behind a stone. It taxed his strength to tear a strip from the hem of the lime yellow toga. With the strip he bound her hands tightly behind her, placing the knot out of the reach of her fingers. As he tightened the knot, his right arm extended, he saw that the tattoo was gone from his upper arm. It was replaced with another area of that pallid healthy skin.

Andro sat a few feet from the woman and waited for her to regain consciousness. He tried to guess what had happened. He still wore the leather and metal battle skirt, but his cape was gone. He remembered tearing it off as it had started to flame, throwing it aside as he picked up the dying girl and carried her through the great smashed place in the hull of his ship. The battle skirt showed signs of having been scorched. The thongs that bound his sandals were blackened, crisped and the hair had been burned from his calves and ankles. The holster at his right side was empty.

The woman's face was toward him as she opened her eyes. Her eyes were a clear grey and they saw nothing. They focused on him and he did not like the look of intelligence that came into them. In face and body he found her pleasing, but the eyes alarmed him. They spoke too clearly of knowledge beyond his own — knowledge that made him feel like a child. He saw her test the strength of the strip that bound her wrists, then sit up awkwardly, throw her head back to swing a heavy strand of her hair away from her face. She smiled at him as a conspirator would smile.

"Who are you?" he asked heavily.

She moved her underjaw from side to side and grimaced. "You are strong, Andro."

"Who are you?"

"Your friend. Your very good friend. My name is Calna."

"Calna," he said, tasting the word carefully. "I was dying. Now I am whole again. I was trapped, and now I am free. If you did that, it is evidence that you are a friend. But your purposes in doing that may make you enemy rather than friend."

She glanced down at her belt. "Untie me, Andro. The bonds are too tight."

He untied her. She stood up, flexing her hands, rubbing her wrists. The top of her shining head was on a level with his eyes. She smiled at him and there was something in the smile he didn't like.

She said, "I'm helpless now because you took the things from my belt?"

"Of course."

She put her hands on him and he tried to strike her again. He cried out in sudden agony as her fingers found pressure points. She did not cease smiling. She touched his elbows in what could have almost been a caress and both arms hung slack and useless. Her hand swept across the side of his throat and he fell heavily. He tried to move and though his effort made the sweat stream from his face, he could not move.

She sat beside him and said softly, "It will go away in a few moments, Andro. And do not let your pride be hurt. Those are methods in which I was carefully trained." She stood up and glanced around. She went unerringly to the stone behind which he had hid the shining things. She picked them up and hooked them casually onto the belt.

Some of the weakness had left him. He sat up and glared at her. She laughed. "Don't look so fierce, Andro. You see, I know you very well. I've known you for four long years. There were five escapes before this last one. Probably you thought they were good luck, or even good judgment. I was helping you, Andro. Six times you should have died, and I helped you. The seventh time occurred while you were unconscious and that was the worst time of all, the most dangerous."

"Why did you help me?"

"I am not from your world, Andro."

"I have guessed that."

"My world was interested in your revolt against Shain. It was to our advantage to help you succeed. We helped in many ways, but not enough. I was following orders given to me. When it was seen that our help was not enough, I was ordered to let you die on Zeran. I disobeyed orders."

"Why?"

Calna frowned. "I . . . I don't really know. I knew that I was becoming emotionally interested in you, but that in itself should not have been strong enough to enable me to act counter to my training. It just became something I . . . I had to do, Andro. Now I am being hunted by my world."

"As I am being hunted by mine?"

"No. Your world believes you are dead."

He stood up as the last increment of his strength flooded back. He looked around.

"Is this your world or mine?"

"Neither."

He stared at her. "What are we to do? How did we come here? I wish to go back to my own world. I left . . . many things unfinished."

"You cannot go back. There is no way."

Andro watched her for a moment. "Until that moment, I believe you told the truth. Now why do you start to lie?"

"Listen carefully and understand, if you can. I will say it as simply as I possibly can, Andro. We tried to help your world without making our presence known. If we did it too obviously, your world would grow out of our reach and we could no longer visit it. If you should go back now, the mere fact of your returning from the dead will put your world out of our reach. So I cannot permit that."

He studied her. "That seems odd, Calna. You say you are being hunted by your world. Can they hunt for you here?"

"Of course."

"Then why not return me to my world. You say it will

place my world out of reach. Then wouldn't that mean safety for you, in my world?"

"Yes, but it is against all my training, all I believe in, and . . ."

He saw her indecision and for the first time he felt that his strength equaled hers. He put his hands lightly on her shoulders, felt her tense under his touch. He looked into her grey eyes until her glance wavered, dropped. She came into his arms with a small cry in her throat that was like a confession of weakness, that was the sign of the transfer to him of the authority for whatever path they would take into the unknown future.

"We will go to my world," he said. He felt her acquiescence. "And before we return," he said, "you will teach me how to use the devices of your world. When I return I shall be stronger than Shain and Larrent and Masec, even with no followers."

She stood a little apart from him then, her head lowered. "My people will be looking for us in your world. They will want to stop us, before the effects of your return have made sufficient change in your world to move it out of their reach."

*At a place which was the essence of no-place, and in a time which, in stasis, was no-time, there was a record of progress in the analysis of paradox, where directed thought maintained the record, where a billion eras moved the record one half-step nearer the point where at last all infinities would become finite. It could not be done on the basis of a controlled experiment, because there is a flaw in that theory. The mere factor of control is an alien factor, a newness added to the other components. Without control, all things must be weighted and all factors considered. The measured counting of high value infinites can only be performed in no-time, and only no-place is vast enough to hold the records.*

*A child awakens and cries in the night. In its simplest sense the impact of that occurrence can be measured through a thousand generations, given all factors for weighing. What complicates it is that cause and effect are*

*expressions of the same factor. It is more delicate to trace
the child's awakening backward for a thousand generations, but still finite and feasible — given enough time and
enough space for the keeping of records. Where it becomes paradoxical is when worlds are bridged and all
probabilities assume equal values, and in ten thousand
co-existent fields of probability where the child awoke at
the same instant, the same track can be plotted backward
for a thousand generations and be identical for ninety-
nine hundred and ninety-nine probabilities, only to diverge at the next to the last generation in the very last of
the ten thousand co-existent webs in the matrix. So go
back and make that last one similar, and the result will be
an increment of divergence which results, most probably,
in no child at all, and, less probably, in a night of unbroken rest for the child.*

*The labor involved makes it essential that the computa-
tions be made in no-time, and the records kept in no-
space.*

*And one facet of the endless computation can be — as
one range of probabilities begin to gain mutual access,
what happens if such access is denied?*

*The finite computation of infinites is possible because
infinity is merely a function of time and space. Only nothingness becomes endless.*

Ever since the dreaded audience with Shain that had been
so miraculously saved from disaster, Deralan was ob-
scurely troubled. It was his nature and his profession to
learn the background of all events and incidents. Long
search for the girl who had handed him the object which
had bought his safety was fruitless. He was almost glad
that he could not find her. They had returned to Rael
from Zeran with all haste possible. Either the object had
been brought back on the pursuit ships, or it had arrived
at Rael by faster means. And Deralan did not see how it
was possible for the object to have been smuggled onto
one of the ships. As to faster means of transport — there
were none.

As he tried to pick up the threads of his responsibilities

that had been disrupted by the revolt of Andro, third son of Shain, he found himself suffering from an inability to give his complete attention to his duties. The capital city was very much like a cage of wild animals. The animals detected the faint inattention of the trainer and crouched a bit lower on their haunches, ready to spring.

When two of his most trusted assistants were torn to bits by a mob, Deralan did not feel the old raw fury with which he had avenged similar previous incidents. His identification, capture and execution of the leaders of the mob was quick and effective, but without heat. His villa, protected almost as well as the very palaces of Shain, no longer was a place of revelry by night. He ceased the entertainment of those close to Shain, and knew that by so doing he was prejudicing his influence at court. He spent more and more time alone, and his thoughts were dark. Many times there was fear in him, but fear of something not quite understood.

He felt that somewhere in the city he would find an answer to all that troubled him. He began to listen more carefully to the talk of odd happenings in the empire. It seemed to be a time of strange occurrences that bordered on the supernatural.

On one sultry afternoon when most of the city slept, Deralan questioned a frightened girl who had been brought to him by his agents. She was a dirty, half-wild creature, seemingly poised on the very edge of flight. Her dark red hair was matted with filth and her tip-slanted eyes were of that distinctive lavender shade of the women of Vereen. Her rags barely covered her body. In her left armpit was the telltale gouge where the mark of the slave had been recently removed. Very recently removed.

Though she was frightened to the very borderline of inconsciousness, she would not speak. And such was her emaciation that it was immediately obvious to Deralan she would die at once if force were used. What intrigued him most was the freshness of the blisters along the calf of her left leg. Those were the distinctive blisters carried by one who has traveled on one of the old ships with their defective shielding.

379

Several isolated bits of information clicked into place in Deralan's mind and convinced him that this girl held a clue to his own bafflement. The increasing numbers of escaped slaves on Rael — the fresh blisters — the girl's obvious fright — the two month delay in customary reports from slave marts — all these things pointed to Simpar, from his agents on that planet of something only she could give him.

Her teeth were small and even and pointed. "Kill me and watch how a Vereen woman can die!" she whispered to him.

"What made you slave?" he asked, forcing a gentleness into his tone.

"I stabbed my husband. The court sentenced me. They said it was without cause. I was shipped to Simpar with hundreds of others."

"And you escaped. How?"

She moved restlessly in the thongs which bound her, and turned her head from him, affecting casualness, though the cords stood out like wires in her lean throat.

"How would it feel," he asked softly, "to be clean once more. To be scrubbed and clean and scented again. To feel the touch of silk. To recline beside a spiced fountain and have rich foods brought to you. Fine fruit from Vereen. Wines from Lell."

She did not move. He saw a tear cut a channel of whiteness through the grime of her cheek.

He called the bored attendants and told them to free her and bring her to his villa. He turned his back on their knowing sneers and left. By the time the girl was brought through the innermost gates of the villa all was ready for her. The maids took her in hand. It was dusk in the wide gardens before she was brought to him. She stood with a new pride, tall and silent and quite lovely.

He watched her eat with the precise, almost vicious hunger of a half-starved animal. The wines were brought. She was wary but after a time she lost wariness and her lips grew swollen and her eyes grew vague and she emptied the glass each time he filled it from the flagon. Night came and he sat with her. She laughed with an empty sound as he caressed her.

"It wasn't hard to escape, was it?" he asked.

"No. Not hard. Not with the gates broken and the guards dead and the ships waiting. Not hard."

"Who broke the gates and killed the guards?"

She giggled. "Oh, but I am not supposed to tell anyon that, yet. Not until he is ready. Not until we receive word."

"You can tell me, Leesha. You will stay here with me in comfort and in peace. There will be no secrets between us. You can tell me." His tone was wheedling.

She giggled emptily again. Her eyes shuttered and she slumped out of the circle of his arm. He grasped her shoulders and shook her hard. "Tell me!" he shouted.

Her head wobbled loosely. He let her fall to the edge of the fountain. She lay on her back and her breathing was loud between her parted lips.

At noon the next day, heavily guarded, Deralan shuffled up the ramp and through the port of the waiting ship. His face was deeply pocked and scarred, unrecognizable. Around him was the wailing of the newly enslaved. The inner door clanged shut. In the confined space Deralan's nose wrinkled with distaste. At take off there was no warning. They slid into a tangled heap at one end of the lightless room.

As he fought free of the others, found a clear space on the floor, Deralan wondered what would become of him if he could not prove his true identity on Simpar.

Once Calna had committed herself to Andro's plan, she resolutely forgot how far she had veered from the paths of her training. The only remaining indication of the extent of the conflict within her was the splitting headaches which blinded her at times, without warning.

Andro had showed surprising aptness as a pupil. At times she felt that he had taken all of her knowledge and combined it with his own to create a strength beyond anything she had ever before experienced. It was he who had selected Simpar as the symbol of everything he detested about Empire.

They had driven the golden ship deep into the planet crust and waited there for the thrum of directed energy which would tell them that they had been detected. Andro, using the device which collapsed the orbital electrons in matter without releasing the energy, had driven the long slanting corridor to the surface. The ship, completely shielded, lay behind them, deep in the skin of Simpar, utterly undetectable.

Together, disguised by his suggestion as slave buyers from Lell, they had visited the pens, the auction blocks. Though inured through training to the misery on savage planets, Calna felt emotionally staggered by the mere weight of the suffering around her.

Andro, his face altered by her careful surgery, stalked through the open slave marts with an unforgiving grimness in his eyes, in the clamp of his jaw. They knew their danger. Were he to announce his presence too quickly, they would be overpowered by Field Teams before his influence could spread enough to cause a probability deviation.

Calna sensed that Simpar, as well as the other main planets of Empire, was under constant, wary scrutiny. She explained to Andro, saying, "We must free them in such a way that it will appear to be a natural revolt. I have been trained in that sort of thing. Yet if I do it too cleverly, my presence here will be suspected."

He thought it over. "Then why not take this step? As we free them, give them ships and send them away to other planets. And, as they leave, tell them that Andro of Galvan has released them, and to keep that information secret until the word is passed. That will give this influence you talk about the widest possible chance to operate."

The director received the report in person. He immediately beamed it to all Field Teams in Era 4, saying, "Slave revolt on Simpar indicates help being given by Ex-Agent Calna. Request immediate Team concentration at Simpar."

Within twenty hours the suspicion was verified by direct

report from Simpar. The Field Team reported, "Ex-Agent Calna and Andro can be immediately eliminated. However, escaped slaves have gone to other planets with information re Andro. Request verification of present probability index, as ship power less responsive than before."

"Index sagging. Approaching danger point. Immediate elimination ordered. Verify. Verify."

There was no verification. The Director waited until the last possible moment before ordering the slip back to a stable era. The city slipped back and communication with all Field Teams was thus cut.

It was night on Simpar. The triple moons, blood red, arced across the night sky. There were no more ships. The freed slaves, eyes wide and wild in the torchlight, raced through the plundered streets. Throughout Solom, the capitol city of Simpar, Andro and Calna could hear distant crashes, faint screams as the last of the traders and buyers were hunted down and murdered. They had underestimated the unreasoning fury of the slaves, and thus found themselves in danger. Slaves dressed in the fineries of the traders and buyers and were themselves killed by their fellows.

Thrice Andro had to stand and fight and kill in order to clear their path through the city. The first scattered revolts on the planet had been orderly, and the freed slaves had been spirited away on the captured ships without incident. But this past night when the last of the fortified marts and pens and mansions of the traders and the government had fallen completely was nightmare.

Andro found a grim humor in having to stand and do battle with slaves who died screaming his name, as though it were a magic incantation.

At last they were out of the city. Fires burned unchecked in the heart of the city. At one place flames rose hundreds of feet into the air. The dark plain was ahead of them, and in the darkness they meant to find the slanting tunnel down to the hidden ship.

"Now have we won?" Andro demanded as he hurried along beside her.

"I'll know when we reach the ship. If we've won, we cannot reach any other known era."

The hidden entrance to the tunnel was less than a mile ahead. They ran on, and the night seemed endless as the clamor of the city faded behind them.

Solin's ship, containing the other agent who had replaced Calna, hung poised and invisible fifty feet above the mouth of the tunnel. The screens were adjusted to make the plain that stretched out toward the city as bright and clear as though it were bathed in sunshine.

He watched the tiny figures approaching. He knew who the first two were. The third one, the one who followed them, was unknown to him.

Solin felt the tiny shudder and turned almost in anger to Arla, the woman Agent who had replaced Calna. "It's pointless to keep trying," he said, "we're beyond the point where we can return."

The woman dropped her hands from the panel and turned toward him. Her expression was bleak and hopeless. Her shoulders sagged. She glanced at the screen. "Soon they'll be near enough."

"There seems to be no point in killing them now," Solin said.

Arla gasped. "But it was an order! Your service with that Calna has made you a poor Agent, Solin. You heard the order."

"We're trapped here in Four. They can't reach us and we can't reach them. So why kill them? The damage is already done."

"It was an order," the woman said.

Solin sighed. He sometimes wondered if the male-female teams were not a mistake. According to Field Team theory, it made for a more flexible unit, increased the time that could be spent by any single Team on any single assignment. But it did give rise to a great many petty irritations.

"We took so long finding the tunnel," the woman said. "That's what trapped us here. We can make it worthwhile now by following orders."

# IV

### *The Might of Deralan*

Deralan, on arrival at Simpar, had been clapped into one of the feeding pens for fattening. He listened to the rumors that brightened the eyes of the one who had been in the pen before his shipment had arrived. Rumors of freedom. Rumors of revolt. They heard violence in the city for many days and nights and at last they were released. The guards were slain and the walls broken down and the gates smashed and the great house where the trader and pen-owner had lived set afire.

Deralan trotted into the city with the rest of them and there he heard the word that he had suspected, that he had not wanted to believe.

"Andro!" they shouted. "Andro of Galvan!" It was a rallying cry, battle cry, blood scream. "Andro!"

With sickness in his throat, Deralan dodged into the mouth of an alley and waited until the running steps had thudded into the distance. Dusk had changed slowly to night before he found a lone slave he could overpower.

"What of this Andro? Quick, while you live!"

"Please! He is said to be in the city. He has come back. His face is changed, but he has come back."

"Where can I find him?"

"I don't know. Believe me, I don't know!"

Deralan made a quick and practiced gesture and then flung the body from him. He joined another wolf pack, snatched a torch, held it high, looked endlessly for a man with the huge strong body of Andro of Galvan.

He found a knife with a blade that suited him. He looted and burned and shouted with the others, but always he searched for Andro. He lost track of the hours. And at last he found a big man who stood with a fair-haired girl behind him and fought well, fought with the skill to be

385

expected of any noble of the House of Galvan. He seemed about to be overpowered when the girl stepped to the side and something gleamed in her hand. The three who still faced the big man folded and dropped into absurdly small heaps on the paving stones.

As the big man turned, the torchlight touched his upper arm. Deralan sucked in his breath as he saw the pale rectangular patch. As they hurried on, Deralan looked at the three bodies. He swallowed hard. Something that swept across them, something the girl had used, had apparently completely removed whole sections of the men's torsos. That was why the huddled bodies looked so small.

He flung the torch aside to gutter out and followed the man and the girl through the smoke drift of the streets, his fingers hard and tight on the haft of the knife.

Deralan followed them out of the city and across the dark plain. The three dark moons stretched three vague shadows of his crouched body as he followed them. As the ground grew more uneven, he shortened the distance between them. He reversed the knife in his grasp. It had a good balance. Andro's back was broad. Deralan raised the knife. He poised it. He hurled it with all his strength. In the fractional part of a second before he released it, a great light bathed the entire plain in green-white brilliance. During the last six inches of the swing of his arm it seemed to Deralan that some great outside force had taken his arm and had given it a whip and power beyond anything any man should possess. The odd power snapped the bones of his arm and hurled him screaming into blackness.

Solin sat with his hand on the port control, completely frozen by an astonishment so vast that he could not move. Arla had asked to perform the actual execution. Solin had been glad to comply as he had no heart for it. He opened the port for her and when she had the hand weapon readied, he lighted the target area for her. Andro and Calna were in perfect range, a hundred yards away and fifty feet below them. In the instant of touching the lights he had seen the third figure in the act of hurling what seemed to be a knife at the pair leading him.

The unknown man had hurled the knife. There had been a keening whistle indicative of high velocity and a full-throated chunk. Arla had fallen dead with the knife in her brain, the guard of the haft flat against her forehead.

No person could throw a knife that way. Yet they had. He had seen it. The thrower lay crumpled on the ground with both Andro and Calna staring at him.

Solin dropped the ship to the ground beside the hidden tunnel entrance. He stepped over Arla's body and out into the now restricted area of green-white light.

Transition rested in Era 3 beside the endless thunder of the space port.

The Socionetics Board had launched a full scale investigation of the circumstances surrounding the loss of Era 4, and the loss of the thirty-odd Field Teams who had been trapped there when the index of probability dropped below the point where Agent ship power could accomplish the return.

The Board was exercising its prerogative of interviewing the staff members, one at a time. The Board met in the huge central chamber with the luminescent mural depicting the eventual merger of twenty-six co-existent worlds. Though now, of course, there were only twenty-four and thus the mural was, in that sense, a rather wry joke.

After three weeks of review and deliberation, the Director was called in to hear the decision of the Board.

The decision was very simple and very direct. It was given to him in the form of an order. Improper controls and criminal laxness have lost us two complete spheres of eventual cultural expansion. There will no longer be a continuing effort to accelerate the extrapolated cultural pattern of all backward eras simultaneously. All Field Teams will be concentrated on one era. All existing equipment will be immediately altered to make only that era, plus the basic three, available to Agent ships. Era 20 is closest to unity status. All effort is to be concentrated there. If, by any chance, Era 20 should be lost to us, all Field Team activities will be cancelled. No further acceleration of cultures will be attempted. All equipment except one master ship will be altered so as to permit only slip between basic eras. Periodic surveys with the master ship will be made. When each peripheral culture has attained proper probability status, then unity will be undertaken, but it will achieve that status in its own way and in its own time.

"And if unity is achieved with Era 20 without trouble?" the Director asked in a low voice.

"Then all effort will be concentrated on the next era closest to a possible unity status."

The Director was permitted to leave. He gave the orders he was required to give. He gave an additional one of his own. He called all remaining Field Teams in for complete indoctrination on Era 20, for retraining, for reanalysis.

Thirty-three Field Teams trapped in Era 4. Count Andro and Calna, and subtract Arla. Sixty-seven persons. So few. So very few.

The golden pyramidial ships sat in a closed circle in such a way that the shields combined to form a cone of silence. The cone rose black and tall near the palaces of Rael.

In the streets they said, in hushed tones, "The Great Ones speak together."

Andro had matured in the past months. Authority was stamped on his face, and dignity was imprinted on each movement.

"It is time to speak," he said after a long silence. "I do not pretend to know how you are trapped here. It has been explained to me. I have been told that my activities caused this era to diverge from some pattern or another. You say that this era has become less probable, in relation to your basic eras. Be that as it may. The damage was done. You were trapped. Through the urging of Solin and Calna you consented to help me impose my will on what is left of Empire. That has been done. There is no more resistance. We are the object of superstitious awe on every inhabited planet of Empire. Now you must feel that your task is ended. I say to you that it is not ended. With your consent, I wish to make you my agents, give each of you an area to govern until such time as self-government is possible. You have been told the things in which I believe. You do not need specific orders. It is not easy to be considered a god, as I now am. If you do your assigned tasks properly, there will come a time when I am no longer considered to be a god. That time will come long after all of us have died. I am urging this course because it seems to me that in this way this era can be gently guided back towards a point where eventually your own people will once again be able to make contact."

The trapped Agents showed no great enthusiasm.

Calna took Andro's place and spoke. "I urge you to accept. Through the incident of Arla's death, we have a piece of knowledge that they do not have back at Transition. We know now that while we were attempting to build backward eras up to the point where unity could be achieved, a stronger force was seeking to make all frames divergent. We do not know what that stronger force is. In my own case, I know I was guided when I set this entire pattern in motion. I suspected it then. I know it now. One thing is puzzling. Why was Deralan made the agent of saving Andro and myself from certain death? Divergence had already been achieved. Why was it done in such a way that we would learn of this outside force which interferes with the achievement of unity for our coexistent eras? There is one possible answer. We were saved so that we could be the focal point of this successful effort of the past few months. We were advised of outside interference so that we should be able to content ourselves with these new limitations."

Solin spoke. "Content ourselves? How is that meant?"

"Through knowledge that we are part of a master plan guided by some race, some civilization whose abilities make ours look like the efforts of children," Calna replied.

"What sort of master plan is it which keeps the basic eras from achieving unity with all sister probability

389

frames? That seems like progress in the worng direction," another Agent said with a note of anger.

"I say," said Solin, "that now that we have given Andro the assistance he asked, we should concentrate on using what skills and talents we have to devise a power source ample enough to enable us to slip back to our own era."

There was a mutter of agreement. Andro turned to Calna and shrugged.

He said to all of them, "I see that Solin's suggestion is your wish. So be it." He looked at Calna. "You will work with them?"

"I made my choice quite a long time ago," she said. Together they went back to the palaces where new laws were being written for a galactic race.

Deralan knew at last that the madness was leaving him. It began to leave when he was willing to admit to himself that he had been mad. Something had swept acrosss his brain, twisting it, convulsing it. At last he recognized his environment, knew with a sense of shock that he was in a cell deep under the main palace, a cell that he had filled and emptied many times in what now seemed like a previous incarnation.

Co-mingled with his weariness and lethargy was a new, odd sense of mental power, as though the twisting force had also liberated areas of his brain that had previously been dormant. Throughout the uncounted days of torment he had heard a constant shrill chorus of thin voices, as though he lay in the midst of a vast throng of children at play. Now he could bring back the voices at will, merely by *reaching* to hear them.

When food was brought, one of the shrill voices separated itself from the others and became so distinct that he could understand scattered phrases, "——should be executed — Andro will decide — so many things changed — the Great Ones——"

And slowly Deralan came to know that he was *listening* to the thoughts of those near him. For a long time he listened. With practice he grew more acute, more certain of this new power. Once, when food was brought on an earthen dish, he willed the movement of opening the fingers of his right hand, not opening them, but willing the movement to open them with all his strength. The guard stared stupidly down at the smashed dish and scattered food. He massaged his fingers for a few moments.

With this start, Deralan began to practice with great care, making sure that what he was doing remained undiscovered. He found he could trip those who walked by the cell. At times he wondered if it was merely madness, but there was the evidence of his eyes and ears to be considered.

When he was certain of himself he caused a guard to leave the cell door unlocked. Deralan walked out. It was simplicity itself to cause every other guard to look the other way. He walked through as though invisible. He climbed the flights of stairs up to ground level and went out through all the gates into the streets of the city. He found a man of his own general build and guided the man into a narrow place between two buildings and caused the man to strip and don the prison garments. The man obeyed with an utterly blank expression, with no sign of confusion or fear.

Suddenly Deralan realized how pointless this attempt at escape was. This inexplicable gift which had been thrust upon him at the moment of hurling the knife was too powerful to be used for such a petty affair as escape. He turned soberly and walked back toward the main palace.

He found Andro and the fair-haired girl of the dark plain in the apartments that had once belonged to Shain. He sent the guards striding woodenly down the corridor and entered through the arched doorway.

Andro stared at him, his eyes widening, "Deralan!" he gasped.

"Where is Shain?"

"Shain is dead by his own hand. Larrent and Masec are in exile."

"You are Emperor?"

"The last one, Deralan. How did you get by the guards?"

"How do you plan to dispose of me?"

"By trial. You'll receive justice."

He stood and listened to their thoughts, first sorting out Andro's, then the woman's. Andro was merely puzzled, not afraid. The woman intrigued him. Two voices seemed to come from her. One from here and now. Another background voice that spoke of far places and wondrous things and skills beyond imagining, of others like her who were nearby. He related it immediately to the thoughts of the guards who had spoken of the Great Ones. He changed his plan immediately. He had intended to kill them both, setting them against each other to kill. But these two were not the real opposition.

"Take me to your people," he said aloud to the woman. She reached for a glittering object which hung from her wide belt. He remembered the three who died so quickly and strangely on Simpar. He made her fling the glittering object into a corner. Her eyes widened with fear and then assumed the familiar blankness. She came with him as he willed her to walk. Andro gave a hoarse cry of alarm and Deralan forced him back into a far corner, left him standing there.

The woman guided him to a place just outside the city where a ring of golden pyramidal objects stood around a building that was new, oddly constructed, covered with hoods and twisted screens of wire.

The woman took him into the building where there were scores of people at work. They stared at him oddly. These were the enemy.

In the center of the floor was the cube on which they worked. Cables as big around as a man's thigh writhed away from the cube. A shining metal column rose upward from the cube through the roof high overhead.

Deralan looked at the cube and he was puzzled. He had a feeling of *wrongness*. He stared at it and saw wrongness, and an obscure clumsiness, and a childish ineffectuality. He walked closer to it and in his mind saw the image of the way it should be. The people were forgotten. Only the power cube was important. He brushed by those who tried to bar the way and reached into the cube where tiny tubes glowed and relays chattered. Slowly at first, and then with increasing dexterity he began to take down circuits. As they tried to pull him away, he turned with impatience and smote them back with a careless easy power of the mind which sent them sprawling. Soon he noted that they were helping him, and he heard his own voice giving instructions that sounded meaningless and yet had a sound of *rightness* as opposed to the *wrongness* he was eliminating.

After fifty hours of ceaseless labor the work was done. The blue cube was like nothing any of the exiled Agents had ever seen before. It utilized only a fractional part of the power they had hooked up to lead into it. It had ceased to be a cube and had become a geometric form which dizzied them as they looked at it. It had nine sides, yet only ten edges. The effect was mildly hypnotic, and the attempt to relate visual evidence to known geometric forms gave it the look of being in constant flux.

Deralan had collapsed the moment the work was finished. They had taken him to a couch. His eyes were wide and he babbled endlessly and sucked at his fingers.

The cables led to one of the Agent ships which had been brought as close as possible to the main entrance to the building.

Calna looked at them all in anger. "Are we to be superstitious children? Are we to be afraid of this? He was used before, by 'them'. Now he has been used again. Once he had fulfilled his purpose, he was discarded."

"What will it do?" Solin asked.

"I say it will do just what it was intended to do. Take us back to our own era," she said.

Hesitation faded. Two Agents stepped into the ship and the port folded shut behind them. The others watched, expecting the mistiness which would indicate that the ship had slipped properly. Instead the ship was just . . . gone. The heavy cables fell to the ground and the air, rushing into the place where the ship had been, made a sound like the cracking of a great whip.

One by one they departed. Solin was last. He left alone in the ship he had shared with Arla. There was one golden ship left. And Calna. Andro had come. He watched her thoughtfully.

"You may go," he said.

"I shall stay here, Andro. I belong now."

She went back to the palace with him.

The long days went by. Often she went to a high window from which she could see the building in which the cube throbbed and shifted. Many times she walked to that place and watched the cube and touched her fingers lightly to the side of the small golden ship.

Andro sensed her discontent. He was busy with the new structure of government which he was building carefully. There was little that they could share.

She remembered other days, and other times, and realized more strongly each day how savage and primitive an era this was.

*In a place that was no-place and in a time that was no-time, the thought record halted and waited. It waited, not in the sense of elapsing time, but in the sense of an endless interruption. Impatience was not known to the intelligence directing the record. Other endless computations continued. But the directing intelligence, which did exist in a finite, though variable, space time, felt a subtle irritation.*

*This particular phase of this particular problem had been completed. The basic questions had been answered. An unseen hand had reached into the remote past, had twisted probabilities to the ultimate degree of distortion. In its simplest sense, false worlds had been created. The historical derivations had been weighed. Cause-effects had been measured in all temporal directions.*

*And now the ultimate step in the problem was held in stasis, merely because of the almost unpredictable whim of a female who, being a structural portion of an experiment in improbability, was herself improbable. . . .*

He came to her as she stood at the high window, and he said, "You must return. I know that. Come back, if it can be done, and if you have the desire. I can keep you a prisoner no longer."

"Not a prisoner, Andro."

"You must go back."

"I will return if I can. But you're right."

They went to the golden ship where the cables were already attached, waiting.

She turned as she entered the port, and lifted her hand slowly. Her eyes were misted. She turned quickly to the controls. The port folded shut.

And thus, with the whip crack of her departure, the universe itself, Andro's time and place and cities and suns and planets and wars and history — snapped out as though a quick finger had touched the light switch, leaving a room in darkness. The webs of probability had been pulled tight, twisted. And now the pressure was released. The record had been kept. The experiment was over.

Probability is like a plastic which is formed with a molecular "memory." It can be distorted but, once released, it will revert.

The reversion will be a function of time, rather than space. Tangential worlds can be artificially created. So long as the artificial pressure is maintained, they will seem to "exist." But with the release of that pressure . . .

The Agent Ship had plunged into the crust of Zeran in Era 4, powerless to save the sole remaining ship, the flagship of Andro's fleet. The crippled flagship swung lower, out of control. Solin, at the controls of the Agent ship, picked up the crippled ship in his screen and swung up through the planet crust in order to be within close range in case anything might be done. He halted the Agent ship twenty feet below ground level just as the crippled ship landed with a tremendous jarring crash.

Calna moved up behind him and watched the screen over Solin's shoulder. A powerful man staggered out through the huge rent in the skin of the ship, dragging an unconscious dark-haired girl. They saw him glance up at the dark skies, his face twisted with fury and anger. He fumbled for a pulse in the girl's throat, then stood silently, shoulders slumped, in stoic grief. Again he searched the blackness overhead, and ran into the city. His wounds had weakened him. He weaved as he ran, but he tugged a weapon from his holster.

"Can we save him once more?" Calna asked calmly.

"Not this time. They've seen him run into the city."

"At least we could follow. Report the end of it."

They took the portable screen from the rack, left the ship standing there, sliced through the depths of the city, following Andro in his blundering run. They saw him take refuge in a blind alley, shadowed by the eternal blue dusk. They saw him brace his shoulders against the wall, waiting for them to find him.

Calna and Solin waited directly below him.

Soon the dying man was spotted. He used the weapon well. His last shot was fired from within the boundary of death itself, the finger tightening in the last convulsion. Deralan came and cautiously inspected the body. He signaled to the other to take the body away.

Solin started back along the fresh tunnel, but Calna did not follow. He turned and stared at her. "What is it?"

"I . . . I don't know. A very odd feeling. As though somehow we have made a mistake that we could not predict. We should have cut up through to him, saved him."

"And turn a decent rebellion into a pseudo-religious revival?" Solin said.

"I know all that. It was just an odd feeling. But strong, Solin. Very strong."


Sarrz, Deputy Director of the Bureau of Socionetics, turned in his chair so that he would not have to look at the face of the female Agent who had asked to speak with him after she and Solin had made a rather disappointing, but unavoidable, report on the demise of one Andro, rebel of Era 4.

"You say you are troubled."

She chose her words carefully. "I wish to request EC, Deputy Director. I have had odd imaginings. Possibly the strain of the last few months in Era 4."

"Do you care to tell me any of them?"

She shrugged. "They are all a bit ridiculous. It seemed that in some other existence we had saved Andro rather than permitting him to be killed. I know how unfortunate a mistake it would have been to save him again. Also, I found myself thinking that we had lost some of the eras by permitting too great a probability divergence from our basic eras. And during the last sleep I dreamed that we have a power source which can cause slip to any era, no matter how divergent."

"Those are concrete examples. But what is your attitude toward them?"

"Awe, I would say. Foreboding. And a feeling of having led other existences."

Sarrz said, "All of us have dreams. I dreamed of dying at this desk. I have dreamed of losing all the worlds."

"And you feel fear?"

"Tension. Doubt. But those, I feel, are the result of our primitive heritage. It is in our blood and our bones to think of only one space and one time. Now we know that there are twenty-six available space-times contiguous to our own which we can reach, and an infinite number of others that we cannot yet reach. I would not worry too much, Agent Calna. We live in a day of oddness, of new philosophic evaluations, of invisible doors which have opened so that we can step through. The first wild dogs that joined savage man in his caves must have had uneasy dreams by the fires of night. And maybe, Agent Calna, we are no higher in our possible evolutionary scale than those dogs were in relation to the man they joined. Even now, at this moment, some inconceivable intelligence from our remote future may be tampering with our acts and the consequences of our acts. Such tampering would leave elusive traces in your mind, in my mind. Possibly every time we enter a strange room and have the feeling that we have been in that room before, it is because we actually *have* been in that room, in some fragmentary part of a vast experiment which was later abandoned. Our present actions, this very conversation, this room . . . it could all be part of an artificially induced environment merely in order to test your reaction and mine. In fact, you may not even exist in the ordinary sense of the word, but only as a manufactured entity thrown into my personal equation as some portion of a test for a solution."

The girl smiled uncertainly. "This begins to sound like one of the conversations planned to disprove the existence of everything except the mind of the beholder."

"I will approve EC if you insist."

"I think I must insist."

"You can report to EC at once, if you wish. I will reassign Solin, and give you a new partner when you return."

The girl left. Sarrz sat in utter stillness for a long time. The girl's request had crystallized some of his own weary doubts as to the rightness of the entire program on which they had embarked.

He sat and felt a sour yearning for the days gone by, the days when man could concern himself with only one environment — back in the functional simplicity of the third atomic era.

*He was willing to blow himself and his strange
weather station—that watched the movement of mil-
lennium-long storms of inter-stellar space—to atoms
to conceal the secret of his people. They were safe,
concealed in the haystack of a hundred trillion stars
—unless he gave a clue!*

●

# CONCEALMENT

## By A. E. van Vogt

The Earth ship came so swiftly around the planetless Gisser sun that the alarm system in the meteorite weather
station had no time to react. The great machine was already visible when Watcher grew aware of it.

Alarms must have blared in the ship, too, for it slowed
noticeably and, still braking, disappeared. Now it was
coming back, creeping along, obviously trying to locate the
small object that had affected its energy screens.

It loomed vast in the glare of the distant yellow-white
sun, bigger even at this distance than anything ever seen
by the Fifty Suns, a very hell ship out of remote space, a
monster from a semi-mythical world, instantly recognizable
from the descriptions in the history books as a battleship
of Imperial Earth. Dire had been the warnings in the histories of what would happen someday — and here it was.

He knew his duty. There was a warning, the age-long
dreaded warning, to send to the Fifty Suns by the non-
directional sub-space radio; and he had to make sure nothing telltale remained of the station.

There was no fire. As the overloaded atomic engines dissolved, the massive building that had been a weather sub-station simply fell into its component elements.

Watcher made no attempt to escape. His brain, with its knowledge, must not be tapped. He felt a brief, blinding spasm of pain as the energy tore him to atoms.

She didn't bother to accompany the expedition that landed on the meteorite. But she watched with intent eyes through the astroplate.

From the very first moment that the spy rays had shown a human figure in a weather station — a weather station *out here* — she had known the surpassing importance of the discovery. Her mind leaped instantly to the several possibilities.

Weather stations meant interstellar travel. Human beings meant Earth origin. She visualized how it could have happened: an expedition long ago; it must have been long ago because now they had interstellar travel, and that meant large populations on many planets.

His majesty, she thought, would be pleased.

So was she. In a burst of generosity, she called the energy room.

"Your prompt action, Captain Glone," she said warmly, "in inclosing the entire meteorite in a sphere of protective energy is commendable, and will be rewarded."

The man whose image showed on the astroplate, bowed. "Thank you, noble lady." He added: "I think we saved the electronic and atomic components of the entire station. Unfortunately, because of the interference of the atomic energy of the station itself, I understand the photographic department was not so successful in obtaining clear prints."

The woman smiled grimly, said: "The *man* will be sufficient, and that is a matrix for which we need no prints."

She broke the connection, still smiling, and returned her gaze to the scene on the meteorite. As she watched the energy and matter absorbers in their glowing gluttony, she thought:

There had been several storms on the map in that

weather station. She'd seen them in the spy ray; and one of the storms had been very large. Her great ship couldn't dare to go fast while the location of that storm was in doubt.

Rather a handsome young man he had seemed in the flashing glimpse she had had in the spy ray, strong-willed, brave. Should be interesting in an uncivilized sort of fashion.

First, of course, he'd have to be conditioned, drained of relevant information. Even now a mistake might make it necessary to begin a long, laborious search. Centuries could be wasted on these short distances of a few light years, where a ship couldn't get up speed, and where it dared not maintain velocity, once attained, without exact weather information.

She saw that the men were leaving the meteorite. Decisively, she clicked off the intership communicator, made an adjustment and stepped through a transmitter into the receiving room half a mile distant.

The officer in charge came over and saluted. He was frowning:

"I have just received the prints from the photographic department. The blur of energy haze over the map is particularly distressing. I would say that we should first attempt to reconstitute the building and its contents, leaving the man to the last."

He seemed to sense her disapproval, went on quickly:

"After all, he comes under the common human matrix. His reconstruction, while basically somewhat more difficult, falls into the same category as your stepping through the transmitter in the main bridge and coming to this room. In both cases there is dissolution of elements — which must be brought back into the original solution."

The woman said: "But why leave him to the last?"

"There are technical reasons having to do with the greater complexity of inanimate objects. Organized matter, as you know, is little more than a hydro-carbon compound, easily conjured."

"Very well." She wasn't as sure as he that a man and

.ıis brain, with the knowledge that had made the map, was less important than the map itself. But if both could be had — She nodded with decision. "Proceed."

She watched the building take shape inside the large receiver. It slid out finally on wings of antigravity, and was deposited in the center of the enormous metal floor.

The technician came down from his control chamber shaking his head. He led her and the half dozen others who had arrived, through the rebuilt weather station, pointing out the defects.

"Only twenty-seven sun points showing on the map," he said. "That is ridiculously low, even assuming that these people are organized for only a small area of space. And, besides, notice how *many* storms are shown, some considerably beyond the area of the reconstituted suns and——"

He stopped, his gaze fixed on the shadowy floor behind a machine twenty feet away.

The woman's eyes followed his. A man lay there, his body twisting.

"I thought," she said frowning, "the man was to be left to the last."

The scientist was apologetic: "My assistant must have misunderstood. They——"

The woman cut him off: "Never mind. Have him sent at once to Psychology House, and tell Lieutenant Neslor I shall be there shortly."

"At once, noble lady."

"Wait! Give my compliments to the senior meteorologist and ask him to come down here, examine this map, and advise me of his findings."

She whirled on the group around her, laughing through her even, white teeth. "By space, here's action at last after ten dull years of surveying. We'll rout out these hide-and-go-seekers in short order."

Excitement blazed inside her like a living force.

The strange thing to Watcher was that he knew before he wakened why he was still alive. Not very long before.

He *felt* the approach of consciousness. Instinctively, he began his normal Dellian preawakening muscle, nerve and

402

mind exercises. In the middle of the curious rhythmic system, his brain paused in a dreadful surmise.

Returning to consciousness? *He!*

It was at that point, as his brain threatened to burst from his head with shock, that the knowledge came of how it had been done.

He grew quiet, thoughtful. He stared at the young woman who reclined on a chaise longue near his bed. She had a fine, oval face and a distinguished appearance for so young a person. She was studying him from sparkling gray eyes. Under that steady gaze, his mind grew very still.

He thought finally: "I've been conditioned to an easy awakening. What else did they do — find out?"

The thought grew until it seemed to swell his brainpan: WHAT ELSE?

He saw that the woman was smiling at him, a faint, amused smile. It was like a tonic. He grew even calmer as the woman said in a silvery voice:

"Do not be alarmed. That is, not too alarmed. What is your name?"

Watcher parted his lips, then closed them again, and shook his head grimly. He had the impulse to explain then that even answering one question would break the thrall of Dellian mental inertia and result in the revolution of valuable information.

But the explanation would have constituted a different kind of defeat. He suppressed it, and once more shook his head.

The young woman, he saw, was frowning. She said: "You won't answer a simple question like that? Surely, your name can do no harm."

His name, Watcher thought, then what planet he was from, where the planet was in relation to the Gisser sun, what about intervening storms. And so on down the line. There wasn't any end.

Every day that he could hold these people away from the information they craved and would give the Fifty Suns so much more time to organize against the greatest machine that had ever flown into this part of space.

His thought trailed. The woman was sitting up, gazing at him with eyes that had gone steely. Her voice held a metallic resonance as she said:

"Know this, whoever you are, that you are aboard the Imperial Battleship *Star Cluster*, Grand Captain Laurr at your service. Know, too, that it is our unalterable will that you shall prepare for us an orbit that will take our ship safely to your chief planet."

She went on vibrantly: "It is my solemn belief you already know that Earth recognizes no separate governments. Space is indivisible. The universe shall not be an area of countless sovereign peoples squabbling and quarreling for power.

"That is the law. Those who set themselves against it are outlaws, subject to any punishment which may be decided upon in their special case.

"Take warning."

Without waiting for an answer, she turned her head. "Lieutenant Neslor," she said at the wall facing Watcher, "have you made any progress?"

A woman's voice answered: "Yes, noble lady. I have set up an integer based on the Muir-Grayson studies of colonial peoples who have been isolated from the main stream of galactic life. There is no historical precedent for such a long isolation as seems to have obtained here, so I have decided to assume that they have passed the static period, and have made some progress of their own.

"I think we should begin very simply, however. A few forced answers will open his brain to further pressures, and we can draw valuable conclusions meanwhile from the speed with which he adjusts his resistance to the brain machine. Shall I proceed?"

The woman on the chaise longue nodded. There was a flash of light from the wall facing Watcher. He tried to dodge and discovered for the first time that *something* held him in the bed, not rope, or chain, nothing visible. But something as palpable as rubbery steel.

Before he could think further, the light was in his eyes, in his mind, a dazzling fury. Voices seemed to push through it, voices that danced and sang, and spoke into his brain, voices that said:

"A simple question like that — of course I'll answer ... of course, of course, of course—— My name is Gisser Watcher. I was born on the planet Kaider III, of Dellian parents. There are seventy inhabited planets, fifty suns, thirty billion people, four hundred important storms, the biggest at Latitude 473. The Central Government is on the glorious planet, Cassidor VII——"

With a blank horror of what he was doing, Watcher caught his roaring mind into a Dellian knot, and stopped that devastating burst of revelation. He knew he would never be caught like that again but — too late, he thought, too late by far.

The woman wasn't quite so certain. She went out of the bedroom, and came presently to where the middle-aged Lieutenant Neslor was classifying her findings on receptor spools.

The psychologist glanced up from her work, said in an amazed voice: "Noble lady, his resistance during the stoppage moment registered an equivalent of IQ 800. Now, that's utterly impossible, particularly because he started talking at a pressure point equivalent to IQ 167, which matches with his general appearance, and which you know is average.

"There must be a system of mind training behind his resistance. And I think I found the clue in his reference to his Dellian ancestry. His graph squared in intensity when he used the word.

"This is very serious, and may cause great delay — unless we are prepared to break his mind."

The grand captain shook her head, said only: "Report further developments to me."

On the way to the transmitter, she paused to check the battleship's position. A bleak smile touched her lips, as she saw on the reflector the shadow of a ship circling the brighter shadow of a sun.

Marking time, she thought, and felt a chill of premonition. Was it possible that one man was going to hold up a ship strong enough to conquer an entire galaxy?

The senior ship meteorologist, Lieutenant Cannons, stood up from a chair as she came toward him across the vast floor of the transmission receiving room, where the Fifty Suns weather station still stood. He had graying hair, and he was very old, she remembered, very old. Walking toward him, she thought:

There was a slow pulse of life in these men who watched the great storms of space. There must be to them a sense of futility about it all, a timelessness. Storms that took a century or more to attain their full roaring maturity, such storms and the men who catalogued them must acquire a sort of affinity of spirit.

The slow stateliness was in his voice, too, as he bowed with a measure of grace, and said:

"Grand Captain, the Right Honourable Gloria Cecily, the Lady Laurr of Noble Laurr, I am honoured by your personal presence."

She acknowledged the greeting, and then unwound the spool for him. He listened, frowning, said finally:

"The latitude he gave for the storm is a meaningless quantity. These incredible people have built up a sun relation system in the Lesser Magellanic Cloud, in which the center is an arbitrary one having no recognizable connection with the magnetic center of the whole Cloud. Probably, they've picked some sun, called it center, and built their whole spatial geography around it."

The old man whirled abruptly away from her, and led the way into the weather station, to the edge of the pit above which poised the reconstructed weather map.

"The map is utterly worthless to us," he said succinctly.

"What?"

She saw that he was staring at her, his china-blue eyes thoughtful.

"Tell me, what is your idea of this map?"

The woman was silent, unwilling to commit herself in the face of so much definiteness. Then she frowned, and said:

"My impression is much as you described. They've got

406

a system of their own here, and all we've got to do is find the key."

She finished more confidently: "Our main problems, it seems to me, would be to determine which direction we should go in the immediate vicinity of this meteorite weather station we've found. If we chose the wrong direction, there would be vexatious delay, and, throughout, our chief obstacle would be that we dare not go fast because of possible storms."

She looked at him questioningly, as she ended. And saw that he was shaking his head, gravely:

"I'm afraid," he said, "it's not so simple as that. Those bright point-replicas of suns look the size of peas due to light distortion, but when examined through a metroscope they show only a few molecules in diameter. If that is their proportion to the suns they represent——"

She had learned in genuine crises to hide her feelings from subordinates. She stood now, inwardly stunned, outwardly cool, thoughtful, calm. She said finally:

"You mean each one of those suns, their suns, is buried among about a thousand other suns?"

"Worse than that. I would say that they have only inhabited one system in ten thousand. We must never forget that the Lesser Magellanic Cloud is a universe of fifty million stars. That's a lot of sunshine."

The old man concluded quietly: "If you wish, I will prepare orbits involving maximum speeds of ten light days a minute to all the nearest stars. We may strike it lucky."

The woman shook her head savagely: "One in ten thousand. Don't be foolish. I happen to know the law of averages that relates to ten thousand. We would have to visit a minimum of twenty-five hundred suns if we were lucky, thirty-five to fifty thousand if we were not.

"No, no" — a grim smile compressed her fine lips — "we're not going to spend five hundred years looking for a needle in a haystack. I'll trust to psychology before I trust to chance. We have the man who understands the map, and while it will take time, he'll talk in the end."

She started to turn away, then stopped. "What," she

asked, "about the building itself? Have you drawn any conclusions from its design?"

He nodded. "Of the type used in the galaxy about fifteen thousand years ago."

"Any improvements, changes?"

"None that I can see. One observer, who does all the work. Simple, primitive."

She stood thoughtful, shaking her head as if trying to clear away a mist.

"It seems strange. Surely after fifteen thousand years they could have added something. Colonies are usually static, but not that static."

She was examining routine reports three hours later when her astro clanged twice, softly. Two messages——

The first was from Psychology House, a single question: "Have we permission to break the prisoner's mind?"

"No!" said Grand Captain Laurr.

The second message made her glance across at the orbit board. The board was aglitter with orbit symbols. That wretched old man, disobeying her injunction NOT to prepare any orbits.

Smiling twistedly, she walked over and studied the shining things, and finally sent an order to Central Engines. She watched as her great ship plunged into night.

After all, she thought, there was such a thing as playing two games at the same time. Counterpoint was older in human relations than it was in music.

The first day she stared down at the outer planet of a blue-white sun. It floated in the darkness below the ship, an airless mass of rock and metal, drab and terrible as any meteorite, a world of primeval canyons and mountains untouched by the leavening breath of life.

Spy rays showed only rock, endless rock, not a sign of movement or of past movement.

There were three other planets, one of them a warm, green world where winds sighed through virgin forests and animals swarmed on the plains.

Not a house showed, nor the erect form of a human being.

Grimly, the woman said into the intership communicator: "Exactly how far can our spy rays penetrate into the ground?"

"A hundred feet."

"Are there any metals which can simulate a hundred feet of earth?"

"Several, noble lady."

Dissatisfied, she broke the connection. There was no call that day from Psychology House.

The second day, a giant red sun swam into her impatient ken. Ninety-four planets swung in their great orbits around their massive parent. Two were habitable, but again there was the profusion of wilderness and of animals usually found only on planets untouched by the hand and metal of civilization.

The chief zoological officer reported the fact in his precise voice: "The percentage of animals parallels the mean for worlds not inhabited by intelligent beings."

The woman snapped: "Has it occurred to you that there may have been a deliberate policy to keep animal life abundant, and laws preventing the tilling of the soil even for pleasure?"

She did not expect, nor did she receive, an answer. And once more there was not a word from Lieutenant Neslor, the chief psychologist.

The third sun was farther away. She had the speed stepped up to twenty light days a minute — and received a shocking reminder as the ship bludgeoned into a small storm. It must have been small because the shuddering of metal had barely begun when it ended.

"There has been some talk," she said afterward to the thirty captains assembled in the captains' pool, "that we return to the galaxy and ask for an expedition that will uncover these hidden rascals.

"One of the more whining of the reports that have come to my ears suggests that, after all, we were on our way home when we made our discovery, and that our ten years in the Cloud have earned us a rest."

Her gray eyes flashed; her voice grew icy: "You may

409

be sure that those who sponsor such defeatism are not the ones who would have to make the personal report of failure to his majesty's government. Therefore, let me assure the faint hearts and the homesick that we shall remain another ten years if it should prove necessary. Tell the officers and crew to act accordingly. That is all."

Back in the main bridge, she saw that there was still no call from Psychology House. There was a hot remnant of anger and impatience in her, as she dialed the number. But she controlled herself as the distinguished face of Lieutenant Neslor appeared on the plate. She said then:

"What is happening, lieutenant? I am anxiously waiting for further information from the prisoner."

The woman psychologist shook her head. "Nothing to report."

"Nothing!" Her amazement was harsh in her voice.

"I have asked twice," was the answer, "for permission to break his mind. You must have known that I would not lightly suggest such a drastic step."

"Oh!" She had known, but the disapproval of the people at home, the necessity for accounting for any amoral action against individuals, had made refusal an automatic action. Now—— Before she could speak, the psychologist went on:

"I have made some attempts to condition him in his sleep, stressing the uselessness of resisting Earth when eventual discovery is sure. But that has only convinced him that his earlier revelations were of no benefit to us."

The leader found her voice: "Do you really mean, lieutenant, that you have no plan other than violence? Nothing?"

In the astroplate, the image head made a negative movement. The psychologist said simply:

"An 800 IQ resistance in a 167 IQ brain is something new in my experience."

The woman felt a great wonder. "I can't understand it," she complained. "I have a feeling we've missed some vital clue. Just like that we run into a weather station in a system of fifty million suns, a station in which there is a human being who, contrary to all the laws of self-preservation, immediately kills himself to prevent himself from falling into our hands.

"The weather station itself is an old model galactic affair, which shows no improvements after fifteen thousand years; and yet the vastness of the time elapsed, the caliber of the brains involved suggest that all the obvious changes should have been made.

"And the man's name, Watcher, is so typical of the ancient pre-spaceship method of calling names on Earth according to the trade. It is possible that even the sun, where he is watching, is a service heritage of his family. There's something — depressing — here somewhere that——"

She broke off, frowning: "What is your plan?" After a minute, she nodded. "I see . . . very well, bring him to one of the bedrooms in the main bridge. And forget that part about making up one of our strong-arm girls to look like me. I'll do everything that's necessary. Tomorrow. Fine."

Coldly she sat watching the prisoner's image in the plate. The man, Watcher, lay in bed, an almost motionless figure, eyes closed, but his face curiously tense. He looked, she thought, like someone discovering that for the first time in four days, the invisible force lines that had bound him had been withdrawn.

Beside her, the woman psychologist hissed: "He's still suspicious, and will probably remain so until you partially ease his mind. His general reactions will become more and more concentrated. Every minute that passes will increase his conviction that he will have only one chance to destroy the ship, and that he must be decisively ruthless regardless of risk.

"I have been conditioning him the past ten hours to resistance to us in a very subtle fashion. You will see in a moment . . . ah-h!"

Watcher was sitting up in bed. He poked a leg from under the sheets, then slid forward, and onto his feet. It was an oddly powerful movement.

He stood for a moment, a tall figure in gray pajamas. He had evidently been planning his first actions because, after a swift look at the door, he walked over to a set of drawers built into one wall, tugged at them tentatively, and then jerked them open with an effortless strength, snapping their locks one by one.

Her own gasp was only an echo of the gasp of Lieutenant Neslor.

"Good heavens!" the psychologist said finally. "Don't ask me to explain how he's breaking those metal locks. Strength must be a by-product of his Dellian training. Noble lady——"

Her tone was anxious; and the grand captain looked at her. "Yes?"

"Do you think, under the circumstances, you should play such a personal role in his subjection? His strength is obviously such that he can break the body of anyone aboard——"

She was cut off by an imperious gesture. "I cannot," said the Right Honourable Gloria Cecily, "risk some fool making a mistake. I'll take an antipain pill. Tell me when it is time to go in."

Watcher felt cold, tense, as he entered the instrument room of the main bridge. He had found his clothes in some locked drawers. He hadn't known they were there, but the drawers aroused his curiosity. He made the preliminary Dellian extra energy movements; and the locks snapped before his super strength.

Pausing on the threshold, he flicked his gaze through the great domed room. And after a moment his terrible fear that he and his kind were lost, suffered another transfusion of hope. He was actually free.

These people couldn't have the faintest suspicion of the truth. The great genius, Joseph H. Dell, must be a forgotten man on Earth. Their release of him must have behind it some plan of course but——

"Death," he thought ferociously, "death to them all, as they had once inflicted death, and would again."

He was examining the bank on bank of control boards

when, out of the corner of his eyes, he saw the woman step from the nearby wall.

He looked up; he thought with a savage joy: The leader! They'd have guns protecting her, naturally, but they wouldn't know that all these days he had been frantically wondering how he could force the use of guns.

Surely to space, they *couldn't* be prepared to gather up his component elements again. Their very act of freeing him had showed psychology intentions.

Before he could speak, the woman said, smilingly: "I really shouldn't let you examine those controls. But we have decided on a different tactic with you. Freedom of the ship, an opportunity to meet the crew. We want to convince you . . . convince you——"

Something of the bleakness and implacableness of him must have touched her. She faltered, shook herself in transparent self-annoyance, then smiled more firmly, and went on in a persuasive tone:

"We want you to realize that we're not ogres. We want to end your alarm that we mean harm to your people. You must know, now we have found you exist, that discovery is only a matter of time.

"Earth is not cruel, or dominating, at least not any more. The barest minimum of allegiance is demanded, and that only is the idea of a common unity, the indivisibility of space. It is required, too, that criminal laws be uniform, and that a high minimum wage for workers be maintained. In addition, wars of any kind are absolutely forbidden.

"Except for that, every planet or group of planets, can have its own form of government, trade with whom they please, live their own life. Surely, there is nothing terrible enough in all this to justify the curious attempt at suicide you made when we discovered the weather station."

He would, he thought, listening to her, break her head first. The best method would be to grab her by the feet, and smash her against the metal wall or floor. Bone would crush easily and the act would serve two vital purposes:

It would be a terrible and salutary warning to the other

413

officers of the ship. And it would precipitate upon him the death fire of her guards.

He took a step toward her. And began the faintly visible muscle and nerve movements so necessary to pumping the Dellian body to a pitch of superhuman capability. The woman was saying:

"You stated before that your people have inhabited fifty suns in this space. Why only fifty? In twelve thousand or more years, a population of twelve thousand billion would not be beyond possibility."

He took another step. And another. Then knew that he must speak if he hoped to keep her unsuspicious for those vital seconds while he inched closer, closer. He said:

"About two thirds of our marriages are childless. It has been very unfortunate, but you see there are two types of us, and when intermarriage occurs as it does without hindrance——"

Almost he was near enough; he heard her say: "You mean, a mutation has taken place; and the two don't mix?"

He didn't have to answer that. He was ten feet from her; and like a tiger he launched himself across the intervening gap.

The first energy beam ripped through his body too low down to be fatal, but it brought a hot scalding nausea and a dreadful heaviness. He heard the grand captain scream:

"Lieutenant Neslor, what are you doing?"

He had her then. His fingers were grabbing hard at her fending arm, when the second blow struck him high in the ribs and brought the blood frothing into his mouth. In spite of all his will, he felt his hands slipping from the woman. Oh, space, how he would have liked to take her into the realm of death with him.

Once again, the woman screamed: "Lieutenant Neslor, are you mad? *Cease fire!*"

Just before the third beam burned at him with its indescribable violence, he thought with a final and tremendous sardonicism: "She still didn't suspect. But somebody

414

did, somebody who at this ultimate moment had guessed the truth."

"Too late," he thought, "too late, you fools! Go ahead and hunt. They've had warning, time to conceal themselves even more thoroughly. And the Fifty Suns are scattered, scattered among a million stars, among——"

Death caught his thought.

The woman picked herself off the floor, and stood dizzily striving to draw her roughly handled senses back into her brain. She was vaguely aware of Lieutenant Neslor coming through a transmitter, pausing at the dead body of Gisser Watcher and rushing toward her.

"Are you all right, my dear? It was so hard firing through an astroplate that——"

"You mad woman!" The grand captain caught her breath. "Do you realize that a body can't be reconstituted once vital organs have been destroyed. Dissolution or resolution cannot be piecemeal. We'll have to go home without——"

She stopped. She saw that the psychologist was staring at her. Lieutenant Neslor said:

"His intention to attack was unmistakable and it was too soon according to my graphs. All the way through, he's never fitted anything in human psychology.

"At the very last possible moment I remembered Joseph Dell and the massacre of the Dellian supermen fifteen thousand years ago. Fantastic to think that some of them escaped and established a civilization in this remote part of space.

"Do you see now: 'Dellian' — Joseph M. Dell — the inventor of the Dellian perfect robot."

*After how many years, how many generations, the
Earthmen were going home—peacefully submitting
to the order of exile. What was the meaning of it all?
Why were the Earthlings letting themselves be ex-
pelled?*

●

# TO CIVILIZE

## By Algis Budrys

There was no moon, there were no stars; the sky was
overcast. The spacefield lights threw up an umbrella of
yellow-white, shot through by the silvered reflections
thrown off by the ship on the takeoff stand. The big
winches at the ship's cargo-hatches creaked their cables
with a disproportionate loudness. Except for the constant
undercurrent of the sound of straining metal, the field was
quiet.

*Is it too quiet?* Deric thought. Was it the silence that
lurks at the van of a storm, waiting to be ripped to tatters
as the sudden wind broke out, as the hurricane spun out
of the tropics and howled?

*Is this how it ends?* Deric leaned his weight against the
rail of the observation-platform, his whiplash body drawn
up into a taut ribbon. The field lights gleamed from the
polished blackness of his hide, glinting on the cropped
silver follicles of his crest. *Is this the way of Earthmen?*

Except for the graceful bodies of his own people as
they operated the silent cargo-carriers streaming out to the
ship, there was no life on the field. Even behind the big

416

doors of the cargo-hatches, there was no sign of movement. Under him, at ground-level, the Galactics waited in their big room for the loading to end. Then there would be a procession of figures, loaded with their personal baggage, walking out across the field to the ship. There would be women holding or leading children, and men walking beside them.

In the beginning, when the order had been published, Deric had thought there might be trouble. The Galactics were not a meek lot. While they were independent enough in their everyday affairs, and even occasionally quarrelsome among themselves, he had seen emergencies weld them into a tight, concerted group that operated at high and heedless efficiency. There was every right to expect some sort of demonstration on their part.

Nothing had happened. The Galactics had sold their holdings to the government without a murmur, and disposed of their other non-essential belongings quickly and quietly. Their children had been withdrawn from any classes or special groups they might have attended; goodbyes had been said; and now, a scant GST month after the issuance of the order by the Voroseii, the Galactics were leaving Voroseith, never to return.

*Never?* Even now, Deric found that impossible to believe. The order was specific, and enforcable, but he had seen other laws relaxed, or evaded with the passage of time.

Or, for that matter, overcome.

Was that it? Deric had heard many stories about the GSN and its big green ships that poured the fire of a sun from their innumerable guns. Were the Earthpeople leaving Voroseith so that the planet would be open to bombardment from outer space?

No, the possibility had been considered before, and rejected. True, no single planet could stand before the Federation. Not even a group of solar systems could do it. The lesson of Ardath Secession was still fresh, and terrible. But Voroseith's protection lay in the very fact that she was a single planet, and relatively unimportant to the Federation as a whole. Compared to the GSN fleet, her

417

own navy was an insignificant handful of ships. But, ship for ship, it was just as deadly, and the price of conquest would be high — too high for the prize it would bring. There would be no war.

Still — why was there no protest? The Galactics had homes and property on Voroseith. The grandchildren of the First-comers were grown and bred on this world. There were friendships, business relations, ties of many kinds by the hundreds. As a lover of the strange composite art form that was opera, Deric would suffer from the loss of new Berkeley libretti, for no one else could work as well with Marto Lihh.

The Federation itself had done nothing beyond dispatching the transport. All reference to the order had been offhand, casual, as a thing that existed without question.

He could not let the Galactics depart and leave him without an answer. He pushed himself back from the rail and slid rapidly down the ramp to the room where the Earthpeople were.

Here, too, there was silence; even the children were quiet. The Galactics sat in rows on benches, facing each other across the narrow aisles. There was no talking, but groups of friends had sat down together, and occasionally there would be a smile or a nod to someone across the aisle.

As Deric entered, several heads turned in his direction. In every case, there was a friendly smile as he was recognized; several people separated themselves from their immediate groups and came over to him.

"Deric!" That was Morris, one of the men who had worked at the museum with him. The Galactic strode up to him rapidly, and laid his hand behind Deric's head with a firm and friendly greeting stroke. Deric gently touched his right hand to the Earthman's own.

"I thought you'd come down," Morris said. His face was regretful at the thought of his leaving.

Now that he was here, among them, Deric felt the strangeness of the situation even more strongly than before. He had never seen a group of Galactics before without seeing his own people among them. It felt strange to suddenly realize that this was the winnowing of all the Galactics on Voroseith — that most of these people knew each other less well than they did the individual Voroseii among whom they had lived and worked; but that, nevertheless, they were suddenly a homogenous and segregated group by mere virtue of the fact that they were all Galactics.

It was possible to consider the entire problem as a sort of intellectual puzzle, to be evaluated in the light of the economic factors that had made the order necessary. But Morris was his friend and co-worker, so the situation became one of losing a good friend, of never seeing his family again, and of learning to remember that Day 184, GST, was no longer Susan Morris' birthday.

"I wanted to see you," Deric said. "I'm not sure I should be here, but——" He stopped, not sure of his words. "Well . . ."

Morris smiled. "Thanks, Deric."

The other Galactics who had come up exchanged greetings with him in turn. Each of them, like Morris, reflected a regret as great as Deric's own.

He saw Berkeley, sitting by himself at the end of a bench, his eyes somber. *How does he feel?* Deric wondered. He turned back to Morris. "I — if it's possible, could I talk to him? You know how much I admire his work."

"Easily done," Morris said. "Come on."

Deric followed his friend across the floor of the waiting room. As he passed among the seated Galactics, he could see the same traces of sadness in their eyes — sadness, but no protest, no rebellion.

Berkeley looked up at Morris' words. "Deric Liss?" He turned his eyes on Deric. "Of course." He reached out and touched Deric's neck warmly. "I've read your *Cultural History*. One of the most valuable texts I've ever seen."

"Thank you," Deric said, his eyes glowing. Completely embarrassed, he felt his body twitch awkwardly. "I've always admired your work," he blurted out, conscious of

419

the clumsiness of the statement. Following Berkeley's compliment as it did, it sounded more like back-scratching than anything like the sincere appreciation he had intended to express.

But Berkeley smiled, his eyes crinkling at the corners. "I'll never have a composer like Marto Lihh to work with again," he said. A trace of his former brooding look returned to his face.

Deric could hold back his puzzlement no longer. He looked up at Morris and Berkeley. "I can't understand this," he said, his voice full of uncertainty. "Why are you leaving? Or, if you must leave, why aren't you . . ." He let the sentence trail off. One doesn't ask a man why he hasn't been resentful of some unjustice you've done him.

"Why aren't we displaying our famous Terrestrial aggressiveness?" Berkeley asked, smiling.

"Yes." Completely disconcerted, he said, "And you — a man who's leaving everything he loves and works for. Aren't *you*, at least, angry at what we've done?"

Berkeley shook his head. "Angry? Your planet's overcrowded. There are no other habitable planets in this system, and we were all competing with you for what room there was. It's only natural that your government has to consider the well-being of its people. After all, we are a foreign race; this is your planet, to do with as you choose. I'd say the order was a very wise move, from the point of view of your people. I'm sure the rest of us feel the same way."

Morris nodded.

"But the Federation . . ."

"The Federation is exactly that — not an empire. You have the privileges of membership — and the rights, as well," Berkeley pointed out. If he himself felt a personal loss, he kept it within himself.

"I still don't understand. When the Ardan group seceded, the remainder of the Federation refused to allow it," Deric said.

Berkeley's face clouded. "The Ardan Secession was an armed insurrection, born of frustrated ambition and a desire for power. It was motivated only by the Ardans' drive to regain control of the Federation."

"But they were as justified in their eyes as we are in ours," Deric protested.

Berkeley cocked his head. "Perhaps — but what about the Ardan dissolutionists? Was that a sign that even all the Ardans were in agreement with their government's policy?"

"I don't approve of our action, either," Deric replied.

Berkeley smiled. "You mean, it strikes you as being somewhat peremptory; and this feeling is augmented by the fact that we're submitting to it without any action that would make it seem emotionally justified. If we fought back, you could at least feel that maybe getting rid of the quarrelsome Terrestrials was worthwhile."

"Yes . . ." Deric admitted slowly, abashed. He had never thought it out that far.

"But you're not actively angry at the order," Berkeley went on. "You sympathize with us, but you don't feel it's an outrageous situation."

The Galactic was right. Deric could feel himself twitching with embarrassment again. "I don't know what to say," he mumbled.

The librettist smiled again. "No need for that," he said warmly. "We've known from the very beginning that this would happen someday. We've accepted it, so it didn't come as a shock."

Deric, once again, felt his puzzlement coming to the fore. "But why did you come at all, then? Look at the history of the last three generations. After we were contacted by the sample ship, your people came here, settled into our culture, and began to live alongside us. More than alongside. You worked for the same goal as we — the progress of Voroseithan culture and civilization. You speak our language. Never once have you done something for the benefit of the Federation, or of Earth. It was as if — as if you were Voroseii yourselves, not as if you were foreigners at all.

"It was difficult to believe. We expected taxes, or levies of *some* kind. We expected you to bring your arts and your sciences, to merge our culture with yours. But none of that happened. And now, though you are Galactics, you are nevertheless Voroseii. If you knew you would someday leave, why did you make Voroseith more truly a home than any other world could possibly be?"

Berkeley, who wrote poetry as a Voroseii would, thinking in terms of a six-tone scale, let a flicker of sorrow cross his face. "Yes, I imagine that would be what you'd expect. It's what the Ardans did, when they guided the Federation. You're right, and yet, you're wrong, as well."

He smiled, almost wistfully. "Yes, Voroseith *is* home to us, and we will miss it. But we were working for the benefit of the Federation, nonetheless. We had to act as though we would always live here — more than act, we had to *believe* we would always live here. We had to devote all our whole-hearted energies to working for Voroseith. It was——" He hesitated, and, for a moment, there was a lost look on his face. "It was a shock when we realized that our job was done, that Voroseith was ready to go out into interstellar space."

"Interstellar space?" Deric felt his back arch in puzzlement.

Morris nodded. "It's coming. That's why you've got your navy. You were working out the necessary techniques."

"But the Federation rules the Galaxy. Will you permit us to go out into your territory?"

Berkeley spoke again. "The Federation doesn't rule anything; you can't impose civilization by force. It's your turn, as a member of a civilizing movement, to go out and pass on what you have to other people. Space is full of worlds, and people. Earth *guides* the Federation, true, but it doesn't run it — no one does. We work with the common bond of civilization between us — but it is civilization as an abstract concept — not as a rigid, universal pattern of some kind, into which each diverse culture has to be hammered and forced, jammed into a mold for which it was never suited."

"We didn't try to make you do things our way, did we?" Morris asked.

Deric waved his arm negatively. "No — no, you didn't. You learned from us, and then you became just so many more individuals working to improve our culture. You brought in a fresh approach to many problems; but it was an approach founded in the roots of our culture, not of yours." He stopped.

The annunciator crackled. "All cargo has been loaded. Passengers will please embark." The dispatcher's voice lost its impersonality. Another Voroseii was saying goodbye to his friends. "Farewell, Earthmen."

The seated rows of Galactics stood up, still quiet despite the shuffle of feet, the scraping of baggage as it was picked up.

"So now we'll be out in space beside you?" Deric asked Berkeley.

The Galactic nodded. "When the groups like ours leave a world, that is the historical sign that another race is going out into the stars, civilized, to civilize."

Deric felt a surge of pride shoot through him. "Then, this was a stage, like the time of the sample ship, during which we were trained."

Morris shook his head. "Not trained. The sample ship was a test, true — but a test designed to measure nothing more than your ability to conceive of other races beyond your own, and your readiness to accept the fact that interstellar travel was an actuality. Why should we train you? Our culture is not superior to yours in any way — and there are far too many diverse races in space, and far too few Earthmen even remotely to justify any attempt to make you do things the way they're done on Earth.

"No, we were just sent here to accustom you to working beside other races. We weren't instructors — we were coworkers."

Most of the Galactics were already through the doors that led out to the field. Morris and Berkeley touched Deric's neck again. "Goodbye, Deric," Morris said.

Berkeley suddenly reached into his pack and pulled out a sheaf of manuscript. "I wish you'd take this, Deric."

Deric looked at the top page. "But — but this is the original manuscript for the Llersthein Epic!"

Berkeley nodded. "Take it. I'll remember it, and nobody will really understand it, where I'm going."

Deric looked up at the Galactic. The somber eyes looked back into his, and, though this was not truly one of his people — theoretically, the facial expressions of one race should be incomprehensible to another — Deric could read what lay in the mind behind the eyes; nor did it occur to him that there was anything remarkable about the fact that he could.

"Thank you," he said, and let the position of his hands and the twist of his body tell Berkeley what emotions lay behind the words.

The two Galactics picked up their packs and swung them over their shoulders, and joined the waiting groups of their families.

Deric stayed where he was, watching them go, still trying to grasp what it was he had half-seen, half-understood. It was important, too, he knew. It explained, more than sadness, the silence that had overlaid the waiting room, the odd feeling that the Galactics were drawn apart into numerous small groups, each of them turning to his family and immediate friends.

As if they were in danger——

Fear! They were afraid! Morris, Berkeley — all of them.

He saw them reach the door and wait for their families to precede them. He coiled his muscles and slid forward in a rapid surge.

"Wait!"

Berkeley and Morris turned back toward him, their faces questioning.

"Where *are* you going?" Deric asked. "What are you going to do?"

"I don't know," Berkeley said. "I don't know," he repeated slowly. "We're being taken to Earth." And now

424

Deric could plainly see the naked uncertainty in their eyes, the hesitation, the clammy tinge of fear.

"We have to get going," Morris said with sudden harshness — the harshness of nerves strained to the point where they sang and vibrated, waiting for the first new burden to snap and lash back with deadly effect.

Berkeley smiled at Deric — but there were white spots along his own jawline. He laid a gentle hand on Deric's neck. "I liked it here," he said wistfully. "I was born here, like my father was." He looked up, through the panes of the exit door, and, at that moment, the overcast finally broke, and the starlight flashed through.

Berkeley winced as though something had struck him. Then he shook himself and grinned — the fighting grin that was the Earthman's trademark. Nevertheless, there was something haunted in his voice as he said, "I wonder what Earth is like."

"Come on!" Morris said, and half-pushed Berkeley through the door. He raised a hand in a last farewell to Deric, and Berkeley, with Morris' hand on his shoulder, half turned, and waved apologetically for their friend's nervousness.

Deric looked after them, feeling the first beginnings of understanding trickle into his consciousness, knowing that the trickle would swell into a live, leaping torrent. When it came, he had better be very, very busy at some work that was unimportant enough to be spoiled by trembling hands, or clouded vision.

What was it the dispatcher had said? "Farewell, Earthmen?" He shook his head in the acquired Terrestrial mannerism, turned, and slipped rapidly up the ramp to the observation platform. He watched the last of the Galactics walk into the waiting ship.

"Farewell, Voroseii," he said softly, as his brothers went unprotestingly into exile.

*Earth's Secret Service kept peace in the Galaxy effi-*
*ciently — very efficiently. I was always there . . .*
*before trouble started!*

•

# BEEP

## By James Blish

# I

Josef Faber lowered his newspaper slightly. Finding the
girl on the park bench looking his way, he smiled the
agonizingly embarrassed smile of the thoroughly married
caught bird-watching, and ducked back into the paper
again.

He was reasonably certain that he looked the part of a
middle-aged, steadily employed, harmless citizen enjoying
a Sunday break in the bookkeeping and family routines.
He was also quite certain, despite his official instructions,
that it wouldn't make the slightest bit of difference if he
didn't. These boy-meets-girl assignments always came off.
Jo had never tackled a single one that had required him.

As a matter of fact, the newspaper, which he was supposed to be using only as a blind, interested him a good
deal more than his job did. He had only barely begun to
suspect the obvious ten years ago when the Service had
snapped him up; now, after a decade as an agent, he was

426

still fascinated to see how smoothly the really important situations came off. The *dangerous* situations — not boy-meets-girl.

This affair of the Black Horse Nebula, for instance. Some days ago the papers and the commentators had begun to mention reports of disturbances in that area, and Jo's practiced eye had picked up the mention. Something big was cooking.

Today it had boiled over — the Black Horse Nebula had suddenly spewed ships by the hundreds, a massed armada that must have taken more than a century of effort on the part of a whole star-cluster, a production drive conducted in the strictest and most fanatical kind of secrecy——

And, of course, the Service had been on the spot in plenty of time. With three times as many ships, disposed with mathematical precision so as to enfilade the entire armada the moment it broke from the nebula. The battle had been a massacre, the attack smashed before the average citizen could even begin to figure out what it had been aimed at — and good had triumphed over evil once more.

Of course.

Furtive scuffings on the gravel drew his attention briefly. He looked at his watch, which said 14:58:03. That was the time, according to his instructions, when boy had to meet girl.

He had been given the strictest kind of orders to let nothing interfere with this meeting — the orders always issued on boy-meets-girl assignments. But, as usual, he had nothing to do but observe. The meeting was coming off on the dot, without any prodding from Jo. They always did.

Of course.

With a sigh, he folded his newspaper, smiling again at the couple — yes, it was the right man, too — and moved away, as if reluctantly. He wondered what would happen were he to pull away the false mustache, pitch the newspaper on the grass, and bound away with a joyous whoop. He suspected that the course of history would not be deflected by even a second of arc, but he was not minded to try the experiment.

The park was pleasant. The twin suns warmed the path and the greenery without any of the blasting heat which they would bring to bear later in the summer. Randolph was altogether the most comfortable planet he had visited in years. A little backward, perhaps, but restful, too.

It was also slightly over a hundred light-years away from Earth. It would be interesting to know how Service headquarters on Earth could have known in advance that boy would meet girl at a certain spot on Randolph, precisely at 14:58:03.

Or how Service headquarters could have ambushed with micrometric precision a major interstellar fleet, with no more preparation than a few days' buildup in the newspapers and video could evidence.

The press was free, on Randolph as everywhere. It reported the news it got. Any emergency concentration of Service ships in the Black Horse area, or anywhere else, would have been noticed and reported on. The Service did not forbid such reports for "security" reasons or for any other reasons. Yet there had been nothing to report but that (a) an armada of staggering size had erupted with no real warning from the Black Horse Nebula, and that (b) the Service had been ready.

By now, it was a commonplace that the Service was always ready. It had not had a defect or a failure in well over two centuries. It had not even had a fiasco, the alarming-sounding technical word by which it referred to the possibility that a boy-meets-girl assignment might not come off.

Jo hailed a hopper. Once inside, he stripped himself of the moustache, the bald spot, the forehead creases — all the makeup which had given him his mask of friendly innocuousness.

The hoppy watched the whole process in the rear-view mirror. Jo glanced up and met his eyes.

"Pardon me, mister, but I figured you didn't care if I saw you. You must be a Service man."

"That's right. Take me to Service HQ, will you?"

"Sure enough." The hoppy gunned his machine. It rose smoothly to the express level. "First time I ever got close to a Service man. Didn't hardly believe it at first when I saw you taking your face off. You sure looked different."

"Have to, sometime," Jo said, preoccupied.

"I'll bet. No wonder you know all about everything before it breaks. You must have a thousand faces each, your own mother wouldn't know you, eh? Don't you care if I know about your snooping around in disguise?"

Jo grinned. The grin created a tiny pulling sensation across one curve of his cheek, just next to his nose. He stripped away the overlooked bit of tissue and examined it critically.

"Of course not. Disguise is an elementary part of Service work. Anyone could guess that. We don't use it often, as a matter of fact — only on very simple assignments."

"Oh." The hoppy sounded slightly disappointed, as melodrama faded. He drove silently for about a minute. Then, speculatively: "Sometimes I think the Service must have time-travel, the things they pull . . . well, here you are. Good luck, mister."

"Thanks."

Jo went directly to Krasna's office. Krasna was a Randolpher, Earth-trained, and answerable to the Earth office, but otherwise pretty much on his own. His heavy, muscular face wore the same expression of serene confidence that was characteristic of Service officials everywhere — even some that, technically speaking, had no faces to wear it.

"Boy meets girl," Jo said briefly. "On the nose and on the spot."

"Good work, Jo. Cigarette?" Krasna pushed the box across his desk.

"Nope, not now. Like to talk to you, if you've got time."

Krasna pushed a button, and a toadstool-like chair rose out of the floor behind Jo. "What's on your mind?"

"Well," Jo said carefully. "I'm wondering why you patted me on the back just now for not doing a job."

"You did a job."

"I did not," Jo said flatly. "Boy would have met girl, whether I'd been here on Randolph or back on Earth. The course of true love always runs smooth. It has in all my boy-meets-girl cases, and it has in the boy-meets-girl cases of every other agent with whom I've compared notes."

"Well, good," Krasna said, smiling. "That's the way we like to have it run. And that's the way we expect it to run. But, Jo, we like to have somebody on the spot, somebody with a reputation for resourcefulness, just in case there's a snag. There almost never is, as you've observed. But — if there were?"

Jo snorted. "If what you're trying to do is to establish preconditions for the future, any interference by a Service agent would throw the eventual result farther *off* the track. I know that much about probability."

"And what makes you think that we're trying to set up the future?"

"It's obvious even to the hoppies on your own planet; the one that brought me here told me he thought the Service had time-travel. It's especially obvious to all the individuals and governments and entire populations that the Service has bailed out of serious messes for centuries, with never a single failure." Jo shrugged. "A man can be asked to safeguard only a small number of boy-meets-girl cases before he realizes, as an agent, that what the Service is safeguarding is the future children of those meetings. Ergo — the Service *knows* what those children are to be like, and has reason to want their future existence guaranteed. What other conclusion is possible?"

Krasna took out a cigarette and lit it deliberately; it was obvious that he was using the manoeuvre to cloak his response.

"None," he admitted at last. "We have some foreknowledge, of course. We couldn't have made our reputation with espionage alone. But we have obvious other advantages: genetics, for instance, and operations research, the theory of games, the Dirac transmitter — it's quite an arsenal, and of course there's a good deal of prediction involved in all those things."

"I see that," Jo said. He shifted in his chair, formulating all he wanted to say. He changed his mind about the cigarette and helped himself to one. "But these things don't add up to infallibility — and that's a qualitative difference, Kras. Take this affair of the Black Horse armada. The moment the armada appeared, we'll assume, Earth heard about it by Dirac, and started to assemble a counter-armada. But it takes *finite time* to bring together a concentration of ships and men, even if your message system is instantaneous.

"The Service's counter-armada was *already on hand*. It had been building there for so long and with so little fuss that nobody even noticed it concentrating until a day or so before the battle. Then planets in the area began to sit up and take notice, and be uneasy about what was going to break. But not very uneasy; the Service always wins — that's been a statistical fact for centuries. *Centuries*, Kras. Good Lord, it takes almost as long as that, in straight preparation, to pull some of the tricks we've pulled! The Dirac gives us an advantage of ten to twenty-five years in really extreme cases out on the rim of the Galaxy, but no more than that."

He realized that he had been fuming away on the cigarette until the roof of his mouth was scorched, and snubbed it out angrily. "That's a very different thing," he said, "than knowing in a general way how an enemy is likely to behave, or what kind of children the Mendelian laws say a given couple should have. It means that we've some way of readng the future in minute detail. That's in flat contradiction to everything I've been taught about probability, but I have to believe what I see."

Krasna laughed. "That's a very able presentation," he said. He seemed genuinely pleased. "I think you'll remember that you were first impressed into the Service when you began to wonder why the news was always good. Fewer and fewer people wonder about that nowadays; it's become a part of their expected environment." He stood up and ran a hand through his hair. "Now you've carried yourself through the next stage. Congratulations, Jo. You've just been promoted!"

"I have?" Jo said incredulously. "I came in here with the notion that I might get myself fired."

"No. Come around to this side of the desk, Jo, and I'll play you a little history." Krasna unfolded the desktop to expose a small visor screen. Obediently Jo rose and went around the desk to where he could see the blank surface. "I had a standard indoctrination tape sent up to me a week ago, in the expectation that you'd be ready to see it. Watch."

Krasna touched the board. A small dot of light appeared in the center of the screen and went out again. At the same time, there was a small *beep* of sound. Then the tape began to unroll and a picture clarified on the screen.

"As you suspected," Krasna said conversationally, "the Service is infallible. How it got that way is a story that started several centuries back. This tape gives all the dope. You should almost be able to imagine what really happened . . ."

# II

Dana Lje — her father had been a Hollander, her mother born in the Celebes — sat down in the chair which Captain Robin Weinbaum had indicated, crossed her legs, and waited, her blue-black hair shining under the lights.

Weinbaum eyed her quizzically. The conqueror Resident who had given the girl her entirely European name had been paid in kind, for his daughter's beauty had nothing fair and Dutch about it. To the eye of the beholder, Dana Lje seemed a particularly delicate virgin of Bali, despite her western name, clothing and assurance. The combination had already proven piquant for the millions who watched her television column, and Weinbaum found it no less charming at first hand.

"As one of your most recent victims," he said, "I'm not sure that I'm honored, Miss Lje. A few of my wounds are still bleeding. But I am a good deal puzzled as to why you're visiting me now. Aren't you afraid that I'll bite back?"

"I had no intention of attacking you personally, and I don't think I did," the video columnist said seriously. "It was just pretty plain that our intelligence had slipped badly in the Erskine affair. It was my job to say so. Obviously you were going to get hurt, since you're head of the bureau — but there was no malice in it."

"Cold comfort," Weinbaum said dryly. "But thank you, nevertheless."

The Eurasian girl shrugged. "That isn't what I came here about, anyway. Tell me, Captain Weinbaum — have you ever heard of an outfit calling itself Interstellar Information?"

Weinbaum shook his head. "Sounds like a skip-tracing firm. Not an easy business, these days."

"That's just what I thought when I first saw their letter-head," Dana said. "But the letter under it wasn't one that a private-eye outfit would write. Let me read part of it to you."

Her slim fingers burrowed in her inside jacket pocket, and emerged again with a single sheet of paper. It was plain type-writer bond, Weinbaum noted automatically: she had brought only a copy with her, and had left the oringinal of the letter at home. The copy, then, would be incomplete — probably seriously.

"It goes like this: 'Dear Miss Lje: As a syndicated video commentator with a wide audience and heavy responsibilities, you need the best source of information available. We would like you to test our service, free of charge, in the hope of proving to you that it is superior to any other source of news on Earth. Therefore, we offer below several predictions concerning events to come in the Hercules and the so-called "Three Ghosts" areas. If these predictions are fulfilled 100% — no less — we ask that you take us on as your correspondents for those areas, at rates to be agreed upon later. If the predictions are wrong in *any* respect, you need not consider us further.' "

"H'm," Weinbaum said slowly. "They're confident

433

cusses — and that's an odd juxtaposition. The Three Ghosts make up only a little solar system, while the Hercules area could include the entire star-cluster — or maybe even the whole constellation, which is a hell of a lot of sky. This outfit seems to be trying to tell you that it has thousands of field correspondents of its own, maybe as many as the government itself. If so, I'll guarantee that they're bragging."

"That may well be so. But before you make up your mind, let me read you one of the two predictions." The letter rustled in Dana Lje's hand. " 'At 03:16:10, on Year Day, 2090, the Hess-type interstellar liner *Brindisi* will be attacked in the neighborhood on the Three Ghosts system by four——' "

Weinbaum sat bolt upright in his swivel chair. "Let me see that letter!" he said, his voice harsh with repressed alarm.

"In a moment," the girl said, adjusting her skirt composedly. "Evidently I was right in riding my hunch. Let me go on reading: '——by four heavily armed vessels flying the lights of the navy of Hammersmith II. The position of the liner at that time will be at coded coordinates 88-A-theta-88-aleph-D and-per-se-and. It will——' "

"Miss Lje," Weinbaum said, "I'm sorry to interrupt you again, but what you've said already would justify me in jailing you at once, no matter how loudly your sponsors might scream. I don't know about this Interstellar Information outfit, or whether or not you did receive any such letter as the one you pretend to be quoting. But I can tell you that you've shown yourself to be in possession of information that only yours truly and four other men are supposed to know. It's already too late to tell you that everything you say may be held against you; all I can say now is, it's high time you clammed up!"

"I thought so," she said, apparently not disturbed in the least. "Then that liner *is* scheduled to hit those coordinates, and the coded time coordinate corresponds with the predicted Universal Time. Is it also true that the

434

*Brindisi* will be carrying a top-secret communications device?"

"Are you deliberately trying to make me imprison you?" Weinbaum said, gritting his teeth. "Or is this just a stunt, designed to show me that my own bureau is full of leaks?"

"It could turn into that," Dana admitted. "But it hasn't, yet. Robin, I've been as honest with you as I'm able to be. You've had nothing but square deals from me up to now. I wouldn't yellow-screen you, and you know it. If this unknown outfit has this information, it might easily have gotten it from where it hints that it got it: from the field."

"Impossible."

"Why?"

"Because the information in question hasn't even reached my *own* agents in the field yet — it couldn't possibly have leaked as far as Hammersmith II or anywhere else, let alone to the Three Ghosts system! Letters have to be carried on ships, you know that. If I were to send orders by ultrawave to my Three Ghosts agent, he'd have to wait three hundred and twenty-four years to get them. By ship, he can get them in a little over two months. These particular orders have only been under way to him five days. Even if somebody has read them on board the ship that's carrying them, they could not possibly be sent on to the Three Ghosts any faster than they're traveling now."

Dana nodded her dark head. "All right. Then what are we left with but a leak in your headquarters here?"

"What, indeed," Weinbaum said grimly. "You'd better tell me who signed this letter of yours."

"The signature is J. Shelby Stevens."

Weinbaum switched on the intercom. "Margaret, look in the business register for an outfit called Interstellar Information and find out who owns it."

Dana Lje said, "Aren't you interested in the rest of the prediction?"

"You bet I am. Does it tell you the name of this communications device?"

"Yes," Dana said.

"What is it?"

"The Dirac communicator."

Weinbaum groaned and turned on the intercom again. "Margaret, send in Dr. Wald. Tell him to drop everything and gallop. Any luck with the other thing?"

"Yes, sir," the intercom said. "It's a one-man outfit, wholly owned by a J. Shelby Stevens, in Rico City. It was first registered this year."

"Arrest him, on suspicion of espionage."

The door swung open and Dr. Wald came in, all six and a half feet of him. He was extremely blond, and looked awkward, gentle, and not very intelligent.

"Thor, this young lady is our press nemesis, Dana Lje. Dana, Dr. Wald is the inventor of the Dirac communicator, about which you have so damnably much information."

"It's out *already?*" Dr. Wald said, scanning the girl with grave deliberation.

"It is, and lots more — *lots* more. Dana, you're a good girl at heart, and for some reason I trust you, stupid though it is to trust anybody in this job. I should detain you until Year Day, videocasts or no videocasts. Instead, I'm just going to ask you to sit on what you've got, and I'm going to explain why."

"Shoot."

"I've already mentioned how slow communication is between star and star. We have to carry all our letters on ships, just as we did locally before the invention of the telegraph. The overdrive lets us beat the speed of light, but not by much of a margin over really long distances. Do you understand that?"

"Certainly," Dana said. She appeared a bit nettled, and Weinbaum decided to give her the full dose at a more rapid pace. After all, she could be assumed to be better informed than the average layman.

"What we've needed for a long time, then," he said, "is some virtually instantaneous method of getting a message from somewhere to anywhere. Any time lag, no matter how small it seems at first, has a way of becoming major as longer and longer distances are involved. Sooner or later we must have this instantaneous method, or we won't be able to get messages from one system to another fast enough to hold our jurisdiction over outlying regions of space."

"Wait a minute," Dana said. "I'd always understood that ultrawave is faster than light."

"Effectively it is; physically it isn't. You don't understand that?"

She shook her dark head.

"In a nutshell," Weinbaum said, "ultrawave is radiation, and all radiation in free space is limited to the speed of light. The way we hype up ultrawave is to use an old application of waveguide theory, whereby the real transmission of energy is at light speed, but an imaginary thing called phase velocity is going faster. But the gain in speed of transmission isn't large — by ultrawave, for instance, we get a message to Alpha Centauri in one year instead of nearly four. Over long distances, that's not nearly enough extra speed."

"Can't it be speeded further?" she said, frowning.

"No. Think of the ultrawave beam between here and Centaurus III as a caterpillar. The caterpillar himself is moving quite slowly, just at the speed of light. But the pulses which pass along his body are going forward faster than he is — and if you've ever watched a caterpillar, you'll know that that's true. But there's a physical limit to the number of pulses you can travel along that caterpillar, and we've already reached that limit. We've taken phase velocity as far as it will go.

"That's why we need something faster. For a long time our relativity theories discouraged hope of anything faster — even the high phase velocity of a guided wave didn't contradict those theories; it just found a limited, mathematically imaginary loophole in them. But when Thor here began looking into the question of velocity of propagation of a Dirac pulse, he found the answer. The communicator he developed does seem to act over long distances,

437

*any* distance, instantaneously — and it may wind up knocking relativity into a cocked hat."

The girl's face was a study in stunned realization. "I'm not sure I've taken in all the technical angles," she said. "But if I'd had any notion of the political dynamite in this thing——"

"——you'd have kept out of my office," Weinbaum said grimly. "A good thing you didn't. The *Brindisi* is carrying a model of the Dirac communicator out to the periphery for a final test; the ship is supposed to get in touch with me from out there at a given Earth time, which we've calculated very elaborately to account for the residual Lorentz and Milne transformations involved in overdrive flight, and for a lot of other time-phenomena that wouldn't mean anything at all to you.

"If that signal arrives here at the given Earth time, then — aside from the havoc it will create among the theoretical physicists whom we decide to let in on it — we will really have our instant communicator, and can include all of occupied space in the same time-zone. And we'll have a terrific advantage over any lawbreaker who has to resort to ultrawave locally and to letters carried by ships over the long haul."

"Not," Dr. Wald said sourly, "if it's already leaked out."

"It remains to be seen how much of it has leaked," Weinbaum said. "The principle is rather esoteric, Thor, and the name of the thing alone wouldn't mean much even to a trained scientist. I gather that Dana's mysterious informant didn't go into technical details . . . or did he?"

"No," Dana said.

"Tell the truth, Dana. I know that you're suppressing some of that letter."

The girl started slightly. "All right — yes, I am. But nothing technical. There's another part of the prediction that lists the number and class of ships you will send to protect the *Brindisi* — the prediction says they'll be sufficent, by the way — and I'm keeping that to myself, to

438

see whether or not it comes true along with the rest. If it does, I think I've hired myself a correspondent."

"If it does," Weinbaum said, "you've hired yourself a jail-bird. Let's see how much mind-reading J. Whatsit Stevens can do from the sub-cellar of Fort Yaphank." He abruptly ended the conversation and ushered Dana Lje out with controlled politeness.

# III

Weinbaum let himself into Stevens' cell, locking the door behind him and passing the keys out to the guard. He sat down heavily on the nearest stool.

Stevens smiled the weak benevolent smile of the very old, and laid his book aside on the bunk. The book, Weinbaum knew — since his office had cleared it — was only a volume of pleasant, harmless lyrics by a New Dynasty poet named Nims.

"Were our predictions correct, Captain?" Stevens said. His voice was high and musical, rather like that of a boy soprano.

Weinbaum nodded. "You still won't tell us how you did it?"

"But I already have," Stevens protested. "Our intelligence network is the best in the Universe, Captain. It is superior even to your own excellent organization, as events have shown."

"It's results are superior, that I'll grant," Weinbaum said glumly. "If Dana Lje had thrown your letter down her disposal chute, we would have lost the *Brindisi* and our Dirac transmitter both. Incidentally, did your original letter predict accurately the number of ships we would send?"

Stevens nodded pleasantly, his neatly trimmed white beard thrusting forward slightly as he smiled.

"I was afraid so." Weinbaum leaned forward. "Do you have the Dirac transmitter, Stevens?"

439

"Of course, Captain. How else could my correspondents report to me with the efficiency you have observed?"

"Then why don't our receivers pick up the broadcasts of your agents? Dr. Wald says it's inherent in the principle that Dirac 'casts are picked up by *all* instruments tuned to receive them, bar none. And at this stage of the game, there are so few such broadcasts being made that we'd be almost certain to detect any that weren't coming from our own operatives."

"I decline to answer that question, if you'll excuse the impoliteness," Stevens said, his voice quavering slightly. "I am an old man, Captain, and this intelligence agency is my sole source of income. If I told you how we operated, we would no longer have any advantage over your own service, except for the limited freedom from secrecy which we have. I have been assured by competent lawyers that I have every right to operate a private investigation bureau, properly licensed, upon any scale that I may choose; and that I have the right to keep my methods secret, as the so-called 'Intellectual assets' of my firm. If you wish to use our services, well and good. We will provide them, with absolute guarantees on all information we furnish you, for an appropriate fee. But our methods are our own property."

Robin Weinbaum smiled twistedly. "I'm not a naive man, Mr. Stevens," he said. "My sevice is hard on naivete. You know as well as I do that the government can't allow you to operate on a free-lance basis, supplying top-secret information to anyone who can pay the price, or even free of charge to video columnists on a 'Test' basis, even though you arrive at every jot of that information independently of espionage — which I still haven't entirely ruled out, by the way. If you can duplicate this *Brindisi* performance at will, we will have to have your services exclusively. In short, you become a hired civilian arm of my own bureau."

"Quite," Stevens said, returning the smile in a fatherly way. "We anticipated that, of course. However, we have contracts with other goverments to consider: Erskine, in particular. If we work exclusively for Earth, necessarily our price will include compensation for renouncing our other accounts."

"Why should it? Patriotic public servants work for their government at a loss, if they can't work for it any other way."

"I am quite aware of that. I am quite prepared to renounce my other interests. But I do require to be paid."

"How much?" Weinbaum said, suddenly aware that his fists were clenched so tightly that they hurt.

Stevens appeared to consider, nodding his flowery white poll in senile deliberation. "My associates would have to be consulted. Tentatively, however, a sum equal to the present appropriation of your bureau would do, pending further negotiations."

Weinbaum shot to his feet, eyes wide. "You old buccaneer! You know damned well that I can't spend my entire appropriation on a single civilian service! Did it ever occur to you that most of the civilian outfits working for us are on cost-plus contracts, and that our civilian executives are being paid just a credit a year, by their own choice? You're demanding nearly two thousand credits an hour from your own government, and claiming the legal protection that the government affords you at the same time, in order to let those fanatics on Erskine run up a higher bid!"

"The price is not unreasonable," Stevens said. "The service is worth the price."

"That's where you're wrong! We have the discoverer of the machine working for us. For less than half the sum you're asking, we can find the application of the device that you're trading on — of that you can be damned sure."

"A dangerous gamble, Captain."

"Perhaps. We'll soon see!" Weinbaum glared at the placid face. "I'm forced to tell you that you're a fee man, Mr. Stevens. We've been unable to show that you came by your information by any illegal method. You had classified documents, and it's your privilege as a citizen to make guesses, no matter how educated.

"But we'll catch up with you sooner or later. Had you been reasonable, you might have found yourself in a very good position with us, your income as assured as any political income can be, and your person respected to the hilt. Now, however, you're subject to censorship — you have no idea how humiliating that can be, but I'm going to see to it that you find out. There'll be no more newsbeats for Dana Lje, or for anyone else. I want to see every word of copy that you file with any client outside the bureau. Every word that is of use to me will be used, and you'll be paid the statutory one cent a word for it — the same rate that the FBI pays for anonymous gossip. Everything I don't find useful will be killed without clearance. Eventually we'll have the modification of the Dirac that you're using, and when that happens, you'll be so flat broke that a pancake with a hare lip could spit right over you."

Weinbaum paused for a moment, astonished at his own fury.

Stevens' clarinetlike voice began to sound in the windowless cavity. "Captain, I have no doubt that you can do this to me, at least incompletely. But it will prove fruitless. I will give you a prediction, at no charge. It is guaranteed, as are all our predictions. It is this: *You will never find that modification.* Eventually, I will give it to you, on my own terms, but you will never find it for yourself, nor will you force it out of me. In the meantime, not a word of copy will be filed with you; for, despite the fact that you are an arm of the government, I can well afford to wait you out."

"Bluster," Weinbaum said.

"Fact. Yours is the bluster — loud talk based on nothing more than a hope. I, however, *know* whereof I speak . . . But let us conclude this discussion. It serves no purpose; you will need to see my points made the hard way. Thank you for giving me my freedom. We will talk again under different circumstances on — let me see; ah, yes, on June 9th of the year 2091. That year is, I believe, almost upon us."

Stevens picked up his book again, nodding at Weinbaum, his expression harmless and kindly, his hands showing the marked tremor of *paralysis agitans*. Weinbaum moved helplessly to the door and flagged the turnkey. As the bars closed behind him, Stevens' voice called out: "Oh, yes; and a Happy New Year, Captain."

Weinbaum blasted his way back into his own office, at least twice as mad as the proverbial nest of hornets, and at the same time rather dismally aware of his own probable future. If Stevens' second prediction turned out to be as phenomenally accurate as his first had been Capt. Robin Weinbaum would soon be peddling a natty set of second-hand uniforms.

He glared down at Margaret Soames, his receptionist. She glared right back; she had known him too long to be intimidated. "Anything?" he said.

"Dr. Wald's waiting for you in your office. There are some field reports, and a couple of Diracs on your private tape. Any luck with the old codger?"

"That," he said crushingly, "is Top Secret."

"Poof. That means that nobody still knows the answer but J. Shelby Stevens."

He collapsed suddenly. "You're so right. That's just what it does mean. But we'll bust him wide open sooner or later. We've *got* to."

"You'll do it," Margaret said. "Anything else for me?"

"No. Tip off the clerical staff that there's a half-holiday today, then go take in a stereo or a steak or something yourself. Dr. Wald and I have a few private wires to pull . . . and unless I'm sadly mistaken, a private bottle of aquavit to empty."

"Right," the receptionist said. "Tie one on for me, Chief. I understand that beer is the best chaser for aquavit — I'll have some sent up."

"If you should return after I am suitably squiffed," Weinbaum said, feeling a little better already, "I will kiss you for your thoughtfulness. *That* should keep you at your stereo at least twice through the third feature."

As he went on through the door of his own office, she said demurely behind him, "It certainly should."

As soon as the door closed, however, his mood became

443

abruptly almost as black as before. Despite his comparative youth — he was now only fifty-five — he had been in
the service a long time, and he needed no one to tell him
the possible consequences which might flow from possession by a private citizen of the Dirac communicator. If
there was ever to be a Federation of Man in the Galaxy,
it was within the power of J. Shelby Stevens to ruin it before it had fairly gotten started. And there seemed to be
nothing at all that could be done about it.

"Hello, Thor," he said glumly. "Pass the bottle."

"Hello, Robin. I gather things went badly. Tell me
about it."

Briefly, Weinbaum told him. "And the worst of it," he
finished, "is that Stevens himself predicts that we won't
find the application of the Dirac that he's using, and that
eventually we'll have to buy it at his price. Somehow I believe him — but I can't see how it's possible. If I were to
tell Congress that I was going to spend my entire appropriation for a single civilian service, I'd be out on my ear
within the next three sessions."

"Perhaps that isn't his real price," the scientist suggested. "If he wants to barter, he'd naturally begin with a
demand miles above what he actually wants."

"Sure, sure . . . but frankly, Thor, I'd hate to give the
old reprobate even a single credit if I could get out of it."
Weinbaum sighed. "Well, let's see what's come in from
the field."

Thor Wald moved silently away from Weinbaum's desk
while the officer unfolded it and set up the Dirac screen.
Stacked neatly next to the ultraphone — a device Weinbaum had been thinking of, only a few days ago, as permanently outmoded — were the tapes Margaret had
mentioned. He fed the first one into the Driac and turned
the main toggle to the position labeled *Start*.

Immediately the whole screen went pure white and the
audio speakers emitted an almost instantly end-stopped
blare of sound — a *beep* which, as Weinbaum already
knew, made up a continuous spectrum from about 30 cycles per second to well above 18,000 cps. Then both the

light and the noise were gone as if they had never been, and were replaced by the familiar face and voice of Weinbaum's local ops chief in Rio City.

"There's nothing unusual in the way of transmitters in Stevens' office here," the operative said without preamble. "And there isn't any local Interstellar Information staff. except for one stenographer, and she's dumb as they come. About all we could get from her is that Stevens is 'such a sweet old man.' No possibility that she's faking it; she's genuinely stupid, the kind that thinks Betelgeuse is something Indians use to darken their skins. We looked for some sort of list or code table that would give us a line on Stevens' field staff, but that was another dead end. Now we're maintaining a 24-hour Dinwiddie watch on the place from a joint across the street. Orders?"

Weinbaum dictated to the blank stretch of tape which followed: "Margaret, next time you send any Driac tapes in here, cut the damnable *beep* off them first. Tell the boys in Rio City that Stevens had been released, and that I'm proceeding for an Order In Security to tap his ultraphone and his local lines — this is one case where I'm sure we can persuade the court that tapping's necessary. Also — and be damned sure you code this — tell them to proceed with the tap immediately and to maintain it regardless of whether or not the court okays it. I'll thumbprint a Full Responsibility Confession for them. We can't afford to play patty-cake with Stevens — the potential is just too damned big. And oh, yes, Margaret, send the message by carrier, and send out general orders to everybody concerned not to use the Dirac again except when distance and time rule every other medium out. Stevens has already admitted that he can receive Dirac 'casts."

He put down the mike and stared morosely for a moment at the beautiful Eridanean scrollwood of his desktop. Wald coughed inquiringly and retrieved the aquavit.

"Excuse me, Robin," he said, "but I should think that would work both ways."

"So should I. And yet the fact is that we've never picked up so much as a whisper from either Stevens or his agents. I can't think of any way that could be pulled, but evidently it can."

"Well, let's rethink the problem, and see what we get," Wald said. "I didn't want to say so in front of the young lady, for obvious reasons — I mean Miss Lje, of course, not Margaret — but the truth is that the Dirac is essentially a simple mechanism in principle. I seriously doubt that there's any way to transmit a message from it which can't be detected — and an examination of the theory with that proviso in mind might give us something new."

"What proviso?" Weinbaum said. Thor Wald left him behind rather often these days.

"Why, that a Dirac transmission doesn't *necessarily* go to all communicators capable of receiving it. If that's true, then the reasons why it is true should emerge from the theory."

"I see. Okay, proceed on that line. I've been looking at Stevens' dossier while you were talking, and it's an absolute desert. Prior to the opening of the office in Rio City, there's no dope whatever on J. Shelby Stevens. The man as good as rubbed my nose in the fact that he's using a pseud when I first talked to him. I asked him what the 'J' in his name stood for, and he said, 'Oh, let's make it Jerome.' But who the man behind the pseud *is*——"

"Is it possible that he's using his own initials?"

"No," Weinbaum said. "Only the dumbest ever do that, or transpose syllables, or retain any connection at all with their real names. Those are the people who are in serious emotional trouble, people who drive themselves into anonymity, but leave clues strewn all around the landscape — those clues are really a cry for help, for discovery. Of course we're working on that angle — we can't neglect anything — but J. Shelby Stevens isn't that kind of case, I'm sure." Weinbaum stood up abruptly. "Okay, Thor — what's first on your technical program?"

"Well . . . I suppose we'll have to start with checking the frequencies we use. We're going on Dirac's assumption — and it works very well, and always has — that a positron in motion through a crystal lattice is accompanied by de

Broglie waves which are transforms of the waves of an electron in motion somewhere else in the Universe. Thus if we control the frequency and path of the positron, we control the placement of the electron — we cause it to appear, so to speak, in the circuits of a communicator somewhere else. After that, reception is just a matter of amplifying the bursts and reading the signal."

Wald scowled and shook his blond head. "If Stevens is getting out messages which we don't pick up, my first assumption would be that he's worked out a fine-tuning circuit that's more delicate than ours, and is more or less sneaking his messages under ours. The only way that could be done, as far as I can see at the moment, is by something really fantastic in the way of exact frequency control of his positron-gun. If so, the logical step for us is to go back to the beginning of our tests and re-run our diffractions to see if we can refine our measurements of position frequencies."

The scientist looked so inexpressibly gloomy as he offered this conclusion that a pall of hopelessness settled over Weinbaum in sheer sympathy. "You don't look as if you expected that to uncover anything new."

"I don't. You see, Robin, things are different in physics now than they used to be in the Twentieth Century. In those days, it was always presupposed that physics was limitless — the classic statement was made by Weyl, who said that 'It is the nature of a real thing to be inexhaustible in content.' We know now that that's not so, except in a remote, associational sort of way. Nowadays, physics is a defined and self-limited science; its scope is still prodigious, but we can no longer think of it as endless.

"This is better established in particle physics than in any other branch of the science. Half of the trouble physicists of the last century had with Euclidean geometry — and hence the reason why they evolved so many recomplicated theories of relativity — is that it's a geometry of lines and thus can be subdivided infinitely. When Cantor proved that there really is an infinity, at least math-

447

ematically speaking, that seemed to clinch the case for the possibility of a really infinite physical universe, too."

Wald's eyes grew vague, and he paused to gulp down a slug of the licorice-flavored aquavit which would have made Weinbaum's every hair stand on end.

"I remember," Wald said, "the man who taught me theory of sets at Princeton, many years ago. He used to say: 'Cantor teaches us that there are many kinds of infinites'. *There* was a crazy old man!"

Weinbaum rescued the bottle hastily. "So go on, Thor."

"Oh." Wald blinked. "Yes. Well, what we know now is that the geometry which applies to ultimate particles, like the positron, isn't Euclidean at all. It's Pythagorean — a geometry of points, not lines. Once you've measured one of those points, and it doesn't matter what kind of quantity you're measuring, you're down as far as you can go. At that point, the Universe becomes discontinuous, and no further refinement is possible.

"And I'd say that our positron-frequency measurements have already gotten that far down. There isn't another element in the Universe denser than plutonium, yet we get the same frequency-values by diffraction through plutonium crystals that we get through osmium crystals — there's not the slightest difference. If J. Shelby Stevens is operating in terms of fractions of those values, then he's doing what an organist would call 'playing in the cracks' — which is certainly something you can *think* about doing, but something that's in actuality impossible to do. *Hoop.*"

"Hoop?" Weinbaum said.

"Sorry. A hiccup only."

"Oh. Well, maybe Stevens has rebuilt the organ?"

"If he has rebuilt the metrical frame of the Universe to accommodate a private skip-tracing firm," Wald said firmly, "I for one see no reason why we can't counter-check him — *hoop* — by declaring the whole cosmos null and void."

"All right, all right," Weinbaum said, grinning. "I didn't mean to push your anology right over the edge — I was just asking. But let's get to work on it anyhow. We can't just sit here and let Stevens get away with it. If this frequency angle turns out to be as hopeless as it seems, we'll try something else."

Wald eyed the aquavit bottle owlishly. "It's a very pretty problem," he said. "Have I ever sung you the song we have in Sweden called 'Nat-og-Dag?' "

*"Hoop,"* Weinbaum said, to his own surprise, in a high falsetto.

"Excuse me. No. Let's hear it."

The computer occupied an entire floor of the Security building, its seemingly identical banks laid out side by side on the floor along an advanced pathological state of Peano's "space-filling curve." At the current business end of the line was a master control board with a large television screen at its center, at which Dr. Wald was stationed, with Weinbaum looking, silently but anxiously, over his shoulder.

The screen itself showed a pattern which, except that it was drawn in green light against a dark gray background, strongly resembled the grain in a piece of highly polished mahogany. Photographs of similar patterns were stacked on a small table to Dr. Wald's right; several had spilled over onto the floor.

"Well, there it is," Wald sighed at length. "And I won't struggle to keep myself from saying 'I told you so.' What you've had me do here, Robin, is to reconfirm about half the basic postulates of particle physics — which is why it took so long, even though it was the first project we started." He snapped off the screen. "There are no cracks for J. Shelby to play in. That's definite."

"If you'd said 'That's flat,' you would have made a joke," Weinbaum said sourly. "Look . . . isn't there still a chance of error. If not on your part, Thor, then in the computer? After all, it's set up to work only with the unit charges of modern physics; mightn't we have to disconnect the banks that contain that bias before the machine will follow the fractional-charge instructions we give it?"

"Disconnect, he says," Wald groaned, mopping his brow reflectively. "The bias exists everywhere in the machine, my friend, because it functions everywhere on those same unit charges. It wasn't a matter of subtracting banks; we had to add one with a bias all of its own, to counter-correct the corrections the computer would otherwise apply to the instructions. The technicians thought I was crazy. Now, five months later, I've proved it."

Weinbaum grinned in spite of himself. "What about the other projects?"

"All done — some time back, as a matter of fact. The staff and I checked every single Dirac tape we've received since you released J. Shelby from Yaphank, for any sign of intermodulation, marginal signals, or anything else of the kind. There's nothing, Robin, absolutely nothing. That's our net result, all around."

"Which leaves us just where we started," Weinbaum said. "All the monitoring projects came to the same dead end; I strongly suspect that Stevens has not risked any further calls from his home office to his field staff, even though he seemed confident that we'd never intercept such calls — as we haven't. Even our local wiretapping hasn't turned up anything but calls made by Stevens' secretary, making appointments for him with various clients, actual and potential. Any information he's selling these days he's passing on in person — and not in his office, either, because we've got bugs planted all over that and haven't heard a thing."

"That must limit his range of operation enormously," Wald objected.

Weinbaum nodded.

"Without a doubt — but he shows no signs of being bothered by it. He can't have sent any tips to Erskine recently, for instance, because our last tangle with that crew came out very well for us, even though we had to use the Dirac to send the orders to our squadron out there. If he overheard us, he didn't even try to pass the word. Just as he said, he's sweating us out——" Weinbaum paused. "Wait a minute, here comes Margaret. And by the length of her stride, I'd say she's got something particularly nasty on her mind."

"You bet I do," Margaret Soames said vindictively.

"And it'll blow plenty of lids around here, or I miss my guess. The ID squad has finally pinned down J. Shelby Stevens. They did it with the voice-comparator alone."

"How does that work?" Wald said interestedly.

"Blink microphone," Weinbaum said impatiently. "Isolates inflections on single, normally stressed syllables and matches them. Standard ID searching technique, on a case of this kind, but it takes so long that we usually get the quarry by other means before it pays off. Well, don't stand there like a dummy, Margaret. Who is he?"

" 'He,' " Margaret said, "is your sweetheart of the video waves, Miss Dana Lje."

"They're crazy!" Wald said, staring at her.

Weinbaum came slowly out of his first shock of stunned disbelief. "No, Thor," he said firmly. "No, it figures. If a woman is going to go in for disguises, there are always two she can assume outside her own sex: a young boy, and a very old man. And Dana's an actress; that's no news to us."

"But — but why did she do it, Robin?"

"That's what we're going to find out right now. So we wouldn't get the Dirac modification by ourselves, eh? Well, there are other ways of getting answers besides particle physics. Margaret, do you have a pick-up order out for that girl?"

"No," the receptionist said. "This is one chestnut I wanted to see you pull out for yourself. You give me the authority, and I send the order — not before."

"Spiteful child. Send it, then, and glory in my gritted teeth. Come on, Thor — let's put the nutcracker on this chestnut."

As they were leaving the computer floor, Weinbaum stopped suddenly in his tracks and began to mutter in an almost inaudible voice.

Wald said, "What's the matter, Robin?"

"Nothing. I keep being brought up short by those predictions. What's the date?"

"M'm ... June 9th. Why?"

"It's the exact date that 'Stevens' predicted we'd meet

451

again, damn it! Something tells me that this isn't going to be as simple as it looks."

If Dana Lje had any idea of what she was in for — and considering the fact that she was "J. Shelby Stevens" it had to be assumed that she did — the knowledge seemed not to make her at all fearful. She sat as composedly as ever before Weinbaum's desk, smoking her eternal cigarette, and waited, one dimpled knee pointed directly at the bridge of the officer's nose.

"Dana," Weinbaum said, "this time we're going to get all the answers, and we're not going to be gentle about it. Just in case you're not aware of the fact, there are certain laws relating to giving false information to a security officer, under which we could heave you in prison for a minimum of fifteen years. By application of the statutes on using communications to defraud, plus various local laws against transvestism, pseudonymity and so on, we could probably pile up enough additional short sentences to keep you in Yaphank until you really *do* grow a beard. So I'd advise you to open up."

"I have every intention of opening up," Dana said. "I know practically word for word, how this interview is going to proceed, what information I'm going to give you, just when I'm going to give it to you — and what you are going to pay me for it. I knew all that many months ago. So there would be no point in my holding out on you."

"What you're saying, Miss Lje," Thor Wald said in a resigned voice, "is that the future is fixed, and that you can read it, in every essential detail."

"Quite right, Dr. Wald. Both those things are true."

There was a brief silence.

"All right," Weinbaum said grimly. "Talk."

"All right, Captain Weinbaum, pay me," Dana said. calmly.

Weinbaum snorted.

"But I'm quite serious," she said. "You still don't know what I know about the Dirac communicator. I won't be forced to tell it, by threat of prison or by any other threat. You see, I know for a fact that you aren't going to send me

452

to prison, or give me drugs, or do anything else of that kind. I know for a fact, instead, that you are going to pay me — so I'd be very foolish to say a word until you do. After all, it's quite a secret you're buying. Once I tell you what it is, you and the entire service will be able to read the future as I do, and then the information will be valueless to me."

Weinbaum was completely speechless for a moment. Finally he said, "Dana, you have a heart of purest brass, as well as a knee with an invisible gunsight on it. I say that I'm *not* going to give you my appropriation, regardless of what the future may or may not say about it. I'm not going to give it to you because the way my Government — and yours — runs things makes such a price impossible. Or is that really your price?"

"It's my real price . . . but it's also an alternative. Call it my second choice. My first choice, which means the price I'd settle for, comes in two parts: (a), to be taken into your service as a responsible officer; and, (b), to be married to Capt. Robin Weinbaum."

Weinbaum sailed up out of his chair. He felt as though copper-coloured flames a foot long were shooting out of each of his ears.

"Of all the——" he began. There his voice failed completely.

From behind him, where Wald was standing, came something like a large, Scandinavian-model guffaw being choked into insensibility.

Dana herself seemed to be smiling a little.

"You see," she said, "I don't point my best and most accurate knee at every man I meet."

Weinbaum sat down again, slowly and carefully. "Walk, do not run, to nearest exit," he said. "Women and childlike security officers first. Miss Lje, are you trying to sell me the notion that you went through this elaborate hanky-panky — beard and all — out of a burning passion for my dumpy and underpaid person?"

"Not entirely," Dana Lje said. "I want to be in the bureau, too, as I said. Let me confront you, though, Captain, with a fact of life that doesn't seem to have occurred to you at all. Do you accept as a fact that I can read the future in detail, and that that, to be possible at all, means that the future is fixed?"

"Since Thor seems able to accept it, I suppose I can too — provisionally."

"There's nothing provisional about it," Dana said firmly. "Now, when I first came upon this — uh, this gimmick — quite a while back, one of the first things that I found out was that I was going to go through the 'J. Shelby Stevens' masquerade, force myself onto the staff of the bureau, and marry you, Robin. At the time, I was both astonished and completely rebellious. I did not want to be on the bureau staff; I liked my free-lance life as a video commentator. I did not want to marry you, though I wouldn't have been averse to living with you for a while — say a month or so. And above all, the masquerade struck me as ridiculous.

"But the facts kept staring me in the face. I *was* going to do all those things. There no alternatives, no fanciful 'branches of time,' no decision-points that might be altered to make the future change. My future, like yours, Dr. Wald's, and everyone else's, was fixed. It didn't matter a snap whether or not I had a decent motive for what I was going to do; I was going to do it anyhow. Cause and effect, as I could see for myself, just don't exist. One event follows another because events are just as indestructible in space-time as matter and energy are.

"It was the bitterest of all pills. It will take me many years to swallow it completely, and you too. Dr. Wald will come around a little sooner, I think. At any rate, once I was intellectually convinced that all this was so, I had to protect my own sanity. I knew that I couldn't alter what I was going to do, but the least I could do to protect myself was to supply myself with motives. Or, in other words, just plain rationalizations. That much, it seems, we're free to do; the consciousness of the observer is just along for the ride through time, and can't alter events — but it can comment, explain, invent. That's fortunate, for none of us could stand going through motions which were truly free of what we think of as personal significances.

"So I supplied myself with the obvious motives. Since I was going to be married to you and couldn't get out of it, I set out to convince myself that I loved you. Now I do. Since I was going to join the bureau staff, I thought over all the advantages that it might have over video commentating, and found that they made a respectable list. Those are my motives.

"But I had no such motives at the beginning. Actually, there are never motives behind actions. All actions are fixed. What we called motives evidently are rationalizations by the helpless observing consciousness, which is intelligent enough to smell an event coming — and, since it cannot avert the event, instead cooks up reasons for wanting it to happen."

"Wow," Dr. Wald said, inelegantly but with considerable force.

"Either 'wow' or 'balderdash' seems to be called for — I can't quite decide which," Weinbaum agreed. "We know that Dana is an actress, Thor, so let's not fall off the apple tree quite yet. Dana, I've been saving the *really* hard question for the last. That question is: *How?* How did you arrive at this modification of the Dirac transmitter? Remember, we know your background, where we didn't know that of 'J. Shelby Stevens.' You're not a scientist. There were some fairly high-powered intellects among your distant relatives, but that's as close as you come."

"I'm going to give you several answers to that question," Dana Lje said. "Pick the one you like best. They're all true, but they tend to contradict each other here and there.

"To begin with, you're right about my relatives, of course. If you'll check your dossier again, though, you'll discover that those so-called 'distant' relatives were the last surviving members of my family besides myself. When they died, second and fourth and ninth cousins though they were, their estates reverted to me, and among their effects I found a sketch of a possible instantaneous communicator based on de Broglie-wave inversion. The material was in very rough form, and mostly beyond my comprehension, because I am, as you say, no scientist myself. But I was interested; I could see, dimly, what such a thing might be worth — and not only in money.

"My interest was fanned by two coincidences — the kind of coincidences that cause-and-effect just can't allow, but which seem to happen all the same in the world of unchangeable events. For most of my adult life, I've been in communications industries of one kind or another, mostly branches of video. I had communication equipment around me constantly, and I had coffee and doughnuts with communications engineers every day. First I picked up the jargon; then, some of the procedures; and eventually, a little real knowledge. Some of the things I learned can't be gotten any other way. Some other things are ordinarily available only to highly educated people like Dr. Wald here, and came to me by accident, in horseplay, between kisses, and a hundred other ways — all natural to the environment of a video network."

Weinbaum found, to his own astonishment, that the "between kisses" clause did not sit very well in his chest. He said, with unintentional brusqueness: "What's the other coincidence?"

"A leak in your own staff."

"Dana, you ought to have that set to music."

"Suit yourself."

"I can't suit myself," Weinbaum said petulantly. "I work for the Government. Was this leak direct to you?"

"Not at first. That was why I kept insisting to you in person that there might be such a leak, and why I finally began to hint about it in public, on my program. I was hoping that you'd be able to seal it up inside the bureau before my first rather tenuous contact with it got lost. When I didn't succeed in provoking you into protecting yourself, I took the risk of making direct contact with the leak myself — and the first piece of secret information that came to me through it was the final point I needed to put my Dirac communicator together. When it was all

456

assembled, it did more than just communicate. It predicted. And I can tell you why."

Weinbaum said thoughtfully, "I don't find this very hard to accept, so far. Pruned of the philosophy, it even makes some sense of the 'J. Shelby Stevens' affair. I assume that by letting the old gentleman become known as somebody who knew more about the Dirac transmitter than I did, and who wasn't adverse to negotiating with anybody who had money, you kept the leak working through you — rather than transmitting data directly to unfriendly governments."

"It did work out that way," Dana said. "But that wasn't the genesis or the purpose of the Stevens masquerade. I've already given you the whole explanation of how that came about."

"Well, you'd better name me that leak, before the man gets away."

"When the price is paid, not before. It's too late to prevent a getaway, anyhow. In the meantime, Robin, I want to go on and tell you the other answer to your question about how I was able to find this particular Dirac secret, and you didn't. What answers I've given you up to now have been cause-and-effect answers, with which we're all more comfortable. But I want to impress on you that all apparent cause-and-effect relationships are accidents. There is no such thing as a cause, and no such thing as an effect. I found the secret because I found it; that event was fixed; that certain circumstances seem to explain why I found it, in the old cause-and-effect terms, is irrelevant. Similarly, with all your superior equipment and brains, you didn't find it for one reason, and one reason alone: because you didn't find it. The history of the future says you didn't."

"I pays my money and I takes no choice, eh?" Weinbaum said ruefully.

"I'm afraid so — and I don't like it any better than you do."

"Thor, what's your opinion of all this?"

"It's just faintly flabbergasting," Wald said soberly.

"However, it hangs together. The deterministic Universe which Miss Lje paints was a common feature of the old relativity theories, and as sheer speculation has an even longer history. I would say that in the long run, how much credence we place in the story as a whole will rest upon her method of, as she calls it, reading the future. If it is demonstrable beyond any doubt, then the rest becomes perfectly credible — philosophy and all. If it doesn't, then what remains is an admirable job of acting, plus some metaphysics which, while self-consistent, are not original with Miss Lje."

"That sums up the case as well as if I'd coached you, Dr. Wald," Dana said. "I'd like to point out one more thing. If I can read the future, then 'J. Shelby Stevens' never had any need for a staff of field operatives, and he never needed to send a single Dirac message which you might intercept. All he needed to do was to make predictions from his readings, which he knew to be infallible; no private espionage network had to be involved."

"I see that," Weinbaum said dryly. "All right, Dana, let's put the proposition this way: *I do not believe you.* Much of what you say is probably true, but in totality I believe it to be false. On the other hand, if you're telling the whole truth, you certainly deserve a place on the bureau staff — it would be dangerous as hell *not* to have you with us — and the marriage is a more or less minor matter, except to you and me. You can have that with no strings attached; I don't want to be bought, any more than you would.

"So: if you will tell me where the leak is, we will consider that part of the question closed. I make that condition not as a price, but because I don't want to get myself engaged to somebody who might be shot as a spy within a month."

"Fair enough," Dana said. "Robin, your leak is Margaret Soames. She is an Erskine operative, and nobody's bubble-brain. She's a highly trained technician."

"Well, I'll be damned," Weinbaum said in astonishment. "Then she's already flown the coop — she was the one who first told me we'd identified you. She must have taken on that job in order to hold up delivery long enough to stage an exit."

"That's right. But you'll catch her, day after tomorrow. And you are now a hooked fish, Robin."

There was another suppressed burble from Thor Wald.

"I accept the fate happily," Weinbaum said, eyeing the gun-sight knee. "Now, if you will tell me how you work your swami trick, and it backs up everything you've said to the letter, as you claim, I'll see to it that you're also taken into the bureau and that all charges against you are quashed. Otherwise, I'll probably have to kiss the bride between the bars of a cell."

Dana smiled. "The secret is very simple. It's in the beep."

Weinbaum's jaw dropped. "The beep? The Dirac noise?"

"That's right. You didn't find it out because you considered the beep to be just a nuisance, and ordered Miss Soames to cut it off all tapes before sending them in to you. Miss Soames, who had some inkling of what the beep meant, was more than happy to do so, leaving the reading of the beep exclusively to 'J. Shelby Stevens' — who she thought was going to take on Erskine as a client."

"Explain," Thor Wald said, looking intense.

"Just as you assumed, every Dirac message that is sent is picked up by every receiver that is capable of detecting it. *Every* receiver — including the first one ever built, which is yours, Dr. Wald, through the hundreds of thousands of them which will exist throughout the Galaxy in the Twenty-Fourth Century, to the untold millions which will exist in the Thirtieth Century, and so on. The Dirac beep is the simultaneous reception of *every one of the Dirac messages which have ever been sent, or ever will be sent*. Incidentally, the cardinal number of the total of those messages is a relatively small and of course finite number; it's far below really large finite numbers such as the number of electrons in the Universe, even when you break each and every message down into individual 'bits' and count those."

"Of course," Dr. Wald said softly. "Of course! But

Miss Lje . . . how do you tune for an individual message? We tried fractional positron frequencies, and got nowhere."

"I didn't even know fractional positron frequencies existed," Dana confessed. "No, it's simple — so simple that a lucky layman like me could arrive at it. You tune individual messages out of the beep by time-lag, nothing more. All the messages arrive at the same instant, in the smallest fraction of time that exists, something called a 'chronon.' "

"Yes," Wald said. "The time it takes one electron to move from one quantum-level to another. That's the Pythagorean point of time-measurement."

"Thank you. Obviously no gross physical receiver can respond to a message that brief, or at least that's what I thought at first. But because there are relay and switching delays, various forms of feedback and so on in the apparatus itself, the beep arrives at the output end as a complex pulse which has been 'splattered' along the time axis for a full second or more. That's an effect which you can exaggerate by recording the 'splattered' beep on a high-speed tape, the same way you would record any event that you wanted to study in slow motion. Then you tune up the various failure-points in your receiver, to exaggerate one failure, minimize all the others, and use noise-suppressing techniques to cut out the background."

Thor Wald frowned. "You'd still have a considerable garble when you were through. You'd have to sample the messages——"

"Which is just what I did; Robin's little lecture to me about the ultrawave gave me that hint. I set myself to find out how the ultrawave channel carries so many messages at once, and I discovered that you people sample the incoming pulses every thousandth of a second and pass on one pip only when the wave deviates in a certain way from the mean. I didn't really believe it would work on the Dirac beep, but it turned out just as well: 90% as intelligible as the original transmission after it came through the smearing device. I'd already got enough from

460

the beep to put my plan in motion, of course — but now every voice message in it was available, and crystal-clear: If you select three pips every thousandth of a second, you can even pick up an intelligible transmission of music — a little razzy, but good enough to identify the instruments that are playing — and that's a very close test of any communications device."

"There's a question of detail here that doesn't quite follow," said Weinbaum, for whom the technical talk was becoming a little too thick to fight through. "Dana, you say that you knew the course this conversation was going to take — yet it isn't being Dirac-recorded, nor can I see any reason why any summary of it would be sent out on the Dirac afterwards."

"That's true, Robin. However, when I leave here, I will make such a transcast myself, on my own Dirac. Obviously I will — because I've *already* picked it up, from the beep."

"In other words, you're going to call yourself up — months ago."

"That's it," Dana said. "It's not as useful a technique as you might think at first, because it's dangerous to make such broadcasts while a situation is still developing. You can safely 'phone back' details only after the given situation has gone to completion, as a chemist might put it. Once you know, however, that when you use the Dirac you're dealing with time, you can coax some very strange things out of the instrument."

She paused and smiled. "I have heard," she said conversationally, "the voice of the President of our Galaxy, in 3480, announcing the federation of the Milky Way and the Magellanic Clouds. I've heard the commander of a worldline cruiser, traveling from 8873 to 8704 along the world-line of the planet Hathshepa, which circles a star on the rim of NGC 4725, calling for help across eleven million light-years — but what kind of help he was calling for, or will be calling for, is beyond my comprehension. And many other things. When you check on me, you'll hear these things too — and you'll wonder what many of them mean.

"And you'll listen to them even more closely than I did, in the hope of finding out whether or not anyone was able to understand in time to help."

Weinbaum and Wald looked dazed.

Her voice became a little more somber. "Most of the voices in the Dirac beep are like that — they're cries for help, which you can overhear decades or centuries before the senders get into trouble. You'll feel obligated to answer every one, to try to supply the help that's needed. And you'll listen to the succeeding messages and say: 'Did we — will we get there in time? Did we understand in time?'

"And in most cases you won't be sure. You'll know the future, but not what most of it means. The farther into the future you travel with the machine, the more incomprehensible the messages become, and so you're reduced to telling yourself that time will, after all, have to pass by at its own pace, before enough of the surrounding events can emerge to make those remote messages clear.

"The long run effect, as far as I can think it through, is not going to be that of omniscience — of our consciousness being extracted entirely from the time-stream and allowed to view its whole sweep from one side. Instead, the Dirac in effect simply slides the bead of consciousness forward from the present a certain distance. Whether it's five hundred or five thousand years still remains to be seen. At that point the law of diminishing returns sets in — or the noise-factor begins to overbalance the information, take your choice — and the observer is reduced to traveling in time at the same old speed. He's just a bit ahead of himself."

"You've thought a great deal about this," Wald said slowly. "I dislike to think of what might have happened had some less conscientious person stumbled on the beep."

"That wasn't in the cards," Dana said.

In the ensuing quiet, Weinbaum felt a faint, irrational sense of let-down, of something which had promised more than had been delivered — rather like the taste of fresh bread as compared to its smell, or the discovery that Thor

Wald's Swedish "folk-song" *Nat-og-Dag* was only Cole Porter's *Night and Day* in another language. He recognized the feeling: it was the usual emotion of the hunter when the hunt is over, the born detective's professional version of the *post coitum triste.* After looking at the smiling, supple Dana Lje a moment more, however, he was almost content.

"There's one more thing," he said. "I don't want to be insufferably skeptical about this — but I want to see it work. Thor, can we set up a sampling and smearing device such as Dana describes and run a test?"

"In fifteen minutes," Dr. Wald said. "We have most of the unit in already assembled form on our big ultrawave receiver, and it shouldn't take any effort to add a high-speed tape unit to it. I'll do it right now."

He went out. Weinbaum and Dana looked at each other for a moment, rather like strange cats. Then the security officer got up, with what he knew to be an air of somewhat grim determination, and seized his fiancee's hands, anticipating a struggle.

The first kiss was, by intention at least, mostly *pro forma.* But by the time Wald padded back into the office, the letter had been pretty thoroughly superseded by the spirit.

The scientist harrumphed and set his burden on the desk. "This is all there is to it," he said, "but I had to hunt all through the library to find a Dirac record with a beep still on it. Just a moment more while I make connections . . ."

Weinbaum used the time to bring his mind back to the matter at hand, although not quite completely. Then two tape spindles began to whir like so many bees, and the end-stopped sound of the Dirac beep filled the room. Wald stopped the apparatus, reset, and started the smearing tape very slowly in the opposite direction.

A distant babble of voices came from the speaker. As Weinbaum leaned forward tensely, one voice said clearly and loudly above the rest:

"Hello, Earth bureau. Lt. T. L. Matthews at Hercules Station NGC 6341, transmission date 13-22-2091. We have the last point on the orbit-curve of your dope-runners plotted, and the curve itself points to a small system about 25 light-years from the base here; the place hasn't even got a name on our charts. Scouts show the home planet at least twice as heavily fortified as we anticipated, so we'll need another cruiser. We have a 'can-do' from you in the beep for us, but we're waiting as ordered to get it in the present. NGC 6341 Matthews out."

After the first instant of stunned amazement — for no amount of intellectual willingness to accept could have prepared him for the overwhelming fact itself — Weinbaum had grabbed a pencil and begun to write at top speed. As the voice signed out he threw the pencil down and looked excitedly at Dr. Wald.

"Seven months ahead," he said, aware that he was grinning like an idiot. "Thor, you know the trouble we've had with that needle in the Hercules haystack! This orbit-curve trick must be something Matthews has yet to dream up — at least he hasn't come to me with it yet, and there's nothing in the situation as it stands now that would indicate a closing-time of six months for the case. The computers said it would take three more years."

"It's new data," Dr. Wald agreed solemnly.

"Well, don't stop there, in God's name! Let's hear some more!"

Dr. Wald went through the ritual, much faster this time. The speaker said:

"Nausentampen. Eddettompic. Berobsilom. Aimkaksetchoc. Sanbetogmow. Datdectamset. Domatrosmin. Out."

"My word," Wald said, "what's all that?"

"That's what I was talking about," Dana Lje said. "At least half of what you get from the beep is just as incomprehensible. I suppose it's whatever has happened to the English language, thousands of years from now."

"No, it isn't," Weinbaum said. He had resumed writing, and was still at it, despite the comparative briefness of the transmission. "Not this sample, anyhow. That, ladies and gentlemen, is code — no language consists exclusively of four-syllable words, of that you can be sure. What's more, it's a version of our code. I can't break it down very far — it takes a full-time expert to read this stuff — but I get the date and some of the sense. It's March 12, 3022, and there's some kind of a mass evacuation taking place. The message seems to be a routing order."

"But why will we be using code?" Dr. Wald wanted to know. "It implies that we think somebody might overhear us — somebody else with a Dirac. That could be very messy."

"It could indeed," Weinbaum said. "But we'll find out, I imagine. Give her another spin, Thor."

"Shall I try for a picture this time?"

Weinbaum nodded. A moment later, he was looking squarely into the green-skinned face of something that looked like an animated traffic signal with a helmet on it. Though the creature had no mouth, the Dirac speaker was saying quite clearly, "Hello, Chief. This is Thammos NGC 2287, transmission date Gor 60, 302 by my calendar, July 2, 2973 by yours. This is a lousy little planet. Everything stinks of oxygen, just like Earth. But the natives accept us and that's the important thing. We've got your genius safely born. Detailed report coming later by paw. NGC 2287 Thammos out."

"I wish I knew my New General Catalogue better," Weinbaum said. "Isn't that M 41 in Canis Major, the one with the red star in the middle? And we'll be using non-humanoids there! What *was* that creature, anyhow? Never mind, spin her again."

Dr. Wald spun her again. Weinbaum, already feeling a little dizzy, had given up taking notes. That could come later. All that could come later. Now he wanted only scenes and voices, more and more scenes and voices from the future. They were better than aquavit, even with a beer chaser.

# IV

The indoctrination tape ended, and Krasna touched a button. The Dirac screen darkened, and folded silently back into the desk.

"They didn't see their way through to us, not by a long shot," he said. "They didn't see, for instance, that when one section of the government becomes nearly all-knowing — no matter how small it was to begin with — it necessarily becomes all of the government that there is. Thus the bureau turned into the Service and pushed everyone else out.

"On the other hand, those people did come to be afraid that a government with an all-knowing arm might become a rigid dictatorship. That couldn't happen and didn't happen, because the more you know, the wider your field of possible operation becomes and the more fluid and dynamic a society you need. How could a rigid society expand to other star-systems, let alone other galaxies? It couldn't be done."

"I should think it could," Jo said slowly. "After all, if you know in advance what everybody is going to do——"

"But we don't, Jo. That's just a popular fiction — or, if you like, a red herring. Not all of the business of the cosmos is carried on over the Dirac, after all. The only events we can ever overhear are those which transmitted as a message. Do you order your lunch over the Dirac? Of course you don't. Up to now, you've never said a word over the Dirac in your life.

"And there's much more to it than that. All dictatorships are based on the proposition that government can somehow control a man's thoughts. We know now that the consciousness of the observer is the only free thing in the Universe. Wouldn't we look foolish trying to control that, when our entire physics shows that it's impossible to do so? That's why the Service is in no sense a thought police. We're interested only in acts. We're an Event Police."

"But why," Jo said. "If all history is fixed, why do we bother with these boy-meets-girl assignments, for instance? The meetings will happen anyhow."

"Of course they will," Krasna agreed immediately. "But look, Jo. Our interests as a government depend upon the future. We operate *as if* the future is as real as the past, and so far we haven't been disappointed: the Service is 100 percent successful. But that very success isn't without its warnings. What would happen if we *stopped* supervising events? We don't know, and we don't dare take the chance. Despite the evidence that the future is fixed, we have to take on the role of the caretaker of inevitability. We believe that nothing can possibly go wrong . . . but we have to act on the philosophy that history helps only those who help themselves.

"That's why we safeguard huge numbers of courtships right through to contract, and even beyond it. We have to see to it that *every single person who is mentioned in any Dirac 'cast gets born.* Our obligation as Event Police is to make the events of the future possible, because those events are crucial to our society — even the smallest of them. It's an enormous task, believe me, and it gets bigger every day. Apparently it always will."

"Always?" Jo said. "What about the public? Isn't it going to smell this out sooner or later? The evidence is piling up at a terrific rate."

"Yes and no," Krasna said. "Lots of people are smelling it out right now, just as you did. But the number of new people we need in the Service grows faster — it's always ahead of the number of laymen who follow the clues to the truth."

Jo took a deep breath. "You take all this as if it were as commonplace as boiling an egg, Kras," he said. "Don't you ever wonder about some of the things you can get from the beep? That 'cast Dana Lje picked up from Canes Venatici, for instance, the one from the ship that was travelling backward in time? How is that possible? What could be the purpose? Is it——"

"*Pace, pace,*" Krasna said. "I don't know, and I don't

care. Neither should you. That event is too far in the future for us to worry about. We can't possibly know its context yet, so there's no sense in trying to understand it. If an Englishman of around 1600 had found out about the American Revolution, he would have thought it a tragedy; an Englishman of 1950 would have a very different view of it. We're in the same spot. The messages we get from the really far future have no contexts yet."

"I think I see," Jo said. "I'll get used to it in time, I suppose, after I use the Dirac for a while. Or does my new rank authorize me to do that?"

"Yes, it does. But, Jo, first I want to pass on to you a rule of Service etiquette that must never be broken. You won't be allowed anywhere near a Dirac mike until you have it burned into your memory beyond any forgetfulness."

"I'm listening, Kras, believe me."

"Good. This is the rule: *The date of a Serviceman's death must never be mentioned in a Dirac 'cast.*"

Jo blinked, feeling a little chilly. The reason behind the rule was decidedly tough-minded, but its ultimate kindness was plain. He said, "I won't forget that. I'll want that protection myself. Many thanks, Kras. What's my new assignment?"

"To begin with," Krasna said, grinning, "as simple a job as I've ever given you, right here on Randolph. Skin out of here and find me that cab-driver — the one who mentioned time-travel to you. He's uncomfortably close to the truth; closer than you were in one category.

"Find him, and bring him to me. The Service is about to take in a new raw recruit!"

Heady stuff, galactic empires, when you identify with the ruling classes. One of the delights of science fiction is the ease with which it changes viewpoints and attitudes. In this section, we are set among the losers.

A word here from Arnold Toynbee comes in appropriately. In his volume *Surviving the Future,* he has this comment on a world state which applies equally to galactic unification: "It is most unlikely, I fear, that it will be established by the will, or even with the acquiescence of the majority of mankind. It seems to me likely to be imposed on the majority by a ruthless, efficient, and fanatical minority, inspired by some ideology or religion." Mack Reynolds has a few words to say on that subject.

The Davidson and Brown offerings are the shortest in the book. Brevity generally makes its point with wit. Avram Davidson, who lives in an exotic part of the world — as does Mack Reynolds — has written a number of amusing stories, often with a Jewish flavour. Fredric Brown was another wit, known to the thriller field for such novels as *The Fabulous Clip Joint,* and to sf readers for his crazy comic novel, *What Mad Universe. Not Yet the End* is the oldest story in this anthology; but it still makes its amusing point.

*When the aliens come, Earth finds itself a mere bar-*
*barian pawn in the game of galactic empire!*

●

# DOWN THE RIVER

## By Mack Reynolds

The space-ship was picked up by Army radar shortly after
it entered the atmosphere over North America. It descended rather slowly and by the time it hovered over
Connecticut a thousand fighter planes were in the air.

Wires sizzled hysterically between captains of State Police and colonels of the National Guard, between Army
generals and cabinet members, between admirals and
White House advisers. But before anything could be decided in the way of attack upon the intruder or defense
against him the space-ship had settled gently into an empty
Connecticut field.

Once it had landed all thought of attack left the minds
of everyone concerned with North American defense. The
craft towered half a mile upward and gave an uncomfortable impression of being able to take on the armed forces
of the United States all by itself, if it so desired, which
seemingly it didn't. As a matter of fact it showed no signs
of life whatsoever for the first few hours of its visit.

The governor arrived about noon, beating the representative from the State Department by fifteen minutes and the delegates from the United Nations by three hours. He hesitated only briefly at the cordon which State Police and National Guardsmen had thrown up about the field and decided that any risk he might be taking would be worth the publicity value of being the first to greet the visitors from space.

Besides, the television and newsreel cameras were already set up and trained upon him. "Honest Harry" Smith knew a good thing when he saw it. He instructed the chauffeur to approach the ship.

As the car came closer, escorted cautiously by two motorcycle troopers and the newsreel and television trucks, the problem arose of just how to make known his Excellency's presence. There seemed to be no indication of a means of entrance to the spectacular craft. It presented a smooth mother-of-pearl effect that was breathtakingly beautiful — but at the same time cold and unapproachable in appearance.

Happily the problem was solved for them as they came within a few yards of the vessel. What seemed a solid part of the craft's side swung inward and a figure stepped lightly to the ground.

Governor Smith's first shocked impression was that it was a man wearing a strange mask and a carnival costume. The alien, otherwise human and even handsome by our standards, had a light green complexion. It tucked the Roman-like toga it wore about its lithe figure and approached the car smilingly. Its English had only a slight touch of accent. Grammatically it was perfect.

"My name is Grannon Tyre Eighteen-Hundred and Fifty-two K," the alien said. "I assume that you are an official of this — er — nation. The United States of North America, is it not?"

The governor was taken aback. He'd been rehearsing inwardly a pantomime of welcome — with the television and newsreel men in mind. He had pictured himself as holding up his right arm in what he conceived to be the universal gesture of peace, of smiling broadly and often and, in general, making it known that the aliens were welcome to the earth and to the United States in general and to the State of Connecticut in particular. He hadn't expected the visitors to speak English.

However he had been called upon to speak off the cuff too often not to be able to rise to the occasion.

"Welcome to Earth," he said with a flourish that he hoped the TV boys got. "This is an historical occasion indeed. Without doubt future generations of your people and mine will look back on this fateful hour and . . ."

Grannon Tyre 1852K smiled again. "I beg your pardon but was my assumption correct? You are an official of the government?"

"Eh? Er —- humph — yes, of course. I am Governor Harry Smith, of Connecticut, this prosperous and happy state in which you have landed. To go on——"

The alien said, "If you don't mind, I have a message from the Graff Marin Sidonn Forty-eight L. The Graff has commanded me to inform you that it is his pleasure that you notify all the nations, races and tribes upon Earth that he will address their representatives exactly one of your Earth months from today. He has an important message to deliver."

The governor gave up trying to hold command of the situation. "Who?" he asked painfully. "What kind of a message?"

Grannon Tyre 1852K still smiled but it was the patient smile you used with a backward or recalcitrant child. His voice was a bit firmer, there was a faint touch of command.

"The Graff requests that you inform all nations of the world to have their representatives gather one month from today to receive his message. Is that clear?"

"Yeah. I guess so. Who——"

"Then that is all for the present. Good day." The green alien turned and strode back to the space-ship. The portal closed behind him silently.

"I'll be double blessed," said Governor Harry Smith a

fraction of a second before the television cameras could cut him off the air.

Never before had there been anything like the following month. It was a period of jubilation and fear, of anticipation and foreboding, of hope and despair. As the delegates from all over Earth gathered to hear the message of the visitor from space tension grew throughout the world.

Scientist and savage, politician and revolutionist, banker and beggar, society matron and street walker, awaited that which they knew would influence the rest of their lives. And each hoped for one thing and feared another.

Newspaper columnists, radio commentators and soap-box speakers dwelt on the possibilities of the message endlessly. Although there were some who viewed with alarm, as a whole it was believed that the aliens would open up a new era for earth.

Scientific secrets beyond the dreams of man were expected to be revealed. Disease was to be wiped out overnight. Man would take his place with this other intelligence to help rule the universe.

Preparations were made for the delegates to meet at Madison Square Garden in New York. It had early been seen that the United Nations buildings would be inadequate. Representatives were coming from races, tribes and countries which had never dreamed of sending delegates to the international conferences so prevalent in the last few decades.

The Graff Marin Sidonn 48L was accompanied to the gathering by Grannon Tyre 1852K and by a score of identically uniformed green complexioned aliens, who could only be taken for guards although they carried no evident weapons either defensive or offensive.

The Graff himself appeared to be an amiable enough gentleman, somewhat older than the other visitors from space. His step was a little slower and his toga more conservative in color than that of Grannon Tyre 1852K, who was evidently his aide.

Although he gave every indication of courtesy, the large number of persons confronting him seemed irritating and the impression was gained that the sooner this was over the more pleased he would be.

President Hanford of the United States opened the meeting with a few well chosen words, summing up the importance of the conference. He then introduced Grannon Tyre 1852K, who was also brief but who threw the first bombshell, although a full half of the audience didn't at first recognize the significance of his words.

"Citizens of Earth," he began, "I introduce to you Marin Sidonn Forty-eight L, Graff of the Solar System by appointment of Modren One, Gabon of Carthis, and, consequently, Gabon of the Solar System including the planet Earth. Since the English language seems to be nearest to a universal one upon this world, your Graff has prepared himself so that he may address you in that tongue. I understand that translating devices have been installed so that representatives of other languages will be able to follow."

He turned to the Graff, held the flat of his right hand against his waist and then extended it toward his chief. The Graff returned the salute and stepped before the microphone.

The delegates arose to their feet to acclaim him and the cheers lasted a full ten minutes, being stilled finally when the alien from space showed a slight annoyance. President Hanford got to his feet, held up his hands and called for order.

The clamor died away and the Graff looked out over his audience. "This is a strange meeting indeed," he began. "For more than four decals, which roughly comes to forty-three of your Earth years, I have been Graff of this Solar System, first under Toren One, and, more recently, under his successor, Modren One, present Gabon of Carthis, which, as has already been pointed out by my assistant, makes him Gabon of the Solar System and of Earth."

Of all those present in the Garden, Larry Kincaid, of Associated Press, was the first to grasp the significance of what was being said. "He's telling us we're property. Shades of Charlie Fort!"

The Graff went on. "In all of this four decals, however, I have not visited Earth but have spent my time on the planet you know as Mars. This, I assure you, has not been because I was not interested in your problems and your welfare as an efficient Graff should be.

"Rather it has been traditional with the Gabons of Carthis not to make themselves known to the inhabitants of their subject planets until these subjects have reached at least an H-Seventeen development. Unfortunately, Earth has reached but an H-Four development."

A low murmur was spreading over the hall. The Graff paused for a moment and then said kindly, "I imagine that what I have said thus far is somewhat of a shock. Before we go on, let me sum it up briefly.

"Earth has been for a longer period than your histories record, a part of the Carthis Empire, which includes all of this Solar System. The Gabon, or perhaps you would call him Emperor, of Carthis appoints a Graff to supervise each of his sun systems. I have been your Graff for the past forty-three years, making my residence on Mars, rather than on Earth, because of your low state of civilization.

"In fact," he went on, half musingly, "Earth hasn't been visited more than a score of times by representatives of Carthis in the past five thousand years. And, as a rule, these representatives were taken for some supernatural manifestation by your more than usually superstitious people. At least it is well that you have got over the custom of greeting us as gods."

The murmur increased within the large auditorium to reach the point where the Graff could no longer be heard. Finally President Hanford, pale of face, stepped before the microphones and held up his hands again. When a reasonable quiet had been obtained, he turned back to the green man.

"Undoubtedly, it will take considerable time for any of us fully to assimilate this. All of the assembled delegates probably have questions which they would like to ask.

However, I believe that one of the most pressing and one that we all have in mind is this——

"You say that ordinarily you wouldn't have made yourself known to us until we had reached a development of, I think you said, H-Seventeen — and that now we are but H-Four. Why have you made yourself known to us now? What special circumstances called for this revelation?"

The Graff nodded. "I was about to dwell upon that, Mr. President." He turned again to the quieted world delegates.

"My purpose in visiting Earth at this time was to announce to you that an interstellar arrangement has been made between the Gabon of Carthis and the Gabon of Wharis whereby the Solar System becomes part of the the Gabon of Wharis Empire, in return for certain considerations among the Aldebaran planets. In short, you are now subjects of the Gabon of Wharis. I am being recalled and your new Graff, Belde Kelden Forty-eight L, will arrive in due order."

He let his eyes go over them gently. There was a touch of pity in them. "Are there any other questions you wish to ask?"

Lord Harricraft stood up at his table directly before the microphones. He was obviously shaken. "I cannot make an official statement until I have consulted with my government but I would like to ask this — what difference will it make to us, this change in Graffs, or even this change in — er — Gabons? If the policy is to leave Earth alone until the race has progressed further it will affect us little, if at all, for the time being, will it not?"

The Graff spoke sadly. "While that has always been the policy of the Gabons of Carthis, your former rulers, it is not the policy of the present Gabon of Wharis. However, I can only say that your new Graff, Belde Kelden Forty-eight L, will be here in a few weeks and will undoubtedly explain his policies."

Lord Harricraft remained on his feet. "But you must have some idea of what this new Gabon wants of Earth."

The Graff hesitated then said slowly, "It is widely understood that the Gabon of Wharis is badly in need of uranium and various other rare elements to be found here on Earth. The fact that he has appointed Belde Kelden Forty-eight L, as your new Graff is also an indication, since this Graff has a wide reputation for success in all-out exploitation of new planets."

Larry Kincaid grinned wryly at the other newspapermen at the press table. "We've been sold down the river."

Monsieur Pierre Bart was on his feet. "Then it is to be expected that this Graff Belde Kelden Forty-eight L, under the direction of the Gabon of Wharis, will begin wholesale exploitation of this planet's resources, transporting them to other parts of the Gabon's empire?"

"I am afraid that is correct."

President Hanford spoke again. "But are we to have nothing to say about this? After all—"

The Graff said, "Even in Carthis and under the benevolent rule of Modren One, the most progressive Gabon in the galaxy, a planet has no voice in its own rule until it has reached a development of H-Forty. You see, each Gabon must consider the welfare of his empire as a whole. He cannot be affected by the desires or even needs of the more primitive life forms on his various backward planets. Unfortunately——"

Lord Harricraft was beet red with indignation. "But this is preposterous," he sputtered. "It is unheard of that a——"

The Graff held up his hand coldly. "I have no wish to argue with you. As I have said I am no longer Graff of this planet. However, I might point out to you a few facts which make your indignation somewhat out of place. In spite of my residence on Mars I have gone to the effort of investigating to some extent the history of Earth. Correct me if I am wrong in the following——

"This nation in which we hold our conference is the United States. Is it not true that in eighteen-hundred-three the United States bought approximately one million square miles of its present territory from the French Emperor Napoleon for fifteen million dollars? I believe it is called the Louisiana Purchase.

"I also believe that at that time the Louisiana Territory was inhabited almost exclusively by Amerindian tribes. Had these people ever heard of Napoleon or the United States? What happened to these people when they tried to defend their homes against the encroaching white man?"

He indicated Lord Harricraft. "Or perhaps I should come closer to home. I understand that you represent the powerful British Empire. Tell me, how was Canada originally acquired? Or South Africa? Or India?"

He turned to Pierre Bart. "And you, I believe, represent France. How were your North Africa colonies acquired? Did you consult with the nomadic peoples who lived there before you took over control of them?"

The Frenchman sputtered. "But these were backward barbarians! Our assuming government over the area was to their benefit and to the benefit of the world as a whole."

The Graff shrugged sadly. "I am afraid that that is exactly the story you will hear from your new Graff Belde Kelden Forty-eight L."

Suddenly half the hall was on its feet. Delegates stood on chairs and tables. Shouts rose, threats, hysterical defiance.

"We'll fight!"

"Better death than slavery!"

"We'll unite for all-out defense against the aliens!"

*"Down with other-world interference!"*

"WE'LL FIGHT!"

The Graff waited until the first fire of protest had burnt itself out, then held up his hands for quiet.

"I strongly recommend that you do nothing to antagonize Belde Kelden Forty-eight L, who is known to be a ruthless Graff when opposed by his inferiors. He strictly carries out the orders of the Gabon of Wharis, who usually makes a policy of crushing such revolts and then removing the population remaining to less desirable planets, where they are forced to support themselves as best they can.

"I can only add, that on some of the Wharis Empire planets, this is quite difficult, if not impossible."

479

The din throughout the hall was beginning to rise again. The Graff shrugged and turned back to President Hanford. "I am afraid I must go now. There is nothing more for me to say." He motioned to Grannoh Tyre 1852K and his guard.

"One moment," the President said urgently. "Isn't there anything else? Some advice, some word of assistance?"

The Graff sighed. "I am sorry. It is now out of my hands." But he paused and considered a moment. "There is one thing I can suggest that might help you considerably in your dealings with Belde Kelden Forty-eight L. I hope that in telling you of it, I don't hurt your feelings."

"Of course not," the president muttered hopefully. "The fate of the whole world is at stake. Anything that will help——"

"Well, then, I might say that I consider myself completely without prejudice. It means nothing to me if a person has a green skin, a yellow one or is white, brown, black or red. Some of my best friends are unfortunately colored.

"However — well, don't you have any races on this planet with a green complexion? Graff Belde Kelden Forty-eight L is known to be extremely prejudiced against races of different colors. If you had some green representatives to meet him——"

The president stared at him dumbly.

The Graff was distressed. "You mean that you have no races at all on Earth of green complexion? Or, at very least, blue?"

*Gently ironic and bearded Avram Davidson is one of the most interesting among the newcomers to the field. A beautiful stylist, Davidson has gained rapid recognition for his sensitive studies of very human and very credible Tomorrows. . . .*

●

# THE BOUNTY HUNTER

## By Avram Davidson

There was a whirring noise and a flurry and part of the snowbank shot up at a 45-degree angle — or so it seemed —and vanished in the soft grey sky. Orel stopped and put out his arm, blocking his uncle's way.

"It's a bird . . . only a bird . . . *get* on, now, Orel," Councillor Garth said, testily. He gave his nephew a light shove. "They turn white in the winter-time. Or their feathers do. Anyway, that's what Trapper says."

They plodded ahead, Orel, partly distracted by the pleasure of seeing his breath, laughed a bit. "A bird outside of a cage. . . ." The councillor let him get a few feet ahead, then he awkwardly compressed a handful of snow and tossed it at his nephew's face when he turned it back. The first startled cry gave way to laughter. And so they came to the trapper's door.

The old fellow peered at them, but it was only a thing he did because it was expected of him; there was nothing wrong with his eyes. Garth had known him for many years,

481

and he was still not sure how many of his mannerisms were real, how many put on. Or for that matter, how much of the antique stuff, cluttering up the cabin, was actually part of the trapper's life and how much only there for show. Not that he cared: the trapper's job was as much to be quaint and amusing as to do anything else.

Orel, even before the introductions were over, noticed the cup and saucer on the top shelf of the cabinet, but not till his two elders paused did he comment, "Look, Uncle: earthenware!"

"You've got a sharp eye, young fellow," the trapper said, approvingly. "Yes, it's real pottery. Brought over by my who knows how many times removed grandfather from the home planet. . . .Yes, my family, they were pretty important people on the home planet," he added, inconsequentially. He stood silent for a moment, warmed with pride, then made a series of amiable noises in his throat.

"Well, I'm glad to meet you, young fellow. Knew your uncle before he was councillor, before you were born." He went to the tiny window, touched the defroster, looked out. "Yes, your machine is safe enough." He turned around. "I'll get the fire started, if there's no objection? And put some meat on the grill? Hm?"

The councillor nodded with slow satisfaction; Orel grinned widely.

The trapper turned off the heating unit and set the fire going. The three men gazed into the flames. The meat turned slowly on the jack. Orel tried to analyse the unfamiliar smells crowding around him — the wood itself, and the fire: no, fire had no smell, it was *smoke;* the meat, the furs and hides . . . he couldn't even imagine what they all were. It was different from the cities, that was sure. He turned to ask something, but his uncle Garth and Trapper weren't attending. Then he heard it — a long, drawn-out, faraway sort of noise. Then the trapper grunted and spat in the fire.

"What was it?" Orel asked.

The old fellow smiled. "Never heard it before? Not even recorded, in a nature studies course? That's one of the big varmints — the kind your uncle and the other big sportsmen come out here to hunt — in season — the kind I trap in any season." Abruptly, he turned to Councillor Garth. "No talk of their dropping the bounty, is there?" Smilingly, the councillor shook his head. Reassured, the trapper turned his attention to the meat, poked it with a long pronged fork.

Orel compared the interior of the cabin to pictures and 3-D plays he had observed. Things looked familiar, but less — smooth, if that was the word. There was more disorder, an absence of symmetry. Hides and pelts — not too well cured, if the smell was evidence — were scattered all around, not neatly tacked up or laid in neat heaps. Traps and parts of traps sat where the old man had evidently last worked at mending them.

"Council's not in session, I take it?" the trapper asked. Orel's uncle shook his head. "But — don't tell me school's out, too? Thought they learned right through the winter."

Garth said, "I was able to persuade the Dean that our little trip was a genuine — if small — field expedition — and that Orel's absence wouldn't break the pattern of learning."

The trapper grunted. *Pattern!* Orel thought. The mention of the word annoyed him. Everything was part of a pattern: Pattern of learning, pattern of earning, pattern of pleasure. . . . Life in the city went by patterns, deviations were few; people didn't even *want* to break the patterns. They were afraid to.

But it was obvious that the trapper didn't live by patterns. This . . . disorder.

"Do you have any children, Trapper?" he asked. The old man said he didn't. "Then who will carry on your work?"

The trapper waved his hand to the west. "Fellow in the next valley has two sons. When I get too old — a long time from now," he said defiantly; "——one of them will move in with me. Help me out. Split the bounties with me.

"I was married once." He gazed into the fire. "City woman. She couldn't get used to it out here. The solitude. The dangers. So we moved to the cities. *I* never got used to *that*. Got to get up at a certain time. Got to do everything a certain way. Everything has to be put in its place, neatly. All the people would look at you otherwise. Breaking the patterns? They didn't like it. Well, she died. And I moved back here as fast as I could get the permission. And here I've stayed."

He took down plates, forks, knives, carved the meat. They ate with relish.

"Tastes better than something out of a factory lab, doesn't it?"

Orel's mind at once supplied him with an answer: that synthetics were seven times more nutritious than the foods they imitated. But his mouth was full and besides, it *did* taste better. Much better. . . . After the meal there was a sort of lull. The trapper looked at Councillor Garth in an expectant sort of way. The councillor smiled. He reached over into the pocket of his hunting jacket and took out a flask. Orel, as he smelled it (even before: after all, everyone knew that the bounty-hunters drank — the flask was part of every 3-D play about them), framed a polite refusal. But none was offered him.

"The purpose of this two-man field expedition," his uncle said, after wiping his mouth, "is to prepare a term paper for Orel's school showing how, in the disciplined present, the bounty-hunters maintain the free and rugged traditions of the past, on the Home Planet . . . let me have another go at the flask, Trapper."

Orel watched, somewhat disturbed. Surely his uncle knew how unhealthy. . . .

"My family, they were pretty important people back on the Home Planet." The Old Trapper, having had another drink, began to repeat himself. Outside — the dusk had begun to set in — that wild, rather frightening, sound came again. The old man put the flask down. "Coming nearer," he said, as if to himself. He got to his feet, took up his weapon. "I won't be gone long . . . they don't generally come so near . . . but it's been a hard winter. This one sounds kind of hungry. But don't you be frightened, young fellow," he said to Orel, from the door; "There's no chance of its eating *me*."

"Uncle . . ." Orel said, after a while. The councillor looked up. "Don't be offended, but . . . does it ever strike you that we lead rather useless lives in the city — compared, I mean, to *him?*"

The councillor smiled. "Oh, come now. Next you'll be wanting to run away and join the fun. Because that's all it is, really: fun. These beasts — the big 'varmints,' as he calls them — are no menace to us any longer. Haven't been since we switched from meat to synthetics. So it's not a truly useful life the old man leads. It's only our traditional reluctance to admit things have changed which keeps us paying the bounty. . . ." He got up and walked a few steps, stretched.

"We *could* get rid of these creatures once and for all, do it in one season's campaign. Drop poisoned bait every acre through the whole range. Wipe them out."

Orel, puzzled, asked why they didn't.

"And I'll tell you something else — but don't put it in your report. The old fellow, like all trappers, sometimes cheats. He often releases females and cubs. He takes no chances of having his valley trapped out. 'Why don't we?' you ask — why don't we get rid of the beasts once and for all, instead of paying bounties year after year? Well, the present cost is small. And as for getting an appropriation for an all-out campaign — who'd vote for it? *I* wouldn't.

"No more hunting — no more 3-D plays about the exciting life in the wild country — no more trappers — why, it would just about take what spirit is left away from us. And we are dispirited enough — tired enough — as it is."

Orel frowned. "But why are we like that? We weren't always. A tired people could never have moved here from the Home Planet, could never have conquered this one. Why are we so — so played out?"

The councillor shrugged. "Do you realize what a tremendous effort it was to move such a mass of people such a distance? The further effort required to subdue a wild, new, world? The terrible cost of the struggle against colonialism — and finally the Civil Wars? We don't even like to think about it — we create our myths instead out of the life out here in the wilds — and all the time, we retreated farther and farther, back into our cities. We are tired. We've spent our energies, we've mortgaged them, in fact. We eat synthetics because it's easier, not because it's healthier."

A gust of cold wind blew in on them. They whirled around. The Old Trapper came in, dragging his kill by the forelimbs. He closed the door. The two city folk came up close. The beast was a huge male, gaunt from the poor hunting which winter meant to the wild creatures.

"See here——" the trapper pointed. "Lost two toes there. *Old* wound. Must've gnawed his way out of a trap one time. *There* — got *these* scars battling over a mate, I suppose. This *here's* a burn. Bad one. When was the last big forest fire we had? — one too big to outrun——" He figured with moving lips. "*That* long ago? How the time does pass. . . . Let me have that knife there, young fellow——" Orel glanced around, located the knife, handed it to him; gazed down in fascination and revulsion. The wild life did not seem so attractive at this moment.

"Watch close, now, and I'll show you how to skin and dress a big varmint," the Old Trapper said. He made the initial incision. "Dangerous creatures, but when you know their habits as well as *I* do . . . Can't expect to wipe them out altogether——" He looked at the two guests. Orel wondered how much he knew or guessed of what had been said in his absence. "No. Keep their numbers down, is all you can expect to do." He tugged, grunted. "I *earn* my bounty, I can tell you." He turned the creature on its back.

Orel, struck by something, turned to the councillor.

"You know, Uncle, if this beast were cleaned up and shaved and——" he laughed at the droll fancy — "and dressed in clothes, it——"

Councillor Garth finished the sentence for him. "Would bear a faint, quaint resemblance to *us?* Hm, yes . . . in a way . . . of course, but their external ears and their having only five digits on each——" He clicked his tongue and stepped aside. The Old Trapper, who didn't care how much blood he got on things or people, worked away, but the Councillor took his nephew closer to the fire to finish what he had to say.

*There was a vacancy for the dirtiest job in the galaxy.
But were those terrestrial layabouts bright enough to
qualify?*

●

# NOT YET THE END

## By Fredric Brown

There was a greenish, hellish tinge to the light within the
metal cube. It was a light that made the dead-white skin of
the creature seated at the controls seem faintly green.

A single, faceted eye, front center in the head, watched
the seven dials unwinkingly. Since they had left Xandor
that eye had never once wavered from the dials. Sleep
was unknown to the galactic race to which Kar-388Y belonged. Mercy, too, was unknown. A single glance at the
sharp, cruel features below the faceted eye would have
proved that.

The pointers on the fourth and seventh dials came to a
stop. That meant the cube itself had stopped in space relative to its immediate objective. Kar reached forward with
his upper right arm and threw the stabilizer switch. Then
he rose and stretched his cramped muscles.

Kar turned to face his companion in the cube, a being
like himself. "We are here," he said. "The first stop, Star
Z-5689. It has nine planets, but only the third is habita-

ble. Let us hope we find creatures here who will make suitable slaves for Xandor."

Lal-16B, who had sat in rigid immobility during the journey, rose and stretched also. "Let us hope so, yes. Then we can return to Xandor and be honoured while the fleet comes to get them. But let's not hope too strongly. To meet with success at the first place we stop would be a miracle. We'll probably have to look a thousand places."

Kar shrugged. "Then we'll look a thousand places. With the Lounacs dying off, we must have slaves else our mines must close and our race will die."

He sat down at the controls again and threw a switch that activated a visiplate that would show what was beneath them. He said, "We are above the night side of the third planet. There is a cloud layer below us. I'll use the manuals from here."

He began to press buttons. A few minutes later he said, "Look, Lal, at the visiplate. Regularly spaced lights — a city! The planet *is* inhabited."

Lal had taken his place at the other switchboard, the fighting controls. Now he too was examining dials. "There is nothing for us to fear. There is not even the vestige of a force field around the city. The scientific knowledge of the race is crude. We can wipe the city out with one blast if we are attacked."

"Good," Kar said. "But let me remind you that destruction is not our purpose — yet. We want specimens. If they prove satisfactory and the fleet comes and takes as many thousand slaves as we need, then will be time to destroy not a city but the whole planet. So that their civilization will never progress to the point where they'll be able to launch reprisal raids."

Lal adjusted a knob. "All right. I'll put on the megrafield and we'll be invisible to them unless they see far into the ultraviolet, and, from the spectrum of their sun, I doubt that they do."

As the cube descended the light within it changed from green to violet and beyond. It came to a gentle rest. Kar manipulated the mechanism that operated the airlock.

He stepped outside, Lal just behind him. "Look," Kar

said, "two bipeds. Two arms, two eyes — not dissimilar to the Lounacs, although smaller. Well, here are our specimens."

He raised his lower left arm, whose three-fingered hand held a thin rod wound with wire. He pointed it first at one of the creatures, then at the other. Nothing visible emanated from the end of the rod, but they both froze instantly into statuelike figures.

"They're not large, Kar," Lal said. "I'll carry one back, you carry the other. We can study them better inside the cube, after we're back in space."

Kar looked about him in the dim light. "All right, two is enough, and one seems to be male and the other female. Let's get going."

A minute later the cube was ascending and as soon as they were well out of the atmosphere, Kar threw the stabilizer switch and joined Lal, who had been starting a study of the specimens during the brief ascent.

"Viviparous," said Lal. "Five-fingered, with hands suited to reasonably delicate work. But — let's try the most important test, intelligence."

Kar got the paired headsets. He handed one pair to Lal, who put one on his own head, one on the head of one of the specimens. Kar did the same with the other specimen.

After a few minutes, Kar and Lal stared at each other bleakly.

"Seven points below minimum," Kar said. "They could not be trained even for the crudest labor in the mines. Incapable of understanding the most simple instructions. Well, we'll take them back to the Xandor museum."

"Shall I destroy the planet?"

"No," Kar said. "Maybe a million years from now — if our race lasts that long — they'll have evolved enough to become suitable for our purpose. Let us move on to the next star with planets."


The make-up editor of the *Milwaukee Star* was in the composing room, supervising the closing of the local page.

490

Jenkins, the head make-up compositor, was pushing in leads to tighten the second last column.

"Room for one more story in the eighth column, Pete," he said. "About thirty-six picas. There are two there in the overset that will fit. Which one shall I use?"

The make-up editor glanced at the type in the galleys lying on the stone beside the chase. Long practice enabled him to read the headlines upside down at a glance. "The convention story and the zoo story, huh? Oh, hell, run the convention story. Who cares if the zoo director thinks two monkeys disappeared off Monkey Island last night?"

# SECTION 3
# DECLINE AND FREE FALL

## *i   All Things are Cyclic*

•

*The sense of the fated incompleteness of all creatures
and of their achievements gave the Galactic Society
of Worlds a charm, a sanctity, as of some short-lived
and delicate flower.*

Olaf Stapledon: *Star Maker.*

One thing we learn from science fiction is that pleasure
can be derived from the worst catastrophe.

Magazine sf — never let it be forgotten — was written
in the main for an underprivileged audience. It was grass
roots literature, a child of the pulp magazines. If you were
under-paid and under-educated and worked in a dingy
office in London or New York, commuting home at the
end of the day to a drab flat in a mean street, then the
fictional destruction of your capital city could be a good
cathartic read. Or write. One of the great nineteenth century disaster novels, *After London,* was written by a nat-
uralist and journalist called Richard Jefferies, who found
himself caught up with London and hated the place. His
evocative novel, which totally erases London, was written
as a kind of revenge.

The man to ask about this subject is Harry Harrison,
who lived many years of his life in New York, only to flee
it forever when he made his first big science fiction sale.
He sat in an elegant house in Denmark and wrought the
ruin of his home town in a now-famous novel, *Make
Room! Make Room!,* later made into a film called Soylent
Green, starring Charlton Heston, which does not do justice to Harrison's panoramic view of urban over-
population.

Harrison specialises in ramshackle worlds which never
quite fall apart; his style is generally unmistakable, in
person as in his books. But the story included here, *Final
Encounter,* is, exceptionally, about a world coming to-

495

gether. It marks, I suppose, the logical end of the galactic empire. The two hands are folded about the apple.

It could be that the same atavistic urge which moves sf writers to destroy what they love or loathe prompts them so often to marry their galactic empire with an extraordinary feudal system, loaded with lords, beautiful ladies, and sweating peasants. Computers are rare; jewels are everyday currency.

In this respect, Gardner Fox's gloriously extravagant story runs true to form, right down to the lovely Moana, of whom it has been said that "the thin stuff of her gown clung to supple haunches and proud breasts." Down in the swill-wet streets, revolt is brewing. We also have superscience and talk of "compulsory interracial wedlock". And we surge symbolically from the mire and filth of Lower City to the clean white reaches of the Citadel. So the cycle of being is completed, as in the Harrison story.

The use of feudalism in so many stories like Fox's is not just caprice. In Volume One we remarked on the minting of steel currency in Isaac Asimov's *Foundation*. Asimov freely admits that he took the Roman Empire as pattern and exemplar for his galactic empire. But in general empires of the skies use such feudal backgrounds as we have described. This of course provides all the trappings of glamour and the contrasts between high life and squalor which are clear to a reader's heart. But there may be a less calculated reason for embracing such an anachronistic model.

For the operation of what Lewis Mumford calls "the invisible machine" or "the megamachine" of human endeavour and achievement, our present culture needs money as the individual needs blood. We are creatures of economics and we must work while we are able or perish, just as did our ancestors generations back; we are ruled by money, the endless necessity for which forms the circuitry that keeps workforce and nation functional. (True, there are rare individuals who stand outside this invisible machine; they are dictators — Stalin, owning Russia, never had a coin in his pocket — royalty, the very rich, or the extremely poor; gipsies are shunned since they contribute no power to the invisible machine.)

The capitalist system enjoys comparatively effective circuitry. That is to say, its pressures are constant but, when its units are functioning smoothly, not all that insistent on the majority.

All the same, it is difficult to imagine any present-day coercion system, not capitalism, certainly not communism, working effectively to embrace several planetary systems light years apart. Relativity, which affects space and time, would certainly affect cash-flow. Cash-flow has two aspects; it works both as coercive and incentive. A more coercive system would be more effective. Like dictatorship. Or even feudalism.

Feudalism was a cruder version of the invisible machine, yet the sort of feudalism practised in Ancient Egypt produced, in the shape of the Great Pyramids, some of the most lasting and impressive monuments on this planet.

The number of nutty attempts to explain the pyramids, or the memorials of the Incas or of any other great vanished race, in terms of some superstitious theory — an example is von Daniken's notion that all the great achievements on our planet were built by galactic astronauts — simply shows lack of understanding of how other invisible machines than ours functioned in the past. All invisible machines make human and/or mechanical energy available in strength where it is needed; under our present system, we all work to accumulate stockpiles of military hardware, as the feudal world worked to accumulate stones for the dead Pharoahs. We can empathise with that world no more than it could empathise with ours.

But we can empathise with the abolition of money! Oh, yes! This is what makes feudal systems attractive in escapist literature. It frees the way for adventure, which has little to do with cash-flow. And I think the sf writers' basic instincts are right: money will have to fade out when we move into the galaxy.

497

Or could it be that those sinister dark pools of energy in *Tonight the Stars Revolt!*, guarded by the ancient god Stasor, are symbolic representations of your local Barclay's Bank?

*In the Black Pools he found the 50,000-year-lost wisdom of the Ancients. For a day Red Angus held victory in his swordhand. But it was too short a glimpse, too elusive a thought to bolster the star-rabble against the Citadel's iron guard.*

●

# TONIGHT THE STARS REVOLT!

## By Gardner F. Fox

*The pools were like the gaping mouth of space itself, dark and fathomless, extending into bottomless wells, the depths of which the people of Karr could only guess. Some said the god Stasor dwelt in the glistening black depths. Others claimed the emptiness was the hollow interior of the planet. None of them was right.*

*All men feared the pools. Only a man fifty thousand years old knew their incredible secret, and he lived in an invisible city. . . .*

Red Angus fled like a frightened hound through the twisted alleys of the Lower City. Dim lamplight from the towering white walls of the Citadel threw glowing brilliance across his naked chest, glinted on the metal studs of his broad leather belt, and on the rippling muscles of his long legs. He skidded on a patch of slops, righted himself and dove for the darkness of an arched doorway. He drew back in the shadows, barely feeling the burn of the new brand on his shoulder that stamped him as a pirate.

Faintly, he heard the shouts and drumming feet of the Diktor's police as they ravened in the streets, hunting him. His heart thudded swiftly under the high arch of his ribcase. Red Angus smiled wryly.

He was a hunted space pirate, just free of the cell blocks below the palace. But he was more than that to the Diktor of Karr. He was a Karrvan noble who had gone bad, who had fled into space and established an eyrie on a wandering asteroid, who had set himself up as a one-man crusade against Stal Tay, ruler of Karr by the grace of the god Stasor.

"I'll find a way," the pirate swore in the shadows, listening to the shouts and running of the guards, the sharp, barking blasts of their heatguns.

There was a faint sound behind the thick oaken door. Angus moved his naked back, still welt and scarred, away from the damp wood. He clenched a big fist and stood silent, waiting.

He was a tall man, lean in the belly and wide about the shoulders. His mouth was thin but curved at the corners as though used to smiling. Close-cropped reddish hair gave his hard, tanned face a fiery look. Dark blue eyes glistened in the half-squint of the habitual spaceman.

The oaken door swung open. A cowled form stood in the darkness of the archway putting out a thin, old hand toward him. Where the cowl hung there was only a faint white dimness for a face.

"The Hierarch will see you, and save you, Red Angus," said the old man. "Come in. He hopes you'll listen to reason."

"The Hierarch?" snorted the lean man in disbelief. "He's hand in arm with Stal Tay. He'd land me back with my ankles in a manacle chain."

The cowled man shook his head and whispered, "Hurry, hurry. There's no time to argue!"

A shout from a street less than sixty feet away decided the half-naked, winded Angus. He moved his shoulders in a bitter shrug and slid inside the door. The latch clicked on the door and a hand caught his. A voice, gentle with age, said softly, "Follow me."

Two hundred feet from the door the walls began to glow. Angus looked at his guide and saw an old man, a member of the Hierarchy, a priestly cult of scientists who were honored and protected by the Diktor. Thirty years before, when the people of the Lower City had been ravaged by disease, they had stormed the block of buildings where the scientists worked.

They had wrecked machines and killed men.

The people of the Lower City were no better than savages and the pagan superstitions they boasted were encouraged by Stal Tay. It pleased the Diktor to believe that science was something only the rich deserved. So Stal Tay stepped in. He withdrew the scientists from the world of men and gave them a little world of their own that was called the Citadel.

Red Angus and the scientist went through corridors that bent and twisted in subtle fashion. It was quiet in this underground tunnel. Once Angus heard the subterranean rush of a hidden river seeking an outlet in the great Car Carolan Sea. Water condensed in oozing droplets on the cold stone walls.

Then they were going up handhewn stone steps toward an archway in which a thick, soot-blackened door was opening. Lights glared beyond the doorway in a large room with a high, groined ceiling.

He saw Tandor first, standing big and massive among the cowled priests, the wall light glinting from his bald head. They had had a time taking him from the Lower City, Angus saw. There were cut marks on him, and the blood here and there on his rough wool tunic had dried.

A tall man in a white cowl that was bordered with purple came toward them. He said, "I saved your man from the Diktor's torturers. Money will do much in the Citadel. Even a pirate's first captain is not as valuable as a handful of *sestelins*."

Red Angus shrugged. "What do you want from me?"

The Hierarch nodded. "They told me you were a sensible man. Tonight I will free Tandor after you do me a service."

"What service?"

The Hierarch studied him carefully. "Kill the Diktor!"

Angus barked derisive laughter. "As well ask me to find the Book of Nard. I'd stand as much chance!"

"I may well ask that too, before you and I are through."

"Suppose I refuse?"

The Hierarch sighed. His black eyes glittered in the shadow of his cowl. "I'll smash your legs so you can't run, and let Stal Tay send his men for you. I'll put red-hot daggers in Tandor's eyes until he confesses your crimes. I——"

Angus scowled. "I thought the Diktor was your friend."

"He keeps us penned in the Citadel as his slaves. The scientific discoveries we make he claims as his own. He sent the diseases that the people blamed on the scientists."

Angus said, "I will kill him." But he thought to himself, I only play for time. It's promise or get my legs broken.

They led Angus to a little room where a cowled man waited for him with garments that were living reds and ochres, braided with gold and ornate with jewels. The scientist said coldly, "You are to impersonate the Ambassador of Nowk. He's red-headed and big with a scar on his face like your own."

The night air was crisp as Angus stepped with the cowled scientist through a stone gateway and into a long, sleek wheeler. He gathered his cloak of black sateenis about him and sank into the foamisal upholstery.

The cowled man whispered, "Everything is arranged. A woman dancer, Berylla by name, will dance for the Diktor. Right after that he plans to call you to his side to discuss the new trade agreement with Nowk. The dancer will give you the signal as she leaves. When you're summoned strike at the Diktor's neck. A divertissement in the form of drunken revellers has been planned. In the excitement, you will be spirited away."

Angus touched the slim dagger at his side and nodded.

The Diktor of Karr was a big man. He was solid in the shoulder and slim at the waist. His head was bald, and there was a jagged scar across his right temple. He sat on his jewelled throne and drummed restless fingers against the hand-carved arm.

Beside him sat a woman with sloe eyes and hair the color of a raven's wing. The thin stuff of her gown clung to supple haunches and proud breasts. She watched the new Ambassador from Nowk thread a path through the guests, unable to decide whether the man was ugly or ruggedly handsome. But he was big, with long, heavily-muscled arms and legs, and he had the look of a fighter.

Moana laughed softly. There was music in her voice and art in the manner of her movement as he drew closer. Her eyes ran over his big frame slowly, slumberously.

Red Angus came to a stop at the base of the dais and bowed low. He was a pirate but he had been in the great capitals of the Six Worlds.

"Your first visit to Karr?" smiled Stal Tay.

"The first, excellency."

"You like the court we keep?"

Red Angus knew of the taverns and swill-wet streets of the Lower City. He knew the people were slaves to the Hierarchy and to the Diktor and his little coterie. Girls danced and pandered to the desires of the rich — if they did not, things were done to them in secret. He knew men grew old before their time, working to pay for the rare jewels that Moana and others like her flaunted.

But he murmured, "Plegasston of Nowk has said, 'For the good of the State, the greatest number of its people must enjoy the greatest amount of its highest rewards.' But Plegasston was a dreamer."

Moana gestured Angus to the golden chair beside her. She let her fingertips brush his hand as he took the seat. "Tell me about yourself, Ben Tal."

Angus grinned, "I'm a relative of his Eminence of Nowk. That explains all about me. But you. You're priestess to the god Stasor. You've gone into the black pool to face him. You've heard his pronouncements."

Moana made a wry face and shrugged. Strains of music

swept down from the fluted ceiling, diffused throughout the room. Her black eyes glowed. "Don't talk religion to me, Ben Tal. Take me in your arms and let us dance."

She was warm and fragrant, following his movements. Her dark eyes enticed as her hands fluttered from his arm to his shoulder to his neck. She made the moments fly. Seated with her at a table, letting her feed him playfully, he almost forgot his mission.

And then. . . .

The room darkened. The hidden musicians made their stringed instruments dance with savage rhythm. And in a circle of golden light, her white flesh gleaming fitfully through a garment of diamonds, a woman swayed out onto the cleared floor.

And Angus remembered. He was here to kill a man.

The woman in the service of the Hierarchs was a fire-flame out there with the jeweled dress cloud of living rainbows swirling about her. She pirouetted, dipped, and leaped. She was motionless — and a storm of movement. She laughed. She wept. She taunted and cajoled. She was everything any woman ever was.

Angus saw her eyes darting, hunting him. They slid over his deep chest and long legs, square jaw and close-cropped red hair many times without recognition. Only toward the end, as the beam of light that spotlighted her dance touched him too, did she know him.

Her surprise made her stumble but she recovered swiftly. She whirled around the room, diamonds tinkling faintly to the stamping of her bare feet. She threw herself into the Dance of the Garland of Gems, and made it a living thing. When she came to the black curtains she posed for an instant, moved her arm in the agreed signal, and was gone.

The Diktor lifted a hand and gestured. Angus bowed to Moana and got to his feet. With all the iron control he had developed on the lonely star-trails he fought to keep his hand from his knife-haft.

He bent to take his seat. Now his right hand was sheltered by his body and he put it on the dagger.

The thin blade whispered, coming out of the scabbard.

Red Angus leaned forward and thrust at the throat before him.

Four hands came out of midair and fastened to his wrist. They dragged him down by surprise and by the weight of their bodies. He went off his chair in a rolling fall, hitting the man to his left, toppling him backwards into Stal Tay.

Men were shouting. A woman screamed. Angus brought his hard left fist up in a short arc, drove it into the stomach-muscles of the man on his right. The man grunted and went backwards. Red Angus stood free, his clean blade still naked in his hand.

He leaped for Stal Tay but other guards had come running. One threw himself before the dagger, both hands catching at it. Another hit the pirate across the legs with his hurtling body. A third man clawed himself to a position astride his back, hooking a hairy forearm under his chin. That was when the rest of them hit him.

Angus went back off his feet into a mass of struggling, cursing flesh. The guards yelped triumphantly but Red Angus had fought in tavern brawls in the Lower City, had wrestled with salt slavers on the desert dunes, had fought fights from Karr to Rimeron. He surged up. His fists went up and down. His right hand flashed out, closing on a guard's wrist. The guard screamed and fell away, moaning.

Angus breathed through distended nostrils, dancing back, fists thudding into rib and jaw. He fought to get room and he almost made it. But a guard left his feet in a wild dive before the pirate could brace himself. The man hit his knees and took them out from under him. Angus went down under a dozen leaping warriors. Grimy, blooded, Red Angus shook his head and gave up.

Moana was standing above him, laughing scorn through the queer, awed light in her eyes. Her white breasts rose and fell swiftly under their scant covering. "The little dancer knew you, Ben Tal. I saw that. But she's never been out of Karr City. And this is your first visit. Who are you?"

Red Angus shrugged as the guardsman lifted him to his feet and sat him roughly down in a chair before the Diktor. He made a wry face. There was a taste like bitter ashes dragging down the corners of his mouth. His belly quivered under the glistening cloth of his breeches. He seemed to hear the Hierarch's drawling voice, "If you fail, you die."

The Diktor waved a hand. The guards lifted him, dragged him behind velveteen drapes and along a stone corridor, into a small room. The Diktor and Moana followed at his heels. It was the Diktor who turned the key in the lock.

"Who sent you?" the stocky ruler asked softly. "Who paid for my death? Tell me that, and you'll walk out of here a free man."

Red Angus shook his head. He met the hazel eyes of the Diktor grimly.

Stal Tay smiled. "Berylla the dancer knows you. I can always have her brought in, you know."

Moana had been walking around Angus. She came close, put a hand on the tunic that fitted his chest like a glove, and ripped. His heavily muscled shoulder was laid bare, where the inflamed interlocking triangles gleamed.

Moana cried out. "A pirate!"

The Diktor opened his eyes wide. "Of course. Now I know you. Red Angus. My men captured you a week ago. But how in Stasor's name did you get free?"

Angus said briefly, "Does it matter?"

"No." Stal Tay went and sat on a curved sigellis-chair and crossed his heavy legs. He drummed short, powerful fingers against the beethel-wood arm. "But the fact that you came back after getting free — that is important. You wouldn't have stayed in Karr City unless you had to. Who made you stay? Certainly you didn't hate me enough to risk your neck on such a long chance."

Angus grinned through the fear in him. "A million people hate you, if you want to know. You keep the lower-city men and women in filthy poverty to buy you and your kind jewels and luxury. You subsidize the Hierarchy, using their science to make your life easier and safer. Why deny those poor devils down below what you could give them so cheaply? Heat. Light. Power to operate a few machines. Let them taste something from life besides slops and sweaty clothes and hard beds."

"Oho," laughed the Diktor softly. "Plegasston of Nowk made a convert. What else did he say, Angus?"

"He said that government and science should serve the people, not enslave them. Doesn't Stasor teach that?"

Moana laughed softly. Her black eyes taunted him. She said, "You want to hear what Stasor says about government and science and people, Angus the Red? Let me take him through the Veil, Eminence. Let the god himself tell the fool."

The Diktor smiled thinly, looking from man to woman. He shook his head. Moana moved to one side of the square-set ruler. Her black eyes bored straight at Angus. He tried to understand their expression.

The Diktor stood up. "I've used reason, Angus. You're a pirate. You've preyed on my space-caravans. You've stolen and plundered from me. I tell you again, I'll forgive all that — even reward you — if you tell me who sent you here this night."

The black eyes burned at him in Moana's pale white face. She touched her full upper lip with a red tongue-tip.

"If I could see Stasor," fumbled Angus, trying to fathom what Moana wanted him to say. When she nodded almost imperceptibly, he went on, "perhaps he could make me change my mind. If Stasor says I've been a fool, why then everything I've believed in will have gone smash. In that case I'd like to serve your Eminence."

Moana's black eyes laughed, silently applauding him. The Diktor scowled thoughtfully. He swung around on the girl. "Will you be his vow-companion?"

Angus knew what that meant. If he found a way to escape, the Diktor would stretch that lovely white body on the rack in place of his own, give those thighs and breasts and face to the red-hot pincers, the nails, the barbed hooks. He would never let her suffer that fate.

Maybe the Diktor knew that. He smiled a little as

Moana promised. He went, without another glance at Angus.

Moana said softly, "It was all I could do, Red Angus. He would have taken you to the Pits tonight if I hadn't delayed it."

"You don't owe me anything," he told her crisply.

"I do, though. My brother angered the Diktor a year ago. He was sent to the salt marshes of Ptixt. You raided the caravan that carried him and set him free. My brother lives safely hidden today in one of your pirate cities. I remember that, Angus. Sometimes good deeds do pay off. What does Plegasston say about that?"

She went past him and through the doorway.

He followed her swaying body along the drape-hung corridors, into small rooms and past oak-beamed doors. She came to a blank wall, reached up and pressed pink fingertips against a rose-red stone.

"The whorls at the tips of my fingers set off a light-switch mechanism within the stone," she explained. "It's better than any key."

Somewhere an engine hummed faintly and the rock wall began to turn. It swung aside to reveal a narrow corridor leading downwards. The walls were coated with a luminescent blueness that glowed brightly, lighting the way.

Angus saw the pool long before he came to it. A round metal collar bordered the glistening blackness, that seemed to press upward as though striving to burst free of whatever held it. It shimmered and quivered. It pulsed and throbbed with something close to life itself.

Angus came to a stop, staring at it. He put out a hand and thrust it into the darkness. It felt light, biting, and he thought it might taste like heady wine.

Moana took his other hand. She whispered, "Come," and stepped down into the pool.

The darkness swam all around Angus. He felt it on his skin, in the pores of his arms and hands and legs. It made him giddy, so that he wanted to laugh. It was like walking on air, to stride in this thing.

They went down into the pool and stood in a strange space, where there was only blackness, unrelieved by light. It was cold. Faintly, Angus could hear what he thought was music.

"Will yourself ahead," he heard a musical voice whisper.

He floated effortlessly.

"Where are we?" he wondered aloud.

"Out of space. Out of time. In the abode of the god. Soon now, we shall see Stasor."

A bright point of red glowed faintly, as a pinhead might gleam when heated in a fire. It grew swiftly to the size of a fist, to the size of a head.

The red glow burst, and sent streamers of flame out into the darkness.

Where the red had been was Stasor.

His face floated in a white mist, ancient and wise and sorrowful. The dimly veined lids were shut. The forehead was high, rounded, surmounted by snowy hair. On either side of the great hawk-nose, high cheekbones protruded. The eyelids quivered, slowly arose.

Angus stared dumbly into living wisdom. He wondered deep inside him how old Stasor must be, to know what those eyes knew; how many worlds he must have gazed on, how many peoples he must have seen grow to statehood, to degeneracy, to death.

"You entered the pool. I felt your emanations. What do you wish?"

Moaná said, "I am your priestess, Stasor. I have brought a man to see you."

"Let the man speak."

Angus wet his lips. He scowled, trying to find words. He mumbled, "I've been sentenced to die for attempting to kill the Diktor of Karr. He's an evil man."

"What is evil, my son? Is a man bad because he opposes your will?"

Angus growled, "He's a curse to his race. He sends disease and death on his people when they disobey him. He keeps improvement from them. He makes them slaves when they might be gods."

"That is your belief. What says the Book of Nard?"

509

Moana whispered, "The Book of Nard is lost, High One."

Stasor was silent a long time. He said, finally, "The Book must be found. In it are the secrets of the Elder Race. Go to the City of the Ancients. There you will find the Book."

"No one today knows where the City is, either. It is lost, with all the secrets of the Elder Race."

"The City lies across the Car Carolan Sea, through the Land of Living Flame. Go there."

The lips closed. The eyelids shut. Swiftly the old face faded into nothingness. The blackness came and pressed around them.

Angus turned slowly, as in a dream. Still in that dream-like trance he found himself staring at three tall, cowled forms that stood like sentinels.

Moana screamed.

One of the cowled figures lifted an arm and gestured assurance. "There is no cause for fear. The Hierarch sent us to bring you before him."

Moana shuddered. Angus felt her cold hand seeking his, trying to hide itself in his palm. Hand in hand they willed themselves after the cowled forms. They swam bodily through the blackness, moving eerily, without muscular movement.

A round curtain of shimmering bluish motes ahead of them was like a glowing patch in the darkness. One of the cowled forms turned and waited. He said, "Another pool, Moana. The pool of the Hierarchy. We, too, know the way into this world."

"What is the blackness?" wondered Angus.

"What man knows? It was formed and built by the Elder Ones before they went on."

They were in the pool, passing upward through its queer surface. It sizzled and bubbled all around them, tingling on the skin.

They passed the pool and stood in a low-ceilinged, bare room.

A cowled man opened a door for them and stood aside. The Hierarch sat in a curved chair ornate with gold edgings. His pale, ascetic face gloomed from the shadow of his big cowl. He stared at them, a thin smile touching his lips. He stared so long that Angus asked impatiently, "What do you want with us? Tandor, is he free?"

Moana gasped, sudden understanding waking her mind. The Hierarch brushed her with his eyes and sighed.

"Tandor is free. I fulfill my promises. You tried and failed, yet you tried. Now——"

He paused, fingertips pressed together, brooding down at Angus.

"Many thousands of eons ago, before our race came into existence, all Karr belonged to the Elder Race. It lived a long time on this world, before it went on."

Angus grinned, "Your priest said that. You and he mean——"

The Hierarch spoke patiently, as if lecturing a child. "It did not die out. It went on, to another plane of existence. Everything must progress. That is the immutable law of nature. The First Race progressed, far beyond our understanding, beyond the natural laws as we know them. They exist today — somewhere outside.

"Stasor, now. Take him, for instance." The Hierarch flicked burning black eyes at Moana. "Some think he is a god. He is a member of the Elder Race."

Moana said harshly. "Blasphemy! You speak blasphemy of Stasor."

The Hierarch shrugged. "I tell you Stasor is a four-plane man, one not bound by our three dimensions. He and his kind have gone on to that other world. They left behind them rules to guide those who came after them. They left the pools. They were a great race, the Elders, and the black pools are their greatest discovery. Those rules they gave us are contained in the Book of Nard. I want that book!"

"Why?"

The Hierarch smiled gently. "With the secrets of the Elders at my fingertips do you think the Diktor could keep us penned here in the Citadel?"

A faint hope burned in Angus' chest. "You mean, you

wouldn't be cloistered any more? That you'd give your science to the people and help them up?"

"Pah!" snapped the Hierarch. "The people? Pigs! They wallow in their filths and love it." His burning black eyes glittered fanatically. "No. I mean I — and not the Diktor — will rule all Karr!"

He is mad, too, thought Angus. He and the Diktor — mad with the lust for power. If the Diktor dies and the Hierarch rules the people will change a bootheel for a mortar and pestle. *Even the stars must revolt against that.*

# II

The street was dark, except for the moonlight shining faintly through the serrated rooftops, and reflected grey and dismal from the rounded edges of the cobblestones. Angus and a cowled man made a short dash, ran into the shadows, and trotted at a slow pace.

Above them a sign creaked on rusty chains. Angus looked behind at the huge stone bulk of the Citadel where it rose from solid rock, wall piled on wall, and turret on tower, and battlement upon bastion. Beyond the Citadel the thin, delicate spires of the palaces towered above the clean, fragrantly perfumed Upper City. Up above, there was no swill. There was no stench of rotting garbage. The patricians did not know what roast derstite looked like on a greasy platter, or how broiled colob smelled or what awful stuff the vintners sold in the big Mart.

Angus said, "I still don't see why the Hierarch bothers sending me after the Book. He has a lot of scientists who'd do a better job of finding it."

The lips of the man twisted in the darkness of the cowl. "How do you think the Diktor keeps us penned in the Citadel, red-man? He has spectragrams of each of us in his palace, attached to central controls. Every once in a while he has his captains check on our locations. When the vibratory beams touch us, they reflect our spectrums on the visi-screens. If one of us is out of place — beyond the limits of Karr City, that is — he sends a patrol to find and capture us. We lost several good men that way before we grew resigned. Once a scientist is captured by the Diktor he is destroyed. Instantly."

"Isn't there anyone else to help you?"

The scientist showed his disdain by a twitch of the lips. "Who? One of the people? They'd run so fast to betray us a theto-hound couldn't catch them. They hate the Diktor, but I think they hate us more."

Behind them the shadow of a man with a zigzag scar on his face disengaged himself from beneath an overhanging cornice and silently followed.

Angus and the scientist went through the narrow streets, down stone steps and across a great square. To one side the red lanterns of the Spotted Stag tavern glowed and the shouts and roistering laughter of men mingled with the shrill excited laughter of a woman.

The scientist glanced about him nervously, wet his lips with his tongue. "I don't like this section. It's too near the wharves. There are other rats than the four-legged kind."

A blackish, blunt instrument in the hand of a half-naked man bounced from the skull of the cowled one. Angus went forward, left hand hooking. He caught the big man on the side of the mouth and drove his head sideways. His right fist was crossing as his left landed. He hit the man with his right hand and the man went backwards into a brick wall.

"Easy, Angus," growled a voice in back of him, with a hint of laughter in it.

Angus whirled, teeth bared. When he saw the bald head of the giant in front of him he laughed harshly.

"By the gods! Tandor. The Hierarch did keep his promise, then!"

"We heard you'd missed killing that scum that lives in the palace by an inch. Tsk! The Hierarch felt that, with luck, Stal Tay would be dead by now. He let me go, yes. As soon as he learned that you and that priestess were in the black pool."

Angus bent and threw back the cowl of the scientist.

There was a swelling lump on the back of his head. Angus said, "I thought you broke his skull when you hit him." He looked at the man stirring against the brick wall. "Sorry, friend. I thought you a footpad."

"Tandor told me you were fast. He wasn't lying." The man grinned ruefully, feeling his jaw.

Tandor shouldered Angus aside and picked up the cowled man. He led the way up through the streets, the limp man's legs and arms dangling inertly. Tandor asked, "Where was he taking you?"

"To a hidden globe-ship. I'm supposed to find the Book of Nard. The Hierarch is holding Moana as hostage for my success."

Tandor whistled softly, eyes round. "He exchanged me for the girl. A smart man, the High Priest!"

Laughter came out at them from the ill-lighted interior of the tavern together with the dry smell of wine and the stench of sweating flesh. Tandor kicked the oak door open and went along the wall with his burden. A girl with a rag around her middle ran for Angus, tipsily pressing wet lips to his. She threw up a wooden goblet, the red wine splashing over its rim, crying, "The Anvil! To Red Angus the Anvil — the only friend we have!"

The roar echoed in his ears as Angus stepped into the little side room. Tandor kicked a chair toward Angus, reaching for a wooden pitcher. He growled, "Are you going hunting for the Book?"

Angus stretched out his legs and dragged a full goblet toward him. He stared at the dark liquor. Finally he said, "Yes, I'm going."

"Why?"

"Because I've seen the way they live in the Upper City. I've seen the life they lead and I've seen the life those people out there in the big room lead."

Tandor made a rumbling sound in his throat. "You don't think they'll appreciate your changing it, do you?"

Angus looked thoughtful. He smiled, "I know what our race is heading toward, now. We will be like Stasor — the man behind the veil — eventually. The longer the Diktor stays in power, and others like them, the longer will the rest of us be kept from that goal."

Tandor grinned like a wolf. "Some men like to be martyrs. It's a weakness of the brain." He scowled, and brought the flat of his ham-like hand down on the wooden tabletop. "I say it's madness. Let the Hierarch and the Diktor slit each other's throats. Let's go back to the star trails, Angus. Out where a man can breathe and stretch himself."

Angus shook his head. "Take the ship yourself. Go raiding, if you want. I stay. I want to answer a question."

"What question?"

"Why is science?"

"Why is—— You're crazy, now. I know it. Of all the stupid questions. Science is an art designed to better the life standards of the patrician class. There. That answer you?"

"I say science is something that would benefit all. Why do we have torches while the Hierarchy and the patricians use illumilamps and incandescent walls? Why don't we have stoves instead of hearths or electronizers instead of percussion guns?"

Tandor smirked. "It's safer."

Angus got to his feet and walked about the smoky, oak-beamed room. In the reddish light his chest and thickly muscled arms seemed coated with crimson. The crop of red hair on his rounded, square-jawed skull added to the illusion. He planted his hands on his hips and stood in front of his lieutenant.

"I turned pirate when the last Diktor executed my father for leniency with his servants. The Diktor said he was undermining governmental discipline. I took my mother and fled into space. I found a safe spot on Yassinan. I built a pirate empire with your help. I'd offer up all that — all the wealth we've amassed in Yassinan — to smash the setup here!"

Tandor spat on his hand and rubbed his palm on the flat of his bald dome. He said drily, "You make me mad, Angus. You aren't satisfied with things. Always you have to change them. Isn't life full enough for you now?"

Angus ignored him. "If I could get the Book of Nard and free Moana and take her away to safety we might stand a chance. If we could develop science undisturbed on Yassinan we could do it."

"Why fret about Moana?"

"She became my vow-companion. You know what that means to somebody like the Diktor." Angus slapped his broad leather belt decisively. "I'll do it. I'll go in his globe-ship and try and find the Book. Tandor, you stay here. Raise men to fight for us."

The big man with the bald head nodded gloomily. He poured wine from the wooden tankard, downed the brimming goblet in one long gulp. He wiped his lips on the palm of his hand and rubbed it dry on his bald head. "I hear you. I think you're mad but I hear you. What are you going to do with that?"

His thumb jerked at the limp scientist in the long cowled robe. Angus shrugged. "He'll come around. When he does I'll pretend I've fought off his assailant. Meanwhile, you find out which globe-ship he means to give me. Can you do that?"

The big man rumbled. "Tandor can do anything. I'll find out without leaving the room." He lifted his voice and bellowed. When the door opened and a face peered in, Tandor grinned, "Find that wharf-rat Plisket and send him in here."

Plisket limped in, grinning at Angus, bobbing his head. His eyes opened when he heard what Tandor wanted. He chuckled, "The hierarchy plot like a pack of fools. Everybody outside the Citadel hates them. It happens I hate the Diktor more. They gave me gold to build a ship."

"The Skimmer?" asked Tandor. "That wonder-boat you were telling me about?"

"It is a wonder-boat. It incorporates the——"

"Never mind the details," rapped Angus, leaning his palms on the table. "Is that the boat the hierarchy want me to use?"

"It must be. It's the only one unchartered. And Angus — if you are to control — remember that it will submerge. And it has four speeds, two more than . . ."

516

Tandor slapped the table with his palm, making the goblets bounce. "Enough, enough. Plisket, your tongue wags like a hound's tail. Angus, are you ready?"

Angus stretched his tall, heavily shouldered body. He went and bent his lean height over the shallow-breathing scientist and swung him up in a fireman's hitch. He walked firmly, steadily, as he headed for the oaken door.

The man with the zigzag scar on his cheek drew back into the darkness of a jutting second storey as a door creaked open down the street. His eyes glittered, watching Angus emerge with a cowled body atop a shoulder. The hidden man touched a glittering knob strapped to his wrist, turned the knob and lifted it to his mouth.

Angus did not see him, did not hear him whisper into the voxbeamer. He heaved up, settling the body on his shoulder. He began to trot, with space-devouring strides. He went by the spot where Tandor's bully had struck down the cowled man. He went ten paces beyond it, and halted. He lowered the man to the ground and began to shake him.

"Wake up . . . he didn't hit you that hard. Come on. Man, stir yourself . . . that's better . . . see me, do you? Who am I? Angus. Good. You're better? All right . . . on your feet . . . I'll give you a hand."

The scientist teetered weakly, tried to smile. "I told you it was a place for rats. What happened?"

"I beat him off. I carried you a bit, thinking he might come back. We've lost some time."

"Sorry. I'll make a report to the Hierarch. He'll be glad to know you didn't run out on him."

Red Angus clipped coldly, "I wouldn't leave Moana to that Diktor devil. The Hierarch knows that."

The cowled man nodded. "Just the same, I'll tell him. I like you, Angus. If I can ever help you, remember Thordad."

"You're all right? Sure you can go on?"

"I can go on. Hurry. Never mind me. I'll make it."

They saw the towering ball of the globe-ship as they broke from the squat buildings framing the square at the waterfront. It was a ball of golden brilliance, riding the slight sea-swell despite its bulk, occasionally rubbing against the soft snubbers attached to the dock. In the moonlight it loomed majestic and awe-inspiring above the wet, rounded stones of the quay. Its soft *slip-slup* motion on the waves made it seem alive in the salt-laden breeze moving in from the sea.

The scientist halted. "I leave you here. You know how to get to the Flaming Land? Good."

Thordad held out his bony hand. Angus grinned and clasped it. He chuckled, "Tell the Hierarch to dust off a shelf in his Literatum. I'll fill it with the Book of Nard."

Thordad smiled, turned on a heel and strode off into the darkness of an alleyway. Angus went on, eyes gleaming up at the hulk of the ship. He heard the wind whistling in the roof-tops, and across the flat stretch of the square. With eyes and ears already occupied, he did not hear the sobbed cry Thordad managed as a hand closed on his throat, nor did he see the dagger dripping crimson in the hand of the man with the zigzag scar, rising to fall again and again in Thordad's body.

Angus went across the gangplank into the curved port. He pressed a stud and the door slid into place. Lights sprang to full illumination, revealing shimmering metal beams and cross-braces, glittering crimson floor, and long banks of control panels. Glowing tubes, slowly warming, flooded the gigantic room with a soft blue color.

Angus studied the meters. He drew down a red-handled lever. Far below the plasticine-sheltered engines throbbed, roared their power. Slowly the great hull of the globe-ship began to revolve, circling the inner ball. The fine margin of air-space, charged with electronically regulated magnets, made a soft, swooshing sound as the outer ball rotated faster. The inner ball, gigantic gyroscope set in a magnetic field, held steady, while the outer globe swirled rapidly.

The globe-ship seemed a huge ball that some giant's hand was shoving through the water. It flipped water from it as it raced. Its bulk, designed for the minimum amount of friction in water, lanced across the waves with terrific speed.

Angus watched the great bulk of swaying, restless water ahead of him, saw combers flee by, watched huge swells come and go, split by the globular hull. He flipped over the light-map and studied his progress, making changes in the directional needle.

He headed out across the heaving Car Carolan Sea toward the Flaming Lands, where no living man had ever gone before.


The Diktor turned from a contemplation of the serried bands of light glistening across the beaded spectragraph screen. A young attendant in golden jacket and breeches touched a button at his command and the screen went dead.

The drapes over the arched doorway at the end of the room billowed aside as an officer entered, clicked heels and bowed. His voice was hoarse. "Teoman has returned, Eminence. He bears news of the pirate."

The Diktor came striding across the floor, sweeping his cloak behind him with a short, thickly muscled arm. He gestured peremptorily and the billowing curtains lifted. A man with a zigzag scar on his cheek bobbed his head up and down, sidling into the room.

"The pirate has gone in a globe-ship across the Car Carolan Sea, Highest One. A scientist of the Dragon Class was assisting him. I daggered the scientist but I could not reach Angus in time."

The Diktor bit his lip. "Moana?"

The spy shook his sparsely-haired head. "No sign of her, Eminence. She was not with him."

The Diktor tossed a bag of coins to Teoman, gestured the man out. He snapped an order and went striding back and forth across the room as the officer hurried out.

The officer came back with two red-clad attendants who wheeled a squat engine, bulbs and gears locked inside a transparent jacket, before them. High on the gleaming metal top of the machine stood a vox-phone.

The Diktor bent and put his lips to the vox-phone. He said irritably, "Subject: the Car Carolan Sea and adjacent territories. Query: What, if anything, of scientific value is reputedly found in that region?"

There was a faint hum of the gears and pistons. A soft, gentle voice replied, "The Flaming Land and the Desert of Dead White Stones border the Car Carolan Sea to the west. To the east is the continent of Karr Major. To the south the ice floes that are barren. To the north, the polar regions. Beyond the Flaming Land is an inland sea fed underground by waters from the Car Carolan. Beyond that sea lies the desert. It is an uninhabited land. There is nothing of scientific import there aside from the volcanic region of the Flaming Land."

The machine clicked and died. The Diktor sighed. He would have to go and see Stasor. He did not want to do that because he had a feeling that the members of the Elder Race did not approve of him and his methods.

Even far out at sea Angus felt the heat coming toward him in surging waves. Mists, formed from water heated to the boiling point, rose like a white pall to shelter the Flaming Lands from his eyes. But here and there, through a breeze-made rift, he could see huge tongues of fire, red and sullen, rising from the ground.

Angus drove the globe-ship into the white fog. Gigantic bubbles broke under it, flung mists and steam up over the ship. Inside the glober the heat was fierce.

Angus was clammy with the sweat running down his cheeks and ribs. It was sapping his energies. When the controls started to blur in his eyes he knew he had enough. His fingers touched the warm control lever and threw it forward.

He fled miles from the mist and slowed to a stop, riding the ocean's swell. He muttered, "I'm through. Finished. I can't go over and I can't go under . . . or can I? Didn't Plisket say something about that? Wait . . . wait . . . sure! He said this thing will submerge."

Angus got up and crossed the room. There was a small literatum inset in the metal wall. He ran his eyes over titles, reached up and brought down a thick book on geophysiology.

He bent, consulting pages on subterranean oceanology. His finger pointed out a paragraph. "From the Car Carolan Sea an underground river feeds the inland sea that lies between the Flaming Lands and the Desert of Dead White Stones'.

It took him a long time, hunting blindly in the heated water all around him. He went deep, trundling across the jagged ocean bottom. The oxygenerators were laboring when he found the great dark orifice looming ahead in his sea-lights.

It was close work, maneuvering the glober through the sea-tunnel. All around was the muted booming of volcanic fires sending up hot jets of molten lava, flame and ashes. Water swirled, black and thickish, past the rounded hull.

When the water lightened, he knew they were out of the tunnel. Angus sent the glober rocketing upward. It burst through the water into clean air. The Flaming Lands lay behind. Ahead, across the bluish expanse that was the inland sea, lay a vast stretch of sand and rock.

Angus anchored the globe-ship. He dove overboard and swam to the whitish sands. The sun was warm above and the hot sand bit through his boots. Angus threw a canteen across his shoulder and fastened a packet of food tablets around his waist.

He walked for two days and a night before he found the half-sunken road that arched across the desert. The road ended four days later, in the barrens. His water was gone and the leathern pocket that had held food tablets was empty.

"I can't turn back," he thought. "I've been gone a whole week from the inland sea."

Angus turned and stumbled on. The sun beat down on his naked shoulders, on the remnants of the sun-worn rags about his middle. With each puff of sand his feet kicked up, something went out of his spirit.

Angus saw a brown rock uplifting its jagged tip from the sand. He ran awkwardly toward it, hoping that from its top he might see the spires of a distant, nebulous city.

But there was only sand and more twisted, curving dunes, and the faint azure tint of the horizon.

He stood on the naked finger of rock and swore. He invoked the olden gods — the fecund Ashtal, goddess of love and sex; Grom who fought with warriors; Jethad who loved the wise. He called on them for their attention and he cursed them, upwards and down, forward and back.

In his rage he took the empty canteen and hurled it.

Choking, he broke off in mid-curse.

*The canteen had disappeared in mid-air!*

The Hierarch made fists out of his taloned hands. The cowled man, bent before his carven chair, trembled. The Hierarch whispered, "Are you sure?"

"We followed his spectragraph in the screen, Excellency. We followed it until it disappeared!"

The black orbs in the thin white face of the chief scientist burned with fanatical ardor. Through thin lips he rasped, "He tricked me. He had those pirates of his pick him up when he was safely out of my hands."

"He went through the Flaming Lands," quavered the cowled man. "We saw him do that. Would he go to all that trouble to be picked up in the desert? He could have escaped from the Car Carolan Sea."

"Evidence of his cunning. He wanted to make sure he was a good distance away from the power of the Diktor."

"The Diktor?"

"You fool! I'm going to the Diktor and turn Moana over to his torturers. I'll tell him Angus planned with Moana to kill him. Ha! The torturers will work over her for a long time, I think. When Angus hears of that . . ."

The Hierarch brooded. He smiled, "I might even turn that into a trap for him. When he returns, having heard what has happened to Moana, I'll be waiting for him."

Angus slid down from the rock with his heart in his mouth. *The canteen flew out into the air,* he thought. *It went high, and as it came down it disappeared!*

There was something just ahead of him. Perhaps a force

field hidden in the shifting and eddying mists rising from the desert lands.

If he could find the canteen and discover what made it invisible . . .

Angus was weak. His knees crumpled as he tried to take a forward step. He summoned the muscles and the nerves of his big, gaunt body. He went forward one step, then two.

At the third step he fell. He put out his hands.

They parted the grey mists in front of him but did not break his fall. His naked knees hit rounded stones and then his palms went out and touched the worn pavings of a city street.

"Gods!" the pirate whispered, lifting his head, blue eyes burning like coals in his tanned face.

The gray mists shifted, fading. From their wisps, as though like the flesh of a naked woman revealed by smoky veils, shone queerly rounded and smoothly curved walls of amaranthine and ochre, red and jonquil yellow. Here and there a dome of pearly champagne stood tipped with a knob of vermilion. The houses on the edge of the city were low, seeming to rise higher and higher toward the center where a tall, slender building reared its spire.

Red Angus drew a deep breath, running his hands down the ridged muscles of his thighs. He turned and stared behind him where the hot sands ought to be. He saw only mists, shifting and shimmering.

Angus went down the street, past empty-windowed buildings, across bare intersections, his foot-falls loud in the stillness of the dead city.

He walked until the entrance to the central towers was in front of him. Crested with heraldic devices — Red Angus recognized the flame-eyed Stallion of forgotten Shallar and the rampant Dragon of Domeer — the wide door was a glittering mass of emeralds embedded in carvings so delicate they seemed sheared from paper.

The doors opened at a touch, revealing red-and-yellow squares of metal stretching forward beneath a glittering dome of translucent jade. In the center of the hall stood a low metal rim about a bubble of grayish green iridescence. He went toward the rim, bent over and stared down.

"One of the black pools!" whispered Angus.

Through the luminescent bubble he could see only blackness, a jet nothingness that seemed alive.

A step sounded on the metal flagging behind him.

Angus whirled.

A man stood there, leaning on a bent staff, smiling gently. He was clad in a loose woollen garment, white as falling snow. His arms and legs were bare and brown. His face, though lined and creased, seemed almost youthful.

"I have waited many years," he said softly, "and no one ever came. Now — at last — there is someone who has found the city. Welcome. I bid you welcome to the Tower of the Ancients!"

"Stasor!" cried Angus in sudden recognition.

"The Stasor you know, yes. One of my race is chosen to spend a hundred years as Guardian of the City, to wait for any who might come to seek its treasures. You are the first who ever found it."

Angus said, "A lifetime of loneliness. Are we worth it?"

The old man laughed. "We do not die — not as your race knows death. It's one of our attainments. Like the blackness where you first saw me."

"The blackness?" Angus turned, stared down at the metal collar encasing the jet black pool. "What is it? It must be all over the planet. No one knows what the pool is."

"It is the greatest product of my race. Many eons ago a scientist discovered that an atom may be split to create ravening energy. For years the mightiest scientists of the Elders studied that fact. Eventually they built machines that could house such awful power. Finally, after many centuries, they developed the pools.

"The pools are nothing more than that atomic radiation — sheer energy — bottled up in vast chambers lined with *stalabasil*. Ready for use at any time.

"In the early days men died from such radioactivity.

As time went on and we handled it more and more, our bodies evolved, so that the painful burns that caused death became as mere tinglings along the nerve-ends. Your own race, that evolved on Karr after the Elders went on, is also immune to it."

"Reservoirs of energy," murmured Angus, rubbing hand on thigh. "If you could harness that energy and turn it into channels of production . . ."

His blue eyes widened as breath caught in his throat. Stasor smiled, his old head nodding. "That's what we Elders used. We powered our machines with it. We needed no fuel, no refilling of bins or tanks. It was always there, ready to tap."

"Does the Book of Nard mention it?"

The old man nodded. "All our secrets are contained in the Book of Nard. Do you want to see it?"

They went up a flight of spiralling steps and into a room where heavy golden drapes hung bright and splendid. On a wooden rest lay a closed book, its covers solid gold, its parchment leaves tinted a pale rose.

"Open it," said the Guardian.

Angus bent and lifted the cover. He gazed on the archaic lettering etched into the thick vellum.

*Each man has in him the seeds of his own immortality. He must progress or he must die. And the race is like the man. Who shall say what path that progression shall take? A man cannot know his own future. Neither does the race. This is the Book of Nard, first of the Elder Race. With encouragement to all peoples who come after us, we leave this short transcript of our past.*

Angus lifted his eyes. He stared at the smiling Guardian, who nodded. Quickly the pirate touched the parchment, spread pages wide. His keen blue eyes scanned the etchings while he read the record of those who had gone on. He scanned mathematical and astronomical formulae, chemical equations, biological charts.

He whispered, "The entire history of the race, told in the achievements of its scientists!"

"It is all that lives."

"I don't understand it, of course. I catch a thought, here and there. But the entire equation . . ."

"You don't understand it?"

"No."

The old man smiled. He said suddenly, "Would you like to see some of those achievements in action? Would you like to see the worlds in three-dimensional space, the island universe, the galaxies, the stars and their planets?"

Angus said, "I've been out among the Six Worlds. I've seen other systems through telescopes."

The old man laughed. It was a spontaneous, happy sort of laugh. "I don't mean that way. Come, let me show you what my race can do." Angus caught him smiling oddly, the corners of his lips drawing down, as though he shared a queer joke only with himself.

They did not use the stairway this time. They stepped into a bare room walled and ceilinged and floored with shining steel. The old man touched a stud on the door.

The room of the book was gone.

In its stead, there was a round chamber with a transparent dome that revealed stars twinkling uncounted miles above. In the middle of the otherwise unfurnished room stood a low, flat dais set with chairs riveted on their curving metal legs into the dais. A bank of controls was set flush in the floor of the platform.

The old man led him to the dais. He smiled, bending over the control panel, "This is the kind of observatory your race will have, someday. You won't have to depend on polished mirrors and light and thick lenses. Basically the principle of the thing is the same as that of the teleport room we used to come over here. We just make use of coordinated space and time factors. It's like steering a boat on an uncharted ocean. If you know where your lodestar is you can go anywhere you want."

He turned and reached for a chair. "We're ready now. You are perfectly safe, no matter what you see, or think you see. Just relax."

The reflected light in the room was fading. Blackness came down through the transparent dome and surrounded

526

them. It was like the Staratarium Red Angus had visited on Mawk — or it was, until Angus saw stars beside and below him.

A nebula that was uncounted light years away came rushing toward them. It was a spinning silver wheel at a distance, but it broke into great blotches of black space to dissolve into just another star system without form or noticeable nebulosity.

They swooped over a reddish planet and dropped through its atmosphere. They studied great buildings of stone and metal that towered high into the clouds. Tiny fliers and great air-freighters dotted the skies. The old man said, "This people used their science wisely. They built a civilization that gives every man all he wants which is, in effect, all he can understand."

They left the red planet, swept light years away and down through heavy mists to a greenish globe whirling majestically in the light of its distant sun. Beneath them lush, tropical jungles lifted fronds and branches to the steaming mists. Somewhere in that massed carpet of vegetation an animal screamed in its dying agonies. Through a break in the trees Angus saw a naked man squat and hairy and with a stone-bladed spear in his hand, fleeing before the bounding fury of a gigantic tiger. The great cat was making its last leap, spreading its talons into the man's shivering flesh, as the mists crept up and hid them.

"A young world," Stasor said softly, "with all its life ahead of it in which to find its destiny."

They went out into space and found a planet where giant insects ruled, where a lumbering thing in the shape of a man, but mindless, was used for heavy labor. Another planet showed lizards dwelling in strangely wrought mansions. A third showed mind-beings that looked like crimson jellyfish hanging in midair by some means of mental suspension.

"All these," explained Stasor with a wave of his palm, "are freaks. Life throughout the whole universe, across all of its uncountable light-years, follows mainly a pattern like our own. Creatures that we call man, with two arms, two legs, two eyes, a nose and mouth, breathing atmosphere into lungs, have been the ruling race because of circumstances like gravity and atmosphere, over which they themselves have no control.

"One more example, then we're done. . . ."

They fled across star galaxies, through sprawling universe where binaries and dwarf stars and red giants alternated against the black void like a spangled curtain. They went through the Megellanic Cluster and the Andromeda nebula. They came swooping down so swiftly that the stars blurred a little, even at their incredible distances, toward another galaxy.

Stasor found a little star. It was surrounded by nine planets. He chose the third planet outward from the star, and dropped his observational platform through the heaviside and ionosphere.

Angus craned forward. He liked this world. It reminded him vaguely of Karr, with its green grasses and rolling oceans.

"Its inhabitants call it the Earth. A peaceful place. Look over there — you can see the city clearer now."

It had graceful spires and round, lovely dwellings. Giant ships rested beside white, sparkling wharves. People went back and forth clad in light, airy garments. There was an air of glowing contentment.

Stasor said, "This is their golden age. It will last a long time. Soon they will colonize other planets near them. In the end — some million years from now — these people will rule almost all the known universes. And yet, compared to ours, their science is just a crawling child."

Angus felt a touch of jealousy. "Why should they rule the worlds? We people of Karr . . ."

"Wait, not yet. I want to show you this world three hundred years ago."

He touched a lever. The world below them grew away, shot backward and out into space. Angus cried out in amazement. "It's receding from us."

"I'm going back in time. Remember, this is an expanding universe. It's come a long way in the past three centuries, going toward the fixed star, Vega. We have to follow it."

This time, there was no lovely world. There was only blackened earth, charred and scorched. Great humps of steel stuck up from the ground like the fire-blackened ribs of some giant fallen in swamp-muck. From the west came seven thin, lean shapes, speeding through the air. From the blackened ground came thinner, smaller shapes to intercept them. The small shapes were like wasps in their darting and their speed. The big shapes never had a chance. They went down in masses of red flame, spinning.

Stasor announced, "This is their Last War. It is to go on ten more years. The seven shapes you saw were bombers loaded to their wings with atomic bombs. The smaller ships were fighters, their armaments mounted with fission-guns, an invention of an American scientist."

"Ten more years!" flinched Angus. "There's only blackened ground for them to live on."

"They live underground," explained Stasor.

Angus mused, "There's such a sharp difference between this world and what it's to be like three hundred years from this time."

"The American who invented the fission-gun," explained Stasor, "will lead their world to that pinnacle. He is going to organize the remnants of the civilization left after the last war, compel interracial wedlock and births. The biological result of that will be, naturally, a new and different race in the course of the years. It is that race that will go out from Earth to the stars."

Angus regarded Stasor thoughtfully. "You're thinking that what the American did with his people, I can do with mine."

The old man shrugged. He reached out and twisted the dials. He murmured, "Karr fights a war just as deadly as the one you see below. There's a difference. Instead of death, Karr's enemies deal it stagnation and degeneration."

"If I could get the Diktor to give the Hierarch's sciences to the people," Angus mused.

"Where there is hope you have new life," smiled Stasor

gently. "Without science to benefit their lives the people of Karr have no hope."

Angus lashed out bitterly, "The Diktor is too powerful. There isn't any way to beat him."

"I will show you a way," murmured the old man.

# III

Stal Tay held court before his ruby throne. He sat with right hand on his knee, bent forward, thin lips smiling. Before him stood the Hierarch, rigid with rage, black eyes burning under the shadow of his white cowl. To the Hierarch's left an almost naked Moana was crumpled on the cold stone floor, manacles rivetted to her wrists and ankles, her white flesh gleaming through torn garments.

Stal Tay taunted, "You come too late, Hierarch. I know where Red Angus went, what he went for, and who sent him."

"It was done in your interests," rasped the scientist. "I brought her to you that you might know the truth."

Stal Tay glanced at the weeping Moana. "So many odd things are done in my supposed interests these days. At that, I'm almost inclined to believe you but what really bothers me is this — did Angus find . . ."

The Diktor snapped off his speech abruptly. He rose half out of his throne, fingers clutching the jeweled arms. The Hierarch whirled. Even Moana turned her head to look, the sobs still racking her body.

A yellow glow was forming in midair a foot above the stone tiles of the Audience Chamber. The yellow glittered, coruscated and faded away. Where the color was now stood a flat black dais with three chairs whose curving legs were rivetted to the floor of the dais. A man turned from the control panel that rose between the seats, a man with red hair and a tanned body. The man looked at them and laughed.

"Angus," whimpered Moana.

"Seize him," raged Stal Tay.

Angus bent and lifted something and held it up. It glittered in the light filtering through the arched windows of the Audience Chamber. Angus said, "This is the Book of Nard. I've come to bargain with you, Stal Tay."

The Diktor sank back into his throne, gesturing his guards aside. He said, "What do you want for the Book?"

"Moana."

"Moana," said the Diktor in surprise. "Is that all? Take her . . . but wait. How do I know this isn't a trick? How do I know I'll get the Book?"

Angus stepped from the dais to the floor of the chamber. He placed the book in its golden covers on the floor. "I went to the City of the Ancients. I met Stasor and took the Book of Nard from him. I came to bring it to you. I see I came just in time to save Moana."

Stal Tay came to his feet. "That thing you ride. What is it? Tell me its secret and I'll pardon you."

Angus laughed in his face. "Stasor calls it a teleportator. It shifts space, draws sectors of space together in an instant. In it a man can move from here to anywhere on Karr. Stasor knows many things, Stal Tay. One of them is how to bring you off that throne!"

The Diktor's face purpled. He started to talk but his eyes caught the golden covers of the Book of Nard and he controlled his anger. "Take her," he said, "before I decide the Book isn't worth your insults!"

Irons clanking, the girl stepped to Angus' side, let him lift her to the dais. Then Angus turned and studied the Diktor through narrowed eyelids.

"I'm giving you the Book now, Stal Tay. But it's only fair to warn you — I'll be back for it!"

He steppepd onto the dais, turned a knob on the control panel. The dais fled and the golden bubble came back, and then that, too, disappeared.

Moana sobbed as the dais fled through shifting white mists. Angus knelt beside her, using his disintegrator on the links of her manacles. She said, "The Diktor will send men for you. He'll never let you get away with this. You've only won a temporary victory."

Angus chuckled. "He'll be too busy with the Hierarch

531

and the Book of Nard to go after me for a while. When he does, it will be too late." He dropped the severed chains to the floor of the dais. "You see, none of the scientists in the Citadel will understand the sciences in the book. They'll tell Stal Tay that and he won't believe them. There'll be a minor war between the Diktor and the Hierarchy. Once a breach between them is made, we'll step into it."

The dais settled on something solid. The golden veil dissipated as before a wind, to reveal the smoke-blackened beams of a tavern room. Tandor was there, a wooden mug in one hand, straining forward from the tableside, his other hand clutching its edge, staring at them.

Angus helped Moana down. Tandor drained the mug and slammed it on the tabletop. He demanded, "Well? Got a bellyful of it? Ready for the star trails?"

"Not yet, Tandor."

Tandor growled and rubbed his palm on his bald head. He grumbled, "You'll be a martyr yet. You watch. You'll see. Red Angus — who died saving nothing!"

The pirate grinned at him, leaning his palms flat on the tabletop. "If I win, you know what'll happen, don't you? You and I will have to rule Karr. You'll be my majordomo. You'll wear fine clothes and make decisions and listen to people bellyache."

Tandor howled, leaping up so suddenly that his chair went skidding. He slammed his palms on the table. "Not me!" he bellowed. "I want no office and no snivelling folk to spoil my days! I——"

Angus moved a hand. He put it flat to Tandor's chest and held it there. The bald giant snapped his lips together. He grew silent as a clam, and as still.

The door was opening.

Something that looked like a man, that was swathed in white bandages from toes to head, with two slits for eyes and a hole for a mouth, was coming in the room. Tandor's hand swooped and lifted with a disintegrator.

"Angus," whispered the apparition. "Red Angus! I need help."

The pirate was across the room, catching the bandaged figure in cradling arms, lowering him to the couch. He whispered, "This is the second time you've been on that couch, Thordad. What happened to you?"

"When I left you at the globe-ship dock one of Stal Tay's spies knifed me and left me for dead. The Hierarch sent men to find me. They doctored me and were carrying me to the Citadel when the Diktor jumped us. He sent me to his torture dungeons."

The man shuddered under the bandages. The eyes, through the slits, were wide with horror and remembered pain. "The Diktor wanted to learn what the Hierarch was after. I wouldn't tell him. Before that he confronted me with the Hierarch who disowned me. He told Stal Tay to do with me what he wanted!"

The raw hate throbbed in Thordad's voice. It sent a cold ripple down Angus' spine. The pirate leaned closer to the bandaged mouth: "The Diktor let his beasts at me for three days. It was horrible. But I got away. I think I went mad with the pain. I crept to my cousin's house and was bandaged and partially healed there. Then I came here. You're the only hope any of us have. You've got to do something — anything — to stop that madman and the Hierarch!"

Angus wiped his hands on his jacket. "You, Tandor. What news have you?"

"I've been busy too," Tandor growled, eyeing Thordad curiously. "I've roused the men and women of the Lower City. I've sent for the pirates on Yassanin, sent for warriors from the cities of Streeth and Fayalat. We've a crew of fighting men with swords and spears and a few disintegrators. But with the scientific might of Stal Tay and the Hierarch we're beaten before we start."

Angus laughed. "Not yet. Stasor has promised help. We're to meet him and get the weapons he told me about. Into the teleportator on the double — all of you."

When they were in the chairs fastened to the dais, Angus threw over the lever. A golden mist formed about them, hardened. There was an instant of coldness . . .

The golden mist disappeared. The teleportator stood before the fountain in the Tower of the Ancients. Angus sprang from the machine. "Stasor, I'm back!"

There was no answer. Only the silence of the dead walls of the dead city replied.

It was Moana who found the blood-stained bit of silk that had been ripped from Stasor's garment. Wordlessly she held it out to Angus.

His belly turned over when he saw it. He looked at the girl, then at Tandor.

"The Diktor's come for him. With Stasor to unravel the secrets in the Book of Nard, Stal Tay can't be beaten!"

Tandor shrugged massive shoulders. "I knew that a long time ago. We'll all die. It's just a matter of when and where."

In the time Angus had allotted him, Tandor had thrown up a small city of tents and wickiups along the stone ridges of the Bloody Cliffs. Here came the pirates from Yassinan, the starved soldiery from the star cities of Fayalat and Kor. Here were half-naked gypsy girls and camp followers, fighting men and muckers. Here were dishonored captains and untried youths who owned swords and a hot hunger to use them.

In the red fire of an armorer's forge, Red Angus handled a ring-barreled gun that was powered by a portable dynamo set up a small, two-wheeled cart.

The armorer said, "It's weak and it's clumsy, but it's the best I could do. The electroray gets its power from the dynamo in the cart. Power travels along the fuel line to the breach. A tiny converter translates it into a thin beam of force. I've seen them in the museums. I made sketches. Given more time I could do better."

Red Angus put a grin on his lips and held it there by sheer will-power. His hand clapped the man on the back. He told him, "You've done fine, Yoth! Keep it up. Turn out as many as you can!"

The armorer shook his head glumly. "They won't be much alongside the disintegrators that Stal Tay will have. Even their sonic-beams will do more damage than this!"

Tandor came swaggering up through the half-naked,

hairy chested men who fought with blunted sabres and war-spears. There was dirt on his face, and runnels of sweat ran on his barrel chest. He planted his legs apart, and glowered at Red Angus.

"You're mad as a priest of Grom. You keep us here when we'd do better by scattering to the six worlds."

Angus said, "These are the toughest fighting men in the galaxy. If they can't take the Citadel no one can. Once we get within sword-sweep of the Diktor's guards . . ."

Tandor bellowed. He went up on his toes and waved his arms, and his veins stood out on his bald head. "As well get within sword-sweep of Ashtal the Shameless!" he roared. "The Diktor will sweep the streets with disintegrator beams when he sees us coming. Maybe you want to play martyr, but I've better uses for my life. Take that gypsy girl . . ."

Angus caught him by the fur of his cloak and shook him. "Forget your gypsy wenches. We go into the Lower City at night. All of us, over a week's time. We bed down in different homes. Loyal homes. A fortnight from now will be the Night of the Serpent. Singing and dancing in the streets. Wine. Women."

Tandor grinned. "Aie, that sounds good."

"At the hour of the Dog we hit the Citadel. There'll be so much roistering going on we'll belt-whip every mother's son into the streets that night, and make 'em yell to cover our movements. No one'll notice us!

"We hit the Citadel from every street. Some of us will get through. Ten streets, ten companies, each of them a flying wedge to get inside and kill Stal Tay. That's our first job. After that . . ."

Red Angus talked on, sketching in the hot sands. He did not see a bandaged Thordad come out of a tent and stand there, watching them, and listening. Thordad turned away after a while and went back into the tent where he sat shivering and staring down at his hands.

Neither did Red Angus see him that night when he daggered a guard and fled on a haml across the desert for Karr City. They found the guard but guessed him a victim of a jealous lover for he had a reputation as a lady's man.

535

The days slid into weeks, and the fires burned and metal glowed, and the forges and the anvils never stopped. Swords and shields and spears, daggers and clumsy electrorays were turned out for eager hands.

They broke camp in the faint mists of an early dawn. On ewe-necked haml and on foot, by cart and by stolen jetcar, they left the base of the Bloody Cliffs. They came into Karr City by twos and threes and hid themselves in the taverns and in the thatch-roofed houses. The city knew them and the city swallowed them, and the city slumbered, waiting.

In the tavern of the Spotted Stag, Red Angus paced the floor. Tandor, an arm around his gypsy girl, was sampling a new tun of imported wine. Moana was white-faced, pale and silent at the table.

Angus said, "I don't like it. I don't like it. I have the feel of a wolf sniffing at the jaws of a trap."

Tandor drew his lips from the gypsy's neck long enough to say, "It's quiet, isn't it. What more do you want?"

"That's just it. It's too quiet. There are no Citadel guards out hunting me. No arrests for five days. No street patrols, even!"

"Good. Then let's call it off and go back to Yassanin. You'll like Yassanin, honey." Tandor nuzzled the girl's throat, "I have a big house there. Much wine. Better wine than this!"

Angus stared at the man through slitted eyes, reached for a goblet and lifted it. His hand poised the goblet, about to throw. Angus swore and buried his nose in the cup. He flung it from him, and it broke against the wall.

The city stayed quiet for five days. On the morning of the Night of the Serpent it exploded with energy. Men and women, in masks and costumes, paraded and sang. They drank and danced and the Citadel brooded down on them.

The day wore on. Tandor and Angus were busy, keeping some semblance of order in their fighting crews, keeping the men from the wine-barrels, readying them for their assignments. Tandor went stalking into the taverns and the wine shops with heavy hands, striking out as he walked, often upending an unfortunate into a wine-tun after knocking in its head with the head of the man he held upside down in his hands.

Red Angus went more circumspectly, fighting off the tipsy women and armed footpads who waxed rich in the torchlight gatherings during the long Night of the Serpent. He rounded up his crews and found them their weapons.

"Tonight the stars revolt!"

At the hour of the Dog ten companies of hard-eyed fighting men came out of the shadows of the ten cobblestoned streets that led by twisting tiers to the Citadel. They went up the curving stone stairs to the smooth Citadel streets and started forward . . .

And then the Diktor struck.

The sonicbeams came first, cutting the front ranks to bloody pulp. Disintors rayed into action. Men went down silently under the lightning-swift impact of purplish lances.

It was a rout.

Here, a naked mercenary from Fayalat would flesh his blade in a few necks as he drove in behind a wall of dead flesh. There, a warrior from Kor might take three of Stal Tay's soldiers with him before he touched hands with his ancestors. But the beams and the rays slew in the darkness and the rabble was driven back.

Where Red Angus fought with an electroray cart, sweeping the ringed nozzle of his weapon in and out of the shadows, the men of the Lower City stood a while. They fought with the ferocity of trapped thots, for the pits of Stal Tay yawned for them.

"Hold firm!" roared Tandor, his sword a sweeping line of death where it circled and darted.

"Fall back," cried Angus. "Back to reform! They've trapped us well, the tricky dogs."

A man with a bandaged face stood out a moment from the shadows, pointing. He cried, "Half a hundred *oblis* to the man who brings down Red Angus!"

"Thordad!" shouted Angus, and he knew now the manner of his betrayal. Thordad had seen a chance for reinstatement and had taken it. He had seen the rabble that served Red Angus and knew the disciplined power of the

Diktor's guards. He had gone with news of Angus' plans. This trap was the result.

Red Angus forgot the others. He sighted the electroray carefully. A thin beam of brilliance lanced out. It touched Thordad on face and neck. A headless corpse rolled at the guards' feet as they came forward.

Their rush caught Angus and the men with him. It swept them backward through the streets, rolled up their flanks. It clubbed the center with sonicbeams until men screamed in the agony of mashed legs and caved-in chests.

Angus fought like a maddened griff. He used the electroray like a broom, sweeping it before him. He kicked the two-wheeled cart ahead for without the dynamo in the cart the electroray was useless.

A sudden rush of guards caught Angus in a maelstrom of cursing, howling men.

They hit him and drove him back against the glittering metal collar of one of the black pools, yawning grim and silent in the cobblestoned square. They hammered him with swordblades and pounded the cart with metal-headed axes.

Angus stumbled, fell. He came up slowly, his back to the cold metal collar of the pool, the ringed barrel of the useless electroray still in his hands.

*It's all over,* he told himself, staring at the swords coming for him. *I've failed, and I'll die, and so will Moana, and Tandor, and all the rest of this motley crew who tried to pull themselves up by their bootstraps.*

Angus clubbed with the ringed barrel and a man fell whimpering at his feet.

"Come on!" the pirate roared. "Here's my last stand, here at the edge of the pool! You're done with Red Angus. See how a free man dies."

Angus broke off, eyes wide.

The pool!

One of the black pools of Karr . . .

What was it Stasor had said of those pools? "The pools are nothing more than atomic radiation — sheer energy —

538

bottled up in vast chambers lined with stalahasil. Ready for use at any time."

Ready for use.

With the savage fury of the barbarian, Angus slammed the ringed barrel at the faces pressing in on him. They wanted him alive and that gave him the precious moment he needed.

He whipped the electroray high in the air, swung it so the weighted powercord flailed high and far over the metal rim of the pool's collar. It dropped down and down into the black depths.

Angus pressed the stud.

A ravening stream of black mist shot from the ringed nozzle. It touched the oncoming soldiers of the Diktor, touched them, and . . .

Ate them!

When the black mist faded the Diktor's soldiers faded, too. They were gone in that desolation of yawning street and crumpled walls. Where the black mist had touched nothing remained.

Tandor bellowed.

The star-pirates roared their glee.

Angus moved the weapon and touched the stud again. The black mist fled outward, up one street, down another. When he was finished there were no soldiers facing them. The streets to the Citadel lay empty, beckoning.

They went forward in a ravening wave of fury, the fury of roused fighting men, who had looked the eyeless sockets of Death's skull in the face and lived. The night held no more terrors for them for their nostrils were tasting the fragrance of victory. Other men came up from the Lower City to join them, men who bore home-made weapons, crude clubs and axes.

Angus caught a sweat-streaked Tandor by the arm. "This gun! The powercord that fell in the black pool. That's what did it. It's a weapon of the Elders. The pool feeds it, gives it power . . ."

"What matters that?" bellowed Tandor, shaking a new sword in his hand. "It worked!"

"But it won't work if I can't keep the powercord inside the pool."

Tandor blinked, grunting as understanding came to him. "Huh. That's different. Pask. Gatl. Sonal. At the double, you riff-raff. To me."

He gave orders crisply, then swung to Angus. "They'll scour the Lower City for copper wire. We'll couple an extension to the cord so you can take it wherever you want."

Angus nodded. "Put a file of men on either side of it. Keep them there. Make them fight for that cord with their lives. If they fail us, we die."

Tandor handpicked his men, big men all, with the scars of many battles speaking their experience. The cord was slit and fitted with gleaming copper cable-lengths, insulated, and welded tightly.

Weapon in hands, Red Angus led his rabble army up the stone-block roadway steps, upward from the mire and filth of the Lower City, upward to the clean white reaches of the Citadel.

The Diktor's personal guards made a sortie against them, but the black mist swept them away. When the Hierarch sent his troops to join those of the Diktor the mist swirled around them once, and then blew away, leaving the Citadel gardens empty of opposition.

It was over.

They walked through the gardens, into the halls and corridors of the Palace. Men stood weaponless, fright tightening the lines of their faces.

Tandor roared, "The Diktor, you foul hounds. Where is he?"

Men pointed and at the end of their fingers loomed the great golden bulk of the Audience Chamber.

The Diktor and the Hierarch stood before the ruby throne. They were beaten men, expecting death, their cheeks washed an ashen gray.

Angus said, "If you've harmed Stasor you'll take a year to die."

The Diktor gestured wearily. "He's in chains, in the lower pits. We haven't harmed him. He would not translate the Book of Nard. But even so, dead he was useless to us. Alive, he might have changed his mind."

He went on to explain how he had traced Angus' journey in the spectragraph, how his men had followed Angus' course in globe ships to bring the god of Karr to the Citadel. He said, "You were beaten. Whipped. My messengers told me that you were hemmed in, your men chopped to thumbits. And yet — yet you come here———"

Madness glinted in the Diktor's eyes. His right hand moved like lightning, and the blue metal of a disintor caught fire from the soft luminescence of the walls.

The Diktor was swift but Tandor was faster. His hand blurred and a glittering longsword jumped the five feet that separated them. It drove the dead body of the Diktor back three steps to the ruby throne. He fell at its base and a pool of blood grew on the floor.

The Hierarch shrugged and put a pellet to his mouth. The poison acted with incredible speed. He was falling as the chamber door opened and a gently smiling Stasor entered, leaning on his staff.

Angus and Moana stood on the heights of the Citadel and looked down at the Lower City. They saw the thatched roofs no longer, but instead tidy houses, clean streets and healthy children. Men and women walked with pride, their bodies clean, enjoying the new life that Stasor and the Book of Nard could bring them. It would take time, all that. But it would come.

Moana moved gently. Her hand caught his. He turned her head up and his lips settled on hers.

A hundred feet away, Tandor grinned. "A martyr, I called him," he told the night.

He thought of a black-haired noblewoman who had been widowed in the night's fighting. Tandor rubbed his head again and chuckled. He tiptoed from the gardens.

*Far in the future, they discovered a new natural law: what goes up must come round. Even Hautamaki came round to the idea.*

●

# FINAL ENCOUNTER

## By Harry Harrison

## I

Hautamaki had landed the ship on a rubble-covered pan of rock, a scored and ancient lava flow on the wrong side of the glacier. Tjond had thought, but only to herself, that they could have landed nearer; but Hautamaki was shipmaster and made all the decisions. Then again, she could have stayed with the ship. No one had forced her to join in this hideous scramble across the fissured ice. But of course staying behind was out of the question.

There was a radio beacon of some kind over there — on this uninhabited planet — sending out squeals and cracklings on a dozen frequencies. She *had* to be there when they found it.

Gulyas helped her over a difficult place and she rewarded him with a quick kiss on his windburned cheek.

It was too much to hope that it could be anything other than a human beacon, though their ship was supposed to be covering an unexplored area. Yet there was the slimmest chance that some *others* might have built the beacon. The thought of not being there at the time of a discovery like that was unbearable. How long had mankind been looking now, for how many time-dimmed centuries?

She had to rest, she was not used to this kind of physical effort. She was roped between the two men and when she stopped they all stopped. Hautamaki halted and looked when he felt her hesitant tug on the rope, staring down at her and saying nothing. His body said it for him, arrogant, tall, heavily muscled, bronzed and nude under the transparent atmosphere suit. He was breathing lightly and normally, and his face never changed expression as he looked at her desperately heaving breast. Hautamaki! What kind of a man are you, Hautamaki, to ignore a woman with such a deadly glance?

For Hautamaki it had been the hardest thing he had ever done. When the two strangers had walked up the extended tongue of the ship's boarding ramp he had felt violated.

This was his ship, his and Kiiskinen's. But Kiiskinen was dead and the child that they had wanted to have was dead. Dead before birth, before conception. Dead because Kiiskinen was gone and Hautamaki would never want a child again. Yet there was still the job to be done; they had completed barely half of their survey swing when the accident had occurred. To return to survey base would have been prodigiously wasteful of fuel and time, so he had called for instructions — and this had been the result. A new survey team, unfledged and raw.

They had been awaiting first assignment — which meant they at least had the training if not the experience. Physically they would do the work that needed to be done. There would be no worry about that. But they were a team, and he was only half a team; and loneliness can be a terrible thing.

He would have welcomed them if Kiiskinen had been there. Now he loathed them.

The man came first, extending his hand. "I'm Gulyas, as you know, and my wife Tjond." He nodded over his shoulder and smiled, the hand still out.

"Welcome aboard my ship," Hautamaki said and clasped his own hands behind his back. If this fool didn't know about the social customs of Men, he was not going to teach him.

"Sorry. I forgot you don't shake hands or touch strangers." Still smiling, Gulyas moved aside to make room for his wife to enter the ship.

"How do you do, shipmaster?" Tjond said. Then her eyes widened and she flushed, as she saw for the first time that he was completely nude.

"I'll show you your quarters," Hautamaki said, turning and walking away, knowing they would follow. A woman! He had seen them before on various planets, even talked with them, but he never believed that there would some day be one on his ship. How ugly they were, with their swollen bodies! It was no wonder that on the other worlds everyone wore clothes, to conceal those blubbery, bobbing things and the excess fat below.

"Why — he wasn't even wearing *shoes!*" Tjond said indignantly as he closed the door. Gulyas laughed.

"Since when has nudity bothered you? You didn't seem to mind it during our holidays on Hie. And you knew about the Men's customs."

"That was different. Everyone was dressed — or undressed — the same. But this, it's almost indecent!"

"One man's indecency is another's decency."

"I bet you can't say that three times fast."

"Nevertheless it's true. When you come down to it he probably thinks that we're just as socially wrong as you seem to think he is."

"I don't think — I *know!*" she said, reaching up on tiptoes to nip his ear with her tiny teeth, as white and perfectly shaped as rice grains. "How long have we been married?"

"Six days, nineteen hours standard, and some odd minutes."

"Only odd because you haven't kissed me in such a terribly long time."

He smiled down at her tiny, lovely figure, ran his hand over the warm firmness of her hairless skull and down her straight body, brushing the upturned almost vestigial buds of her breasts.

"You're beautiful," he said, then kissed her.

# II

Once they were across the glacier the going was easier on the hard-packed snow. Within an hour they had reached the base of the rocky spire. It stretched above them against the green-tinted sky, black and fissured. Tjond let her eyes travel up its length and wanted to cry.

"It's too tall! *Impossible* to climb. With the gravsled we could ride up."

"We have discussed this before," Hautamaki said, looking at Gulyas as he always did when he talked to her. "I will bring no radiation sources near the device up there until we determine what it is. Nothing can be learned from our aerial photograph except that it appears to be an untended machine of some kind. I will climb first. You may follow. It is not difficult on this type of rock."

It was not difficult — it was downright impossible. She scrambled and fell and couldn't get a body's-length up the spire. In the end she untied her rope. As soon as the two men had climbed above her she sobbed hopelessly into her hands. Gulyas must have heard her, or he knew how she felt being left out, because he called back down to her.

"I'll drop you a rope as soon as we get to the top, with a loop on the end. Slip your arms through it and I'll pull you up."

She was sure that he woudn't be able to do it, but still she had to try. The beacon — it might *not* be human made!

The rope cut into her body, and surprisingly enough he could pull her up. She did her best to keep from banging into the cliff and twisting about: then Gulyas was reaching down to help her. Hautamaki was holding the rope . . . and she knew that it was the strength of those corded arms, not her husband that had brought her so quickly up.

"Hautamaki, thank you for——"

"We will examine the device now," he said, interrupting her and looking at Gulyas while he spoke. "You still both stay here with my pack. Do not approach unless you are ordered to."

He turned on his heel, and with purposeful stride went to the outcropping where the machine stood. No more than a pace away from it he dropped to one knee, his body hiding most of it from sight, staying during long minutes in this cramped position.

"What is he doing?" Tjond whispered, hugging tight to Gulyas' arm. "What is it? What does he see?"

"Come over here!" Hautamaki said, standing. There was a ring of emotion in his voice that they had never heard before. They ran, skidding on the ice-glazed rock, stopping only at the barrier of his outstretched arm.

"What do you make of it?" Hautamaki asked, never taking his eyes from the squat machine fixed to the rock before them.

There was a central structure, a half sphere of yellowish metal that clamped tight to the rock, its bottom edge conforming to the irregularities beneath it. From this projected stubby arms of the same material, arranged around the circumference close to the base. On each arm was a shorter length of metal. Each one was shaped differently, but all were pointing skywards like questing fingers. An arm-thick cable emerged from the side of the hemisphere and crawled over to a higher shelf of rock. There it suddenly straightened and stood straight up, rearing into the air above their heads. Gulyas pointed to this.

"I have no idea what the other parts do, but I'll wager that is the antenna that has been sending out the signals we picked up when we entered this system."

"It might be," Hautamaki admitted. "But what about the rest?"

"One of those things that's pointing up towards the sky looks like a little telescope," Tjond said. "I really believe it is."

Hautamaki gave an angry cry and reached for her as she knelt on the ground, but he was too late. She pressed one eye to the bottom of the tube, squinted the other shut and tried to see.

"Why — yes, it is a telescope!" She opened the other eye and examined the sky. "I can see the edge of the clouds up there very clearly."

Guylas pulled her away, but there was no danger. It was a telescope, as she had said, nothing more. They took turns looking through it. It was Hautamaki who noticed that it was slowly moving.

"In that case — all of the others must be turning too, since they are parallel," Gulyas said, pointing to the metal devices that tipped each arm. One of them had an eyepiece not unlike the telescope's, but when he looked into it there was only darkness. "I can't see a thing through it," he said.

"Perhaps *you* weren't intended to," Hautamaki said, rubbing his jaw while he stared at the strange machine, then turned away to rummage in his pack. He took a multi-radiation tester from its padded carrying case and held it before the eyepiece that Gulyas had been trying to look through. "Infra-red radiation only. Everything else is screened out."

Another of the tube-like things appeared to focus ultraviolet rays, while an open latticework of metal plates concentrated radio waves. It was Tjond who voiced the thought they all had.

"If I looked through a telescope — perhaps all these other things are telescopes too! Only made for alien eyes, as if the creatures who built the thing didn't know who, or what, would be coming here and provided all kinds of telescopes working on all kinds of wavelengths. The search is over! We . . . mankind . . . we're not alone in the universe after all!"

"We mustn't leap to conclusions," Hautamaki said, but the tone of his voice belied his words.

"Why not?" Gulyas shouted, hugging his wife to him in a spasm of emotion. "Why shouldn't we be the ones to find the aliens? If they exist at all we knew we would come across them some time! The galaxy is immense — but finite. *Look and you shall find.* Isn't that what it says over the entrance to the academy?"

"We have no real evidence yet," Hautamaki said, trying not to let his own growing enthusiasm show. He was the leader, he must be the devil's advocate. "This device could have been human made."

"Point one," Gulyas said, ticking off on his finger. "It resembles nothing that any of us have ever seen before. Secondly, it is made of a tough unknown alloy. And thirdly it is in a section of space that, as far as we know, has never been visited before. We are light-centuries from the nearest inhabited system, and ships that can make this sort of trip and return are only a relatively recent development. . . ."

"And here is *real* evidence — without any guesswork!" Tjond shouted, and they ran over to her.

She had followed the heavy cable that transformed itself into the aerial. At the base, where it was thickened and fastened to the rock, were a series of incised characters. There must have been hundreds of them, rising from ground level to above their heads, each one clear and distinct.

"Those aren't human," Tjond said triumphantly. "They do not bear the slightest resemblance to any written characters of any language known to man. They are *new!*"

"How can you be sure?" Hautamaki said, forgetting himself enough to address her directly.

"I know, ship master, because this is my specialty. I trained in comparative philology and specialized in abbicciology — the study of the history of alphabets. We are probably the only science that is in touch with earth——"

"Impossible."

"No, just very slow. Earth must be halfway around the galaxy from where we are now. If I remember correctly, it takes about four hundred years for a round-trip communication. Abbicciology is a study that can grow only at the outer fringes; we deal with a hard core of unalterable fact. The old Earth alphabets are part of history and cannot be changed. I have studied them all, every character and every detail, and I have observed their mutations through the millennia. It can be observed that no matter how alphabets are modified and changed they will retain elements of their progenitors. That is the letter 'L' as it has been adapted for computer input." She scratched it into the rock with the tip of her knife, then incised a wavy character next to it. "And this is the Hebrew *lamedh,* in which you can see the same basic shape. Hebrew is a proto-alphabet, so ancient as to be almost unbelievable. Yet there is the same right-angle bend. But these characters — there is *nothing* there that I have ever seen before."

The silence stretched on while Hautamaki looked at her, studied her as if the truth or falsity of her words might be written somehow on her face. Then he smiled.

"I'll take your word for it. I'm sure you know your field very well." He walked back to his pack and began taking out more test instruments.

"Did you see that," Tjond whispered in her husband's ear, "he *smiled* at me."

"Nonsense. It is probably the first rictus of advanced frostbite."

Hautamaki had hung a weight from the barrel of the telescope and was timing its motion over the ground. "Gulyas," he asked, "do you remember this planet's period of rotation?"

"Roughly eighteen standard hours. The computation wasn't exact. Why?"

"That's close enough. We are at about 85 degrees north latitude here, which conforms to the angle of those rigid arms, while the motion of these scopes . . ."

"Counteracts the planet's rotation, moving at the same speed in the opposite direction. Of course! I should have seen it."

"What are you two talking about?" Tjond asked.

"They point to the same spot in the sky all the time," Gulyas said. "To a star."

"It could be another planet in this system," Hautamaki

said, then shook his head. "No, there is no reason for that. It is something outside. We will tell after dark."

They were comfortable in the atmosphere suits and had enough food and water. The machine was photographed and studied from every angle and they theorized on its possible power source. In spite of this the hours dragged by until dusk. There were some clouds, but they cleared away before sunset. When the first star appeared in the darkening sky Hautamaki bent to the ocular of the telescope.

"Just sky. Too light yet. But there is some sort of glowing grid appearing in the field, five thin lines radiating in from the circumference. Instead of crossing they fade as they come to the centre."

"But they'll point out whatever star is in the centre of the field — without obscuring it?"

"Yes. The stars are appearing now."

It was a seventh-magnitude star, isolated near the galactic rim. It appeared commonplace in every way except for its location with no nearby neighbours even in stellar terms. They took turns looking at it, marking it so they could not possibly mistake it for any other.

"Are we going there?" Tjond asked, though it was more of a statement than a question that sought an answer.

"Of course," Hautamaki said.

# III

As soon as their ship had cleared atmosphere, Hautamaki sent a message to the nearest relay station. While they waited for an answer they analyzed the material they had.

With each result their enthusiasm grew. The metal was no harder than some of the resistant alloys they used, but its composition was completely different and some unknown process of fabrication had been used that had compacted the surface molecules to a greater density. The characters bore no resemblance to any human alphabet. And the star towards which the instruments had been pointed was far beyond the limits of galactic exploration.

When the message arrived, *signal recorded,* they jumped the ship at once on the carefully computed and waiting course. Their standing instructions were to investigate anything, report everything, and this they were doing. With their planned movements recorded they were free. They, *they,* were going to make a first contact with an alien race — had already made contact with one of its artifacts. No matter what happened now, the honour was irrevocably theirs. The next meal turned naturally into a celebration, and Hautamaki unbent enough to allow other intoxicants as well as wine. The results were almost disastrous.

"A toast!" Tjond shouted, standing and wobbling just a bit.

"To Earth and mankind — no longer alone!"

*No longer alone,* they repeated, and Hautamaki's face lost some of the party gaiety that it had reluctantly gained.

"I ask you to join me in a toast," he said, "to someone you never knew, who should have been here to share this with us."

"To Kiiskinen," Gulyas said. He had read the records and knew about the tragedy that was still fresh in Hautamaki's thoughts.

"Thank you. To Kiiskinen." They drank.

"I wish we could have met him," Tjond said, a tendril of feminine curiosity tickling at her.

"A fine man," Hautamaki said, seeming anxious to talk now that the subject had been broached for the first time since the accident. "One of the very finest. We were twelve years on this ship."

"Did you have . . . children?" Tjond asked.

"Your curiosity is not fitting," Gulyas snapped at his wife. "I think it would be better if we dropped . . ."

Hautamaki held up his hand. "Please. I understand your natural interest. We Men have settled only a dozen or so planets and I imagine our customs are curious to you; we are only in a minority as yet. But if there is any embarrassment it is all your own. Are you embarrassed about being bisexual? Would you kiss your wife in public?"

"A pleasure," Gulyas said, and did.

"Then you understand what I mean. We feel the same way and at times act the same way, though our society is monosexual. It was a natural result of ectogenesis."

"Not natural," Tjond said, a touch of colour in her cheeks. "Ectogenesis needs a fertile ovum. Ova comes from females; an ectogenetic society should logically be a female society. An all-male one is unnatural."

"Everything we do is unnatural," Hautamaki told her without apparent anger. "Man is an environment-changing animal. Every person living away from Earth is living in an 'unnatural' environment. Ectogenesis on these terms is no more unnatural than living, as we are now, in a metal hull in an unreal manifestation of space-time. That this ectogenesis should combine the germ plasm from two male cells rather than from an egg and a sperm is of no more relevancy than your vestigial breasts."

"You are being insulting," she said, blushing.

"Not in the least. They have lost their function, therefore they are degenerate. You bisexuals are just as natural — or unnatural — as we Men. Neither is viable without the 'unnatural' environment that we have created."

The excitement of their recent discovery still possessed them, and perhaps the stimulants and the anger had lowered Tjond's control. "Why — how dare you call me unnatural — you——"

"You forget yourself, woman!" Hautamaki boomed, drowning out the word, leaping to his feet. "You expected to pry into the intimate details of my life and are insulted when I mention some of your own taboos. The Men are better off without your kind!" He drew a deep, shuddering breath, turned on his heel and left the room.

Tjond stayed in their quarters for almost a standard week after that evening. She worked on her analysis of the alien characters and Gulyas brought her meals. Hautamaki did not mention the events, and cut Gulyas off when he tried to apologize for his wife. But he made no protest when she appeared again in the control section, though he reverted to his earlier custom of speaking only to Gulyas, never addressing her directly.

"Did he actually want me to come too?" Tjond asked, closing her tweezers on a single tiny hair that marred the ivory sweep of her smooth forehead and skull. She pulled it out and touched her brow. "Have you noticed that he really has eyebrows? Right *here*, great shabby things like an atavism. Even hair around the base of his skull. Disgusting. I'll bet you that the Men sort their genes for hirsuteness, it couldn't be accident. You never answered — did he ask for me to be there?"

"You never gave me a chance to answer," Gulyas told her, a smile softening his words. "He didn't ask for you by name. That would be expecting too much. But he did say that there would be a full crew meeting at nineteen hours."

She put a touch of pink make-up on the lobes of her ears and the bottoms of her nostrils, then snapped her cosmetic case shut. "I'm ready whenever you are. Shall we go see what the shipmaster wants?"

"In twenty hours we'll be breaking out of jump-space," Hautamaki told them when they had met in the control section. "There is a very good chance that we will encounter the people — the aliens — who constructed the beacon. Until we discover differently we will assume that they are peacefully inclined. Yes, Gulyas?"

"Shipmaster, there has been a good deal of controversy on the intentions of any hypothetical race that might be encountered. There has been no real agreement . . ."

"It does not matter. I am shipmaster. The evidence so far indicates a race looking for contact, not conquest. I see it this way. We have a rich and very old culture, so while we have been searching for another intelligent life form we have also been exploring and recording with ships like this one. A poorer culture might be limited in the number of ships that they could apply to this kind of occupation. Therefore the beacons. Many of them could be easily planted by a single ship over a large area of space. There are undoubtedly others. All of them serve to draw attention to a single star, a rendezvous point of some type."

"This doesn't prove peaceful intentions. It could be a trap."

"I doubt it. There are far better ways to satisfy warlike tendencies than to set elaborate traps like this. I *think* their intentions are peaceful, and that is the only factor that matters. Until we actually encounter them any action will have to be based on a guess. Therefore I have already jettisoned the ship's armament——"

"You *what?*"

"——and I'll ask you to surrender any personal weapons that you might have in your possession."

"You're risking our lives — without even consulting us," Tjond said angrily.

"Not at all," he answered, not looking at her. "You risked your own life when you entered the service and took the oath. You will obey my instructions. All weapons here within the hour; I want the ship clean before we break through. We will meet the strangers armed only with our humanity. . . . You may think the Men go naked for some perverse reason, but that is wrong. We have discarded clothes as detrimental to total involvement in our environment, a both practical and symbolic action."

"You aren't suggesting that *we* remove our clothes as well, are you?" Tjond asked, still angry.

"Not at all. Do as you please. I am just attempting to explain my reasons so we will have some unanimity of action when we encounter the intelligent creatures who built the beacon. Survey knows now where we are. If we do not return, a later contact team will be protected by mankind's complete armoury of death. So we will now give our aliens every opportunity to kill us — if that is what they are planning. Retribution will follow. If they do not have warlike intentions we will make peaceful contact. That, in itself, is reason enough to risk one's life a hundred times over. I don't have to explain to you the monumental importance of such a contact."

The tension grew as the time for break-through approached. The box of handguns, explosive charges, poisons from the laboratory — even the large knives from the kitchen — had long since been jettisoned. They were all in the control area when the bell pinged softly and they broke through, back into normal space. Here, at the galactic rim, most of the stars were massed to one side. Ahead lay a pit of blackness with a single star glowing.

"That's it," Gulyas said, swinging back the spectral analyzer, "but we're not close enough for clear observation. Are we going to take another jump now?"

"No," Hautamaki said, "I want a clevs observation first."

The sensitive clevs screen began to glow as soon as the pressure dropped, darkening slowly. There were occasional bursts of light from their surface as random molecules of air struck them, then this died away. The forward screen deepened to the blackness of outer space and in its centre appeared the image of the star.

"It's impossible!" Tjond gasped from the observer's seat behind them.

"Not impossible," Hautamaki said. "Just impossible of natural origin. Its existence proves that what we see can — and has — been constructed. We will proceed."

The star image burned with unreality. The star itself at the core was normal enough — but how to explain the three interlocking rings that circled it? They had the dimensions of a planetary orbit. Even if they were as tenuous as a comet's tail their construction was an incredible achievement. And what could be the significance of the coloured lights on the rings, apparently orbiting the primary like insane electrons?

The screen sparkled and the image faded.

"It could only be a beacon," Hautamaki said, removing his helmet. "It is there to draw attention, as was the radio beacon that drew us to the last planet. What race with the curiosity to build spaceships could possibly resist the attraction of a thing like that?"

Gulyas was feeding the course corrections into the computor. "It is still baffling," he said. "With the physical ability to construct that why haven't they built an exploring fleet to go out and make contacts — instead of trying to draw them in?"

555

"I hope that we will discover that answer soon. Though it probably lies in whatever composes their alien psychology. To their way of thinking this might be the obvious manner. And you will have to admit that it has worked."

# IV

This time when they made the transition from jump-space the glowing rings of light filled the front ports. Their radio receivers were on, automatically searching the wavelengths.

They burst into sound on a number of bands simultaneously. Gulyas lowered the volume.

"This is the same kind of broadcast we had from the beacon," he said. "Very directional. All of the transmissions are coming from that golden planetoid, or whatever it is. It's big, but doesn't seem to have a planetary diameter."

"We're on our way," Hautamaki told him. "I'll take the controls, see if you can get any image on the video circuits."

"Just interference. But I'm sending out a signal, a view of this cabin. If they have the right equipment there they should be able to analyse our signal and match it. . . . Look, the screen is changing! They're working fast."

The viewscreen was rippling with colour. Then a picture appeared, blurred, then steadied. Tjond focused and it snapped into clear life. The two men looked, stared. Behind them Tjond gasped.

"At least no snakes or insects, praise fortune for that!"

The being on the screen was staring at them with the same intensity. There was no way to estimate its relative size, but it was surely humanoid. Three long fingers, heavily webbed, with an opposed thumb. Only the upper part of its figure was visible, and this was clothed so that no physical details could be seen. But the being's face stood out clearly on the screen, golden in colour, hairless, with large, almost circular eyes. Its nose, had it been a human one, would be said to be broken, spread over its face, nostrils flaring. This, and the cleft upper lip, gave it a grim appearance to human eyes.

But this yardstick could not be applied. By alien standards it might be beautiful.

"S'bb'thik," the creature said. The radio beacons carried the matching audio now. The voice was high-pitched and squeaky.

"I greet you as well," Hautamaki said. "We both have spoken languages and we will learn to understand each other. But we come in peace."

"Maybe we do, but I can't say the same thing for these aliens," Gulyas interrupted. "Look at screen three."

This held an enlarged view taken from one of the forward pickups, locked onto the planetoid they were approaching. A group of dark buildings stood out from the golden surface, crowned with a forest of aerials and antennae. Ringed about the building were circular structures mounted with squat tubular devices that resembled heavy-bore weapons. The similarity was increased by the fact that the numerous emplacements had rotated. The open orifices were tracking the approaching ship.

"I'm killing our approach velocity," Hautamaki said, stabbing the control buttons in rapid sequence. "Set up a repeater plate here and switch on a magnified view of those weapons. We'll find out their intentions right now."

Once their motion relative to the golden planetoid had been stopped, Hautamaki turned and pointed to the repeater screen, slowly tapping the image of the weapons. Then he tapped himself on the chest and raised his hands before him, fingers spread wide, empty. The alien had watched this dumb show with glistening, golden eyes. It rocked its head from side to side and repeated Hautamaki's gesture, tapping itself on the chest with its long central finger, then pointed into the screen.

"He understood at once," Gulyas said. "Those weapons — they're turning away, sinking out of sight."

"We'll continue our approach. Are you recording this?"

"Sight, sound, full readings from every instrument.

We've been recording since we first saw the star, with the tapes being fed into the armoured vault as you ordered. I wonder what the next step is?"

"They've already taken it — look."

The image of the alien reached off the screen and brought back what appeared to be a metal sphere that it held lightly in one hand. From the sphere projected a pipe-like extrusion of metal with a lever half way up its length. When the alien pressed the lever they heard a hissing.

"A tank of gas," Gulyas said. "I wonder what it is supposed to signify? No — it's not gas. It must be a vacuum. See, the pipe is sucking up those grains sprinkled on the table." The alien kept the lever depressed until the hissing stopped.

"Ingenious," Hautamaki said. "Now we know there is a sample of their atmosphere inside that tank."

There was no mechanical propulsion visible, but the sphere came swooping up towards their ship where it swung in orbit above the golden planetoid. The sphere stopped, just outside the ship and clearly visible from the viewports, bobbing in a small arc.

"Some sort of force beam," Hautamaki said, "though nothing registers on the hull instruments. That's one thing I hope we find out how to do. I'm going to open the outer door on the main hatch."

As soon as the door opened the sphere swooped and vanished from sight and they saw, through the pickup inside the air lock, that it fell gently to the deck inside. Hautamaki closed the door and pointed to Gulyas.

"Take a pair of insulated gloves and carry that tank to the lab. Run the contents through the usual air examination procedures that we use for testing planetary atmosphere. As soon as you have taken the sample evacuate the tank and fill it with our own air, then throw it out through the lock."

The analysers worked on the sample of alien air, and presumably the aliens were doing the same with their tank of ship's atmosphere. The analysis was routine and fast, the report appearing in coded form on the panel in control.

"Unbreathable," Gulyas said, "at least for us. There seems to be enough oxygen, more than enough, but any of those sulphurated compounds would eat holes through our lungs. They must have rugged metabolisms to inhale stuff like that. One thing for certain, we'll never be in competition for the same worlds. . . ."

"Look! The picture is changing," Tjond said, drawing their attention back to the viewing screen.

The alien had vanished and the viewpoint appeared to be in space above the planetoid's surface. A transparent bulge on its surface filled the screen and while they watched the alien entered it from below. The scene shifted again, then they were looking at the alien from inside the clear-walled chamber. The alien came toward the pickup, but before reaching it the alien stopped and leaned against what appeared to be thin air.

"There's a transparent wall that divided the dome in half," Gulyas said. "I'm beginning to get the idea."

The pickup panned away from the alien, swept around to the opposite direction where there was an entrance cut into the clear fabric of the wall. The door was open into space.

"That's obvious enough," Hautamaki said, rising to his feet. "That central wall must be airtight, so it can be used for a conference chamber. I'll go. Keep a record of everything."

"It looks like a trap," Tjond said, fidgeting with her fingers while she looked at the invitingly open door on the screen. "It will be a risk. . . ."

Hautamaki laughed, the first time they had ever heard him do it, as he climbed into his pressure suit. "A trap! Do you believe they have gone to all this to set a trap for me? Such ego is preposterous. And if it were a trap — do you think it possible to stay out of it?"

He pushed himself free of the ship. His suited figure floated away, getting smaller and smaller.

Silently, moving closer together without realizing they

did so, they watched the meeting on the screen. They saw Hautamaki drawn gently in through the open doorway until his feet touched the floor. He turned to look as the door closed, while from the radio they heard a hissing, very dimly at first, then louder and louder.

"It sounds like they are pressurizing the room," Gulyas said.

Hautamaki nodded. "Yes, I can hear it now, and there is a reading on the external pressure gauge. As soon as it reaches atmospheric normal I'm taking my helmet off."

Tjond started to protest, but stopped when her husband raised his hand in warning. This was Hautamaki's decision to make.

"Smells perfectly breathable," Hautamaki said, "though it has a metallic odour."

He laid his helmet aside and stripped his suit off. The alien was standing at the partition and Hautamaki walked over until they stood face to face, almost the same height. The alien placed his palm flat against the transparent wall and the human put his hand over the same spot. They met, as close as they could, separated only by a centimetre of substance. Their eyes joined and they stared for a long time, trying to read intent, trying to communicate. The alien turned away first, walking over to a table littered with a variety of objects. It picked up the nearest one and held it for Hautamaki to see. *"Kilt,"* the alien said. It looked like a piece of stone.

Hautamaki for the first time took notice of the table on his side of the partition. It appeared to hold the identical objects as the other table, and the first of these was a lump of ordinary stone. He picked it up.

"Stone," he said, then turned to the television pickup and the unseen viewers in the ship. "It appears that a language lesson is first. This is obvious. See that this is recorded separately. Then we can programme the computor for machine translation in case the aliens aren't doing it themselves."

The language lesson progressed slowly once the stock of simple nouns with physical referents had been exhausted. Films were shown, obviously prepared long before, show-

560

ing simple actions, and bit by bit verbs and tenses were exchanged. The alien made no attempt to learn their language, he just worked to ensure accuracy of identity in the words. They were recording too. As the language lesson progressed Gulyas's frown deepened, and he started to make notes, then a list that he checked off. Finally he interrupted the lesson.

"Hautamaki — this is important. Find out if they are just accumulating a vocabulary or if they are feeding a MT with this material."

The answer came from the alien itself. It turned its head sideways, as if listening to a distant voice, then spoke into a cup-like device at the end of a wire. A moment later Hautamaki's voice spoke out, toneless since each word had been recorded separately.

"I talk through a machine . . . I talk my talk . . . a machine talk your talk to you . . . I am Liem . . . we need have more words in machine before talk well."

"This can't wait," Gulyas said. "Tell them that we want a sample of some of their body cells, any cells at all. It is complex, but try to get it across."

The aliens were agreeable. They did not insist on a specimen in return, but accepted one. A sealed container brought a frozen sliver of what looked like muscle tissue over to the ship. Gulyas started towards the lab.

"Take care of the recordings," he told his wife. "I don't think this will take too long."

# V

It didn't. Within the hour he had returned, coming up so silently that Tjond, intent on listening to the language lesson, did not notice him until he stood next to her.

"Your face," she said. "What is wrong? What did you discover?"

He smiled dryly at her. "Nothing terrible, I assure you. But things are very different from what we supposed."

"What is it?" Hautamaki asked from the screen. He had heard their voices and turned towards the pickup.

"How has the language progressed?" Gulyas asked. "Can you understand me, Liem?"

"Yes," the alien said, "almost all of the words are clear now. But the machine has only a working force of a few thousand words so you must keep your speech simple."

"I understand. The things I want to say are very simple. First a question. Your people, do they come from a planet orbiting about a star near here?"

"No. We have travelled a long way to this star, searching. My home world is there, among those stars there."

"Do all your people live on that world?"

"No, we live on many worlds, but we are all children of children of children of people who lived on one world very long ago."

"Our people have also settled many worlds, but we all come from one world," Gulyas told him, then looked down at the paper in his hands. He smiled at the alien in the screen before him, but there was something terribly sad about this smile. "We came originally from a planet named Earth. That is where your people came from too. We are brothers, Liem."

"What madness is this?" Hautamaki shouted at him, his face swollen and angry. "Liem is humanoid, not human! It cannot breathe our air!"

"*He* cannot breathe our air, or perhaps she," Gulyas answered quietly. "We do not use gene manipulation, but we know that it is possible. I'm sure we will eventually discover just how Liem's people were altered to live under the physical conditions they do now. It might have been natural selection and normal mutation, but it seems too drastic a change to be explained that way. But that is not important. *This* is." He held up the sheets of notes and photographs. "You can see for yourself. This is the DNR chain from the nucleus of one of my own cells. This is Liem's. They are identical. His people are as human as we are."

"They can't be!" Tjond shook her head in bewilderment.

"Just look at him, he is so different, and their alphabet —
what about that? I cannot be wrong about that?"

"There is one possibility you did not allow for, a totally
independent alphabet. You yourself told me that there is
not the slightest similarity between the Chinese ideographs
and western letters. If Liem's people suffered a cultural
disaster that forced them to completely reinvent writing
you would have your alien alphabet. As to the way they
look — just consider the thousands of centuries that have
passed since mankind left Earth and you will see that his
physical differences are minor. Some are natural and some
may have been artificially achieved, but germ plasm cannot lie. We are all the sons of man."

"It is possible," Liem said, speaking for the first time. "I
am informed that our biologists agree with you. Our points
of difference are minor when compared to the points of
similarity. Where is this Earth you come from?"

Hautamaki pointed at the sky above them, at the star-
filled sweep of the Milky Way, burning with massed stars.
"There, far out there on the other side of the core, roughly
half way around the lens of the galaxy."

"The galactic core explains partially what must have
happened," Gulyas said. "It is thousands of light-years in
diameter and over 10,000 degrees in temperature. We
have explored its fringes. No ship could penetrate it or
even approach too closely because of the dust clouds that
surround it. So we have expanded outwards, slowly circling
the rim of the galaxy, moving away from Earth. If we
stopped to think about it we should have realized that
mankind was moving the other way too, in the opposite direction around the wheel."

"And sometime we would have to meet," Liem said.
"Now I greet you, brothers. And I am sad, because I
know what this means."

"We are alone," Hautamaki said, looking at the massed
trillions of stars. "We have closed the circle and found
only ourselves. The galaxy is ours, but we are alone." He
turned about not realizing that Liem, the golden alien —

the man — had turned at the same time in the same manner.

They faced outwards, looking at the infinite depth and infinite blackness of intergalactic space, empty of stars. Dimly, distantly, there were spots of light, microscopic blurs against the darkness, not stars but island universes, like the one at whose perimeter they stood.

These two beings were different in many ways: in the air they breathed, the colour on their skins, their languages, mannerisms, cultures. They were as different as the day is from the night: the flexible fabric of mankind had been warped by the countless centuries until they could no longer recognize each other. But time, distance and mutation could not change one thing; they were still men, still human.

"It is certain then," Hautamaki said, "we are alone in the galaxy."

"Alone in *this* galaxy."

They looked at each other, then glanced away. At that moment they measured their humanness against the same rule and were equal.

For they had turned at the same instant and looked outward into intergalactic space, towards the infinitely remote light that was another island galaxy.

"It will be difficult to get there," someone said.

They had lost a battle. There was no defeat.

## ii  *Big Ancestors and Great Descendants*

•

It was not just starships and communication and pageantry which flashed across the galaxy from planet to planet. It was also a stream of blood. In that stream of blood was born man's genetic inheritance, shaping him even as he shaped his heritage.

As the stream of blood carried the taste of the primaeval ocean from which life was born, it also carried the message from which future life — unimaginable and perhaps incomprehensible to us — would spring.

What is our place in the galaxy? It is a serious question, and no very serious answer is attempted in this volume. Olaf Stapledon attempted a serious answer and for those who are interested his mighty chronicle-novel, *Star Maker*, is strongly recommended. It is the great fictional work about the galaxy and the universe, and the destiny of mankind.

Working in a much lighter vein, Roger Dee and F. L. Wallace present opposed speculations on the subject. In Dee's story, an Earthman speaks: "A hundred thousand races from rim to rim of the galaxy — the least of them, so far as Clowdis had seen, older and wiser and infinitely stronger that his own upstart culture — suspended opinion when the T'sai spoke." The T'sai are the galactic masters. Note how the cyclic pattern once more imposes itself.

At least indirectly, *The Interlopers* is about what we may become, and so forms a fitting conclusion to our history. In contrast, *Big Ancestor* looks back on what we are — and by so doing reflects on our future role in galactic terms. A nice story, and as nasty as they come.

Both these stories run on logic, lubricated by a little prejudice. Whereas *Lord of a Thousand Suns* is an extravagant emotional exercise in the youthful Poul Anderson's best vein. It is crammed full of those mythopoeic archetypes to which our friendly reviewer, previously quoted, made mention. "I who was Daryesh of Tollogh, lord of a thousand suns and lover of Ilorna the Fair, immortalized noble of the greatest empire the universe has ever seen — I am now trapped in the half-evolved body of a hunted alien, a million years after the death of all which mattered . . ."

We all experience, on one level or another, similar dualities in our being. Perhaps that is what attracts us to galactic empire-building in the first place. The hope of establishing against the loneliness and majesty of the cosmos a few humble warm-blooded, human institutions appeases the two sides of our nature — the individual side which responds with affection to other individuals, and the evolutionary side which we can never properly know, since its time-scale is not ours, as it burns like a green fuse towards whatever remote destiny awaits humankind on whatever remote mountainside.

Blood's a rover, as they say. Where it will take us is anyone's guess.

*A Man without a World, this 1,000,000-year-old Daryesh! Once Lord of a Thousand Suns, now condemned to rove the spaceways in alien form, searching for love, for life, for the great lost Vwyrdda.*

●

# LORD OF A THOUSAND SUNS

## By Poul Anderson

"Yes, you'll find almost anything man has ever imagined, somewhere out in the Galaxy," I said. "There are so damned many millions of planets, and such a fantastic variety of surface conditions and of life evolving to meet them, and of intelligence and civilization appearing in that life. Why, I've been on worlds with fire-breathing dragons, and on worlds where dwarfs fought things that could pass for the goblins our mothers used to scare us with, and on a planet where a race of witches live — telepathic pseudohypnosis, you know — oh, I'll bet there's not a tall story or fairy tale ever told which doesn't have some kind of counterpart somewhere in the universe."

Laird nodded. "Uh-huh," he answered, in that oddly slow and soft voice of his. "I once let a genie out of a bottle."

"Eh? What happened?"

"It killed me."

I opened my mouth to laugh, and then took a second

glance at him and shut it again. He was just too dead-pan serious about it. Not poker-faced, the way a good actor can be when he's slipping over a tall one — no, there was a sudden misery behind his eyes, and somehow it was mixed with the damnedest cold humor.

I didn't know Laird very well. Nobody did. He was out most of the time on Galactic Survey, prowling a thousand eldritch planets never meant for human eyes. He came back to the Solar System more rarely and for briefer visits than anyone else in his job, and had less to say about what he had found.

A huge man, six-and-a-half feet tall, with dark aquiline features and curiously brilliant greenish-grey eyes, middle-aged now though it didn't show except at the temples. He was courteous enough to everyone, but shortspoken and slow to laugh. Old friends, who had known him thirty years before when he was the gayest and most reckless officer in the Solar Navy, thought something during the Revolt had changed him more than any psychologist would admit was possible. But he had never said anything about it, merely resigning his commission after the war and going into Survey.

We were sitting alone in a corner of the lounge. The Lunar branch of the Explorer's Club maintains its building outside the main dome of Selene Center, and we were sitting beside one of the great windows, drinking Centaurian sidecars and swapping the inevitable shop-talk. Even Laird indulged in that, though I suspected more because of the information he could get than for any desire of companionship.

Behind us, the long quiet room was almost empty. Before us, the window opened on the raw magnificence of moon-scape, a sweep of crags and cliffs down the crater wall to the riven black plains, washed in the eerie blue of Earth's light. Space blazed above us, utter black and a million sparks of frozen flame.

"Come again?" I said.

He laughed, without much humor. "I might as well tell you," he said. "You won't believe it, and even if you did it'd make no difference. Sometimes I tell the story — alcohol makes me feel like it — I start remembering old times . . ."

He settled farther back in his chair. "Maybe it wasn't a real genie," he went on. "More of a ghost, perhaps. That was a haunted planet. They were great a million years before man existed on Earth. They spanned the stars and they knew things the present civilization hasn't even guessed at. And then they died. Their own weapons swept them away in one burst of fire, and only broken ruins were left — ruins and desert, and the ghost who lay waiting in that bottle."

I signalled for another round of drinks, wondering what he meant, wondering just how sane that big man with the worn rocky face was. Still — you never know. I've seen things out beyond that veil of stars which your maddest dreams never hinted at. I've seen men carried home mumbling and empty-eyed, the hollow cold of space filling their brains where something had broken the thin taut wall of their reason. They say spacemen are a credulous breed. Before Heaven, they have to be!

"You don't mean New Egypt?" I asked.

"Stupid name. Just because there are remnants of a great dead culture, they have to name it after an insignificant valley of ephemeral peasants. I tell you, the men of Vwyrdda were like gods, and when they were destroyed whole suns were darkened by the forces they used. Why, they killed off Earth's dinosaurs in a day, millions of years ago, and only used one ship to do it."

"How in hell do you know that? I didn't think the archeologists had deciphered their records."

"They haven't. All our archeologists will ever know is that the Vwyrddans were a race of remarkably humanoid appearance, with a highly advanced interstellar culture wiped out about a million Earth-years ago. Matter of fact, I don't really know that they did it to Earth, but I do know that they had a regular policy of exterminating the great reptiles of terrestroid planets with an eye to later colonization, and I know that they got this far, so I suppose our planet got the treatment too." Laird accepted his fresh drink and raised the glass to me. "Thanks. But now do be a good fellow and let me ramble on in my own way.

"It was — let me see — thirty-three years ago now, when I was a bright young lieutenant with bright young ideas. The Revolt was in full swing then, and the Janyards held all that region of space, out Sagittari way you know. Things looked bad for Sol then — I don't think it's ever been appreciated how close we were to defeat. They were poised to drive right through our lines with their battle fleets, slash past our frontiers, and hit Earth itself with the rain of hell that had already sterilized a score of planets. We were fighting on the defensive, spread over several million cubic light-years, spread horribly thin. Oh, bad!

"Vwyrdda — New Egypt — had been discovered and some excavation done shortly before the war began. We knew about as much then as we do now. Especially, we knew that the so-called Valley of the Gods held more relics than any other spot on the surface. I'd been quite interested in the work, visited the planet myself, even worked with the crew that found and restored that gravitomagnetic generator — the one which taught us half of what we know now about g-m fields.

"It was my young and fanciful notion that there might be more to be found, somewhere in that labyrinth — and from study of the reports I even thought I knew about what and where it would be. One of the weapons that had novaed suns, a million years ago——

"The planet was far behind the Janyard lines, but militarily valueless. They wouldn't garrison it, and I was sure that such semi-barbarians wouldn't have my idea, especially with victory so close. A one-man sneakboat could get in readily enough — it just isn't possible to blockade a region of space; too damned inhumanly big. We had nothing to lose but me, and maybe a lot to gain, so in I went.

"I made the planet without trouble and landed in the Valley of the Gods and began work. And that's where the fun started."

Laird laughed again, with no more mirth than before.

There was a moon hanging low over the hills, a great scarred shield thrice the size of Earth's, and its chill white radiance filled the Valley with colorless light and long shadows. Overhead flamed the incredible sky of the Sagittarian regions, thousands upon thousands of great blazing suns swarming in strings and clusters and constellations strange to human eyes, blinking and glittering in the thin cold air. It was so bright that Laird could see the fine patterns of his skin, loops and whorls on the numbed fingers that groped against the pyramid. He shivered in the wind that streamed past him, blowing dust devils with a dry whisper, searching under his clothes to sheathe his flesh in cold. His breath was ghostly white before him, the bitter air felt liquid when he breathed.

Around him loomed the fragments of what must have been a city, now reduced to a few columns and crumbling walls held up by the lava which had flowed. The stones reared high in the unreal moonlight, seeming almost to move as the shadows and the drifting sand passed them. Ghost city. Ghost planet. He was the last life that stirred on its bleak surface.

But somewhere above that surface——

What was it, that descending hum high in the sky, sweeping closer out of stars and moon and wind? Minutes ago the needle on his gravitomagnetic detector had wavered down in the depths of the pyramid. He had hurried up and now stood looking and listening and feeling his heart turn stiff.

*No, no, no, — not a Janyard ship, not now — it was the end of everything if they came.*

Laird cursed with a hopeless fury. The wind caught his mouthings and blew them away with the scudding sand, buried them under the everlasting silence of the valley. His eyes travelled to his sneakboat. It was invisible against the great pyramid — he'd taken that much precaution, shoveling a low grave of sand over it — but, if they used metal detectors that was valueless. He was fast, yes, but almost unarmed; they could easily follow his trail down into the labyrinth and locate the vault.

Lord if he had led them here — if his planning and

striving had only resulted in giving the enemy the weapon which would destroy Earth——

His hand closed about the butt of his blaster. Silly weapon, stupid popgun — what could he do?

Decision came. With a curse, he whirled and ran back into the pyramid.

His flash lit the endless downward passages with a dim bobbing radiance, and the shadows swept above and behind and marched beside, the shadows of a million years closing in to smother him. His boots slammed against the stone floor, *thud-thud-thud* — the echoes caught the rhythm and rolled it boomingly ahead of him. A primitive terror rose to drown his dismay; he was going down into the grave of a thousand millennia, the grave of the gods, and it took all the nerve he had to keep running and never look back. He didn't dare look back.

Down and down and down, past this winding tunnel, along this ramp, through this passageway into the guts of the planet. A man could get lost here. A man could wander in the cold and the dark and the echoes till he died. It had taken him weeks to find his way into the great vault, and only the clues given by Murchison's reports had made it possible at all. Now——

He burst into a narrow ante-chamber. The door he had blasted open leaned drunkenly against a well of night. It was fifty feet high, that door. He fled past it like an ant and came into the pyramid storehouse.

His flash gleamed off metal, glass, substances he could not identify that had lain sealed against a million years till he came to wake the machines. What they were, he did not know. He had energized some of the units, and they had hummed and flickered, but he had not dared experiment. His idea had been to rig an antigrav unit which would enable him to haul the entire mass of it up to his boat. Once he was home, the scientists could take over. But now——

He skinned his teeth in a wolfish grin and switched on the big lamp he had installed. White light flooded the tomb, shining darkly back from the monstrous bulks of things he could not use, the wisdom and techniques of a race which had spanned the stars and moved planets and endured for fifty million years. Maybe he could puzzle out the use of something before the enemy came. Maybe he could wipe them out in one demoniac sweep — just like a stereofilm hero, jeered his mind — or maybe he could simply destroy it all, keep it from Janyard hands.

He should have provided against this. He should have rigged a bomb, to blow the whole pyramid to hell——

With an effort, he stopped the frantic racing of his mind and looked around. There were paintings on the walls, dim with age but still legible, pictographs, meant perhaps for the one who finally found this treasure. The men of New Egypt were shown, hardly distinguishable from humans — dark of skin and hair, keen of feature, tall and stately and robed in living light. He had paid special attention to one representation. It showed a series of actions, like an old time comic-strip — a man taking up a glassy object, fitting it over his head, throwing a small switch. He had been tempted to try it, but — gods, what would it do?

He found the helmet and slipped it gingerly over his skull. It might be some kind of last-ditch chance for him. The thing was cold and smooth and hard, it settled on his head with a slow massiveness that was strangely — *living*. He shuddered and turned back to the machines.

This thing now with the long coil-wrapped barrel — an energy projector of some sort? How did you activate it? Hell-fire, which was the muzzle end?

He heard the faint banging of feet, winding closer down the endless passageways. Gods, his mind groaned. They didn't waste any time, did they?

But they hadn't needed to . . . a metal detector would have located his boat, told them that he was in this pyramid rather than one of the dozen others scattered through the valley. And energy tracers would spot him down here . . .

He doused the light and crouched in darkness behind one of the machines. The blaster was heavy in his hand.

A voice hailed him from outside the door. "It's useless, Solman. Come out of there!"

He bit back a reply and lay waiting.

A woman's voice took up the refrain. It was a good voice, he thought irrelevantly, low and well modulated, but it had an iron ring to it. They were hard, these Janyards, even their women led troops and piloted ships and killed men.

"You may as well surrender, Solman. All you have done has been to accomplish our work for us. We suspected such an attempt might be made. Lacking the archeological records, we couldn't hope for much success ourselves, but since my force was stationed near this sun I had a boat lie in an orbit around the planet with detectors wide open. We trailed you down, and let you work, and now we are here to get what you have found."

"Go back," he bluffed desperately. "I planted a bomb. Go back or I'll set it off."

The laugh was hard with scorn. "Do you think we wouldn't know it if you had? You haven't even a space-suit on. Come out with your hands up or we'll flood the vault with gas."

Laird's teeth flashed in a snarling grin. "All right," he shouted, only half aware of what he was saying. "All right, you asked for it!"

He threw the switch on his helmet.

It was like a burst of fire in his brain, a soundless roar of splintering darkness. He screamed, half crazy with the fury that poured into him, feeling the hideous thrumming along every nerve and sinew, feeling his muscles cave in and his body hit the floor. The shadows closed in, roaring and rolling, night and death and the wreck of the universe, and high above it all he heard — laughter.

He lay sprawled behind the machine, twitching and whimpering. They had heard him, out in the tunnels, and with slow caution they entered and stood over him and watched his spasms jerk toward stillness.

They were tall and well-formed, the Janyard rebels — Earth had sent her best out to colonize the Sagittarian worlds, three hundred years ago. But the long cruel struggle, conquering and building and adapting to planets that never were and never could be Earth, had changed them, hardened their metal and frozen something in their souls.

Ostensibly it was a quarrel over tariff and trade rights which had led to their revolt against the Empire; actually, it was a new culture yelling to life, a thing born of fire and loneliness and the great empty reaches between the stars, the savage rebellion of a mutant child. They stood impassively watching the body until it lay quiet. Then one of them stooped over and removed the shining glassy helmet.

"He must have taken it for something he could use against us," said the Janyard, turning the helmet in his hands; "but it wasn't adapted to his sort of life. The old dwellers here looked human, but I don't think it went any deeper than their skins."

The woman commander looked down with a certain pity. "He was a brave man," she said.

"Wait — he's still alive, ma'm — he's sitting up——"

Daryesh forced the shaking body to hands and knees. He felt its sickness, wretched and cold in throat and nerves and muscles, and he felt the roiling of fear and urgency in the brain. These were enemies. There was death for a world and a civilization here. Most of all, he felt the horrible numbness of the nervous system, deaf and dumb and blind, cut off in its house of bone and peering out through five weak senses . . .

Vwyrdda, Vwyrdda, he was a prisoner in a brain without a telepathy transceiver lobe. He was a ghost reincarnated in a thing that was half a corpse!

Strong arms helped him to his feet. "That was a foolish thing to try," said the woman's cool voice.

Daryesh felt strength flowing back as the nervous and muscular and endocrine systems found a new balance, as his mind took over and fought down the gibbering madness which had been Laird. He drew a shuddering breath. Air in his nostrils after — how long? How long had he been dead?

His eyes focused on the woman. She was tall and handsome. Ruddy hair spilled from under a peaked cap, wide-

576

set blue eyes regarded him frankly out of a face sculptured in clean lines and strong curves and fresh young coloring. For a moment he thought of Ilorna, and the old sickness rose — then he throttled it and looked again at the woman and smiled.

It was an insolent grin, and she stiffened angrily. "Who are you, Solman?" she asked.

The meaning was clear enough to Daryesh, who had his — host's — memory patterns and linguistic habits as well as those of Vwyrdda. He replied steadily, "Lieutenant John Laird of the Imperial Solar Navy, at your service. And your name?"

"You are exceeding yourself," she replied with frost in her voice. "But since I will wish to question you at length . . . I am Captain Joana Rostov of the Janyard Fleet. Conduct yourself accordingly."

Daryesh looked around him. This wasn't good. He hadn't the chance now to search Laird's memories in detail, but it was clear enough that this was a force of enemies. The rights and wrongs of a quarrel ages after the death of all that had been Vwyrdda meant nothing to him, but he had to learn more of the situation, and be free to act as he chose. Especially since Laird would presently be reviving and start to resist.

The familiar sight of the machines was at once steadying and unnerving. There were powers here which could smash planets! It looked barbaric, this successor culture, and in any event the decision as to the use of this leashed hell had to be his. His head lifted in unconscious arrogance. *His!* For he was the last man of Vwyrdda, and they had wrought the machines, and the heritage was his.

He had to escape.

Joana Rostov was looking at him with an odd blend of hard suspicion and half-frightened puzzlement. "There's something wrong about you, Lieutenant," she said. "You don't behave like a man whose project has just gone to smash. What was that helmet for?"

Daryesh shrugged. "Part of a control device," he said

577

easily. "In my excitement I failed to adjust it properly. No matter. There are plenty of other machines here."

"What use to you?"

"Oh — all sorts of uses. For instance, that one over there is a nucleonic disintegrator, and this is a shield projector, and——"

"You're lying. You can't know any more about this than we do."

"Shall I prove it?"

"Certainly not. Come back from there!"

Coldly, Daryesh estimated distances. He had all the superb psychosomatic coordination of his race, the training evolved through millions of years, but the subcellular components would be lacking in this body. Still — he had to take the chance.

He launched himself against the Janyard who stood beside him. One hand chopped into the man's larynx, the other grabbed him by the tunic and threw him into the man beyond. In the same movement, Daryesh stepped over the falling bodies, picked up the machine rifle which one had dropped, and slammed over the switch of the magnetic shield projector with its long barrel.

Guns blazed in the dimness. Bullets exploded into molten spray as they hit that fantastic magnetic field. Daryesh, behind it, raced through the door and out the tunnel.

They'd be after him in seconds, but this was a strong long-legged body and he was getting the feel of it. He ran easily, breathing in coordination with every movement, conserving his strength. He couldn't master control of the involuntary functions yet, the nervous system was too different, but he could last for a long while at this pace.

He ducked into a remembered side passage. A rifle spewed a rain of slugs after him as someone came through the magnetic field. He chuckled in the dark. Unless they had mapped every labyrinthine twist and turn of the tunnels, or had life-energy detectors, they'd never dare trail him. They'd get lost and wander in here till they starved.

Still, that woman had a brain. She'd guess he was making for the surface and the boats, and try to cut him off. It would be a near thing. He settled down to running.

It was long and black and hollow here, cold with age. The air was dry and dusty, little moisture could be left on Vwyrdda. How long has it been? How long has it been?

John Laird stirred back toward consciousness, stunned neurones lapsing into familiar pathways of synapse, the pattern which was personality fighting to restore iself. Daryesh stumbled as the groping mind flashed a random command to his muscles, cursed, and willed the other self back to blankness. Hold on, Daryesh, hold on, a few minutes only——

He burst out of a small side entrance and stood in the tumbled desolation of the valley. The keen tenuous air raked his sobbing lungs as he looked wildly around at sand and stone and the alien stars. New constellations — Gods, it had been a long time! The moon was larger than he remembered, flooding the dead landscape with a frosty argence. It must have spiraled close in all those uncounted ages.

The boat! Hellblaze, where was the boat?

He saw the Janyard ship not far away, a long lean torpedo resting on the dunes, but it would be guarded — no use trying to steal it. Where was this Laird's vessel, then?

Tumbling through a confusion of alien memories, he recalled burying it on the west side . . . No, it wasn't he who had done that but Laird. Damnation, he had to work fast. He plunged around the monstrous eroded shape of the pyramid, found the long mound, saw the moongleam where the wind had blown sand off the metal. What a clumsy pup this Laird was.

He shoveled the sand away from the airlock, scooping with his hands, the breath raw in throat and lungs. Any second now they'd be on him, any instant, and now that they really believed he understood the machines——

The lock shone dully before him, cold under his hands. He spun the outer dog, swearing with a frantic emotion foreign to old Vwyrdda, but that was the habit of his host, untrained psychosomatically, unevolved—— There they came!

Scooping up the stolen rifle, Daryesh fired a chattering burst at the group that swarmed around the edge of the pyramid. They tumbled like jointed dolls, screaming in the death-white moonlight. Bullets howled around him and ricocheted off the boat-hull.

He got the lock open as they retreated for another charge. For an instant his teeth flashed under the moon, the cold grin of Daryesh the warrior who had ruled a thousand suns in his day and led the fleets of Vwyrdda.

"Farewell, my lovelies," he murmured, and the remembered syllables of the old planet were soft on his tongue.

Slamming the lock behind him, he ran to the control room, letting John Laird's almost unconscious habits carry him along. He got off to a clumsy start — but then he was climbing for the sky, free and away——

A fist slammed into his back, tossed him in his pilot chair to the screaming roar of sundered metal. Gods, O gods, the Janyards had fired a heavy ship's gun, they'd scored a direct hit on his engines and the boat was whistling groundward again.

Grimly, he estimated that the initail impetus had given him a good trajectory, that he'd come down in the hills about a hundred miles north of the valley. But then he'd have to run for it, they'd be after him like beasts of prey in their ship and John Laird would not be denied, muscles were twitching and sinews tightening and throat mumbling insanity as the resurgent personality fought to regain itself. That was one battle he'd have to have out soon!

Well — mentally, Daryesh shrugged. At worst, he could surrender to the Janyards, make common cause with them. It really didn't matter who won this idiotic little war. He had other things to do.

Nightmare. John Laird crouched in a wind-worn cave and looked out over hills lit by icy moonlight. Through a stranger's eyes, he saw the Janyard ship landing near the downglided wreck of his boat, saw the glitter of steel as they poured out and starting hunting. Hunting *him*.

Or was it him any longer, was he more than a prisoner in his own skull? He thought back to memories that were not his, memories of himself thinking thoughts that were not his own, himself escaping from the enemy while he, Laird, whirled in a black abyss of half-conscious madness. Beyond that, he recalled his own life, and he recalled another life which had endured a thousand years before it died. He looked out on the wilderness of rock and sand and blowing dust, and remembered it as it had been, green and fair, and remembered that he was Daryesh of Tollogh, who had ruled over whole planetary systems in the Empire of Vwyrdda. And at the same time he was John Laird of Earth, and two streams of thought flowed through the brain, listening to each other, shouting at each other in the darkness of his skull.

A million years! Horror and loneliness and a wrenching sorrow were in the mind of Daryesh as he looked upon the ruin of Vwyrdda. A million years ago!

Who are you? cried Laird. What have you done to me? And even as he asked, memories which were his own now rose to answer him.

It had been the Erai who rebelled, the Erai whose fathers came from Vwyrdda the fair but who had been strangley altered by centuries of environment. They had revolted against the static rule of the Immortals, and in a century of warfare they had overrun half the Empire and rallied its populations under them. And the Immortals had unleashed their most terrible powers, the sun-smashing ultimate weapons which had lain forbidden in the vaults of Vwyrdda for ten million years. Only — the Erai had known about it. And they had had the weapons too.

In the end, Vwyrdda went under, her fleets broken and her armies reeling in retreat over ten thousand scorched planets. The triumphant Erai had roared in to make an end of the mother world, and nothing in all the mighty Imperial arsenals could stop them now.

Theirs was an unstable culture, it could not endure as that of Vwyrdda had. In ten thousand years or so, they would be gone, and the Galaxy would not have even a memory of that which had been. Which was small help to

581

us, thought Laird grimly, and realized with an icy shock that it had been the thought of Daryesh.

The Vwyrddan's mental tone was, suddenly, almost conversational, and Laird realized what an immensity of trained effort it must have taken to overcome that loneliness of a million years. "See here, Laird, we are apparently doomed to occupy the same body till one of us gets rid of the other, and it is a body which the Janyards seem to want. Rather than fight each other, which would leave the body helpless, we'd better cooperate."

"But — Lord, man! What do you think I am? Do you think I want a vampire like you up there in my brain?"

The answer was fierce and cold. "What of me, Laird? I, who was Daryesh of Tollogh, lord of a thousand suns and lover of Ilorna the Fair, immortalized noble of the greatest empire the universe has ever seen — I am now trapped in the half-evolved body of a hunted alien, a million years after the death of all which mattered. Better be glad I'm here, Laird. I can handle those weapons, you know."

The eyes looked out over the bleak windy hillscape, and the double mind watched distance-dwarfed forms clambering in the rocks, searching for a trail. "A hell of a lot of good that does us now," said Laird. "Besides, I can hear you thinking, you know, and I can remember your own past thoughts. Sol or Janya, it's the same to you. How do I know you'll play ball with me?"

The answer was instant, but dark with an unpleasant laughter. "Why — read my mind, Laird! It's your mind too, isn't it?" Then, more soberly: "Apparently history is repeating itself in the revolt of the barbarians against the mother planet, though on a smaller scale and with a less developed science. I do not expect the result to be any happier for civilization than before. So perhaps I may take a more effective hand than I did before."

It was ghostly, lying here in the wind-grieved remnants of a world, watching the hunters move through a bitter haze of moonlight, and having thoughts which were not one's own, thoughts over which there was no control. Laird clenched his fists, fighting for stability.

"That's better," said Daryesh's sardonic mind. "But relax. Breathe slowly and deeply, concentrate only on the breathing for a while — and then search my mind which is also yours."

"Shut up! Shut up!"

"I am afraid that is impossible. We're in the same brain, you know, and we'll have to get used to each other's streams of consciousness. Relax, man, lie still; think over the thing which has happened to you and know it for the wonder it is."

Man, they say, is a time-binding animal. But only the mighty will and yearning of Vwyrdda had ever leaped across the borders of death itself, waited a million years that that which was a world might not die out of all history.

What is the personality? It is not a thing, discreet and material, it is a pattern and a process. The body starts with a certain genetic inheritance and meets all the manifold complexities of environment. The whole organism is a set of reactions between the two. The primary mental component, sometimes called the ego, is not separable from the body but can in some ways be studied apart.

The scientists had found a way to save something of that which was Daryesh. While the enemy was blazing and thundering at the gates of Vwyrdda, while all the planet waited for the last battle and the ultimate night, quiet men in laboratories had perfected the molecular scanner so that the pattern of synapses which made up all memory, habit, reflex, instinct, the continuity of the ego, could be recorded upon the electronic structure of certain crystals. They took the pattern of Daryesh and of none other, for only he of the remaining Immortals was willing. Who else would want a pattern to be repeated, ages after he himself was dead, ages after all the world and all history and meaning were lost? But Daryesh had always been reckless, and Ilorna was dead, and he didn't care much for what happened.

Ilorna, Ilorna! Laird saw the unforgotten image rise in his memory, golden-eyed and laughing, the long dark hair flowing around the lovely suppleness of her. He remem-

bered the sound of her voice and the sweetness of her
lips, and he loved her. A million years, and she was dust
blowing on the night wind, and he loved her with that
part of him which was Daryesh and with more than a little of John Laird . . . O Ilorna . . .

And Daryesh the man had gone to die with his planet,
but the crystal pattern which reproduced the ego of
Daryesh lay in the vault they had made, surrounded by all
the mightiest works of Vwyrdda. Sooner or later, sometime in the infinite future of the universe, someone would
come; someone or something would put the helmet on
his head and activate it. And the pattern would be reproduced on the neurones, the mind of Daresh would live
again, and he would speak for dead Vwyrdda and seek to
renew the tradition of fifty million years. It would be the
will of Vwyrdda, reaching across time — But Vwyrdda is
*dead,* thought Laird frantically. Vwyrdda is gone — this
is a new history — you've got no business telling us what
to do!

The reply was cold with arrogance. "I shall do as I see
fit. Meanwhile, I advise that you lie passive and do not
attempt to interfere with me."

"Cram it, Daryesh!" Laird's mouth drew back in a
snarl. "I won't be dictated to by anyone, let alone a ghost."

Persuasively, the answer came. "At the moment, neither of us has much choice. We are hunted, and if they
have energy trackers — yes, I see they do — they'll find
us by this body's thermal radiation alone. Best we surrender peaceably. Once aboard the ship loaded with all the
might of Vwyrdda, our chance should come."

Laird lay quietly, watching the hunters move closer,
and the sense of defeat came down on him like a falling
world. What else could he do? What other chance was
there?

"All right," he said at last, audibly. "All right. But I'll
be watching your every thought, understand? I don't think
you can stop me from committing suicide if I must."

"I think I can. But opposing signals to the body will
only neutralize each other, leaving it helplessly fighting itself. Relax, Laird, lie back and let me handle this. I am

584

Daryesh the warrior, and I have come through harder battles than this."

They rose and began walking down the hillside with arms lifted. Daryesh's thought ran on, "Besides — that's a nice-looking wench in command. It could be interesting!"

His laughter rang out under the moon, and it was not the laughter of a human being.

"I can't understand you, John Laird," said Joana.

"Sometimes," replied Daryesh lightly, "I don't understand myself very well — or you, my dear."

She stiffened a little. "That will do, Lieutenant. Remember your position here."

"Oh, the devil with our ranks and countries. Let's be live entities for a change."

Her glance was quizzical. "That's an odd way for a Solman to phrase it."

Mentally, Daryesh swore. Damn this body, anyway! The strength, the fineness of coordination and perception, half the senses he had known, were missing from it. The gross brain structure couldn't hold the reasoning powers he had once had. His thinking was dull and sluggish. He made blunders the old Daryesh would never have committed. And this young woman was quick to see them, and he was a prisoner of John Laird's deadly enemies, and the mind of Laird himself was tangled in thought and will and memory, ready to fight him if he gave the least sign of——

The Solarian's ego chuckled nastily. Easy, Daryesh, easy!

Shut up! his mind snapped back, and he knew drearily that his own trained nervous system would not have been guilty of such a childishly emotional response.

"I may as well tell you the truth, Captain Rostov," he said aloud. "I am not Laird at all. Not any more."

She made no response, merely drooped the lids over her eyes and leaned back in her chair. He noticed abstractedly how long her lashes were — or was that Laird's appreciative mind, unhindered by too much remembrance of Ilorna?

They sat alone, the two of them, in her small cabin aboard the Janyard cruiser. A guard stood outside the door, but it was closed. From time to time they would hear a dull thump or clang as the heavy machines of Vwyrdda were dragged aboard — otherwise they might have been the last two alive on the scarred old planet.

The room was austerely furnished, but there were touches of the feminine here and there — curtains, a small pot of flowers, a formal dress hung in a half-open closet. And the woman who sat across the desk from him was very beautiful, with the loosened ruddy hair streaming to her shoulders and the brilliant eyes never wavering from his. But one slender hand rested on a pistol.

She had told him frankly, "I want to talk privately with you. There is something I don't understand . . . but I'll be ready to shoot at the first suspicion of a false move. And even if you should somehow overpower me, I'd be no good as a hostage. We're Janyards here, and the ship is more than the life of any one of us."

Now she waited for him to go on talking.

He took a cigarette from the box on her desk — Laird's habits again — and lit it and took a slow drag of smoke into his lungs. *All right, Daryesh, go ahead. I suppose your idea is the best, if anything can be made to work at all. But I'm listening, remember.*

"I am all that is left of this planet," he said tonelessly. "This is the ego of Daryesh, of Tollogh, Immortal of Vwyrdda, and in one sense I died a million years ago."

She remained quiet, but he saw how her hands clenched and he heard the sharp small hiss of breath sucked between the teeth.

Briefly, then, he explained how his mental pattern had been preserved, and how it had entered the brain of John Laird.

"You don't expect me to believe that story," she said contemptuously.

"Do you have a lie detector aboard?"

"I have one in this cabin, and I can operate it myself."

She got up and fetched the machine from a cabinet. He watched her, noticing the grace of her movements. You died long ago, Ilorna — you died and the universe will never know another like you. But I go on, and she reminds me somehow of you.

It was a small black thing that hummed and glowed on the desk between them. He put the metal cap on his head, and took the knobs in his hands, and waited while she adjusted the controls. From Laird's memories, he recalled the principle of the thing, the measurement of activity in separate brain centers, the precise detection of the slight extra energy needed in the higher cerebral cortex to invent a falsehood.

"I have to calibrate," she said. "Make up something I know to be a lie."

"New Egypt has rings," he smiled, "which are made of Limburger cheese. However, the main body of the planet is a delicious Camembert——"

"That will do. Now repeat your previous statements."

*Relax, Laird, damn it — blank yourself! I can't control this thing with you interfering.*

He told his story again in a firm voice, and meanwhile he was working within the brain of Laird, getting the feel of it, applying the lessons of nerve control which had been part of his Vwyrddan education. It should certainly be possible to fool a simple electronic gadget, to heighten activity in all centers to such an extent that the added effort of his creative cells could not be spotted.

He went on without hesitation, wondering if the flickering needles would betray him and if her gun would spit death into his heart in the next moment: "Naturally, Laird's personality was completely lost, its fixed patterns obliterated by the superimposition of my own. I have his memories, but otherwise I am Daryesh of Vwyrdda, at your service."

She bit her lip. "What service! You shot four of my men."

"Consider my situation, woman. I came into instantaneous existence. I remember sitting in the laboratory under

587

the scanner, a slight dizziness, and then immediately I was in an alien body. Its nervous system was stunned by the shock of my entry, I couldn't think clearly. All I had to go on was Laird's remembered conviction that these were deadly foes surrounding me, murderous creatures bent on killing me and wiping out my planet. I acted half-instinctively. Also, I wanted, in my own personality, to be a free agent, to get away and think this out for myself. So I did. I regret the death of your men, but I think they will be amply compensated for."

"H'm — you surrendered when we all but had you anyway."

"Yes, of course, but I had about decided to do so in all events." Her eyes never lifted from the dials that wavered life or death. "I was, after all, in your territory, with little or no hope of getting clear, and you were the winning side of this war, which meant nothing to me emotionally. Insofar as I have any convictions in this matter, it is that the human race will best be served by a Janyard victory. History has shown that when the frontier cultures — which the old empire calls barbaric but which are actually new and better adapted civilizations — when they win out over the older and more conservative nations, the result is a synthesis and a period of unusual achievement."

He saw her visibly relaxing, and inwardly he smiled. It was so easy, so easy. They were such children in this later age. All he had to do was hand her a smooth lie which fitted in with the propaganda that had been her mental environment from birth, and she could not seriously think of him as an enemy.

The blue gaze lifted to his, and the lips were parted. "You will help us?" she whispered.

Daryesh nodded. "I know the principles and construction and use of those engines, and in truth there is in them the force that molds planets. Your scientists would never work out the half of all that there is to be found. I will show you the proper operation of them all." He shrugged. "Naturally, I will expect commensurate rewards. But even altruistically speaking, this is the best

588

thing I can do. Those energies should remain under the direction of one who understands them, and not be misused in ignorance. That could lead to unimaginable catastrophes."

Suddenly she picked up her gun and shoved it back into its holster. She stood up, smiling, and held out her hand.

He shook it vigorously, and then bent over and kissed it. When he looked up, she stood uncertain, half afraid and half glad.

*It's not fair!* protested Laird. The poor girl has never known anything of this sort. She's never heard of coquetry. To her love isn't a game, it's something mysterious and earnest and decent——

I told you to shut up, answered Daryesh coldly. Look, man, even if we do have an official safe-conduct, this is still a ship full of watchful hostility. We have to consolidate our position by every means at hand. Now relax and enjoy this.

He walked around the desk and took her hands again. "You know," he said, and the crooked smile on his mouth, reminded him that this was more than half a truth, "you make me think of the woman I loved, a million years ago on Vwyrdda."

She shrank back a little. "I can't get over it," she whispered. "You — you're old, and you don't belong to this cycle of time at all, and what you must think and know makes me feel like a child — Daryesh, it frightens me."

"Don't let it, Joana," he said gently. "My mind is young, and very lonely." He put a wistfulness in his voice. "Joana, I need someone to talk to. You can't imagine what it is to wake up a million years after all your world is dead, more alone than — oh, let me come in once in awhile and talk to you, as one friend to another. Let's forget time and death and loneliness. I need someone like you."

She lowered her eyes, and said with a stubborn honesty, "I think that would be good too, Daryesh. A ship's captain doesn't have friends, you know. They put me in this service because I had the apitude, and that's really all I've ever had. Oh, comets!" She forced a laugh. "To space with all that self-pity. Certainly you may come in whenever you like. I hope it'll be often."

They talked for quite a while longer, and when he kissed her goodnight it was the most natural thing in the universe. He walked to his bunk — transferred from the brig to a tiny unused compartment — with his mind in pleasant haze.

Lying in the dark, he began the silent argument with Laird anew. "Now what?" demanded the Solarian.

"We play it slow and easy," said Daryesh patiently — as if the fool couldn't read it directly in their common brain. "We watch our chance, but don't act for a while yet. Under the pretext of rigging the energy projectors for action, we'll arrange a setup which can destroy the ship at the flick of a switch. They won't know it. They haven't an inkling about subspatial flows. Then, when an opportunity to escape offers itself, we throw that switch and get away and try to return to Sol. With my knowledge of Vwyrddan science, we can turn the tide of the war. It's risky — sure — but it's the only chance I see. And for Heaven's sake let me handle matters. You're supposed to be dead."

"And what happens when we finally settle this business? How can I get rid of you?"

"Frankly, I don't see any way to do it. Our patterns have become too entangled. The scanners necessarily work on the whole nervous system. We'll just have to learn to live together." Persuasively: "It will be to your own advantage. Think, man! We can do as we choose with Sol. With the Galaxy. And I'll set up a life-tank and make us a new body to which we'll transfer the pattern, a body with all the intelligence and abilities of a Vwyrddan, and I'll immortalize it. Man, you'll never die!"

It wasn't too happy a prospect, thought Laird skeptically. His own chances of dominating that combination were small. In time, his own personality might be completely absorbed by Daryesh's greater one.

Of course — a psychiatrist — narcosis, hypnosis——

"No, you don't!" said Daryesh grimly. "I'm just as fond of my individuality as you are."

The mouth which was theirs twisted wryly in the dark. "Guess we'll just have to learn to love each other," thought Laird.

The body dropped into slumber. Presently Laird's cells were asleep, his personality faded into a shadowland of dreams. Daryesh remained awake a while longer. Sleep — waste of time — the Immortals had never been plagued by fatigue——

He chuckled to himself. What a web of lies and counterlies he had woven. If Joana and Laird both knew——

The mind is an intricate thing. It can conceal facts from itself, make itself forget that which is painful to remember, persuade its own higher components of whatever the subconscious deems right. Rationalization, schizophrenia, autohypnosis, they are but pale indications of the self-deception which the brain practices. And the training of the Immortals included full neural coordination; they could consciously utilize the powers latent in themselves. They could by an act of conscious will stop the heart, or block off pain, or split their own personalities.

Daryesh had known his ego would be fighting whatever host it found, and he had made preparations before he was scanned. Only a part of his mind was in full contact with Laird's. Another section, split off from the main stream of consciousness by deliberate and controlled schizophrenia, was thinking its own thoughts and making its own plans. Self-hypnotized, he automatically reunited his ego at such times as Laird was not aware, otherwise there was only subconscious contact. In effect a private compartment of his mind, inaccessible to the Solarian, was making its own plans.

That destructive switch would have to be installed to satisfy Laird's waking personality, he thought. But it would never be thrown. For he had been telling Joana that much of the truth — his own advantage lay with the Janyards, and he meant to see them through to final victory.

It would be simple enough to get rid of Laird temporarily. Persuade him that for some reason it was advisable to get dead drunk. Daryesh's more controlled ego would remain conscious after Laird's had passed out. Then he could make all arrangements with Joana, who by that time should be ready to do whatever he wanted.

Psychiatry — yes, Laird's brief idea had been the right one. The methods of treating schizophrenia could, with some modifications, be applied to suppressing Daryesh's extra personality. He'd blank out that Solarian ... permanently.

And after that would come his undying new body, and centuries and millennia in which he could do what he wanted with this young civilization.

The demon exorcising the man — He grinned drowsily. Presently he slept.

The ship drove through a night of stars and distance. Time was meaningless, was the position of the hands on a clock, was the succession of sleeps and meals, was the slow shift in the constellations as they gulped the light-years.

On and on, the mighty drone of the second-order drive filling their bones and their days, the round of work and food and sleep and Joana. Laird wondered if it would ever end. He wondered if he might not be the Flying Dutchman, outward bound for eternity, locked in his own skull with the thing that had possessed him. At such times the only comfort was in Joana's arms. He drew of the wild young strength of her, and he and Daryesh were one. But afterward——

"We're going to join the Grand Fleet. You heard her, Daryesh. She's making a triumphal pilgrimage to the gathered power of Janya, bringing the invincible weapons of Vwyrdda to her admiral.

Why not? She's young and ambitious, she wants glory as much as you do. What of it?"

We have to escape before she gets there. We have to steal a lifeboat and destroy this ship and all in it soon.

All in it? Joana Rostov, too?

Damn it, we'll kidnap her or something. You know I'm in love with the girl, you devil. But it's a matter of all Earth. This one cruiser has enough stuff in it now to wreck a planet. I have parents, brothers, friends — a civilization. We've got to act!

All right, all right, Laird. But take it easy. We have to get enough of a demonstration to allay their suspicions. Joana's the only one aboard here who trusts us. None of her officers do.

The body and the double mind labored as the slow days passed, directing Janyard technicians who could not understand what it was they built. Laird, drawing on Daryesh's memories, knew what a giant slept in those coils and tubes and invisible energy-fields. Here were forces to trigger the great creative powers of the universe and turn them to destuction — distorted space-time, atoms dissolving into pure energy, vibrations to upset the stability of force-fields which maintained order in the cosmos. Laird remembered the ruin of Vwyrdda, and shuddered.

They got a projector mounted and operating, and Daryesh suggested that the cruiser halt somewhere that he could prove his words. They picked a barren planet in an uninhabited system and lay in an orbit fifty thousand miles out. In an hour Daryesh had turned the facing hemisphere into a sea of lava.

"If the dis-fields were going," he said absent-mindedly, "I'd pull the planet into chunks for you."

Laird saw the pale taut faces around him. Sweat was shining on foreheads, and a couple of men looked sick. Joana forgot her position enough to come shivering into his arms.

But the visage she lifted in a minute was exultant and eager, with the thoughtless cruelty of a swooping hawk. "There's an end of Earth, gentlemen!"

"Nothing they have can stop us," murmured her exec dazedly. "Why, this one ship, protected by one of those space-warp screens you spoke of, sir — this one little ship could sail in and lay the Solar System waste."

Daryesh nodded. It was entirely possible. Not much energy was required, since the generators of Vwyrdda served only as catalysts releasing fantastically greater forces. And Sol

593

had none of the defensive science which had enabled his world to hold out for a while. Yes, it could be done.

He stiffened with the sudden furious thought of Laird: *That's it, Daryesh! That's the answer.*

The thought-stream was his own too, flowing through the same brain, and indeed it was simple. They could have the whole ship armed and armored beyond the touch of Janya. And since none of the technicians aboard understood the machines, and since they were now wholly trusted, they could install robotcontrols without anyone's knowing.

Then — the massed Grand Fleet of Janya — a flick of the main switch — man-killing energies would flood the cruiser's interior, and only corpses would remain aboard. Dead men and the robots that would open fire on the Fleet. This one ship could ruin all the barbarian hopes in a few bursts of incredible flame. And the robots could then be set to destroy her as well, lest by some chance the remaining Janyards manage to board her.

*And we — we can escape in the initial confusion, Daryesh. We can give orders to the robot to spare the captain's gig, and we can get Joana aboard and head for Sol! There'll be no one left to pursue!*

Slowly, the Vwyrddan's thought made reply: *A good plan. Yes, a bold stroke. We'll do it!*

"What's the matter, Daryesh?" Joana's voice was suddenly anxious. "You look——"

"Just thinking, that's all. Never think, Captain Rostov. Bad for the brain."

Later, as he kissed her, Laird felt ill at thought of the treachery he planned. Her friends, her world, her cause — wiped out in a single shattering blow, and he would have struck it. He wondered if she would speak to him ever again, once it was over.

Daryesh, the heartless devil, seemed only to find a sardonic amusement in the situation.

And later, when Laird slept, Daryesh thought that the young man's scheme was good. Certainly he'd fall in with it. It would keep Laird busy till they were at the Grand Fleet rendezvous. And after that it would be too late. The

Janyard victory would be sealed. All he, Daryesh, had to do when the time came was keep away from that master switch. If Laird tried to reach it their opposed wills would only result in nullity — which was victory for Janya.

He liked this new civilization. It had a freshness, a vigor and hopefulness which he could not find in Laird's memories of Earth. It had a tough-minded purposefulness that would get it far. And being young and fluid, it would be amenable to such pressures of psychology and force as he chose to apply.

Vwyrdda, his mind whispered. Vwyrdda, we'll make them over in your image. You'll live again!

Grand Fleet!

A million capital ships and their auxiliaries lay marshaled at a dim red dwarf of a sun, massed together and spinning in the same mighty orbit. Against the incandescent whiteness of stars and the blackness of the old deeps, armored flanks gleaming like flame as far as eyes could see, rank after rank, tier upon tier, of titanic sharks swimming through space — guns and armor and torpedoes and bombs and men to smash a planet and end a civilization. The sight was too big, imagination could not make the leap, and the human mind had only a dazed impression of vastness beyond vision.

This was the great spearhead of Janya, a shining lance poised to drive through Sol's thin defense lines and roar out of the sky to rain hell on the seat of empire. They can't really be human any more, thought Laird sickly. Space and strangeness have changed them too much. No human being could think of destroying Man's home. Then, fiercely: All right Daryesh. This is our chance!

Not yet, Laird. Wait a while. Wait till we have a legitimate excuse for leaving the ship.

Well — come up to the control room with me. I want to stay near that switch. Lord, Lord, everything that is Man and me depends on us now!

Daryesh agreed with a certain reluctance that faintly puzzled the part of his mind open to Laird. The other half, crouching deep in his subconscious, knew the reason: It was waiting the posthypnotic signal, the key event which would trigger its emergence into the higher brain-centers.

The ship bore a tangled and unfinished look. All its conventional armament had been ripped out and the machines of Vwyrdda installed in its place. A robot brain, half-alive in its complexity, was gunner and pilot and ruling intelligence of the vessel now, and only the double mind of one man knew what orders had really been given it. *When the main switch is thrown, you will flood the ship with ten units of disrupting radiation. Then, when the captain's gig is well away, you will destroy this fleet, sparing only that one boat. When no more ships in operative condition are in range, you will activate the disintegrators and dissolve this whole vessel and all its contents to basic energy.*

With a certain morbid fascination, Laird looked at that switch. An ordinary double-throw knife type — Lord of space, could it be possible, was it logical that all history should depend on the angle it made with the control panel? He pulled his eyes away, stared out at the swarming ships and the greater host of the stars, lit a cigaret with shaking hands, paced and sweated and waited.

Joana came to him, a couple of crewmen marching solemnly behind. Her eyes shone and her cheeks were flushed and the turret light was like molten copper in her hair. No woman, thought Laird, had ever been so lovely, and he was going to destroy that to which she had given her life.

"Daryesh!" Laughter danced in her voice. "Daryesh, the high admiral wants to see us in his flagship. He'll probably ask for a demonstration, and then I think the fleet will start for Sol at once with us in the van. Daryesh — oh, Daryesh, the war is almost over!"

Now! blazed the thought of Laird, and his hand reached for the main switch. Now — easily, casually, with a remark about letting the generators warm up — and then go with her, overpower those guardsmen in their surprise and head for home!

And Daryesh's mind reunited itself at that signal, and the hand froze . . .

No!

*What? But——*

The memory of the suppressed half of Daryesh's mind was open to Laird; and the triumph of the whole of it, and Laird knew that his defeat was here.

So simple, so cruelly simple — Daryesh could stop him, lock the body in a conflict of wills, and that would be enough. For while Laird slept, while Daryesh's own major ego was unconscious, the trained subconscious of the Vwyrddan had taken over. It had written, in its self-created somnambulism, a letter to Joana explaining the whole truth, and had put it where it would easily be found once they started looking through his effects in search of an explanation for his paralysis. And the letter directed, among other things, that Daryesh's body should be kept under restraint until certain specified methods known to Vwyrddan psychiatry — drugs, electric waves, hypnosis — had been applied to eradicate the Laird half of his mind.

Janyard victory was near.

"Daryesh!' Joana's voice seemed to come from immensely far away; her face swam in a haze and a roar of fainting consciousness. "Daryesh, what's the matter? Oh, my dear, what's wrong?"

Grimly, the Vwyrddan thought: Give up, Laird. Surrender to me, and you can keep your ego. I'll destroy that letter. See, my whole mind is open to you now — you can see that I mean it honestly this time. I'd rather avoid treatment if possible, and I do owe you something. But surrender now, or be wiped out of your own brain.

Defeat and ruin — and nothing but slow distorting death as a reward for resistance. Laird's will caved in, his mind too chaotic for clear thought. Only one dull impulse came: I give up. You win, Daryesh.

The collapsed body picked itself off the floor. Joana was bending anxiously over him. "Oh, what is it, what's wrong?"

Daryesh collected himself and smiled shakily. "Excitement will do this to me, now and then. I haven't fully mastered this alien nervous system yet. I'm all right now. Let's go."

Laird's hand reached out and pulled the switch over.

Daryesh shouted, an animal roar from the throat, and tried to recover it, and the body toppled again in a stasis of locked wills.

It was like a deliverance from hell, and still it was but the inevitable logic of events, as Laird's own self reunited. Half of him still shaking with defeat, half realizing its own victory, he thought savagely:

None of them noticed me do that. They were paying too much attention to my face. Or if they did, we've proved to them before that it's only a harmless regulating switch. And — the lethal radiations are already flooding us! If you don't cooperate now, Daryesh, I'll hold us here till we're both dead!

So simple, so simple. Because, sharing Daryesh's memory, Laird had shared his knowledge of self-deception techniques. He had anticipated, with the buried half of his mind, that the Vwyrddan might pull some such trick, and had installed a posthypnotic command of his own. In a situation like this, when everything looked hopeless, his conscious mind was to surrender, and then his subconscious would order that the switch be thrown.

Cooperate, Daryesh! You're as fond of living as I. Cooperate, and let's get the hell out of here!

Grudgingly, wryly: You win, Laird.

The body rose again, and leaned on Joana's arm, and made its slow way toward the boat blisters. The undetectable rays of death poured through them, piling up their cumulative effects. In three minutes, a nervous system would be ruined.

"Too slow, too slow. Come on, Joana. Run!"

"Why——" She stopped, and a hard suspicion came into the faces of the two men behind her. "Daryesh — what do you mean? What's come over you?"

"Ma'm . . ." One of the crewmen stepped forward. "Ma'm, I wonder . . . I saw him pull down the main switch. And now he's in a hurry to leave the ship. And none of us really know how all that machinery ticks."

Laird pulled the gun out of Joana's holster and shot him.

The other gasped, reaching for his own side arm, and Laird's weapon blazed again.

His fist leaped out, striking Joana on the angle of the jaw, and she sagged. He caught her up and started to run.

A pair of crewmen stood in the corridor leading to the boats. "What's the matter, sir?" one asked.

"Collapsed — radiation from the machines — got to get her to a hospital ship," gasped Daryesh.

They stood aside, wonderingly, and he spun the dogs of the blister valve and stepped into the gig. "Shall we come, sir?" asked one of the men.

"No!" Laird felt a little dizzy. The radiation was streaming through him, and death was coming with giant strides. "No——" He smashed a fist into the insistent face, slammed the valve back, and vaulted to the pilot's chair.

The engines hummed, warming up. Fists and feet battered on the valve. The sickness made him retch.

O Joana, if this kills you——

He threw the main-drive switch. Acceleration jammed him back as the gig leaped free.

Staring out the ports, he saw fire blossom in space as the great guns of Vwyrdda opened up.

My glass was empty. I signalled for a refill and sat wondering just how much of the yarn one could believe.

"I've read the histories," I said slowly. "I do know that some mysterious catastrophe annihilated the massed fleet of Janya and turned the balance of the war. Sol speared in and won inside of a year. And you mean that you did it?"

"In a way. Or Daryesh did. We were acting as one personality, you know. He was a thoroughgoing realist, and the moment he saw his defeat he switched wholeheartedly to the other side."

"But — Lord, man! Why've we never heard anything about this? You mean you never told anyone, never rebuilt any of those machines, never did anything?"

Laird's dark, worn face twisted in a bleak smile. "Certainly. This civilization isn't ready for such things. Even

Vwyrdda wasn't, and it'll take us millions of years to reach their stage. Besides, it was part of the bargain."

"Bargain?"

"Just as certainly. Daryesh and I still had to live together, you know. Life under suspicion of mutual trickery, never trusting your own brain, would have been intolerable. We reached an agreement during that long voyage back to Sol, and used Vwyrddan methods of autohypnosis to assure that it could not be broken."

He looked somberly out at the lunar night. "That's why I said the genie in the bottle killed me. Inevitably, the two personalities merged, became one. And that one was, of course, mostly Daryesh, with overtones of Laird.

"Oh, it isn't so horrible. We retain the memories of our separate existences, and the continuity which is the most basic attribute of the ego. In fact, Laird's life was so limited, so blind to all the possibilities and wonder of the universe, that I don't regret him very often. Once in a while I still get nostalgic moments and have to talk to a human. But I always pick one who won't know whether or not to believe me, and won't be able to do much of anything about it if he should."

"And why did you go into Survey?" I asked, very softly.

"I want to get a good look at the universe before the change. Daryesh wants to orient himself, gather enough data for a sound basis of decision. When we — I — switch over to the new immortal body, there'll be work to do, a galaxy to remake in a newer and better pattern by Vwyrddan standards! It'll take millennia, but we've got all time before us. Or I do — what do I mean, anyway?" He ran a hand through his gray-streaked hair.

"But Laird's part of the bargain was that there should be as nearly normal a human life as possible until this body gets inconveniently old. So——" He shrugged. "So that's how it worked out."

We sat for a while longer, saying little, and then he got up. "Excuse me," he said. "There's my wife. Thanks for the talk."

I saw him walk over to greet a tall, handsome red-haired woman. His voice drifted back: "Hello, Joana——"

They walked out of the room together in perfectly ordinary and human fashion.

I wonder what history has in store for us.

*Man's family tree was awesome enough to give every
galactic race an inferiority complex—but then he
tried to climb it!*

●

# BIG ANCESTOR

## By F. L. Wallace

In repose, Taphetta the Ribboneer resembled a fancy
giant bow on a package. His four flat legs looped out and
in, the ends tucked under his wide, thin body, which constituted the knot at the middle. His neck was flat, too,
arching out in another loop. Of all his features, only his
head had appreciable thickness and it was crowned with
a dozen long though narrower ribbons.

Taphetta rattled the head fronds together in a surprisingly good imitation of speech. "Yes, I've heard the legend."

"It's more than a legend," said Sam Halden, biologist.
The reaction was not unexpected — non-humans tended
to dismiss the data as convenient speculation and nothing
more. "There are at least a hundred kinds of humans,
each supposedly originating in strict seclusion on as many
widely scattered planets. Obviously there was no contact
throughout the ages before space travel — *and yet each
planetary race can inter-breed with a minimum of ten*

*others!* That's more than a legend — one hell of a lot more!"

"It is impressive," admitted Taphetta. "But I find it mildly distasteful to consider mating with someone who does not belong to my species."

"That's because you're unique," said Halden. "Outside of your own world, there's nothing like your species, except superficially, and that's true of all other creatures, intelligent or not, with the sole exception of mankind. Actually, the four of us here, though it's accidental, very nearly represent the biological spectrum of human development.

"Emmer, a Neanderthal type and our archaeologist, is around the beginning of the scale. I'm from Earth, near the middle, though on Emmer's side. Meredith, linguist, is on the other side of the middle. And beyond her, toward the far end, is Kelburn, mathematician. There's a corresponding span of fertility. Emmer just misses being able to breed with my kind, but there's a fair chance that I'd be fertile with Meredith and a similar though lesser chance that her fertility may extend to Kelburn."

Taphetta rustled his speech ribbons quizzically. "But I thought it was proved that some humans did originate on one planet, that there was an unbroken line of evolution that could be traced back a billion years."

"You're thinking of Earth," said Halden. "Humans require a certain kind of planet. It's reasonable to assume that, if men were set down on a hundred such worlds, they'd seem to fit in with native life-forms on a few of them. That's what happened on Earth; when Man arrived, there was actually a manlike creature there. Naturally our early evolutionists stretched their theories to cover the facts they had.

"But there are other worlds in which humans who were there before the Stone Age aren't related to anything else there. We have to conclude that Man didn't originate on any of the planets on which he is now found. Instead, he evolved elsewhere and later was scattered throughout this section of the Milky Way."

603

"And so, to account for the unique race that can interbreed across thousands of light-years, you've brought in the big ancestor," commented Taphetta dryly. "It seems an unnecessary simplification."

"Can you think of a better explanation?" asked Kelburn. "Something had to distribute one species so widely and it's not the result of parallel evolution — not when a hundred human races are involved, and *only* the human race."

"I can't think of a better explanation." Taphetta rearranged his ribbons. "Frankly, no one else is much interested in Man's theories about himself."

It was easy to understand the attitude. Man was the most numerous though not always the most advanced — Ribboneers had a civilization as high as anything in the known section of the Milky Way, and there were others — and humans were more than a little feared. If they ever got together — but they hadn't except in agreements as to their common origin.

Still, Taphetta the Ribboneer was an experienced pilot and could be very useful. A clear statement of their position was essential in helping him make up his mind. "You've heard of the adjacency mating principle?" asked Sam Halden.

"Vaguely. Most people have if they've been around men."

"We've got new data and are able to interpret it better. The theory is that humans who can mate with each other were once physically close. We've got a list of all our races arranged in sequence. If planetary race F can mate with race E back to A and forward to M, and race G is fertile only back to B, but forward to O, then we assume that whatever their positions are now, at one time G was actually adjacent to F, but was a little further along. When we project back into time those star systems on which humans existed prior to space travel, we get a certain pattern. Kelburn can explain it to you."

The normally pink body of the Ribboneer flushed

slightly. The colour change was almost imperceptible, but it was enough to indicate that he was interested.

Kelburn went to the projector. "It would be easier if we knew all the stars in the Milky Way, but though we've explored only a small portion of it, we can reconstruct a fairly accurate representation of the past."

He pressed the controls and stars twinkled on the screen. "We're looking down on the plane of the Galaxy. This is one arm of it as it is today and here are the human systems." He pressed another control and, for purposes of identification, certain stars became more brilliant. There was no pattern, merely a scattering of stars. "The whole Milky Way is rotating. And while stars in a given region tend to remain together, there's also a random motion. Here's what happens when we calculate the positions of stars in the past."

Flecks of light shifted and flowed across the screen. Kelburn stopped the motion.

"Two hundred thousand years ago," he said.

There was a pattern of the identified stars. They were spaced at fairly equal intervals along a regular curve, a horseshoe loop that didn't close, though if the ends were extended, the lines would have crossed.

Taphetta rustled. "The math is accurate?"

"As accurate as it can be with a million-plus body problem."

"And that's the hypothetical route of the unknown ancestor?"

"To the best of our knowledge," said Kelburn. "And whereas there are humans who are relatively near and not fertile, they can always mate with those they were adjacent to *two hundred thousand years ago!*"

"The adjacency mating principle. I've never seen it demonstrated," murmured Taphetta, flexing his ribbons. "Is that the only era that satisfies the calculations?"

"Plus or minus a hundred thousand years, we can still get something that might be the path of a spaceship attempting to cover a representative section of territory," said Kelburn. "However, we have other ways of dating it.

On some worlds on which there are no other mammals, we're able to place the first human fossils chronologically. The evidence is sometimes contradictory, but we believe we've got the time right."

Taphetta waved a ribbon at the chart. "And you think that where the two ends if the curve cross is your original home?"

"We think so," said Kelburn. "We've narrowed it down to several cubic light years — then. Now it's far more. And, of course, if it were a fast-moving star, it might be completely out of the field of our exploration. But we're certain we've got a good chance of finding it this trip."

"It seems I must decide quickly." The Ribboneer glanced out the visionport, where another ship hung motionless in space beside them. "Do you mind if I ask other questions?"

"Go ahead," Kelburn invited sardonically. "But if it's not math, you'd better ask Halden. He's the leader of the expedition."

Halden flushed; the sarcasm wasn't necessary. It was true that Kelburn was the most advanced human type present, but while there were differences, biological and in the scale of intelligence, it wasn't as great as once was thought. Anyway, non-humans weren't trained in the fine distinctions that men made among themselves. And, higher or lower, he was as good a biologist as the other was a mathematician. And there was the matter of training; he'd been on several expeditions and this was Kelburn's first trip. Damn it, he thought, that rated some respect.

The Ribboneer shifted his attention. "Aside from the sudden illness of your pilot, why did you ask for me?"

"We didn't. The man became sick and required treatment we can't give him. Luckily, a ship was passing and we hailed it because it's four months to the nearest planet. They consented to take him back and told us that there was a passenger on board who was an experienced pilot. We have men who could do the job in a makeshift fashion, but the region we're heading for, while mapped, is largely unknown. We'd prefer to have an expert — and Ribboneers are famous for their navigational ability."

Taphetta crinkled politely at the reference to his skill. "I had other plans, but I can't evade professional obligations, and an emergency such as this should cancel out any previous agreements. Still, what are the incentives?"

Sam Halden coughed. "The usual, plus a little extra. We've copied the Ribboneer's standard nature, simplifying it a little and adding a per cent here and there for the crew pilot and scientist's share of the profits from any discoveries we may make."

"I'm complimented that you like our contract so well," said Taphetta, "but I really must have our own unsimplified version. If you want me, you'll take my contract. I came prepared." He extended a tightly bound roll that he had kept somewhere on his person.

They glanced at one another as Halden took it.

"You can read it if you want," offered Taphetta. "But it will take you all day — it's micro printing. However, you needn't be afraid that I'm defrauding you. It's honoured everywhere we go and we go nearly everywhere in this sector — places men have never been."

There was no choice if they wanted him, and they did. Besides, the integrity of Ribboneers was not to be questioned. Halden signed.

"Good," Taphetta crinkled. "Send it to the ship; they'll forward it for me. And you can tell the ship to go on without me." He rubbed his ribbons together. "Now if you'll get me the charts, I'll examine the region toward which we're heading."

Firmon of hydroponics slouched in, a tall man with scanty hair and an equal lack of grace. He seemed to have difficulty in taking his eyes off Meredith, though, since he was a notch or so above her in the mating scale, he shouldn't have been so interested. But his planet had been inexplicably slow in developing and he wasn't completely aware of his place in the human hierarchy.

Disdainfully, Meredith adjusted a skirt that, a few inches shorter, wouldn't have been a skirt at all, revealing, while doing so, just how long and beautiful a woman's legs could be. Her people had never given much thought to physical modesty and, with legs like that, it was easy to see why.

Muttering something about primitive women, Firmon turned to the biologist. "The pilot doesn't like our air."

"Then change it to suit him. He's in charge of the ship and knows more about these things than I do."

"More than a man?" Firmon leered at Meredith and, when she failed to smile, added plaintively, "I did try to change it, but he still complains."

Halden took a deep breath. "Seems all right to me."

"To everybody else, too, but the tapeworm hasn't got lungs. He breaths through a million tubes scattered over his body."

It would do no good to explain that Taphetta wasn't a worm, that his evolution had taken a different course, but that he was in no sense less complex than Man. It was a paradox that some biologically higher humans hadn't developed as much as lower races and actually weren't prepared for the multitude of life-forms they'd meet in space. Firmon's reaction was quite typical.

"If he asks for cleaner air, it's because his system needs it," said Halden. "Do anything you can to give it to him."

"Can't. This is as good as I can get it. Taphetta thought you could do something about it."

"Hydroponics is your job. There's nothing I can do." Halden paused thoughtfully. "Is there something wrong with the plants?"

"In a way, I guess, and yet not really."

"What is it, some kind of toxic condition?"

"The plants are healthy enough, but something's chewing them down as fast as they grow."

"Insects? There shouldn't be any, but if there are, we've got sprays. Use them."

"It's an animal," said Firmon. "We tried poison, and got a few, but now they won't touch the stuff. I had electronics rig up some traps. The animals seem to know what they are and we've never caught one that way."

Halden glowered at the man. "How long has this been going on?"

"About three months. It's not bad; he can keep up with them."

It was probably nothing to become alarmed at, but an animal on the ship was a nuisance, doubly so because of this pilot.

"Tell me what you know about it," said Halden.

"They're little things." Firmon held out his hands to show how small. "I don't know how they got on, but once they did, there were plenty of places to hide." He looked up defensively. "This is an old ship with new equipment and they hide under the machinery. There's nothing we can do except rebuild the ship from the hull inward."

Firmon was right. The new equipment had been installed in any place just to get it in and now there were inaccessible corners and crevices everywhere that couldn't be closed off without rebuilding.

They couldn't set up a continuous watch and shoot the animals down because there weren't that many men to spare. Besides, the use of weapons in hydroponics would cause more damage to the thing they were trying to protect than to the pest. He'd have to devise other ways.

Sam Halden go up. "I'll take a look and see what I can do."

"I'll come along and help," said Meredith, untwining her legs and leaning against him. "Your mistress ought to have some sort of privileges."

Halden started. So she *knew* that the crew was calling her that! Perhaps it was intended to discourage Firmon, but he wished she hadn't said it. It didn't help the situation at all.

Taphetta sat in a chair designed for humans. With a less flexible body, he wouldn't have fitted. Maybe it wasn't sitting, but his flat legs were folded neatly around the arms and his head rested comfortably on the seat. The head ribbons, which were his hands and voice, were never quite still.

He looked from Halden to Emmer and back again. "The hydroponics tech tells me you're contemplating an experiment. I don't like it."

Halden shrugged. "We've got to have better air. It might work."

"Pests on the ship? It's filthy! My people would never tolerate it!"

"Neither do we."

The Ribboneer's distaste subsided. "What kind of creatures are they?"

"I have a description, though I've never seen one. It's a small four-legged animal with two antennae at the lower base of its skull. A typical pest."

Taphetta rustled. "Have you found out how it got on?"

"It was probably brought in with the supplies," said the biologist. "Considering how far we have come, it may have been any one of a half a dozen planets. Anyway, it hid, and since most of the places it had access to were near the outer hull, it got an extra dose of hard radiation, or it may have nested near the atomic engines; both are possibilities. Either way, it mutated, became a different animal. It's developed a tolerance for the poisons we spray on plants. Other things it detects and avoids, even electronic traps."

"Then you believe it changed mentally as well as physically, that it's smarter?"

"I'd say that, yes. It must be a fairly intelligent creature to be so hard to get rid of. But it can be lured into traps, if the bait's strong enough."

"That's what I don't like," said Taphetta, curling. "Let me think it over while I ask questions." He turned to Emmer. "I'm curious about humans. Is there anything else you can tell me about the hypothetical ancestor?"

Emmer didn't look like the genius he was — a Neanderthal genius, but nonetheless a real one. In his field, he rated very high. He raised a stubble-flecked cheek from a large thick-fingered paw and ran shaggy hands through shaggier hair.

"I can speak with some authority," he rumbled. "I was born on a world with the most extensive relics. As a child, I played in the ruins of their camp."

"I don't question your authority," crinkled Taphetta. "To me, all humans — late or early and male or female — look remarkably alike. If you are an archeologist, that's enough for me." He paused and flicked his speech ribbons. "Camp, did you say?"

Emmer smiled, unsheathing great teeth. "You've never seen any pictures? Impressive but just a camp, monolithic one-story structures, and we'd give something to know what they're made of. Presumably my world was one of the first they stopped at. They weren't used to roughing it, so they built more elaborately than they did later on. One-story structures and that's how we can guess at their size. The doorways were forty feet high."

"Very large," agreed Taphetta. It was difficult to tell whether he was impressed. "What did you find in the ruins?"

"Nothing," said Emmer. "There were buildings there and that was all, not a scrap of writing or a tool or a single picture. They covered a route estimated at thirty thousand light-years in less than five thousand years — and not one of them died that we have a record of."

"A faster-than-light drive and an extremely long life," mused Taphetta. "But they didn't leave any information for their descendants. Why?"

"Who knows? Their mental processes were certainly far different from ours. They may have thought we'd be better off without it. We do know they were looking for a special kind of planet, like Earth, because they visited so many of that type, yet different from it because they never stayed. They were pretty special people themselves, big and long-lived, and maybe they couldn't survive on any planet they found. Perhaps they had ways of determining there wasn't the kind of planet they needed in the entire Milky Way. Their science was tremendously advanced and when they learned that, they may have altered their germ plasm and left us, hoping that some of us would survive. Most of us did."

"This special planet sounds strange," murmured Taphetta.

"Not really," said Emmer. "Fifty human races reached space travel independently and those who did were scattered equally among early and late species. It's well

611

known that individuals among my people are often as bright as any of Halden's or Meredith's, but as a whole we don't have the total capacity that later Man does, and yet we're as advanced in civilization. The difference? It must lie somewhere in the planets we live on and it's hard to say just what it is."

"What happened to those who didn't develop space travel?" asked Taphetta.

"We helped them," said Emmer.

And they had, no matter who or what they were, biologically late or early, in the depths of the bronze age or the threshold of atomic — because they were human. That was sometimes a frightening thing for non-humans, that the race stuck together. They weren't actually aggressive, but their total number was great and they held themselves aloof. The unknown ancestor again. Who else had such an origin and, it was tacitly assumed, such a destiny?

Taphetta changed his questioning. "What do you expect to gain from this discovery of the unknown ancestor?"

It was Halden who answered him. "There's the satisfaction of knowing where we came from?"

"Of course," rustled the Ribboneer. "But a lot of money and equipment was required for this expedition. I can't believe that the educational institutions that are backing you did so purely out of intellectual curiosity."

"Cultural discoveries," rumbled Emmer. "How did our ancestors live? When a creature is greatly reduced in size, as we are, more than physiology is changed — the pattern of life itself is altered. Things that were easy for them are impossible for us. Look at their life span."

"No doubt," said Taphetta. "An archeologist would be interested in cultural discoveries."

"Two hundred thousand years ago, they had an extremely advanced civilization," added Halden. "A faster-than-light drive, and we've achieved that only within the last thousand years."

"But I think we have a better one than they did," said the Ribboneer. "There may be things we can learn from them in mechanics or physics, but wouldn't you say they were better biologists than anything else?"

Halden nodded. "Agreed. They couldn't find a suitable planet. So, working directly with their germ plasm, they modified themselves and produced us. They *were* master biologists."

"I thought so," said Taphetta. "I never paid much attention to your fantastic theories before I signed to pilot this ship, but you've built up a convincing case." He raised his head, speech ribbons curling fractionally and ceaselessly. "I don't like to, but we'll have to risk using bait for your pest."

He'd have done it anyway, but it was better to have the pilot's consent. And there was one question Halden wanted to ask; it had been bothering him vaguely. "What's the difference between the Ribboneer contract and the one we offered you? Our terms are more liberal."

"To the individual, they are, but it won't matter if you discover as much as you think you will. The difference is this: *My* terms don't permit you to withhold any discovery for the benefit of one race."

Taphetta was wrong; there had been no intention of withholding anything. Halden examined his own attitudes. *He* hadn't intended, but could he say that was true of the institutions backing the expedition? He couldn't, and it was too late now — whatever knowledge they acquired would have to be shared.

That was what Taphetta had been afraid of — there was one kind of technical advancement that multiplied unceasingly. The race that could improve itself through scientific control of its germ plasm had a start that could never be headed. The Ribboneer needn't worry now.

"Why do we have to watch it on the screen?" asked Meredith, glancing up. "I'd rather be in hydroponics."

Halden shrugged. "They may or may not be smarter than planetbound animals, but they're warier. They don't come out when anyone's near."

Lights dimmed in the distant hydroponic section and the screen with it, until he adjusted the infra-red frequencies. He motioned to the two crew members, each with his own peculiar screen, below which was a miniature keyboard.

"Ready?"

When they nodded, Halden said: "Do as you've rehearsed. Keep noise at a minimum, but when you do use it, be vague. Don't try to imitate them exactly."

At first, nothing happened on the big screen, and then a grey shape crept out. It slid through leaves, listened intently before coming forward. It jumped off one hydroponic section and fled across the open floor to the next. It paused, eyes glittering and antennae twitching.

Looking around once, it leaped up, seizing the ledge and clawing up the side of the tank. Standing on top and rising to its haunches, it began nibbling what it could reach.

Suddenly it whirled. Behind it and hitherto unnoticed was another shape, like it but larger. The newcomer inched forward. The small one retreated, skittering nervously. Without warning, the big one leaped and the small one tried to flee. In a few jumps, the big one caught up and mauled the other unmercifully.

It continued to bite even after the little one lay still. At last it backed off and waited, watching for signs of motion. There was none. Then it turned to the plant. When it had chewed off everything within reach, it climbed into the branches.

The little one twitched, moved a leg, and cautiously began dragging itself away. It rolled off the raised section and surprisingly made no noise as it fell. It seemed to revive, shaking itself and scurrying away, still within range of the screen.

Against the wall was a small platform. The little one climbed on top and there found something that seemed to interest it. It sniffed around and reached and felt the discovery. Wounds were forgotten as it snatched up the object and frisked back to the scene of its recent defeat.

This time it had no trouble with the raised section. It leaped and landed on top and made considerable noise in doing so. The big animal heard and twisted around. It saw and clambered down hastily, jumping the last few feet. Squealing, it hit the floor and charged.

The small one stood still till the last instant — and then a paw flickered out and an inch-long knife blade plunged into the throat of the charging creature. Red spurted out as the bigger beast screamed. The knife flashed in and out until the big animal collapsed and stopped moving.

The small creature removed the knife and wiped it on the pelt of its foe. Then it scampered back to the platform on which the knife had been found — *and laid it down.*

At Halden's signal, the lights flared up and the screen became too bright for anything to be visible.

"Go in and get them," said Halden. "We don't want the pests to find out that the bodies aren't flesh."

"It was realistic enough," said Meredith as the crewmen shut off their machines and went out. "Do you think it will work?"

"It might. We had an audience."

"Did we? I didn't notice." Meredith leaned back. "Were the puppets exactly like the pests? And if not, will the pests be fooled?"

"The electronic puppets were a good imitation, but the animals don't have to identify them as their species. If they're smart enough, they'll know the value of a knife, no matter who uses it."

"What if they're smarter? Suppose they know a knife can't be used by a creature without real hands?"

"That's part of our precautions. They'll never know until they try — and they'll never get away from the trap to try."

"Very good. I never thought of that," said Meredith, coming closer. "I like the way your primitive mind works. At times I actually think of marrying you."

"Primitive," he said, alternately frozen and thawed, though he knew that, in relation to her, he was *not* advanced.

"It's almost a curse, isn't it?" She laughed and took the curse away by leaning provocatively against him. "But barbaric lovers are often nice."

615

Here we go again, he thought drearily, sliding his arm around her. To her, I'm merely a passionate savage.

They went to his cabin.

She sat down, smiling. Was she pretty? Maybe. For her own race, she wasn't tall, only by Terran standards. Her legs were disproportionately long and well shaped and her face was somewhat bland and featureless, except for a thin, straight, short nose. It was her eyes that made the difference, he decided. A notch or two up the scale of visual development, her eyes were larger and she could see an extra colour of the violet end of the spectrum.

She settled back and looked at him. "It might be fun living with you on primeval Earth."

He said nothing; she knew as well as he that Earth was as advanced as her own world. She had something else in mind.

"I don't think I will, though. We might have children."

"Would it be wrong?" he asked. "I'm as intelligent as you. We wouldn't have subhuman monsters."

"It would be a step up — for you." Under her calm, there was tension. It had been there as long as he'd known her, but it was closer to the surface now. "Do I have the right to condemn the unborn? Should I make them start lower than I am?"

The conflict was not new nor confined to them. In one form or another, it governed personal relations between races that were united against non-humans, but held sharp distinctions themselves.

"I haven't asked you to marry me," he said bluntly.

"Because you're afraid I'd refuse."

It was true; no one asked a member of a higher race to enter a permanent union.

"Why did you ever have anything to do with me?" demanded Halden.

"Love," she said gloomily. "Physical attraction. But I can't let it lead me astray."

"Why not make a play for Kelburn? If you're going to be scientific about it, he'd give you children of the higher type."

616

"Kelburn." It didn't sound like a name, the way she said it. "I don't like him and he wouldn't marry me."

"He wouldn't, but he'd give you children if you were humble enough. There's a fifty per cent chance you might conceive."

She provocatively arched her back. Not even the women of Kelburn's race had a body like hers and she knew it.

"Racially, there should be a chance," she said. "Actually, Kelburn and I would be infertile."

"Can you be sure?" he asked, knowing it was a poor attempt to act unconcerned.

"How can anyone be sure on a theoretical basis?" she asked, an oblique smile narrowing her eyes. "I know we can't."

His face felt anesthetized. "Did you have to tell me that?"

She got up and came to him. She nuzzled against him and his reaction was purely reflexive. His hand swung out and he could feel the flesh give when his knuckles struck it.

She fell back and dazedly covered her face with her hand. When she took it away, blood spurted. She groped toward the mirror and stood in front of it. She wiped the blood off, examining her features carefully.

"You've broken my nose," she said factually. "I'll have to stop the blood and pain."

She pushed her nose back into place and waggled it to make sure. She closed her eyes and stood silent and motionless. Then she stepped back and looked at herself critically.

"It's set and partially knitted. I'll concentrate tonight and have it healed by morning."

She felt in the cabinet and attached an invisible strip firmly across the bridge. Then she came over to him.

"I wondered what you'd do. You didn't disappoint me."

He scowled miserably at her. Her face was almost plain and the bandage, invisible or not, didn't improve her appearance any. How could he still feel that attraction to her?

617

"Try Emmer," he suggested tiredly. "He'll find you irresistible, and he's even more savage than I am."

"Is he?" She smiled enigmatically. "Maybe, in a biological sense. Too much, though. You're just right."

He sat down on the bed. Again there was only one way of knowing what Emmer would do — and she knew. She had no concept of love outside of the physical, to make use of her body so as to gain an advantage — what advantage? — for the children she intended to have. Outside of that, nothing mattered, and for the sake of alloying the lower with the higher, she was as cruel to herself as she was to him. And yet he wanted her.

"I do think I love you," she said. "And if love's enough, I may marry you in spite of everything. But you'll have to watch out whose children I have." She wriggled into his arms.

The racial disparity was great and she had provoked him, but it was not completely her fault. Besides . . .

Besides what? She had a beautiful body that could bear superior children — and they might be his.

He twisted away. With those thoughts, he was as bad as she was. Were they all that way, every one of them, crawling — upward out of the slime toward the highest goal they could conceive of? Climbing over — no, *through* — everybody they could coerce, seduce or marry — onward and upward. He raised his hand, but it was against himself that his anger was turned.

"Careful of the nose," she said, pressing against him. "You've already broken it once."

He kissed her with sudden passion that even he knew was primitive.

There were no immediate results from the puppet performance and so it was repeated at intervals. After the third time, Firmon reported, coming in as Halden pored over the meager biological data he'd gathered on the unknown ancestor. Wild guesses mostly, not one real fact in all the statistics. After two hundred thousand years, there wasn't much left to work with.

Firmon slouched down. "It worked," he said. "Got three a few hours ago."

Halden looked at him; he had hoped it wouldn't work. There was satisfaction in being right, but he would rather face something less intelligent. Wariness was one thing, the shyness and slyness of an unseen animal, but intelligence was more difficult to predict.

"Where are they?" he asked.

"Did you want them?" Firmon seemed surprised at the idea.

Halden sighed, it was his own fault. Firmon had a potentially good mind, but he hadn't been trained to use it and that counted for more than people thought. "Any animal smart enough to appreciate the value of a knife is worth study on that account. That goes double when it's a pest."

"I'll change the cremation setting," said Firmon. "Next time, we'll just stun them."

The trap setting was changed and several animals were taken. Physically, they were very much as Halden had described them to Taphetta, small four-legged creatures with fleshy antennae. Dissection revealed a fairly large brain capacity, while behaviour tests indicated an intelligence somewhat below what he had assumed. Still, it was more than he wanted a pest to have, especially since it also had hands.

The biological mechanism of the hands was simple. It walked on the back of the front paws, on the fingers of which were fleshy pads. When it sat upright, as it often did, the flexibility of the wrists permitted the forepaws to be used as hands. Clumsy, but because it had a thumb, it could handle such tools as a knife.

He had made an error there. He had guessed the intelligence, but he hadn't known it could use the weapon he had put within reach. A tiny thing with an inch-long knife was not much more dangerous than the animal alone, but he didn't like the idea of it loose on the ship.

The metal knife would have to be replaced with something else. Technicians could compound a plastic that would take a keen edge for a while and deteriorate to a soft mass in a matter of weeks. Meanwhile, he had actually given the animal a dangerous weapon — the concept of a tool. There was only one way to take that away from them, by extermination. But that would have to wait.

Fortunately, the creature had a short life and a shorter breeding period. The actual replacement rate was almost negligible. In attaining intelligence, it had been short-changed in fertility and, as a consequence, only in the specialized environment of this particular ship was it any menace at all.

They were lucky; a slightly higher fertility and the thing could threaten their existence. As it was, the ship would have to be deverminized before it could land on an inhabited planet.

Halden took the data to the Ribboneer pilot and, after some discussion, it was agreed that the plastic knife should supplant the metal one. It was also decided to allow a few to escape with the weapon; there had to be some incentive if the creature was to visit the trap more than a few times. Besides, with weapons there was always the chance of warfare between different groups. They might even exterminate each other.

Gradually, over a period of weeks, the damage to hydroponics subsided; the pests were under control. There was nothing to worry about unless they mutated again, which was unlikely.

Kelburn scowled at the pilot. "Where are we now?" he challenged, his face creased with suspicion.

"You have access to all the instruments, so you should know," said Taphetta. He was crouching and seemed about to spring, but he was merely breathing relaxedly through a million air tubes.

"I do know. My calculations show one star as the most probable. We should have reached it two days ago — and we're nowhere near it."

"True," admitted Taphetta. "We're heading toward what you would consider the fifth or sixth most likely star."

620

Kelburn caught the implication. They all did. "Then you know where it is?" he asked, suspicion vanishing.

"Not in the sense you're asking — no, I'm not sure it's what you're looking for. But there was once a great civilization there."

"You knew this and didn't tell us?"

"Why should I?" Taphetta looked at him in mild astonishment. "Before you hired me, I wouldn't tell you for obvious reasons. And afterwards — well, you engaged all my skill and knowledge and I used them to bring you here by the shortest route. I didn't think it necessary to tell you until we actually arrived. Is that wrong?"

It wasn't wrong; it merely illustrated the difference in the way an alien mind worked. Sooner or later, they would have found the place, but he had saved them months.

"What's it like?" Emmer asked.

Taphetta jiggled his ribbons. "I don't know. I was passing near here and saw the planet off to one side."

"And you didn't stop?" Emmer was incredulous.

"Why should I? We're great navigators because we do so much of it. We would never get very far if we stopped to examine everything that looks interesting. Besides, it's not a good policy in a strange region, especially with an unarmed ship."

They wouldn't have that problem. The ship was armed well enough to keep off uncivilized marauders who had very recently, reached the spaceship age, and only such people were apt to be inhospitable.

"When will we land?" asked Halden.

"In a few hours, but you can see the planet on our screens." Taphetta extended a head ribbon toward a knob and a planet came into view.

There weren't two civilizations in the Milky Way that built on such a large scale, even from the distance that they could see it. Great, distinctive cities were everywhere. There was no question as to what they had found.

"Now you'll learn why they ran away," said Taphetta.

"A new theory," Kelburn said, though it wasn't, for they *had* left. "What makes you think they were afraid?"

"No air. If your calculations are right, there must have

been an extensive atmosphere a few hundred thousand years ago and now there isn't any. A planet this size doesn't lose air that fast. Therefore, it's an artificial condition. Who takes the trouble to leave a planet uninhabitable except someone who's afraid others will use it — and who else runs away?"

"They may have done it to preserve what they left," suggested Halden.

"Perhaps," said Taphetta, but it was obvious he didn't think so.

The lack of air had one thing to recommend it — they needn't worry about their pests escaping. The disadvantage was that they had to wear spacesuits. They landed on top of a great building that was intact after thousands of years and still strong enough to support the added weight. And then——

Then there was nothing.

Buildings, an enormous number and variety of them, huge, not one of them less than five stories high, all with ramps instead of stairs. This was to be expected, considering the great size of the people who had lived there, and it followed the familiar pattern.

But there was nothing in those buildings! On this airless world, there was no decay, no rust or corrosion — *and nothing to decay or corrode.* No pictures, tools, nothing that resembled sculpture, and while there were places where machines had stood, none were there now. Here and there in inaccessible locations were featureless blobs of metal. The implication was clear: Where they hadn't been able to remove a machine, they had melted it down on the spot.

The thoroughness was bewildering. It wasn't done by some enemy; he would have stood off and razed the cities. But there was no rubble and the buildings were empty. The inhabitants themselves had removed all that was worth taking along.

A whole people had packed and moved away, leaving behind only massive, echoing structures.

There was plenty to learn, but nothing to learn it from.

Buildings indicate only so much and then there must be something else — at least some of the complex artifacts of a civilization — and there was none. Outside the cities, on the plains, there were the remains of plants and animals that indicated by their condition that airlessness had come suddenly. Sam Halden, the biologist, had examined them, but he discovered no clues. The unknown ancestor was still a mystery.

And the others — Emmer, the archeologist, and Meredith, the linguist — had nothing to work on, though they searched. It was Kelburn who found the first hint. Having no specific task, now that the planet was located, he wandered around in a scout ship. On the other side of the planet, he signaled that there was a machine and that it was intact!

The crew was hurriedly recalled, the equipment brought back into the ship, and they took off for the plain where Kelburn waited.

And there was the machine, immense, like everything on the planet. It stood alone, tapering toward the sky. At the base was a door, which, when open, was big enough to permit a spaceship to enter easily — only it was closed.

Kelburn stood beside the towering entrance, a tiny figure in a spacesuit. He gazed up at it as the three came near. "All we have to do is open it," he said.

"How?" asked Meredith. She seemed to have forgotten that she disliked him. He had made a chance discovery because he had nothing to do while the others were busy, but she regarded it as further proof of his superiority.

It was hard to watch the happiness that her face directed toward Kelburn. Halden turned away.

"Just press the button," he said.

Emmer noticed his expression. "It's such a big button," he objected. "It's going to be hard to know when we find it."

"There's an inscription of some sort," said Kelburn loftily. "This thing was left for a purpose. Somewhere there must be operating instructions."

"From here, it looks like a complex wave-form," a voice

crinkled in their radio — Taphetta from the spaceship. "All we have to do is find the right base in the electromagnetic spectrum and duplicate it on a beam broadcast and the door should open. You're too close to see it as clearly as I can."

Perhaps they were too close to the big ancestor, decided Halden moodily as they went back. It had overshadowed much of their thinking, and who really knew what the ancestor was like and what had motivated him?

But the Ribboneer was right about the signal, though it took several days to locate it. And then the huge door swung open and air whistled out.

Inside was another disappointment, a bare hall with a ramp leading upward, closed off at the ceiling. They could have forced through, but they had no desire to risk using a torch to penetrate the barrier — in view of the number of precautions they'd already encountered, it was logical to assume that there were more waiting for them.

It was Emmer who found the solution. "In appearance, it resembles a spaceship. Let's assume it is, minus engines. It was never intended to fly. Listen.

"There's no air, so you can't hear," said Emmer impatiently. "But you could if there were air. Put your hands against the wall."

A distinct vibration ran through the whole structure. It hadn't been there before the door opened. Some mechanism had been triggered. The rumbling went on, came to a stop, and began again. Was it some kind of communication?

Hastily rigged machines were hauled inside the chamber to generate an air supply so that sounds would be produced for the recorder. Translating equipment was set up and focused and, after some experimentation with signals, the door was slowly closed. No one remained inside; there was no guarantee that it would be as easy to get out as it had been to get in.

They waited a day and a half while the sounds were being recorded. The delay seemed endless. The happiest of the crew was Kelburn. Biologically the highest human on the expedition, he was stimulated. He wandered aimlessly and smiled affably, patting Meredith, when he came to her, in the friendliest fashion. Startled, she smiled back and looked around wanly. Halden was behind her.

If I had not been there, thought Halden — and thereafter made it a point to be there.

Meredith was excited, but not precisely happy. The work was out of her hands until the translating equipment was retrieved. As the second highest biological type, she, too, was affected, until she pointedly went to her room and locked it from the inside.

Halden kept himself awake with anti-fatigue pills, in part because Meredith could change her mind about Kelburn, and because of that locked door.

Emmer tried to be phlegmatic and seemed to succeed. Taphetta alone was unconcerned; to him, it was an interesting and perhaps profitable discovery, but important only because of that. He would not be changed at all by whatever he learned.

Hours crawled by and at last the door opened; the air came rushing out again. The translating equipment was brought back to the ship and Meredith was left alone with it.

It was half a day before she admitted the others to the laboratory.

"The machine is still working," she said. "There seems to have been some attempt to make the message hard to decode. But the methods they used were exactly the clues that the machine needed to decipher it. My function as a linguist was to help out with the interpretation of key words and phrases. I haven't got even a little part of the message. You'll know what it is as soon as I do. After the first part, the translator didn't seem to have much trouble."

They sat down facing it—— Taphetta, Kelburn, Meredith, Halden and Emmer. Meredith was midway between Kelburn and himself. Was there any significance in that, wondered Halden, or was he reading more in her behaviour than was actually there?

"The translation is complete," announced the machine.

"Go ahead," Meredith ordered.

"The words will be speeded up to human tempo," said the translator. "Insofar as possible, speech mannerisms of the original will be imitated. Please remember that it is only an imitation, however."

The translator coughed, stuttered and began. "We have purposely made access to our records difficult. If you can translate this message, you'll find, at the end, instructions for reaching the rest of our culture relics. As an advanced race, you're welcome to them. We've provided a surprise for anyone else.

"For ourselves, there's nothing left but an orderly retreat to a place where we can expect to live in peace. That means leaving this Galaxy, but because of our life span, we're capable of it and we won't be followed."

Taphetta crinkled his ribbons in amusement. Kelburn frowned at the interruption, but no one else paid any attention.

The translator went on. "Our metabolic rate is the lowest of any creature we know of. We live several thousand revolutions of any recorded planet and our rate of increase is extremely low; under the most favourable circumstances, we can do no more than double our numbers in two hundred generations."

"This doesn't sound as if they were masters of biological science," rustled Taphetta.

Halden stirred uneasily. It wasn't turning out at all the way he had expected.

"At the time we left," the message continued, "we found no other intelligent race, though there were some capable of further evolution. Perhaps our scout ships long ago met your ancestors on some remote planet. We were never very numerous, and because we move and multiply so slowly, we are in danger of being swept out of existence in the foreseeable future. We prefer to leave while we can. The reason we must go developed on our own planet, deep beneath the cities, in the underworks, which we had ceased to inspect because there was no need to. This part was built to last a million generations, which is long even for us."

Emmer sat upright, annoyed at himself, "Of course! There are always sewers and I didn't think of looking there!"

"In the last several generations, we sent out four expeditions, leisurely trips because we then thought we had time to explore thoroughly. With this planet as base of operations, the successive expeditions fanned out in four directions, to cover the most representative territory."

Kelburn stiffened, mingled pride and chagrin on his face. His math had been correct, as far as he had figured it. But had there been any reason to assume that they would confine their exploration to one direction? No, they would want to cover the whole Milky Way.

Taphetta paled. Four times as many humans to contend with! He hadn't met the other three-fourths yet — and, for him, it wasn't at all a pleasant thought.

"After long preparation, we sent several ships to settle one of the nearer planets that we'd selected on the first expedition. To our dismay, we found that the plague was there — though it hadn't been on our first visit!"

Halden frowned. They were proving themselves less and less expert biologists. And this plague — there had to be a reason to leave, and sickness was as good as any — but unless he was mistaken, plague wasn't used in the strict semantic sense. It might be the fault of the translation.

"The colonists refused to settle; they came back at once and reported. We sent out our fastest ships, heavily armed. We didn't have the time to retrace our path completely, for we'd stopped at innumerable places. What we did was to check a few planets, the outward and return parts of all four voyages. In every place, the plague was there, too, and we knew that we were responsible.

"We did what we could. Exhausting our nuclear armament, we obliterated the nearest planets on each of the four spans of our journeys."

"*I wondered* why the route came to an end," crinkled Taphetta, but there was no comment, no answer.

"We reconstructed what had happened. For a long time,

the plague had lived in our sewers, subsisting on wastes. At night, because they are tiny and move exceedingly fast, they were able to make their way into our ships and were aboard on every journey. We knew they were there, but because they were so small, it was difficult to dislodge them from their nesting places. And so we tolerated their existence."

"They weren't so smart," said Taphetta. "We figured out that angle long ago. True, our ship is an exception, but we haven't landed anywhere, and won't until we determinize it."

"We didn't guess that next to the hull in outer space and consequently exposed to hard radiation," the message went on, "those tiny creatures would mutate dangerously and escape to populate the planets we landed on. They had always been loathsome little beasts that walked instead of rolling or creeping, but now they became even more vicious, spawning explosively and fighting with the same incessant violence. They had always harboured diseases which spread to us, but now they've become hot-houses for still smaller parasites that also are able to infect us. Finally, we are now allergic to them, and when they are within miles of us, it is agony to roll or creep."

Taphetta looked around. "Who would have thought it? You were completely mistaken as to your origin." Kelburn was staring vacantly ahead, but didn't see a thing. Meredith was leaning against Halden; her eyes were closed. "The woman has finally chosen, now that she knows she was once vermin," clicked the Ribboneer. "But there are tears in her eyes."

"The intelligence of the beast has advanced slightly, though there isn't much difference between the highest and the lowest — and we have checked both ends of all four journeys. But before, it was relatively calm and orderly. Now it is malignantly insane."

Taphetta rattled his ribbons. "Turn it off. You don't have to listen to this. We all are of some origin or other and it wasn't necessarily pretty. This being was a slug of some kind — and are you now what it describes? Perhaps mentally a little, out of pride, but the pride was false."

"We can't demolish all the planets we unthinkingly let it loose on; there are too many and it lives too fast. The stars drift and we would lose some, and before we could eliminate the last one, it would develop space travel — it has little intelligence, but it could get that far — and it would escape ahead of us. We know an impossible task when we see it. And so we're leaving, first making sure that this animal will never make use of the products of our civilization. It may reach this planet, but it will not be able to untangle our code — it's too stupid. You who will have to face it, please forgive us. It's the only thing that we're ashamed of."

"Don't listen," said the Ribboneer and, bending his broad, thin body, he sprang to the translator, shook it and banged with his ribbons until the machine was silent. "You don't have to tell anyone," crackled Taphetta. "Don't worry about me — I won't repeat it." He looked around at the faces. "But I can see that you will report to everyone exactly what you found. That pride you've developed — you'll need it."

Taphetta sat on top of the machine, looking like nothing so much as a huge fancy bow on a gift-wrapped package.

They noted the resemblance vaguely. But each of them knew that, as a member of the most numerous race in the Milky Way, no longer feared for their mysterious qualities — despised, instead — wherever they went, there would never be any gifts for them — for any man.

*There's a great difference between potential and developed power. The one is clearly visible and can be awe-inspiring. The other may take a demigod to recognize.*

●

# THE INTERLOPERS

## By Roger Dee

For the brief time that the intercepting craft hung on the ship's foreign-body screen, Clowdis felt himself pulled taut as wire with the strain of uncertainty. When the expected finger of the communications beam reached across the distance and he saw the reddish reptilian face of the other commander, and the faces of others like him ranked in the alien control room behind, his sigh of relaxing tension was not an expression of relief but of resignation.

"Korivians," Vesari said, unnecessarily, from the navigator's place beside him. "T'sai bodyguards — and from the number of them, there's bound to be some T'sai aboard. We're going to meet the galactic masters at last, Ed."

Without turning his head, Clowdis called: "Shassil!"

Their Cetian interpreter came forward at once, his oddly angled body tensing and his narrow goatish face taking on the galactic's inevitable air of deference when he saw the faces on the screen.

"Find out what they want of us," Clowdis said.

The Cetian touched his beard respectfully — not to himself, Clowdis noted, but to the Korivian captain on the screen — and spoke in a swift rush of sibilance. The Korivian answered in turn, beaked lizard-face expressionless as reddish stone.

Shassil touched his caprine beard again and turned from the screen. "You are to shut down the ship's engines," he said to Clowdis, "and gather all hands below."

Neither Clowdis nor Vesari, knowing themselves as far out of their depth as kittens in a computing room, considered demanding why. But Vesari paused at the downspiraling ramp of a companionway and Clowdis, feeling a curiously unreal sense of experiment, paused with him.

"What do you think they want, Shassil?" Vesari asked.

The Cetian considered him gravely with long-pupiled eyes. "When a T'sai is near," he said, "I do not think at all."

A literal truth, Clowdis thought as he went with Vesari down the steep twist of helicline, and not one confined to Shassil nor to Cetians alone. A hundred thousand races from rim to rim of the galaxy — the least of them, so far as Clowdis had seen, older and wiser and infinitely stronger than his own upstart culture — suspended opinion when the T'sai spoke.

As if the T'sai were not flesh like other creatures, but gods. But *were* they flesh?

Clowdis smothered an incipient flare of resentment by reminding himself that he was after all a newt in strange waters, a minnow among sharks.

*When in Rome one does as the Romans do*, he told himself wryly. *When in space——*

"First things first," he said aloud. "We'd better break the news to Buehl in the engine room before we see Barbour and the colonists."

Powermaster Buehl took the T'sai order with a bellicose impatience that was an index to his temper. A thick-bodied and heavy-minded man of middle age, given when off duty to solitary drinking and deadly serious absorption in his collection of Wagnerian tapes, he was devoted to his atomic charges with a singleness of soul which Clowdis, who had gone to space for the sheer restless love of seeing, had never been able to understand.

"Draw my men from their stations?" Buehl demanded angrily when Clowdis found him at his engine-room desk. "Damp the piles, kill the ship?"

He had an incredulous mental picture of the ship not driven but drifting, helpless as a crippled fish in treacherous waters, an image sharply defined within the familiar bounds of his power section but growing vaguer when extended to minor reaches of cargo holds and crew quarters and many-tiered bunking cubicles filled with chattering, cow-eyed colonists. Control section and hydroponics, galley and hospital bay did not register at all in Buehl's regard because they lay in the seldom-visited and dispensable upper level; the power that drove the ship like a metal thunderbolt through space was everything to him, and he would no more have throttled it voluntarily in midflight than he would have taken a blade to his own throat.

"This is the moment we've dreaded since we first touched at Sirius ten years ago," Clowdis reminded him. "There are *T'sai* out there, Buehl. Get your men to crew quarters on the double, or I'll iron you and put Simmonds on the engines."

The threat defeated Buehl as no other could have, as Clowdis had known it must. The powermaster gave the order from his desk communicator, but did not follow when his puzzled subordinates filed past him out of the power room. He remained in place, glowering through the uneasy silence that followed the sudden cessation of engine noise, long after the others had gone.

And slowly he began to realize something of the gravity of their position, piecing it together gradually from those accumulated bits of experience that had reality for him. The aesthetic had no existence for Buehl beyond his instinctive response to Wagnerian clamor; the social and economic intricacies of alien cultures left him as unmoved as did those of his own, and for the emotional drives that made men and not-men what they were he had only contempt.

But Buehl respected Power. He thought of it as an entity spelled out in upper-case symbols, a name synonymous with deity.

For Buehl was powermaster in his own sphere, and he had seen power beyond imagining.

His first stunning surmise as to what power could be like had come at the end of man's initial stellar jump — Buehl had been an engine-room member of that original expedition, but the glory of pioneering meant nothing compared to the feeling of mastery over the surging forces under his hands — to the far-swinging Sirian worlds. He recalled vaguely a swarming society of upright anthropoids, disturbingly manlike for all their chitinous jointure and wonderfully, if incuriously, courteous.

The engines he remembered better.

The Sirians had outgrown atomic energy millennia before. Somehow they tapped the force reservoirs of their giant sun, and a single monolithic station on each planet supplied power that could have pulverized a world but which instead drove their beautifully mechanized economy with the purring smoothness of a fine chronometer.

The Eridanians had used subatomic binding forces to make a perpetual paradise of their single slow-freezing world, and the Cetians, Shassil's people, drew limitless energy from the strain-currents that permeated space. A single building there housed a power more formidable than the totel output of Earth's straining generators.

The hundred thousand other peoples of whom Earthmen had heard, but into whose spatial backyards they had not yet penetrated, had power as great and as varied. And over them all loomed the T'sai, the masters and mentors, the teachers and governors, who owned the secret of instantaneous transfer and who ruled with a word.

What, Buehl wondered, was power to the T'sai?

To the T'sai his own shining converter plant would be more primitive than Hero's steam engine. To them he was not a powermaster but a savage, squatting vacantly over the first-kindled spark of atomic force.

For the first time in his career Buehl, with his beloved

engines silent under his feet, felt the frustration of utter insignificance.

Rumors of the emergency had already reached Barbour in his quarters, and he was — as Clowdis had expected, understanding as he did the agile thoroughness of his psychologist-propagandist's mind — busily organizing a program to reassure crew and colonists alike.

"We expected to meet the T'sai eventually," Barbour said. He was a tall man, stooped and spectacled and balding, his mild light eyes normally veiled with habitual introspection. "As well get it over with now as later, Ed."

"They'll know about us from cultures we've visited already," Clowdis pointed out. "We're going to be weighed and judged and perhaps fitted into their scheme of things, Frank. The lot we draw is going to be largely up to you."

Barbour sighed. "I know, Ed, I wish they had caught us earlier, before we started to bring out colonists—— we're trespassers to begin with, and to unload our surplus population out here without T'sai permission may prejudice them against us."

Clowdis shrugged. He had anticipated such a development from the first and had opposed the colonization project; but political pressure at home, the necessity of justifying the enormous expense of interstellar exploration, had defeated his objections.

"We had to make the try, with that perfect oxy-nitrogen planet of Regulus lying unclaimed," he said. "And we'll have to do the best we can with the T'sai now."

Clowdis moved on to the task he hated most, explaining to the colonists what might be expected of them.

Barbour, left alone, took off his spectacles and wiped them thoughtfully, his trained mind running carefully over the possibilities. Barbour, like Clowdis, had come to space under the lash of curiosity; not in his case to satisfy any restless yearning for adventure, but to push his investigations into the minds and manners of alien races as he had pursued them into his own society. The fact that intelligence was galaxy-wide instead of confined to his own insular sphere had fired his imagination from that first flight to Sirius — that that intelligence should follow such divergent paths, yet should always arrive at the same conclusion in the end, at once challenged and perplexed him.

Each culture they had touched, he considered, was older and wiser and immensely more powerful than Earth's, so far superior as to put his own handful in the position of a canoe-load of savages paddling wide-eyed through the harbors of a great city.

Yet these aliens were different after a fashion the nature of which had persistently eluded him.

The galactics traveled widely in pursuit of trade, making jumps of a magnitude inconceivable to an Earthman's mind. They lived in comfort and peace, without want or war, each society presenting a new variation of Utopia which only emphasized the homogeneity of the whole.

The nature of that unity came to Barbour now of itself, and he cursed himself with academic invective for not having seen it earlier.

There was no real progress out here — and had been none, obviously, for millennia. Each culture was balanced precisely to suit the demands of its own peculiar mores, but he had yet to skirt the fringes of an alien philosphy which was not founded on fatalism and *laissez-faire* resignation.

The galaxy was static. And what made it so?

The T'sai.

The realization brought Barbour a feeling of profound depression. So many promising beginnings intercepted and channeled to ultimate mediocrity by the super-race, so many vaulting young ambitions crushed to compliance with superior will!

And Earth?

Earth, Barbour thought, was the newest entrant to this cosmic kindergarten, the downiest yokel coming afoot in brash ignorance daring to blink at the bright lights of civilization. To be monitored and graded and assigned a niche, if found worthy of the trouble, in the T'sai economy.

To Barbour the truth behind the universal resignation he had seen was suddenly and chillingly clear. Why struggle, why toil and sweat for an ideal when the striving is doomed to failure from the start?

Earth, again.

Men, reckless of odds and intolerant of opposition, were never a docile people. Taken in hand by the T'sai, they might resent such regimentation forcibly. And then——

Barbour, like any good psychologist, knew when to drop a line of thought and close his mind to an unpleasant conclusion.

Clowdis was waiting with Shassil and the others at the conference-room table — Vesari fidgeting over an unwanted cigarette, Buehl a little drunk and more surlily taciturn than usual, Barbour humped moodily with his mild eyes fogged in thought — when Wilcox hurried in to take his place.

"Sorry to be late," Wilcox said. His voice betrayed an habitual diffidence, an unconscious surprise that he should have been chosen to sit in consultation with the powers of the ship. "I've been elected to represent the colonists, sir. I'll do the best I can."

Clowdis accepted his presence without comment, avoiding his eyes because the man's meekness was somehow offensive to a spaceman's sense of fitness. Wilcox was a small, pale man with neutral hair and troubled eyes, a former hydroponics operator who had sold his job-registry rights in Greater Pittsburgh to raise fare for his wife and himself to Regulus. He had been chosen now, Clowdis knew, for the reason that Wilcox *was* the average colonist — anxious to please, inoffensive and without initiative or ambition beyond his own small interest.

"Good enough," Clowdis said, and looked across the table at Shassil. "What can you tell us now, Shassil?"

The Cetian sighed, revealing twin rims of cartilage that served him in lieu of teeth. "Little, beyond the fact that the T'sai will board us soon for an interview. After that——"

"After that," Buehl interrupted, "the little gods of space will give us their word, and the word is Power." There was a growl in his voice which he did not try to conceal.

"Easy," Clowdis cautioned, "we've passed on sufferance

so far, Buehl, only because none of the peoples we've visited had orders from the T'sai to stop us. We'd be mad to make trouble now."

Barbour looked up, his mild eyes sharp with interest. "You said *the* T'sai, Shassil. Does that mean there's only one of them aboard the Korivian ship?"

The Cetian nodded. "The T'sai travel seldom, and then singly. But the T'sai are not as we others — to them one is all and all are one."

He rose from the table. "My presence constrains conversation, I think. I shall wait for the T'sai in the control room."

He left, for all his galactic politeness, without touching his beard in the Cetian gesture of respect. Clowdis, thinking of that goatish creature holding solitary sway over *his* control room, felt a quick surge of anger and quelled it as quickly.

"He's right, you know," Barbour said. "It's our problem, Ed, and we couldn't talk freely with Shassil sitting in."

"What is there to talk about?" Vesari demanded fretfully. "If we can't *do* anything, what's the use of talking at all?"

"We're not planning to do anything," Clowdis pointed out. "We're only here to assess the possibilities, and to wait."

"The possibilities are soon numbered," Barbour said dryly. "They can kill us or imprison us, send us packing home again or ignore us."

Clowdis said positively, "They won't ignore us. I've made a hearsay study of the systems we haven't visited yet, and every one is an integral part of the T'sai realm. Personally, I can't see that we'd fit into such a scheme of things — I think we'll be lucky if they let us go home again."

"Is it really as bad as that?" Wilcox asked in alarm. The face he turned on Clowdis had gone even paler than usual. "I mean — we *can't* go back, we colonists. There's no place for us!"

Clowdis kept the annoyance from his face with an effort. "The conditions of this Regulus expedition were carefully explained before the flight, Wilcox. Your people understood from the start that we were on shaky ground out here. You knew the chances you took when you signed away your job-rights."

The colonist subsided, blinking. He was thinking at the moment not of galactic rights and powers but of his wife, of the child to be born to them in half a year and of the seventy-odd other couples waiting in the lower level for his report. To be turned back now meant more than a return to the desperately crowded warrens of Earth; with the surrender of their rights they held no status whatever, and the only course open was compulsory migration to a drab and driven existence, infinitely worse, in the domes of Mars or Venus or the moons of Jupiter.

The soft green planet of Regulus that lay short hours ahead was heaven by contrast. To give it up now, when they were so near——

They felt the presence of their inquisitor even before Shassil presented him, the slightest feather-touch of exploratory thought that was like a momentary, not unpleasant, itching at the roots of the mind.

The Cetian interpreter sidled into the conference room with a hand at his beard, his long-pupilled eyes down-cast.

"The T'sai," Shassil said reverently.

They rose together, incredulous, stunned by the unsuspected possibilities opened by their first sight of a galactic master.

The T'sai was a man.

A small man, smaller by a head than even Wilcox, but looming like a Titan through the aura of power that hung about him.

"You think yourselves worthy of claiming our empty worlds," the T'sai said. "Prove it."

And left them alone with their problem.

". . . Not of the same species as ourselves," Barbour said. Even an hour later he found the truth overwhelming, the wonder of it still blinding to reason. "It's impossible! The straining of coincidence——"

"He's no oxygen breather," Clowdis said. He felt like a

man struggling up from drugged sleep, regaining the sharp use of his senses with slow labor. "There was a sort of force envelope around him that held his air. The ears were different, and the hair, and he had more than five fingers to the hand . . . I think."

He turned to Barbour in sudden suspicion. "You don't think what we saw was an illusion, Frank? A projection of some kind?"

"I doubt that he'd go to the trouble," Barbour said slowly. "But it's so hard to realize——"

"Power," Buehl burst out, astonishing them all until they saw that he had retreated to his own thoughts. "With such power, they can do anything."

It was Wilcox, who understood less of the wonder of it but whose problem was more personally immediate, who brought them back to reality.

"Man or not, he left us no better off," Wilcox said. "Do you remember what he said, commander?"

Clowdis' brain felt like an eye blinded by a light too powerful to bear, but he remembered.

"He suggested that we prove ourselves worthy of claiming the world we're reaching for."

"It wasn't a suggestion," Barbour corrected. "It had the sound of an order, Ed. And he said *worlds.*"

"Power," Buehl muttered. He stared hungrily at fingers that twitched for the feel of bottle and glass.

The others sat lost in blank surmise.

"He as much as said we'd have a free hand out here if we can prove ourselves," Vesari said. "What scares me is that he didn't say what happens if we can't."

"Precisely," Barbour said. He ran a palm over his balding scalp and was surprised to find it damp. "If we can prove our worth. The problem is — *how?*"

They digested the issue in uneasy silence, facing it squarely for the first time and marshaling up, each after his own nature, the possibilities of satisfying it.

Clowdis moved first, linking his conference-room screen with the control-room. Shassil answered promptly, his goatish face blandly uncommunicative.

"Is every new race that develops space flight put to this test?" Clowdis asked. "And what happens if they fail, Shassil?"

The Cetian shrugged oddly-jointed shoulders. "The T'sai have always sought out the new cultures. You are the first to the T'sai."

They looked at each other uncomprehendingly. To Barbour the information held a tantalizing hint of greatest significance, but he could not pin it down.

"Then the T'sai gave these other races their start," he said. "They must have——"

"Beside the point," Clowdis cut in. "What we want to know is this, Shassil: *What will the T'sai do if we fail?*"

The Cetian raised a hand to his own screen's control. "I do not know. The T'sai do not confide in the minor cultures, nor do we expect it."

The blanking out of the screen left them, Clowdis thought, precisely where they had begun. Barbour felt differently, but his nagging sense of significance concealed would not define itself for analysis.

"I'm out of my depth here," Wilcox said, and stood up. "With your permission, commander, I'll get back to my friends."

Clowdis hesitated, foreseeing a risk more immediate than T'sai action. The ship's crew, including himself, numbered seventeen, while below decks a hundred and fifty colonists were already muttering uneasily among themselves. If they panicked, any chance of survival was gone at the outset.

He considered holding Wilcox until some plan of action should be agreed upon, and dismissed the thought because he knew from experience that no leaderless body of men could be kept for long in uncertainty without demanding reassurance.

"Go ahead," Clowdis said. "But remember this, Wilcox — our chances of surviving this thing depend as much on yourself as on us. If you can't help us, then keep your people out of our hair."

When Wilcox had gone, Clowdis and Vesari and Barbour looked at each other doubtfully in a silence broken only by Buehl's heavy breathing.

"Maybe they won't panic," Barbour said finally, without conviction. "Not one of them can have any accurate idea of what we're really up against here."

Clowdis shrugged helplessly. "Have *we*, Frank?"

Wilcox went directly below and found the colonists' bay astir with rumour and apprehension. Men converged upon him the instant he set foot in the long metal room, voices clamoring for reassurance.

Surprisingly, he found it in himself to give it to them. The role of leader had been thrust upon him against his will, but their obvious dependence upon him now lent him a strength he had not known he possessed.

"We're being delayed for examination," he told them. "A kind of immigration clearance we must pass before we can claim the Regulian planet we're bound for. There's no danger. Commander Clowdis has the situation under control."

But later, when the others had drifted away to talk in animated knots, Wilcox sat with his wife in their cramped cubicle and discovered that his specious assurance had deceived her not at all.

"You're holding back something, Carl," his wife said. She was younger than Wilcox, in her late twenties, dark-haired and moderately pretty even in her emigrant's cheap and sober clothing. "They're going to turn us back, is that it?"

He shook his head helplessly. "I don't know, Alice. None of us knows, not even the commander. This T'sai looks like a man, but he's more like a god. There's no way of guessing what he may do if we fail to prove ourselves."

She tilted her head to look at him shrewdly, sensing with a perception clearer than his own something of the issues at stake behind their arrest in space.

"The T'sai never did this before. Carl, do you suppose they're going to judge the whole human race by this one ship-load?"

He flinched from the thought. "I hope not! The responsibility——"

Inevitably the possibilities rose to chill him: themselves rejected, wiped out or driven back to Earth; other scheduled expeditions banned from space; men restricted forever, perhaps, to their own barren overcrowded little ring of worlds.

But as inevitably, because he was from birth a simple cog in a complex economic machine and as such was experienced only in his immediate circle of concerns, his thought went back to himself and his wife and their unborn child and to the other colonists who had burned thier bridges to make this venture into space.

They could not go back. There was no place for them on Earth, and the colonies were bitter hells for outcasts worse off than slaves.

*We may as well die out here,* he told himself. The thought took root and fanned to flame the smoldering spark of resentment that had burned in him, unaware, from the beginning.

"We're only trying to *live,*" he said aloud, and did not know that he spoke. "The T'sai have no right to deny us that. They've no use for that planet, or they'd have colonized it long ago. There's no reason why we shouldn't have it."

His wife put a hand on his arm and the touch brought him, as always, the warmth of more than physical support.

"I understand," she said. "I think the other colonists will understand too, Carl. If we can't settle out here, after sacrificing the little we had, there's no point in going on."

They sat quietly after that while resolve built up in Wilcox.

"I think I'd better tell the others the truth," he said finally. "We'll give Commander Clowdis and his group every chance, but if they can't come up with a solution——"

Clowdis and Barbour, sitting alone in the conference-room when Wilcox came up again an hour later, had arrived at no sort of conclusion. Buehl had long ago given up a task for which he had no qualifications, and had gone to his quarters for whiskey and Wagner. Vesari had followed suit from sheer weariness, and was at the moment sleeping the sleep of the unimaginative in his bunk.

"We're no better off than when you left," Barbour said irritably in answer to Wilcox's question. "There's a gulf between the T'sai psychology and our own that makes it impossible to guess what he wants. He's not a man, for all his likeness, and there's no knowing how his mind runs. It may be a matter of ethics, and the proof he demands may hinge on a facet of personality unfamiliar to us.

"Suppose one of our ancient Earthly aborigines had asked admission to our own society — he'd have had to pass an immigration board, and his ethical code would have had to correspond nearly enough to ours before he could be considered compatible. Suppose he came from a culture that ate human flesh — would that sort of conditioning be acceptable? It would not, and you know it. It would make him unfit for citizenship, and the fact that he understood nothing of that unfitness would not sway us for a minute in denying him."

"And if he tried forcible entry we'd deport or kill him," Clowdis added. He lit his hundredth cigarette and scowled at the colonist with strain-reddened eyes. "Frank is right, Wilcox. We've seen a dozen cultures at close range out here, and there's hardly a point of similarity between ourselves and any of them. Don't you agree, Wilcox?"

Wilcox was a little surprised at his own steadiness when he said, "Surely we ought to know how long we're given to produce our proof. Have you asked Shassil?"

Clowdis and Barbour looked at each other in disgust.

"Out of the mouths of babes," Barbour said. Clowdis reached for the activator button that lit his conference-room screen.

Shassil's answer had less meaning to them at the moment than the empty expanse of foreign-body plate behind him.

"You have until sunset of the present day on the Regulian planet for which you were bound," the Cetian said. "Some twelve hours from this moment, by your time."

Clowdis ignored the information. "Where's the T'sai ship?"

"The T'sai has gone to confer with his council. He will return at the appointed time."

They looked at each other helplessly when the Cetian's screen went dark.

"Instantaneous transference," Clowdis said faintly. "Across the galaxy and back in twelve hours, with a conference thrown in. What's the use, Frank? Why don't we admit we're whipped?"

Barbour turned his hands palm up in silent defeat.

"But we've twelve hours to ourselves," Wilcox said. "We can reach Regulus in ten."

He went on defiantly when Clowdis whirled on him. "We're going to land on that planet, commander, if we die for it."

They had no chance to argue. At Wilcox's call three colonists came into the room with heat guns broken from the below-decks small-arms store, and as quickly as that the ship changed hands.

Shassil, with his unshakable air of galactic resignation, took the new order without a murmur. With a heat gun at his back he sat before the commander's control board and took over the handling of the ship as readily as if the Korivian craft with its T'sai passenger had never appeared.

Wilcox and his contingent, now that the die was cast, seemed relieved of strain and as resigned as the Cetian interpreter.

"I suppose you're right, sir," Wilcox said once when Clowdis cursed him for bringing annihilation upon them. "But we're probably slated for execution anyway, and we colonists would rather die here than go back to Earth and be shipped out to the domes on Mars or Venus or the Jovian moons. You've seen those installations yourself, and know what it's like there."

Clowdis did know. He knew, too, the bitter monotony of shuttling back and forth between those dreary hellholes on the planetary runs he had followed before the advent of the interstellar drive freed him. Considering that the T'sai at best must have returned him to that drab routine awoke a certain sympathy in him for the colonists' stand, but failed utterly to compensate for the death he saw in the offing.

They brought Vesari up from his quarters, partly to check on Shassil's navigation and partly to keep Clowdis company, but Buehl they were forced to confine to his room. The powermaster had rushed to the engine room the moment the atomics came to life, and in his bull-like fury had to be bound hand and foot to prevent his interfering with the engine-room crew.

Twelve hours could be a wonderfully brief time when it measured the span of a man's life, Clowdis thought. Yet the flight dragged interminably; the ship seemed not to be flashing at twice light-speed through space, but stalled straining and motionless. Seated with Barbour and Vesari on a spare acceleration couch, Clowdis relaxed for the first time in hours and found himself nodding with exhaustion before he realized the strain he had been under.

He slept the flight through. When he roused, it was to see the soft green sweep of the Regulian planet rising under the ship, horizons rushing up with sudden dizzying speed to change from convex to concave.

"We're landing," he said stupidly, blinking away sleep.

"As we set out from Earth to do," Wilcox agreed. His wife stood at his elbow, her warm femininity startlingly out of place in the functionally male realm of control room, her eyes fixed on the clean sweep of hills and meadow below. "Let the T'sai come and blast us now if they like. We've begun what we came here for."

"Fools," Clowdis growled. "If you had to commit sui-

645

cide, why didn't you bring the atomics up to critical mass and get it over with?"

But he thrilled a little nevertheless when the engines thundered in last-minute deceleration and the ship stood like a tall silver candle on the green plain.

"Now," Wilcox said. His voice trembled.

Someone opened the locks below decks, and Clowdis could feel the stale air of the ship drifting out and smell the clean fragrance of growing things stealing in to take its place.

"We'll give you back your ship," Wilcox said, "as soon as we can get our supplies and gear unloaded."

Clowdis looked at Barbour, who shook his head wonderingly.

"Men," Barbour said. "I've studied them for a lifetime, Ed, and I've never been further from understanding them."

But both of them, while they watched the colonists hastily passing out their meager possessions, felt an unexpected tug of envy.

"I think we've been to space too long, Ed," Barbour said when the last colonist left the ship. "We've been too much interested in hunting out new worlds and investigating alien puzzles to appreciate our own species."

Clowdis, lacking the psychologist's trained capacity for empathy, still felt a shattering change of perspective.

He *had* been out of touch. He had forgotten the pull of men toward the soil, the drive that made men fight and die for possession of a few square yards of it. He and Barbour and Vesari were in their own way pioneers, latter-day Boones and Houstons and Carsons, cramped when they saw the figurative smoke of other human occupation. To them in large measure was due the credit for man's early leaping across the spatial frontier, but now, as always, it was the settlers who carried with them the dogged unyielding spirit of humanity. Those poor idealistic fools going to their deaths out there were of the same breed that had slogged patiently in the steps of all pioneers, to hold the conquered land in perpetuity for their children and their children's children forever.

*But not this time,* Clowdis thought. *The T'sai*——

Wilcox appeared briefly upon the trampled grass below, turning a flushed face up to Clowdis and Barbour at the open port.

"You'd better take the ship away, commander," he called. "The deadline——"

Clowdis threw a glance toward the sunset washing the low hills to the west, and flinched when the T'sai ship sprang into view and blocked out the sun. His immediate reaction, curiously, was not the belated panic he had anticipated but a blast of red anger against the T'sai.

"Damned if I'll try to lift her now," he said.

Then, before Barbour could move to prevent, he dropped down the personnel ladder to where Wilcox had stood.

"Here we are," he shouted. He shook his fist at the lowering ship. "Blast the lot of us and be——"

The T'sai appeared beside him like a solid projection that denied transit time, tiny face inscrutable behind his force field.

"Watch," the T'sai said.

The alien ship grounded, feather-soft, on the grass. Korivian police marched out upon the meadow like orderly ranks of reddish reptilian automatons and bore down upon the huddled colonists. Clowdis caught the glint of late sunlight on enigmatic weapons, and stiffened with a sick chill of horror when he saw that the few colonists who had clung to their commandeered heat guns had aligned themselves before the rest.

He saw Wilcox in the forefront, keeping his wife behind him so that his body shielded her own. Her own and the other life not due for half a year, the unborn son or daughter they had confidently expected to inherit their share of the new Earth.

The T'sai raised a hand and the Korivians stopped like snouted statuary.

The colonists shifted uneasily and stilled. For a moment the tableau held fast in static suspense, a dragging eternity in which Clowdis forgot to breathe.

Then the Korivians turned as if on prearranged signal and marched back to their ship.

"The proof is sufficient," the T'sai said. His voice, amplified without apparent mechanism, carried the length of the meadow. "The world is yours."

And left them alone with their victory.


The ship did not lift that night. Clowdis got roaring drunk with Barbour and Vesari and Buehl on the powermaster's whiskey, and put off questioning Shassil until late the next day.

The Cetian made explanation when they were sober, his lucid monlogue falling with clear logic even upon their dulled minds.

"The T'sai ruled the galaxy," Shassil said, "before the first life crawled up from the sea of your world. They ruled because they, of us all, possessed both intelligence and initiative, the restless drive toward perfection that was somehow left out of the lesser races. The T'sai sought us out one by one and helped us up the long path to self-sufficiency, but they had despaired of finding another race with purpose like their own until you appeared.

"They watched over you from the beginning but without interfering; if your species was to prove itself worthy it would find its way to the T'sai when the time was right, and the T'sai would weigh it and pronouce judgment. You passed their test because your kind possesses the same initiative and idealism that made the T'sai what they are, the loyalty and belligerence necessary to make you their proper successors."

They stared at him unbelievingly. *"Sucessors?"* Clowdis repeated. "What——"

"The T'sai have grown old in fulfilling their obligations to the rest of the galaxy," the Cetian said. "And a renewal of lost racial virility depends upon their finding new fields to explore. Other galaxies are waiting for them, as this one waited for you. The T'sai will go when you are ready to step into their place."

And in leaving their presence Shassil, for the first time, touched his goatish beard in respect.

# EPILOGUE

Before and after man's troubled life we saw other humanesque races rise in scores and hundreds, of which a mere handful was destined to waken beyond man's highest spiritual range, to play a part in the galactic community of worlds. These we now saw from afar on their little Earth-like planets, scattered among the huge drift of the star-streams, struggling to master all those world-problems, social and spiritual, which man in our "modern" era is for the first time confronting. Similarly, we saw again the many other kinds of races, nautiloid, avian, composite, and the rare symbiotics, and still rarer plant-like beings. And of every kind only a few, if any, won through to utopia, and took part in the great communal enterprise of worlds. The rest fell by the way.

Olaf Stapledon: *Star Maker*

# A Selection of Legend Titles

| | | |
|---|---|---|
| ☐ Eon | Greg Bear | £4.95 |
| ☐ The Infinity Concerto | Greg Bear | £3.50 |
| ☐ Wolf in Shadow | David Gemmell | £3.50 |
| ☐ Wyrms | Orson Scott Card | £2.95 |
| ☐ Speaker for the Dead | Orson Scott Card | £2.95 |
| ☐ The Misplaced Legion | Harry Turtledove | £2.95 |
| ☐ An Emperor For the Legion | Harry Turtledove | £2.99 |
| ☐ Falcon's of Narabedla | Marion Zimmer Bradley | £2.50 |
| ☐ Dark Lady | Mike Resnick | £2.99 |
| ☐ Golden Sunlands | Christopher Rowley | £2.99 |
| ☐ This is the Way the World Ends | James Morrow | £5.50 |
| ☐ Emprise | Michael Kube-McDowell | £3.50 |

Prices and other details are liable to change

---

ARROW BOOKS, BOOKSERVICE BY POST, PO BOX 29, DOUGLAS, ISLE OF MAN, BRITISH ISLES

NAME.........................................................................

ADDRESS......................................................................

..............................................................................

..............................................................................

Please enclose a cheque or postal order made out to Arrow Books Ltd. for the amount due and allow the following for postage and packing.

U.K. CUSTOMERS: Please allow 22p per book to a maximum of £3.00.

B.F.P.O. & EIRE: Please allow 22p per book to a maximum of £3.00

OVERSEAS CUSTOMERS: Please allow 22p per book.

Whilst every effort is made to keep prices low it is sometimes necessary to increase cover prices at short notice. Arrow Books reserve the right to show new retail prices on covers which may differ from those previously advertised in the text or elsewhere.